FOR WHOM THE BELLE TOLLS

— HELL'S BELLES BOOK ONE —

FOR WHOM THE BELLE TOLLS

JAYSEA LYNN

SAGA PRESS

LONDON NEW YORK TORONTO
AMSTERDAM/ANTWERP NEW DELHI SYDNEY/MELBOURNE

SAGA PRESS
AN IMPRINT OF SIMON & SCHUSTER, LLC

1230 AVENUE OF THE AMERICAS, NEW YORK, NEW YORK 10020

For more than 100 years, Simon & Schuster has championed authors and the stories they create. By respecting the copyright of an author's intellectual property, you enable Simon & Schuster and the author to continue publishing exceptional books for years to come. We thank you for supporting the author's copyright by purchasing an authorized edition of this book.

This book is a work of fiction. Any references to historical events, real people, or real places are used fictitiously. Other names, characters, places, and events are products of the author's imagination, and any resemblance to actual events or places or persons, living or dead, is entirely coincidental.

First Saga Press trade paperback edition May 2025

SAGA PRESS and colophon are trademarks of Simon & Schuster, LLC

Simon & Schuster strongly believes in freedom of expression and stands against censorship in all its forms. For more information, visit BooksBelong.com.

For information about special discounts for bulk purchases, please contact Simon & Schuster Special Sales at 1-866-506-1949 or business@simonandschuster.com.

The Simon & Schuster Speakers Bureau can bring authors to your live event. For more information or to book an event, contact the Simon & Schuster Speakers Bureau at 1-866-248-3049 or visit our website at www.simonspeakers.com.

Interior design by Meryll Preposi
Maps: Jamie Noble Frier at The Noble Artist

Manufactured in the United States of America

1   3   5   7   9   10   8   6   4   2

Library of Congress Cataloging-in-Publication Data is available.

ISBN 978-1-6682-0875-5
ISBN 978-1-6682-0876-2 (ebook)

For anyone who has ever felt temporary.
And for the nerds.

AUTHOR'S NOTE

For Whom the Belle Tolls is a humorous fantasy romance set in the After-life, and deals with death in the liveliest-possible way. In addition to the lighter moments, the story includes elements that might not be suitable or palatable for all readers. Blood and gore, violence, battle, serious injury, religious trauma, and terminal illness are all shown on the page, as well as multiple explicit sex scenes. Torture, child abuse, sexual assault, self-harm, and suicide are referenced and/or discussed.

Readers who may be sensitive to these subjects, please take note.

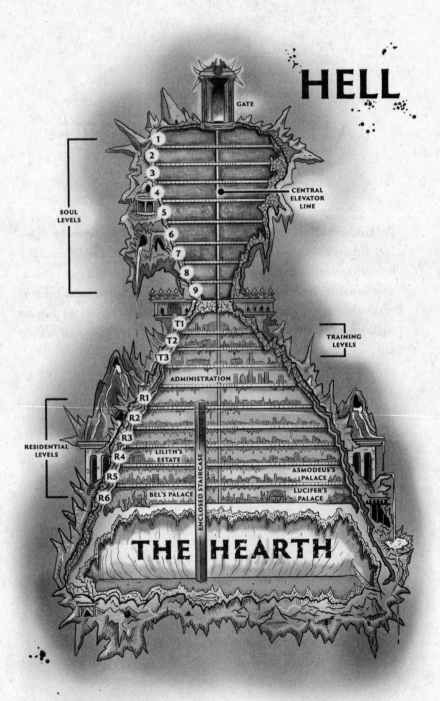

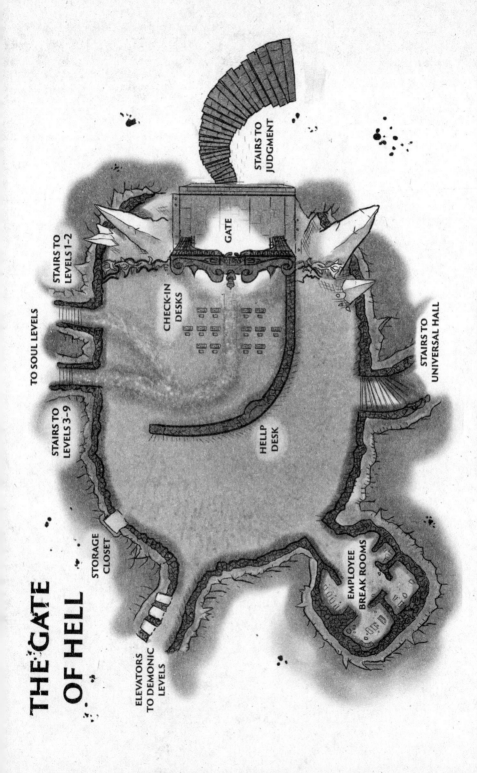

THE GATE OF HELL

STAIRS TO JUDGMENT

STAIRS TO LEVELS 1-2

GATE

TO SOUL LEVELS

CHECK-IN DESKS

STAIRS TO LEVELS 3-9

HELP DESK

STAIRS TO UNIVERSAL HALL

STORAGE CLOSET

ELEVATORS TO DEMONIC LEVELS

EMPLOYEE BREAK ROOMS

1

DIAGNOSIS

Lily

Lily knew the cancer was going to kill her when her car wouldn't start. The battered but usually reliable old Corolla had turned over a couple of times but never caught, leaving her sitting numbly in the driver's seat, the pounding of her heartbeat too loud in her ears.

Her heart had been pounding all day. From the moment she'd woken up, while she'd sipped her coffee in fretful silence, as she'd driven to the doctor's office and sat in the chair with its scratchy blue fabric. Pounded right up until the doctor walked in, sympathy in his eyes and a clipboard in his hands.

The antiseptic clinic smell had suddenly been too sharp, and the cool air went biting, the scratchy fabric of the chair like sandpaper against her skin. The doctor's too-calm tone and quiet words had been somehow shatteringly loud as he'd laid it all out for her plainly.

Her heart had started racing then, pumping blood and adrenaline through her system, preparing her for a fight that would never come. One she'd already lost.

Lily sat helpless and alone, gripping the steering wheel and staring down at her hands, the sleeve of tattoos snaking up her left arm going blurry as her eyes burned. She'd been told countless times that getting tattoos was like putting a bumper sticker on a Bentley, and each time, she'd laughed them off and joked that she was a Corolla at best. What a self-fulfilling prophecy that had been. A single gasp of breathless, unfunny laughter escaped as she tried to blink away the tears. She clapped a hand over her mouth, even though no one was around to hear.

She was in shock. She knew that. Panicking? Probably. Why not add hysterical to the mix?

It bubbled up her throat and escaped around her palm, until finally she gave up the pretense and let her hand drop. She laughed and laughed, horrible, desperate laughter, at her diagnosis, at her car that wouldn't start, at her whole ridiculous life. Her throat tightened, and she gripped the steering wheel with both hands until her knuckles turned white and her laughter started to sound and feel suspiciously like sobs.

"Fuck," she choked out. The mirthless humor washed away in an instant, replaced by a familiar burn of anger. Fury.

"Fuck! FUCK!" She slammed her hands on the wheel, the sting and jolt of impact shuddering up her hands and arms. "*FUCK!*" She screamed so loudly that a woman getting into an SUV four spots over startled and dropped her keys.

Lily slumped, pressing her forehead to the wheel, long auburn hair falling forward to shroud her from the world, hands clasping the back of her head as she took deep, shuddering breaths. Her heart pounded so hard she could hear it in her ears, like it was trying to reassure her that she and it were still alive.

The doctor had given her options, of course. Options to prolong. To ease. But options were for people with money.

People whose cars would start.

She sucked in a long, slow breath, focusing on the sweet rush of air into her lungs, lightly scented with amber and sandalwood thanks to her air freshener. She'd known in the doctor's office, from the moment he'd told her that not only did she have cancer, but it had metastasized everywhere. She'd run through every option, every variable again, then once more just in case, and reached the same conclusion.

She was going to die.

The knowledge sank into her soul like a stone. She wanted to panic, to completely lose it, to let herself *finally* fall to pieces. To let herself cry, scream, beg, and rage. To shatter into shards so small she wouldn't see herself in any of them. But, damn it, she just wasn't built that way. She wasn't built to break, no matter how much she wanted to, and she silently and half-heartedly cursed that fucking part of her that wouldn't—couldn't—let her be that vulnerable, even alone.

Lily pressed her fingers to her eyes so hard she saw stars. She'd be dead in less than a year with no treatment. With aggressive chemo, she could buy herself some more time . . . miserable, painful time. And debt.

Why did it always come down to fucking money? Her job paid reasonably well, and she got a week of paid time off each year—with no accumulation of paid time off from year to year, of course. But benefits? Too expensive for a company that would rather pad their bottom line. She'd been scrolling through job listings in every spare moment of time at work, and damn near none of them offered benefits. Most of the ones that did sounded awful and soul-sucking, but she'd applied to the few that didn't sound completely intolerable.

She'd always been careful with her money, trying to walk the fine line between financial responsibility and allowing herself to enjoy life, but her savings wouldn't pay for the *first* round of chemo. She could afford a hospital gown and a high five from an overworked nurse, but those wouldn't keep the cancer from killing her.

Nothing would.

Her phone buzzed in the center console, and she squeezed her eyes shut, her heart aching so fiercely it made her breath catch. She knew without looking who the text was from, and horror for her family clawed at her throat. The cancer might kill her, but her death might kill her parents. Oh hell, her brothers . . .

A hot tear burned down her cheek.

Her hand shook when she reached for her phone, and it took twice as long as it should have to unlock it and open the text from her mom.

Mothership: *So?*

Lily's heart lurched. "Fuck." She choked, dropping her head back. Her backpack sat in the passenger seat, packed for a weekend at her parents' house. She'd hoped it would be a celebratory visit. Self-loathing and fear rose like a tide, threatening to drown her. In a surge of helpless, defiant rage, Lily reached for the key, twisting it mercilessly hard. With a pause and a whine of effort, the engine started and purred quietly. She briefly wondered if it was a hopeful omen before dismissing the idea and just being thankful for the small mercy.

"Okay," she said quietly. Then again, with more conviction. "Okay."

She sat up, swiping at her eyes, and took a deep, steadying breath, then another. She checked herself in the rearview mirror, hating the truth she saw in her own hazel eyes. She had a couple of hours on the road to think, and she would need every second of them.

Her response to her mom was brief, but it was all she could manage.

Lily: *I'll tell you when I get there. See you in a bit. Love you.*

2

PASSING

Lily

In the end, dying was both a massive pain in the ass and a relief.

As the symptoms progressed, she'd tried to explain to her friends and family that, while the physical pain was omnipresent and did indeed royally suck, the knowledge that the pain would eventually end was comforting. Only a few of them were able to get it.

For most, like her parents and brothers, the situation was still too raw for them to be able to take that observation in, and they'd told her not to think so negatively. Part of her had wanted to scream.

She was losing everything. Wasting away, bit by bit, she ached down to her bones with a chronic pain that over-the-counter medications couldn't hope to touch. She sat with the knowledge that all of her dreams, her goals, and her hopes had died long before her body would. If she took comfort in the end, it didn't mean that she loved them any less, that she didn't hate knowing the pain her death would cause them.

Didn't they know that? Didn't they know she would stay if she could?

The utter unfairness of it made it hard to bite her tongue, but she tried. If she could get through the conversations that immediately followed her diagnosis—some of the most painful of her life—she could do this too. She knew that it was her pain and fear that had her quietly resenting every mournful or overly positive comment and every long look they gave her. All she had to do was die, and with death would come the end of the pain, but they would have to live with the memory of it. Of her. So, she'd swallowed the bitterness and rage down—mostly—and tried to give them as many good days and things to remember her by as she could.

She'd written letters for them, especially for her brothers, sat and talked with her mom for hours, marathoned all the old Godzilla movies with her dad. She'd cleared her apartment and didn't tell anyone how she'd drifted through the rooms, numbly wondering what to sell, who to leave certain things to, what she would need or want to the end, before she'd laughed and sobbed over the memories and hopes attached to different items. She tried not to burden them when she had the choice, painfully aware of how she'd had to move back in with her parents to prepare for the inevitable and rapidly approaching decline to the end.

She tried to be cheerful for them.

Her genial attitude had its limits, however, and those limits made themselves rather abruptly known every time one of her religious relatives or her parents' well-meaning church friends pushed the idea of faith healing on her or urged her to reconvert before her death. In a particularly ballsy move, a former college roommate named Kaitlyn had emerged from the depths of social media and taken the opportunity to tout the healing abilities of her essential oils. She'd been more than happy to offer to sell Lily a bottle or twelve and stated that it worked best when combined with prayer. Lily's temper had definitely slipped the leash then, and she'd spent the rest of that week trying to be as pleasant as possible to everyone around her to make up for it.

It crept up on her though, until she wasn't strong enough to hide it anymore. The pain. The fatigue. The way breathing had grown more and more difficult. Her utter lack of appetite and frequent bouts of nausea had made her body weak and skeletal, any movement sapping what little strength she had. She didn't want to go, but she didn't want to linger in the prison of her failing body either.

A deep, primal part of her felt it coming one evening. Her heart had beat a little bit harder in defiance of the inevitable but had stayed steady until the end. She'd hugged her parents a little tighter that night.

When death came for her, it was bittersweet.

But nothing hurt anymore.

3

CELESTIAL LOBBY

Lily

Lily stared into the swirling expanse of everything and nothing for a few seconds, for an eternity, and felt . . . nothing.

Odd.

She was supposed to feel too much. After all, that had always been the problem before. She remembered struggling to express her feelings, but she'd never lacked them.

In any of her lifetimes.

Oh. She remembered those, vaguely.

A child, huddled against the sharp bite of cold until it wasn't so sharp or cold, but she was so tired. A young woman with flames licking up her skirt, skin melting, acrid air searing her lungs. A teenage girl in rags, starving, starving, starving. The newest face, her face, older than she'd ever been, but sick and thin and pale.

What fucking bullshit. She hadn't managed to grow old at least once? Unacceptable.

There. Not a feeling, but something. Enough to propel her toward a door that had always and never been there. It swung open soundlessly, revealing . . . she didn't know, but she stepped through it anyway.

She blinked. Blinked and—oh thank fuck—*felt*. Emotions and sensations washed over her like a cooling rain, grounding her, reminding her that she still *was*. The apathy of the in-between hadn't been bad, but it hadn't been good either. It, like her, hadn't been anything.

Lily pressed her palm against her chest, searching for the reassuring pulse of life, but it was nowhere to be found. A hollow, jarring quiet sat in its place, her heart still beneath her hand. Grief, potent and swift, stole the air from her lungs in a rush.

She'd been no more or less aware of her heartbeat than anyone before her diagnosis, but ever since she'd found out that her beats were more numbered than she'd thought, she'd savored each one. The silence under her palm was just another reminder of the fight she'd lost, of her failure.

Lily dropped her hand, squeezing her eyes closed. *Breathe in. Hold. Breathe out.*

When she felt a little more like herself again, she opened her eyes and took in her oddly familiar surroundings. It was reminiscent of a cathedral, though it was built on a scale that human hands could never hope to achieve, with a ceiling towering so high above her that its shape and details were hopelessly obscured. The shifting golden light emanating nebulously from it was pretty, gilding the edges of delicate puffs of mist that wafted like clouds high above.

Sounds trickled into her awareness, and she pulled her gaze from the ceiling just in time to see a man in a suit appear next to her, walking through a door that quickly disappeared. He looked around for only a second before reaching up and tugging his tie loose, striding forward with languid ease. Lily watched him go, then studied the room. Eclectic rows of seating stretched into the distance, armchairs, pews, cushions, prayer mats, benches, some of them occupied by people—souls, she realized—who were, for whatever reasons, waiting. On the far side of the space, she could make out a line of what looked like, and what instinct told her were, desks.

Lily took one step forward, then another, marveling at how easy it was to move again. Missing heartbeat aside, she felt like she had in her late twenties when she'd been at her most athletic and moving her body had been *fun*. Damn, it had been so long since she'd had fun.

Some of the seated souls who she passed had a crackling, angry energy to them. Others were so serene that peace radiated from them like light. Still others were twitchy, or stunned, or sad, or looking around curiously.

Lily didn't stop to talk to any of them, just kept heading toward those oddly important desks that weren't actually that far at all.

Stretching in an unbroken line from the wall on her right to a set of pillars framing the entrance to a massive hallway off to her left, the desks were a hive of voices and activity. They were set up like bank teller desks, with rich, dark wood and solid dividers separating the desks and their occupants from their neighbors. People of all ages, nationalities, and, seemingly—if their attire was an indication—time periods sat behind the desks, talking to the equally diverse souls who sat in the lush, comfortable-looking wingback chairs before them.

A red-faced man slammed his meaty fist on the desk of a woman in Victorian dress, who simply arched an unimpressed eyebrow over her oversized mug of tea and repeated herself in a crisp, no-nonsense voice.

A little boy, barely more than a toddler, hugged a teddy bear tightly to his side, staring wide-eyed but unafraid at the androgynous person who held his hand and spoke gently to him as they walked toward an elevator made of light.

"It takes a moment to get used to, I know," a soft, cheerful voice said.

Lily looked down, startled to find herself standing directly in front of one of the desks.

A Middle Eastern woman wearing a hijab in a delicate shade of pink smiled up at her, gesturing to the wingback chair. "You're welcome to sit if you like and take as long as you need to process."

Lily sank down, dimly noting that it would make a wonderful reading chair. "I remember this. A bit."

The woman smiled. "It's not so bad if you've done it before, is it?"

Lily smiled back. "Not bad at all. I'm Lily."

"I know." The woman chuckled, holding up a file. "I'm Siedah."

"Nice to meet you, Siedah." The chair really was comfortable.

"I'll help guide you through your options for the Afterlife when you're ready. I'm happy to answer any questions you might have if you need immediate answers to help you adjust, or we can just sit together for a time."

Oh, she had questions. But as she considered which to ask, a vague recollection came to her about her previous deaths.

"If my memory serves me right, this process is fairly thorough and self-explanatory. Though"—Lily frowned, annoyed that her memories were so hazy—"I can't quite remember what that process or explanation is."

"That's very normal," Siedah assured her warmly. "You'll find that impressions and feelings of past lives are going to be far more prevalent than details or fully formed memories . . . unless you are looking through your soul file, of course. Your most recent life will remain clear to you until you decide to reincarnate."

Lily nodded, eyes dropping to the file in Siedah's hand.

Her soul file. A tangible, unfettered manifestation of everything she'd ever been.

Not exactly light reading.

"Then can you remind me of the process, please? I'm a 'more rather than less information' type."

Siedah smiled before answering. "Your options are as varied as the beliefs of humanity. There are a few, shall we say, *umbrella* beliefs— Christianity for example, with all of its different denominations and offshoots and adaptations. There isn't a dedicated Judgment system and Afterlife for each, but there is a generalized process based on the core, essential values outlined by the Universe and in the case of *that* belief, God. This keeps things like cults from gaining legitimacy for their corrupt values and actions."

Lily tilted her head back, absorbing the implications of what Siedah had just said. "So, in the case of, say, Hinduism, does the Universe work with the Hindu deities to decide the Judgment system and process?"

Siedah brightened. "Yes, precisely." She tilted her head slightly to the side. "Although, while each belief system has its own system of Judgment, there are a few Universal Constants, such as valuing kindness and condemning extreme cruelty.

"There is also Universal Judgment, which is based on no specific faith or creed, but leads to the same basic results as anything else. The realm of Paradise doesn't have any particular faith attached to it, and souls who reside there have their own unique Paradise." Siedah paused, smiling softly. "It's easier to see it than to have it explained, but does that make sense so far?"

"It does. So, all the deities and beliefs in history . . ." Lily trailed off, looking at Siedah expectantly.

She beamed. "If you can think of it, it's here, as long as it wasn't based in cruelty."

The white-knuckled grip Lily had on the armrests loosened a little. The confirmation that the Greek pantheon actually existed, and that the Polynesian pantheons did too, was pretty fucking cool. She'd wondered if all religions had been a little right and a little wrong. "Okay, so what happens after Judgment?"

"After passing through Judgment, souls who have been judged well will go to the 'paradise realm' of their preference. Using the example of Islam, this would be the levels of Jannah. For Christianity, it would be Heaven, and so on. That is, unless the soul prefers otherwise. These souls are free to move about the Afterlife and its many realms as they wish, within the bounds of respect and courtesy, of course.

"Think of it as a neighborhood. You have your own home, your perfect dream home, and you can walk out the front door and visit a friend or a different neighborhood anytime. If you find a neighborhood you'd like to live in more, you can move there. If you are judged well, there are very few places that you cannot go."

"Such as?" Lily asked.

"Well—"

A loud clatter interrupted her. Two desks down, a chair had toppled over backward when the woman occupying it had stood abruptly. Clearly upset, she stood with her hands pressed to her face. Lily raised her eyebrows and braced for a possible tantrum.

"I can't deal with anything else until I find out what's going to happen to my dog! I don't have an automatic feeder for him, and I lived on my own, and now he's all alone and I can't . . . I . . . *please*."

Oh. That was a fairly reasonable thing to be concerned about.

The attendant said something that seemed to calm the woman down enough that she righted the chair and sat.

Siedah cleared her throat. "Are you all right?"

Lily nodded, hoping the woman's dog would be okay. "Yeah, I'm good. So, where can't souls go?"

"The Void, which is a final option for all, regardless of how they are judged." A thread of sadness entered Siedah's tone. "The Void is where souls go to stop existing, as much as they are able. Often those who choose the Void are souls who have lived hundreds of lives, or souls who have lived many hard lives and find themselves tired in the way that only souls can be. Sometimes souls who have lived perfectly normal lives choose to go there, because it's their peace. Some atheists choose to go there because that is what they believed in. If you are judged favorably, you can go there temporarily; some find comfort in not *being* for a short while. That's the only place in the Afterlife that you cannot visit someone. Contact between the other Universes is exceptionally rare, but they are off-limits as well, unless you are an ambassador to one."

Lily decided to inquire about the "other Universes" bit later, focusing on the information at hand. "So, it really is all a choice?"

"Oh yes, the Universe is quite big on choice. Now, you can't choose to go to one of the paradise realms this very moment. You can choose how you wish to be judged, and then if you go to a paradise, then you can choose which one. Most souls stay within their beliefs, but some like to shake it up a bit."

Lily studied her. The mental picture Siedah had painted was intriguing, but there were a few glaring omissions from her explanation that had prickles itching up her spine.

She steeled herself before asking, "And if I don't go to Paradise?"

Siedah's smile grew sad. "Souls who are judged unfavorably can make a limited choice. They are given a handful of options of so-called punishment realms to choose from. If they refuse to choose in an attempt to avoid consequences, they will be sent to Hell. Much like Paradise, its existence predates all religions and myths. It has long served as the faith-neutral realm of justice."

She set Lily's soul file on the desk and clasped her hands on top of it. "So, there technically is a choice, but there is no way to escape consequences. Full freedom of choice is reserved for souls who won't abuse that power."

"Good," Lily said.

Siedah's eyebrows lifted. Her dark, pretty eyes were considering.

Lily shrugged, once-agonizing memories merely aching as they flickered through her mind. "Too many people abuse the power of choice. Too many people take the power of choice away from others. I like justice. Especially when it can't be argued."

Siedah studied her for a long moment. Lily held her gaze, not sure what the other woman was seeing or what she already knew.

Siedah looked at the file on the desk. "I haven't read this, you know. I only get the first page, which is your basic information and outstanding notes. I don't know your story, and I won't pretend to know you." Siedah gently slid the file across the desk. The glimmering metallic letters of Lily's name shimmered in a kaleidoscope of colors across the smooth, dove-gray paper. She nodded at the file. "Your story is yours to keep. Yours to share."

"Thank you," Lily said.

"I would like to, though," Siedah added softly.

Lily frowned up at her.

"Know you, I mean." The other woman inclined her head slightly, her hijab rustling as it moved over her shirt. "I believe I would like to know your story too. This is Eternity, and you can never have too many friends."

Lily shot her a wry grin. "I could be a terrible person. Like, a Universally certified terrible person, depending on how this next part goes. I'll be the first to tell you that I can be mouthy."

Siedah cocked her head, amused. "Mouthy doesn't automatically make you a bad person. If it did, I would have far fewer coworkers."

An Asian man leaned around the divider behind the desk, grinning impishly. "How boring would that be? You would miss us."

"I would," Siedah agreed, waving him back to his side of the divider before returning her attention to Lily. "Terrible sometimes doesn't mean terrible all the time. I'm not the Universe, or even a deity, but even I can tell that you aren't truly terrible."

Lily reached to pull her file closer, the dove-gray paper warm under her fingertips. "I appreciate the vote of confidence."

"We all need one sometimes," Siedah said. "I certainly did when I arrived."

Lily hummed in agreement, tracing the letters of her name with her left hand, which looked—

Ice rushed through her veins, freezing her in place, and sucking the air out of her lungs. She shoved the sleeve of her shirt up, a new wave of horror hitting with every inch of revealed skin.

No.

Her tattoos were gone. They had been one of the first things in her life she had done purely for herself, and getting them had helped heal her in ways that she hadn't anticipated. They had been a celebration of her passions, of her interests, of *her*. She'd had them all done in black and gray, and had spent years carefully curating the ones on her arm to be a cohesive patchwork.

A delicate filigree, woven from wrist to shoulder, to help the designs tie together. The stack of books twined with her favorite flowers on her forearm. The illustration of a dragon and a mountain from *The Hobbit*, as well as a round door with a little backpack beside it. A line from one of her favorite songs near the crease of her elbow. The Evenstar from *Lord of the Rings* on her inner biceps. A quote from one of her favorite books above that. The snake coiled among lines of filigree and stargazer lilies trailing along the outside of her upper arm.

She didn't need to look to confirm that her back, ribs, hip, and thigh were all missing the ink she'd loved so much.

All of them. Gone.

A slender brown hand settled over hers, snapping her out of her spiraling grief.

Siedah's eyes were understanding but firm. "Tattoos?"

Lily nodded, not trusting her voice.

"You can get them back after Judgment. They can be the same, or they can be different, and you can change them at will. As a soul, your appearance isn't as fixed as it was when you were alive. But only after Judgment."

"Well, that's a relief." Lily forced herself to relax and flash a smile. "And a hell of an incentive."

"I once had a man come through who had been heavily tattooed and was inconsolable for an hour before I managed to explain the situation to him. I've never seen someone leave the chair so quickly. I saw him in the Universal Hallway some time later, happy as a clam and covered in his art again. Personally, my incentive was the potential of limitless spice cakes." Siedah grinned.

Lily's smile turned genuine. If Judgment went well, what awaited her? What would coffee be like in the Afterlife? Oh, the *books*. There had to be so many new books!

She picked up her file, a thrum of reality disrupting her hopeful train of thought. She knew herself, who she had been, who she had become. The good, the bad. All of it. Siedah seemed to have faith that she would be judged favorably, but Lily wasn't so sure.

She sucked in a deep breath that she didn't need, but the habit sure felt good.

Fuck it.

"In that case, I'll go with Universal Judgment."

Siedah beamed. "Excellent. Would you like some company?"

4

A BIT JUDGMENTAL

Lily

Lily waited for Siedah at the pillars framing the massive hallway, gazing at some of the souls who sat waiting. An elderly man sat quietly on a park bench, a peaceful smile on his weathered face, hands clasped in his lap. His file—thicker than Lily's—rested beside him, but he just calmly watched the souls at the line of desks as if they were pigeons at the park. He must have caught her staring, because he met her eyes with a smile and a nod before going back to watching the souls.

"He's waiting." Siedah's voice drew her attention to where the other woman stood at her side.

Lily was unsurprised to find that she towered over the other woman. At six feet tall, and with a fondness for high heels, she'd seldom had to look up at someone.

"He's not ready to be judged yet?" Lily asked.

"Yes and no. He's received his file, and he's selected his method of Judgment, but he's waiting for his wife." Siedah smiled. "It was their third lifetime together. Their stories are beautiful ones. Powerful. Sometimes heartbreaking."

"Three lifetimes?" Lily's silent chest ached, as if her useless heart still had the capacity to break.

"I know. We're all very fond of him. He's very sweet. Would you like to talk to him?"

Three lifetimes together. What would that kind of love and devotion even look like? *Feel* like? No one had ever wanted her like that, and certainly not in her last lifetime. Her romantic life had been a short string of hookups, unrequited crushes, and politely declining offers from people she just hadn't clicked with. Before that . . . all she had were dim flickers of memory from old lifetimes.

An arranged marriage to a man she didn't love, but who had been decent enough. He'd loved someone else. The blacksmith's daughter maybe? But her husband had never strayed physically or beaten her. She didn't think he'd mourned her when she'd been falsely accused of being a witch and burned at the stake. Had he ever married the woman he actually wanted, or had his first wife's alleged witch-ness ruined his chances?

In another lifetime, she vaguely remembered being hungry and wondering if she really had feelings for the young man with the chestnut cart, or if she'd just wanted the food he sold.

The memories from her most recent life flared hot and bright. Most prominently, a drunken moment of honesty from some frat guy at a party in college. *You're good enough for a quick hookup, but not worth the effort of dating, you know? You're hot but a lot.* He'd been so pleased with his inadvertent rhyme that he'd taught it to others, and "hot but a lot" had followed her for months.

She'd known it was a horseshit sentiment from the moment it was said, but for the rest of her life, in weak moments, there had been an insidious little voice in her mind that had whispered that maybe he had been right. Maybe she was too much. Too sharp, too sarcastic, too independent, took things too seriously, had feelings that were too big. She'd worked so damn hard to grow, to overcome her traumas, to smooth the roughest of her edges and dull the worst of her sharp tongue. It had never seemed to make a difference in the ways she'd wanted it to.

Three lifetimes.

Her longest "relationship" had been a monthlong friends-with-benefits situation with a woman from her Rhetorical Criticism class whom she'd never seen again.

"No," she choked, then cleared her throat. "No, thank you."

Siedah gestured to the hallway without a hint of pity or judgment. Lily fell into step beside her, adjusting her stride to match the shorter woman's as they left the cavernous main room behind. Souls walked with them, heading to various doors, arches, and gates set into walls that shifted and moved like pastel clouds under glass. A few souls walked against the flow of people, nodding a greeting to Siedah as they passed.

"Coworkers?" Lily asked.

"Some of them; others work elsewhere and are just running errands. All souls pass through the Front Desk, so if there is a paperwork issue with a soul, we tend to deal with it."

"Someone missed a golden opportunity to call it the Front Death-k," Lily mused, watching a soul peer up at a pearlescent arch before walking into the golden mist inside it.

Siedah laughed. "I'll add it to the name suggestions in the break room. People will love it."

Before either of them could say anything else, a set of elevator doors dinged open. A being walked out with an armful of stapled papers, looking harried. Towering over everyone in the hallway, Lily included, they appeared to be female, with fine features, an aquiline nose, and a body built along powerful, athletic lines. Smooth, navy-blue skin was offset by a dark-gray shirt, black jerkin, and leggings, all decorated with intricate embroidery along the hems and paired with immaculately buffed, calf-high boots. A pair of spiraling black horns near her temples gleamed in the shifting golden light, their bases hidden in the being's straight, blue-black hair.

"Moura," Siedah said, surprise coloring her tone. "Everything all right?"

The being—Moura, apparently—stopped mid-stride with an exasperated sigh.

"No. Fucking souls. They've been judged by the system *of their choosing*. Sent to Hell by that system. And yet, they still have the mortal audacity to complain and blame us, whose only job at the gate is to guide them to where they need to go." She scoffed. "This morning, we had a group of them claim that we managed to steal them and drag them down there. Drag them! As if they don't *take the stairs themselves*. The more they complained, the longer they held up the whole process, the busier we got, and then this happened." Moura hefted the armful of paperwork. "Souls who actually *needed* guidance didn't get it, and now we have to go find them and figure out where they're supposed to be."

A long, tapered tail the same color as Moura's skin lashed behind her, reminding Lily of an annoyed cat. She found herself nodding along in sympathy. After spending her whole working life in some form of customer service, she could relate all too well to the miserable frustration of trying to deal with people who had seemingly little common sense and more than their fair share of audacity. She hadn't expected to relate so well to what she suspected was a demon, but the Afterlife seemed to be full of surprises.

Moura adjusted the stack of paperwork on her arm. "These are the reports for the ones that I could track down today, but I just know some poor soul is sitting down there—probably on Level Nine, knowing our luck—throwing off someone else's paperwork. Universe help them if they *are* on Level Nine. He *hates* it when—"

The elevator dinged again, and an equally tall but slightly younger-looking demon stepped out, holding yet more paperwork. His cherry-red skin and bull-like horns fit the traditional idea of a demon, but between his short white hair and the gray T-shirt he wore under his jerkin, he looked far more . . . human. His handsome, sculpted features were almost *too* sculpted, but a quick grimace animated his otherwise imperious face.

"A few more, Captain," he said apologetically.

Siedah hummed, glancing back toward the Front Desk. "Marcus should be getting back from his break right about now. He loves fussing over these kinds of problems, and I'll lend a hand when I'm done here."

Both demons turned their eyes, green for her and gold for him, onto Lily. The instinctive flash of intimidation faded as she took a moment to really look at them. For all their height and horns and fangs, which she'd seen peeking through their lips as they spoke, they were just like her. How many times had she and her coworkers bitched about ridiculous customers and even more ridiculous requests and demands? How many times had she grimaced the exact same way over the prospect of more paperwork? Customer service was a bonding experience. She got it.

She offered a wave, immediately feeling like an idiot, but committing to it anyway. *You can get away with a lot of things if you do them with confidence.*

"If I knew the solution to dealing with idiots, I'd share it with you. Sadly, I just had to vent to friends and soothe myself with wine or chocolate. It didn't solve the problem, but it sure made me feel better."

Moura's face brightened into a grin, and a passing soul flinched and took several running steps away. Lily grinned back.

The red demon chuckled. "It's nice to remember not all souls are complete fuckwits."

"Eh." Lily shook her hand back and forth. "You caught me on a good day."

The demons laughed outright, and even Siedah gave a little chuckle. The irreverent banter and vague camaraderie with other service workers were as familiar as breathing.

As their laughter eased, Moura's eyes gentled as she looked at Lily. "Are you heading for Judgment?"

Throat tight, Lily nodded, trying for a *what-can-I-say* smile.

Moura clapped her lightly on her shoulder with a large hand. The unexpected heat and familiarity of her touch made Lily blink.

"If you make it through on the decent side, come have that glass of wine with us. We can swap stories." Her hand dropped away, and her smile dimmed. "And if you do end up on the other side, well, do us a favor and don't make a fuss."

"I'll see what I can do." Lily smiled, though her voice sounded strange to her own ears.

With friendly nods and farewells, the two demons strode away, tails flicking absently as they spoke to each other. A male soul walking toward them practically leapt to the side to get out of their way, pressing himself flat to the wall.

Siedah's smile was kind as she turned to Lily. "Thank you for being so nice to them. The demons get a bad rap from mortals, and sometimes the uninitiated souls they encounter can be . . ."

"Judgmental?" Lily supplied wryly.

"Quite. They're different, but they're a lovely people. They usually avoid the Entrance Hall to keep from, uh, causing a scene."

Lily glanced in the direction they'd walked, watching their horns moving into the distance. The souls parted around them like a school of fish avoiding a shark.

If I'd known demons looked like that, I wouldn't have had such an irrational fear of letting my foot hang over the edge of the bed. Hell, I might've done it on purpose.

Lily mused over the thought, curious. Hopefully, having a high sex drive wasn't a bad thing when it came to the Universe's idea of right and wrong, though she couldn't fathom why it might be.

So, she'd read some particularly filthy monster romances in the name of— Fuck! Her reading history! Oh *fuck*, her search history! She'd had the presence of mind to throw away her collection of vibrators and toys before she'd gotten really sick, not wanting to traumatize her family any more than she already had. But oh, oh *no*, her little library of monster and kinky romance novels . . . Shit, her mom *absolutely* would have seen those—

A soft hand on her arm snapped her attention back to the present.

"It's okay, really." Siedah's face was kind. "Judgment isn't that bad; the Universe has a sense of humor."

For a brief, horrifying moment, Lily wondered if Siedah was some kind of Afterlife mind reader.

"Even if I'm wrong and you don't get your Paradise, if you choose to go to Hell, I promise you that the demons are just. They can be terrifying, but they are not needlessly cruel. Hell is a place of justice and, for those who are willing, growth."

It seemed that the years of practice keeping her face neutral, even while reading toe-curling smut in public, had paid off. Siedah had mistaken her nerves for something more benign.

Lily dipped her head in acknowledgment and murmured a thank-you, following quietly when Siedah kept walking.

A man stepped out of an elevator with a cell phone that Lily didn't recognize pressed to his ear. ". . . of course I'd be interested in running a new D&D campaign, but if the Monkey King is involved, I want nothing to do with it. Having Loki as a rogue in that one campaign was enough trickster god experience for one eternity . . ."

Lily twisted and walked backward for a few steps to watch him hustle toward the Front Desk, still talking into his phone. *They have D&D here?* She turned back around, watching souls line up and go through various arches and doors that all opened into different swirling mists. A few souls sat petulantly against the walls, and a couple in the middle of the floor, like toddlers protesting nap time.

"What happens with them?" she asked, nodding to a particularly huffy-looking woman.

"They sit there until they get bored enough to go through with Judgment. They can always go to the Void, of course, but otherwise, unjudged souls cannot leave the Front Desk or the Entrance Hall until they go through some form of Judgment."

"Seems like a waste of eternity," Lily murmured mostly to herself as they passed the woman.

Siedah stopped in front of an arch set into the swirling wall. The stone was smooth and undecorated, unlike most of the arches they'd passed, but danced with a vibrant rainbow of color. Through the arch itself, nothing was visible but a solid gray haze. The noise and bustle of the hallway around them faded, Lily's attention pinpointed on the arch.

What a simple thing. What a simple culmination of life and death and experience and loss. Decades of *being* and all the lifetimes before that, all to stand before an arch filled with gray. The file in her hand suddenly seemed heavy. She knew what was in it, in her. The moments of kindness and cruelty. The mistakes, the triumphs, the sheer dumb luck, the motivations behind actions.

What if—

She shut the thought down hard before it had a chance to fully form. The Universe wouldn't care that she'd never been wanted like that, loved like that. Romantic love, or the lack of it, didn't make a person better or worse at their core. *She* was to be judged. *Her* life, *her* actions. She wasn't unlovable. She'd loved her family and friends with her whole heart, and they had loved her, each in their own way.

She'd known love, and she'd known herself.

Tearing her eyes away from the arch, she looked at Siedah. Her smile was gentle, eyes bright and understanding against the soft pink of her hijab. She offered Lily one slim hand. Lily gripped it, probably too hard, but Siedah simply squeezed back.

Lily sucked in a deep breath and stared into the gray. It didn't move. Gave nothing away. Might as well have been a solid wall.

But there was *something* on the other side of that gray. She knew it. What it was, she didn't have the faintest idea, but it called her. Beckoned and dared her to come see, to open a book with no description and a blank cover and see where the story would take her.

Hand slipping from Siedah's, she stepped forward into the gray.

Running through the yard as a child, long auburn hair bright in the sun, a fistful of daisies clutched in one pudgy little hand.

The kitchen light turning on as her parents caught her in the act of climbing down from the counter with the bag of chocolate chips.

Calling the girl she hated for stealing her colored pencils a "butthead," the foulest word in her vocabulary, and getting a letter sent home to her parents. The spanking afterwards.

Curling against her dad's side while he read to her at bedtime, his voice pitching lower for Gandalf's dialogue.

Stealing wine from her parents as a teenager.

The endless refrain of "going to Hell, going to Hell, going to Hell" screaming though her mind whenever she did something her youth pastor had strictly told them not to do, but especially when she showed skin below her collarbones and especially—especially—when she'd made out with the cute skater boy behind the track shed.

Saying "fuck" for the first time, and liking how it felt.

Making her mom cry during a fight.

Reading a book out loud to the kids she babysat and doing funny voices to make them giggle.

Taking a blade to her skin when the guilt and pain had been too much to keep in her head.

Being the getaway driver for a friend escaping an abusive boyfriend.

Wearing a string bikini in public for the first time and being so scared that she would instantly trapdoor to Hell that she'd thrown up in the bathroom.

Her first tattoo, and the singing relief of feeling a piece of her click into place.

Searing jealousy that the bitchy, hyper-religious girl from youth group had gotten married before she did.

Flirting with a woman at a party for the first time and loving it, but waking up in a cold sweat that night, terrified that she'd secured her place among the damned.

Quietly crawling into her mom's lap—despite being twenty-seven and nearly a foot taller than her mother—when that same bitchy girl had had her first baby and she'd felt so lonely and hopeless that she'd just needed to be held.

Hating herself for the building resentment of celebrating all her friends for their weddings, babies, and homes, and never being the one who was celebrated. Knowing it was stupid, feeling hollow inside anyway.

The savage glee of verbally sparring with her friend's aunt, Linda. Being outlandish to prove a point and make Linda's lesbian daughter feel a little less alone.

Watching her mom's heart shatter in the kitchen when she'd revealed her diagnosis.

Hours of Mario Kart with her brothers when the cancer had begun to take its toll, wishing she could watch them grow as men, grow old, and poke fun at each other as only siblings could, knowing she was ripping their hearts out with her decision.

Hours and a lifetime spent working on herself, fighting to be better, failing sometimes, her sharp tongue slicing like a knife, even as her brain begged her to shut up.

Trying to live. Trying to die, once. Trying to be kinder. Trying to be worse. Trying to make an impact. Trying to not make things worse. Trying to love better. Trying to heal.

Trying.

5

FRESH OUT
OF FUCKS

Lily

The scents hit her first.

Fresh air, wildflowers, cut grass, good food, woodsmoke, all carried by a warm breeze that tickled over her skin and tugged at her hair.

Paradise.

She'd made it to Paradise.

Lily opened her eyes and squinted, adjusting to the bright, cheerful sunshine. A bird twittered as it swooped past, its mate dancing along on the breeze behind it, the pair of them flying away over lush, rolling green hills dotted with trees, the roofs of cottages, and smoking chimneys, some set right into the ground. A wide, clear stream burbled happily in the distance, cutting right through the center of an idyllic little village full of trees and what looked like canals. A rugged line of small mountains stretched up toward the sky in variegated shades of blue, purple, gray, and green, dropping down to a sparkling fjord, reminding her of home.

Focus shifting to her immediate surroundings, Lily looked down. She stood in a vibrant patch of grass, surrounded by a garden of thriving plants: vegetables, fruit trees, pots and beds of flowers. Bees buzzed as they went from bloom to bloom. A wooden fence stood proudly between her and a well-worn cobbled road, the gate a delicate swirl of wrought iron.

A familiar purring chirp that she hadn't heard in more than a decade had her whipping around in disbelief.

Her childhood cat, Max, trotted out of a patch of strawberries, his black-on-white fur gleaming in the sun, fluffy tail straight up in greeting. He mashed his little head against her shin before she could react, rubbing his whole body against her leg and purring with all his might. Eyes stinging, Lily scooped him up and buried her face in his sun-warmed fur, laughing and crying all at once.

"I knew you'd be here," she told him, grinning as he shoved his head against her cheek affectionately. She'd been six when they'd brought him home as a kitten, and twenty-three when she'd had to put him down to ease his pain.

"Sweet boy," she told him, scratching under his chin the way he'd always liked. "You were my best boy."

Hours of homework and agonizing over writing various essays had been spent and eased with Max's weight on her lap or curled behind her on the seat. She'd missed him every day, and often considered getting another cat, but she'd been unwilling to put them through her frequent moves.

A tear rolled down her cheek, dripping to gleam on Max's fur as she loosed a sigh of relief.

It's okay. I'm *okay.*

Lily turned in search of the house that would go with the garden and burst out laughing. Painted her favorite shade of deep purple and decorated with elegant swirls of wrought iron, an iconically round door beckoned her to explore the house half set into a hill. Wisteria tumbled around a span of large windows to her left, the reflection of the distant mountains keeping her from seeing inside. Her feet skimmed over the stone path that led to the door, and she half expected the whole scene to fade away into nothing at any moment. The sun-warmed metal of the doorknob was solid under her touch. A faint hum of something pleasant went up her arm, followed by a wash of peace. Like she was finally home after a long journey.

The door swung open soundlessly, revealing an entryway with

smooth, wide-planked wood floors and parchment-colored walls stretching up to high barrel-vaulted ceilings. Ahead of her and to the left, a wide, arched doorway led into what looked like a living room, and straight ahead lay a pair of double doors with a hallway to the left of them. A closet door was tucked into the wall on her right, the wood polished but lightly worn, and directly on her left a cushioned bench offered a convenient place to put on and take off shoes. Hanging above the bench was a picture that stole her breath and nearly made her drop Max.

It was a moment there had been no real picture of, but she remembered every detail of it all the same.

She and her brothers had hiked out to some cliffs overlooking the sea and ended up scrambling down to a lower level to feel the spray on their faces as the waves crashed against the rocks. It had been ridiculous and reckless, and they'd all sworn never to tell their parents, despite the fact that they'd all been in their twenties. After some playful roasting of each other, and one or two or six threats to shove each other over the edge of the cliff, they'd ended up standing next to each other, laughing at a seagull trying and failing to eat a starfish.

The picture hanging on the wall had captured that moment: the three of them laughing next to each other, their hair gleaming in the sun, each a different shade of red, faces wet with sea spray, eyes bright with adventure and the joy of being *alive*. She stared at her brothers' frozen, laughing faces, wondering for the millionth time if she had done more harm than good.

"Don't you know those things will kill you?" Ryan said, dropping down next to her on the roof of their parents' house. He held his hand out for the cigar Lily had swiped from their dad's secret stash. Stealing it was a petty retaliation after a conversation turned fight, and she was smoking out of spite. Just like they all had as teenagers. She held it out of his reach.

"I knew there was something I was forgetting," Lily drawled, taking a long inhale of smoke. She didn't even like it really, but what the hell, she was already dying. She blew out a stream of smoke, rolling the fat cigar between her fingers and wondering if Ryan would be more receptive than their dad.

"Do shots at my funeral. That's what I want," she said, tipping her head

back to look at the stars. "I mean, it doesn't have to be shots, but don't let the stupid thing turn into this boring recital of reverent bullshit where everyone lies about how wonderful of a person I was. Tell all the stories I told you never to tell Mom. Put the 'fun' in funeral. Get good cake. I will haunt your asses if you have bad cake at my funeral."

"So, the opposite of Grandma's funeral, got it," Ryan said, stealing the cigar from her before she could react.

They sat in silence, passing the cigar back and forth until she snubbed it out, tendrils of smoke wafting up toward the stars.

Ryan's tight hug came out of nowhere and took her aback. Her youngest brother wasn't really affectionate.

"You don't have to haunt me full-time, but haunt me sometimes, okay?" he murmured, wiry arms squeezing her a little tighter.

She hugged him back, throat tight and mind spinning. "I will. Tell you what, just to keep you on your toes, I'll—"

A tear burned its way down her cheek, jerking her out of the past. She swiped at it, turning away to deposit Max on the floor, where he insisted on rubbing against her legs like a menace.

A happy day. This was a happy day, and she would face that particular guilt when she was ready. If she was ever ready. She took a deep breath, laden with the scents of flowers and freshly baked bread, held it, savored it, and released it slowly, along with the torrent of less savory emotions.

A happy fucking day, Lily.

Emotions under control, she turned her focus to exploring. Her suspicions about the room to the left had been correct. The arched doorway led into a bright, comfortable living room with plush, cozy-looking furniture and an abundance of blankets. The large windows she'd noticed outside allowed sunlight to spill in, and the sweeping views they offered were stunning enough to make her breath catch. Opposite the windows, a large fireplace with a merrily crackling fire drew her attention. The flames seemed to dance on top of the wood rather than consume it, almost like a gas fireplace, but it smelled and behaved like wood fire. Max had abandoned his plea for attention and taken up residence on the stone hearth, stretched out and absorbing the heat, blinking lazily at her.

To her delight, a trio of already full bookshelves were nestled against the walls, and she recognized a few of the spines at a glance.

Beyond the living room, through another arched doorway, lay the kind of kitchen she'd only ever dreamed about: open and airy, but still cozy, with wood beams on the ceiling, gray stone countertops, and deep teal cabinets. She touched the handle of the double oven reverently before breaking into a laugh. Her favorite dish towel, one that her mother had despised because of the language, hung from the handle of the lower oven. It had been the fastest $12.99 she'd ever spent. Nestled among the beautiful spray of purple and teal and gold flowers, incongruously elegant script declared: *fresh out of fucks*.

Still chuckling, Lily continued. A little dining table was tucked into the sunny back corner of the kitchen, with windows looking out over the hills behind the house, and to the right of the table lay the other end of the hallway she'd glimpsed from the door. Two doors studded the left side, one opening into a decent-sized guest bedroom, perfectly made up and waiting. Eager to see what had to be her room, Lily pushed the next door open.

"Oh," she breathed, swaying a little.

She registered the purple-gray walls and crisp white trim first, shortly followed by the massive rustic mirror in the corner, stretching nearly to the ceiling. The bed, perched on a luxe faux-fur rug, drew her attention next: a king-sized frame with a beautifully upholstered headboard, black comforter and sheets, contrasted by a chunky cream-colored knit throw tossed over the bottom. Every inch of it was a decadent invitation.

Lily took a running leap onto the bed, bouncing once with a laugh before nestling into the puff of blankets.

Divine.

She rolled onto her side and paused, looking at the mirror. Looking *into* the mirror. She arched an eyebrow, pushing herself up to kneel in the middle of the glorious bed, watching her reflection as she did so. *What a perfect angle.*

"Damn, I hope there's sex in the Afterlife," she murmured, pushing her hair back.

As if the house had heard her, something appeared on the sheets before her. A vibrator.

Lily stared at it, then glanced up at the ceiling, feeling only a little insane. "Okay, then. Thanks, I guess?"

A slight rumble shuddered through the house, reminding her of when a truck had driven by her old apartment. Instinct told her that both the rumbling house and the magically appearing vibrator were part and parcel of Paradise, but a mortal lifetime of avoiding anything resembling the beginning of a horror movie had her freezing in place. When nothing else happened and no internal alarm bells went off, she relaxed, scooting off the bed to peer into the adjoining bathroom that, although lacking a toilet, was somehow both luxurious and cozy.

She wandered back out into the hall, toward the one door left unopened. The house was perfectly sized, spacious without being cavernous, cozy but not cramped. Every detail felt right, her familiar favorites and fantasies blended together to create a space that spoke of safety and security and peace. She would have called the house perfect, she mused, pushing open the double doors, if not for the lack of a . . .

She gasped, pressing one hand to her throat as she stepped slowly into the space, turning to look around and verify that she was actually seeing what she thought she was seeing.

The library was twice the size of her living room and soared two stories high, up to a ceiling that swirled with patterns of blue and green and white, like an abstraction of the coast that she'd called home. Two wrought-iron, spiral staircases led up to the second balcony level, and each full bookcase had a sliding ladder just waiting to fulfill her childhood fantasy. The far wall was dominated by a massive floor-to-ceiling mullioned window, with a bed-sized window seat piled with pillows, and a small selection of loungers and cushy chairs were carefully arranged in the central open area. A trio of equally tall but far narrower windows broke up the right wall, allowing more soft light to filter in.

A library. She had a *library*.

She drifted toward the nearest bookcase, running her fingers along the spines, most of them familiar and beloved, old friends that had entertained and amused and hurt and comforted and aroused and in-spired. She paused, staring at her extended hand. Her left hand. Her bare left arm.

I want . . .

The thought had only just fully formed when shadows and lines appeared on her skin, as crisp and vibrant as if they had been freshly tattooed, but without the accompanying redness.

"That's better," she murmured, running her opposite hand over the newly inked skin. The sigh of relief seemed to come from her toes.

She tugged a particularly filthy romance novel, one of her old favorites, off the shelf and headed for a chair to celebrate.

6

A MALL TO DIE FOR

Lily

Lily sat in one of the perfect loungers in the library, toying idly with Max's ear as he dozed in her lap. Steam curled up from the nearly empty mug of tea on the side table as rain tapped lightly on the windows, the restive atmosphere doing nothing to soothe the persistent sensation that she was missing something. It had been little more than a week since she'd arrived in her Paradise, and she'd spent most of it in her library, reading books from authors who had kept writing after their deaths.

She had taken some time to explore a bit of the Paradise beyond her gate. While she wasn't the only one to have the spectacular fantasy land as her Paradise, each home was kept magically private for each resident. They might see each other's chimneys and gates, but they were physically unable to intrude on each other's gardens, unless the person was open to visitors. The picturesque little village and its collection of shops, pubs, and restaurants was mostly a neutral area, with a few pockets of more urban-style Paradise living. The streets often bustled with a wide assortment of people, and Lily had enjoyed chatting with everyone she'd met, but the connections had felt fairly surface level.

She'd texted Siedah, whose contact information had simply appeared in her phone one day, and asked if she wanted to get together. Siedah had responded enthusiastically, congratulating her on her Paradise, but explained that they had a lot of unexpected trainees that she was helping with, and asked for a rain check.

Beyond her driving need to *do* something, curiosity about the rest of the Afterlife had become a constant thought. Siedah had mentioned other realms, like the Underworld and the Summerland, and then there was the standing invitation for wine with the demon Moura, if she hadn't been kidding.

Committing the grave sin of disturbing a cat at rest, Lily gently rearranged Max as she slipped away, leaving him to stretch on the lounger while she downed the last of her tea, excitement trickling through her veins. The dirty mug disappeared from her hand as she headed for the hall, thanks to the house's magic, and she patted the doorframe in acknowledgment.

Shucking off her baggy T-shirt and boxer shorts, she squinted into the closet before deciding not to strive for greatness, pulling out leggings and a charcoal-gray V-neck shirt. She paused in the entryway to pull on some comfortable boots and a lightweight zip-up hoodie, then grabbed the Paradise version of her favorite black leather jacket, which didn't have patches of wear and a hole in the pocket.

She pulled up her hood and stepped outside, the smell of rain curling around her senses as she surveyed the gray skies and damp garden, eyes snagging on a massive new addition. A near-perfect replica of her front door was set into the fence beside her front gate. She glanced behind her to confirm. The only difference was that the door in the fence was inlaid with silver instead of wrought iron.

Paradise Gate.

She blinked. The information came to her from everywhere and nowhere, a flood of information and something she'd always known.

Oh. It was like the door to her apartment versus the door to her apartment *building*.

She closed the door of the house with a click and grinned, boots squeaking on the wet stone pathway. The silver doorknob on the new door twisted smoothly, and Lily stepped through into a massive field that, with different lighting, could easily have passed as the set of a horror movie.

Sourceless golden hour sunlight radiated from a sky that shifted in patchy shades of pastels, but the most striking feature of the new land-scape was the doors—hundreds and thousands of them, scattered over the flat ground and stretching endlessly into the distance.

A dozen paces to her left stood a traditionally shaped door, painted a bright, cheerful red. A similar distance ahead of her stood a door covered in neon spatters of paint. White doors, blue doors, multicolored doors, medieval doors, oddly shaped doors, frames with blankets or beads hanging over them, all freestanding on the lush, verdant grass, with no other buildings in sight. Wide paths of hard-packed soil cut through the grass, weaving to and between each door, joining together and branching apart apparently at random.

Lily turned. Her closed door stood alone, and she peered around the outer edge, only to see the reverse side of the door. She reached for the knob and cracked it open, the scent and sound of rain slipping out. She closed it again.

"Well, that's trippy," she muttered, slowly letting the magnitude of what she saw sink in.

Each door led to a person's Paradise. Not just a Paradise *realm*, but someone's unique, perfect Paradise. Siedah had been right to use the analogy of a neighborhood, though Lily felt that she might have over-simplified it. The overall realm of Paradise wasn't the metaphorical apart-ment building, it was a *neighborhood* of apartment buildings and, more likely than not, completely isolated "houses," for those whose Paradise involved solitude.

Footsteps made her turn, only to see a slim-built man in full hippie garb sauntering down a path nearby.

He slid his round yellow-lensed glasses down his nose. "First time out?"

Lily shrugged and offered a grin, pushing her hood back. "Caught me."

"Well, let's get shaking, I'll show you out. It's simple, you just walk, and then you get there."

Lily fell into step beside him, not in the least bit enlightened but will-ing to roll with it. "Sounds about right," she murmured.

The endless field of doors should have felt creepy. While it didn't feel particularly comfortable, and certainly didn't invite lingering, it didn't make her spine prickle with the sense of *wrongwrongwrong* that she'd sometimes gotten in certain places or rooms in the mortal world.

The man's name was Jason, and they chatted aimlessly as they wove around doors. His Paradise was a shared one, as it turned out, a commune.

"One that won't ever end up getting weird," he told her cheerfully.

She laughed. "Were you ever in a commune in Arizona? My uncle was, back in the day, and he would've gone to Woodstock, but apparently the commune he was on had really good food, so he stayed there and missed out."

"Right on." Jason nodded sagely. "I'd been eating old cans of cat food, so I didn't have any holdups about going to Woodstock, which was a fucking *experience*. We were gonna have an Afterlife Woodstock, but I guess there's an issue with the pocket realm we wanted to use— Oh, here we are."

A monumental white stone arch towered three stories high, set into a patch of sky that dipped down to touch the earth. Beyond it, a gargantuan hallway, at least as wide as a football field, stretched away into a gradual curve. From what she could see through the limited view of the arch, it vaguely reminded her of a single-level mall, given all the bustle and activity, but built on an impossible scale. Slightly roughened walls of striated stone reached up hundreds of feet toward an indistinct ceiling of hazy golden light. It had an old look to it, vaguely medieval in the way her favorite fantasy stories were, except it felt modern too. The timelessness of it made sense—it was the *Universal* Hallway, the community hub of all activity and connection point of all realms in the Afterlife.

Lily moved to the edge of the arch to get a better view. Instead of department stores, a few grand doorways and arches were set into each wall that she could see, offering glimpses of the realms within. Shops were built into large depressions in the stone walls, clearly a part of the Hall, and not a gateway to another place.

Thousands of figures moved along the Hall, stepping into shops, entering and exiting the arches, and—Lily's mouth dropped open before she could catch herself—a few even flying high above the crowds. One such figure swooped down to dip below the peak of the arch she and Jason were approaching, wings moving like a hummingbird's. The person waved as they buzzed overhead, their pale-blue skin shimmering with iridescence, then they zipped up and away, moving purposefully toward something in the distance.

"The Fae are trippy," Jason said casually. "Personally, I find them a little creepy, but hey, different strokes for different folks, right? Non-souls don't usually come into Paradise unless they, like, know someone here, so if they creep you out too, don't worry, they won't be in here much. See you around, Red!" He bumped her arm with his elbow before sauntering toward a group of people waiting in the Hall nearby.

Lily ventured into the Hall herself, trying not to stare at some of the more unusual people. The Paradise arch was situated on a slight convex curve of the hallway, so while it looked straight down the main line of the Hall, when she exited it, she saw that it continued to the right, narrowing a bit. The Paradise arch was noticeably larger than other arches Lily could see, though they were all dwarfed by the scale of the Hallway. Perhaps the neutrality of Paradise was a more common choice than faith-specific Afterlives.

The Hall seemed wider and busier straight ahead, so, with a bracing breath, she headed out. A woman in a flowing chiton talked animatedly with a Middle Eastern man in pristine white robes, while a child sitting at her feet played with a carved toy that looked a bit like a dog. Lily's eyes lingered on the child for a moment. Logically, she knew that young souls would be in the Afterlife, but something about the child seemed slightly *other*. She'd have to ask Siedah about that when they met up.

A man with arms covered in colorful tattoos stepped out of a Celtic-style arch, nodding as the ethereally beautiful woman next to him read aloud from a heavy leather-bound book, her delicate dragonfly wings shimmering with each step. Another woman, who could have stepped off the set of a show based on the Middle Ages, strode up to them, waving another book in disgust.

"It was so many reincarnations ago she barely remembers, but I've checked her old notes *six* times, and there is nothing to indicate that the phases of the moon would affect that particular . . ."

". . . the damnedest thing, everyone who was there said it was like an earthquake, but more like an earth-shiver? Someone probably set off one of those magic fireworks again . . ." a powerfully built man said into his phone, a small dog tucked into his other arm.

Lily stuck to the main Hall, though she peered down the narrower offshoots at each intersection she passed. Two of them had been short and ended with a cul-de-sac of realms. One had narrowed significantly and seemed devoid of anyone or anything, meandering around a corner that she didn't want to go past. There were only a couple of major intersections along the length of the main Hall, making it feel a bit more like a small city center instead of an incomprehensible maze. It reminded her of maps she'd seen of old European cities, with a main street as the central vein and then a bit of a chaotic layout branching out from it—growing organically as they went, rather than neatly.

The arches to different Afterlives or realms were impossible to miss; each one thrummed with power and was carved or decorated in a unique style. The name of each realm floated in glowing letters above each entrance, some familiar, some she'd never heard of: Valhalla, the Summerland, Garden of the Gods, Rarohenga. After some exploring, she even found the arch for the Underworld, which was busier than she'd expected.

Farther down the Hall, Lily rounded a corner and stepped closer to the wall to get out of the way of a group of muscular women.

"You Amazons aren't fucking around with arm day. I almost cried lifting my coffee this morning," one woman said.

"I have no sympathy," a tall, Grecian woman drawled back. "Just hearing the phrase 'Valkyrie leg day' makes my thighs go all weak."

"Aww *sæta*, you know what will fix that? Hitting leg day more often," another woman teased as they passed by.

"Plus, if the weird stuff from the last report turns into an actual conflict, we'll need all the muscle we can get . . ." the first woman said, their conversation fading into the general chatter.

Lily frowned after them, wondering what could possibly cause conflict in a place that seemed to be a bastion of chaotic harmony.

Shaking the thought away, she peered down a side hallway and stopped in her tracks, comprehension an icy wash over her senses, a sick ache twisting through her silent chest.

Heaven.

The archway of solid mother-of-pearl was striking in its simplicity, the soft golden light of the realm within casting a warm glow out into the Hall. It didn't feel sinister—the opposite in fact—but she wished that it did.

Unable to tear her eyes away from the arch, she felt like a stain on the landscape of the Afterlife. An inky, smudgy dark, wrong *blot*. And small. So very small. Like she was five years old in her little church dress, learning about sin and Hell for the first time.

Hands gripping too tight, begging for mercy, for help, for forgiveness. So scared, so worried about how she might mess it all up.

A flash of shame from her preteen years, curious and confused and desperate to know, to understand.

Questioning God will get you sent to Hell, Lily, is that what you want?

Tired and sick and in pain, trying to seem calm and happy for others when all she wanted was comfort.

Please, Lily, it's not too late to accept God again. I don't expect him to cure your cancer, but please don't sentence yourself to an eternity of suffering.

Fighting the childish urge to pull her hood up, Lily spun on her heel and headed back to the main Hall, fighting to keep her steps even and unhurried and her expression neutral, despite the nausea and fury roiling in her gut.

"Okay," she muttered, stepping into a little alcove and leaning against the wall, "so we don't go down that hall unless we can't help it." She ran a hand through her hair, swallowing the snarl of emotions down. It was just a stupid arch. Just a place. She'd earned her Paradise, though a part of her was waiting to realize that it was as ephemeral and temporary as she and her heartbeat had been.

Lily eased out of the alcove, determined to continue her exploration.

She followed the slight curvature of the Hall and had stopped to admire a dress on a mannequin when yelling drew her attention.

A disheveled man burst out of an arch farther up the Hall, pursued by two towering figures with horns. Several people laughed or clapped when demons secured the man by the arms and began frog-marching him back in the direction they'd come from, and more than a few shook their heads before carrying on.

"Trainees," an older woman said fondly as she sauntered past Lily, the aura of power around her making Lily's skin itch. "They're trying, bless them."

Lily frowned and rolled her shoulders to shake the feeling, fairly certain that some manner of deity had just gone by. The man twisted and nearly escaped, but was quickly caught by the frazzled trainees, who gave up on marching him and instead held him off the floor, carrying him while he screamed obscenities that made Lily's eyebrows lift.

"I WAS A PASTOR!" the man bellowed, kicking at the air. "GET THEE BEHIND ME, SATAN!"

"My name," grunted one, a gangly-looking demon with ochre skin, "is Lamech."

The man wailed like a husky being forced into a bathtub.

Lily covered her mouth, trying desperately not to laugh. Her early days as a teenage cashier at a grocery store had been confusing while she'd learned how to deal with customers, some not too far removed from the hopeful escapee. People like that had been awful, but through controlled exposure to their awfulness, she'd become immune to the outlandish behavior. Like getting a flu shot.

Lily winced as the man spat a slur at one demon, then turned to threaten the other with an exorcism, trying to bite at their hands on his arms before they carried him through the arch. It seemed the trainees were getting one hell of a dose.

The yelling echoed and faded, and activity in the Hall resumed as if nothing had happened, but Lily slipped through the flow of people to stand before the arch of polished obsidian etched with swirling designs. Inside, red-gold filaments of light on the ceiling and walls softened the darkness, illuminating a tunnel and stairs, as well as the closed doors of an elevator.

Wicked girls go to Hell.

Dressed like that, you'll end up in Hell.

You're going to Hell if you keep acting like that.

You're going to Hell.

You're going to Hell.

You're going to Hell.

Those four words swelled into a chorus in her memory. The hundreds—the thousands—of times she'd been warned of and threatened with Hell. Warned, then as she'd grown up and purposefully left the faith, condemned.

She shook her head to clear it, like resetting a mental Etch A Sketch, and turned her attention back to the arch. The delicate artistry of the obsidian almost made her breath catch, swooping and curling in some places, glinting with sharp edges in others. Pleasantly warm air wafted out of the arch, too warm for her two jackets, but perfect for what she considered T-shirt weather.

Come have that glass of wine with us. We can swap stories.

She straightened, a smile playing at her mouth.

Some people thought she was going to Hell? Fine. She would prove them right, on *her* terms, and with a glass of wine in hand. Then she would go home to Paradise.

❦

7

DEMONIC RETAIL

Lily

Lily strode down the sweeping, circular stairs, excitement and nerves swirling in her stomach with every step. The red-gold light had turned out to be veins of magma peeking through the black stone, growing thicker and more numerous the farther down she went, until the tunnel was woven with an arched lattice of warm light. With each step, the dull roar of voices grew louder.

She squared her shoulders.

What was the worst that could happen, really? If either of the demons she'd met weren't there, she'd leave a message or something. If they told her to get lost, back up the stairs she'd go. It wasn't like she could get stuck down there.

Could she?

Just as that lovely little thought made its appearance, the stairs leveled out into a short but cavernous hallway with the elevator on one side, and then—

"Holy *shit*," Lily breathed, turning in a circle to take it all in.

It barely registered as something "underground." Like the main Hall, the ceiling of the cavern was so high that the details of it were obscured, yet it glowed with soft red-gold light. Cragged stone walls delineated the space, with gleaming veins of magma set in the stone offering more light. To her right, a fence more than fifty feet high sprouted out of the rock wall and cut directly across the space, the metal twisted in a style reminiscent of the arch in the Hall. Lily stepped closer, curious. If it *was* metal, it was unlike any metal she'd ever seen, as it was closer in appearance to half-cooled lava somehow keeping shape.

On the other side of the fence lay a barren, featureless stretch of stone, save for the behemoth entryway looming like the gaping maw of an animal, complete with a jagged line of fang-like stalactites. She couldn't see into its black depths, but the sounds of feet scuffing on stairs echoed out of it in an endless cacophony. She watched as souls emerged into the light and followed the flow of people toward the fence. That was the entrance to Hell for the souls sent here, then.

Lily followed the line of the fence to the source of all the activity. There, towering as tall as the fence, yet far more ornate, stood the gate that had inspired millennia of stories and religious fear. Both halves were swung open, allowing souls to enter and go to one of two dozen freestanding little desks lined up in alternating rows that began at the edges of the gate and formed a funnel into a lobby-like space. The desks were manned by demons who seemed to look at their files and talk briefly with them, a bit like the security check at an airport.

After the desks, souls were directed to a pair of tunnels carved into the wall. They were guided—or, perhaps more accurately, corralled—by a chest-high ridge of black rock curving in an arc from the fence, almost all the way to the tunnels. Two parallel lines of several dozen demons stood guard along either side of the route, and they, along with the half wall, were clearly meant to keep the souls from deviating from the path. Many of the demons had spears propped on their shoulders, or sheathed weapons within easy reach. Most souls walked quietly, but a few . . .

Lily bit her lip to keep from laughing.

Customer service looked the same dead and alive apparently.

A few raised voices carried from the area with the desks, and someone slammed their hand down. A man stormed out of line, purple-faced with rage, and screamed at a female demon who towered over him, asking if she had any idea who he was. Many of the demons guarding the souls within the gate, not a single one of them under six and a half feet tall, bore expressions ranging from annoyed to verging on open violence.

It looked like retail during the holidays. Demon retail.

For a moment, Lily wondered if she should come back another time, but other than the screamer, nothing seemed particularly out of control. She headed to the end of the stone half wall, moving toward the tunnels before pivoting to round the wall and walking to the gate, boots thudding on floors that looked suspiciously like cooling magma under glass. A few of the demons guarding the gap noticed her approach, shooting her curious but not unfriendly looks and nudging each other. She was nearly in line with the desks when a faintly familiar red-skinned demon left his position by the gate and jogged her way, face lifting into a grin so wide she could see his fangs.

"You made it through!"

Lily grinned back and sketched a bow. "As if there was any doubt."

So, so much doubt.

"None at all," he assured her, bracing the end of his spear on the ground and leaning on it. "Well, welcome to Hell, uh . . ." His face fell slightly.

"Lily."

"Crocell," he said, pressing a clawed hand to his chest, then gesturing around them. "Well, what do you think?"

A dim flicker of memory, walking through the gleaming gate, past towering horned figures, into the tunnels and down to a level, soft understanding voices and kind words.

I've been here before. Once. A long, long time ago.

The memory was so hazy it raised more questions than answers, but the overall sensation it left behind wasn't unpleasant. It had been her . . . second life? Yes, that felt right. When she'd been falsely accused of being a witch. She'd been convinced that she'd deserved it, hadn't she? That there was a good reason why her neighbors had burned her. She'd been all jagged, ragged edges then. She'd been sent to Hell so they could *help*. And they had.

She blinked away the soul-deep memory.

"Much nicer than I was led to believe. Also smaller," Lily said, the dim echo of gratitude soothing the edges of her lingering anxiety.

"Ah, common misconception. The mortal writer Dante got almost everything wrong about Hell, but he got the idea of levels right. The meaning of each level? Not so much. This is the smallest level, the lobby, if you will. Those tunnels"—he pointed to the tunnels the souls went into—"lead to the actual levels for the souls. The one closest to the fence leads to the first and second levels, the other is for levels three through nine. The elevators to the levels, and to the demon levels below, are through that tunnel there, the big one." He pointed to a tunnel on the wall farthest from the gate. "And the other tunnel goes to the break room, bathrooms, and some other communal areas."

"This is amazing," she told him sincerely. Her curiosity flared at the idea of "demon levels," but the endless line of souls was a tempering reality. "Well, I didn't mean to drag you away from your job—"

"Please," another demon cut in as they walked past, tail drooping to the floor in defeat, "*please* drag us away from our jobs. Something is in the air today. They're awful."

"Do you guys have a moon here? Full-moon madness is real, just ask anyone who worked in emergency medicine."

The demon rubbed at their eyes. "Maybe in the mortal world it's a full moon? I don't know, mortal time is weird."

"Take a break," a woman's voice—Moura's—cut in. She clapped her hand on the defeated demon's shoulder. "We've got it covered for now. Mortal! You made it! Time for wine, eh?"

"Please." Lily grinned. "Though it looks like you all have your hands full."

"We have a bit longer on shift, but you are welcome to come back in a bit. You can wander if you like. As a visiting soul you can pretty much go anywhere, within reason obviously."

Lily watched the crowd of souls, a funny feeling in her chest.

A woman had the audacity to poke her finger into the chest of a demon nearly twice her size. The demon flung her hand back at her with a snarled response, pointing toward the tunnel. Another soul, sensing the distraction, hurried back toward the gate, only to be put back in line by a female demon with the kind of muscular physique that powerlifters would envy. Did they think going back to Judgment would help them? Or were they trying to sneak somewhere better?

Demon customer service apparently had at least one perk over mortal customer service: The workers could fight back.

Oh, and wasn't that the dream.

"You guys get to talk back to the souls?" she asked.

"Of course," Moura said, confusion coloring her tone. "I doubt any of us would be sane if we couldn't. Sometimes it's amusing, but sometimes . . . we just get tired."

Lily hummed in sympathy, but her mind whirled, genuine excitement skittering through her body. She loved her Paradise, loved the peaceful refuge of it, but she'd spent too long working and fighting the battles of life to feel complete just resting.

"Could I help?"

Both demons went utterly still, and the ones standing guard near them turned to stare at her.

Crocell peered down at her, concern written all over his face. "Why in all the realms would you want to do *that*?"

Lily chuckled, playing with the hem of her sleeve. "I worked customer service, with people, my whole life. How much do you know about mortal customer service?"

The demons exchanged a befuddled glance before Crocell answered.

"I know people work in stores and restaurants and stuff, like some souls do here, but in the mortal world, they have prices and money."

"That's true," Lily said. "In the mortal world, people who work in those jobs deal with entitled people all the time, but *we* generally weren't allowed to be rude or talk back, and we definitely weren't allowed to get physical, even when they were awful to us, because we were supposed to keep the customer happy. I'm sure whoever decided to abbreviate the phrase 'the customer is always right in matters of taste' is down here somewhere."

The fucker. Maybe if she asked nicely, she'd be allowed to kick him in the dick on behalf of service industry workers everywhere.

"You"—Moura looked horrified—"you couldn't *say* anything? You couldn't fight back?"

"We were supposed to avoid it as much as possible. Sometimes you could get away with setting a boundary, but the managers probably wouldn't, or couldn't, back you up on it. I used to get candy bars thrown at me because people were mad about the prices, and I would just have to ring them up like normal."

"What the fuck," Crocell murmured, gripping his spear a little tighter. "That's barbaric!"

"That's customer service, and I have two decades of rage from that that I would be more than happy to put to use somehow." She looked over the line of souls. "I mean, getting to talk back? Could be fun."

Please let me do something, I'm so . . . bored. Just let me run my mouth a little or flip someone off. Please?

"Shit, do you want a knife or something?" Moura asked, reaching for one of the blades sheathed at her hips.

The flare of temptation took her by surprise. She'd never really been violent, except for the times when she'd come to the defense of a friend in a bar. Or the notable occasion when she'd slapped a guy who had grabbed her ass at a concert. She'd hit him so hard he'd dropped like a lead balloon.

It wasn't like she hadn't thought about violence before.

Hit her creepy coworker with her car. Whack every hand that had been slammed on her desk or counter. Punch every shitty, smarmy hypocrite. Cut the dick off her assaulter and make him wear his own balls as earrings. Find the guy who had left her friend a shattered shell of herself, bruised and crying on a bathroom floor, see how much he liked begging for his life.

"Maybe later," she said finally, shrugging out of her leather jacket and unzipping her hoodie. "So where would I be most useful? I could distract the really shitty ones for you."

"That would make sorting easier," Moura mused, watching the souls thoughtfully.

Lily did too. Some people looked angry or dangerous, one or two downright evil, but most just tired and lost and confused.

"What's their thing? The . . . quiet ones?"

"So, Levels Three through Nine are punishment levels, increasing in intensity as they go down, but souls *can* work their way up. Though, usually the ones beyond Level Five never do. The souls you're talking about are Level Ones and Twos," Moura explained. "Healing levels. Therapy levels really. Souls who weren't good, but were truly sorry, or who had no opportunity to be better, the ones who just need a bit of support so they can grow and change. Most of the time, a soul just needs a chance, needs help. It's not always comfortable, but the point of all of it is to grow."

"I know how uncomfortable that can be," Lily said, silent chest aching a little more.

A flurry of activity drew all of their attention to the line, where a male soul had attacked a female one and seemed to be attempting to use her as a hostage. A demon stepped forward, yanking him away and shaking him like a maraca before shoving him toward another demon, who dragged him to the tunnel on the left. The demons clearly had the capacity to be brutal and uncompromising. But . . . Lily slid her gaze to a truly massive demon with olive-green skin and a broken horn, hunched nearly double as he spoke quietly to the weeping female soul. He offered her an arm that was nearly as thick as her waist, helping her up and walking slowly with her toward the tunnel on the right. His scarred face should have been terrifying, but there was an obvious gentleness there, genuine compassion for what the soul had been through.

Lily's nose stung, a warning sign of imminent tears. She dug her nails into her palm.

Kind. The demons were kind, in their own way. Even after seeing the worst of humanity, they *cared*.

Something seemed to click into place inside, a knot in the fabric of her soul unraveling as her lifelong fear of Hell withered in the light of reality. Sure, it could be a brutal place, but it wasn't needlessly so. They wanted to help.

So did she.

Swallowing around the lump of emotion, she forced a note of hopefully carefree cheer into her voice. "Do you guys have a pen and a big piece of paper or cardboard or something? And a chair? I have an idea."

"Do you mean a foldable one? Like they use in mortal cage fighting?" Crocell asked.

Lily laughed. "I mean, sure, if that's all you have, but I plan on sitting in it."

"And the paper and pen?" Moura's face slowly eased into a grin.

"I'm going to make a sign. 'Customer Service' or 'Complaints' or something. It'll draw them in."

"Why?" Crocell frowned, looking between her and Moura. "You can't do anything to change where they're going."

"No, and I don't expect to," Lily said, trying to decide how to explain. "There's a certain kind of person who is going to have everything explained to them by the Front Desk, go through the Judgment of their choosing, come out on this side of it—where I'm guessing things get explained to them again—and then *still* complain about it. I'm willing to bet that they're the ones giving you guys the most grief, and they're going to think that, because I'm a soul, I'll be easier to intimidate or coerce."

Moura snorted.

Lily appreciated the vote of confidence as she continued. "If I can either get them to understand, or not be little bitches about it, then problem solved. If I can't, well, at least they're not clogging up the main line, and things might go more smoothly."

"But"—Crocell scratched at the base of one of his horns—"they'll think they're getting their way. They'll be . . . They'll treat you like . . ."

"Have you ever expected something and then suddenly had it yanked away from you? Or realized that it was never actually going to happen, and you'd been lying to yourself the whole time? It's a shitty feeling."

Insurance. Healthcare. A long life. A family. Children with bright eyes and a contagious laugh. To watch my brothers and friends grow old.

Lily coughed to loosen her too-tight throat. "And for people who are clearly deeply entitled, it will sting that much more. Plus, I'll get to fight back this time. I still want to be kind, but I don't want to have to be *nice* anymore."

Crocell looked skyward, eyes darting left and right as he worked through her explanation, sweet concern all over his face.

Wait. Shit. Was she even allowed to help?

"Sorry, I know I'm asking this out of the blue. Do you need to run this by someone? Please let me know if I'm overstepping here. I'd just like to help you guys out."

Moura grinned so broadly that Lily could see fangs, and waved over another demon. "In no way are you overstepping. We get to decide how and when to accept help up here. No need to involve the fancy management. Crocell, we've got that folding table in the storage closet, and didn't Vepar dump his old gaming chair in the break room? It might be a little big, but it'll be comfortable."

A slender, midnight-blue demon reached them, and Moura rested her hand on his shoulder. "Zagan here will whip up a sign for you quick-like. Nothing fancy, Zag. We just need souls to take it seriously. 'Customer Service' should work, right?"

"Sounds good to me," Lily said, watching Crocell hurry off. "Oh, wait! How about 'Help Desk,' but spelled with two L's? *Hell*p Desk?"

"Punny, I like it." Moura laughed, gesturing toward a spot on the inside curve of the half wall that was in easy eyeline of the souls as they walked away from the desks, but well before the line of guards began in the gap. "Let's get you set up over there, that's a nice midpoint."

Fifteen minutes later, Lily was grinning so hard her face hurt. The chair they'd found was, predictably, a bit large, but they'd put it down to a lower height. The break room she'd helped them retrieve it from was comfortable and eclectic, with a large kitchen and plenty of chairs and tables. A whiteboard with dozens of notes and notices took up the far wall. It had a cozy feel to it.

Zagan had made a sign big enough to reach from the tabletop to the ground, with *Hell*p Desk spelled out in clean, elegant letters.

"Zagan, you have the most gorgeous penmanship I've ever seen," Lily told him, tracing the *H* with a fingertip.

The demon ducked his head, cheeks staining a deeper shade of blue. "Thank you. Um . . . here." He held out the black metal baseball bat he'd brought over with the sign. "Just in case. It's from Agares." He pointed toward one of the admission desks at the gate. "She's dating a soul from the Summerland, and said that a lot of mortal women used bats as protection, so you might be familiar with it."

The bat was solid and well-balanced in her hand, the weight of it reassuring, but not as much as the intention of the gift itself. "That's so sweet, thank you! Please tell her thank you for me as well."

Zagan blushed even deeper and nodded. Lily smiled. It wasn't fair for a seven-foot-tall demon with fangs and horns to be so precious, but Zagan was a purehearted cutie.

"HEY! Finally, someone to listen to me," a man snarled, marching toward her table, face mottled in frustration.

"Showtime." Lily smiled at Zagan, tapping a finger on the smooth handle of the bat. She settled into the chair, anticipation coiling in her stomach.

"Good luck," Zagan murmured, tail lashing as he scurried away before the soul reached the table.

The soul threw his arms out to the sides. "What the fuck is this?"

"Hell," Lily said calmly, fingers curling around the bat for reassurance.

"Yeah, got that part, but this is bullshit! I'm not even Christian. I'm agnostic."

"You also either willfully forgot everything they told you, or you didn't pay attention. Let me guess . . . Universal Judgment?" Lily asked, watching him carefully. She knew posturing when she saw it, and the man was too twitchy and furious for there to be an actual mistake. She'd bet her Paradise on it.

"Of course," he bit out.

She chose her words carefully. "Okay, and when you got to the other side of that, were you then presented with a list of options for where you could go to work on yourself?"

The man scoffed and leaned over her table. "You mean be *punished*?"

"Why would you say that?" Lily asked innocently.

"Because I was asked which *punishment realm* I wanted to spend my time in."

Got him.

"So you admit that you chose to be here?"

The man's mouth opened, then snapped shut, jaw muscles clenching. "Fine, I chose Hell because I didn't think it would actually be like this," he gritted out.

"Real?"

"Yeah. Fuck. Listen, it sounds bad, but all I did was—"

Lily held up a hand. "Ahh, hold on. If you're about to try to explain why whatever you did to be down here 'wasn't actually that bad,' then all that tells me is that you know *exactly* why you're down here. It also says that you either don't understand or willfully ignore that actions have consequences."

"I don't *want* to be in Hell!"

"I didn't want to die. But we don't always get what we want, do we?"

The man slammed a fist on the table, making it jump, before storming away without another word.

Zagan appeared at her side, copper eyes wide. "Are you all right?"

"That"—Lily took a long, steadying breath—"felt *so* good."

Before Zagan could say anything else, a wire file basket appeared on the table. Lily yanked her hand back as if it was a spider. She hadn't expected unseen assistance outside her Paradise.

"Oh, that's good." Zagan gave her a cautious grin. "It looks like you're hired, so to speak."

"What?"

"We get to choose our personnel, but not everyone is immediately granted the ability to see soul files without the soul's permission. It's an honor and a responsibility, and it looks like you earned both."

"Is this a Hell thing or a Universe thing?" Lily asked cautiously, looking up at him.

"Both?" Zagan shrugged.

"*Excuse* me!" A female voice tore their attention back to the line, where a woman stomped toward them. Zagan scurried away before she got too close.

The soul came to a puffing halt in front of Lily's makeshift desk, and oh, it was just too perfect.

Her bleached and highlighted hair had been cut into a long bob, and a pair of oversized sunglasses perched on top of her head. Blue eyes that would have been pretty if they hadn't been lit with contempt glared down at her. Lily was almost impressed. If there had been a pamphlet for Karen Identification, this soul would have been Exhibit A. The Prime Karen. The audacity to which all others could only aspire.

Excellent.

A mud-brown file popped into existence on her little desk, the dull lettering spelling out the woman's wonderfully ironic name.

"Wow, a true Karen," Lily mused, reaching for the file curiously. "This ought to be good."

"Do *not*," Karen spat, shoving her finger in Lily's direction, "pull that shit with me. You *people* seem to think you are so clever, but guess what, you're not."

"Mmhmm." Lily flipped open the file. The first page seemed to be basic information about the woman's life, and Lily ran her finger down each line.

Children: two daughters, one son.

I wonder how she treated . . . oh.

No sooner did she start to wonder than the page shimmered before her eyes and the information flashed through her brain. She lifted her finger away from the page in shock, and the information and images faded into the background of her thoughts, like the afterimage of a flash at night. She touched the page again and—there.

She loved her children, or at least thought she did. She liked to use them to further her own wants and desires, as canvases on which to project her own insecurities and failures. Her youngest daughter had always been, in Karen's opinion, pudgier than she should have been, and she never missed an opportunity to remind her daughter of that fact. She claimed that she only wanted the best for her, that she said things out of love, but it was a lie. Her youngest daughter looked the most like her, and she'd resented her for her youth, for her differences. Her youngest daughter had married a good man but had cried on her wedding day when her mother, swirling champagne in the dressing room right before the ceremony, had said, "It's just that that dress makes you look fatter. You really should have gone for something with sleeves. When I got married, I was a size two. But I suppose at least you know he's marrying you for the right reasons."

Her daughter had looked so beautiful on her wedding day, eyes bright with hope and promise, skin glowing with health, her gown a delicate sweep of chiffon and lace. Poor sweet baby.

Karen was full of shit.

And vindictiveness. And homophobia. And not a small amount of racism and bigotry. The information and context scrolled through Lily's mind at lightning speed until she lifted her hand from the page.

Karen huffed, leaning across the table. "Are you even listening to me? Hello?" She snapped her fingers in Lily's face.

Lily's hand whipped up so fast that it surprised her, but she kept her expression neutral as she tightly gripped Karen's wrist. Karen's eyes went wide.

"Snap your fingers in my face again," Lily said conversationally, as if discussing the weather, "and I will snap them *off* and feed them to you one, by, one."

"How *dare*—"

"Stop talking." Lily poured every ounce, every shred of contempt into her voice.

Karen's mouth snapped shut, still furious but clearly rattled.

How many times had Lily been at the beginning of this script and played it out with different variables? How many times had she apologized and catered to someone who had screamed at her, sworn at her, thrown things, grabbed her arm, made her afraid, all because that was what the service standard had required of her?

The deference and apologies that had been branded into her mind to use with angry customers sat on the tip of her tongue. But she wasn't sorry that this woman was upset. She wasn't sorry that the woman hadn't "enjoyed her experience."

Karen was treating her badly.

And Lily refused to apologize for someone else's bad behavior. No more. Never again.

Lily cocked her head, watching the woman's eyes, searching for any hint of understanding, of regret. "What possible reason could you have for speaking to me that way?"

Karen's eyes bulged, and her mouth flew open with an indignant gasp.

"I suggest," Lily said mildly, tightening her grip on the woman's wrist, "that you consider making what you say next very polite."

"Or else what?"

Lily smiled. "Don't fuck around if you're not willing to find out." She released the woman's hand and sat back, waiting.

She touched a finger to the pages of the file again, hoping that this interaction was the result of extreme duress.

Karen's adult life had been a trail of hundreds of abused service industry workers. She enjoyed it. Enjoyed flexing the perceived power she felt she lacked in her own life. When she'd found out that her husband had cheated on her—again—she'd gone shopping at the mall and made four young employees in different stores cry, and had gotten one fired. A teenager, working to help support her family, who all lived in poverty. She didn't know, couldn't have known, but even if she had, she wouldn't have cared. She held poor people, especially poor people of color, in such low regard that they barely registered as human to her. The satisfaction she'd gotten from her trip had lasted only until she'd gotten to her car. Then the humiliation of her husband's infidelity had threatened to drown her in her own tears.

Lily blinked the information away, glancing down at the page.

LEVEL FIVE, printed at the top of every page.

"You can't treat me this way! No one should be treated this way!" Karen sputtered, twisting her fingers together.

Lily looked up. "You didn't seem to have a problem treating people a lot worse than I'm treating you right now."

"What people are y—"

"If you want to waste your eternity listening to me list each and every one of them, so be it. But for every name, I will use this bat." Lily laid it across the desk. "Or you can shut up, get back in line without a fuss, and go down to Level Five, where I presume they will be more merciful than I will be if you don't pull your shit together. You have no power here. You forfeited that right with the decisions that you made. Actions have consequences. These are yours."

Karen took a step back, color draining from her face as she stared at Lily.

Lily held that gaze and, for the first time in her existence, wasn't afraid.

Karen swallowed hard and gave a tiny nod, shoulders drooping. Suddenly, she looked . . . like just a person, and not a persona. A person who had been too small-minded and cowardly to brave discomfort for the sake of change and was now wondering if maybe she should have.

Moura had said Level Fives stood a chance, right? The least chance, but a chance nonetheless.

Lily touched the page again, then leaned across the table, trying to temper her tone. "Listen, Level Five doesn't have to be forever. If you want another shot at life, it's going to be a long road, but it's not an unending one. Your kids had hope for you, even after everything. Maybe think about that on your way down."

Karen twitched, genuine pain flaring in her pretty eyes. She pressed her lips together and turned without a word, walking quietly back toward the line. A few of the demons watched her as she passed, glancing back to Lily with shocked faces. One of them flashed her a thumbs-up.

Lily sucked in a deep breath and puffed out her cheeks, wiping her sweaty, shaky hands on her leggings. She was glad she'd pulled back at the end, but it had felt so damn good to match the energy and stand up for herself.

Lily placed Karen's file into the wire tray, and it glinted with a faint sparkle of light before fading away.

Another file, blue and slightly creased, appeared in the center of her desk.

Lily looked up. A short line of souls had formed, the man at the head of it scowling down at her expectantly. The demons, apparently confused and delighted, watched avidly. The giant demon with one horn even gave her a two-fingered salute, his craggy face lit with a quiet smile.

Her hands steadied. She reached for the new file, brushing her fingers across the pages. He pitched a spectacular hissy fit for only being sent to Level Two for some intensive therapy and caved quickly.

The souls came in quick succession after that, blurring together in varying degrees of awfulness and ridiculousness and opportunities for witty or sardonic comebacks. Thankfully, not all of them were hideously awful, and most of them took one look at the bat resting across her lap and didn't try to make things physical. A few slammed their hands on the desk in an act of intimidation, only to get their hand whacked with the bat.

Their lives were fascinating and frustrating and heartbreaking and cruel. The more souls she dealt with, the more thankful she was that the memories of their lives faded from her own mind. She kept her impressions of them, but the full weight of what she'd seen lifted as soon as the soul files disappeared.

Finally, a sickly orange file appeared on her desk, the cover oddly oily to the touch. The man to whom it belonged smiled calmly down at her.

Something about his presence set off every primal alarm bell she had and had her gripping the handle of the bat. The eerie mystery of the soul evaporated as the man's life flashed through her mind.

Perhaps the bat would be fully put to use for this one.

8

❦

SEVEN DEADLY

Lily

Lily flopped into the oversized gaming chair, panting, the bat slick in her hand. She'd honestly tried to talk to him first.

And he'd smiled.

Smiled as he'd first lied, then tried to manipulate, despite the fact she held an account of his soul in her hands. He'd stopped smiling when she hadn't tried to soothe him. When she'd called him out on his twisted bullshit, he'd laughed.

It was the laughter that had made her snap.

The oily file had shown her the children, their fear of him, the pain he'd inflicted on them, the damage he'd done to them.

A child huddled under their bed, shaking in fear as the door to their room crept open, his footsteps heavy on the carpet. The man's malicious glee as he saw the empty bed, saw the edge of a blankie peeking out from under it. It was so much more fun for him when they were scared, when they cried . . .

She'd never *liked* violence. But the reverberation of impact that had juddered up the bat and her arm had been damn near euphoric.

He'd stopped laughing then. She imagined that it was hard to laugh without teeth.

Or a functioning lower jaw.

Lily studied the blood trickling down the bat and regretted nothing.

Her quiet chest felt wrong though. Her heart should have been pounding a mile a minute.

"Good form," said a voice so deep it nearly rattled her bones.

Bones. Did she have bones anymore? She was dead but it felt like she had bones . . .

"Thanks," she rasped, and swallowed hard. "I had incentive."

"Murderer?" A giant figure appeared beside the desk, crouching down slowly. It was the demon with the broken horn, at least eight feet tall and built like a mountain.

"Child molester." Lily angled the bat to keep gore from dripping onto her leggings.

Maybe the Universe had made a mistake in giving her a Paradise, because what she'd just done didn't bother her. What bothered her was that she didn't feel *worse* about what she'd done. She should have felt awful and cruel, shouldn't she? But she didn't.

Evil. He'd been pure evil.

And now he was a pulpy, person-shaped mess on the floor. One that wheezed and twitched.

Echoes of a little girl, crying, crying, crying. He'd wanted her to cry harder.

A hand nearly the size of a serving tray held out a handkerchief that could have easily passed as a small towel. She took it, murmuring a thanks, and wiped the bat.

"He'll regenerate," the demon rumbled, watching her with knowing black eyes. "He will wish that he didn't, but he will, and then Gregorith will make you look like a mortal saint." The demon glanced at the mess on the other side of the desk, raised his eyebrows, and quirked his mouth in a smile. "Well, maybe not a saint, but certainly the kinder of two options."

"Level Nine doesn't fuck around, huh?"

"No." The demon shuddered slightly. "They don't."

"You've worked there?"

"No, my niece works down there, and they all take their jobs very seriously. I thought about it when I was younger, but I found that the structure and work of the legions appealed to me, for a time anyway. Working at the gate offers a certain kind of challenge and requires a level of discipline that I enjoy. It can be difficult, like all work. But so can life, yes?"

Lily finally dragged her eyes away from the reasonably clean bat to study him. His rough-hewn features would never qualify him as classically handsome, but he was far from terrifying. His nose had been broken and badly set a few times, and a gnarled scar as wide as her thumb split his hair, running from the broken horn down across his face, slashing over one eye and narrowly missing his nose and mouth. His body, even crouched and hunched in an attempt to make himself smaller and less intimidating, was built for brutal power. The tail he'd carefully curved to drape over his feet was blunted and too short, the end a long-healed mass of scars.

Her eyes had never been that kind. She'd never radiated peace and security like he did. She couldn't see him as anything other than a gentle, capable giant. Her friend Anna's dad had been like that, a bruiser of a man who no one ever suspected of caring diligently for a flower garden that could have won awards, or fussing over a bee that he'd found lying exhausted on the pavement.

The demon tilted his head, and a tiny, messy braid with a glitter-encrusted bead at the end slid out from the mass of his hair to tap against his thick neck.

"My little girl," he explained with a chuckle, tucking it behind his pointed ear. "She is learning how to braid and decided that I needed a 'bravery bead.'" His features grew serious. "Do not feel sorry for him, for what you've done. Justice and mercy are not the same, and sometimes, especially here, they cannot coexist. As a father, I thank you. You did well. And not just with him, but with all the others. It was the quietest shift I've ever had."

"It felt good," Lily admitted quietly, watching the line of souls moving smoothly from the gate to the tunnels. "To be helpful and to not be the punching bag."

"You handled yourself well."

She smiled, then sat up guiltily. "I'm so sorry, I just realized I don't know your name."

"No apology needed, I'm Krun. You are Ms. Lily, yes?"

"Just Lily." She laughed.

"All due respect, I don't think there is anything 'just' about you. Few mortals venture down here of their own free will, let alone offer to help us at the gate. For that, you have all of our thanks."

Lily opened her mouth to say . . . what? That it was nothing? It wasn't, and she knew it. Effective help in the service industry was like cold water on a hot day. To question the lack of mortal help offered to them? She hated that she believed it, was ashamed of it, but also understood completely. Fear was an easy deterrent.

Going to Hell. Going to Hell. Going to Hell.

Joke's on you, I did it and rather enjoyed myself.

"You're welcome," she said softly.

"Come on, Ms. Lily." Krun straightened, knees popping, and offered her his arm with a grin. "We're all very excited to grab that drink with you and share stories, as well as show off our home. Also, are you much into gaming?"

Lily stood and took his arm, feeling cartoonishly small for the first time in her existence. "What kind of gaming?"

"What do you mean you all play *Invaders*?" Lily asked, trying not to spill her drink—the best margarita she'd ever had—in excitement. The online multiplayer game set in a colony on Mars had been one of the few she'd played frequently during her life. The social aspect of it had appealed to her, as well as the ridiculous ways that people tried to defend or condemn themselves during the "trial" that was held every time someone found the body of a murdered "settler."

"Well, not all—"

"Some of us are more into Dungeons and Dragons."

"*Minecraft*, motherfucker."

". . . not really a gamer, but my partner and I like to go to the neighborhood board game night . . ."

"I don't game, but there's a brewery in the Universal Hallway that hosts 'Ales and Ideas' every week . . ."

The demons, many of them verging on—if not already—drunk,

started talking over each other, bickering cheerfully and striking up conversations about everything and nothing. Lily had achieved a pleasant level of buzzed, which in her mortal life was where she would have called it a night. She leaned against the table, sucking down the rest of the sinfully delicious margarita she'd been served in a demon-sized glass, and reached for the basket of golden-brown fries.

They hadn't needed to start drinking to swap stories. No, that had started long before they'd ever reached their destination, a delightful and apparently very popular pub called Seven Deadly on one of the demon residential levels. Despite the size of the pub, the architecture was stunningly delicate, featuring rib-vaulted ceilings painted and carved with frescoes in rich colors and bas-relief sculptures. But glorious ceiling aside, it was comfortable and unpretentious, with a long bar made of some kind of dark, glittery stone and an abundance of tables. The entertainment stage sat empty, though a small area had been left open for dancing.

It was busy, but not packed; demons of all heights, colors, and professions gathered together in a dull roar of conversation and laughter over music. It was a veritable forest of horns, some twisted, some perfectly straight, some forked, some broken, some with elaborate adornment, some plain. The odd set of wings stood out here and there, leathery and bat-like, tipped with a spike at the apex. No one wore particularly bright colors, but there certainly wasn't an *absence* of colorful clothing. In addition to the apparently very popular black and gray attire that made her feel right at home, a rainbow of jewel tones and deep shades tantalized the eye.

It was *beautiful*.

"Please say you'll join our *Invaders* lobby at least once," Crocell begged. "Krun and his wife play with us."

"Only after the kids are in bed," Krun said. "But yes, please do join us. It's very fun."

"I'm down, if I can find a computer to play on."

Crocell drained his drink, gagged, and set the glass on the table with a flourish. "It's been a while since I was in school, but isn't the saying

'Paradise provides' or something? Like stuff just kind of happens there, right?"

"I mean, yeah?" Lily said slowly, wondering how the hell she was supposed to ask her Paradise for a computer. Ha! How the *hell* . . .

"Cool. I'm gonna get another drink, wanna come?" Crocell asked, only slurring slightly.

Lily was halfway off her stool before he'd finished asking. Three other demons slipped free of their seats with them, moving toward an empty section of the bar in a drunken herd. Lily only noticed a few curious glances aimed her way, probably thanks to the fact that she'd glimpsed one or two other mortal souls—at least what she thought were mortal souls—in the crowd at one point.

One of the bartenders, a turquoise-skinned female demon, stopped in front of them, drying a glass with a cloth. She was so stunningly pretty that Lily's mind went completely blank.

"New round?" she asked.

"Yes, please," Crocell said flirtatiously, bracing his forearms on the bar. "What do you recommend, Dialen? We're celebrating."

One of Dialen's perfect dark eyebrows arched upward, her diamond-fire eyes glittering with amusement. "I noticed," she said dryly, just as a roar of laughter came from their table. "There's not much to celebrate at the gate, so what gives?"

One of the other demons threw an arm around Lily's shoulder, and she swayed.

"We're celebrating *her*. She—*hic*—pulled some stunt with a sign and *helped* us. Masterful work with the bat and the words, the very good words, and the"—they waved a hand at her—"the yes."

"I have a talented tongue," Lily said to clarify. Then realized—then didn't care. She grinned a little flirtatiously.

Dialen's smile turned feline, and her voice grew sultry, her eyes tracing a slow path down Lily's body, then back up. "I'll bet you do, kitten."

Heat pooled low in Lily's belly and nearly shocked her into sobriety.

She hadn't felt horny since . . . too damn long ago, and she hadn't felt *sexy* or *desirable* for a lot longer than that. Double work shifts, long hours, stress, the chronic fatigue that should have been a clue, and not having a reason or energy to dress nicely, they'd all taken a toll.

Dialen was a seductive, glorious dream, with sly intelligence and humor glittering in those impossible eyes.

But something didn't feel quite right. Emotionally anyway. It felt a bit like when she'd sprained her ankle as kid and tried to run on it a week before the doctor was supposed to give her the all clear. Healed, but not quite. Still a bit to go.

She leaned back, following that line of thought.

She'd always used sex as a pleasurable enough distraction even though she'd craved the intimacy of, well, *actual* intimacy. It had been a hollow comfort for her, but a comfort nonetheless.

Aha, that was the issue at hand. She didn't want a distraction or some kind of erotic emotional Band-Aid, however pleasurable. She wanted it to *matter*.

Oh. She wrinkled her nose at herself, watching Dialen's nimble hands fly as she made a cocktail.

Damn it all. Being horny again was a *gift*, a thrill she thought she'd never get to experience again. But it wasn't enough on its own anymore. If she leapt into the physical side of things, even if she *thought* that actual intimacy could grow, she knew she'd more than likely fall into old habits.

Annoying, that.

She could still flirt though.

"Dialennn," complained a wiry, androgynous demon with burgundy skin. "You can flirt with Ms. Lily later. We're trying to celebrate an *easy shift*. Well, easy-ish. Eashish? Shishish?"

"No, there's gotta be an *e* in there somewhere," their friend pointed out.

Dialen pointed a manicured nail at them. "I should cut you both off for that little speech alone."

"Nooooo!" they wailed in near-perfect unison.

"I'll be good!"

The other demons joined together in a plaintive chorus, assuring Dialen that they'd never done anything wrong a day in their very long lives and would never dare misbehave in a pub, no matter how drunk they got.

Lily might have been drunk, but not nearly drunk enough to believe a word out of their mouths. She laughed anyway, lighter than she'd been in a long time, and it had nothing to do with the alcohol.

Moments later, Dialen plunked a giant glass full of shimmering gold-and-purple liquid in from of her.

"It's called the Permanent Vacation, and it creeps up on you like a motherfucker." Dialen's sly grin softened slightly, and she leaned over the bar. "My brother works on Level Six, and he used to work at the gate. He doesn't tell me much, but he's told me enough to know that whatever you did today? Shit, the fact that you even *wanted* to help? That makes you a hero. To them, to him, and by extension, me. Even if it was a one-time thing, thank you."

Odd, to be serious and drunk at the same time.

"I don't think I did anything all that special," Lily said honestly. It was easier to be honest and drunk than serious and drunk. Serious and honest and drunk and—oh, she hoped hangovers weren't a thing in the Afterlife. "I just tried to help by, I dunno, I was my smart-ass self, I guess. Customer service can suck, and I wanted to help. That's not very heroic. Or at least, I don't feel very heroic."

"Being yourself—really, authentically yourself—that's a heroic feat, yeah?" Dialen cocked her head to the side, the inky silk of her ponytail sliding over her shoulder. "Universe knows I've struggled with it." She clinked a nail against the base of the glass, then chucked Lily's chin with a wink. "Drink up, *Ms. Lily*, it's okay to be celebrated sometimes."

9

---෴---

INVADERS

Lily

Lily stared at the laptop that had appeared in her living room.

The night before, she'd staggered home from Hell, drunk off her ass, giggling like a lunatic, and singing old ABBA songs under her breath. Max had blinked at her disapprovingly for interrupting his nap in front of the fire. She'd whisper-yelled an apology before leaving a trail of clothes to her room, flopping on top of the sheets naked and passing out within seconds.

When she'd woken up well into the morning, memory told her that she should be waking up with the kind of raging hangover that would result in at least a year of fearful sobriety and a lifelong aversion to whatever liquor or cocktail had tried to ruin her liver.

Nausea. Puking. Headache. Weirdly sweaty—especially her lower back. Why did her lower back always get sweaty? She'd mentally calculated the distance from her bed to the bathroom, which, granted, didn't have a toilet, but what the hell, she'd puke in the tub and then *never* drink again—

"Wait a fucking second."

When she'd opened her eyes, the light hadn't felt like an ice pick boring into her brain. She'd sat up. No swooping stomach, no blurry vision, no sweaty—ah shit, her lower back *was* a little sweaty, but was that it? She'd wiggled free of the blanket that had appeared from somewhere and stood, toes buried in the plush rug.

Nothing.

"Holy *shit*, that's lucky!"

The ball of fur on one of the pillows had shifted with a half-awake little *brrrp* of sound.

She'd laughed mid-stretch. "Guess this is Paradise, huh, Maxy-Max? No praying to the porcelain god for me."

Only after a lengthy shower and a hearty breakfast had she noticed the computer. It had no logo or marking of any kind, and it, like the phone that had appeared beside her bed one morning, was unlike any make or brand she recognized, but it was perfectly navigable all the same. Plus, it was damn near instantaneously fast.

The search engine had a list of suggested sites, including something called MortalTube that she clicked on and almost immediately exited out of. Livestreams of mortal events, of political debates, of concerts, of *people*. A banner at the top of the page gave the caveat: *All livestreams are censored for modesty and are not available at all times.* One nausea-inducing search bar had been specifically to find loved ones left behind.

Lily stuck to the Afterlife-specific pages after that, searching for events and scrolling through the lists of coffee shops, curious about one called Common Grounds that seemed to be very popular.

A message popped up in the corner of her screen from Crocell, an invite to an *Invaders* lobby that evening. Like with Siedah's contact in her phone, she assumed that the Universe connected people who wanted to connect. Cool.

She read the message.

Crocell: *It's a partially open lobby, so there will be some random people from Hell, but Krun and his wife, Naamah, will be in it, as well as a few other demons from our shift. Please join us. Show us how mortals can kick ass but, like, nicely.*

Lily grinned.

Hazy twilight had draped itself over the landscape by the time Lily settled in front of the computer with a mug of cocoa, *Invaders* already glowing on her screen. Her fingers hovered over the keyboard, half considering using her old social media handle, *LilyPad*, as her username.

But this was a new world, and she was funny. And a nerd.

She typed out then erased half a dozen options, nibbling on her lower lip in concentration before inspiration struck.

Nearamir.

Chuckling to herself, she picked from the available skins for her character—purple—added a little flower as decoration, and spawned into the lobby, pulling on her headphones while it loaded.

"Oh, hey, new person," username Croaky said, sounding suspiciously like Crocell.

"Hey, thanks for the invite," Lily said, scanning the names and snickering.

"How about we introduce ourselves? Username only?" Croaky suggested. There was a chorus of agreement, then the names came hard and fast.

Stabby was a smooth male voice, who spoke with quiet precision. A bubbly female voice belonged to TacoTime. Fezzik had to be Krun, she was damn sure of it, especially when the username Buttercup introduced herself right after with a soft, gentle voice. Theirs were the only matching usernames in the lobby. NotGuilty was definitely female and sounded vaguely familiar, WohnJick's voice was unfamiliar and male, but cheerful, and ObiWonton had a crisp, androgynous voice and seemed rather reserved.

Then the final player, a hot-pink little figure with bat wings, spoke up. "Hey, this is FruitBat; I'm friends with Stabby and TacoTime."

Lily sat up so fast she nearly spilled her cocoa. The voice was unmistakably male: deep, resonant, slightly growly, and sexy as *shit*. Krun's voice was deep, but this voice . . . this voice was hot.

She wasn't alone in her surprise either; half the lobby reacted with gasps or laughter or sounds of disbelief. She set her cocoa on the safety of the side table.

Is it a voice kink if it's just for one voice?

Then he chuckled. FruitBat chuckled, and it stroked along her skin, thudding through her chest like a phantom heartbeat.

All control over her mouth seemed to be in the hands of her hormones, which was why she heard her own awed voice cutting through the murmur of other people. "Okay, listen, that is the sexiest voice I have ever heard, what the *fuck*?"

Bel

Bel laughed again, even as his face heated. More like went supernova. His ears *burned*. Half the lobby cackled openly, this time at the woman's awestruck tone. A few, Greg included, groaned.

"Here we go again," Angel chortled gleefully.

"Every time," Greg muttered. "It happens *every* time."

Another voice, sounding a bit smug, said, "He's not the deepest voice in the lobby."

The original voice, smooth and female, chimed back in. "Sorry, Kru—uh, Fezzik, you have the deepest voice here, but FruitBat has the sexiest, in my opinion anyway."

"Sexy is so subjective. But as a baseline, I'd say he's all right," Angel put in.

"Is it possible to be attracted to a voice?" a different speaker, possibly NotGuilty, asked.

There were resounding and discordant responses of "Yes."

"Hey, FruitBat," the original woman said, her tone carrying a serious note, "is this making you uncomfortable? We can stop."

"Speak for yourself," someone muttered.

"If it makes him uncomfortable, we stop." The pretty voice had an edge to it.

Yes, yes, it was possible to be attracted to a voice. Bel shifted in his chair, stretching his wings around the specially designed back. "I appreciate you checking . . . who is this?"

"Nearamir."

Bel cocked his head, smile creeping over his lips when he found the little purple figure. "Like Faramir? From *Lord of the Rings*?"

He could hear the grin in her voice. "Yeah, but closer."

Bel laughed so hard his stomach ached. Whoever she was, he liked her.

Lecti, his head housekeeper, appeared in the doorway with an unidentifiable expression. He pointed to the computer in explanation, and she nodded slowly, a series of emotions he couldn't quite make out flitting over her face before she left, glancing over her shoulder with a soft smile.

His laughter wasn't that rare these days, was it?

"That doesn't even make any sense," someone said. "Wouldn't, like, Uglyamir be better?"

"Phonetically maybe, but it's spelled F-A-R-amir, not F-A-I-R-amir, so's more of a visual play on it," Nearamir explained.

Bel leaned forward, still chuckling. "It's an elite-level nerd joke, and I salute it. I don't mind the reaction to the voice; I know it's deep."

There was a beat of silence before someone muttered something unintelligible. His phone lit up.

Greggles: *If I'm the invader I'm killing you first, just to keep the thirsting to a minimum.*

Bel: *You're just jealous, she sounds cool*

Greggles: *Half the lobby is horny for you right now.*

Bel: *Touchy touchy*

"Are we doing proximity chat?" Bel asked, setting his phone aside, screen down.

"I vote yes, if only to keep listening to you, big guy," Nearamir crooned teasingly, a hint of laughter in her voice.

Bel smirked.

"How do you know he's big?" Croaky asked.

"Just his vibe. Plus, I haven't seen a demon yet that I would classify as 'small.'"

Demon. Yet. Small.

"Wait." Bel hunched toward his screen, staring at the little character with the flower on its chest as if he could see through to the person controlling it. "Are you *mortal?*"

A brief pause.

"Mortal soul, yeah."

A ripple of disbelieving noise quickly turned into a warm chatter of greetings. This *Invaders* lobby was fairly private, and mainly comprised of Hell denizens. Most mortal souls were skittish around demons, but she must have befriended a demon to know about it. Or be dating one.

Bel glanced at the little character again, curious.

His phone glowed around the edges as someone texted him. Probably Greg or Angel. Then again, it might be work. He checked the screen, saw the flash of Greg's name, and put it down again.

"Well," Krun cut in, "let's get this game going, shall we? Good luck, everyone!"

The lobby faded away to reveal his character and WohnJick as the invaders. His grin went feral.

Nearamir was safe, from him anyway. It would be her welcome-to-the-Afterlife present. Greg, however . . .

Oh, Greggles, where are yooouuu?

Lily

Two rounds later, Lily shook her head, cheeks hurting from smiling so hard as she guided the ghost of her character around the screen. She couldn't remember the last time she'd laughed so hard or so often, and FruitBat, who also seemed to have a nerdy streak of his own, had the best jokes. They'd gotten into the habit of telling each other a stupid joke or one-liner every time they crossed paths.

Nine bees made their way to Mordor. It was the Fellowship of the Sting.

Did you hear that Godzilla destroyed a cheese factory? De-brie was everywhere.

What is Gandalf's favorite band? The Eagles.

What's the first thing a bat learns at school? The alpha-bat.

After he'd told that last one, she wondered if he had wings, and would have asked him if an emergency meeting hadn't been called and immediately gone sideways.

All of the players were good, but none were better than Stabby. No one seemed to be able to tell when he was lying, he'd elevated social manipulation into an art form, and he knew the game inside and out. He'd killed her while she'd been feeding the weird space fish.

She'd been grumpy about it right up until FruitBat had found her body and began the trial with: "Who the *fuck* killed my nerd wife?!"

It had been the most romantic thing she'd ever heard.

Stabby had lied like a damn rug, gotten Buttercup exiled for it, and made everyone suspicious of Croaky. Now he was on the hunt again.

FruitBat stood at the cartoon hydroponics array, oblivious of the doom coming his way. Lily guided her ghost up and down the hallway, waiting for the inevitable. Barely pausing, Stabby killed FruitBat and darted into the nearest elevator, just in time for FruitBat's ghost to appear in the middle of a rant.

". . . knife-happy, *short*, grumpy—"

"Hey, Batty."

"Nerd wife!" His rumbling voice lit up, and she laughed, guiding her ghost over to his and making a little smooching noise.

"Nerd hubby. I told you he was the invader when he killed WohnJick."

"Bastard. Did he kill you too?"

"Yeah, at the weird fish."

"Double bastard. I need to finish doing the plant thing that I started before I was unjustly murdered."

"I still have a task on the far side of the map."

"Fair enough," he said. "Hey, what do demons eat for breakfast?"

Lily hummed thoughtfully. "If the answer isn't deviled eggs, I'm going to riot."

"You're good," he said, the delight in his tone sending tingles down her spine.

She kissed at him again, quipping, "Only sometimes," before zooming away, a fuzzy warmth spreading through her chest.

She liked this. This nerdy, faceless flirting.

An hour and one loss, one win, later, Lily said good night to her new friends and faceless, nameless acquaintances and closed the laptop.

It had been *fun*. The kind of carefree, guiltless fun she hadn't ever really had. Time had always been a precious, finite resource to be carefully budgeted between work and basic needs. But now? Eternity stretched ahead. Peaceful, abundant, and . . . empty. She could, in theory, spend eternity just wandering, exploring the many realms, meeting countless souls and Afterlife denizens, perhaps even deities, though she doubted any of them would deign to talk to her. Money didn't exist in the Afterlife. Goods didn't have prices, people made, grew, and offered things because it made them happy to share them. She certainly would never have to worry about her health again, given the whole "dead" thing.

But she hated her silent chest, missed life and all its potential. She had dreams she'd never managed to achieve. Things she still wanted to do.

Thinking about reincarnation made her flinch, but perhaps it was like sex. Maybe she just wasn't ready for either yet.

Time. She needed time, and, for once, she had it.

She pushed herself to her feet and stretched, padding toward the bedroom, where Max had already taken over one of the pillows. Though she didn't need to anymore, she still enjoyed the familiar little ritual of brushing her teeth and washing her face before bed. She stripped naked and crawled into the pleasantly warm sheets, snuggling down with a contented sigh.

I hope the souls at the gate weren't super weird today.

10

COMMON GROUNDS

Lily

Lily sauntered into the busy coffee shop nestled into a large indentation off the main Hall, the olfactory siren-song of quality caffeine and baked goods overriding the flash of uncertainty inspired by the assortment of souls, denizens, and a handful of beings who seemed to glow slightly with power. She'd set off that morning with no real plans beyond further exploration, locating the Universal Library, and a possible visit to Hell. It had only taken one whiff of coffee to lure her away from the vine-covered archway of Tír na nÓg.

She'd followed her nose with the intensity of a bloodhound. Growing up in the Pacific Northwest had meant there were a few things in abundance, one of which had been rain. Another had been coffee. And *oh*, she'd missed it.

Sure, her Paradise could make a cup of coffee appear, but she was convinced that coffee made by a person had a little extra oomph. Plus, she liked seeing all the people.

The wide brick entryway that separated the shop from the rest of the Hall opened to a courtyard dotted with tables, and near the far wall, a glossy countertop separated the baristas from the orderly lines of patiently waiting customers. Most of the tables were occupied, and happy chatter filled the air. Lily craned her neck to peer at the front of the line, toward the glass cases filled with—

She moaned. "Holy *shit*, I'm home."

Pastries. Baked goods. *Bread.* Oh, she would commit war crimes for some good, fresh bread. She'd slather it with a little butter . . .

"I highly recommend the morning buns, though the bougatsa is also delicious," said a stunningly beautiful woman, laughing.

Lily turned around to look at her, taking in her sparkling brown eyes and smooth, dark skin. Freckles scattered over her cheeks and Grecian nose lent her a friendly air when her beauty and faint glow of power would have made her otherworldly. If not for the cell phone in her hand, she would have looked like she'd stepped straight from the pages of a history book in her emerald-green chiton, embroidered along the edges with little orange flowers.

"I love it when there're no bad options. I love your chiton, by the way. That color is gorgeous." Lily grinned back.

"Thank you! It has pockets, see?" The woman excitedly demonstrated by shoving both hands into said pockets. "I know it's not necessarily traditional, but damn is it convenient. I like your look too." She grinned up at her. "'Effortless badass' is a timeless and much-appreciated classic."

"It's the height and the resting bitch face, I think." Lily chuckled, fighting the urge to roll her shoulders at the tickle of unearthly energy dancing over her skin.

"Hey, if it works, it works."

They laughed together for a moment before the woman held out her hand, a strand of black hair sliding over her shoulder.

"I'm Persephone."

"Nice to meet you, I'm Lily," she said, shaking her hand, slightly taken aback by the faint calluses on the other woman's palm. Between the name and the aura of power around the other woman, a hint of suspicion flickered at the back of her mind.

It must have shown on her face as well, because Persephone tilted her head knowingly. "Yes, *that* Persephone." She waved a hand and continued. "Lily is a lovely name. Lovely flowers too. You'd think they'd be fussy, but I find they just grow where they feel like it."

Lily nodded a few too many times.

Holy shit. Holy shit, holy shit, holy shit.

She'd been caught practically lusting over pastries by the Greek goddess of spring. She'd barely put any effort into her hair that morning, blow-drying it, pulling it half back, and calling it a day. Now she was standing in front of a fucking goddess. She'd read erotica novels about Hades and Persephone. She'd shaken *Persephone's* hand. That hand had probably shaken Hades's cock at some point—

Nope. Do not go there.

Please don't let there be any mind readers here. Please, Universe, in your mercy give me that . . .

"Really?" Lily said lightly. "I can't say that I ever tried to grow them myself. My mom always had a pot of them on the deck, but I just assumed she babied the hell out of them."

There. That sounded appropriately *not completely stupid.*

She just needed to be chill and not fuck up her coffee order. Persephone was being nice. She'd started the conversation, and she probably liked being treated fairly normally.

"Oh, they absolutely appreciate a bit of babying now and then, but who among us doesn't?"

"This particular Lily flourishes best with books, baked goods, caffeine, and I'd never turn down an orgasm or two."

I am an absolute heathen. This isn't some drunken girls' night.

Well, if the goddess decided to smite her, then her debate about reincarnation wouldn't fucking matter.

It'd been a nice, albeit short, Afterlife.

"Mm, or seven." Persephone's grin was wicked.

Lily raised her eyebrows, surprised. Persephone was beautiful *and* fun? No wonder Hades was allegedly smitten with his wife.

A part of Lily relaxed, concern about her initial lack of a filter fading.

"Seven?" She sighed regretfully. "Now that is a level of stamina that was rarely seen in the mortal world, and it certainly wasn't in my experience. How does it feel to live the dream?"

"You sleep really well. And you're late to things . . . often." The goddess's smirk was positively feline.

Lily moved up in line. "'Goddess of spring,' my ass. More like the goddess of sexual satisfaction. You should change your brand."

Persephone laughed so loudly that a few people turned to look. "Perhaps I'll make it a private title. After all, there's only one worshipper I want kneeling at that particular altar." She turned to speak to the barista as they stepped up to the counter. "A medium lavender vanilla iced latte and a regular mocha, please, and two morning buns."

The barista looked at Lily.

"Large white mocha with Irish cream flavoring, hot, no whip, and a morning bun, please."

"You got it." The barista smiled, hands flying into action.

"So, Lily, what are you up to today? Just exploring?" Persephone asked as she finished texting someone.

"I've wandered a bit already, but I . . ." *I miss feeling like a part of something. I miss working.* "I think I'm going to head down to Hell for a bit, see if they want a hand again."

"What?" Persephone shoved her phone into her pocket. "What do you mean 'if they want a hand again'?"

Lily shifted her weight to one leg. "I stopped by a couple days ago just to see what it was like and ended up helping the demons at the gate out with some of my, uh, customer service experience."

The goddess stared at her, stunned. "And you're going to do it *again*?" *I'm sensing a theme here. Has no one ever helped them out?*

Lily slid her hands into the pockets of her leather jacket and shrugged. "Yeah, the demons are sweet. Plus, I liked the work."

The barista slid two paper bags across the counter, along with two drinks in a carrier, and a single cup for Lily.

Persephone picked up her bag and drinks, shaking her head. "It has been a long time since I've been truly surprised by a mortal soul, for a good reason, anyway."

"Why is it so surprising?" Lily asked. "That I'd want to help, I mean."

"Because no mortal soul has thought to help at the gate. Let alone *asked* to do so."

"Ah." She'd been right. Her stomach gave a sad twist.

"The Underworld is less busy than it used to be, but we still see all kinds. Hell, though, they've always been busy. Ever since the early Middle Ages when Christianity really took off, they've been *ridiculously* busy, and no one envies them for it. They do such amazing work, meting out justice and helping those who are willing to be helped, but I've seen how nasty souls can be, and theirs is often a thankless task. You seeing that and wanting to help them? That's more than surprising. And I'm sure they love the help." Persephone smiled at her warmly. "I have to go, but I'll see you around, Lily. Maybe on another coffee run?"

"Sure." Lily fiddled with the edge of the cup's lid. "I'd love that."

"Excellent. I'll keep an eye out for you!" Persephone said, before weaving away through the crowd.

Lily picked up her bag and cup, thanking the barista quietly, more than a little starstruck by the whole conversation.

What . . . the fuck just happened?

"You okay? You look a little shell-shocked," Moura asked.

Lily leaned against the half wall and stared ahead, unseeing. "I just met Persephone. An actual no-shit goddess. Moura, I made a *sex joke*. To—and I cannot overstate this enough—a *goddess*."

The mortification had fully sunk in when she'd replayed the conversation in her head on the way down the stairs.

"Really? Did she laugh?"

"Yeah," Lily said, wonderingly, "believe it or not."

"I believe it. Now, you're back for a real visit this time, right? Did you want to explore the residential levels?"

Lily finally sipped her coffee and bit back a full-fledged moan. There was good coffee, and there was whatever-the-fuck-magic-that-was coffee. She closed her eyes, savoring the roll of flavors over her tongue, the soothing warmth radiating out through her whole body. She sipped it again, just to be sure it would be as delicious as the first. It was. Bolstered by the caffeine, she braced herself.

"I was actually wondering if you guys wanted some help again. For a few hours, anyway."

"Do we . . . want help," Moura repeated slowly. "Are you serious?"

"Yeah." Lily pulled a piece off of the still-warm morning bun and popped it into her mouth. Delicious. "Is that okay? I know I got cosmic approval or whatever, but if I'm more of a hinderance than a help, I can go."

Krun appeared beside the still-silent Moura, clapping her on the shoulder and giving Lily a kind look. "You are a wonderful help, and on behalf of all of us, we'd be happy to have you. The table is in the storage closet. Your sign is in there too. Zagan wouldn't let us get rid of it, 'just in case.'"

Lily beamed, making a mental note to thank Zagan when she saw him. The big blue sweetie.

Moura snapped out of her frozen shock, waving Krun off. "Right. Yes. Your chair is in the break room," she explained, "and if you're going to help out again, take a breather in the break room whenever you need to."

Lily nodded, heading off to get her chair. "I will."

"And Lily?" Moura called. Lily turned expectantly, walking backward. A bright smile had taken over Moura's face. "Thank you."

Lily inclined her head, then grinned and nodded toward the storage closet. "Is the baseball bat in there too?"

Moura's smile shifted into a grin.

Her chair required a little lifting to retrieve, but once it was down on its wheels, she pushed it toward the line of souls while Moura retrieved the table, sign, and bat. Once it was set up, they surveyed their work, pleased.

"If you make this a habit, you're probably going to start receiving offers of marriage. Shit, you're probably going to start getting them today."

Lily scoffed.

But Moura's warning about receiving proposals hadn't been wrong. Three separate, exasperated demons offered to marry her on the spot after dealing with a series of particularly nasty souls. Two more had offered to kiss her when she'd smacked a low-level politician.

Lily chuckled to herself as she put her chair back the break room. A trio of young guards had serenaded her, enthusiastically off-key, on their way back to their posts as a thank-you, and she could tell that it would be stuck in her head for days.

She had fun in Hell.

She felt *good* in Hell.

I like this. I think I'll do this for a while.

11

F.A. & F.O.

Lily

There was a desk in Hell.

An honest-to-shit desk, halfway along the half wall of black rock that guided souls from the gate to the tunnels. Made of the same stone as the rest of the wall and looking as if it had just grown into shape, it bulged outward in a crescent, disrupting the otherwise smooth arc of the wall. A cushy, human-sized gaming chair waited behind it, along with a laptop, a neat arrangement of office supplies, and a small weapons rack built into the nearby wall, which, other than the baseball bat, sat empty.

Lily had almost dropped her coffee in shock. "How did you . . . ?"

"We didn't," Moura said. "We just came in yesterday and there it was. One of the other shifts said that it just appeared. One second it wasn't there, the next it was. Scared the shit out of some of the trainees. They figured that based on the size and proximity to where you usually set up, it had to be for you."

"Which shift?"

"Ahriman's."

"Oh. They're sweeties," Lily murmured absently, running her fingers over the supple leather of the chair.

Her chair.

She couldn't believe it. Though, she had become a regular at the gate, hadn't she?

For the last couple of months, Lily spent a few days a week down in

Hell, sitting behind her makeshift desk and dealing with souls. The rest of her time remained her own. She still played online games, not only with the demons, but with a wide variety of other people too. No matter what other games she joined or tried, *Invaders* remained a favorite, and not just for the social chaos of it. FruitBat had become a faceless, nameless friend, one who chuckled at her sarcasm and made her laugh with silly dad jokes.

Though he had to fucking know what that voice *did* to people. Especially when he rumbled things like *that's my girl* and *nerd wife* or laughed softly. Nerd wife, oddly, got her every time. Maybe the "wife" bit was what did it, but it also could have been the fond tone. She couldn't decide which.

One slow day, she asked Krun if he knew who the voice belonged to, but he'd just shrugged and told her that it could be any one of a few billion demons.

"Deep voices aren't exactly uncommon down here." He'd smiled, tapping his own chest. She hadn't elaborated further. After meeting all the shifts at the gate and wandering briefly through Residential Level Three, where Seven Deadly was located, she knew that deep voices were common and could confirm that they were pretty much universally hot. But they weren't quite like *that* one.

When she wasn't working or relaxing at home, she made a point to continue exploring. She visited the Summerland, eating fruit on the bank of a creek while a band of witches gave a concert under the trees. There was a popular Irish pub in the Hall that had live music each night and served amazing stew.

One day, to her absolute delight, she found the Universal Library— which was a whole realm unto itself—and accidentally spent three days there before leaving with a small stack of borrowed books.

She and Persephone had struck up a coffeehouse friendship and chatted amicably whenever they saw each other. Persephone introduced her to a few nymphs, and would have introduced her to Freyja, but the Norse goddess had been deep in conversation with a bearded man. Lily had caught pieces of their conversation as she'd waited for her coffee . . .

something about negotiations and increasing training, the tension on both their faces at odds with the general atmosphere of the Afterlife. She'd been tempted to ask Persephone if she knew about who they were negotiating with and what they were training for, but she didn't want to admit to eavesdropping. Especially if the conversation was between two deities.

In all her explorations, there remained one arch that she avoided. She'd tried once, making it as far as the middle of the Hall before she'd been unable to make her feet move any farther. She'd watched as people came and went through the Heaven arch. They'd seemed friendly and kind, greeting each other with smiles and nods. They'd smiled at her as they headed toward the main Hall. One had even asked her if she needed directions. Good people. People who truly loved others. People who were the opposite of the environment she'd grown up in. She'd always known that Christians like them existed, but they had been so few and far between in her life that she considered them the exception and not the rule.

She'd stood there for ten minutes. Unable to move. Her mind a sickening whirl of guilt and shame.

Furious with herself, and cursing her own weakness, she'd spun on her heel and gone straight to Hell, where her makeshift desk sat waiting. She pointed out one logical fallacy after another, imploring, sassing, threatening, listening, one soul at a time, until Krun brought her some muffins that his wife had made and asked if she wanted to sit with him in the break room for a bit. She'd barely talked, and he hadn't asked her to, but he'd told her about his daughter and their pet hellhound while she ate and listened until her chest didn't feel so hollow anymore.

That was one of the reasons she kept coming back—the demons. They always cared.

And, admittedly, she loved getting to mouth off on a regular basis. The opportunity for a brilliant one-liner was a matter of *when* not *if*.

"I'll let you settle in," Moura said, startling her back to the present. A shrill voice cut through the air by the gate.

"Looks like we have a problem child at admissions," Moura said, frowning toward the lines of desks before walking away.

"Hey, does this have Zagan's sign?" Lily called after her.

Moura turned, walking backward for a few steps. "Even better, take a look."

Not wanting to waste time walking all the way around the end of the half wall, and realizing the desk was too wide to comfortably lean over, Lily climbed over the top of it.

There, in bold letters carved directly into the stone, in a perfect match to Zagan's writing:

HELLP DESK

Then below that, smaller:

F.A. & F.O.

Lily mouthed the letters, confused, running through all the acronyms she could think of until—

She laughed. *Fuck around and find out.* A worthy sentiment for the desk. Still chuckling, she climbed back over the desk and crouched to inspect the drawers, which turned out to be mostly empty, but did hold a few interesting little finds. A mini cleaning kit. A binder with basic procedures, as well as restaurant recommendations—

"The desk meets your approval?" A new voice interrupted her perusal of one menu. She put the binder back and stood, then blinked like an idiot at the newcomer.

Devastatingly handsome was too pale of a description for him, but it was the best her befuddled brain could come up with. If every hot-as-fuck-please-ride-me businessman from every erotica novel ever written had merged together, then added a healthy dash of fantasy, he would have been the result. Nearly seven feet tall, with a sveltely powerful build, neat dark hair, striking bone structure, and pearlescent copper skin. Oh, and wings. Glorious, feathered black wings that glimmered with filaments of white gold.

Might be time to end that dry spell. We can break in the desk.

"Um," she said brilliantly.

The newcomer smiled, white teeth flashing. "Apologies, I forget my manners. My name is Lucifer." He held out a hand.

She returned his firm handshake with a smile, all while mentally slapping the shit out of herself. *If I can survive telling a sex joke to Persephone, I can handle this. No sex jokes. I don't even know what sex is.*

"Lily." Good, she still remembered her own name.

"I've heard quite a bit about you, Ms. Lily."

"Hopefully they left out the bit about the karaoke night."

His eyes, a vivid, glacier blue, lit up. *Actually* lit up. Glowed. The thrum of what she had at first mistaken as her own excitement over the desk increased to a palpable sensation over her skin, though it wasn't as unpleasant as some other deities she'd crossed paths with.

"They did, the bastards. We shall have to remedy that someday. I personally have recused myself from any and all karaoke after the 'Tequila' incident."

"Ah, tequila, a fickle mistress. I know her well. Got to know my toilet bowl fairly well because of her too."

"Fortunately, I cannot relate, but I have heard the stories. No, it was the song, not the drink, that was the last straw."

Lily let out a surprised laugh. "The one by the Champs?"

Lucifer nodded with dramatic solemnity. "I sang 'Don't Stop Me Now,' and Asmodeus—the smart-ass—chose to sing 'Tequila' right after, somehow winning our little competition. Personally, I think his soldiers cheated, but that's irrelevant." He shook his head. "What are your thoughts about the desk? That's what I came to ask."

"I— Thank you, so much. It's beautiful." It really was.

His perfect lips quirked up in a pleased smile. "I had heard so much from the captains and staff of the gate about how you have helped smooth the process here. Your assistance, your work, has not gone unnoticed or unappreciated. If there is anything that we, or I, can do to help you, please let us know."

Lily swallowed, studying his eyes for any trace of performance or trick and finding nothing but honesty. The urge to deflect the praise and turn it into a palatable joke reared its head. She pushed it aside.

"You're welcome. Honestly, I feel like I should thank you for allowing me to spend time down here, let alone change anything about your process," she said. The polished black curve of the desk gleamed in the corner of her eye. The edges of the surface were rounded for comfort and would be perfect for kicking her feet up during lulls. "I hope you don't mind that I've been reading on the job when things are quiet."

Lucifer snorted, waving a hand. "This isn't one of those bullshit mortal jobs where, for some reason, they expect you to be one hundred percent productive one hundred percent of the day. If you can make your work easier, do so. If you have nothing to do, relax. If you want to go home, do so. The shifts function as a team to support and cover for each other, but your position is a more solitary one. You decide the time you spend here." Something powerful, like grief or loneliness, flickered over his face. "Eternity is a long time. There is time for everything."

His eerily beautiful eyes had never once wavered from hers, but she found herself calmly meeting his stare. He was being genuine.

"That's very understanding of you."

"Hell is a place of justice and, above all, understanding. For the souls, yes, but for its denizens too. We are all people with feelings and lives."

His obvious respect for the demons at the gate and their work, for her and her work, was unexpected. The casual delivery of his speech belied the obvious passion he held for the topic. She studied him, try-ing to see past the seductive exterior to the person beneath. Lucifer, like the demons, cared. For the souls, for the mortal world, for justice, brutal though it could be. Something eased within her.

A male soul ran up to the new desk, bracing his hands on the polished surface as tears ran down his face. His disheveled appearance only em-phasized the frazzled desperation in his watery eyes.

"Please," he choked out when they both looked at him. "I didn't know what else to do. You can't punish me for just trying to survive." The fear on his face twisted to anger as, before Lily could move, Lucifer stepped toward the desk and towered over him, the picture of composure. "If you think you can threaten me into submission, you can't!"

"Your fear and fury are justified, though your target for them is mis-placed," Lucifer said kindly. "This place is not a prison sentence; it is an opportunity to get the help you wanted and needed in your mortal life.

As you will discover on Level Two, healing can be uncomfortable, but it is only a punishment if you choose to think of it as such."

Lucifer hadn't looked at the soul file, but perhaps as the ruler of Hell his power allowed him to see souls' assignments unassisted. The soul's jaw flexed, mistrust in every line of his body, but eventually he walked stiffly toward the tunnels, leaving them in thoughtful silence.

Lily studied Lucifer, mulling over everything she'd been told in her mortal life and everything she'd learned in death. If she hadn't seen Hell in action, she never would have believed it. In every interaction with a soul, no matter how lost, or rude, or cruel, the demons approached from a place of empathy, but did not allow that empathy to temper the justice they were there to mete out. She'd watched a man shove at Crocell, only to accept his embrace when Crocell had calmly explained that he would not face his healing journey alone. How many souls had she dealt with, like the first woman, who had absolutely deserved their Judgments, but clearly just needed help that they didn't have in their lives? Very few souls were marked irredeemable, and those who were, were cruel beyond measure.

"How did humans get Hell so wrong?" she asked softly.

Lucifer turned back to her, and his smile went rueful, his wings rustling as they shifted, glinting in the warm light. He spread his arms and angled his head. "Did they? With few exceptions, such as yourself, souls who come to Hell are sent here. Souls are given the opportunity and support to grow and change, but as I suspect you know, healing can be an arduous process. When they grow enough to earn their reincarnation, they return to the mortal world with no *true* memories, but their souls remember."

His tone darkened. "They remember not being a guest of Hell, but an inmate of it, and that is not a pleasant thing to be. Mortals, wonderful creatures that they are, or can be, naturally spun these deep memories and impressions into stories. Stories that then became foundations for beliefs, beliefs that became foundations for entire cultures and civilizations. Were they entirely factual? No. But the best stories have nuggets of truth, yes? Thus"—he angled his head—"the not entirely unjustified vilification of Hell."

She smiled sadly. "I spent a lifetime being terrified of this place. The mortal stories of Hell might have started out as cautionary, but now they're mostly a method of control through fear. I never would have come down here if I hadn't been motivated by spite, but I have been thankful every day that I did. You and the demons don't deserve to be thought of as equal-opportunity monsters because you've had to do terrible things in the name of justice. I'm sorry that there's not a way to set the record straight."

Lucifer's eyes grew even more serious, glow intensifying as they surveyed each other. The quiet stretched between them, the only noise the dull murmur of conversation and footsteps. "It has been a very long time since I have met a soul like you," he said finally.

Aiming for respectfully blasé, she shrugged and grinned. "I keep hearing that from deities, and I'm not sure whether to be flattered or concerned. It's good for you guys to be shaken up a bit, life—er, existence—would get so boring otherwise."

Lucifer's rich laugh boomed through the air, and he patted her on the shoulder, sending a pulse of power jolting through her body. "That is very true. It looks like you have company, so I won't hold you." He nodded to the forming line of grumpy souls.

"Lovely. Well, this will be one way to break in the desk." She smiled at him. "Thank you, Lucifer."

"You are very welcome, Lily." He shot a downright terrifying glare at the waiting line of souls, sending a third of them scampering back toward the main line. He winked as he turned. "Perhaps you'll be able to get some reading in today."

Lily was still grinning when an Asian man stormed up to the desk, cussing a blue streak.

12

FUCKING LUCIFER

Bel

Bel scrubbed his hand over his face, sighing at the mountain of paperwork still left on his desk. Legion reports to be read, training and drill schedules to approve, intelligence reports to read through . . .

"Six," Asmodeus said. His cousin lounged on one of the couches in his office, the portrait of boredom.

"What?"

Asmodeus tucked a hand behind his head, muscles shifting beneath his slate-gray skin. "You've sighed six times in the last, I don't know, ten minutes? Fifteen? Maybe, just maybe, you should do something crazy, like take a break?"

"You don't *have* to be in my office," Bel pointed out, reaching for the next paper: an incident report from the training exercise in the Underworld. *Joy.* Hades had texted him about it.

"Your couches are so much more comfortable than mine though. Plus, my office has paperwork in it."

"Universe forbid." Bel grinned, leaning back and stretching his arms above his head. He hadn't had time to fully stretch after his morning training session, and that, combined with the stress of slogging through paperwork—his least favorite everyday task in his role as a general—had his shoulders feeling extra tight. He flared his wings slightly as he rose from the chair, then tucked them close to his back, careful not to disturb the papers with a breeze. He ruffled Asmodeus's hair as he passed by, dodging his retaliatory swipe, and headed toward the floor-to-ceiling windows.

The Admin Level stretched into the distance, red-gold light glinting off the ornate architecture and many windows of the small city. Bridges arched over the wide river of lava that wound through the buildings, a small lavafall throwing up sparks and clumps of molten earth that glowed ethereally against the black rock.

Beautiful.

It was something his mother had taught him from the time he was old enough to understand: how to find beauty everywhere he went.

Beauty feeds the soul, my sweet boy. It takes many forms, some of them obvious, like a flower in bloom or the laughter of a child, but sometimes it is hidden, though it is never absent. Find beauty.

Sometimes the exercise was easier said than done, but he always managed to find something that made his heart settle.

Bel glanced over his shoulder at his desk and grimaced.

Hard to find beauty in *paperwork*, though sometimes the signatures were lovely. Thankfully, unless something catastrophic happened, it rarely grew overwhelming. Unless he ignored it for too long.

A clean desk. That was the beauty he would strive for.

"Azzy, exactly how long have you been putting off your office job?"

"Well," Asmodeus drawled, propping a boot on the arm of the couch, "I've mostly been shoving papers out of the way so that I can bend Sariah over my desk. I made an exception yesterday with Lev's memo about"—he made air quotes with his fingers—"'the importance of not sullying professional spaces with sex.' We made a point to fuck on top of that."

Bel chuckled, shaking his head. Asmodeus and his wife were famously infatuated with each other and had been from their first meeting. Bel had learned the importance of listening, *then* knocking, with all of his regular acquaintances, but especially with Asmodeus.

Except Lev. The meticulous demon had been fairly uninterested in carnal activities since they'd been young. Hence, the now-infamous memo.

Bel had nearly laughed himself sick when it had landed on his desk, shortly followed by spending a solid chunk of time wondering who he could call to fuck in his office out of sheer spite.

He hadn't been able to come up with a valid option.

"Thanks for taking one for the team," Bel said dryly, turning back to the window.

An adult demon flew carefully, far above the city, the tiny figure next to them flapping clumsily along, dipping every now and then before recovering. A ghost of a smile tugged at Bel's lips. He'd helped teach little ones how to fly before, and while he might have outwardly exuded calm confidence, his heart had stopped every time one of them dropped a little too fast, or they'd banked a little too hard or too close to something. He'd still savored every moment.

"Hey, Grumpus," Asmodeus called.

"Fuck you." Greg's smooth response was venomless.

"Didn't even hear you come in," Bel said, turning to greet one of his oldest friends.

Nearly as tall as Bel, with short, spiraling horns, neat black hair, and burgundy skin, Greg had a coolly collected presence that even other demons could find eerie. Where Bel preferred comfortable, athletic clothing, Greg favored a slightly more mortal style, akin to mortal businessmen in movies—if those businessmen ran the most extreme punishment level in Hell, and arguably one of the most intense in the entire Afterlife. His crisply laundered, black button-down shirt lacked any telltale signs of his sleeves being rolled up, suggesting he hadn't been required to exact his expertise yet that day. The tailored black pants tucked into polished knee-high boots also bore no sign of Greg's skill set. His tail swayed lazily behind him, a dead giveaway that he was bored and not bothering to hide it.

Greg shot Bel a droll look and eased himself onto the empty couch across from Asmodeus. "Sneaking in isn't hard when you've got this one making a racket."

Asmodeus beamed and flipped him off.

"Any news on the disturbance in that pocket realm?" Greg asked Bel, aiming his own middle finger at Asmodeus.

"Just what I've heard in passing. Sounds like another Universe might be trying to make contact. They probably gave me a report, but I haven't gotten to it yet." Bel sighed, running a hand over his face.

Greg barely glanced at his cluttered desk and arched a brow. "Too busy flirting with your *nerd wife?*"

"Shut up."

"Ooooo," Asmodeus cooed, sitting up and nearly knocking over a picture frame on the side table with his wing. "Right, tell me about this mortal soul who kicked Greg's ass."

"Is that really more interesting to you than the fact that Bel is finally flirting with someone again?"

"It's only been, what? Almost a century since . . . what was her name? Or no, you never dated her, you just hooked up for like a month, right? Or was that the guy before that?" Asmodeus asked.

"He hasn't actually dated anyone since before you *met* Sariah," Greg said. "See why your priorities are skewed?"

"Both things can be interesting at once. And I met Sariah a century ago, so I'm not entirely off base. How did it feel to lose?" Asmodeus brightened suddenly and turned to Bel. "Hey, speaking of her, maybe she'd be your spite fuck for this memo thing."

"No." Bel's tone brooked no argument.

Not that he hadn't thought about it. He had no idea what she looked like, but he liked her voice, liked her sense of humor and quick wit, liked the way she'd cackled when she'd won as an invader that one time. He especially liked the way she crooned her silly pet name for him, had even begun to crave the way it made him shift in his chair.

Hey, nerd hubby, here's one for you: What do you get when you cross a bat and a man? A ban. Specifically, a lifetime ban from all genetics labs, as well as a visit from the ethics committee.

He'd retold that one in a meeting with the leaders of his aerial legions, and they'd cracked up.

"Is the 'memo thing' about Lev's memo?" Greg asked.

Bel grunted an affirmative.

Greg adjusted the cuff of his shirt. "I won't lie and say that I wasn't tempted to have the same reaction, but a series of billionaires just arrived, so I've been rather busy."

"So has Azzy," Bel drawled.

Asmodeus smirked and laced his hands together behind his head. "It's celebratory. Sariah can't get any *more* pregnant."

"Animals, both of you," Greg said.

Bel couldn't help but laugh at that. "I'd like to remind you of a certain drunken story you once told me about when you went to Faerie for that solstice party—"

"Shut up," Greg mumbled, much to Asmodeus's delight. Before Bel's cousin could ask the question that they all knew was coming, the heavy door to Bel's office swung open once more.

"What are we plotting, gentlemen?" Lucifer's voice was light as he strode through the door, a hint of power rolling through the room. Greg sat imperceptibly straighter, his tail stilling. Asmodeus shifted his wings, but otherwise remained sprawled indolently on the couch.

Bel inclined his head slightly as the ruler of Hell sauntered toward him. Bel took in the easy way Lucifer carried his wings, the hands in his pockets, the glint in his brilliant eyes.

He wanted something.

Whatever it was, Bel hoped it wasn't from him, though the evidence suggested otherwise. He had work to do.

"Not plotting," he said as Lucifer came to a halt beside him, "just taking a break and annoying each other. Lovingly. What have you been up to?"

"Oh, this and that."

Shit. Definitely up to something.

"I had a meeting with your mother this morning, a video conference with Heaven, and I'm working on some preparation for the big meeting later. But that's not why I'm here." Lucifer smiled innocently. "I wondered if you would be able to run an errand for me?"

Asmodeus barely choked back a laugh, instead making a noise like a hellhound whose tail had been stepped on.

Bel blinked. *He cannot be serious.* "An errand," he said slowly.

"Yes."

"That you want *me* to run."

"Yes."

"For you."

"Yes."

"What are you up to, sir?" Greg's voice had slipped into the smooth, even register he used when he was working. Sometimes—not that Bel would ever tell him—it made even his spine prickle.

"Who says I'm up to anything?" Lucifer asked mildly. "I just need Beleth to run a very important errand. What's so strange about that?"

Beleth? He was getting full-named? Really?

"You don't just ask generals or princes or heads of levels to run errands. You make the interns do it. What has Bel done now?" Greg said.

Shit, what *had* he done now?

Did the meeting with his mother have anything to do with it? Perhaps Lucifer just wanted him to stop working for a bit. He had been dropping subtle hints about "easing the fuck up with work" and "developing a hobby." Maybe he'd gotten tired of Bel ignoring him and decided to make a point.

Even if that wasn't the case, Greg's point was valid. While Lucifer was the ruler of their entire realm—inherently linked to it through his power, like all deities—he delegated the more day-to-day and specialized responsibilities to trusted and qualified people, stepping in when necessary to achieve a result. Micromanaging wasn't his style.

Lucifer cocked his head and smiled, daring anyone to try to pry the truth out of him. "Don't you want to know what the errand even is?"

Torn between desperately wanting to finish his paperwork and wanting to avoid it for as long as possible, Bel scowled.

"I seem to have left one of the short swords I got from Brigid in the weapons closet . . ."

You've got to be shitting me.

". . . by the gate, and I was wondering if you would be able to find it for me?" Lucifer nearly batted his eyelashes in innocence.

"By the *gate*? Really?" Bel folded his arms, tail lashing, growing more amused than annoyed by how hard Lucifer was pushing this, but a tendril of unease still curled through his belly. Lucifer always seemed to do things for a reason, even if that reason took several hundred years to make itself known. Could this be one of those times? Or was this exactly what it felt like: bullshit.

"I just don't know what I was thinking, leaving it up there."

"Why not have one of the guards find it and send it down? I'm sure they'd be happy for the break."

Bel had never interned at the gate, like many demons did in their youth, and had only ever seen the controlled chaos of it on his way to the Universal Hallway. The demons who worked at the gate were renowned throughout Hell for their seemingly thankless but critical work, but he suspected that the collective awe didn't help them feel better when they were up to their horns in morons.

"I'd hate for them to mistake a Hephaestus or Goibniu blade for one forged by the Lady Brigid. I don't want to bother them more than I have to. You know all of the great smiths' work so well, you'd never mistake one deity's craftsmanship for another."

Asmodeus seemed to be pinching his nose shut in an effort to keep from laughing, and even Greg was trying to hide his smirk.

Traitors.

"Is that all?"

"If you wouldn't mind making sure that the new addition to the gate is doing all right, I'd appreciate it."

"What new addition," Bel said flatly, claws digging into his biceps.

"Oh"—Lucifer waved a hand—"just a new feature to the entry process. I'm sure everything's fine, but it couldn't hurt to check."

"What. New. Addition."

"Don't overthink it. You'll be able to tell if your assistance is required."

Asmodeus giggled. All seven-plus feet of hardened warrior, general, and prince of Hell giggled.

Fucker.

"Would you like me to get you coffee too?" Bel asked, not meaning it in the slightest.

"No, no, just the blade." Lucifer beamed, heading for the door. He glanced at Asmodeus, who was holding his breath and mottling a deeper shade of blue. "Don't you have paperwork to do?"

"He's been too busy doing his wife," Greg muttered.

"Oh please," Lucifer said, halfway out the door. "Haven't you met dear Sariah? It's far more likely *she's* been doing *him*."

"'You're the only one who can tell craftsmanship apart.'" Bel mimicked under his breath, waiting for an elevator.

Nonsense. He knew several retired warriors who worked at the gate, all of whom were older than him and could probably tell blades of different craftsmanship apart by the sounds they made cutting through the air.

Thankfully, the elevator car was empty when it arrived, and he swatted at the *Gate* button before resting his hand on the knife hilt at his hip. As the elevator started moving, he lashed his tail so hard that it smacked into the wall, sending a jolt of pain up his spine.

It didn't help his mood.

Not that he'd been in a great mood lately anyway.

Maybe he did need a vacation. He loved his role as a general, training with the legions, leading them. Sure, the paperwork was annoying, but in the end, it was just part of the job. His role as a prince, though . . . he did his best to ignore it, keep its presence in his life to a minimum. That title didn't matter—not to him anyway. He'd been both wanted and rejected for his title before, which he found simultaneously understandable and ridiculous. It wasn't the lack of sex making him edgy either; he'd gone longer without before, and his hand was adequate to take the edge off.

The ding of the elevator interrupted his train of thought, the doors sliding open and allowing distant voices to fill the air. He clamped his wings tightly to his back; he hated when anyone touched the sensitive membranes without permission.

Except little ones who didn't know better.

His nieces and nephews had once attacked him with affection when he'd arrived during a finger-painting session at his mother's house. He'd had colorful little handprints and smudges on the outer edges of his wings for weeks. He hadn't minded.

He *did* mind when he walked through the Hall and someone, always a mortal soul, touched his wings without so much as saying a word to him. The souls probably wouldn't be close enough to touch him, but he'd rather be safe than sorry.

Bel stalked through the tunnel into the cavernous area of the gate. It looked like a busy day; every intake desk had a line, and the crowds moving toward the levels were dense. There was another line, discordant with his memory of the place, that must be the "new addition" Lucifer had referenced.

The weapons closet lay closer to the tunnels to the levels for the convenience of the working demons, and he made his steps purposeful. One of his old soldiers, Krun, raised a heavy arm in welcome, and Bel dipped his head in acknowledgment, watching the veteran warrior drop back into his role, scowling at the screeching woman waving her arms at him. Krun was more than twice Bel's age and had fought in the last great war between their Universe and an invading one. He had retired a few decades after Bel had risen to general. Bel hadn't known him especially well, but he'd certainly known of him and had been pleased to hear the warrior was doing well.

Bel ducked into the spacious and highly organized weapons closet, which felt like an understatement as the room was nearly the size of his palatial office. A smile tugged at his mouth, recognizing the work of the soldiers who had retired to the gate. Every weapon was in pristine condition, every surface neat and clean, the organization a picture-perfect example of how all weapons rooms should be organized. The sole, glaring exception lay casually on a table. Every inch of the blade practically screamed that it was Brigid's work: A serpent was embossed in rose gold on the black leather of the hilt, and the pommel was carved with a raven. The black scabbard was embossed in the same rose gold, in elegant patterns of clearly Irish origin.

Fucking Lucifer.

The blade's balance was exquisite. The weight and size too light and small for his preference, though it would suit Lucifer's more elegant fighting style. Scabbard clenched in his fist, Bel headed for the elevators and made it two steps out the door before a flurry of motion caught his eye by the strange new line.

He did a double take.

A mortal soul, a woman with deep auburn hair, was mercilessly and enthusiastically beating the ever-loving shit out of a soul that palpably radiated evil. She was tall for a mortal, athletic and curvy, wearing a fitted black T-shirt, leggings, and boots. He thought he glimpsed tattoos on one arm, but distance and her motion made it difficult to tell.

She straightened, flipped a loose piece of hair over her shoulder, and dropped the bat in her hand before winding up to aim a kick at the other soul's stomach.

Bel's mouth went dry.

She was glorious. She was *magnificent*.

She was . . . closer.

He dimly noted that his feet had carried him toward her as he soaked up every detail. Her face was still tilted down toward the soul. He wanted to see it.

As if she'd heard the thought, she looked up.

The hum of voices and the shuffle of feet faded away.

Blood, not her own, was spattered on her cheek when she glanced at him with beautiful hazel eyes, then gave him her full attention.

She was a warrior queen.

And she was looking at him.

13

FRUITBAT AND NEARAMIR

Lily

Lily had snapped when the third evil shithead, this time a perpetrator of genocide, had come through her line. Arguably the worst yet, and absolutely the most arrogant, she'd decided to revoke his teeth privileges with extreme prejudice. A swing of her bat and they littered the floor, but that wasn't enough for this asshole. One of the great perks of the solid desk, she'd discovered, was the ability to leap onto and over it and not have to go around for fear of knocking it over.

She let the images the file had shown her fuel her strikes. *Begging, crying, children screaming, gunshots*—she wound up for a World Cup–worthy kick that would have thrown her back out for a week if she'd still been alive.

Worth it.

So she did it again.

Hands, he didn't need those. She'd seen the atrocities he'd enacted, the lives he'd signed away with those hands—

Something—or someone—large loomed at the edge of her vision, Krun probably, to help or drag the soul away.

She glanced up and did a double take.

Holy fuck.

It was *not* Krun.

His skin was a deep shade of purple-gray, and he had to be at least seven feet tall and powerfully built. His sleeveless, gray, athletic-style tunic showcased arms thick with muscle, and stretched over a broad chest. She had a sense that every inch of him was solid, functional muscle—none of that "muscles for appearances only" nonsense. Bat-like wings tipped with a black talon at each apex poked over his broad shoulders. Long inky-black hair gleamed in the warm light, pulled half back and cascading past his shoulders, framing his ruggedly handsome face.

His features were rough-hewn. His nearly straight nose had a small bump in it, probably from being broken a time or two, and his jawline was clean, save for a pair of dull little spikes on his square chin, like a little demonic goatee. He looked to be in his early to midthirties, though given the immortality of demons, he was likely far older than that.

Black goatlike horns the size of her hand added to his impressive height, arcing up and backward in a smooth curve. A scar sliced through one of his thick eyebrows, making him look even sexier and more dangerous, sending a bolt of awareness between her thighs.

His eyes . . . Her breath caught. Black sclera, a less common trait that she'd noticed, offset his silvery irises. Unusual, beautiful eyes. And they were fixed on her.

The soul at her feet, the thousands of souls shuffling by, along with all the other demons, ceased to matter.

He was . . . incredible.

He hadn't spoken, but something in the way he carried himself, in the expression in his glorious eyes, radiated safety. Kindness. Steadiness.

He opened his mouth, then closed it and swallowed hard before holding his hand out, offering her a beautiful short sword.

She took the weapon, resting the sheathed blade against her shoulder, and smiled up at him. It felt like the most natural thing in the world.

The handsome demon's answering smile warmed her skin like a beam of sunlight on a spring day. She sucked in a deep, oddly satisfying breath, as if it was the first full breath she'd taken in a long time.

"Hi," she said, watching those unusual, glittering eyes crinkle a little in the corners with his smile. He seemed to be watching her just as closely.

"Hi." His deep voice rumbled, familiar in a way she couldn't quite place until he continued, sounding slightly awed. "You have great form."

The Universe seemed to still around them.

"Holy shit, *FruitBat*?"

His rugged features slackened. He blinked once. Twice. "Nerd wife?!"

She nodded as he loosed a booming laugh, hopping excitedly, wings flaring a bit. Lily laughed so hard and so free that something in her silent, hollow chest sparked.

She opened her arms to her nerd hubby.

His hug lifted her feet effortlessly off the ground, his body solid and warm and practically thrumming with excitement. She threw her arms around his neck, gripping his heavy shoulders a little tighter so that she wouldn't brush his wings and trying not to whack him with the sheathed sword. She'd read enough fantasy and monster romances to be overly cautious about the potential sensitivity of wings.

"Look at you, Nearamir, kicking ass in real life and online!" he said gleefully, his voice—*the* voice—rumbling through his chest and into her bones.

Stop. Ignore, ignore, ignore.

He set her down with more care than she'd expected, large hands settling on her shoulders as he beamed down at her with that glorious smile.

"Aw." She chuckled, reaching up to squeeze a thick wrist affectionately. "You caught me on a good day. What are you doing here—wait, shit, I don't even know your real name! I'm Lily." She held out her hand, thoughts spinning at a million miles an hour.

He ran a hand down his face and grimaced. "Oh, yeah, we kinda skipped that part, didn't we? I'm Beleth, but everyone just calls me Bel." His hand dwarfed hers, his palm warm and callused, his grip firm but not crushing. "Nice to meet you officially, Lily."

"Nice to meet you too, Bel." She couldn't stop smiling and couldn't bring herself to care about it. He was as ridiculously attractive as his voice, but that wasn't what mattered. He was here. Her friend. As his hand lingered in hers, a knot seemed to ease in her soul, one that she hadn't been aware of until that moment. "Do you like coffee?"

Lily yelled to Moura that she was shutting the desk down for a bit, leaving the bloody remains of the soul moaning on the floor and taking the arm Bel offered her as they headed toward the Universal Hallway.

She had experienced that kind of instant connection only once or twice before when she'd met some of her best friends. Something on some deep level had told her that, whoever they were, in some way, they were going to be important to her.

Bel felt important.

Their conversation flowed easily and nonstop, save for breaking down in peals of laughter every so often. Apparently, they'd both frequented Seven Deadly for some of the same events, and had probably missed running into each other half a dozen times. He told her about a bar on one of the lower residential levels that was one of his favorites, mostly because it hosted a weekly trivia night.

"Though," he said conspiratorially, "if you want the best trivia night in the Afterlife, Luckyleaf, the Irish pub over by Tír na nÓg, is hands down the winner. It's a massive place, but during monthly trivia it gets *packed*."

"I love trivia!" Lily exclaimed, mind already whirring with the possibilities presented by a trivia night run by immortals and souls. "I think it's a side effect of reading so much."

"It's also a nerd thing, and we're always trying to curate the best team for the theme. We get pretty competitive about it on the Admin Level."

"I wouldn't have pegged you as a full-fledged nerd," Lily mused.

Bel's eyes gleamed wickedly, mouth opening before he bit his lips, cheeks staining a deeper shade.

Her breath caught, utterly distracted by that wicked gleam, before shoving the feeling aside. What had she said again?

Pegged . . .

Well, shit.

Lily covered her hot face with a hand, groaning. "I sure opened the door for that one."

"One? There were *so* many options for that." Bel laughed, easing the tension enough for her to chuckle too.

"Sorry," he said a moment later. "I, uh, have a penchant for dirty humor."

"Oh thank fuck," Lily sighed, squeezing his arm. "I do too, so please don't hold back on my account. I'll probably think it's funny as hell. Literally."

His eyes twinkled, the faint creases at their corners deepening.

She continued. "Actually, when I met Persephone for the first time, I might have accidentally told her a sex joke within, like, two minutes."

A deep laugh burst out of Bel, making a cluster of people nearby jump in surprise, their eyes raking warily over the horns, the wings, the powerful frame. Their skepticism rankled her, so she smiled at Bel while shooting them a challenging look.

"You have a friend forever in her now. She loves filthy humor," Bel informed her, guiding her around a glowing wisp the size of a car. "She's sweet, and good for Hades. They're good for each other really."

"You know them well?" she asked, trying not to sound too incredulous.

"Oh yeah. Hades is an old friend of mine. He lets us train in the Underworld sometimes, and he and Persephone always host great parties. If you get an invite, go. It's worth it."

Lily cocked her head. "Train? So you're a part of the armies?"

A hint of tension crept into his expression, and the arm that she still held. "Ah, yes. A general actually. Eighty-five legions."

Oh.

It explained a lot—the steadiness, the sense of reliability, his powerful build and the athletic way he moved, the calluses on his hands, and the scar on his face. He still smiled, but the warm, crinkly lines by his eyes were gone, replaced by a slight furrow between his thick eyebrows.

"I told a sex joke to a goddess," she reminded him, "so if you're worried about me being all deferential, I promise you that's not going to be a problem."

Bel stopped walking again and gawked at her, blinking for several seconds. She shrugged and smiled.

Please don't let my mouth get me into trouble again. I don't want to lose a not-online friend so soon.

He cleared his throat, furrow between his brows disappearing as a smile teased the corners of his mouth. "You've also told the master of Level Nine, as well as the goddess Hel, to go fuck themselves during a game. Separate occasions."

It was Lily's turn to blink. She *had*?

Warmth enveloped the hand she had on his arm, his other hand covering hers. She dimly registered that his nails weren't just painted black, they were simply naturally black and tipped with points. Claws. They were claws.

"I don't know why I ever worried," he said, the corners of his eyes crinkling again.

Old insecurities twisted their way free of the mental cage she'd shoved them in.

He's a freaking general, and I'm just a retail worker. He's so kind, and I'm not . . .

Batting them back into the shadows was easier than it had been before. She was doing a job that no one else had thought to do, and she was good at it, even if she sometimes worried that she was *too* good at it. She had friends, more friends than she'd ever had in her lifetime. She had faced down some of the worst kinds of monsters ever produced by the mortal world, and made them cower.

Bel was a friend, and he didn't seem to care about all that, He guided the conversation back toward her and her work.

As they joined the line at Common Grounds, Lily explained how she'd started working in Hell, with Bel listening intently.

"I really like the new desk," she said eventually. "It feels more . . . professional. Like I actually belong there, instead of just being temporary, like I've always been before."

Jobs, apartments, romantic relationships, life . . .

Bel covered her hand with his again, shaking his head in wonder. "Nothing about you feels temporary."

Lily ducked her head with a smile, grateful her hair covered her burning ears. "Thank you," she murmured. "So, are things still tense with Heaven? It seems like the army is a big deal in Hell."

Bel tilted his head. "No and yes. I mean, yes, the armies are large, and an integral part of Hell. We're one of the primary fighting forces in the Afterlife, but it's not because of Heaven. We're on good terms with them and everyone else now, and have been for a very long time. No, the primary source of potential trouble is other Universes. Most of them are chill, but the others . . ." Shadows flickered across his expression, his silvery eyes going distant.

Lily tried to remain nonchalant, but she studied him. She'd had friends who had served, and she'd seen that look before. The toll of combat carved itself into the bones of those who had seen it.

He shook himself out of his reverie. "Others are the reason we train so hard. They're more of a deadly annoyance than anything else at the moment."

Deadly?

"You can die?" she asked.

He met her gaze, nodding. "Souls regenerate, though not without cost, and they have more limitations on what they can do. As beings of the Afterlife, the rules are different for us. We are born, grow up, and live pretty much indefinitely unless we are killed or"—he cleared his throat—"or if we choose to go to the Void. If we die, our souls become part of the fabric of the Universe, which is why we all cherish and respect our surroundings so much. We have lives and families, like living mortals, just on a longer timescale than in the mortal world. But all that to say: Yes, we can die."

Lily had known about the denizens and their lives, but the limited reading she'd done hadn't mentioned dying. It *had* mentioned that souls couldn't have children. Souls formed new partnerships all the time, but reproduction was for the living. She could understand and respect that, but it hadn't stopped a pang from shooting through her chest. The pain of that moment paled in comparison to the stomach-twisting horror of Bel's words.

Demons can die.

"Well, as a favor to a new friend, try not to die anytime soon, okay?" she said lightly, or tried to.

Bel's smile was impish. "No promises, but I'll give it a go. On a lighter note, what's your Paradise like?"

"It's straight out of a fantasy novel." Lily grinned, happy for the new topic. "There's this cool little village with tons of stuff to do, and the mountains are stunning. My house is the best part, though. Not only does it have the most amazing round door, it's got the coolest fucking library, you have no idea!"

"A round door? Like in *Lord of the Rings*?" Bel lit up like a firework. "Not only do you live in a literal fantasy land, you have a *hobbit door*? Tell me everything! Does it have Gandalf's mark on it? Is it green? Do you even like green?"

"I like green, but my door is purple," Lily rushed on, practically fizzing with excitement. "I thought you just *liked Lord of the Rings*, not that you were huge fan of it!"

"Please," Bel scoffed, the effect ruined by his thousand-watt grin. "You didn't think I knew that many of those jokes and was just casual about it? What else do you read? I like a lot of fantasy, but sci-fi has some great stuff too . . ."

Bel

The barista had to physically wave a hand between them to get their attention. They each gave their orders, then shuffled off to the side to resume their animated conversation. At the mention of books, Lily lit up.

It was a glorious sight, and also a problem. If Bel had had a hard time keeping his eyes off her before, it had become damn near impossible once that lighter-than-air smile had taken over her features and made his heart kick in his chest.

Beautiful. She was beautiful.

She smirked to herself halfway through detailing a disastrous book-to-movie adaptation she'd seen, and his attention snagged on her lips.

His skin heated, and he pushed back the swell of long-forgotten desire. He cut his eyes back up to hers, thankful she hadn't seemed to notice.

He had other pretty friends. Not pretty like her, but he was friends with Angel, a *succubus*, for Universe's sake. It would be fine. He could be normal. Totally normal. Just Bel.

They found a table with stools instead of chairs and settled across from each other. The little line between her eyebrows disappeared when she sipped her coffee, the corner of her pretty mouth tipping upward.

"Still the best coffee I've ever had, and where I'm from, being a coffee snob is practically a requirement," she said.

"Oh? Where?"

"How familiar are you with mortal geography? Like, the United States?"

"Familiar enough, but I don't think I could name a lot of the states."

"Gotcha. I'm from the Pacific Northwest, it's beautiful, but known for getting a lot of rain. All that seasonal depression and cool weather is best handled with lots of coffee." She cradled the cup in both hands. "Are you much of a coffee guy, or is this a treat for you?"

"I'm typically a tea guy, but I get coffee once or twice a week, depending on what's going on. If you don't mind my asking, what was your mortal life like?"

A lifetime of gauging opponents' minute movements, of reading the tiny expressions in combat or conversation, made the shift obvious. A darkness flitting across those bright eyes, the barest stiffening of her posture, the tiny instinctual intake of breath, lips tightening ever so slightly.

He could practically feel the walls she pulled up around herself, and he didn't believe the practiced smile she shot his way, nor the too-casual shrug, for a second.

Pain. That was old pain in her eyes.

"I'm sorry," he said gently. "I didn't mean to pry."

"It's fine. That's what friends do, right? Ask about each other's lives? It's a valid question. I was pretty inconsequential in my mortal life. Worked. Paid my bills. Got through it, just like everyone else." Her tone had the hint of an edge to it. Like a naked blade, benign until it had to be put to use. "How about you? Did you always want to be a general?"

He watched her for a moment, keeping his demeanor nonchalant and calm. "Yes and no. I always aspired to be worthy of a command position, not necessarily a general. I went to school like everyone else, but I've been training to fight since I could walk. It's kinda my thing." He pretended to flick his hair over his shoulder and preen. She snorted, the threads of tension slipping away into nothing. "I've always been pretty busy with the armies."

"Training?"

He nodded, sipping his coffee. "Always. And patrols, and assignments, and paperwork. And a battle or war, when we don't have a choice, though thankfully we haven't had a *major* war since I became a general."

"So, only a little on your plate, then."

He laughed. "But outside of that, I like spending time with my friends, and apparently getting my ass kicked in *Invaders*."

She laughed outright. "You and me both. Do you have any idea who Stabby is?"

"That would be Gregorith. He's my best friend, has been since we were little. He never really gamed much, but he latched onto *Invaders* when it came out and has been wiping the floor with pretty much all of us ever since, the bastard. He's also the one who runs Level Nine."

It was always a little odd to refer to Greg by his full name, but he introduced himself to people as Gregorith, and had once corrected someone who had heard someone else call him Greg. Ever since then, Bel had made a point to only refer to him as Greg in front of people who knew him as such.

"Oh, *he's* the one who runs Level Nine. I feel slightly bad for telling him to fuck himself with a cactus now."

"Still bitter about that game he had a triple kill?"

Lily growled into her coffee. "Aren't you?"

"He tried to win me back over with a pie."

"And?"

"Well," Bel said conspiratorially, thrilled when Lily leaned in slightly, "in battle, it is very helpful to know your opponent. Sadly, Gregorith knows that I have a weakness for his mom's blackberry pie."

Lily gasped theatrically, placing a hand on her chest. "Oh no, you traitor."

"I would do terrible things for one of Morgen's blackberry pies. Apparently including forgiving Gregorith for that heinous display of violence and manipulation."

"Well, I didn't get a piece of pie. Permission to continue grousing at your friend for being a little too good at *Invaders*, General?"

Her playful tone had him swallowing hard. *Fuuuck. Pull it together and don't make it weird, you jackass.*

"Permission enthusiastically granted. Tell you what, you sass the shit out of him, and I'll think it's hilarious and share the next pie. Win-win for both of us."

She grinned. "Tricky. I like it. You have a deal."

They tapped their coffee cups together and took a drink.

As they walked back, Bel listened as Lily described a bonfire party in her Paradise that had spiraled quickly into a mead-fueled "who can slide down the mud hill the fastest" competition. She was a vivid storyteller, with a wry comedic timing that had him threatening to spew coffee out of his nose more than once.

As Lily spoke, every fiber of his being sat up and took notice of this mortal soul with a certain incandescence about her. It came in flashes, that brightness. Like it slipped out when she wasn't paying attention, or her guard was down. Authenticity. That's what he suspected it was. The moments that she seemed to light up were Lily unfiltered, but, for some reason, she kept a lock on it. He itched to find out why. To understand it, understand her, to let himself bask in the brilliance of her.

Lily.

He dimly wondered if Lucifer had hoped for this and almost instantly realized he didn't give a damn. It didn't matter how he'd gotten to meet Lily, only that he had. She was bright and witty and sharp and sarcastic and lovely, even more so in person than online. She carried a pain within her, though, some discordant note in her song, and it only made him want to know her more.

He'd meant it when he'd told her that she didn't feel temporary. Not only did she move through Hell and the Afterlife like she'd been born to it, but it felt like they'd been friends for years. He wanted to just *be* around her.

They sauntered down the staircase to Hell while he told her about the time, as teenagers, he and Asmodeus had tried to steal a piece of a pie cooling on Morgen's windowsill, and Greg had nailed them with his sister's crafting glitter from an upstairs window.

"I swear I still find glitter from it. I was cleaning my armor the other day, and I have no idea how it got there, but there was a speck of blue glitter in the seam of my vambrace. Sure, it might have been from something else, but I'm doomed to wonder." He smiled, the bracelets around his wrist leaping to the forefront of his mind.

"It's been how many years?" Lily laughed.

Bel puffed out his cheeks and exhaled slowly. "Three hundred in Afterlife years, give or take?"

"That tracks for glitter. Hell, I'm *dead* and I'm pretty sure in the shower yesterday I found remnants of the body glitter I used back in college."

His knee-jerk reaction to wonder about the "body glitter" and "shower" parts of her statement was violently overridden by the pang that shot through his chest. He'd known obliquely, but the full implication of it had finally sunk in.

Dead. Lily was *dead.*

She'd had a life. She'd been a whole, living person, had seen and experienced things in the mortal world that he couldn't hope to ever see or experience. Now she was dead. A mortal soul in the Afterlife like so many others. Everyone had a family, and families could be fucking complicated, but had she loved hers? What about her friends? Did she miss them? Miss them like he missed—

He shut that thought down hard, just like he always did.

Maybe that was part of her guardedness. That pain he'd seen in her eyes . . . maybe she was grieving the life she'd left behind.

Thankfully, their conversation had lapsed enough that his quiet realization went unnoticed. The last few steps out of the tunnel and into the open air of the gate spurred him back into action. A line of souls already waited at her desk. A few quailed and scurried back to the main line as Bel approached the desk beside her.

Bel touched her arm. "It's trivia night tomorrow at Luckyleaf. Would you like to be on our team? You can meet my fathead cousin Asmodeus and his cool wife, Sariah. Then it's just me, Lucifer, Thanatos, Ishtar, and Chesma. I can introduce you to Gregorith and Angel, and some of the other people you've gamed with, but they're on different trivia teams."

Lily's eyes gleamed. Without looking away from him, she flipped off a soul who was waving their hand and snapping for her attention.

"I would love to! I might not be much of an asset, but I'm so there." She jerked her head toward the line of souls and shot him a rueful smile. "It's my incentive to stay sane until then."

Do not say it's a date. It is not a date.

He couldn't remember the last time he'd smiled so much. "Awesome! Can I text you?"

"Of course! Memes and jokes are not required, but they are appreciated."

He knew without looking that her number had just appeared in his phone as soon as she'd agreed. Despite his best efforts, he couldn't come up with an excuse to hang around after that. She had work to do, and so did he.

He cautiously held his arms out.

Shit, maybe she's not a hugger. Maybe the hug before had been a mistake or just a result of enthusiasm or something. I should have asked—

She stepped forward into his embrace as if they'd done it a million times before, sliding her palms across his back under his wings and

squeezing. He wrapped her in his arms, basking in her warmth and softness and sweet floral scent.

Before he wanted it to end, she pulled back, a finger barely brushing
against the base of his left wing. Tension and heat lanced through his
whole body, all of his awareness narrowing down on that tiny touch. He
couldn't stop the soft inhale, but he did manage to swallow the groan
that threatened to escape, his mind screaming at him to not make things
awkward.

She jerked back, face burning almost as red as Greg's skin, mortification and apology written all over her face as she held up her hands
between them. "I am *so sorry*! I didn't— I assume they're sensitive and
private and—"

Ignoring the fading electricity that danced under his skin—because
he was going to be a gentleman, damn it—Bel gently clasped her hands,
and she stopped talking.

"It's okay," he said with a smile, more than a little impressed that she
had pieced together more basic wing etiquette than most souls he met.
"Accidents happen. They *are* sensitive and private, but they're also damn
big and can get in the way when you're trying to hug someone, yeah?"

Lily nodded, hands relaxing in his grip as a little smile returned to her
lips. "Thank you. We'll figure out the hugging Tetris eventually, right?"

"Obviously. Between the two of us, we'll get this thing pegged." He
winked. "In the meantime, O Great Lady of the Desk, looks like we've
both got work to do." He let go of her hands with a grin, walking backward for a few steps and pointing to the blade she'd propped against her
chair. "See you tomorrow, and be sure to use that blade!"

Lucifer's sharp blue eyes zeroed in on Bel's smile the moment the elevator doors slid open.

"Have you been waiting this whole time?" Bel asked, walking past him.

Lucifer paced beside him, ignoring the question. "So?"

"She's amazing," Bel said, swirling the last of his coffee in the cup. The
skin of his back still tingled where her hands had been.

"Did you get me a coffee?"

"Nope." Bel took a sip.

"Where's my sword?"

"Gave it to Lily."

Lily, who beat the shit out of a soul of Level Nine–degree evil with gorgeous form and feral beauty. Lily with the pretty eyes. Lily, who told sex jokes to goddesses and generals and told anyone who deserved it to go fuck themselves. Lily, who liked sugary coffee—a white mocha with Irish cream—and hid herself behind walls.

"You *what*?!" Lucifer squawked.

Bel just laughed.

14

TRIVIAL

Lily

L ily stood in her underwear, staring into her closet.

"It's just trivia night," she explained to Max, who continued grooming himself on the bed. "So I don't need to go balls to the wall fashion-wise." She squinted. "Right?"

The cat ignored her.

How helpful.

She riffled through the seemingly endless array of clothing that appeared and disappeared from the closet at will, pausing on a slinky black cocktail dress. The silk was so fine that it almost looked sheer but seemed to be fully opaque when she held her hand underneath it. The cut of it would bare plenty of skin while draping and pooling over the curves and hollows of her body.

A "fuck-me" dress if ever she'd seen one.

She pushed it aside, along with the flushed curiosity of what clawed hands would feel like skating across the skin the dress would reveal.

Not what I'm here for. Truly.

It really wasn't. She had always craved connection and had always been a naturally tactile person. Despite the raging sex drive she'd had in her life, she had usually preferred the ease and convenience of a vibrator to the potential of a heady physical release and the quietly emotionally shredding nature of a casual hookup or fling. She hadn't been built for hookup culture, but it had been the only real option she'd had at the time for something more fulfilling than silicone.

Nothing about you feels temporary.

She knew she'd be hearing those words in his warm, rumbly, sexy-as-hell voice in her head for a long time. Her fingers stilled on the long sleeve of a shirt in such a dark shade of purple it was nearly black.

Permanence.

That was what she really wanted, wasn't it? She didn't just like the new desk, she loved it. She didn't just want mind-blowing sex, she wanted mind-blowing sex with someone who wanted *her*. Not just the orgasm, or fulfillment of a redhead fantasy, or a way to kill time, or whatever else she, or more accurately her body, represented.

So, yes, she wanted to have sex. But she wasn't going to immediately ruin a perfectly good—possibly great—new friendship based on burgeoning mutual trust and connection and humor just because she wanted to climb him like a tree.

Bel was a friend. Maybe *someday* he could be more, but she would not make them fuck buddies.

There. Decision made. Problem solved.

She pulled on a pair of buttery soft leggings, then tugged the purple shirt over her head. Simple and sexy, with a touch of elegance, the shirt's V-neck just showed the upper swell of her breasts and fitted her torso without being too tight. She headed to the bathroom to add a touch of mascara to her lashes and fiddle with her long fall of hair. Surveying her efforts in the mirror, she happened to catch her own eye.

You fucking coward.

She blinked. Scowled.

You push everyone away. You always push everyone away, just like you did when things were fine, but you were scared of being seen, just like you did when you were sick. It could be more. You're just too scared to let it.

"Shut up," she snarled at the mirror. Max, dozing on the heated tile floor, startled and stared at her with wide eyes. "I'm fine," she snapped at him.

Max blinked slowly at her, then flopped onto his back, purring hard enough to be mistaken for a small engine and clearly begging for belly rubs.

"I'm fine, you little shit." She'd aimed for pissy, but it had come out rather sad. She sighed, crouching down to give him the attention he wanted and smoothing his soft fur in apology. "Sorry, buddy. Not even Paradise can fix some things, huh?"

Paradise was supposed to fix everything.

Max just purred.

Lily hurried through the field of doors toward the Hallway, hand curled around the phone tucked into the pocket of her leather jacket. A taller-than-most-mortals figure with the telltale shape of wings looming behind him lurked just outside the stone arch.

He squinted up at the arch, hands in his pockets, tail swishing idly behind him. His clothes had barely changed from the day before: boots and black pants—on the slightly distracting side of snug—over his powerful thighs. As she got close enough to pick out more detail, she realized that in place of his sleeveless tunic, a faded black Metallica T-shirt stretched over his broad chest and hugged his thick biceps. His hair was haphazardly half pulled back and looked slightly damp.

He looked less like a demon general and more like a normal man who happened to be a demon.

"Trying to figure out if you could fly through it?" she called, grinning when his eyes snapped to hers.

He snorted. "Of course I could fly through it." He threw one thick arm around her shoulders in a side hug, then left it draped there. "I was just trying to figure out if I could do a barrel roll through the narrowest part."

She glanced up at the arch, leaned back to peer at his wings, which, even folded, seemed massive, then dragged her gaze up his athletic body to look at his rugged face. "I'd put money on you."

"And you'd win," he said cheerfully, steering her down the Hall and letting his arm fall to his side. She matched his pace, delighted to not have to shorten her strides, keeping just enough distance between them to be friendly.

"Did you deal with any interesting souls today?" he asked.

Lily wrinkled her nose. The details of the soul files always faded, but sometimes the broad strokes of their actions would linger in her memory, like a movie she saw once and only vaguely remembered the plot of.

"There was a guy who hunted and ate people's dogs . . . for twenty years."

Bel stopped in his tracks, gagging, horror scrawled over his broad features. "He *what*?"

"Yeah, he got off on seeing how desperate they were looking for their dogs, and then how heartbroken they were when they were never found. All while eating—*ugh*. *Creepy* fucker. He did some other stuff that doesn't bear repeating, but yeah, his ass got sent down to Level Six."

"Good."

Lily shivered at the memory of touching the soul's file. She'd kept going to the break room to scrub at her hands, but her skin had still felt greasy. "Hope the drinks are good at Luckyleaf. I'll need one to get over that particular encounter."

"They are," Bel murmured, tail lashing as he started walking again. "Yuck. I mean, I've heard and learned about some shit, so hunting people's beloved pets for sport isn't the worst thing I know of, but what gets me is the complaining about it. Did he honestly try to convince you that he shouldn't be there?"

"Nah, he tried flirting his way into a lighter assignment. If leering at my tits and telling me he had a 'Jessica Rabbit fantasy' counts as flirting, which, for the record, it does not."

"Duly noted. So how many pieces did you leave him in?"

"Just the one. Oh, wait, two if you count the finger, but that was an accident. The sword is great, by the way! Very sharp."

"Brigid does beautiful work. It used to be Lucifer's, but he didn't need it anymore."

Something in his tone made her look up.

A self-satisfied smirk looked good on him. She made a mental note to make sure his gift of her new favorite weapon wasn't going to cause problems for him at some point.

She stole glances at him as they walked. He seemed happier than the day before, but beyond that, her memory hadn't really done him justice. Sure, she remembered the lines of his face and the color of his hair, skin, and eyes, but the more she looked, the more fine details sprang out at her. His horns were neatly polished and unchipped. There was a little scar that cut down by the curve of his jaw and below his pointed ear—an ear that had vaguely geometric tattoos on the shell and tip. The bulge of his ridiculously muscled arms, which also had some meat on them, and—

"What's this?" She hooted, touching the pair of aggressively glittery beaded bracelets that seemed to barely wrap around his wrist. Bel beamed and struck a pose like a woman showing off an engagement ring. "These are the masterful creations of two of my nieces, Nimué and Lezabel. They're twins and had a bracelet-making competition. I was the judge."

"And?"

"Well, Nimmie's is the purple one. She said that she thinks my skin is a pretty color and wanted to make a bracelet to match." He pointed to the bracelet of neon-purple glittery beads interspersed with shades of lavender and pink that looked wildly out of place on his dusky, purple-gray wrist. "Lezzie decided that matching was boring and wanted to take an avant-garde approach." The other bracelet had no discernible pattern and was composed entirely of lurid colors and enough sparkle to put a diamond to shame. "I couldn't pick, so they both won. Naturally, being my sister's children, they weren't satisfied with that, so they demanded that I wear both bracelets, and whoever's bracelet falls off first is the loser."

Lily nodded, impressed. "Smart kids. I like the way they think."

Bel smiled down at the bracelets with such tenderness and obvious pride that Lily's empty chest *ached*. She slid her hand into her pocket and dug her nails into her palm.

"I do too. Though it turns out they're better bracelet makers than I originally anticipated. It's been almost a year," Bel said wryly, dropping his arm. His glance turned into a look, a little furrow appearing between his thick brows.

Oh no you don't. Don't try to get a read on me like that. You won't like it.

"I don't know if I'm more impressed with the durability of the bracelets or your commitment to wearing them," Lily said, aiming for light and carefree and almost nailing the bullseye. "Do your nieces have wings too?"

"Nah," he drawled, flaring those wings slightly. "Kasdeya, my sister, their mom, is technically my half sister. We have different dads. Our mom isn't one for monogamy, and none of her partners are either." He said it factually, with no hint of judgment or shame, only love and pride. "I'm the only one of my siblings with these sweet, sweet wings, and thus, am usually in the running for the title of favorite uncle. As long as I keep taking the kiddos for flights, anyway."

Bel loved his family. Openly. Unapologetically. Enthusiastically. She might not know much about him in the grand scheme of things, but she suddenly knew that with complete certainty. There was a big old softie under that hard warrior's physique. Sexy and sweet, a dangerous combination. Hopefully, she prayed to whatever powers were listening—the Universe, she supposed—hopefully he wasn't nearly as perceptive as she suspected him to be. Because if he was, and he really got to know her, really saw her, he probably wouldn't like what he saw. No one else who'd ever gotten remotely close had.

But what if he did?

Well, she wouldn't have the first idea how to handle that.

15

BATTLE NUGGETS

Lily

Lily asked for a chicken wing from a god of death, and pointed it at a prince of Hell, threatening him with bodily harm if he even thought about changing the answer on the trivia sheet.

"There are twenty-eight properties on a Monopoly board. Not thirty-two. Twenty. Eight. Period. That is a statement of fact."

Asmodeus pursed his lips and gave a hum of doubt. "I'm pretty sure it's thirty-two."

Lily leaned over the table and wielded her chicken wing like a little sword, silently daring the blue-gray demon to make a move toward their much-debated answer sheet.

Asmodeus held up his hands in defeat. "The answers will prove who is right—me—and who is wrong."

"Doubt it," Bel rumbled next to her, reaching for Thanatos's tray of wings only for the god to slide them out of his reach. "Aw, come on, why is Lily the only one who gets to threaten Azzy with chicken?"

Thanatos just shrugged, a smile tugging at his lips, nonchalantly dipping a wing in sauce.

Lily hadn't quite understood that the Thanatos who Bel had referenced was actually the Greek god of peaceful death, but it turned out that the two of them were quite good friends. A zip of anxiety had hit her upon the realization. She wondered if the god knew, or at least suspected, the effect he had on mortal souls, given the reserved way he'd held himself back when Bel had introduced them. It was a primal thing, hardwired into every living creature: the desire to avoid death.

But she'd figured that she couldn't get any more dead and had offered her hand and a smile.

Thanatos had seemed a bit taken aback but had shaken her hand. His hand was huge, warm, and gentle. His timeless dark eyes held a sense of quiet kindness, tempered with seriousness and wisdom. She liked him.

She liked Asmodeus too, who was an equally tall but leaner version of Bel, with slate-colored skin, spike horns, and more refined bone structure. His wife, Sariah, had delicately swooping horns, striking features, and an ever-so-slightly rounded stomach under her "Summerland Fun Run" shirt. Lucifer was just as charming and blindingly handsome as she remembered, though he'd traded his formal attire in for something equally polished but more relaxed. Chesma, a female Turkic demon with catlike ears peeking out of her hip-length, glossy silver hair, chatted animatedly to Sariah. She had a kind of ethereal beauty that was only amplified by the shimmering, scalelike pattern on her skin, but her effervescence and lively chatter had quickly helped Lily form an easy camaraderie with her.

Ishtar, like Bel, Asmodeus, Lucifer, and Thanatos, had wings, a gorgeous amalgamation of feathers in warm browns and creams. Ishtar as a person was just as warm, with an underlying ferocity that reminded Lily of her friends when they'd become mothers. The Mesopotamian goddess occasionally engaged Thanatos in quiet conversation, but otherwise seemed content to listen to the ridiculous sporadic bickering.

Bel laughed at Lily's side, a half-full glass of some kind of cocktail held easily in his clawed hand. The glittery bracelets on his other wrist sparkled from where his hand rested on his thick thigh.

Thighs that she was not going to look at. He had thick thighs. He was a solidly built guy. She didn't need to check repeatedly to confirm that.

Cheeks strangely hot, Lily nibbled the last bit of chicken off the bone and surveyed the packed pub.

All things considered, their wing-heavy group was one of the least unique tables. Mortal souls were interspersed with denizens and beings from different realms, including a fair number of demons. The variety of shapes, colors, sizes, horns, antlers, wings, scales, claws, tails, heads, and other features had been overwhelming at first, but the longer she looked, the more normal it felt.

A fairy the size of a water bottle zipped past, wings humming as she carried a plate of nachos in a sling below her. A white wisp of light and mist that would have fit in Lily's palm hovered next to a green wisp the size of a horse, flickering as they seemed to communicate with each other. Somewhere on the far side of the pub, if she craned her neck, she could see what looked like a flaming wheel covered in eyes floating next to a table packed with people. The last time she'd gone up to the bar, she'd squeezed in next to a being who was eight feet tall and covered in bark. It had taken a concerted effort not to ask if they were an Ent.

It was wonderful. The chatter. The laughter. The friendly chaos of it all. They were all just . . . people. Just like the demons. Just like the souls she'd met, good and bad. Just like her.

She shifted in her chair.

She was *happy*, and for a moment it was so damn foreign that she almost shut it down on instinct. Like white blood cells attacking a virus.

Something brushed her arm—Bel—and she met his dark eyes. So unusual, those eyes. Gray irises, striated with a metallic silver, made even more striking with black sclera. They might have been unsettling if not for the soul behind them, if not for Bel. He tilted his head the tiniest bit, and she could practically hear him asking if she was all right.

Suddenly, she was.

She gave him a genuine smile and, on impulse, shot him a playful wink. Because that's what friends did.

His eyes gleamed, that hint of concern evaporating. He bumped her shoulder with his.

She poked his side—and promptly hurt her finger.

"What the actual fuck?" she asked, shaking her hand out and tapping him again, with all her fingers this time.

Solid. There was a slight give, but fucking hell, underneath that . . .

"What is in the water in Hell, and where can I get some?"

The entire table laughed. Asmodeus linked his hands behind his head and half flared his wings, which would have been impressive had he not nearly knocked over a passing soul, who squawked and scrambled to save their beer.

"Oops, sorry, sorry." Asmodeus tucked his wings in tight, hurrying to apologize and make sure they were all right.

Turning back to the table with cheeks and ears stained a darker shade of blue than before, he shrugged and cleared his throat. "One of the perks of being in the legions? It's a great way to work out."

Lily reached for her drink, still marveling over how solid Bel was, and wrinkled her nose up at Bel. "Remind me never to pick a fight with you, big guy."

Bel chuckled and gently poked at her not-nearly-as-solid side. "Uh-huh, you ever try a pick a fight with me, I'm hauling ass in the opposite direction. I've seen you at work, remember?"

"I'll accept it." She clinked her glass with his.

Everyone at the table watched them with varying degrees of amusement. Lucifer, in particular, looked as if he were watching the last few minutes of a sporting match.

Lily took a long pull of her drink, just as Bel did the same.

Thankfully, the speakers cracked to life, and the collective chatter died down immediately to listen for the correct answers. Sariah, their scribe, hovered over the paper with her pen, her golden eyes focused with laser-like intensity on the emcee.

Lily listened along, flipping Asmodeus a triumphant middle finger when it was confirmed that the standard Monopoly board did, in fact, have twenty-eight properties. Thanatos handed her another chicken wing. Ishtar clapped her on the back with bone-rattling force.

She really was *happy*. That odd, empty-but-tight, snarled-up feeling in her chest still lingered, but . . . less.

Sariah totaled up their points with a cackle. "We've only missed the one so far."

Chesma wrinkled her perfectly straight nose. "Who was possibly going to know that 'barani,' 'rudolph,' and 'randolph' were techniques in *trampolining*?"

"People who are interested in trampolining," Thanatos said mildly, swirling his drink.

"Do we know the next category?" Lily asked, leaning to peer at the screen projected onto a wall.

"It's the mystery category. If we put the clues together right, it should be our time to shine," Bel said. "And if we didn't, then this might suck."

The speakers made everyone take a collective breath. Lily didn't have the faintest idea what the clues had been, or if she would be remotely helpful, but she realized it didn't matter. It was fun.

"Beginning in a few minutes, the topic of the next round will be 'wings and flight.'"

The entire pub erupted into a mixture of cheers and groans. The winged members of their group leaned forward, Bel practically vibrating with excitement. Sariah shot Lily a bemused glance and fondly reached down to pat her equally excited husband's thigh.

Chesma scooted her chair back, rolling her shoulders. "Perfect, just in time for a refill. Need anything, mortal?"

"Lily," Lily said at the same time as someone else.

Multiple someones.

She stared at Lucifer and Thanatos, then Bel, who was the portrait of affable ease unless she looked closely.

And she did. She felt like it was important to look closely. An undercurrent of tension hummed through him.

Chesma winced and met Lily's eyes squarely, apology written all over her striking face. "I'm sorry, I meant no offense. Would you like anything, Lily?" Her smile was tentative, cautious.

Lily hoped her expression was as reassuring as she wanted it to be. "Names can be a pain in the ass. I've been craving a Fuzzy Navel, for some reason, so if they have them, I'll take one. If not, feel free to expand my horizons."

Bel choked on his drink. "You've been craving a *what*?" He coughed.

Ishtar grinned into her drink and nodded knowingly, while Chesma barked a laugh, weaving away through the crowd.

"A Fuzzy Navel. It's a cocktail with a terrible name, I know." Lily hooked her arm over the back of her chair so she could watch the horror spread across his face.

Beside him, Lucifer looked slightly ill. "And I thought Sex on the Beach was an odd name."

"Terrible idea, sex on the beach." Lily shivered. "Sand gets in places sand should *never* be."

Sariah gagged. "Oh, Universe, *no*, I never even thought of that! We're taking that one off the list." She said the last to Asmodeus, who nodded fervently.

"First question!" The speaker drew all of their attention, and they huddled over the table to conspire if needed.

"What is the only mortal mammal that can fly?"

"It's those little squirrel things, right?" Sariah asked lowly.

Lily shook her head. "Bats. Even though they're called flying squirrels, technically they glide."

"Atta girl," Bel murmured, bumping her shoulder. Warmth radiated from their point of contact.

She bumped him back. "Just managed to squeak that answer out."

The corners of his eyes crinkled. "We didn't even have to flap around for it."

"Nah, we just winged it a little."

"For fuck's sake," Asmodeus groaned. "There're two of them. Now they'll both think they're funny."

"Watch your battitude, dude. We're gonna miss the next question." Lily smirked, bumping her fist against Bel's as half the table groaned.

"Uh-uh! Get your own!" Lily cried, pushing Bel's hand as it crept up on her glass. As it turned out, Luckyleaf *did* serve Fuzzy Navels. As it also turned out, it'd been a hit with Bel and Chesma, whom she'd let sample it, and she'd ended up spending half her time protecting her drink from the buzzards. Drinks, more accurately. Her face was pleasantly warm, a happy buzz filling her veins.

"But mine's empty. Just a sip." Bel pouted. She would have thought it impossible for a seven-foot-tall, winged, horned, and fanged demon with a warrior's physique and bearing to pout with any efficacy, but damn if he hadn't figured out a way to make it work.

"I'm beginning to see why you go by FruitBat."

"It's actually because he's a slut for grapes," Asmodeus drawled, handing his new cocktail to Sariah so she could sniff it wistfully.

"Has been since he started solid foods," Lucifer confirmed, chin propped on his hand. "His parents used to carry a whole cluster of them so they could keep him happy during meetings. Any fruit would work, but grapes worked the *best*."

"I'm a man of taste." Bel sniffed, nodding at the half-full glass on the table. "And those taste pretty delicious."

Lily laughed, rolling her eyes and pouring a smidge of liquid from her glass into his, catching a stray drop with her finger and licking it off. Bel's hand paused briefly in midair before bringing the glass to his lips. He threw a beefy arm over the back of her chair and nudged her knee with his.

"Thanks, Lils." His voice was deeper, more gravelly than it had been a moment earlier, and she felt it like a caress.

Or maybe that was the alcohol.

She flopped her head back so that it rested on his arm, warm and buzzy and happy and content. "You're welcome, big guy."

Someone tapped the mic, and the pub went eerily silent. Lily lifted her head.

Competitive was an understatement for many of the trivia players.

"Third place, the Celestial Croissants!"

A table on the far side of the pub erupted into whoops and cheers.

"Second place, the Battle Nuggets!"

Holy shit, that's us—

Their table nearly flipped. Had she still been alive, her eardrums would have ruptured. They all screamed and roared. Chesma stood on her chair, hooting and whirling her shirt above her head like a lasso. Lily had the briefest moment to laugh at Asmodeus, who had Sariah held nearly over his head while she cackled, until she herself was swept up in a bone-crushing hug. Bel lifted her clear off her feet with one arm, while his other wrapped around Thanatos's shoulders, the quiet deity's smile brilliant against his dark beard.

Lily threw one arm around Bel's neck and pumped her other fist in the air, howling like a wild thing. Her fingers tangled in the collar of his shirt, brushing the extra-warm, smooth skin beneath.

She wanted to lick it.

No. She didn't, that was just an intrusive thought brought on by alcohol. She jerked her hand away and gripped his fabric-covered shoulder instead.

Fuck.

She'd always been a horny drunk. She knew that. She'd also hoped that that particular trait had died with her mortal body. Apparently not.

Not when Bel held her so snugly around the waist, pressed against his body. They were pressed so close that his pounding heartbeat beat against her own ribs, against her own silent chest—

Did he notice? Did it bother him? *Would* it bother him?

Her lack of a heartbeat, of *life*.

It was amazing how quickly alcohol could burn away in the Afterlife.

She slid down the length of his body, smile plastered in place, even though her skin sizzled at the contact. Everyone was still cheering and whooping, so she shoved it all down so it didn't affect her anymore, stepping away from Bel to laugh with Ishtar and fist-bump Lucifer before they all settled back into their seats. She reached for her drink, waiting to hear who had taken first place.

She didn't want to put a damper on the night. No one wanted to hear her complain, or sort through her own snarled emotions, least of all herself. It would be fine.

One way or another. Eventually.

"First place is the Ornithologists!"

A different table erupted into cheers, and the rest of the pub cheered for them too. Lily clapped until her hands stung, reaching for that happy, hazy feeling again. Maddeningly, it remained just out of reach.

Their table dispersed to chat with various friends and acquaintances, except Bel, who waved at someone.

"You want to meet some of the people from game nights?" he asked her.

"Sure!"

"Excellent." Bel grinned as a pair of demons headed their way. "They should know who is going to be beating them for the foreseeable future."

"Let's split it, fifty-fifty, keep them on their toes."

Bel looped his arm around her shoulders, and without thinking, she slid hers around his waist, careful not to brush his wings again.

"Damn right we will. Lily, this is Angel." He gestured to a stunningly gorgeous female demon with a pert nose, large crimson eyes, skin the exact shade of a pink rose, and an abundance of perfectly white hair with an ombré to black at the ends. Angel's smile was brilliant, and her delicate horns, reminiscent of a springbok's, were adorned with twisted and polished wire, the little metal flowers along the strands glittering in the light. She was only slightly taller than Lily and lushly curvy, a fact emphasized by her skintight pants and lacy crop top.

Angel bounced in place and waved. "Hi! I've heard so much about you!" Her voice was bubbly and sweet. Lily liked her immediately.

She waved back with her free hand.

"And this," Bel said, "is Gregorith, master of Level Nine." The male demon was slightly shorter than Bel, with angular, handsome features. Despite being built along leaner lines than Asmodeus, he radiated quiet strength and menace. Something about him sent chills up her spine in a way she hadn't encountered before.

All demons were dangerous, sure, but this one . . . The danger in him lurked closer to the surface than in most. His deep red skin was smooth, and his eyes, a few shades lighter than his skin, revealed nothing other than vague curiosity. Not a piece of his immaculately tailored black clothing was out of place. In fact, the only imperfection in his presentation was a strand of black hair, on the longer side of short, that flopped over his forehead.

Gregorith dipped his head and murmured a greeting. His voice, midrange and smooth, reminded her of cream poured over ice.

Level Nine. Where the worst souls went. It made sense that the master of that level would have to have a certain way about him. But he was also friends with Bel and the bubbly Angel, so there was a heart in there. Somewhere.

"So," Lily began, "master of Level Nine? I've had a few souls for Nine come through, and they make my skin crawl."

"I'd think they would."

"Does it annoy you when they come down in pieces?"

The corner of Gregorith's mouth twitched. "Souls regenerate."

"Mm." Lily angled her head. "One arrived yesterday . . . he probably would have still been missing his teeth"—and the lower half of his face, if she was being honest—"by the time he got down to you. What's going on with him?"

Beside her, Bel stiffened, tail twitching. Angel's bright smile dimmed a bit, eyes rounding with what looked like worry as she looked between Gregorith and Lily.

Gregorith's tail moved slowly behind him, but his face may as well have been carved from stone. She held his gaze. His presence was intense and eerie in the way of a predator on the hunt, like a lion stalking a gazelle. She could understand why Bel and Angel seemed nervous that she'd asked him the seemingly innocuous question. But she wanted to know, and Gregorith wasn't nearly as terrifying as that doctor's office had been. She still had nightmares about that scratchy blue chair and the word *metastasized*.

"He's currently suspended by his innards over a lake of fire. He's been relieved of his skin. He won't be needing it for a while."

"Perfect," Lily said. "I'm glad to know you're good at what you do. I'd hate to think that the worst part of a soul's stay in Hell would be what I do to them if they come through my line."

Gregorith's expression thawed slightly. *Slightly.* "Believe me, it isn't."

"Excellent."

Bel let out a relived sigh, tension seeping out of his posture. Angel pressed her hand over her chest and puffed out her cheeks, relief and curiosity in her gorgeous red eyes as she looked at Lily like she was seeing her for the first time.

Gregorith inclined his head and smiled. Not with teeth, but the ice of his expression melted away to reveal a hint of the warmth she suspected he kept hidden.

She smiled back. "And for the record, killing me by the fish was un-fucking-fair, Stabby, you bastard."

Gregorith's neat eyebrows twitched upward a moment before a hint of a smile curled his lips. "Was it? You're not too bad yourself, Nearamir."

Angel giggled brightly, her fangs flashing. "If we're doing other intro-ductions too, I'm TacoTime . . . aka, not really a threat."

"Don't sell yourself short," Bel said. "You can be ruthless when you feel like it."

Angel batted her eyes. "It's true, and you somehow never see it com-ing. Greg—Gregorith—does, but he's snoopy that way."

Bel and Gregorith exchanged an amused glance.

"I love playing with you all." Lily smiled, but the whirlwind of social-izing and Bel and her own confusing emotions had weariness suddenly tugging at her mind if not her body. "And I hope I get to talk to both of you more soon, but I'm feeling like it's time for me to head home. I've got a lifetime of missed sleep I'm trying to catch up on."

Angel stepped forward and shooed Bel away before wrapping Lily in a warm hug, her silky hair tickling her nose. Angel hugged with her whole being, and Lily couldn't help but like her more for it.

"We'll have to get coffee or lunch sometime. I want to know every-thing about how you started working in Hell!" Angel said when she pulled back, the metal adorning her horns gleaming in the light.

"That would be great!" Lily grinned, glancing over her shoulder toward Bel, who watched her with a crooked smile, his hands shoved into his pockets. "You can stay and hang out with everyone. You don't have to walk me back if you don't want to."

"I want to."

Apparently, there was still enough alcohol in her system to keep her on the horny side of drunk, because muscles clenched in her lower ab-domen that had no business clenching.

Right as they wove their way around the last group of people near the door, someone called her name. Siedah waved from a nearby group, beaming beneath her turquoise hijab. Lily hurried over, grinning so hard her face hurt.

Siedah wrapped her in a quick hug, careful not to spill the smoothie she held in one hand. "I haven't seen you to say congratulations in person! Congratulations! I knew you'd make it. It's always better to hear that in person than through text, isn't it? I'm sorry I've been so busy, but I've heard a bit about what you've started in Hell, and I have so many questions!"

"Hey, don't worry about it! Are you still busy with the trainees? Maybe I could swing by your desk sometime. I'd love to just talk more."

"Absolutely, we'll text and figure it out. It's so good to see you! Have a good night!" Siedah squeezed her hand in farewell.

Lily headed toward the door, where Bel waited outside, talking to a woman whose entire being screamed *Valkyrie*. He said a quick farewell to the woman when he spied Lily, and sauntered over.

"So, what do you think? How did it compare to mortal trivia nights?"

"This was so much better! Mortal trivia nights were"—she cleared her throat—"they were fun, but nothing like that."

"I never thought I would say this." He chuckled as they meandered in the direction of Paradise. "But I like Fuzzy Navels."

Lily smirked and patted his arm. "Don't worry, big guy, I don't kink shame."

She squealed when he pinched her side, and he made a strangely delicate *beep* of sound when she jabbed her finger in his armpit, made even funnier by his baritone voice.

They laughed and razzed each other the entire way to the Paradise arch.

Bel

Bel lay flat on his back in bed, wings carefully spread over the sheets, staring up at the glittering mural of stars on the ceiling. One hand tucked behind his head while the other rested on his stomach, clutching his phone.

His smile had yet to fade.

Lily.

She'd looked so happy, laughing and making him forget how to speak. Threatening Asmodeus with a chicken wing. Making Thanatos smile. Meeting Greg and Angel and treating them like people, though he hadn't expected anything less. She hadn't been afraid or seemed remotely intimidated by Greg, even though he had been his grumpy, guarded self and tried to shock her. But he'd suspected that Lily could handle it, and she had. They were both more faceted than people realized, and Lily had looked Greg in the eye without flinching. Something most people found difficult to do for too long.

His armpit ached from where she'd poked him. His smile broadened.

It had taken actual concentrated effort not to kiss her forehead when she'd flopped her head against his arm. He'd always been tactile within the bounds of propriety, but the impulse, like every moment with her, had felt natural.

Kissing her . . . what would that feel like? What would she taste like? If he'd kissed her in that moment, would she have tasted like that delicious fruity drink with the horrible name? Would it have been infinitely better because it had been on her lips? Would she have arched into him? Answered his moan with one of her own? What would all that pretty skin feel like? Her clothing hinted maddeningly at the dips and curves of her body, sending his imagination into overdrive. Unsurprisingly, his cock rose to attention, straining against the blanket covering his legs.

Ah, fuck.

He sucked in a deep breath, held it, and let it go slowly, fighting back the flash of arousal.

They'd known each other—actually known each other—for barely a day. She'd given him no real indication that she was looking for anything physical. Besides, they just *clicked.* His interest in her appearance paled in comparison to the interest in *her*, the mind behind those eyes, the kind heart he'd seen flashes of. What stories could she tell? What monsters was she fighting?

His heart clenched. Lily was hurting inside, deeply and quietly. Why? Could he help?

The buzz of his phone pulled him out of his reverie. He'd half expected the call, though a text had been more likely.

He answered with a swipe of his finger. "Hey, Greggles."

"She's going to break your heart, Bel."

That wasn't quite what he'd been expecting.

"What do you mean?"

"She seems great, and normally, for what it would be worth, I'd approve. I don't care if you're just getting to know each other, I haven't seen you this excited about anything for a long time." He paused. "But she's a soul, and souls reincarnate."

"Not all of them. Not always."

The words sounded hollow even to him. His throat grew tight at the idea. Maybe she'd go back to the mortal world and fall in love, have kids if that's what she wanted. Go live a beautiful and unique life that was all the more precious because it was finite. Sure, Lily would return to the Afterlife after that, but she'd be different. She'd half remember her old life, her old self, old Paradise, but maybe not him.

While he would always be in Hell. Always remembering her, or who she had been.

"Yeah," Greg said softly. "Not all of them. Listen, I don't want to be a killjoy, I just . . . don't want you to get left behind."

The *again* at the end of his statement went unsaid, but Bel heard it anyway.

"I know. I appreciate the warning, but I'm gonna have to figure this one out on my own, yeah?"

Something tapped on the other end of the phone, and Greg sighed. "I'm not against it, you know. If you decide to go for it. For her."

"I'm going to focus on the whole 'being friends' and 'getting to know each other' thing first."

"Sounds like a plan, *General*." He could hear Greg's smirk through the phone.

"Fuck you, *Master of Level Nine*." He cooed Greg's title like a child teasing another over a crush.

Greg barked a laugh and wished him good night before the phone went silent, leaving Bel alone in the dark with a mural of stars and a maelstrom of what-ifs.

Familiar bands of emotion wrapped around his throat and squeezed.

He'd never been worthy of the kind of love and devotion he craved before; what reason did he have to think that had changed? His love and affection hadn't been good enough when it mattered. When he'd been placed on the scales of choice, they'd tipped in the other option's favor with apparent ease.

With few exceptions, his role in relationships had been temporary at best, which was why he'd avoided romantic partnerships for so long. His former relationships had ended on good terms, but they'd still driven home what he'd begun to believe—he wasn't worthy of the kind of love that lasted.

But Lily . . . She felt different. For the first time in too long, he wondered if things had changed.

16

PIE-RATES

Lily

Bel of the Ball: *Is it super obvious that I'm throwing this game?*

Flower Power: *Hopefully he thinks you're just exceptionally out of it today*

Bel of the Ball: *So that's a yes*

Flower Power: *You've been scanning for asteroids for, like, five minutes. To be fair, I've been doing fuck all by solar farm thing and hoping he's feeling like living up to his name*

Bel of the Ball: *Fair*

Bel of the Ball: *My mom says hi*

Flower Power: *Hi Mom! (What's your mom's name?)*

Bel of the Ball: *So, about that . . .*

Flower Power: *Please tell me I haven't told your mom to go fuck herself during a game*

Bel of the Ball: *HA! No, she's a little old-school, she doesn't game*

Flower Power: *You're stalling big guy. It's kinda weird, I learned about some of the alleged Big Bad Demons when I was alive, but we never talked about lady demons much, except Lilith*

Bel of the Ball: *Bingo*

He answered on the second ring.

"Bullshit," she said.

Bel chuckled and she heard his chair creak, as if he'd shifted around. Nervous?

"Nope, that's my mom. *The* Lilith. She's pretty cool. She's not here. She just texted to ask if I was busy and said to tell everyone hello."

Lily stared down at her phone as if she could see him through it. He sounded nonchalant, but she'd gotten to know him well enough over the last few weeks to catch the hint of twitchiness. Like when he'd told her he was a general. She smiled softly at the phone.

Sweet man. Demon. De-man.

"Well, tell her I say hi back, and that her son is doing a shit job of being bait."

"It's the damnedest thing," Bel mused. "He's always telling me how punchable I am. Maybe he's onto us."

"Methinks Gregorith is projecting slightly. I mean, I've met you and haven't found you punchable in the least. I know it when I see it, because at least one comes through the desk every d— *What the fuck?*" Lily scowled at the *Invaders* screen where Stabby had just killed her character.

On the other end of the phone, Bel hooted. "Finally! Brace yourself, princess, I'm about to give the dramatic performance of my life and earn us some pie."

"Wait, hold on. It won't work if I'm the one who got killed. He won't believe that you'd be upset enough about that to warrant a forgive-me pie."

"Oh?"

Her cheeks heated, so she moved on. "Princess?" she asked. He hadn't said it with mockery, but with genuine affection, which was odd, considering that nothing about her honestly said "princess."

"Oh." Bel coughed and seemed to fumble for an answer. "Yeah, that just kind of slipped out. Like, a warrior princess, fierce and capable and braver than an army, you know? I, uh, I thought it the first time I saw you. And ever since. I'm sorry, I didn't mean to make you uncomfortable. I won't say it again."

"No, no, I actually like it," Lily said slowly, rolling it over in her mind.

The first time he'd seen her she'd been beating a deeply despicable soul to a pulp. So, sure. Warrior princess in that moment, maybe. But "ever since"? Ever since, she'd just been . . . herself. He thought she was fierce and capable and brave?

Nothing about you feels temporary.

It had only been a few weeks, but it seemed like they'd known each other so much longer than that. They talked almost every day, either on the phone or in person. She'd almost invited him to come see her Paradise after he asked her more about it, his dark eyes bright with curiosity. She'd swallowed the offer down at the last moment for fear that he'd see something. See *her*. She'd convinced herself that it had been mostly because she wasn't sure he'd fit through the door, but after Bel had practically bounced in place after she'd described the round door and the library, she suspected that he wouldn't mind a bit.

One memorable day, she'd lured him up to the break room with the offer of taste-testing a bread recipe she'd tried. He'd hustled up in no time, still sweating and panting a bit from his time on the training fields, his gray muscle shirt—which would have looked right at home on a frat boy—hysterically at odds with his tough dark pants and boots. She'd laughed her ass off.

"Business on bottom, party on top, it's a clothing mullet." He'd grinned, poking around in the cupboards, trying to find the bread she'd hidden. He'd wiggled—*wiggled*—when she'd cut him a slice. He'd proceeded to inhale it, groaning in a way that sent a shiver down her spine and dampness between her legs, and then ask for more.

They'd stood in the kitchenette while Bel had eaten half the loaf, slice by slice, interspersing rave reviews with stories of his soldiers. He knew them, not all by name of course, but he knew so many more of them than she'd expected . . . and not just those in command. He'd explained that he rotated through each legion, and within those, each company, and whenever he could, the platoons. He talked to everyone, not just about their prowess or training, but their lives.

It had hit her like a lightning bolt that Bel was nothing if not passionate. About his soldiers, about his family, his friends, about his hobbies and interests, about *life*. He had spent his entire existence in the Afterlife, and he was a walking embodiment of *living*.

"What?" he'd asked.

She'd realized she'd been staring at him and shrugged one shoulder. "I like seeing people get excited about stuff. Happy is a good look on you."

His pointed ears had gone a deeper shade of purple, but he'd smirked, flexing one thick arm. "It's actually the muscle shirt, makes me look even sexier."

"Oh, is that it?" She'd laughed, thankful they'd veered into lighter—if equally dangerous—territory for the rest of her break.

He'd really loved her bread. She'd taken to giving him some whenever she baked, and looked forward to—

"Lily," Bel said, jolting her back to the present, where she'd been completely zoned out.

"Yeah?"

"You don't have to like it."

Princess.

She smiled. "I like it."

"Well, then," Bel said, "it's official. Princess it is."

His voice had a slightly rougher quality to it that made her swallow and think of doing taxes. Washing dishes. Anything other than . . .

Lily pressed her hands to her flaming face and sat back, not bothering to guide her ghost around the screen while she waited for someone to find her body.

Friends.

But oh, what would it be like to be the focus of that passion? To be the *source* of it? The kind of passion that had souls finding each other in every lifetime so they could love each other in new ways every time. The kind of passion that had an old man waiting patiently in the lobby of the Afterlife for his love, so that, come what may, they would face it together?

She could see that written all over Bel. Despite the harsh-looking exterior, the warrior body and soul, he had a tremendous capacity and ability to love. That giant heart drew her in like a bee to honey.

It scared the shit out of her that she could mess it all up. That she could lose the incredible friendship she had now in the hope of having what she'd never been able to have before.

The screen flashed when someone found her character's body and called for a murder trial.

The moment the trial opened, Bel's voice boomed through both the computer and their phone call. "Which one of you UTTER BASTARDS *murdered my girl?*"

Lily clamped a hand over her mouth to smother the laughter that threatened to give them away. She fumbled for her phone and hung up, eyes watering with mirth. He sounded so completely indignant, and if she didn't know any better, legitimately pissed. But she did know better, so she laughed herself sick while the other players scrambled to defend themselves. Bel did an admirable job of interrogating a player called Ha-deez-nuts before turning his attention to their target.

"Stabby," Bel growled with enough menace to make her breath catch mid-laugh. "What do you have to say for yourself?"

"What do *you* have to say for yourself, FruitBat?" Gregorith countered, smooth malice dripping from every syllable. "You've been doing such a great job going after everyone else, but what about you? Suspicious that it took you that long to scan for asteroids."

"I kept doing it too fast," Bel said.

"Story of your life," Gregorith said with a smile she could hear.

Lily nibbled on her lip, humming. Fast didn't seem like Bel's style. Rough, maybe. Hard. He'd probably fuck like he seemed to do everything else: with passion and ferocity and a surprising amount of creativity—

Nope.

She grabbed her mug and headed for the kitchen. Tea. Tea was the solution.

Princess . . .

Definitely more tea.

By the time she returned to her chair, Max had taken up residence on the cushion, forcing her to perch delicately on the edge. Gregorith led the charge against a player called They, and the vote for their banishment was almost unanimous.

Her phone buzzed.

Bel of the Ball: *One of my finest performances if I may say so myself.*

Flower Power: *I was laughing so hard I had to hang up! Think it was pie worthy?*

Bel of the Ball: *I just texted him "my couches are off limits, with love, fuck you" to seal the deal. Now we wait.*

Flower Power: *Couches?*

Bel of the Ball: *My office has great couches, it's a good hangout spot for people when I'm not busy. So I banned him.*

Flower Power: *The horror!*

Bel of the Ball: *Fear me, and my desire for us to get this pie.*

17

CARPE NATEM

Lily

A hand waved in Lily's face, the woman so mad she was nearly spitting.

"Are you listening? This is the problem with your generation, you all think that you're the center of the universe, that your feelings matter more than your job. In my day—"

"When dinosaurs roamed the earth," Lily said mildly.

The woman gasped so hard that she choked. "How dare you?"

Lily considered that, leaning back in her chair. "Honestly? I never gave much thought as to 'how.' It just kinda happens. The gift of sass, I suppose."

"You can't just say things like that! What is wrong with you?"

"We're dead and staring eternity in the face, and we still don't have time to answer that question," Lily drawled. "Well, we *do*, but I don't want to waste all that time."

"You've got a mouth on you," the woman hissed.

"I've been told it's one of my best features. Level Three. Quietly." Lily pointed to the line, putting every bit of steel she could muster into her stare.

The woman stomped away, rushing past Crocell and another demon without even looking at them. Crocell shot Lily a thumbs-up before sauntering along the line, whistling a jaunty tune.

Her phone lit up. She smiled, wondering if Siedah was ready for that cup of coffee after a busy few days.

Bel's contact picture, one she'd snapped of him a week earlier, popped up next to a text message. He'd been sneaking a cluster of grapes out of the fruit bowl in the break room, and had turned with his mouth full when he'd heard the laugh she hadn't been able to smother. The picture caught him mid-turn, grapes in hand, looking about as guilty as a person could look.

It made her smile every time she saw it.

Bel of the Ball: *WE'VE GOT PIE BABY!*

Beneath the text was a picture of a truly mouthwatering pie that she half imagined she could still see steaming. Since there were no souls in line, she bolted for the elevator so fast she left her office chair spinning at her desk.

Bel sent directions to his office while the elevator carried her down to the Admin Level, but she couldn't help but pause when she stepped out. The stone streets of the small city were immaculately clean, lined with beds of flowers that glowed in a kaleidoscope of bioluminescence. The buildings were all in the demonic style, a hybrid of Gothic and art nouveau, with glorious panels of stained glass; frescoes in bold, rich colors; and sculptures unlike anything she'd ever seen. Demons who walked from place to place obviously didn't have the same concerns for practical attire that the demons at the gate did, their fashions ranging from modern, mortal-style attire to elegant, flowing robes, and everything in between. Less humanoid beings moved about as well. A towering being who seemed to be made of stone hunched over a phone that was proportional to their size, but still looked like a pain to text on. A female demon wearing a power suit walked a hellhound the size of a pony on a leash, the hellhound's double tails wagging furiously as they passed by.

Lily checked her directions and followed the street, fascinated by everything and silently promising herself to explore the residential levels of Hell more. A male demon with wings like Bel's was crouched down and talking to a child. *His* child, if their similar coloring and features were anything to go by. The child's watery eyes and wobbling lip were explained by the scuff on their elbow that their father was examining.

"Did you feel what went wrong?"

"I lost the air." The child sniffed.

"Yep, it's scary when that happens, huh? You did a good job recovering, buddy. See, when you bank too hard when you're going slow, there's not enough air moving over your wings to keep you up," the father explained gently. He reached back to hold the child's wings out in a specific position. "So, when you hold your wings like this . . ."

Their conversation faded away as she walked, but the smile that had found its way to her face remained.

Cute. Like learning to ride a bike.

She checked her phone against the name of the building in front of her, then slid it into her pocket, confident she'd be able to find his office from there. Her confidence evaporated the second she set foot inside and realized the scale of the building.

"Well, fuck." She reached for her phone again.

"Can I help you?" a male demon asked coolly. He was built similarly to Gregorith, though slightly more wiry, with rich, olive-green skin that shimmered under the lights. Burnt-orange eyes squinted at her with obvious suspicion. His horns were simple and goatlike, a bit like Bel's, but wrapped in smooth leather. She'd learned from conversations that horn fashion wasn't an indicator of status or position, simply a matter of personal preference.

"Hi." She smiled. "I'm looking for Bel's office?"

The demon drew himself up, expression cooling further. "It is of utmost importance that we do not sully our working spaces with sex. It is disrespectful to our stations and our neighbors, not to mention that it would be highly distracting for someone whose focus is required on more pressing events."

Lily's mouth moved before she knew what would come out of it. "Well, fucking Bel wasn't on the to-do list, but I suppose it'll have to be now."

Shit. Well, that was . . . something to say.

The demon's mouth dropped open.

She winced. "I'm sorry, still in work mode. Smart-assery has been the name of the game all day. I'm not here to, uh . . . sully anyone's workspace. I'm just here to visit a friend. I'm Lily." She held out her hand as a peace offering.

The demon stared at her hand, then at her face, then back at her hand. His handshake was firm. "The famous Lily."

Famous?

"My name is Leviathan, Prince of Hell, but you may call me Lev. Your work at the gate seems to have had a demonstrable effect on the efficiency of the Soul Management System. Would you mind typing up a report?"

"Uh, I don't know about typing up a report, but I'd be happy to chat about it sometime. Or you're welcome to come up and see for yourself. You might notice or understand things that I don't, and we can talk about any questions you might come up with."

Lev frowned. "All I want is a brief overview of your established method. I understand from our management meetings that your methods differ from standard procedure, but you must have a clearly defined protocol. The changes that you have made have been wholly positively received on the administrative side. That . . . doesn't just . . . happen."

"Sorry, Lev." Lily smiled, fighting the urge to squirm. "I'm pretty casual. I didn't think it through beyond what my experience taught me and what I noticed. I acted on a hunch, and it happened to work. There's no set method. Every soul is different. Some need sass, some need—or more accurately *deserve*—a little smack. Some just need a little help. I'm sorry I can't be more specific than that."

Lev furrowed his perfect eyebrows and considered her for a long moment. "I suppose . . ." He trailed off and shook his head. "Never mind. I would like to observe your process sometime though. I hope to find it enlightening."

"Anytime. Now, Bel's office is . . . ?"

"Oh, stairs." He pointed to the sweeping main staircase. "Top floor, turn left, two doors down."

She thanked him, boots thudding dully on the polished black stone. Bel's explanation of how the title of prince worked in Hell made the dichotomy of personality between Lev and Asmodeus slightly less jarring.

As she understood it, Lucifer was like a CEO, and the princes were more specialized in their responsibilities, therefore allowing someone like Asmodeus to have equal, if different, responsibilities than Lev. The soul levels of Hell apparently worked on a similar principle, though the master of each level was more akin to a regional manager. She still had a bit of trouble thinking of Asmodeus and Lev as equal in responsibility.

Any lingering concern she had about the validity of Lev's directions was washed away by the names and titles carved into each door.

She raised her fist to knock, then paused, reading the door in its entirety.

PRINCE BELETH

GENERAL, 85 LEGIONS

Every thought eddied out of her head. She read it again. A sticky note was pasted to the door just below the carving, the words in elegant script.

PARI PASSU

She took a deep breath.

Flying off the handle never solved anything nor did anyone any good. She knocked.

Bel's "Come in" was muffled.

She swung open the door and went inside, momentarily distracted by the sensation that she'd entered a small castle. To her left, Bel sat at a massive desk on a dais, in front of a series of floor-to-ceiling windows framed with luxurious charcoal drapes. The seriousness dropped from his features as he grinned and reached for a box sitting on his desk.

"Well, I have no idea what 'pari passu' means," Lily said lightly, strolling toward him, "but I *do* know what 'prince' means."

Bel froze.

Oh, she hated it.

Hated the way the happiness bled out of his expression, the way tension snaked into every line of his body. Especially hated the flicker of some awful, deep *hurt* in those eyes. His hand fell to the desk, short of the pie box.

For the first time since she'd met him, Bel's eyes dropped away from hers to stare at the desk, jaw clenched.

Lily stepped onto the dais and rounded his desk to stand beside him. He still wouldn't look at her.

He should have felt dangerous. With his size and a physique built and honed for combat clearly humming with tension, she should have wanted to put distance between them. But she didn't.

Lily wasn't afraid of Bel. He'd never hurt her.

She studied him again. He didn't seem angry. He seemed . . . ashamed. For lying or for something else?

She stepped closer, careful not to brush his rigid wings.

"Bel?" she said softly, irritation evaporating.

He swallowed hard and kept looking at the desk.

She didn't know why she did it. Perhaps because it just felt right. Perhaps because she knew they both liked touch, and she always craved the grounding of physical contact in those moments when she felt lost or out of control.

She gently cradled his jaw with one hand, the dull little spikes on his chin pressing into her palm, and turned his face toward her.

His skin was warm, noticeably warmer than hers, and smooth. Soft. His pulse hammered in his throat, against her fingers. His head turned without resistance, breath hitching slightly before his eyes turned as well and met hers.

So beautiful, his eyes.

Something in her chest tweaked.

"Talk to me," she murmured, running her thumb over his cheek. His lashes, longer and thicker than any man's had a right to be, dipped slightly.

"I'm sorry. It was a lie of omission," he rasped.

"Okay." She kept tracing her thumb over his cheek. "Why?"

"I . . ." His breathing went a bit ragged, eyes darting around her face. "I'm not proud of it. I hate the way that it makes me feel."

She waited.

"It's not mine. I did nothing to earn it, it shouldn't even be mine, but . . . it doesn't mean anything to me. Not like being a general. I earned that. That matters." It came out of him in a rush.

Gentle, she reminded herself. Bel, seemingly indestructible, cheerful Bel, needed her to be gentle.

"Why doesn't it mean anything? If it shouldn't be yours, then why is it?" She kept her tone quiet, stroking her thumb over his skin, noting the coiling tension humming through his body.

His jaw tightened under her hand. "Because. It's essentially a useless title. A formality. Just a reminder that . . . just a reminder." His tone had grown harsher, the look in his eyes one she recognized. Somehow, she was skating close to a wound he wasn't ready or able to face yet. She saw that expression in the mirror every day. She felt that rawness whenever someone brought up a topic a little too close to home.

Raw. Exposed. That's how he had to be feeling.

The silence between them stretched.

Ah, fuck.

Ignoring the part of her that screamed to not let anyone in, not let anyone see, she sucked in a deep, bracing breath, and spoke. "I died fairly young, at thirty-four. From cancer."

Bel blinked, harshness evaporating in an instant. His heavy brows furrowed as he waited.

Her throat tightened and she dropped her hand to her side, palm tingling with residual warmth from his skin. His much larger hand wrapped around hers as it dangled at her side.

"The cancer itself wasn't my fault." She couldn't help a bitter laugh. *It wasn't, but everything else was.* Her failings clawed at her throat, threatening to strangle her from the inside out. "But I could have done things in my life differently. I could have been more responsible in my spending or job choices instead of doing things because they were fun or enjoyable. My choices meant that I didn't have the resources to take care of myself when it mattered. That I didn't have options. This—" She tapped her silent chest with her free hand. "This is a constant reminder of that, and sometimes I hate the way it makes me feel too."

Bel's eyes widened in understanding, then softened. His thumb traced over the delicate skin of her wrist, the lines of her tattoos there. Every synapse in her brain zeroed in on that touch. Clung to it.

Her lungs loosened enough to take a full breath.

Bel nodded. She nodded back in a silent agreement to move past the moment.

"'Pari passu' means 'on equal footing' or 'in equal step,'" he said. "It's my mother's motto. It's a running joke with everyone to put different mottos on my door because I never chose one. She stopped by yesterday and put it there."

Lily squeezed his hand. "I might have to make my contribution before I leave."

"Oh?"

"It'll be a surprise. I don't know how to say 'Bel lies about the quality of pie' in Latin, so you'd better be telling the truth about how good this pie is."

"Princess, I never lie about the quality of pie." He reached for the box again and cracked open the lid, releasing a waft of fresh, warm, delicious pastry and sweet blackberries. "Besides, our mottos don't have to be in Latin. Asmodeus never bothered to translate his."

"What is it?"

"'For hearth and home.' Now, do you want to eat right out of the box?"

Lily gave his hand a squeeze, hurrying over to the kitchenette in the corner to retrieve plates and forks. Bel cut them each a generous slice and guided her off of the dais.

"These couches are pretty great," Lily said, bouncing on her cushion. Bel settled next to her, handing her a plate and draping his wings over the specially designed low back.

"Cheers, princess," he said, holding up his fork. She clinked it with hers and scooped up a piece of pie. The flavors burst over her tongue in waves, sweet with the perfect touch of tartness, hints of warm spices, perfectly buttery and flaky pastry.

She and Bel moaned in unison, and she tipped her head back, letting the dessert perfection soothe the ragged edges of her emotions.

"Holy shit, that is . . ." She took another mouthful and hummed again.

"Right?" Bel said around his fork. "I told you Morgen's pies are worth committing atrocities for."

"Why has she not been made into a goddess? Goddess of Pie. I'd take up religion again to worship her. Every day. Wholeheartedly."

"I'll mention it again at the next meeting."

Lily sighed, mouth full of possibly the best pie ever made. "If we keep this up, Lev's gonna think I lied and we're actually having sex in your office."

Bel coughed and jerked upright. "What?" He gasped, then coughed again.

"If you choke on this pie, I'll finish your slice and then call for help." Lily warned. "I ran into Lev—Leviathan—in the lobby; he thought I was lost. I asked him for directions to your office, and he told me that 'it's very important that we do not defile our offices with sex because it's disrespectful to our neighbors,' or something along those lines." She shook her head and dug into her rapidly disappearing slice.

Bel laughed so hard he had to set his plate on the seat next to him. "Of course he did, the bastard. What did you say?"

"How do you know I said anything?"

Bel leveled her a bemused look.

The blush spread up her neck, across her face, and up her ears. She pointedly gathered up crumbs with her fork.

"Lily," Bel teased, leaning against her shoulder. "Come on, princess, what did you say? Am I going to get another sexy memo from Lev?"

"I told him," Lily said primly, focusing on her pie, "that fucking you wasn't on my to-do list, but it would have to be now."

There was a beat of silence, then Bel howled.

"It was a reflex," she said, fighting back her own laughter.

Bel laughed harder, lying back, hands pressed to his face, legs curled up as his whole body shook with mirth. Lily couldn't help it, she laughed with him. They laughed until tears streamed from their eyes and her lungs ached.

"He's gonna—" Bel giggled, wiping his eyes. "He's gonna come into my office with a black light."

"If he's *coming* into your office, then he's part of the problem." Lily cackled, and off they went again.

The pie was nearly gone. They had each flopped on a couch, Lily on her back, Bel on his stomach, pushing the pie box back and forth as they chatted about less sensitive topics.

"So, what exactly is wing etiquette? Because I googled it—or whatever the search engine is—and I got a whole lot on the care and keeping of pet birds, and the general rule of 'do not touch the wings,' which I get. I saw a dad and his kid on the way here, though, and it looked like it was okay for the dad to touch to correct his form." Lily pushed the pie box back to him.

Bel stretched his wings out with a leathery rustle, and the one nearest her flared wide enough that he could have laid the tip over her. The light filtered through the membrane, delineating the bones, warming the black with shades of gray and purple and cream. She propped herself up on her elbows to get a better look. It looked incredibly strong, and as if it might be slightly velvety. He half folded it again and draped it on the ground.

"Not touching is a good rule for the masses. Different areas are more acceptable than others. The top edge for example, where we brush against things when they're folded, that's more of a friends-and-family area. We don't tend to let that touch linger. It's a brush or a pat, something brief, you know? The claw"—he gestured to the black spike at the apex of his wing before pushing the pie box back over—"that's the least sensitive. We can grab that and yank each other around with no problem. If you have to touch a wing, try the claw. Everything else is . . . intensely personal, essentially for committed lovers only. The inside edge, where they join our backs, is, by far, the most sensitive."

She'd touched him there. Entirely by accident that first time they'd met in person. The mortification was present but had lessened with time. But now, just now, she remembered his sharp intake of breath and wondered what it would be like for him to invite her to touch him there intentionally. What his wings would feel like under her hands. What noises would he make if she ran her hands over those sensitive, forbidden parts of his wings? Would he gasp? Groan? Growl into her neck, those fangs raking delicately over her skin?

Her skin heated as she looked away from his wings and met his eyes. He was silent, lips slightly parted, as if he was also remembering that accidental touch, or perhaps wondering about the same thing. Her breath hitched. The silence stretched, his eyes dropping to her lips.

Then he looked away and cleared his throat. "Now you know. So if and when Lev accuses you of fucking in my office, you'll know what to tell him to make him believe you."

His voice was a bit deeper than usual, and Lily fought to plaster a cocky grin on her flaming face. "I'll tell him you put on a milkmaid outfit and mooed like a cow when you climaxed."

There. A joke.

Safer territory.

Bel huffed a laugh and pushed himself up onto his elbows. "I'll tell him you spanked me like a pro and couldn't get off unless you spoke in a French accent."

Lily arched an eyebrow and rolled onto her side. "I'll tell him you expressed a fetish for memos about being told not to have sex in your office."

"I'll tell him you had to inspect my toes before you even considered seeing me naked."

"I'll tell him you're sexually attracted to beans."

"I'll tell him—fuck." Bel scrubbed a hand over his face.

"I get the sense that would have the same effect, honestly." Lily scooped up another forkful of pie. "He was a bit uptight, but nice enough. He asked me to write a report on the Hellp Desk."

"He did not," Bel said incredulously.

"He did." Lily pushed the box back. "I told him no. I haven't had to write a full procedural report since I was in my twenties. I said he's welcome to stop by and observe anytime. Does he have a sense of humor?"

"A bit, why?"

Lily tapped her bottom lip with her fork. "I don't know if he's going to think the name of the desk is all that funny if he's super into professionalism. I think it's a stroke of genius, but Lev might think I just had a stroke."

Bel laughed. He had such a great laugh.

"Puns, like dad jokes and dirty jokes, are peak humor. Lev is very literal, so he might get it immediately, but if he doesn't and you take the time to explain things to him, he'll get it."

Lily adjusted her position, groaning as the full and glorious impact of eating half an incredible pie hit her system. "I would say that I'm pleasantly full."

"Mm, 'pleasant' seems like an insult to that pie."

She hummed in agreement just as her phone chirped. "Oh, sweet."

Bel gave an inquisitive grunt.

"Siedah wants to get together for coffee tomorrow. I've been looking forward to that." She sighed and eased herself up. "I should probably get going. The line hasn't been too bad today, but you never know when a really annoying one is going to come through. How's work been for you?"

"Not as relaxed as I'd like it to be. Nothing serious has happened yet, but I'm a little on edge about it," Bel said.

Curiosity nibbled at her, but he didn't offer more. She wasn't sure if she should or shouldn't ask and decided that he'd share more when he needed or wanted to. He pushed to his feet, taking her plate and cleaning up their mess. Lily snagged a pen and a sticky note, scribbling out some of the only Latin she knew and tucked it into the side pocket of her leggings.

"Thanks, big guy," she said, walking into his arms for a hug. His warm, musky scent enveloped her like a second embrace. She held him a little longer, a little tighter, an apology and support.

He rested his cheek on top of her head. "We're here for each other, princess. And thank *you*."

She gave him a little squeeze, definitely didn't sneak a quick inhale, and shot him a wink before walking out the door, pausing only to put the new sticky note over the old one.

Lily panted, pressing her hand to the stitch in her side and leaning back against her desk as a pair of demons dragged the kicking serial killer away.

"So much pie . . . so fucking worth it," she gasped, squinting at her phone and grinning when she saw the picture of Bel and the grapes.

Bel of the Ball: *What does "carpe natem" mean?*

Flower Power: *It means "seize the butt cheek" or "seize the ass."*

Bel of the Ball: *HAHAHAHAHAHA!*

18

PINKIE PROMISE

Lily

Siedah's gentle kindness was palpable as she squeezed Lily's waist. "You have one heck of a story to tell, girl! You go from wondering if you were going to make it to Paradise to being on a trivia team with multiple deities?"

"I contain multitudes." Lily chuckled, squeezing her back. "Trust me, I have no idea how that happened either, I'm just rolling with it."

Siedah shook her head as they linked arms and walked down a bustling side hall toward a coffee place Siedah had suggested and Lily hadn't explored yet. Lily listened as Siedah described in greater detail what happened at the Front Desk, and the highs and lows of dealing with a wider range of souls than Lily had in Hell. Her friend moved through the Afterlife with a sweet, quiet assurance that Lily couldn't help but envy.

"You're so confident here," Lily said during a lull in conversation as they waited in line. The coffee place was much smaller than Common Grounds and looked and smelled amazing.

"So are you."

Lily blinked down at her, waiting for the laugh.

Siedah smiled and squeezed her arm. "I was just admiring *your* confidence. My confidence stems from familiarity. Yours seems to come from here." She tapped her own chest. "I've been in the Afterlife much longer than you, and I've had other lifetimes before this. Every time I've returned here, it feels like my eternal home. I work here, have friends and family here. I enjoy being here. But," she said with a sly grin that was at odds with her soft features, "even I, familiar as I am, have never dared venture into a punishment realm out of curiosity. Especially not Hell. *Working* at the Front Desk is intimidating enough, let alone the idea of *starting* one in Hell. Please give yourself some credit."

Lily tried to laugh it off and move forward in line, but Siedah held her arm.

"We don't go until you give yourself credit," Siedah said sweetly. "No coffee. No pastries. And they are delicious pastries; we'll have to get some boxed to take back to the Front Desk."

Lily winced. She could smell very well how delicious the baked goods would be. The warm, familiar, earthy scent of freshly ground, high-quality coffee caressed her senses like silk.

"You realize this is torture?"

"Of course."

Lily waited.

Perhaps she would get bored?

Siedah waited.

Fuck.

"It didn't seem very gutsy at the time, I just did it. Admittedly, there was some spite involved, but I mostly wanted to see what was down there, and I figured that the worst thing they would do would be to kick me out."

"You're discrediting yourself. Please try again." Siedah smiled innocently. "You know, they have the best blueberry muffins here."

"Cruel."

"A perfect ratio of berry to muffin."

Lily shook her head, rolling her shoulders and reaching for the hard-won self-confidence that still sometimes scared her. "I did something that most people wouldn't think of doing, and I have a lot of fun doing it. Most of the time. All things considered. The people I work with and the people I've met make even the worst parts worth it."

"Excellent!" Siedah led her forward through the vibrantly colorful lit-tle shop. "So, what is it exactly that you do? I know there's already an established intake program . . ."

Lily explained how she had started working in Hell, and the still evolving nature of the Hellp Desk, a name that had Siedah giggling into her tea. Lily hid her self-satisfied grin with her cup.

The chatter from the surrounding patrons was light and happy, the occasional burst of laughter a cheerful staccato among the melody of voices. A child with feathered wings and brown hair tugged at her father's arm, pointing to a cupcake frosted like a ball gown. A table of souls chat-ted in old Gaelic, though Lily somehow understood it.

The bite she took of the berry cobbler she'd ordered was very, very good, but paled in comparison to the ecstasy of the pie she'd shared with Bel. Or what touching him in the smallest of ways had been like.

The memory of his smooth, warm skin against her fingers, the kick of his pulse, his warm scent, like leather and cloves, came to her unbidden. She'd only held his face, yet the moment had kept her up last night. His silver eyes meeting hers, holding hers, like he could see into the fibers of her being. Steady, patient, curious. For a mind-bending moment, she'd thought that if, someday, Bel *saw* her, all of her, he wouldn't be disgusted with what he saw. Wouldn't realize she was too much work, required too much effort, and turn away.

But then reality had kicked in. Bel was wonderful and kind and loyal, a prince and a general, with a family who he loved and who loved him. Maybe Bel wanted his own family, wanted children. The desire for her own family and children had been the dream of her life, and still burned bright. They could never share that together.

And all of that was assuming that he felt even vaguely the same way she did. Emotionally, anyway. She was pretty sure he recognized the ten-sion humming between them. Surely, he felt the . . . chemistry.

She sure fucking did.

Once she'd finally fallen asleep, her dreams had been filled with hot skin and growled words she couldn't understand, typical dream gob-bledygook, but damn if she hadn't woken up with her hand between her slick thighs, wishing it was someone else's fingers making her gasp instead.

She shouldn't have thought about how his hand had felt on her wrist, shouldn't have imagined his heavy, warm weight above her, shouldn't have wondered how his bulk would feel between her thighs.

She'd come apart when she'd remembered his gravelly voice calling her *princess.* A title, she'd realized, gasping in the rolling aftershocks of her orgasm, she deserved to be called about as much as he wanted to be called a prince.

She took a too-large gulp of coffee and forced herself back to the present, then nibbled on another bite of cobbler, hoping that her poker face had kept Siedah from sensing her filthy reverie.

"Do you want to come down and see the desk sometime? I promise Hell isn't nearly as bad as you think. The souls can be a pain in the ass, but most of them just need a little . . . guidance to grow."

"That would be great." Siedah sipped her tea. "It's much less intimidating when you have a guide."

"The demons would have taken care of you, the big sweeties."

"Of course they would," Siedah agreed, then rested her hand on the table, her eyes gentle. "Has this always been your superpower?"

"My superpower is the ability to make my presence a punishment, according to my brothers. If you ask my mom, it's the ability to leave a mess wherever I go."

"Those are minor powers at best." Siedah's eyes twinkled. "I think your superpower is that you *see* people. Even when they're not 'normal' people, you see them for *them.* It's beautiful."

The urge to brush the observation off or turn it into a joke clawed its way up Lily's throat. But she'd already learned that Siedah wasn't one to let her get away with that.

"Thank you." It felt icky to say it, but she did.

And I thought I'd gotten better at accepting compliments.

Lily blew a raspberry and smiled, hoping it wasn't as awkward as it felt. "Guess I'll have to get used to a soul-baring existence, seeing as I'm, ya know, literally a soul."

Siedah nodded knowingly. "If you stick around long enough, you get rather used to it. Getting to just *be* can be rather nice. Though sometimes"—she leaned in—"it can still scare the pants off you."

"Depending on who's scaring me and how attracted to them I am, they can get the pants off me anytime, no scaring required." Lily grinned and took a drink.

Siedah laughed and snorted, clapping her hand over her mouth with wide eyes. Lily tried to spill her sip of coffee back into her cup and was only mostly successful, shaking with laughter of her own. Her Achilles' heel of stoicism: people who snorted and laughed. She loved it.

They cackled together, and just as they were about to pull themselves together, Siedah would snort, and they'd set off again. The table of souls next to them started to catch the giggles too, which didn't help matters.

Humor. One of the great unifiers.

Lily eventually wiped her eyes with a napkin, stomach and cheeks aching. "That was good."

"It was," Siedah agreed breathlessly, pressing a steadying hand to her chest. "I haven't laughed that hard since the comedy show."

"Where?"

"The Theater, the most unoriginal name for a place in the entire Afterlife. The story is that no one could agree on a name, so they just called it what it was: The Theater. They hold lectures, classes, plays, readings, concerts, comedy shows, all sorts of stuff. It's run by souls, but all are welcome."

Lily opened her mouth, then chuckled. "I almost just asked if it was free."

"Oh." Siedah's face grew serious, though her brown eyes sparkled. "I should mention it *can* be rather exclusive."

Lily raised an eyebrow.

"People are just *dying* to get in."

Lily barked out a laugh, smiling wide. "You actually almost had me."

"I've been waiting to use that line!"

Lily adjusted the stack of pastry boxes in her arms.

"Crocell and Zagan, bless them, found a hacky sack who knows where, and they kept it in the air for a solid hour, just bopping it back and forth over the line of souls. The problem was, this one soul decided to get in Zagan's face over something, right as Crocell sent the hacky sack to him. Fortunately, everyone had gotten invested in keeping it going, so we ended up with this, like, forty-demon hacky sack game. I was laughing so hard I could barely deal with the souls in my line, just watching this stupid little thing fly through the air at the most random times."

"Can we get a hacky sack?" a guy carrying a stack of files asked.

"I'm down! I am so down!" another Front Desk worker, a woman, said, spinning in her chair.

"A moment," another man said seriously. "Are those pastries from Brewhaha?"

Every Front Desk worker in hearing range who wasn't occupied with a soul whipped their heads toward them.

"Yes," Siedah said, ignoring the rush of pumped fists, high fives, and subtle exclamations. "They'll be waiting in the break room. No repeats of the croissant incident this time, please."

"The croissant incident?" Lily asked, following her.

"Don't ask. Half of us didn't speak to each other for days."

Where Hell's break room was all dark elegance mixed with casual comfort (and an assortment of misplaced weaponry), theirs was a vibrant and eclectic patchwork of different cultures and styles. A kotatsu with a trio of cats sleeping on it sat on a gorgeous Moroccan rug. An Indigenous woman played cards with a man who looked like he'd stepped off the pages of a Swedish ski ad. A Filipino man reheated something that smelled like adobo.

"Come on," Siedah said, "I want to show you what the other side of the desk looks like. Plus, I have some sticky notes you might enjoy."

Lily followed her, taking time to look at the lobby without the echoing confusion of being freshly dead. The elderly man still sat on his bench, still peacefully smiling, still radiating serenity, still waiting for his beloved.

The twisty, hollow feeling was back in her chest.

She turned her focus to the full spectrum of humanity arriving at the desk. All races, genders, and ages.

"Sometimes it takes a moment for a soul to settle enough to take the appearance they're most comfortable with. For the little ones, well, if they stay, they have a chance to mature, and if not, they can immediately reincarnate," Siedah explained when Lily asked. "Here we are! I got a new set of animal sticky notes, which one would you like?" She slid open a drawer filled with neatly organized stationery and office supplies, as well as a half-finished embroidery project.

"Dinosaurs, definitely," Lily said, immediately enamored with the set of multicolored cartoon T-Rexes.

Siedah handed them over. "It's a little different from this side, huh?"

"Way less intimidating," Lily agreed. "Though, I think I'd like to see it from the other side, but with some confidence this time." She hopped over the desk in a fluid motion that was becoming startlingly familiar.

Siedah laughed, leaning her hip against her desk. "I can't believe confidence has ever been your problem. I heard a rumor that you introduced a new drink to multiple deities and two princes of Hell?"

"Oh yeah, the Fuzzy Navel. They almost had a fit before they tasted it. You should've seen Lucifer's face—"

"Excuse me?" a voice asked. Lily automatically turned to look, and saw nothing. Then the voice registered. How small it was. Unsure. Young.

Lily looked down. If she'd had a working heart, it would have cracked.

A little girl with a wild mop of shaggy blond hair and large, uncertain blue eyes looked up at her from under the hood of a shark onesie. She had a snub little nose and a round face, and carried herself hunched, like she was trying to minimize the space she took up. She hugged her midsection and swayed slightly—self-soothing—meeting Lily's eyes hesitantly, frequently looking down in the general area of her shirt.

"I think I'm lost."

Oh, baby . . .

Lily crouched down and found that they were nearly the same height, despite the fact that the kid seemed older than her size would suggest. The girl took a tiny step backward and hunched smaller on reflex.

Whoever scared this kid is going to get dragged down to Nine by their eyeballs when they show up.

"Really? Do you know what happened to get you here?" Lily asked gently.

The girl swayed a little, staring at the floor. "I don't want to get in trouble."

"You won't get in trouble, hon, I promise."

The kid looked up at her, suspicion and hope all over her little face. Lily reached for the most powerful tool in her arsenal.

She held out her pinkie finger.

"I pinkie promise you that you won't get in trouble for telling me. Do you know what they say about pinkie promises?"

"No?" The kid's voice was a whisper.

Lily nodded solemnly. "A pinkie promise is sacred. It's unbreakable. Isn't that right?" She looked up at Siedah.

"Absolutely unbreakable. No one ever breaks a pinkie promise," Siedah confirmed with a firm nod.

"So when I pinkie promise that you will be okay, I mean that," Lily said.

The girl looked at her dubiously, then down at her outstretched pinkie.

Come on, Baby Shark, let me help you. It's okay.

She slowly reached out and hooked Lily's pinkie finger with her own.

"I snuck out of the house to go to the aquarium for my birthday," she whispered in a rush. "Then there was a car and a loud noise and then I was here. My foster mom is going to be *really* mad at me if I'm not back in the house soon."

Lily swallowed hard, hoping that her voice betrayed none of the tightness in her throat. She tightened the grip of her pinkie finger. "Remember the pinkie promise while you listen to me, okay?"

"Okay." It was barely a whisper. The girl started shaking like a leaf, but she stared at Lily with wide eyes.

"The good news is, you're gonna be okay. It might be a little confusing, maybe even a little scary, but I promise it'll be okay." Lily kept her tone and expression reassuring.

"Pinkie promise?"

"Pinkie promise." *Don't cry, you fucking marshmallow. Cry later, help Baby Shark now.* "The . . . other news is that you're not going to go back to that house, because you died, sweetie. It's okay; I'm dead, she's dead, we're all dead, and this is the Afterlife. Do you know anything about that?"

"I'm dead?" Baby Shark's eyes were huge.

Ah, fuck, this is why the Universe never let me have kids. I suck at this.

"Yeah, baby, but pinkie promise, remember? I'm here with you. You're okay."

"Oh." Baby Shark looked at their hands, then up, up, up at the indistinct ceiling, then back at their hands. "I have to go to Hell. Do you know where that is?"

Well. Lily hadn't expected that. She looked up at Siedah in concern.

Siedah held a blue-green file and shook her head, mouthing *Paradise or reincarnation.* Lily huffed a sigh of relief and looked back at the kid, who seemed scared. And determined.

"Actually, you don't. You have options. You can either go to Paradise, which is super, super cool. That's where I live. Or you can go back to the mortal world and get born again as a new person and live a whole new life. You won't have to go back to your foster mom. You get a clean slate."

"No, I *have* to go to Hell! My foster mom and Mr. Pastor always said that when I died I was going to go to Hell, and that I better do as I was told. I *have* to go to Hell, or I'm going to get into trouble, and I don't want to get into trouble!" She grew more panicked with every word. Fear, real fear, was in those blue eyes.

Icy fury shot through Lily's veins, even as her soul melted for this child who was clearly so sweet and so scared.

Fuck the rules. I'm going to make sure this kid is okay if I have to rip this whole place apart to do it.

She wasn't sure if it would work, or if she was going to overstep every boundary in existence, but she had to try. No innocent child should think they belonged in Hell. She knew all too well the damage that particular belief could cause.

"Okay," Lily said soothingly. Siedah's eyes bored into the side of her head, but she ignored her, focusing on the child in front of her. "Well, you're in luck, Baby Shark, because I happen to work there, so I can take you with me. In fact, I can take you down to the big cheese himself, and we can get this all sorted out, okay?"

"The big cheese?"

"The person in charge."

"Satan?" Baby Shark whispered.

"He prefers Lucifer, but I call him Luci. He's nice, you'll see. Hey—" Lily shook their linked pinkie fingers. "I pinkie promised that you'll be okay. I know you don't know me, but can you trust my pinkie promise?"

Baby Shark considered it, glancing up at Siedah, who smiled. She looked back at Lily. "Okay," she whispered.

"Awesome. Well then, Baby Shark, let's get you to Hell."

Lily stood, letting their hands separate. She glanced at Siedah with a loaded but hopefully reassuring look. Siedah nodded and handed over the file, and Lily tucked it against her side, looking down at the girl.

"Baby Shark?" The kid sounded a little excited.

Oops.

"Yeah, 'cause of the onesie. Which, by the way, is very cool. You don't have to go by Baby Shark, I just don't know your name. I'm Lily."

"Hi, Lily." Baby Shark squirmed a little, eyes brighter than Lily had yet seen them. "My name's Zoe . . ." She trailed off. The bright eyes, the little squirms, the way she fiddled with the floppy sleeve of her onesie. *Snuck out to go to the aquarium . . .* This kid loved fish. Or sharks.

"Do you *want* to be called Zoe? I can call you whatever you want."

"Really?"

"Oh yeah. One of my best friends calls me princess, even though I'm not one."

"Maybe not Baby Shark. I'm not a baby."

"A fair and valid point. You like the 'shark' bit though, huh?"

"Yeah . . . What about Sharkie?"

"Sounds cool to me. Nice to meet you, Sharkie." Lily held out her free hand. Sharkie shook it with the uncertainty of a kid who'd seen a handshake, but never been taught how to give one. "Now, if you'll follow me, we've got places to go," Lily said with an element of forced cheer.

She walked slowly, every fiber of her being focused on the kid at her side. Sharkie stayed close, hood shifting as she looked around with wide eyes. Learned fear. It had to be. The kid seemed like she hummed with natural curiosity, but there was a conditioning there that made Lily's grip tighten on the file. She wouldn't pause to let her fingers brush the pages inside while they were in such a public place, and probably not where Sharkie would notice. The last thing she wanted to do was violate the kid's privacy, but she didn't want to misstep by saying something accidentally cruel either. Just the basics, then she would let Sharkie share the rest in her own time. If she stayed.

As they walked through the pillars of the Entry Hall, a little body brushed her leg. Sharkie's curiosity had disappeared. Her eyes were huge and watery, her steps uneven, shoulders up by her ears.

Lily held her hand out. Sharkie stared at it, then up at her, chewing on the edge of her sleeve.

Her little hand was clammy when it slid into Lily's palm.

"Pinkie promise," Sharkie whispered, huddling close to Lily's side.

Just like that, the last piece of Lily's silent heart melted.

"Pinkie promise," Lily said, squeezing her hand. Together, they walked toward Hell.

19

SHARK WEEK

Lily

Sharkie stayed glued to Lily's side while they walked down the Judgment Hall toward the elevator available to residents. As always, it was filled with souls. A man stood pressed against the wall near one of the arches, unmoving and scowling fiercely at everyone who passed. Sharkie's grip tightened on her hand. Lily squeezed back, locking eyes with him and letting him see exactly what she would do to him if he dared make the child at her side more uncomfortable.

He shifted his eyes away quickly. Hopefully, he was just scared and confused, not some raging asshole that she'd possible have to deal with at the Hellp Desk after his Judgment.

They arrived at the elevator just as it opened with a ding, and they waited for the various residential souls and Afterlife denizens to exit.

Sharkie's little grip grew clammy, but she didn't say a word or so much as twitch. Frozen. Lily rubbed the back of her hand with her thumb, leading her forward and hitting the button for Hell. Mercifully, they were alone when the doors slid shut and the car eased into a smooth downward motion. Lily shot off a quick text, slipped her phone back into her pocket, and pulled Sharkie's file from where she'd clamped it between her arm and her side. She counted to five, then surreptitiously slipped a finger inside to brush one of the pages.

A battered mobile over a crib, little shark figurines that looked jaunty despite their wear and tear. A woman's thin, ragged face with a beautiful smile that felt like home and magic and sunshine. Crying. So much crying. Yelling too. People slamming things. A woman, the woman—Mom—wailing.

A new house. A new woman. A new man. Children with suspicious eyes and pinching fingers. Hungry. So, so hungry. The woman didn't feed her if she cried, but she couldn't stop crying because she was so hungry. Locked in a dark closet by the older kids, throwing her tiny body against the door until she hurt too badly to try again, curling up behind the hanging clothes and humming a song she remembered from a show with bright, colorful cartoon figures.

Another house. The man liked it when she sat on his lap. She didn't like to sit on his lap. His hands left bruises and his words made her shake if she resisted. So she sat. Watched the TV. Which wasn't so bad, because he liked to watch nature shows, and her favorites were the ones about the ocean. About sharks. She remembered sharks, sharks were from home. Not that . . . she really knew what home was. Then he started to come into her room and cuddle. It made her feel icky and scared, and there was no TV or sharks to distract her.

Another house. She'd pitched a fit as soon as she'd walked in, clinging to the lady who brought her there. She didn't like it. It felt wrong. The woman's eyes were too sharp, too mean. The way the man looked at her made her feel icky again. He watched her and told her that she was such a pretty little doll. She stayed away from him whenever she could.

She hated the church they took her to. The lady said that only abominations hated church, only wicked, evil, wrong children hated church. The pastor listened carefully to the lady's concerns, then took Sharkie into the bad room. His office. He seemed nice at first, speaking with a soft voice and hard eyes.

But every time she answered a question wrong, asked a wrong question, said something wrong, fidgeted, sighed, made a wrong eye movement, recited the Bible wrong . . . he laid her hands on the desk and slapped them. With his hands at first, then a ruler. Then he spanked her. Hand, then ruler, then some floppy rigid paddle thing that stung so badly that, when she sat, she would try to hold herself up by pressing her hands down into the seat. Over her clothes. Then on bare skin. She sat naked in the cold, bad room one day. He'd turned the heat off and put on a sweater, and made her read aloud from the Bible before lecturing her on appropriate interests for a girl. Sharks were not appropriate for a girl. Sharks were for boys.

This was stupid, because she was a girl and she liked sharks, so obviously they weren't just for boys. It made no sense. She told him so through chattering teeth. He'd spanked her and had her stand facing the corner for what felt like hours. Until he had her get dressed, prayed over her like he did every time, then sent her out to meet the foster lady.

The lady started doing some of the things Mr. Pastor did. Sharkie didn't understand all of it—any of it—but she knew what certain words and phrases and things meant. Both the foster lady and Mr. Pastor were adults, and had assured her that they knew best, even though Sharkie didn't think so. They thought sharks were for boys, after all. But they'd both solemnly assured her time and time again, for years, that she was a wicked, willful child who would go to Hell. Sharkie knew that was bad, but she'd heard it was warm, hot even. Maybe when the Hell people made her take her clothes off, it wouldn't be cold. That would be nice.

After Sharkie's eighth birthday—the day after—she'd snuck out of the house. She'd seen a flyer for an aquarium at school and wanted to go. They had a new shark exhibit. She figured that, since she was eight and clearly almost an adult (even if she was a bit smaller than she expected, but maybe her growth spurt was delayed), she could walk to the aquarium, sneak in— because she was small—and then sneak home in time for dinner.

The foster lady had always taken a specific route to go into the town, so Sharkie started walking. And walking. Until tires screeched and an engine revved as a truck came hurtling around a corner, swerving wildly before veering out of control and lurching toward Sharkie.

Drunk driver, the file whispered. Lily jerked her finger off the page, biting the inside of her lip so hard she should have tasted blood. It had been the work of a second for the file to share its secrets. They'd barely gone down more than a floor.

The abuse Sharkie had suffered was in an entirely different class than what she herself had gone through, but too much of it held a note of familiarity. The uncomfortable sexualization from a young age, the attempts to curb a boundless curiosity, the fear of misbehaving and being punished for eternity, those were all experiences that hit so close to home that nausea raged through her gut. She knew what that felt like, and how no one deserved to feel or be treated that way, and she couldn't imagine what this child, who had been through far worse, felt. Sharkie sure as shit never should have been exposed to even a fraction of what she'd gone through. The fact that she had . . . Primordial rage so violent it almost scared her jolted through her system.

This kid is mine. No one hurts her anymore.

She fought to keep the torrent in her head from showing. Sharkie needed stability. Lily could redefine vengeance later. Perhaps Bel would help. Or Gregorith. He seemed to have the skills necessary to make nightmares a reality.

The floors slid by, Sharkie's grip growing tighter and tighter. Lily looked down at her, trying to seem calm and casual, but at the sight of the raw panic on the child's face, at the barely heard whimper, casual went out the window. She swore on reflex, jabbed the "Halt" button, and dropped to her knees.

"Oh, honey—"

"I don't want to go to Hell! But I don't want to get in . . . in trouble," Sharkie sobbed, hunching deeper into her hood, rocking back and forth.

"Do you want a hug, sweetheart?"

Lily barely finished the question before Sharkie flung herself into her arms. Lily wrapped her up and twisted to sit on the floor and cradle her in her lap. She rested her cheek on the soft flannel of Sharkie's hood and rocked her as she cried.

Poor spunky sweetheart.

"I know, bug, I know. You don't have to go to Hell, I promise—"

Sharkie cringed into her, little hands fisting in the material of Lily's shirt as she let out a distressed, panicked wail. "I don't wanna get in trouble! I don't wanna get in trouble! It *hurts!*"

The fragments of Lily's unbeating heart ground themselves into dust. A glimmer of understanding from the file flickered through her mind. They'd hurt her when she'd gotten into "trouble." Too much "trouble-making" at home had resulted in a trip to Mr. Pastor. Too much trouble with Mr. Pastor . . .

Oh, my darling.

"Okay, bug, we'll go to Hell, and you won't get into trouble. I promise. Pinkie promise." Anyone who had studied child psychology would probably kick her ass halfway across the Afterlife if they saw how badly she was fumbling this, but it was all Lily had. She silently begged the Universe that it would be enough to help, even a little.

"Pinkie . . . promise," Sharkie sobbed into her shoulder. Lily held her a little closer, ignoring her own nose stinging as a warning of looming tears.

Who could hurt a child like that? Any child? Who could hurt a child like the one in her arms, who had clearly been born vibrant and curious and sweet and uniquely wonderful? It was like taking a rare wildflower and crushing it for the very things that defined it. But worse. So infinitely worse.

"I've got you, sweetheart, I've got you," Lily murmured, running a hand up and down Sharkie's shaking back. "It's okay to cry. It's okay to be scared. It's *okay*. I've got you. I'm here."

Time didn't matter. Lily just held her girl and murmured comfort as she cried and shook. Her phone buzzed at one point. She ignored it, pressing her cheek into the messy blond hair revealed when Sharkie's hoodie fell back. Eventually, the sobs turned to sniffles and the shaking eased to the occasional tremor, but Sharkie's hands remained clenched in Lily's shirt.

Once upon a time, Lily had read a story, allegedly from a former Snow White character actor, where she'd said that "when you are hugging a child, always be the last one to let go. You never know how long they need it." Lily didn't think the advice was broadly applicable, given the number of creeps out there, but in this instance, she took it to heart.

Sharkie shifted her head on Lily's shoulder and sniffed. "You stopped the elevator," she whispered.

"Yep, we needed a moment."

"You're not supposed to do that," Sharkie said in a small voice.

"Oh really? Says who?"

Sharkie was quiet for a moment. "The . . . rules?"

"I don't follow stupid rules," Lily said, and Sharkie twitched. "Lots of rules are there for a good reason, most rules are there to make the world a better place, but some rules are just stupid. Thankfully, there's no rule that says I'm not allowed to stop an elevator in the Afterlife so that my new friend can have a good cry and not be so scared. Actually, I'm following the rule of 'basic decency,' which is to take care of each other."

Lily resisted, barely, the impulse to say "be excellent to each other," but she sensed the reference to *Bill & Ted's Excellent Adventure* would go unnoticed.

"I'm still scared," Sharkie whispered into her neck.

Lily gave her a squeeze. "That's okay. You can be scared, as long as you know that you're not alone, and I won't let anything bad happen to you while we're down there."

Sharkie held up her pinkie. Lily looped it with hers.

"Okay."

"Okay," Lily said, recalling a few other warnings the kid might like to have. "You know how I work in Hell?"

"Yeah."

"Do you want me to tell you about it?"

Lily felt her nod.

"It's warm, and I think it's really pretty. Where I work, there's a big gate and lots of really cool people. The demons might look a little scary, but I *promise*"—Lily tightened her pinkie—"they're really nice. They're really tall, and they have cool horns, and they come in a bunch of colors like blue, and green, and yellow, and everything in between. Most of them have tails. Some of them have wings. I think you'll like them." Lily tried to inject a little cheer into her voice, conscious of her tendency to get serious and stay serious for too long.

It seemed to be working. Sharkie relaxed a bit, then sat up on her lap. Her little face was blotchy, red, and smeared with tears, but her bright eyes were curious. Lily gently wiped the worst of the tears away and offered her a smile.

"Are they nice like you?" Sharkie asked softly.

"Some of them are probably nicer. But I'm the only *me*. And you're the only you. There's nothing wrong with any of that."

A sniffle. "Are there sharks?"

"Not that I've seen, but you know, sharks might not be super happy down there with all the fire and lava instead of water. It doesn't mean there aren't sharks somewhere else in the Afterlife."

"True."

Lily squeezed her hand. "You've got this, bug. You'll be okay. Whenever you're ready to go, we'll go, but not until then, all right?"

Sharkie nodded, wiggling off her lap to sit beside her and rest her head against Lily's arm. Lily put her arm around the girl's slender shoulders and focused on taking deep, steady breaths. She could feel Sharkie mimicking her breathing, and bit by bit by tiny bit, the worst of the tension in her little body eased away.

Sharkie tugged up her hood. "I'm ready." Sharkie's voice was steady but small.

Warmth and pride washed through Lily. They both stood, and Lily pressed the button to get them moving again. Sharkie slipped her hand into hers as the doors slid open with a cheerful ding.

The warm, organized chaos of the gate was both jarring and comforting after their moment in the elevator. Sharkie's head tipped all the way back, staring at the distant ceiling with red-rimmed, awestruck eyes. The moment her inherent curiosity overwhelmed the learned fear was like watching the sun come out from behind the clouds. Sharkie's whole being shifted, lit up. She kept a firm hold of Lily's hand, but her eyes darted gleefully over everything.

Crocell stomped around the half wall with his spear in one hand, the other wiping at a thick, red liquid sprayed across his face and soaking his shirt. When he spied them, his murderous expression evaporated into a curious grin, and he changed his trajectory.

Sharkie went rigid with a whimpered gasp.

"Who do you have there?" he called, oblivious to or forgetting the gory mess on his face.

Lily stepped in front of Sharkie, blocking Crocell's view. He slowed, confusion flickering over his features.

Lily softened the action with a smile, even as she squeezed Sharkie's hand behind her back. "Hey, Crocell, this is a personal space moment."

Understanding broke across his face like a sunrise. "Oh shi-oot, my bad. Sorry, little shark person!" A glob of thick red dripped from his jaw to his shirt, apparently reminding him of the mess. He winced and backed away, wiping at his face faster. "A soul stole Bebi's smoothie and threw it at me. It's strawberry, not, um, blood."

"Good to know."

She turned and found Sharkie staring up at her, something like awe in her eyes.

"You're safe," Lily assured her, guiding her toward the elevators and waving off a few curious stares from the other demons. She stole a glance at her phone.

Luci: *Use code 1412 in the elevator, & I will meet you in the hallway outside the double doors.*

No questions, no playfulness, no "I'm the ruler of Hell and I'm not dealing with some kid."

Bless him. She'd have to make him cookies.

The second elevator ride was far less eventful than the first, except for a disconcerting moment when the elevator seemed to move sideways for a bit. The doors slid open in a part of Hell unlike any other that she'd seen. Despite the same warm temperature, the energy of the place was cooler. Less magma, more smooth stone, as if it was older.

A towering stone hallway stretched away on either side of them, far from the scale of the Universal Hallway, but imperious nonetheless. Unlike everywhere else, the ceiling didn't glow with sourceless light. Instead, the space was illuminated with hundreds of sconces. Little alcoves with benches were spaced evenly down each wall, along with doors of differing colors and styles of scrollwork. She wondered what, if anything, the scrollwork meant. Almost directly across from the elevator, a pair of double doors were set nearly seamlessly into the stone wall, discernible only by their gleaming handles and the golden scrollwork threaded across their surfaces.

They didn't have to wait long. The doors swung open soundlessly and apparently without being touched. Voices spilled out into the hall, chatting casually over each other. Sharkie shuffled slightly behind Lily. She squeezed her hand.

Demons she didn't recognize filed out of the meeting room, carrying binders and papers and sleek-looking bags. A few shot glances their way, and a couple even smiled and nodded at Lily.

She dampened her surprise and nodded back.

"Princess!" Bel's rumbling voice jerked her attention back to the door. His tailored black pants had extra stitching up the sides in subtle black-on-black designs, and his shirt—sleeveless, per his usual preference—was of a finer make and cut than she'd ever seen on him, shimmering with a scalelike pattern. His inky hair seemed especially sleek, and even his horns gleamed, as if he'd polished them.

He looks more delicious than the pie.

No. Stop it.

That pie was delicious, not Bel . . .

His eyes crinkled at the corners with his unfairly handsome smile.

Her chest went all warm and fuzzy.

Fine. Bel looks pretty delicious too. But she wasn't supposed to be thinking about that.

"What are you doing down here? Who's this?" His voice shifted with his second question going gentle.

Lily looked down at Sharkie, who, despite the death grip she had on her hand, peered around her side curiously. She glanced up at Lily, as if verifying that Bel was safe. At Lily's smile, she relaxed a bit.

"This is Sharkie. She has a few questions for Lucifer. Sharkie, this is my friend Beleth, but we just call him Bel."

Bel crouched, spreading his wings enough to keep them from jabbing into the ground, rugged features softening. "Hey, Sharkie, nice to meet you."

Lily had never doubted his love for his nieces and nephews, or that he deserved his place as one of the favorite uncles. But seeing him in action? Seeing the tiny details of his bearing that he managed to shift to make himself less intimidating, the pure kindness that he let shine out of every fiber of his being?

Another crack spread through the foundation of her decision to keep him from seeing the battered, paradoxical entirety of herself. The little voice in the back of her head whispered, dared her to let him see, certain in the knowledge that he would be different. That he wouldn't scare so easily.

She mentally shook herself. *Not thinking about that now.*

"You're Lily's 'princess' friend," Sharkie said, slinking around to stand beside Lily again.

Bel's eyebrows twitched upward.

"As in, you call me princess sometimes," Lily clarified, fighting the urge to fidget.

The look Bel shot her twinkled with mischief before he returned his focus to Sharkie. "She's the princess of our hearts." Bel grinned. "Don't you think she's a princess?"

Beleth, I am going to kill you. Affectionately.

Sharkie squinted up at her. "I guess. I thought princesses wore poofy dresses and stuff though."

Bel looked up at her entirely too innocently.

I'll kill him quickly, because I like him. But I will very much kill him.

"Poofy dresses are annoying to sit in, and I like being comfortable."

"Oh, yeah, that makes sense. You're a new kind of princess, then," Sharkie said matter-of-factly.

Bel beamed.

"Hello, Lily." Lucifer's smooth baritone interrupted. Bel straightened, stepping to the side as Lucifer strode up to them, not a thread of his neat black suit and crisp white shirt out of place. His wings were held with languid precision, feathers gleaming.

Glacier-melt eyes dropped down to Sharkie, who stared from where she'd glued herself to Lily's side. Something flickered in their depths.

Lucifer smiled softly at her. "Hello, Sharkie. My name is Lucifer, ruler of Hell. I understand you think you belong here?"

Sharkie might as well have been a statue, but then she gave a jerky nod.

"I see. May I?" Lucifer asked, holding out his hand for the file.

Lily had no idea what he saw in her face, but she saw the grim understanding and protectiveness in his. A knot eased between her shoulders.

Lucifer flipped open the file, running a finger along the page, eyes going distant. His wings and fingers stiffened minutely before his eyes refocused, pulsing with more light. He shut the file carefully, sinking into an effortless crouch.

"Sharkie, I would like to speak with you privately, if that's all right? We would sit in that alcove right over there so that you can still see Lily, and Lily can still see you. I promise that you are not in trouble, and that I mean you no harm. I only wish to speak."

Sharkie nibbled her lip, looking between Lily, Lucifer, and the alcove. Then she looked at the ruler of Hell and held out her pinkie.

Please let Lucifer know what a pinkie promise is, please, please, please . . .

Lucifer linked his much-larger pinkie with Sharkie's, a slow smile softening his handsome features. He offered her his other hand. Sharkie stepped away from Lily with only a second of hesitation, taking it and following him to the alcove.

Lily leaned back against the wall, sucking in a deep breath. Bel leaned beside her, his face serious.

"How bad is bad?"

Lily's nose stung, the tears she'd fought back in the elevator threatening to spill over. "Bad." Her voice broke. She closed her eyes and tipped her head back against the stone.

Bel threaded his fingers through hers, calluses scraping lightly over her palm.

She wasn't sure whether it was weakness or recklessness that motivated her to lean against him and rest her head on his shoulder. Perhaps she was just tired of all of it. Bel was kind and strong, and part of her wanted—needed—to borrow some of that kindness and strength for herself.

He rested his cheek on top of her head. "Share it with me?"

Keeping an eye on the alcove, she briefly explained the contents of the file. Bel graciously ignored when her voice cracked. She could feel his fury in the twitch of his muscles, the accelerated pounding of his pulse at his wrist, but he stayed quiet, letting her speak.

"I knew it was bad when a child insisted they come to Hell, but fuck. You handled it well," he said when she finished.

"Thanks. Now what? She doesn't want to go back, or at least, she didn't express any interest in it. She clearly has a Paradise waiting for her, and Siedah said something about how young souls can mature, but she's so little. Is she just . . . what? Left alone to grow up? There's no way that will work."

"From what I know, little souls who don't want to reincarnate are always put in a community setting or with a guardian, so they can grow up—'maturing' we call it—in the Afterlife up to the point when they feel physically comfortable. Then they're just like everyone else."

"Ah." Lily frowned. She'd have to find a way to check on Sharkie wherever they set her up.

Bel cleared his throat. "But maybe, to get her started, she can stay with you? Only if you're both okay with it, but she seems to trust you."

Lily started. "With me?"

"Yeah, with you. I doubt she'll want to be far from you, based on what I've just seen."

"I've got a guest room she's more than welcome to have . . ." Lily trailed off, closing her eyes again, unsure of how to say the rest.

Bel shifted. "I'm sensing a 'but,' and not the sexy kind."

She resisted the urge to pinch him for making her say it. "But maybe I'm not the right person to help her. I wasn't . . . I never got to be a mom. I studied basic child development and parenting stuff in my spare time, but Sharkie is going to need better guidance and care than that." She swallowed. "Maybe it's better for her to be with someone more experienced, maybe they'll be able to give her more than I could."

There was a breath of silence, then, "Bullshit."

Bel pushed himself off the wall to stand in front of her calmly.

Lily stared at him, annoyance prickling up her spine. Okay, so maybe he didn't listen as well as she thought. What did he mean, "bullshit"?

"I doubt that anyone in the entire Afterlife could *care* more for that child than you."

Oh.

"Look me in the eye and tell me that you weren't fully prepared to rip Lucifer to shreds if he'd been a dick about this." He raised his eyebrows, waiting.

Lily arched an eyebrow of her own and said nothing.

"You've told deities to shove a cactus up their own asses because of a *game*, and you think that you aren't able to show Sharkie what it's like to be loved and protected? Bull. Shit. Utter bullshit."

"Maybe," she relented. "But it's not just love or protection, it's knowing how to handle everything she's been through the right way. It's knowing how to parent and then some."

He looked at her for a moment. "So you have no practical experience. You'll learn. So you might mess up sometimes. What parental figure doesn't? So you might not immediately know the answers to everything. Who does?"

He gave her a half smile. "If it's an answer you can find, you're a nerd, and a damn fine one at that. You'll do what nerds do best, and research. You'll stick that pretty nose in a book or sit in front of a computer until you figure it out, and then you'll do your best. How do I know? Because it's *you*."

She stayed silent, even as hope hesitantly prickled through her. Could she do it, if Sharkie wanted her?

"If you want to help her, and she wants to trust you, I can't imagine anyone better for the job. You don't have to worry about changing the whole world, princess, that's too big for anyone. But if anyone can change *that child's* world, it's you. So, don't turn it down because you think you're not qualified. There are resources here for her, but love and safety are what she needs more than anything else. You'll tackle the rest too. I know you will."

Lily's head spun. It was a good thing that breathing was more of a habit than a necessity; she'd stopped breathing at some point. Of course he'd been listening. Somehow, he'd managed to say just the right things to make her remember who and what she was.

"Okay," she said, meeting his eyes.

His big hand brushed her cheek, wiping away a tear she hadn't noticed. His voice was soft and earnest. "You've *got* this, princess. And we'll be backing you up every step of the way. You aren't doing this alone."

Since kissing him was—regrettably—out of the question, and even if it had been in the question, would have been deeply inappropriate given the circumstances, Lily wrapped her arms around his solid waist and pressed her cheek to his chest. He curled himself around her, blocking out the world.

"Thank you." It was a paltry response, but it was all she could say. She squeezed him tighter. "*Thank you.*"

He slid his hand down her spine. "I've got you, princess."

I know.

She smiled against his shirt, almost in disbelief at the conversation they'd just had and the decision she'd made. "Who is this 'we' who's supposedly backing me up every step of the way?"

"Me. Lucifer, probably. Everyone. We'll figure it out. Does she actually like sharks, or is it just a 'onesie of convenience' kind of thing?"

"Loves sharks. Do you know anything about them?"

"They exist in oceans, and they're usually the bad guy in boat movies. That's about it. You?"

"Not much better," she admitted, refusing to let go of him. "I know a few different types, but that's all."

Bel loosened his hold, reaching for his back pocket and pulling out his phone. Lily stepped back a bit, missing his warmth.

"Who would know something about sharks?" he muttered, scrolling through his contacts.

Lily pulled out her own phone. "What mortal souls might still be in the Afterlife who could help?"

"Good thinking. Oh, Angel, she surfs, she might know something . . ."

"Steve Irwin maybe? Is he still here? Wait, holy shit, documentaries!

There've gotta be some good documentaries about sharks. Heck, I could just watch Shark Week."

"What's Shark Week?"

"A week of TV shows all about sharks. Documentaries, studies, that kind of thing. There're these great white sharks that launch themselves into the air to catch prey. It's pretty crazy. There you go, a shark fact."

"I . . ." Bel frowned, clearly concerned. "I don't like that. How high into the air? Isn't there a movie about flying sharks?"

"*Sharknado*. Not factual in the slightest, but it's a cultural icon. All, what, eight of them now? We'll add it to the list."

Lily glanced over to the alcove, where Sharkie had her hood pushed back, listening to Lucifer intently, occasionally saying something that Lily couldn't hear. Lucifer had his jacket unbuttoned, dutifully and gently responding to everything.

"Gregorith sent me a link to an article called '10 Great Documentaries About Sharks,'" Bel said excitedly.

"Gregorith?" Lily asked, bringing her focus back to him.

"Yeah, I asked in a bunch of group chats, and people are starting to respond. Cthulhu says 'Sharks are delicious treats, if a bit crunchy.' Not helpful, but I appreciate the effort."

Cthulhu. He's kidding, right?

Lily stared at a literal demon prince while standing in Hell for all of two seconds before she realized that he wasn't.

He hunched over his phone, lips pursed in concentration, a little furrow between his thick brows as he swiped and scrolled through responses. She rubbed at her chest.

"Would you like me to add you to these group texts? They're pretty cool mostly. Just be yourself, they'll love you. Plus, it takes a village to raise a kid, right? Presto, a village." He caught her staring at him. "What?"

Oops.

She just smiled.

20

BANDIT PRINCE

Lily

"Obviously lemon sharks don't taste like lemons," Lily said, looking up from a particularly helpful article about supporting traumatized children. "Was he seriously surprised by that?"

Bel rolled his eyes. "Even I knew that. Though according to this article, lemon sharks do occasionally get possessive over certain divers and get jealous when that diver gives other sharks attention."

"Relatable," Lily said, stretching her back. They'd ended up sitting on a nearby bench, doing what they, as nerds, did best. Bel had offered to research shark facts and documentaries, as well as sift through the flood of text messages from the group chats for valuable advice and information. While he handled that, Lily researched child trauma and general caregiving advice. With every article she felt, if not more qualified for the task at hand, at least slightly more prepared.

She texted Siedah an update and asked if she had any information about child-specific counseling services in the Afterlife, figuring that the Front Desk would know that kind of thing. Lily knew how much counseling could help a person, but she didn't want to overwhelm Sharkie with it too soon, if she ever chose to go. It wouldn't hurt to know what resources were out there though.

Every so often, Bel held up his phone to show her a cute picture of a shark or read a particularly funny joke, text exchange, or interesting fact.

Apparently, Poseidon and Lir were arguing over the best shark, while Cthulhu was offering a "foodie's review" of different shark species.

She leaned her head back, letting out a slow breath. *I've got this. It might not be perfect, but it will be my best. No one had it all figured out.*

"Lily?"

"Mm?"

"It really doesn't bother you? When I call you princess?"

She lolled her head to the side to meet his eyes at the unexpected question. "I wouldn't say I liked it if I didn't mean it."

He gave an amused huff. "I know. But earlier you looked . . . uncomfortable. Not just the fun kind of annoyed."

How had she ever doubted his perceptiveness? "I *do* like it. I just . . . don't think I deserve it, that's all."

An almost sad smile ghosted over his lips. "You do. You might not be a 'poofy dress princess,' but you're still a princess. You could be called a queen, even."

"*Fuck* no." Lily gagged dramatically, rewarded by his deep, rolling laugh. "That's entirely too much responsibility. Plus, it's princesses who have all the fun—going on adventures, kissing bandits who turn out to be naughty princes in disguise, discovering secret powers they somehow never knew they had. That's princess stuff. It's still a huge amount of responsibility, but it sounds like a lot more fun. In movies and books anyway, not historically."

"What princess movies have this 'kissing bandit prince' trope you speak of? I may need to take notes."

"That one would be found in romance books. Everyone loves a secret prince, especially if he's a bad boy with a heart of gold. And has a great ass."

"I'm going to need a list of book recommendations." Bel grinned. "It'll be good for me to branch out."

Lily couldn't help the wicked grin she aimed at him. If only he knew what he was asking for. Her Paradise library had turned out to have not only her favorite smutty romance novels, but some fantastic new ones as well—ones that made even her toes curl and had her reaching for the bedside drawer full of fun toys.

Bel arched an eyebrow, running his tongue along the tip of one fang, mischief lighting up his features. "What kind of books are you reading to put that look on your face? Naughty, naughty princess," he tsked.

They both danced close to that invisible line now. Flirting with Bel wasn't just *flirting*. It was something else.

"You know how much I love research. I want to be prepared for any and all scenarios that may . . . arise," she teased.

He sucked in a barely perceptible little breath, gaze darkening as it flickered down to her lips and back to her eyes.

He might as well have traced her lips with his touch. His heat radiated through his pants and her leggings where their thighs touched. It would be easy, so easy to press her leg just a little harder . . .

A young voice floated down the hallway, answered by Luci's deeper one, fracturing the spell.

She looked back at her phone, the text on the screen gently detailing the kinds of behaviors caregivers could expect from children who had been through deeply traumatic experiences. Guilt soured her stomach, the sexual heat curdling at the realization of how selfish the moment had been—

She immediately quashed that line of thought.

It wasn't selfish. It was *human*.

Connection could be a comfort. She knew that as well as anyone.

She'd once read studies on the prevalence of sex after funerals, how people clung to the things that made them feel alive, even in the midst of death. Remembered how, after her diagnosis, she'd gone out and hooked up with an old booty call, just to feel alive one last time before she'd gotten too sick to enjoy much of anything at all.

That moment with Bel had been heated and real and natural, not selfish. Selfish would have been abandoning Sharkie so that they could go fuck in the newly vacated conference room. While that was a *deeply* pleasing mental image, she'd never do it, and neither would Bel.

Which was part of why it was so *easy* with him. She knew down to the tiniest fiber of her soul that Bel was *good*. Sexier than he had any right to be, but good, first and foremost.

"Bel?"

"Hm?"

She opened her mouth, met his gaze, and thought better of it. Then thought again.

He needed to know. It was important that he know.

"I know you don't feel like you earned being a prince," she said.

He stiffened so completely that even his tail stilled. *Shit.*

She forged on. "But you're a prince to me. Not in the shitty paperwork, 'you got assigned to be a prince of Hell' way, but in the 'you have a good heart' way."

He didn't say anything, didn't even seem to breathe, just stared at her with a stunned look on his face. She wondered if it was possible to melt into the floor.

Could she fade into the wall? No, she couldn't leave Sharkie. Well then, they'd just have to sit in awkward silence until he left or Luci and Sharkie had finished their conversation.

Bel didn't so much as twitch.

Maybe his hatred of being a prince ran deeper than she realized, and she, like an idiot who wanted to be stupid and poetic—and okay, maybe a little romantic—had said the worst possible thing. This was why she just read romance novels and was never the heroine of her own.

"You're still a pretty kick-ass general though. If that . . . makes you feel any better." If Cthulhu could exist and be a nautical food critic, surely she could know when to shut up.

But then Bel's arm slid around her shoulders, pulling her tightly against his side. His breath ghosted over her ear before he pressed a lingering kiss into her hair.

She melted in relief, eyes drifting shut, the hollow tension in her chest replaced with something silky and calm. She'd always assumed that when people described moments as "quiet," they'd literally meant "without sound." They hadn't. Inside her head could be so damned *loud*, but in that moment it went quiet. Peacefully, gently, comfortably quiet.

They were simply there. Together. Side by side, sharing warmth and breath and comfort and affection.

She leaned into him, reaching up to cover the hand on her shoulder with her own. He lifted his lips and rested his cheek on top of her head, letting out a slow breath that riffled her hair.

"Thank you, princess," he murmured.

She squeezed his hand, not opening her eyes, just soaking it all in, comforting him and letting herself feel comforted, their research abandoned. Luci and Sharkie continued their unintelligible conversation. An elevator farther down the hallway dinged. Voices murmured and faded again. She was happy to stay right where she was. Possibly for the foreseeable future.

"So," his voice was rough against her temple, "can I be one of those bandit princes, or does the quality of my ass not meet the standard?"

She clamped her free hand over her mouth in time to muffle what would have been a deeply inappropriate laugh and managed to restrict it to a nasal wheeze. Bel fought his own battle to snicker quietly, his body shaking. She patted him on the thigh with a quiet chuckle.

"With your ass, big guy, I think you could be whatever kind of prince you want."

He grinned into her hair. "Being a prince to you is fine by me."

She turned her head to look at him with a smile, then fought to remember how to breathe. A scant few inches separated their noses. She could see every striation in his irises, the texture of his soft lips, the minute details of his skin, the tiny strands that had escaped the braided portion of his hair to wisp over his face. His breath fanned over her skin, her too-sensitive lips. So close.

She mentally slapped herself but couldn't bring herself to back away.

"Lily," Bel said, his voice rough.

"Bel," she replied, desperately grasping for the threads of their conversation. "You sure you want to be a prince to me? I have very stringent requirements for the quality of royal ass."

His cocky little smile nearly lit her on fire. "Perfect. It'll be an incentive not to slack off in training."

She wrinkled her nose at him.

He stuck his tongue out at her.

Lucifer coughed.

She blushed down to her toes at the sight of Luci standing directly in front of them, looking like the cat that got the canary, with Sharkie holding his hand and watching them with careworn eyes that were brighter than they had been. A little smile even tipped the corners of her mouth.

"Did you guys have a good talk?" Lily asked, sitting up a little straighter at the same time as Bel.

"Yeah. Did you?" Sharkie asked.

Bel coughed, and Lily wondered exactly how brilliantly red her ears had to be at that moment. "Yeah, Bel was very helpful."

"I'll bet he was." Lucifer smirked.

Don't kill him with your eyes, Lily, Sharkie is watching. And he's the ruler of Hell. But mostly, Sharkie's watching.

"So," Lily said, "what did you guys get figured out?"

"Mr. Luci says I don't have to stay in Hell because my foster mom was"—Sharkie lowered her voice as if the bitch would hear her all the way from the mortal world—"*wrong.*"

Lily just nodded.

"He also said, um . . ." Sharkie looked up at him for reassurance. All traces of his smugness evaporated when he looked down at her with a tender smile and an encouraging nod. "He also said that I can ask to stay with you. If that's okay."

"Of course it is," Lily said, simultaneously relieved and nervous. "I have a room that you can make completely your own."

Sharkie's eyes went wide. "Really?"

"Really."

"Okay." Sharkie seemed to waver between excited and dubious. Lily didn't blame her. Consistency, patience, kindness, and respect. Those were going to be the name of the game in helping Sharkie heal and feel safe.

Lucifer leaned toward Sharkie. "Do you mind if I speak to Lily for a moment?"

"Okay . . ." Sharkie said slowly, glancing at Bel, then Lily.

"He's nice, I promise. He doesn't bite," Lily said, rising to her feet.

Bel shot her a look that had liquid heat dripping through her veins and curling through her abdomen, before aiming a cheerful and completely benign grin at Sharkie, bracing one elbow on a knee and holding the pinkie of his other hand out to her.

With that tiny gesture, Lily realized that she was utterly fucked. What she felt for Bel in that moment was so far outside the realm of "only friends" that she had no idea how she'd keep a lid on it.

But she'd deal with that later.

Maybe.

"I'm not so bad," Bel said. "Besides, I hear you like sharks. Do you have a favorite kind? Like lemon sharks?"

Sharkie's gasp of delight had Lily's lips tipping up as she followed Luci farther up the hall. He shot a fond look behind them, where Sharkie had clambered up beside Bel and pointed at something on his phone, talking more animatedly by the second.

"Thank you for bringing her down," he said when they stepped into an alcove.

"Thank you for taking the time to talk to her. I don't know what you said, and I don't need to know, but it seemed to help."

All semblance of warmth disappeared, Lucifer's eyes glowing brighter than she'd ever seen them. Raw power radiated from him in a nauseating buzz, a bit like standing outside when lightning was about to strike. The primal, instinctual screech of *wrong* and *run* jolted through her system, but she steeled herself. Lucifer was beyond furious, but not at her.

"I've been the master of Hell from the beginning, since before it was known as Hell," he began, a strange double-timbre quality to his voice. "I have seen all the worst monsters that humanity has thus far produced. Yet the monsters who prey on children remain among the vilest."

Lily said nothing. She had only worked in Hell for a blip of time in the grand scheme of anything, had only gotten a small taste of exactly the kind of putrid evil that could be found in it, and she agreed with him.

"You looked in the file?" he asked.

"Briefly. I wanted to get a sense of what happened so that I wouldn't say or do anything to accidentally hurt her. I left the rest for her to tell in her own time."

"Good." His voice made her teeth ache. The glow of his eyes dimmed until she only felt vaguely nauseated instead of moments from throwing up. "She wasn't the first child that woman abused. Nor that pastor. Nor those men. And," he snarled, eyes flaring, "she wasn't the last."

He seethed for a moment, jaw clenched as he stared out into the hallway. Lily waited, watching the emotions rage in his eyes.

Lucifer heaved a long, weary sigh, power dimming down, rage fading into exhaustion. He adjusted his tie, fixing those glowing eyes on her. "I'm sorry, I'm sure that was very unpleasant for you. I didn't mean to expose you to that."

Lily held his gaze, letting the mask drop, letting the monster she'd kept caged at the bottom of her soul show a bit. "Luci, there's nothing you could do that will be more unpleasant than seeing what was in that file. I don't care how vicious you are."

He looked so tired.

"I'm sorry," she said gently.

Confusion flashed across his face. "Why are you apologizing to me?"

"Because I know. I know that if anyone were to find out about what those monsters have done, what they will do, they'll blame it on 'Satan's influence.' I'm sorry because they'll never see *this*. They'll never see that Lucifer, ruler of Hell, took time out of his day to comfort a child and be enraged on their behalf. They'll credit you for the evil things that happen, not the justice you represent, and I'm sorry. However, when the fuckers who did this get down here, and it's time for them to reap what they sowed, I'm sorry for that too. Because I will do my level best to make you look like an amateur at the job you created."

Lucifer's power rippled, a slow smile easing onto his lips. "Ms. Lily, I believe that sounds like a challenge."

Lily smiled back. "Think you're up to it?"

"Against you and the justice you'd deliver for that child?" He studied her, assessing the cold fury she was certain was in her eyes. "I will admit to having my doubts that I could do any better."

He rubbed his forehead, mirth fading. "That child, Sharkie, she is special. Such wonder in her heart . . . and such fear too. Luckily, you are special too. Don't"—he held a hand up before she could open her mouth—"argue with me. Please. Life has wounded you in its own way, but that does not diminish who you are, and who you could be, if you only stop being afraid of yourself." His tone was gentle but firm.

Lily felt tremendously itchy.

Standing in front of a rabidly furious ruler of one of the most infamous punishment realms was one thing. Accepting compliments about herself—multiple times in one day no less—was entirely another.

"She trusts you," Luci said. "The only reason she spoke with me was because you had promised to keep her safe." He gestured down the hall, where Sharkie's sweet little voice contrasted with Bel's deep rumble. "The only reason she is so open with Bel is because you trust him. Perhaps there is more there than just trust—"

"Lucifer."

"Your business is your own," he assured her. He angled his head, humor fading into gentle seriousness again. "However, if I may just say this: Home and family may not always look the way we imagined that they would. If you need anything, especially when it comes to helping the child, I am at your disposal. She is very smart, and quite blunt. I enjoy that, and others will as well. Other deities will be happy to offer their assistance. It is one of our Universal Constants to never harm children, but I understand that fears from the mortal world may carry over."

Lily chuckled, thinking of the flashes of Sharkie's wide-eyed wonder. "Honestly, Luci, I think once Sharkie learns how *not* to be afraid, she's probably going to run the place. Or at least explore every inch of it."

Lucifer's smile was brilliant. "Perhaps. Though I think she may get sidetracked by some of the more oceanic realms. There are things in that water that give me the creeps. She'll love them."

Bel

"I believe this goes without saying, but whatever resources she wants or needs, she gets," Lucifer said in his office an hour later, typing away on his phone.

Bel snorted, reaching for a leftover dumpling. "Way ahead of you. I already told Lily backup was only a call away."

The ruins of their lunch were scattered across Lucifer's massive desk. After Lily had finished her conversation with Lucifer and asked Sharkie if she was ready to go to Paradise, Bel had given her a supportive wink and watched her gently take Sharkie's offered hand as they headed toward the elevators.

Lily might not fully believe it yet, but Bel knew that Sharkie was in the best possible hands. If anyone could protect and guide that girl, it was Lily. She had the patience and kindness and fierce protectiveness to help the terrified child feel safe again, and begin what Bel knew could be the long process of healing.

Pride swelled in his chest, and not just because of Lily's incredible strength of character and Sharkie's little flashes of personality breaking through her fear. He was . . . proud of *himself*. Lily had called him a prince, and instead of carving into his soul like a curse, it had settled over him like a warm blanket.

Lucifer stiffened, a hum of power rippling through his office.

"What?" Bel asked, wariness stilling his thoughts.

"She'll have the backup she needs, but for the next few days, it won't come from you." Lucifer handed over his phone, all the spark inspired by his conversation with Sharkie gone.

Bel scanned the screen, cursing. The small incursion from the unfamiliar Universe didn't seem to be staying small. It wasn't an army yet, but it didn't look friendly either. He couldn't bemoan the fact that it had to happen when it was *his* legions' on-call rotation—everyone had things that they didn't want to miss—but he'd allow himself a flare of annoyance before focusing.

He wanted to be there for Lily, for these first days with Sharkie. He wanted to be her backup. Her emotional support, if she needed it.

Bel let himself loose a single sigh, then let the feelings fade and cleared his head.

"I'll gather my legions." He stood, handing Lucifer back his phone.

Lucifer nodded, brow creased as Bel headed toward the door of his office.

He paused on the threshold, turning back. "Lucifer—"

"Whatever she needs, Bel. I promise."

With a short nod, Bel left, shutting the door behind him.

21

CARL

Lily

"Your door is very round," Sharkie said as they stepped through the portal door into Lily's front garden.

"Yeah, isn't it cool? It's like a hobbit door."

"What's a hobbit?"

"It's from one of my favorite books, see?" She showed her the door tattooed on her arm. "I think you'd like it; it's got dragons and dwarves and magic in it." Lily pushed open the door, following Sharkie inside and bending to pull off her boots. "This is home. Do you want to see your room first, or would you like to explore?"

When Sharkie didn't answer, Lily turned to find her staring up at the picture of her and her brothers. Lily wiped her hands on her leggings, hoping that the perceptive kid wouldn't perceive too much.

"Is that your family?" The question was innocent, curious, and punched a hole in her chest. The resulting tide of guilt and shame and love and grief threatened to drown her, pull her down to that cold place that hurt so badly.

She took a deep breath, Lucifer's and Bel's words echoing in her mind, and for the first time tried to swim instead of letting herself sink.

"Yeah, part of it. Those are my brothers, Tommy and Ryan." Did her voice sound as distant to Sharkie as it did in her own ears? Maybe it sounded so odd because she hadn't said their names since she'd died.

"You all have red hair?" Sharkie sounded impressed, her little grin sweet.

"Yeah," Lily choked out. "We got a lot of attention when we went out together because it was unusual to see a pack of redheads."

We couldn't get away with anything, we were too easy to spot. I used to threaten them with murder if they touched my leftovers, but I would have killed for them in a heartbeat. I pretended to be asleep toward the end when Tommy came into my room and said all those sweet things he never would have said if I'd been awake. Or would he have?

I hope they don't miss me as much as I miss them.

"I'm sorry, I didn't mean to make you upset! I'm sorry!" Sharkie's curiosity evaporated into the all-consuming fear from the Front Desk. Lily cursed herself silently for letting the mask slip.

"No, no, bug, it's okay," she soothed, dropping into a crouch. "I'm not mad, it's okay. I promise."

Sharkie's breathing was uneven, hands twisted up in her sleeves, but she listened and nodded. "You looked sad," she whispered.

Lily offered her hands; Sharkie took them. "Yeah, I was, but it wasn't your fault. Sometimes you can be sad for a reason that isn't bad. My brothers are still alive, and I miss them. That's all. Do you want to take a few deep breaths with me?"

Sharkie nodded.

Lily took a slow breath, held it, and let it go, Sharkie following her lead as they repeated the pattern a few times.

"Better?" Lily asked.

"Yeah. You?"

"Yep. Now, room or exploring?"

"I'd like to see my room, please—oh, you have a cat!"

Max sauntered around the corner from the living room, chirping a greeting. Within seconds, Sharkie was sitting cross-legged, holding out her hand for him to sniff. He inspected her fingers for only a moment, then crawled into her lap, rubbing his face against hers and purring so loudly Lily heard him by the door.

She smiled. *That's my good boy.*

"His name is Max, and he's the best."

Sharkie cooed to him, her round little face lighting up with a genuine, unrestrained smile for the first time. "He's so nice!" She giggled as Max flopped onto his side in her lap, politely demanding belly rubs.

Lily wondered when Sharkie had last smiled and giggled so freely. She cooed over Lily's ridiculous and beloved cat with such pure glee that Lily found herself protective of that sweet joy. Maybe Sharkie wasn't technically her kid, but Lily knew she would love her as if she were.

Max was all too happy to be cradled in Sharkie's arms for the short trip to the guest room, which Lily was mildly surprised to see had transformed itself into a shark-themed haven. Sharkie, on the other hand, nearly dropped the cat.

Lily crouched down again, the sense of occasion making her choose her words carefully. "This room is yours."

"All mine?"

"You got it." Lily grinned, then held out her pinkie. Once Sharkie had set Max down and hooked it with her own, Lily continued. "Because this is your room, I will never go in it unless you ask me to, or you give me permission. *No one* will go into your room without your permission."

Sharkie looked between her and the room, doubt and fear dimming what Lily had quickly come to think of as the Sharkie Shine. She waited for that quick little mind go to work.

"You promise?"

Lily wiggled their joined pinkies. "Promise. Hey, House, do you hear that? We promise, right?"

To her utter shock, the house groaned in response. Since the little welcome rumble when she'd arrived, it had been otherwise silent while it worked its housekeeping magic. If she'd been alive, she would have hauled ass outside, calling her witchy friends and asking them to cleanse it.

"Cool!" Sharkie jumped up and down excitedly and patted the doorframe like it was a dog. "Hi, House! Does the house have a name?"

"Um . . . House?"

"It needs a name! We should call it Carl."

The house groaned . . . happily?

"I think we should keep calling it 'House,'" Lily said, trying to convince herself that an apparently semi-sentient house was the least freakout-worthy thing to have happened since she got up that morning.

Shark wrinkled her nose doubtfully, taking a few cautious steps into her room before turning around, a question brewing in her eyes. "Can we, um, test it? The room thing?"

Lily frowned, not following.

"The house is going to keep people out of my room too, right? Can we test that?"

"I'm not—"

The house creaked.

Well, okay then.

"Of course we can test it." Lily stood. She made it to the threshold of the door before she hit an invisible barrier that stretched across the doorway. It had a bit of give to it, so walking into it wasn't painful, then she was gently pushed back into the hallway. She grinned at Sharkie, then tried and failed to reach through with her hand.

She expected Sharkie to be as gleefully delighted as she'd been when the house—which, semi-sentient or not, Lily flatly refused to call Carl—had groaned in response. Instead, what she saw on her face nearly broke her.

Relief. Pure, simple, unfettered *relief*.

"You're safe," Lily said. Sharkie's blue eyes brimmed with tears. "You're *safe*, Sharkie."

Sharkie ran through the doorway and wrapped her arms around Lily's hips, burying her face into her stomach with a sob.

Lily cradled a steaming mug of tea, peering through the cracked door at the lump on the bed, breathing deep and even. Max, purring in a perfect loaf by Sharkie's feet, stood guard. He blinked slowly at Lily and resumed his watch.

She smiled, tiptoeing down the hall and easing into the dimly lit library, where the window bed beckoned. She'd ignored her phone since arriving home, but she'd seen it lighting up with a barrage of texts while she got Sharkie settled in. Easing into the bed with a sigh, she scrolled through the bewildering number of messages. Some, like Luci's, she'd expected.

Luci: *I might have spread the word about Sharkie a bit. Bel is rather annoyed with me. How is she?*

Others came from more shocking sources.

Gregorith: *We'll be ready for the ones who hurt her. Swell sharks have bio-fluorescent properties that let their skin glow green in the dark.*

Luci's definition of "a bit" seemed like rather an understatement as she read dozens—hundreds—of messages from multiple deities, from multiple pantheons—including several sweet ones from Persephone, from half the Front Desk, a truly astounding number of demons, Cthulhu, Kanaloa, and finally, Bel.

Bel of the Ball: *Hey, princess, Lucifer got gossipy (well-intentioned but still). I'm sure you've figured that out by now. I'm sorry, I didn't know what he was doing until it was too late. She's going to be one loved kid. I have to leave tonight for an unexpected patrol, but I'll be thinking of you and Sharkie the whole time. I won't have my phone, so I'll look forward to talking with you when I get back. Remember: I'm proud of you. You've got this. Kick ass and look good doing it.*

"I want to kiss you," she whispered into the quiet privacy of the library, the words sounding dangerous and electric, like admitting it out loud would manifest it into being. She wasn't sure how much longer she'd be able to fight that particular truth.

Home and family may not always look the way we imagined they would.

Lily sipped her tea, wondering for the first time if her home and family, wherever and whatever it may be, would be better than she could have imagined.

22

GROW BREAD GROW

Lily

Sharkie slept through two days and three nights.

While initially concerned, Lily reasoned that she was probably experiencing the soul equivalent of the let-down effect. Poor kid had been running in survival mode for so long, it was no wonder that her soul needed to shut down for a bit. She figured that if anything were wrong that she couldn't sense, either the house or the cat would alert her to it.

Max maintained a vigil on Sharkie's bed, with brief, infrequent forays out for attention from Lily. She texted updates to Luci, informed the gate demons that she would be absent for a little while, and resisted the urge to leave a million text messages for Bel. Luci had been oddly cagey about the patrol, telling her only that "If all went well, it would only last a few days."

Luci's reluctance to tell her more, along with the way people got weird when she asked about it, made her suspect that it was more than just a simple patrol. She didn't expect to know everything, of course, and she trusted Bel to tell her what she needed and was allowed to know . . . but she didn't like it.

Still, all Lily could do was wait. She filled the first day by hunting down new recipes and watching as many shark documentaries as she could stand. The second day was spent researching child development and trauma, reading, and convincing herself that she was not at all stressed.

A lie that she had to confront on the third morning, when she found herself scrubbing the edges of the entryway floor with a toothbrush for no reason other than she'd thought of it.

Stress cleaning. Her biggest tell.

She suspected that the house, which had been entirely self-cleaning up to that point, dirtied itself so that she could feel more productive. Everywhere she decided to clean went from spotless to vaguely grimy before she got there. Only vaguely though, as if the house couldn't stand to make itself truly dirty.

She stood, blowing a piece of hair out of her face, watching the grime she'd left behind disappear into thin air.

"A little dirt won't kill you," she said.

The house grumbled.

She grinned. "It's just extra minerals."

The house didn't make a noise, but she got the distinct impression that it was pouting. She patted the nearest wall.

"Thanks for letting me clean, though. I feel better."

She looked around the entryway, fiddling with the toothbrush restlessly. Sunlight peeked through the mist that had blanketed them overnight, washing everything in a pale glow. A breeze danced through a window she'd cracked open, carrying the fresh scent of dew and grass and the faint perfume of damp flowers.

Fresh bread. That's what the morning was missing. Good, hearty bread. She turned to head for the kitchen but paused.

The picture haunted her. In a friendly, familiar, wonderful kind of way, but a haunting was a haunting. Why, in a place supposed to be her safe haven, her literal Paradise, was there a picture that made her feel like a wineglass spiderwebbed with cracks, still technically holding its form but only a jostle away from shattering? She was done with the sensation. She'd store the picture in a closet or something. The idea of getting rid of it made her sick, but hiding it was fine.

She marched over to it and made to lift it carefully off the wall.

It wouldn't budge.

She dug her nails between the frame and the wall and pulled, then yanked at it. The damn thing might as well have been set into concrete for all it moved.

Lily glowered at it, then the ceiling, and the walls and the floor and the whole fucking house that clearly thought it was *so* clever.

"I don't want that picture up anymore. I'm not going to get rid of it, I just don't want to see it, so if you could please just—" She grunted, trying to pry it off. "I asked nicely!" she hissed, trying different angles.

The hammer from a drawer had no effect, not even scuffing the frame or the wall.

Scraping it off with a butter knife didn't work either.

She hung from it by her fingertips, trying to use her body weight to rip it off the wall, bouncing for extra leverage.

She bargained with the house, promising to never make it pretend to be dirty again, promising to call it Carl or whatever the fuck it wanted.

At one point, she managed to get her fingers behind it near the top and braced both feet on the wall, heaving with every muscle and ounce of spite she possessed to get. it. off.

Half an hour later, panting and dripping with sweat, she threw the toothbrush at it uselessly and gave up.

"Fuck this." She gasped, stomping toward the kitchen, telling herself that the stinging in her eyes was sweat.

Just sweat.

She fixed her hair, washed her hands, put on some music, and threw herself into making not only bread, but cinnamon rolls. If she couldn't stress clean, she'd stress bake. Fuck the house.

By the time she poured hot water into the dry ingredients and started preparing the yeast, her pique had faded enough for her to get philosophical.

Her feelings had always been too intense, for her and certainly for her parents. The conclusion she'd come to as a child was that because dealing with her emotions was such an unsavory prospect, her emotional needs were best ignored. As she got older, she realized that emotional vulnerability was downright dangerous, at least in their community. When things had gotten too overwhelming, she'd found an outlet of some kind and let off some steam.

She mindlessly swirled the spoon through the mixture, waiting for it to cool enough, trying to recapture the peaceful optimism she'd found a few nights before in the library, but it eluded her.

If anyone else bottled everything up, I'd see how unhealthy it is. Why is it so different when it's me?

She almost dropped the spoon as the answer hit her with such clarity that she damn near heard it.

Seeing herself as unimportant was safe. Unimportance was safe, being a disappointment was safe. There were no expectations, no standards, no more pedestals to fall from.

Ensconced in the safety and clarity of the Afterlife, she allowed herself to realize how deep that particular wound was. It had hurt so badly when she'd fallen from the grace of their religious community. Letting herself acknowledge the depth of that pain felt like admitting weakness, admitting that she'd *cared* about their reactions.

It had gutted her when the community she'd always known, the community she'd always believed would be there for her, had thrown her away when she'd dared to ask uncomfortable questions about God's grace, especially after she'd read the book of Job. When she'd gone to them for help after her assault. When she had the audacity to be different, listening to secular music and reading fantasy books, something acceptable at home but not in the church.

The unconditional love she'd been told to expect had had some conditions after all.

She'd never regretted her decision to walk away from the evangelical community, but she remembered the look in her cousin's eyes when she'd told Lily that she wasn't comfortable with her holding her baby anymore. The way her mom's eyes had been pained whenever the topic of faith had come up between them. The little remarks from adults who had always crooned over her, lauded her as everything a good Christian girl should be, until she'd deviated from their expectations. Then their words had grown barbed, their eyes cool and pitying.

She'd already fallen from one pedestal, and it had hurt down to her core, leaving indelible marks on her soul. The last thing she wanted was to fall from another, especially in the eyes of someone whose opinion mattered to her.

Like Bel.

She itched to check her phone or text him something meaningless, but instead forced her hands into motion, adding the yeast to the mixture.

How many times had she told her friends that no one's opinion of them mattered more than their own? She'd cheered for them as they learned to care for themselves, to see themselves as wonderful and flawed and complicated and unique, convincing herself that while others deserved to take up space in the world, she was inherently too much, required too much space and effort. She never knew where the line of rejection would be drawn, which activities she enjoyed or which parts of her personality would be deemed inconvenient or unsavory, and that fear had, in many ways, kept her from *living*.

She kneaded the dough with a bit too much force. Turn, knead. Add some flour. Turn, knead. More flour.

Afraid. I spent my entire life afraid. What a fucking waste.

She worked the dough, muttering under her breath, "It's too early to be growing as a person, the tea hasn't even kicked in yet—"

"What are you making?" Sharkie's drowsy voice asked. She blinked in confusion from the side entrance of the kitchen, wearing rumpled pajamas and clutching a round shark plushie. Free from the confines of her hood, her hair stuck up in a snarled nest around her head. Lily's fingers itched to comb through it.

"Good morning, sleepyhead. We've got cinnamon rolls about ready to come out of the oven, and I'm making bread. We have other options for breakfast too, if you're hungry."

"You can make bread?" Sharkie inched closer to peer into the bowl.

Lily angled it to show her the contents. "Sure can. I'm almost done with this part, but you can sit on the counter and watch if you want."

All traces of sleep evaporated from Sharkie's face, blue eyes growing wide. "I can do that?!"

Lily chuckled, wiping her floury hands on her apron. "I can help you up, or you can drag a chair over."

Sharkie scampered over to the dining nook and pushed over a chair, climbing up with palpable glee to settle herself on the counter. She clutched the shark plushie tighter, taking in the world from her new perspective.

Out of the corner of her eye, Lily caught a flash of black-and-white fur, reflexively reaching out with one hand to scoop Max up just as his paws touched the countertop.

"Oh no you don't. Not on the counter," she admonished. He hadn't tried that since he'd been a kitten. She didn't care what else he climbed on, but the counters and the table were, and had always been, off-limits.

He meowed, unrepentant. Lily set him on the chair, pointed a warning finger at him, and rinsed her hands.

"Why are you making bread?"

"Just felt like it. Figured you'd be hungry when you woke up, plus it seemed like a good bread day. You've been out for quite a while, kiddo."

Sharkie wrinkled her nose. "Really?"

"Yep." Lily offered her a pinch of dough. "It's been a couple of days. Do you feel better?" She certainly looked a bit better. There was a new light in her eyes, a quiet, cautious kind of light. Lily suspected having an impenetrable stronghold to escape to helped. Sharkie's own mini-Paradise.

Safety could do a hell of a lot for a person.

She hoped Bel was safe.

"I guess so," Sharkie said. "Thank you for letting me stay with you."

"You're welcome. It's an honor." Lily sprinkled in some flour and resumed kneading. The mouthwatering scent of the cinnamon rolls filled the kitchen, and she caught Sharkie's eyes darting to the oven.

"Do you have anything you want to do today? We could go exploring, or stay home, watch movies?"

"I don't know." Sharkie shifted. "I was only allowed to go to church or school. Before."

Lily made a mental note to send another text to Gregorith; she was updating her plans.

"Well, now you get to decide what you'd like to do. And there're a lot of options."

Sharkie stayed quiet, looking at the floor.

"Did you like school?"

"Yeah," Sharkie said, looking up hesitantly.

"Luci said there is a school you're welcome to attend if you feel like it, and there're a bunch of other schools for Afterlife kids if you want to try those too."

"I want to stay with you," Sharkie said in a rush, fear limning every line of her body.

"Then you stay with me, bug."

Sharkie nodded, relaxing by degrees.

"A friend told me about a realm with an ocean in it, so we could walk on the beach or see if there's a boat or something."

"Your Bel friend?"

"No, a different friend; you haven't met them yet."

"Where's Bel?"

Lily masked her sudden involuntary inhale with a stretch, rolling her shoulders. "I don't know. He's a general—do you know what that is?"

Sharkie nodded uncertainly.

That's a no.

"He's in charge of a lot of people in Hell's army. They don't fight wars all the time like we're used to in the mortal world. They go on patrols and train and stuff most of the time. That's where he is, on some supersecret patrol mission."

I'm worried about him.

I miss him.

She hadn't realized how used to their casual texting and phone calls she'd gotten, how much she looked forward to seeing whatever goofy selfie or picture he'd sent, or his reactions to her own pictures and terrible jokes. The debates they had over such serious topics as what foods counted as a sandwich and which ones were salads—pizza was abso-fucking-lutely a salad—or the legitimately serious ones when a particularly shitty soul came through her line or when Bel got an odd, distant quality to his voice that told her that he was getting lost in the shadows of his own head.

She missed him.

And yes, she lusted after him a bit. It was hard not to when he was so sweet and filthy and unfairly attractive. She'd replayed certain moments so many times that they were almost as familiar as her own name. That day in his office. At trivia night. All the times he'd leaned his hip against her desk, or his shoulder against the doorframe in the break room. The way they'd laughed and teased each other over Lev's stupid memo. The moments between them in that hallway. That heated look.

"What about Luci?" Sharkie asked.

Lily's smile crept over her face. "Luci's not on patrol. He's down in Hell, and he's been asking about you. He'll be excited to hear that you're awake."

"Oh."

Lily glanced at her, double-checking the meaning of that "oh," relieved to see it seemed to be one of acknowledgment. She flipped the dough one last time and absently patted the top of it gently three times, just like she always did.

"Grow bread grow," she muttered, reaching for a towel to clean her hands.

"What?" Sharkie asked.

"What?"

"Why did you pat the bread and tell it to grow?"

"Oh." Lily wiped her hands in the towel. "It's something my mom did with me when we made bread together, especially as a kid. She'd have me pat the bread and say 'grow bread grow.' She said it made the bread better. Want to give it a pat?"

Sharkie leaned over, gave the bread a gentle *pat, pat, pat*, softly telling it to grow. Lily winked at her, put the bowl into the second oven to proof, then pulled the golden-brown cinnamon rolls out of the other oven.

A short while later, they both sat on the counter, eating fresh cinnamon rolls drizzled with icing and swinging their feet while Sharkie asked a thousand questions, mostly about the Afterlife. Max perched on the chair, staring accusingly at Lily as if to tell *her* to get off the counter. Birds chirped and sang outside as the world finished waking up, the mist burning away to bathe the kitchen in sunshine.

The combination of Sharkie finally waking up, the beautiful morning, and the delicious cinnamon rolls helped ease the lingering ache of Lily's earlier realization. Sharkie leaned down to let Max lick some icing off her finger, and Lily had another epiphany.

We'll be okay. I'll be okay. And . . . maybe I don't want to be afraid anymore.

Sharkie put her onesie back on before they left the house, perhaps as a form of comfort. Lily didn't comment on it, wanting her to do whatever she needed to feel secure. They only ventured as far as the village that day, and Lily had taken her at a time when it tended to be the quietest. Sharkie had stuck close to her, but the moments when her curiosity overrode her caution grew more frequent throughout the day, and Lily loved seeing those snippets of Sharkie just being a child. They ended up sitting in the backyard to watch the sun go down.

The next day, they did the village again, but when it was busier. Sharkie seemed more relaxed, like she'd decided that Paradise was okay, though she periodically glanced at Lily to gauge her state of ease. Midway through their lunch of chicken strips, Sharkie had squared her shoulders and announced that she wanted to see the field of doors again.

They'd gone all the way to the arch to the Universal Hallway, where Lily had expected Sharkie to want to turn around and go home, but with another look at Lily, Sharkie had tugged them forward into the Hall. After a bit more exploration, something caught Sharkie's eye.

Sharkie pushed her hood back and let go of Lily's hand so that she could play tag with a trio of multicolored wisps the size of basketballs, which drew the attention of other kids. Eventually, forty or so souls—Lily included—denizens, and creatures were all running around the Hall, laughing and out of breath. People wove through the game, calling out advice and encouragement, while others formed a small crowd that clapped when they were done. A rumbling, wailing chortle from something more massive than Lily was willing to consider had echoed out of a large archway nearby. Sharkie had waved at it before taking Lily's hand and skipping along down the hall. They'd gotten cocoa after that, and Sharkie had charmed the baristas at Common Grounds.

The day after that, Sharkie hadn't woken up until late afternoon, as if the adventure had burned through some battery of hers. When she'd emerged from her room, she'd been quiet, but asked if they could stay home. Lily suggested a movie night. So, she made cocoa—something Sharkie could have every single day, as far as Lily was concerned—and settled into a nest of blankets and pillows on the couch. Just as the opening credits rolled, a large bowl of fresh popcorn appeared between them. Sharkie had giggled a thank-you to the house around a mouthful of buttery perfection, and they'd stayed like that until darkness fell and they went to their respective rooms to sleep.

Sharkie had woken up early and refreshed the next morning, asking if they could explore more realms. Lily agreed, but, cautious after the day that had resulted in burnout, explained they should have a secret code so Sharkie could signal her at any time. They'd agreed on hand signals: Thumb down meant *help immediately*, thumb in the middle meant *I'm ready to go*, and thumb up meant *I'm having fun*. With that established, Lily took her to the Summerland, where they'd eaten pasties and gravy, then moved on to Valhalla.

The denizens and resident souls of Valhalla welcomed them, a small group forming after their arrival. After a bit of a wobble where Sharkie had pulled her hood up and made herself small, Lily had stepped between her and the others immediately. A man with tattoos all over his bare scalp had shooed everyone off before kneeling down a few feet away to wait.

After a moment, Sharkie peered around Lily to look at him with big eyes. He introduced himself as Ivan and explained calmly about how they liked to spar for fun and training there, offering to show her whenever she was ready. He'd even set her up on his shoulders for the best view, if she wanted. Sharkie had studied him for a long moment, then looked to Lily, who told her both were good choices, but it was entirely up to her. Slowly, she'd stepped out from behind Lily and told the kneeling man that she didn't want to be lifted up, but she did want to see the sparring.

Together, the three of them ended up cheering for the bouts of (mercifully bloodless) sparring in one of the many fighting rings. Lily had tried her hand at some basic sparring on an earlier visit and quickly realized that her technique wasn't so much lacking as it was nonexistent.

Bel could teach me.

The thought popped into her head, and she glanced at her phone for the millionth time. She wondered how Bel might instruct her. How he might laugh and adjust her grip or stance in that sweet way of his.

After a time, when Sharkie had unsurprisingly been adopted by more warriors, Lily retreated contentedly to a nearby banquet table and piled a plate with savory meat and garlic potatoes. She maintained an observation of the warriors and kept an eye out for Sharkie, but she wanted to give Sharkie the chance to be comfortable without Lily directly at her side. According to her research, small steps like that were important.

Lily sipped her mulled wine, bemusedly watching as a horde of warriors crouched down to teach Sharkie the basics of Viking-style combat. Sharkie looked around periodically to check in with Lily, but her eyes were bright with curiosity.

Lily gave her a smile, gesturing up and down with her thumb. Sharkie returned her smile and so far had only given a thumbs-up.

Someone eased into the seat next to her. An old man with a long, flowing beard fixed his single, piercing eye on her, leaning his spear against the table. Lily kept her face neutral, holding his gaze as the hum of his power tingled over her skin.

"Hello, Allfather," Lily said. *I will not be afraid anymore. If I'm not afraid of a god, then I won't be a complete weenie when I'm eventually vulnerable with someone.*

Not just someone.

Bel.

"Lily," Odin said, his voice roughened with age but in no way weak. "I was not here when last you visited my hall. Beleth speaks highly of you, as do others."

"Thank you. Your hall is beautiful. Sharkie seems to be enjoying herself."

They both looked to where three men who wouldn't have been out of place in a biker bar had collaborated to show Sharkie how to make a proper fist. Sharkie mimicked them intently.

A smile tipped Odin's lips. "A true warrior, that one." He fixed his gaze back on Lily. "And a true warrior in you. You would have made a fine addition to my hall. Should you ever wish to quit Paradise, you would be most welcome here."

She hadn't been lying to Odin when she'd complimented his hall. It was stunning—grand in scale and decoration, but warm and hearty in feel. There was a certain primal energy there, but . . . wisdom too. Fitting for a hall of true warriors.

"Thank you. But my battle was less noble than the kind that earns souls a place in your hall."

"All battles have the capacity to be noble," Odin said, casting his gaze over the crowded hall. Not everyone fought. There were plenty who simply relaxed at the tables or wandered through doorways to places Lily couldn't see. "Cancer may not be sung about in songs, or woven into a tapestry, but that does not make the heart and fight required to combat it a lesser thing."

Lily kept her instinctive flinch to just a blink.

"There are many battles worthy of Valhalla, no matter what the stories may say. I'm sure you're aware by now the nuances of reality when it comes to the Afterlife. Not all the souls who find belonging in my hall spilled blood, and not all of them reside here permanently. You are no less a warrior than any soul in this hall, Lily of the Hellp Desk, and you are always welcome." He rose with a languid ease that belied his apparent age. "As is the little one. We'll teach her a trick or two."

"Who knows, Allfather," Lily said, swirling her wine and looking to where Sharkie was biting the ear of a warrior who had gently grabbed her up, giving her an opportunity to practice whatever defensive maneuver they'd been teaching her. "Maybe she'll return the favor."

Odin lightly thumped the butt of his spear on the ground, watching the scuffle. The man, ear bleeding, had quickly set her down and rushed to reassure a suddenly cautious Sharkie, beaming as he heaped praises on her for her creative technique. Other warriors did the same, and bit by bit, Sharkie relaxed. Her eyes found Lily's, and she held her thumb up. Lily returned the gesture as Odin laughed.

"Maybe she will."

23

A SWEARING
SITUATION

Lily

The day after their trip to Valhalla, Sharkie surprised Lily by having *more* energy, not less, after their explorations, and requested to go see Luci. The realization that there was no pattern to Sharkie's healing was a stupidly obvious one, given her own experiences, and she'd resolved to simply be observant and responsive instead of aspiring to some psychological formula.

Admittedly, it took a weight off. She'd never been good at following formulas anyway.

Lily brought her down to Hell to show her the Hellp Desk and to meet the gate demons in a calmer context. While she was initially hesitant, the demons were beyond respectful of her personal space, and within half an hour, she was giggling at their antics. She still stayed close to Lily though. The demons answered all of her questions about working at the gate, and when the questions about the operation of Hell began, they kept their responses age-appropriate and nongraphic.

Eventually, Lily and Sharkie ended up in the break room with a small "committee" of demons huddled around the whiteboard while they explained the layout of Hell. The picture Zagan drew resembled an hourglass, with the levels for the souls taking up the top half and the demon levels on the bottom, separated by an exceptionally thick layer of rock.

Lily found herself equally fascinated by the information, asking questions of her own.

The upper three levels of the demons' part of Hell were training fields, followed by an administrative level, then six residential floors. As Lily understood it, each residential level was like a different county, with their own subcultures and schools. Finally, the largest and lowest level of Hell was simply labeled "The Hearth." Moura explained that it was where they took their dead to become part of the fabric of the Afterlife.

Lucifer showed up at that point, offering to escort them on a tour of the town he lived in on the lowest residential level, known as R6. Sharkie accepted, but then glanced at Lily for reassurance. Lily counted it as progress.

Her decision to hang back during the tour of the town and their time spent at an arcade was a conscious one. She wanted Sharkie to have another familiar adult she could trust, and the foundations of her relationship with Lucifer had already begun to solidify. The two of them grinned at each other during a dance battle game, silly and free. Lily snapped a picture of Sharkie and Lucifer and sent it to Bel. She hoped it would make him laugh when he saw it.

Afterward, they headed toward the central hub of elevators, but Sharkie pointed at a large building.

"What's that?"

"That's one of the schools," Lucifer explained. "Would you like to see inside?"

Sharkie scrunched up her nose, glancing at Lily. "Is this the school I could go to?"

Lily looked to Lucifer for that information.

"It is," he said. "You are free to attend school on any level you like."

"What do you think?" Sharkie asked, looking up at her.

Lily grinned and shrugged. "Why not?"

After checking in with the office, by luck they poked their heads into a classroom in the middle of science class. Sharkie was so immediately enraptured that Lily and Lucifer ended up leaning against the back wall, listening to the kids learn about the life cycle of frogs. Beyond bioluminescence, a fifty-year lifespan, and immediately dissolving into nothing upon death, Afterlife frogs and mortal frogs seemed to be pretty much the same. Sharkie's eyes had lit up with curious wonder anyway.

At the end of the lesson, before the kids had filed out for what Lily assumed was the equivalent of recess, a demon girl paused by Sharkie to ask her about where she was from (Paradise), why she was visiting (she knew Luci), and if she liked frogs (she did). The girl beamed at the last, then waved and said goodbye.

Sharkie was quiet and fidgety for the rest of the day, but Lily waited until they were at home and making dinner to start asking questions.

"What are you thinking, Sharkie?" Lily asked, nonchalantly checking the sweet potatoes in the oven.

"I want to go to school." It came out in a rushed blend of excitement and nerves, her natural curiosity warring with her conditioned fear.

"Sweet," Lily said, closing the oven. "Do you want to go to that one, or do you want to check out the other ones first?"

Sharkie pulled her legs up onto her chair, hugging her knees. "I liked that one. It's on Luci's level. Luci's nice."

"Yeah, he is. When do you want to start?"

"Can I go tomorrow?"

Lily smiled and handed her a plate. "I don't see why not."

"Really?" The soft hope in her voice made Lily's chest ache. How often had the simplest things been denied to her?

"Really," Lily said. As Lily pulled the sweet potatoes out of the oven and set them on a trivet, Sharkie spoke again, this time even quieter.

"And what if I want to come home?"

Lily turned around, tugging off the oven mitts and meeting her eyes. "Then I'll come get you and bring you home."

When Sharkie held out her pinkie, Lily was already halfway there.

Sharkie spun around in Lily's office chair, recounting her day at school while Lily sat cross-legged on the warm floor and organized the new built-in tool rack that had appeared next to the Hellp Desk.

"It kinda sucks that I'm so much smaller than everyone, but the combat teacher, Mr. Damien, had a whole bunch of tricks just for me! He said that anyone can be fierce, no matter how big or small they are. Do you believe that?"

Lily leaned back on her hands, grinning up at her. "Of course. I think it's actually cooler to be small and fierce."

"'Cause people don't expect it?"

"Exactly."

Sharkie spun in the chair a few more times. Her voice was small when she asked, "Can you still be fierce even if you're scared?"

Lily's stomach twisted at the wobble in her tone.

She got up to sit on the desk, facing Sharkie. "Yes," she said simply. "If you're scared and choose to be fierce anyway, that's called being brave."

"But you don't get scared, and you're brave." Sharkie seemed confused.

Lily smiled at her. "Want to know a secret?"

Sharkie's eyes lit up.

"I used to be scared all the time. Especially when I was alive. All kinds of things scared me. Sometimes they were silly things, like spiders, but the things that *really* scared me? Those weren't silly. I still get scared, kiddo." Lily huffed out a breath. "I was scared when I arrived in the After-life, and I thought I would end up down here. I didn't know about the therapy levels, or that it's a place of justice and growth, so I was scared. When I met Bel I was scared, because I didn't want him to *see* me and decide I wasn't worth knowing. When I met you I was scared, because I didn't want to say or do the wrong thing and hurt you by accident. But I had to trust myself and my ability to figure things out. I had to *try*."

And I have to keep trying. No more being afraid all the time.

Sharkie scooted the chair closer and climbed up next to Lily, pulling her feet up to sit cross-legged. "That just sounds like you cared. When the souls are angry at you that doesn't scare you, because you don't care what they think . . . Oh wait, but aren't you scared they'll hurt you?"

That just sounds like you cared . . .

"Not really. I know the demons will always protect me if I need it, and even if the souls do hurt me, I'll regenerate. Pain doesn't scare me, because . . . it ends." Those last few weeks in bed, her body shutting down, the shooting pain, the primal fear of life trickling away . . . then blessed nothing. "One way or another, it ends."

Sharkie opened her mouth, then shut it, her little shoulders curving up and in. She pulled the mittens of her onesie over her hands. Tucked her head farther back into her hood.

Lily silently held out her hand in offering and Sharkie took it. Her palms were clammy through the soft fabric of the mittens.

"Was I scared of Mr. Pastor because I cared?"

Fuck. Way to go, Lily. You sure nailed that one, you jackass.

"No," Lily said immediately and firmly. "You were scared of him because he hurt you, because he wanted to make you scared. Because he was bad. He was evil and fucked up."

A little gasp. "You said a bad word."

"There're no such thing as bad words, baby, just words that need to be used in context. There are words that some people aren't allowed to say ever, but swear words are just words that need to be used in certain situations and not used in others."

"Oh. So . . . but if *he* was bad, then why was *I* scared? I don't understand."

Lily took a moment, sifting through everything she knew about Sharkie's past, about the way that brilliant little mind worked, her own life experiences.

"I think you were scared because you cared about *yourself*. You didn't want him to hurt you, and you didn't like not being able to protect yourself."

"I think . . . I think you're right," Sharkie said quietly. A moment later, she huffed, looking up at Lily solemnly. "This is very complicated."

"Life usually is."

"But we're dead."

"Existence usually is," Lily amended, a surge of affection for her clever girl washing through her.

Sharkie seemed to accept that.

"I don't know *what* you think you're doing," a female soul shrieked behind them, and they both turned to look at her, "but I will have you know that this is UNACCEPTABLE!" Her eyes were wild, and she looked seconds away from launching a physical attack.

"Lily," Sharkie said.

"Yeah?"

"Is this a swearing kind of situation?"

"Yeah."

"Fuck."

24

TURBO NERD MODE

Bel

Everything ached.

Bel washed the grime off, then cranked the water up as hot as it would go, letting it pound his weary muscles as he closed his eyes and braced his hands against the wall. The scuffs on his wings stung under the spray. Minor, annoying injuries in the grand scheme of things, but with the weight of the new information from their patrol, they burned like an omen of what could come.

Hopefully, they'd done enough to prevent it.

He switched off the water, wringing out his hair and wrapping a towel around his waist, stepping out onto the black tile. His phone glowed by the sink, a stream of messages taking up most of the screen, and he reached for it with a sigh.

He was home; he was exhausted from ten increasingly difficult days, but his restless thoughts had him keyed up. The last thing he wanted was to dig into a pile of messages about logistics and reports, but he'd texted Lily before his shower and had an incentive to face the wall of messages. Thankfully, it seemed to be his family welcoming him home, a single middle-finger emoji from Greg, and finally . . .

Princess: *Thank fuck you're okay!*

Princess: *ARE you okay? Like, not physically?*

Princess: *Sharkie says hi, she's been asking about you (she's on an overnight*

*nature walk/field trip to a park on RS, but I was supposed to say hi if you got
back before she did)*

Princess: *Call if you want, I'd like to hear your voice.*

His heart picked up speed as he stared at those last few words. She'd
sent them only moments before he picked up his phone, and the time
stamp for all the texts except that one were close, as if she'd typed them
out one after the other but then paused. Maybe rewritten it a few times
before sending.

He hit the "call" button, putting it on speaker as he headed for his room.

She answered on the second ring.

"Bel?"

Something in him eased. "Hey, princess. I wanted to hear you too."

She exhaled, voice softening. "You sound ragged, big guy. Are you
okay?"

Bel tugged a pair of sweatpants out of the dresser in his closet, debating how to answer. Yes, physically? Yes, but worried? No? No, come kiss
it better?

He ran a hand over the back of his neck. He was usually better at keeping a lock on what he really wanted to say to her, even in his own head.

And he was *supposed* to keep a lock on it, wasn't he?

Except the last time they'd been together, she'd looked at him like
maybe they weren't just friends anymore. They'd nearly kissed even. Unless . . . that had just been another moment of tension between them.
They'd always had chemistry, but they also had always been careful to be
friends. And only friends.

I'd like to hear your voice. That wasn't something that friends said to
each other, was it? Greg had certainly never said it—

"You there, big guy?" Lily said, sounding worried.

"Sorry, princess, didn't mean to go silent on you. I'm . . . a little scuffed
up, but it wasn't bad."

The other Universe hadn't just vaguely tried to make contact this time.
They'd sent scouts and spies through a rift. Bel and his patrol had had
to round them up and forcefully send them back. Hopefully, the other
Universe had gotten the message.

"Scuffed up?" Lily asked.

"Only a bit. Hopefully, we dissuaded the problem from growing, which is the important thing. What are you doing without Sharkie there?"

"I dropped her off not that long ago, and Luci volunteered to chaperone to keep an eye on her. So I just showered and was planning on doing a face mask and eating cinnamon rolls while watching Shark Week until I pass out. Really howling at the moon over here. Wanna join? Or do you need to rest? I'm sure you're pretty worn out."

A thrum of excitement temporarily wiped away the lingering weariness. "Is there a dress code for this wild night we're having?"

"Sweatpants or jammies. If you show up looking formal, you're sitting on the floor, and I'm giving you the weird face mask," she said cheerfully.

"Define weird."

"It's yellow and has these lumps in it, I'm not a fan—" She was interrupted by the sound of timbers groaning. "It's not *personal*, it's just not for me, okay? I like the rest of them," she said to someone—or something—away from the phone, exasperation dripping from her voice. "Sorry about that, the house likes to be opinionated."

The house?

There was a whole row of semi-sentient showers in one of the bathhouses on the training fields, so he supposed that a quirky house wasn't outside the realm of normal.

"No worries. Sweatpants it is. Need me to bring anything?"

"Just you. I'll wait for you by the Paradise gate. Be warned, my jammies are *pretty* sexy, so control yourself upon your arrival or we'll be getting a memo from Lev."

"Damn." Bel grinned, hunting for a specific shirt that he knew would make Lily smile. "There go my evil plans for the evening. I do love a good memo." He threaded his horns through the neckline.

"Ha ha," Lily said dryly before her voice softened in a way that made his breath catch. "I can hear how tired you are, big guy. You sure you're okay? We can hang out another time."

"Lily." He quit fiddling with the closures around his wings, staring at the phone. "I want to see you. Tonight. And your fancy Paradise. In that order. I might crash on your couch at some point, but just stick a cinnamon roll under my nose and that'll perk me right up."

It was half true. He suspected that once he finally crashed, he'd be out for a while. Though he'd never turn down a good sniff of a cinnamon roll, conscious or not.

She chuckled. "Get here when you can, big guy."

Bel rushed to rub a towel through his damp hair, hunt down a pair of extra-thick socks that he liked to wear at home, and shove his feet into some slippers that Angel had picked up for him in the mortal world as a joke.

He couldn't get to Paradise fast enough.

Lily

Lily leaned against the stone of the archway, scanning for a pair of arcing horns and dark wings among the crowd of equally unique and interesting features. When she did spy Bel, she smiled . . . until she spotted his slippers. Then she laughed outright.

He held his arms out, spinning in a slow circle and strutting toward her like he was walking a runway, striking a pose.

The obviously well-worn black sweatpants nearly made her eyes skip over the fuzzy gray slippers with cutesy little bat faces and wings. Through giggles, she dragged her eyes up his powerful body to the faded gold lettering on his sleeveless black shirt listing hobbit mealtimes.

He made a show of covering his eyes with one hand. "The sex appeal is too much. I don't think I'll be able to control myself!"

Lily grinned as she mimed flipping a piece of hair over her shoulder, her own hair safely up in a messy bun.

"I warned you. It's a deadly combination." She gestured to her equally ridiculous attire. The purple shorts had little cartoon dinosaurs riding skateboards all over them, and the oversized shirt proclaimed "Lord of the Cats," with the Fellowship of the Ring reimagined as cartoon cats playing around the central text. In a delightful accident, they'd ended up with coordinating shirts.

"It's a wonder we both haven't been nailed for public indecency." Bel grinned, dropping his hand away from his eyes, revealing dark smudges beneath them. The smile slipped from her face as she studied him, concerned. He held himself in a weary, careful kind of way, each movement stilted in a manner completely at odds with his usual grace.

Protectiveness surging, she took his hand, tugging him forward. "Come on, big guy, let's get you out of here before we have to flee a horde of your ravenous suitors."

His fingers threaded through hers, sending a warm rush through her system. "Don't sell yourself short. At least half would be yours."

She scoffed, following the dirt path through the endless field of doors.

"This is beautiful, but I'm not gonna lie," Bel said a moment later, "it's also kinda creepy."

"I've always thought that the only thing keeping it from looking like a horror movie for the ages is the lighting. Thankfully, the walk never takes too long." She spied their target and shifted paths, towing Bel behind her.

"Wait," Bel said when she reached for the handle. "I need a moment. I'm about to see not only a Paradise, but *your* Paradise, and I need to prepare so that I can appreciate it fully." He closed his eyes, breathing deep.

Lily leaned against her door, amusement warring with the nerves twisting her stomach.

A pair of women walked down a nearby path behind him and one of them did a double take. She paled, grabbing her companion's arm. Both women froze, eyes raking over him from horns to tail, then flicking between him and Lily.

Her blood iced over at the judgment and fear in their eyes.

Are you okay? the first woman mouthed at her.

Lily smothered her irritation so they wouldn't misinterpret it as a cry for help. They obviously meant well, and normally, she'd appreciate the potential backup, but she knew their reaction was based purely on the fact that Bel was a demon. She smiled, throwing them a thumbs-up. They moved on, glancing back occasionally until they were out of sight.

Bel let out a long exhale and opened his eyes.

"Nerd mode activated?" she asked.

"Nerd mode is always activated. Turbo nerd mode is now engaged."

She grinned, twisted the handle, and stepped through, standing aside for Bel and spending an inordinate amount of time making sure the door was latched behind him, then wiping at an imaginary speck of dust on the wood.

Would he be disappointed? Would he even fit through the door? Could demons be allergic to cats? Did he have allergies? What would he think about the picture? She should have covered it. Would he even notice?

She toyed with the hem of her shorts, calling herself six kinds of ridiculous and three kinds of coward before mustering the courage to turn and see his reaction.

He stood with his mouth open, arms slack at his sides. Even his wings and tail were limp.

Think brave, be brave, Lily.

Oh boy.

25

STARING CONTEST

Bel

It was the most beautiful place he'd ever seen.

The sun had set behind distant mountains, the last vestiges of twilight fading on the horizon. Lights from other houses dotted the hills like golden stars, while fireflies danced among them and in her lush fenced-in garden. Laughter floated up the hill from the little village, along with strains of jaunty music, while out on the smooth waters of a fjord, the lanterns of rowboats twinkled. The light from Lily's home illuminated the garden and stone path leading to a round front door cracked open just enough to explain the presence of the cat sitting on the doorstep. The drool-worthy scent of cinnamon rolls wafted temptingly into the cooling air.

It felt like *home*.

The small palace he'd spent his whole life in was comforting in its familiarity and precious for the memories it held, but something about Lily's Paradise sank into his bones, filling him with a sense of peace both familiar and foreign.

"Initial thoughts?"

Was she nervous? He tried to find the words, wishing he had his sister Annika's talent for eloquence, and deciding that simple honesty would have to do.

"It feels like you," he said quietly. Her lips parted in surprise. "Not the version of you that works at the Hellp Desk, but the *real* you. I like it. A lot."

So very much.

His heart rate kicked up, but he was spared from waiting for her response by something brushing against his ankle. The cat had emerged from the house to sniff at his sweatpants, its long fur glossy and well kept.

"Max?"

Lily nodded fondly. "For the record, I left the door shut so that I could give you a warning before the little turd decided to introduce himself."

"That's okay." He crouched down, ignoring the protest of his aching muscles. Max bolted away to hide behind Lily's legs, which only drew Bel's attention to the smooth, tantalizing stretch of skin, the intricate black-and-gray tattoos on her thigh, the athletic lines of her calves leading down to—

He barked out a laugh, glanced at her footwear again, and had to put a hand on the ground to balance while he dissolved into a fit of giggles.

Her clog-like shoes were the ugliest piece of footwear he'd ever laid eyes on, and the glittery black surface did nothing to assuage that fact.

"Those are," he managed once he caught his breath, "not something I expected you to have."

Lily held out her leg like a model showing off couture footwear. "Aren't they hideous?" She beamed. "They're so stupid, I love them. Plus, they're comfy. Now shoo, go make a new friend." She said the last bit to the cat, who had already begun creeping out to inspect him once more.

A cursory sniff of Bel's extended hand resulted in an enthusiastic mashing of his head against Bel's palm.

Success.

He lavished attention on Max, who purred so hard that Bel wondered how he managed to stand, until Lily scooped the cat up, shaking her head.

"You can schmooze him later," she told the cat, kissing its head and smiling at Bel. "Come on, big guy, let's get you onto a couch."

"Well, damn." Bel grinned, pushing to his feet. "At least buy me dinner first."

Lily bumped his hip with hers. "What do you think the cinnamon roll is for?"

"In that case, lead the way."

Hanging flowers draped around her round door, their light perfume lingering in the air. Lily pushed the door fully open, depositing the cat onto the floor, and Bel was delighted to realize that he didn't have to duck to follow her. Tidy and clean without being sterile, the whole place was lived in and cozy, with elegant touches that somehow fit perfectly.

His eyes snagged on a large picture by the door, and everything in him stilled.

Lily stood with two young men who shared similar features and red hair in different shades. Her brothers. They had to be. They stood on a cliff overlooking a crashing sea, laughing and wild. Lily's features were softer, younger, but her beautiful eyes still drew him in, an unfamiliar caution in their hazel depths.

Lily came to stand beside him, and the silence stretched.

"That was a good day," she murmured, a waver in her tone that he'd only heard once before. "We had no business being there, and we all promised to never tell our parents how reckless we'd been, but it was a good day."

Bel could see that. There was a joy there that couldn't be faked. "What were their names?"

"Are. Their names are Tommy, the taller one, and Ryan. I was the oldest." The quiet pain in her voice tore his gaze away from the picture. He didn't know the exact kind of grief spilling over her face, but he knew all too well how choking grief could be.

He slipped his hand into hers, only momentarily surprised by the strength of her grip. She studied the picture while he studied her, memorizing the delicate slope of her nose and the sweep of her wet lashes.

He didn't overthink it, simply reached up with his free hand to brush his knuckles down her satiny cheek, smoothing away the track of wetness.

"I left them," she said softly. "I didn't want to, and I hope they know that." She chuckled wetly and without humor. "I lied to them when I was sick, you know. Especially toward the end. It was stupid, and I knew I was making promises I couldn't keep, but they needed *something* to hold on to to make things . . . easier."

"How did you lie?" It took every ounce of control not to wrap her in his arms and soothe, but the moment felt important. What she was feeling and sharing was important.

"Lots of ways. They'd ask me how I was feeling or ask if I wanted to watch a movie with them. All I wanted to do was lay in bed and cry, but I'd go watch whatever they wanted. I knew I couldn't make it easier to watch me die; all I could do was leave them with memories."

She smiled a little. "I told them I'd steal their socks from the other side. I figured that every time they did laundry and one of their socks went missing, they'd think of me. I said it as a joke, but they made me promise, even though I knew I was lying. We were supposed to watch each other get old. Mourn our parents together. Annoy the shit out of each other for another few decades at least. Teach their kids how to swear and tell them stories about when we were kids. We weren't particularly close, but we were *always* there for each other. I'm the oldest; I was supposed to look out for them. I haven't even looked them up on MortalTube since I got here. I . . . I can't," she said, referring to the video site that many souls used to check in on living loved ones or keep up with current events.

Bel brought his hands up to cradle her face, the picture forgotten. He'd been wondering where they stood. Perhaps the fatigue and stress and worry of the last few days had worn away his caution, or perhaps it was him deciding the bounds of friendship were simply not enough, but he ran the pad of his thumb over the arch of her cheekbone soothingly, watching for her reaction. If she was surprised or shocked by his closeness, she didn't show it . . . or reject it. Instead, she held his gaze as if it were a lifeline.

"Grief isn't linear. There's no formula to it, and sometimes you feel guilty for feeling or not feeling a certain way. That's okay." He paused, battling hundreds of years of habit and pain. *Lily needs to hear this. I need to say it.* "In the equation of grief, as one of the people who has been left behind and had to mourn, I promise you that your brothers know. You loved them. You still love them. If they know nothing else, they know that, princess. Just like they know that you did the best you could while you were there."

He saw the exact moment that sharp mind of hers processed that he'd once lost someone dear to him, and he waited for the pity. He knew he wasn't giving her the full story, wasn't telling her the how or why and the complications of both in his heart. But he did know the pain of that kind of grief, of being left behind, and he could give her this comfort. Because no matter how raw it was for him, he understood that you could know someone loved you and tried their best, even as you grieved their leaving you.

His heart raced and stuttered. Few beings he knew in the Afterlife could understand, and he'd never before been close enough with a mortal soul to bring it up. Part of him braced for her pity or her scorn, but he didn't want Lily to see him as weak. He wanted her to see his weakness and not think less of him for it.

Didn't everyone want the same?

The moment stretched, a precious juncture of intimacy between two people. It scared the shit out of him, all while hope made his heart ache. Lily looked up at him, not with pity or scorn.

With understanding.

Fear loosened its hold on his lungs.

She stepped forward, holding him as if he were the precious one, and he wrapped her in his embrace, burying his nose in the curve of her neck.

A paw batted the tip of his tail, followed by a long, plaintive meow.

They laughed. He loved her laugh, loved the way her body moved against his when they laughed.

It felt right to have her in his arms. Felt right to be in hers.

Neither of them let go.

Max meowed again.

"It's a conspiracy to drive me insane. First the house, now the cat," Lily said into his chest.

"What's the house done now?"

The house groaned, and adrenaline jolted up his spine. He stared at the nearest wall. *Okay*, so it was different than the row of showers, and slightly disconcerting to stand inside the thing making all the conversational noise.

"Yeah," Lily sighed, "that was about my reaction too." She grimaced up at the ceiling. "I'm sure you're being helpful, but it doesn't always sound like it."

The house groaned again.

"Maybe it's trying to tell you something?" Bel suggested, eyeing the coat hooks warily.

It was Paradise, so it wouldn't hurt anyone. Right?

Just in case, he began cataloging everything that could be used as a weapon or shield.

Just in case.

"That's a journey of discovery that'll have to happen another day. I'm tired, you're exhausted—don't lie to me, Beleth, I see how you're moving *and* the bags under your eyes." She held up a warning finger. "I called you hoping we could have a chill evening being dorks and watching movies. So, here." She scooped up the cat winding between her legs and handed it to him. "Take the fur ball, let the power of purring heal you, and get your butt on the couch. We're going to get at least one cinnamon roll in you before we pick a show and pass out."

Bel adjusted the cat so that he held him like a baby, running a finger through the soft fur of his belly. Max closed his eyes in ecstasy. Bel smiled, wondering what the two of them had been like as mortals.

A flicker of movement was his only warning before Lily's hand cupped his cheek. He looked up in surprise.

"If or when you are ready to tell the story, or if you just need someone to listen, I'm here." Her smile was soft. "I see you, big guy."

Lily

Bel had inhaled half a dozen cinnamon rolls, then nibbled on a seventh as they turned the living room into a cozy nest. The couch had morphed before their eyes, the back shifting to accommodate Bel's wings, and the seats growing deeper so that they could both stretch their legs. The little wince as he eased onto the couch, as well as the sigh he tried to hide, told her everything she needed to know.

Armed with notepads, ensconced in a few of her softest blankets, and cradling mugs of tea, they settled next to each other a safe distance apart, as usual. But she'd never felt that distance so acutely. They'd held each other in the entryway. He'd cradled her face. She wanted that closeness back desperately, even as her mind warred over it.

Being brave and opening up to a friend was one thing. Moving beyond friendship? No matter how much she wanted him, wanted all of him, and even with her resolution to no longer shackle herself with fear, it wasn't just her fear that was the problem.

It was that the time she could give Bel was limited.

Lily swallowed a sigh. Max, looking cartoonishly fluffy and small, seemed to have decided that Bel was simply a large heating pad with the ability to give attention, and remained perched on his lap while they watched a docuseries on sharks.

As some point, Bel got up to use the bathroom, something Lily no longer had to deal with. The house conveniently sprouted a bathroom with a toilet in the hallway by their bedrooms. When he sat back down, their shoulders brushed. Later, Lily pulled her blanket up and shifted to a more comfortable position, and their thighs touched. Neither of them commented on it or made any move to get away.

The bare skin of his arm seared against hers. As she made a note about the sleeping habits of reef sharks, she caught herself writing *rest close together under hot, smooth*—and hurriedly scribbled out the last two words—*under caves and ledges.*

Lily gave up on taking notes, her focus zeroed in on each point of contact. They were innocent, casual touches, but she *burned*. The temptation to straddle his lap and see if he knew how to kiss in a way that was distinctly outside the bounds of friendship was so intense that she mentally shoved herself.

I should really move away.

She didn't.

The heavy grittiness of her eyes saved her from the dilemma altogether.

She caught herself nodding off a few times, the fight back to consciousness only growing more difficult each time.

She woke up at some point to find her head propped on Bel's shoulder, the weight on her hair dimly registering as his cheek. Every muscle in his body had grown lax, his breathing deep and even. The lights had dimmed themselves and the TV had gone dark.

His mostly empty mug tilted precariously in his loose grip, but before she could do more than raise her arm, it disappeared. She murmured a drowsy thank-you to the house, snuggled into Bel's side, and let sleep pull her under.

Waking up was like swimming through honey, a heavy, slow approach to consciousness that resulted from a deep rest.

Lily cracked an eye enough to register the golden light diffusing through the windows, wondered why her room was so bright, then snuggled back into the delicious cocoon of warmth she'd found herself in. She pulled her body pillow closer, pleased that it seemed firmer than usual. Something thudded steadily under her ear, as reassuring as a heartbeat. She nuzzled into her body pillow—

Her body pillow that was breathing.

It all came back. Bel's silly bat slippers, the revelations in the entryway, the gradual progression of cuddling on the couch. She couldn't bring herself to regret a second of it.

Her eyes eased open as she took a catalog of their bodies. They must have shifted to lay lengthwise on the couch, which seemed to have morphed again to make them more comfortable.

She lay between Bel and the back of the couch, one of her legs between his, an arm thrown over his side, fingers brushing the hot skin of his back where his shirt had ridden up. Her other arm was folded between them, hand resting by her cheek, one finger hooked in the collar of his shirt. Bel lay on his side with his back to the room, one arm resting heavily over her waist, his hand pressed to her back like he held her to him even in sleep. She could feel his other arm beneath the pillow both their heads rested on, guessing that the spot of heat on her upper back was his hand.

Something warm and smooth was coiled around her calf of the leg resting between his. His tail, maybe? She didn't want to move to find out. A gentle bulge pressed against her thigh, sending liquid heat trickling through her veins. His chin and lips were pressed into her hair, each exhalation ruffling the half-loose strands. Her nose was barely an inch away from the strong column of his neck, and all she could smell was his warm, slightly musky scent, touched with the clove soap he'd showered with the night before. She'd never been so attracted to anyone before.

She ran her fingertips over the satiny skin of his neck, wondering what it would be like to trace the hollows and lines with her lips.

Dangerous. Dangerous and selfish.

He was sweet and kind and sly and funny, with a bone-deep steadiness to him that soothed a part of her she hadn't known needed soothing. Not only did each moment in his presence feel like a breath of fresh air, he made her already healthy sex drive threaten to go into overdrive. It wasn't just his heavy, solid body that she *absolutely* appreciated; it was *him*. She'd been attracted to his mind long before she'd ever laid eyes on his body.

She followed the line of his collarbone with the faintest of touches, a familiar, hollow ache yawning open in her chest. Even if they ended up together—an idea that sent a quiet thrill through her—she couldn't offer him anything beyond companionship and love, and she would have to surrender part of a dream.

She'd always, in all of her lifetimes, wanted to be a mother. She'd known the effects that pregnancy would have on her body. Known about the exhaustion, known that she wouldn't be a perfect parent, but damn, she would have tried. She would have *loved* her children, just as she already loved Sharkie.

She'd kept the desire quiet in her last life. Motherhood had seemed so . . . limiting when she'd been growing up in the church. In her church, it had been considered the pinnacle of achievement for all women. No matter how much she'd wanted to be a mother, she'd always thought that idea was horseshit. Had they *met* women? Had they listened to and seen the glorious ideas and dreams and stories and drive they had? The pinnacle of a woman's achievement was determined by each woman themselves. Who was the church to limit them to a reproductive role?

Even after she'd left religion, she'd kept her desires close. Out of spite at first, then out of pain. When she'd hit thirty without a single serious relationship, friends and family had stopped making pitying, "helpful" comments, and started giving her somber looks. Then, once she'd found out about the cancer, she'd hoped that it would happen for her in a future lifetime, if such a thing existed.

The longer she was in the Afterlife, the muddier her desire became. She loved her Paradise, her work, and now Sharkie. Then there was everything she felt for Bel. However, she hated her silent chest, the nagging sense of something missing, the guilt of failure. The mortal world, fucked up though it could be, was full of wonder. Beautiful things and moments were made all the more special because of the ephemeral nature of mortality. She still thought about going back. But her series of short, painful lives were a testament to the fact that nothing in life was guaranteed, and that had cooled her urgency for another try.

Bel had a heart that, even in the Afterlife, was rare and incandescent. He'd once joked that he didn't half-ass anything, he full-assed it or no-assed it. He full-ass loved his family, his friends, his work as a general, his *life*. Bel had already lost someone once, somehow, and it had clearly devastated him. He didn't deserve any more of that pain, and that was exactly what would happen if she let things progress and someday left to reincarnate.

Bel shifted, pulling his head back and moving down so that their faces were even and their noses nearly brushed.

It wouldn't be fair to him, to either of us, she tried to rationalize, to resist the spell that settled over them.

The understanding and desire in his silver eyes had the whole room, the whole Afterlife, falling away. His hand left her waist to cradle her face and neck, thumb running over her cheek in a tantalizingly slow motion.

She could feel his want, pulsing as strongly as her own. Her fingers moved of their own accord, running up to his chin, touching the blunted spikes there and making his eyelashes dip.

There would be no coming back from this moment, she realized. After this, neither of them could pretend their feelings were completely platonic and they were just friends anymore.

"I'm a mortal soul, Bel," she whispered. Maybe he could help her be reasonable. He knew what her being a soul meant.

"I know," he murmured back.

"I . . . I'll reincarnate someday."

His eyebrows twitched together for a moment, but his eyes remained soft, his thumb still moving maddeningly over her skin. "I know."

"I don't want to hurt you. You don't deserve that."

He looked at her steadily. "Do you think I deserve to be happy?"

"Yes," she breathed.

His nose brushed hers, and her breath caught in her throat. He was *right there*. His fingers ghosted over the sensitive spot on her neck, and she bit back a whimper. "I want to be happy with you, princess. For as long as you'll let me. Whatever time we have together will be a greater gift than I deserve. And when you go back to the mortal world"—his voice grew raspy—"I will be cheering for you every step of the way, honored that, even for a short time, I got to call you mine."

She swallowed. "I'd be being selfish."

"Why? Because you know it will end? If I've learned anything from grief, it's that we should all love like mortals." He paused, breath fanning over her lips, his fingers soft on her skin. "Forever is never guaranteed, not even here, princess."

She pulled back slightly to scan his eyes, to see the honesty there, the heat, and the powerful feelings she was too scared to identify, even if she knew he saw them mirrored in her own eyes.

"Love like mortals?" she asked quietly, cautious hope blooming in her chest.

"Yes," he murmured.

Lily eased forward, brushing his lips with hers. Her eyes drifted shut at the ecstasy of even that simple touch. His hand tightened on her cheek, lips parting on a gasp.

There was a brief moment when they both seemed to reorient themselves to the new paradigm of the Universe, then Bel's lips were on hers again, gently, the faint taste of the cinnamon rolls a heady companion to the taste of *him*.

The kiss was sweet, tender in a way that made her fears vanish entirely, even if just for the moment. His lips softened, and hers parted ever so slightly. It didn't need to build to anything now. No, that would come later. Nor was it the time for any great exploration of each other. This incandescent moment was for *them*. The simple, perfect intimacy of sharing their breath, of softly touching lips and gentle caresses, of *being* together.

When they eased apart, Lily smiled softly at him. Bel's expression was wondrous.

"This better not be a dream," he rumbled, fingers tracing aimless, soothing patterns on her back.

"Not a dream," she murmured, brushing a loose strand of his hair back and running her fingers over the rugged line of his jaw.

"What are you doing?" Sharkie asked.

They froze, the world rushing back in. Sunlight. Couch. Birds. Morning. Kid in a shark onesie home from a field trip. They locked eyes.

Busted.

I think?

"Staring contest," Lily said, proud that her voice sounded even and nonchalant.

Bel's eyes crinkled and gleamed with new mischief. "I'm winning," he said without looking away.

"Why are you lying down though?" Sharkie sounded skeptical.

Lily could *hear* the funny, scrunched-up expression that Sharkie made when she wasn't buying whatever she was being told.

"We were sitting up, but we got tired," Lily explained. It wasn't technically a lie . . .

"That's a long staring contest. Can I shower and then can we have breakfast? I don't like yogurt and granola."

Bel snorted, not looking away.

Well now we really are having a staring contest. And I'm going to win.

"Is that what they were serving on the trip?"

"Yeah." Sharkie sounded disgusted. "Luci brought me home because we have cinnamon rolls here, so why would I eat *granola*?"

Lily chuckled. "Fair and valid. Go shower. I'll have the cinnamon rolls heated up and waiting by the time you're done."

She heard Sharkie scamper away, but remained focused on Bel's eyes, gleaming with competition.

"You gonna go get those cinnamon rolls started?" he asked.

"Sure. Once I've won this staring contest." She grinned.

26

BUY ME DINNER FIRST

Lily

"You cheated," Bel said flatly, bracing his free hand on the countertop beside her thigh and glowering at her.

Lily adjusted her position on the counter and sipped her tea. "The rules of engagement were hazy at best. You licked my nose. I pinched you. It was that or seduce you, and I didn't want to horrify Sharkie."

He huffed, eyes darkening in a way that had her shifting her position again. Now that she knew what his lips felt like when he was being sweet, she couldn't help but wonder how they'd feel when he let loose a little. Or a lot.

"I'll accept that logic. Though, speaking of which—" He stepped closer and set his mug down beside her. "What, if anything, do you want to tell Sharkie?"

His expression was neutral, still a bit sleep rumpled, with faint shadows lingering under his eyes. There, a hint of vulnerability in those eyes.

She traced the heavy line of his eyebrow before cradling his cheek. He leaned into the touch.

"The truth, if that's fine with you. I have nothing to hide, and you're a little big for me to carry over my head like a trophy, so I'll have to settle for claiming you however I can."

He pressed a kiss to her palm, before leaning in to brush a soft kiss to her lips, warmth and lightness suffusing her body.

Am I . . . happy?

"I—" He kissed her again, moving so that he caged her against the cabinets with his body, her knees cradling his hips. "Am more than fine with that. How do you feel about PDA?"

"Big fan in theory, as long as it's within reason. I like it when you touch me, but I've also seen people get way too comfortable in public. You?" She fiddled with a strand of hair that had escaped the haphazard bun he'd thrown his hair into.

"I'm pretty sure I like it when you touch me too," he said, his innocent tone completely at odds with the impish gleam in his eyes.

She raised a hand to his collarbone, tracing it through his shirt, then lightly scraping her nails down his chest. "Only pretty sure?"

He grunted, impishness swapping to something hungrier. "Upon review, I'm *very* sure. And we're on the same page about PDA too."

She smirked. "I thought so."

He checked over his shoulder and lowered his voice. "While we're on the subject, what are your thoughts on intimacy?"

Her stomach swooped and twisted. She played with his hair again, watching herself twirl his hair around her finger while she considered the question. She wanted him, badly. Obviously. But her old habits of using sex as a patch for emotional intimacy had her veering annoyingly toward caution. What if she stopped growing their emotional connection without even realizing it? What they had was precious, and she didn't quite trust herself yet.

"I'm not opposed to some sexy exploration, but I want to make sure we get *us* a little more figured out before I start fully having my wicked way with you."

He guided her chin up so she was looking at him, and relief washed over her at the mischief written all over his handsome face. "If I had pearls I'd be clutching them, princess. Explore all you want, but beyond that, you'll have to buy me dinner first."

"What, the cinnamon rolls aren't good enough?" She feigned indignation but couldn't stop her smile.

I love joking with him. I love that I can joke with him and it's still safe.

Bel tsked sadly. "Unfortunately, I require enthusiastic consent and at least two food groups."

"They have icing."

"I'll take it into consideration. But seriously, I'm more than fine with that. Let's just keep an open dialogue with each other about it, yeah? We're important, and we can take all the time we need."

His fingers traced up the bare skin of her arm, following her tattoos and leaving goose bumps in their wake, moving over her shirt to lightly circle her throat. Her breath hitched, lips parting on a gasp.

"Is this okay?" he murmured. At her nod, he smirked and brushed his nose against hers, deep voice rumbling in his chest. "Good. Once we have us figured out and you've had your wicked way with me, brace yourself, princess, because I'm planning on having my wicked, *wicked* way with you."

No one had ever called her bluff and challenged her like that. It was an entirely new sensation. And she *craved* it.

"Let's plan on missing work for a few days, then."

His thumb stroked up the side of her neck, finding the sensitive spot just below her ear. She fisted his shirt, panting.

"So responsive, princess." He breathed against her mouth, holding himself just out of reach for a span of his heartbeats, then kissed her, reached for his tea, and stepped back.

Fucking tease. She was on fire.

"Have you been staring at each other this whole time? Are the cinnamon rolls cold?"

Ah, he'd heard Sharkie before she had.

Lily wrinkled her nose at Sharkie, who had changed into pajama pants and a T-shirt with a grinning shark and bold letters stating *Caution: will bite.* Her blond hair was wet from her shower and tangled in a way that told Lily she'd forgotten to brush it again.

"Of course not. I won. The cinnamon rolls are toasty warm; they're in the foil on the table. Do you want cocoa?"

"Yes please!"

"She cheated," Bel added. "Cocoa mix is in that cupboard, yeah?"

"Yep, second shelf," Lily confirmed, sliding off the counter.

"Thought I saw it in there. How was the field trip?"

Sharkie launched into an enthusiastic retelling of her adventure, while Lily and Bel joined her at the table, sipping their tea and asking questions when appropriate. Lily let her knee rest against his. He curled his tail around her calf, the sensation odd but not unpleasant, much like the warm lightness in her body that had yet to fade.

Max leapt onto the table, both Sharkie and Lily letting out indignant squawks the moment he landed. Bel picked him up, settling him onto his lap, where Max immediately began kneading his thigh. The cat blinked slowly at Lily in a way that could only be described as smug, rubbing his cheek against Bel's stomach and purring with all his might.

"He's very loud for being so small," Bel said over his mug.

"Are there cats in Hell?" Sharkie asked, a smear of frosting on her chin.

"There are, but hellcats are a little different than mortal cats; bigger, for one. There's a mortal cat that showed up a century ago and decided to attach itself to the Fourteenth Legion. Her name is Pumpkin, follows them everywhere. Well, almost." A shadow darted over his expression, but he took a quick forkful of steaming cinnamon roll and seemed to carefully ignore the fact that Lily was staring at him.

Something, probably the reason for his over-a-week-long, supersecret mission, had him worried. That, combined with the apparent tenderness of his body, made a wave of protectiveness surge through her.

"Excuse me, um, Bel?" Sharkie's voice had a note of vulnerability that had both of them snapping their attention to her. She rubbed at the frosting on her chin with the back of her hand. "When you're done eating, can you help me test something?"

"Sure." He shoveled the last piece of the cinnamon roll into his mouth, drained his mug, and stood. "What do you need me to do?"

Sharkie wiggled off her chair, gesturing for him to follow her down the hallway. Lily cleared the table, flipping off the ceiling as the last plate vanished before she could touch it.

"Let me do *something*," she hissed, holding the plates a little tighter. "At least let me put them in the sink, or so help me, I will host a mud-wrestling competition in the living room. On the rug."

The house gave a little shudder.

Sharkie yelled down the hallway, "Stop arguing with Carl! It doesn't like it!"

"Carl?" Bel rumbled.

Lily set the dishes in the sink, rolling her eyes. *Not him too.*

A muffled *thump* and a grunt sounded in the hallway.

"One more?" Bel asked. Sharkie said something unintelligible. Another *thump*. A small sigh of relief.

Lily melted. Testing the door. They had to be. Until she'd decided to go on the field trip, Sharkie had consistently and quietly gone straight to her room as soon as darkness fell and stayed within the protective confines of it until morning, when she would emerge bright-eyed and ready to take on the Afterlife. Lily hadn't commented on it, wanting her to have personal time and space, while hopefully providing the attention and patience she needed in the daylight hours.

She headed into the living room, folding their abandoned blankets and smoothing her hand over the dip Bel's head had left in the pillow. The odd indentation of his horn made her smile.

The door to the library closed, and Sharkie and Bel appeared in the living room a moment later, a stack of books in Bel's arm.

Lily pointed at them, baffled.

"Sharkie showed me your library." His eyes gleamed, the big nerd. "Is it okay if I borrow a few?"

"Um," Lily said brilliantly, fairly certain she'd hidden the vibrator she'd brought into the library for when a book was particularly well written. "Sure? Which ones did you go for?"

They were both regulars at the Universal Library, and there wasn't a single book she had that it didn't, but hers was curated to her personal tastes.

Bel's grin shot right past impish and went directly to wicked. "I looked for the ones with the most broken-in spines; I figured you must have particularly liked those. Plus, Sharkie pointed out a few she's seen you reading too."

"Smart," she said neutrally.

A demon prince and experienced general of eighty-five whole-ass legions of Hell had an armful of filthy smut. A trilogy of BDSM romance, one of her favorite fantasy romances, and several monster romances, all with well-worn spines. Particularly in certain places.

Is that the one with the tail scene? Shit. Curse my love of paperbacks. Hardcovers would have hidden the evidence better.

Screw it. They'd built a friendship on trust and honesty, even if they both had wounds they weren't ready to bare yet. Why not build a romantic relationship on the same?

"Are you okay? You're really red," Sharkie asked, glancing between her and Bel. "Is she okay?"

"Yeah, I think she's just protective of her books. Isn't that right?" He couldn't have looked smugger if he tried.

"You got it. Take good care of them, please." *Think of me while you read certain scenes.*

"I plan on taking notes. Our favorite books say a lot about us, don't you think?"

"Absolutely. I'd love to read a few of your favorites too." Not a lie. She wanted a peek into what made that mind of his tick, what made him happy, made him curious. Her eyes dropped to the fuzzy bat slippers on his feet. "Are you heading out?"

His smile dimmed, wings shifting with a soft rustle. "Yeah, I have some . . . reports to start on."

She raised an eyebrow and tucked that information away to analyze later, along with all the other shreds and pieces she'd gathered along the way.

"Do you want a bag for the books?"

He shook his head.

"I'll walk out with you. Sharkie, want to come?"

"Yeah! Five minutes!" She scurried to her room.

Lily joined him in the entryway, searching his eyes for clues. His smile turned rueful.

"I don't need to know," she began. "I *want* to know, but I respect that there're things you don't want to—or can't—share about what you do. I've been hearing some weird things around the Afterlife, so I know there's something going on and it's not as small as I thought. But what the fuck is out there that can rough *you* up, big guy? You were gone ten days, and you came back stiff and sore, and still worried about something. And *I'm* worried about *you.*"

For a moment, despite the ridiculous outfit and the messy hair, he was every inch the general, responsibility and capability draping over him like a cloak. He seemed to briefly wrestle with something, then nodded.

"Keep secrets, princess," he said, the corners of his mouth going tight. "Just not from me, yeah?"

So it wasn't common knowledge yet.

"Okay?"

He checked for Sharkie, leaning in until his mouth brushed her ear, the potential eroticism of the gesture utterly lost to the seriousness of the moment as he spoke quietly.

"I've told you that we mainly defend against other Universes. Well, at the moment, at least one isn't friendly with ours. They broke through in one of the fringe realms. A small incursion, apparently an exploratory mission."

Her mind whirled, pieces falling into place to form a picture she didn't like. "What do they want?"

"As far as we know, they have depleted the inherent power of their Universe and are after the power generated by the souls in ours. Remember what I said about how our souls become part of the Universe? That's what they're after. And it's not just denizens. When mortal souls find their final peace, they become part of it too."

The implications of what was at risk hit her like a train. "They can take that power?"

"No, not without—" His jaw flexed. "Not easily. And we reiterated that, because we mounted a defense and won, but it was *hard* won. I'm worried because we don't know yet if it was enough to discourage further attempts. We hope so, but there is still a rift there, so we're still patrolling and guarding the area just in case."

Lily took a breath and touched his thick wrist. "Thank you for telling me."

Bel nodded. "Avoid the fringe realms altogether for a while. If anything happens and you see something *wrong*—trust me you'll know when something doesn't belong to this Universe—get yourself and Sharkie to Paradise if you can. It was the first stronghold of the Afterlife, and it's the most powerful. If not, get yourselves to Hell and go deep. I'm not trying to scare you, but I feel better knowing you're prepared."

Lily committed every word, every inflection of his warning to memory. She didn't realize she'd gripped his shirt until he'd finished talking.

"Souls regenerate," she murmured, glancing over her shoulder.

"True." He winced, rubbing at his shoulder with the opposite hand, the same shoulder she'd seen him favoring since he'd arrived. "But it'll be agony. It doesn't just *hurt*, it's soul-changing pain. I don't want that for you. For anyone, but *especially* not for you or Sharkie."

Her grip on his shirt tightened. "Bel, *you* don't regenerate."

"No." His voice was guarded.

She met his eyes, searching, processing everything she'd just learned. Her soul ached at the idea of an Afterlife, of a Universe, without Bel in it. It was on the tip of her tongue to demand that he keep himself safe, to do whatever it took to get home, including running for his life. But that wasn't realistic. Those kinds of speeches belonged in the sappy romance novels he held, and Bel was *proud* of what he did; he loved being a general and all that came with it. He'd never run from that responsibility before, and he never would.

"I won't ask you to be less than who and what you are. Ever." She breathed. A little furrow formed between his brows. "I'm selfish, but I'm not that selfish. Be safe. Go be a kick-ass general, do what you have to do to keep us all safe. But please be as safe as you can too. I want to be able to smack your ass in front of Lev and listen to him gasp like a scandalized grandmother. I'll feel heinously guilty if I'm smacking the ass of a corpse."

A bit of the intensity evaporated, the crinkles returning around his eyes. "You'll still do it though, right?"

"Of course, I'll cop one last feel, knowing it's what you would have wanted. It won't be as satisfying if you're not there to savor the moment with me though. So. Be. Fucking. Safe." She kissed him lightly. "Please."

Joking about being irreverent at his funeral was one thing, but she'd never do it. The grief of her life, her family, her friends was enough. Grieving her best friend, the person she might find real happiness with on top of it all? Too much.

"I'll be safe," he said. "And feel free to cop a feel any time, just don't grab my ass in front of Lucifer."

"Why?"

"He's a little too excited about me breaking my single streak, and I don't want to give him the satisfaction," he said darkly.

She snorted.

Sharkie gleefully interrogated Bel about the shark documentary they'd watched the night before as they walked toward the stone arch. Lily ignored the twist of nerves, reaching for his hand as soon as they'd walked outside. He laced their fingers together and gave her hand a squeeze that made all the nerves melt away.

She'd known about the other Universes, and known that Universal defense was the primary point of Hell's armies, but she hadn't realized how real it was.

"Lily, can we go to Hell today?" Sharkie asked.

"Yeah, you still want to go to school, right?"

Sharkie nodded so hard her hood flopped back.

"Sweet. I'll get some work done while you're busy." She'd already received several respectful but slightly pathetic messages from at least a dozen of the gate demons, Crocell chief among them when it came to verging on whining. Apparently, it had been a spectacularly dramatic few days for souls, and they all missed her.

Sweeties. She'd bring them the rest of the cinnamon rolls.

Bel squeezed her hand when they reached the archway, callused fingers slipping away. He raised an eyebrow at her, playful smile dancing over his lips.

"Sharkie," Lily said. Sharkie pulled her attention away from the activity outside the arch, curiosity written all over her face. "Just so you know, Bel and I are together now."

"Like a couple," Bel clarified, shifting the stack of books under his arm.

Sharkie looked at them like they were idiots. "Well, *yeah*. Haven't you always been?"

Lily's mouth dropped open, but then she laughed.

"I'm going to kiss Lily now," Bel told Sharkie, who made a face similar to the one she'd made when a woman in the Summerland had convinced her to eat steamed broccoli.

Lily shook her head, already reaching to grab the collar of Bel's shirt. "Not if I kiss you first," she told him a moment before her lips landed on his. It was brief and wonderful, gloriously novel in its unfamiliarity, but warmly comforting.

Bel knelt to give a one-armed hug to Sharkie, fixing her hood for her before striding through the halls, unbothered about his outfit. Lily watched him go, chuckling as more than a few people turned to watch him pass, confusion written all over their faces. *Work it, big guy.*

"I don't know why you guys thought it was some big secret," Sharkie said, coming to lean against her side. Lily wrapped an arm around her shoulders. "It's not like you guys were *subtle*."

27

SEX APPEAL

Lily

"Do you have *any* idea who I am?" the soul snarled as Lily swirled her tea. "I am not someone to be trifled with, and when your superiors hear about your smarmy attitude—"

"They'll be utterly unsurprised and more annoyed with you than they ever will be with me."

A smarmy rich person who wasn't rich-rich but was wealthy enough to have brushed up against the seedier side of the higher tax brackets. He hadn't just dipped a toe into that pool of debauchery either, he'd swan-dived into it with Olympic form, evading various civil suits and complaints leveled against him by former employees by abusing his power and connections. Then there was the endless stream of mistresses and escorts of dubious age, his favorite of which had looked rather like his daughter . . .

She masked her gag with a sip of tea.

Some days it felt insurmountable and demoralizing, both the number of souls who came through her line and their myriad twisted decisions and actions. Thankfully, their thoughts rarely factored into their Judgment and were seldom shown in the files. She'd asked Zazzenaag, a cheerful nonbinary demon who worked one of the intake desks, about it once. They'd explained with knowing yellow eyes and a dimpled smile that thoughts only mattered if souls acted on them, indulged them, dwelled on them.

"We all have terrible thoughts, yes? Sometimes they leap into our minds out of nowhere, other times they creep out of crevices in ourselves we were unaware of or tried to forget. This is normal. It is a condition of life, of *being*, that our minds shock us sometimes. But this is where we define ourselves: we are either horrified or confused or disgusted by these thoughts and work to change them, or we let them rule us. Our first thoughts about a situation are seldom what we actually believe. They are what we have been conditioned to think, or sometimes they truly are random spits of consciousness. But our second thoughts, ah, that is where *we* are. It has helped me, working in this position, to forgive myself for my terrible first thoughts, and to pay more attention to my *second* thoughts."

Lily glanced to where Zazzenaag used their fork to scrape every last smidge of icing off their plate in between souls stepping up to their desk. They had been one of the first to swarm around Sharkie as she'd helped carry the plate of cinnamon rolls around to the demons, who had been thrilled to get a treat twice in one week.

Kindness. That was what helped keep the shadows at bay and kept the shitty souls from being so overwhelming. Kindness and humor and simple understanding.

The stupid hacky sack still got kicked around every so often. They exchanged commiserating looks when someone particularly taxing came through. Sometimes the demons would have little dance-offs when things got a little slow. They'd all cheered like lunatics when a certain politician arrived and hurried toward the stairs without further fuss, all the way down to Level Nine and the tender mercies of Gregorith.

The lesson of kindness clearly hadn't stuck with the soul on the other side of her desk, and they launched into yet another vitriolic tirade. Zagan shuffled behind them, arching an eyebrow and doing an apathetic Macarena. He gave a stripper-quality swing of his narrow hips before he turned and began the process again.

Lily sucked her lips into her mouth.

"Are you *laughing at me*?" The soul spit. Literally spit. The droplets landed across her desk but hit an invisible barrier before they could touch her.

Fucker.

Lily tapped a finger against her steaming mug. "I cannot be bought. I cannot be threatened. I cannot be bargained with. None of us can. None of us have even the faintest desire to listen to you." She tilted her head. "However, if you refuse to shut up and go down to Level Seven as ordered, we would *love* to make you feel as afraid and helpless as you made everyone in this file feel. Your employees. Your wife. Your mistresses. The escorts you treated as subhuman. Your children."

The soul went from cherry red to sickly white with every word.

"Truly. We would love that. *I* would love that. Alternatively, you can be a good boy and do as you're told. It'll save the trainees from having to clean the floor again."

One of the trainees, a gangly young female demon with pale ochre skin and ram horns that she'd painted with glitter, glanced at the cleaning closet with a wince and hurried off to a new position.

The soul's mouth worked for a few moments before they finally turned and scuttled away. Zagan paused his dance as soon as the soul had turned, and leaned on his spear with a squint. "Why are rich people so touchy?"

"They're typically used to getting their way. This is probably the first time some of them have faced actual consequences. It's a *hell* of a learning curve," Lily said, wiping away the lingering droplets of spit with a rag. "Nice moves, Beyoncé. They teach that in guard school?"

"It was that or basket weaving. Figured I could use the cardio."

Lily laughed and set the soul's file in the little basket, where it promptly disappeared, following the soul to their destination.

The flow of souls from the gate to the stairs was lighter than usual, and few of them had wanted to go out of their way to fuss. A fact she was thankful for, leaning back in her chair to stare up at the hazy ceiling and think.

It had been three whole days.

Three days of rubbing her chest every so often, wondering if the sensation of lightness within would ever fade. Three days of having lunch with Bel, once in the break room, once in his office, and once in the training fields.

Oh, the training fields.

They'd kept the physicality of their relationship careful enough. Sitting with their thighs touching, looping an arm around each other whenever they were near, holding hands for any reason, chaste kisses to say hello and goodbye—well, chaste *enough*. They'd been careful by Lily's standards, and she suspected Bel's as well. Which was impressive—commendable, even—given that their attraction, once openly admitted and claimed, felt a bit like a genie they couldn't put back in the bottle. All things considered, they'd been doing well, but the day before on the training fields had been damn near more temptation than she'd been able to take.

Bel had strode over with a grin, sheathing his sword as he went. And if that hadn't been erotic enough to her fantasy-loving mind (or to anyone with eyes and taste), he'd been panting heavily and gleaming with sweat, his damp, inky hair pulled back in a loose knot. She'd wondered—had been fairly certain—that he would look similarly after a good fuck and had been tempted to find out on the spot—audience of several thousand demons be damned.

To make matters worse—and her underwear more soaked—he'd done *the thing* . . . using the hem of his faded gray muscle shirt to wipe his sweaty face, flashing his solid, faintly ridged abdomen, one of his heavy pectorals, and most distracting of all, the line of crisp, black hairs trailing down from his navel to disappear into his well-worn black pants.

Her mouth had gone dry. *I will climb him like a fucking tree. I will follow that line of hair with my tongue and do things to him that would make a succubus blush. I will do it. Fuck waiting, it's unfair when he looks like that.*

She'd still been rallying her brain to form a coherent, not-horny thought, reminding herself that waiting was good and they'd both agreed to it when he'd stopped a short distance away.

"Hey, princess. I'd kiss you, but I'm all sweaty."

Excuse me?

She'd crooked her finger at him. "I like you sweaty. C'mere."

His eyes had flashed with heat, and he'd been deliciously cocky as he stepped forward and gave her possibly the most chaste kiss of her life.

He'd smirked at her little noise of complaint and pressed another, slightly rougher kiss to her lips that had her swaying toward him.

"Behave, princess, or I'll be having a very different kind of meal."

"Funny, I was just about to say the same to you."

He'd groaned and laced his fingers with hers, leading her over to the spectator seating. "Don't. Do you have any idea how hard it is to fight with *tight pants*?"

She'd kissed his shoulder, ignoring the soldiers who poked each other and stared their way. "Just making sure you work *hard*, big guy."

After that, they'd subsided, inhaling their respective lunches as they'd watched soldiers sparring with various weaponry. Even Lily could see the difference between seasoned soldiers and new recruits. Bel had answered all her questions, pointing out tiny details she never would have noticed, much less appreciated.

He was *happy*. Bel in his office was Bel at work. Bel with his soldiers was Bel at his calling. She'd let him steal her apple and watched him light up explaining the various techniques, strategies, dangers, uses, and drawbacks of everything. His passion, as much as anything, drew her to him like a moth to flame. Eventually, he'd convinced her to grab a practice sword and spent the rest of their time teaching her the basics.

As she'd suspected, she'd loved Bel teaching her. And, from the lightness in his features, he'd loved it too.

Asmodeus's arrival heralded the end of their break. He'd strutted up all arrogance and mirth, his shirt rolled up and slung around his neck like a towel. Lily had moved her sword slowly through a new motion, absently noting that while Asmodeus and Bel were built along vaguely similar lines, Asmodeus was leaner, his muscles more defined. She sent a mental *get it girl* to Sariah for having a hot-ass husband and felt deliciously smug that people might be similarly inclined to congratulate her on having a hot-ass boyfriend. Bel's body, built for power, sang to her.

Glancing at Asmodeus again, she'd decided that she wouldn't want to go against either of them in any form of combat more physical than a thumb wrestling match though.

The clang of a dropped spear jolted Lily back to the present, and she hoped she hadn't let her thoughts play over her face.

A teenage demon walked from the elevators toward the stairs to the Universal Hallway, hands in his pockets.

He nodded to her bashfully. "Hi, Ms. Lily."

"Hey." She smiled. It wasn't until he disappeared that she wondered how he'd known her name. Maybe he'd been in one of the student groups doing career tours? She shook the thought away, reaching for her current book and kicking her feet up on the desk.

Several chapters later, she'd only had to look up once to glare at a soul that had quickly rethought their plan. As she turned the page, a slender arm draped over her shoulders, followed by the scent of flowers and fresh grass washing over her senses.

Persephone, who must have come down the stairs from the Universal Hallway while Lily had been absorbed in her book, grinned down at her, along with another woman who was among the most beautiful Lily had ever seen. The new woman had soft features; large, dark eyes; olive skin; and wondrously curly red-brown hair that was half up in ornate braids, with the rest spilling loose over her shoulders. Her casual, modern, cream-colored maxi dress was at utter odds with the aura of lush power that trickled over Lily's skin like honey.

"That's a good book! Have you read it before?" Persephone beamed.

Lily set her book down and hugged her friend, sitting back on the edge of her desk. "Nope, I'm on a new adventure."

"Lucky," Persephone sighed. "I'd love to read that again for the first time. Lily, I'd like you to meet Aphrodite." She gestured to the other woman, who gave a radiant smile.

"Nice to meet you, Lily. I've heard so much about you."

Act cool, it's just another fucking goddess, no big deal, just another day at the office.

"Nice to meet you too. What brings you down here?" Lily asked, hoping her voice didn't sound as weird as she thought it did. She'd had a little plastic replica of the Venus de Milo in her apartment for years, had often stared at it in moments of insecurity, reminding herself that she and the statue had similar body types, and the statue version of Aphrodite had once been considered the pinnacle of beauty. The real Aphrodite shared the statue's basic body type, but her curves were lusher, her figure fuller in a way that Lily admired and slightly envied. Of the many things Lily brought to the table, an absolute beauty of an ass was not one of them.

That was Bel's contribution.

"You, actually." Persephone grinned slyly.

Aphrodite's eyes glittered with mischief. Lily wondered what exactly she was getting into.

"Oh?"

"Trivia night is coming up soon," Aphrodite said, toying with a perfect curl, "and we've decided to play dirty."

Lily couldn't keep the smirk from her face. She had no idea what exactly these two powerful, gorgeous ladies had in mind, but she could already tell that she'd like it.

"Do tell," she purred, curling her fingers around the edge of the desk.

Persephone shot Aphrodite a triumphant look. "We've got this in the *bag*." She turned to Lily, practically bouncing with energy. "So, we're putting a team together for sexual psychological warfare, and we are going to kick all the ass."

"And get plenty of it too, if you're into that," Aphrodite put in.

"Yes, but that's a perk for *after*," Persephone said, more to herself than to anyone else. "I'm talking lingerie, I'm talking hair and makeup, I'm talking whatever makes you feel like you could conquer the Afterlife with your sex appeal and gets your partner so hot and bothered they won't be able to think. We have tried this before."

"And it worked?"

"More or less." Persephone blushed.

"They have a nine-year-old," Aphrodite said in a droll voice. "Guess when we tried this last."

"Aphrodite didn't even make it to the end of the night." Persephone sniffed.

"It's true, Heph dragged me out of there halfway through the sixth round. We found out later that our team scored higher than his, so I considered it a worthy sacrifice."

"Noble of you," Lily said.

"Anyway," Persephone plowed on, "we've been planning this for some time and were going to ask you anyway, but now that you're dating Bel, it's even *better*. One of the categories is weaponry, so hopefully, he'll be too distracted to be useful."

"We also have Sariah, who has promised to make sure that Asmodeus contributes absolutely nothing for the entirety of the evening," Aphrodite said.

"Except his sperm in her later," Lily drawled without thinking.

Is this my curse? Meet a deity, make a sex joke?

"I like her," Aphrodite said.

"I told you," Persephone crowed, throwing her arm around Lily. "We might not win, but we'll beat the guys, and that's all that matters. Also, Melinoe, my daughter, is—on Mommy and Daddy's suggestion—having a sleepover that night and would like to invite Sharkie. We have a phenomenal trio of sitters we've used for millennia who will take great care of them."

"I'll ask her. I think she'll like that."

"Do you need anything for the night?"

"Such as?"

Aphrodite waved a causal hand. "Clothes, or advice, or help with hair and makeup?" She tilted her head, considering. "I have some great ideas for your coloring and build, though of course it's also about what you're comfortable and confident in too."

Lily took a moment to look at the goddess, really look, beyond the unearthly beauty. Lily had never considered herself a stone-cold stunner, but she'd ticked enough boxes on the list of conventionally attractive traits to turn heads on occasion. She knew how quickly people could write an entire person off as simply "pretty."

Aphrodite was grounded in a way that reminded Lily of the women she'd most admired in her mortal life, carrying herself with a sense of calm, self-assuredness, confidence, and grace. Sure, there was a hint of the raw sexuality that would have Hephaestus, and anyone with a sex drive, incapable of speech on trivia night, but like most women, Aphrodite was clearly more than that.

"I'll take any advice I can get, and I'd love some help with hair and makeup. It's not my strongest skill, and I'd hate to let down our cause." Lily grinned.

"Bel won't know what hit him," Aphrodite promised, eyes twinkling.

Persephone clapped her hands together, a wicked smile lighting up her lovely face. "Excellent. Now, what, if anything, do you think can be done about Lucifer?"

———❧❦❧———

28

GREGGLES

Bel

Bel blocked Greg's blade—barely—with a clang that jarred up his arm, and shoved him back.

"You're distracted," Greg said coolly.

"Figured I'd give you a sporting chance this time."

"Ha." Greg flipped his blade in his hand, red eyes seeing everything. "Is this about the mortal?"

"*Lily.*"

"Lily. The mortal soul. Or is it the kid? Both?"

Something in Greg's tone had Bel's temper flaring. He took hold of it, controlling it, understanding it, thinking around it. He exhaled, settling into a stance that was as familiar to him as walking.

"Worried about me?"

"Usually." Greg feinted left before striking right, and their conversation paused as they exchanged a flurry of strikes and counterstrikes. They broke apart, breathing heavily.

"She makes you happy." It wasn't a question.

"I'm sensing you have something else to say about that."

"I told you that if you decided to go for it, I'd support you." Greg wiped at his forehead with the back of his hand. "And I do."

"But?"

"Not a 'but' exactly. Have you had the conversation about reincarnation yet?"

Bel sheathed his blade and reached for the bottle of water resting on a nearby rock. "We have."

Greg waited silently.

Bel finished his drink, clearing his throat and hoping Greg would think it was because of the water. "She's going to go back someday."

Greg's brows furrowed, confusion written all over his face. Written in tiny script, little micro expressions Bel had gotten very good at reading over the years, but written all over his face, nonetheless.

"I don't understand."

"What is there to understand?" Bel growled, patience fraying.

"She *is* going to break your heart," Greg said. "Why risk that? Why get left behind again? Is this some kind of . . . self-punishment for what happened before?"

Bel flexed his hand, watching the muscles and tendons play under his dusky purple skin. His coloring had always favored his mother, but his build was just like his father. They had the same hands. Now, anyway. He remembered being a child—wasn't *that* a long time ago—and trying to hold his father's sword, which had been taller than he was at the time. His father's powerful hands had been steady and so much larger than his own as he'd helped Bel grasp the hilt.

He relaxed his hand, letting it drop. "I'm well aware that it'll hurt like fuck when she leaves. Things that end hurt, but they're all the more precious *because* they end. Mortals' whole lives are so short, and yet they pack so much into them. They don't take partners and spend the whole time thinking about how much it will hurt when it ends. I want to be happy with her and with Sharkie. For however long I can."

Greg sheathed his blade and folded his arms, locking that entirely too perceptive gaze on Bel, who folded his own arms and stared back.

"Okay," Greg said slowly.

Bel waited.

And waited.

His tail lashed.

"And?"

The moment stretched. A cluster of demons glanced at them as they passed by. Bel and Greg ignored them.

"Don't hit me."

Bel kept his mouth shut, tension shooting through his body. Greg had said nothing about throwing something at him. A shoe maybe. Perhaps a knife if what Greg had to say was spectacularly stupid and out of character.

Fucking bring it, Greggles.

"Does she know?"

"For fuck's sake, Greg, know *what*?"

"Know about your history of getting *left behind*? Because if she does and she still entered a relationship with you, then she's incredibly selfish—"

Bel snarled.

"But if she doesn't, then I don't understand. I thought you valued communication and honesty in relationships?"

"I do, but telling her would make me feel like a manipulative asshole. An honest manipulative asshole, but a manipulative asshole. No matter how I phrase it, it would sound like I was trying to guilt her into staying. Lily's just as perceptive as you are. She'd see right through me."

Greg frowned. "So tell her that you don't want to guilt her into staying. If she is as perceptive as you say, and you are as serious about her as I think you are, eventually she'll start asking questions about certain aspects of your life. Lily isn't stupid, and she's got a backbone made of titanium. Plus, she's nicer than I am."

"Well, she's certainly a better kisser than you are," Bel said loftily, trying to lighten the mood.

"It was *one time*, and I was under duress. Hardly my finest work. I don't know what your excuse is." Greg smirked.

"I rocked your little beanpole emo world."

"You did not." Greg tilted his head, amusement fading. "Tell her. You might get lucky. Metaphorically anyway. Maybe someday she'll take pity on you, and you'll finally get to second base—do *not* bring my mother into this."

Bel shut his mouth and flipped him off.

Greg shook his head, drawing his long knife and spinning the handle in his palm a few times. "I'm happy for you. You've been different in a good way. Even if you'll be utterly useless on trivia night."

"What? The categories don't look too bad. Why would I be useless?" Bel drew his own blade and rolled his shoulder, careful with it after his minor injury. It seemed fine.

"Not just you in particular, but a significant portion of the population, you included. Not me. Remember the Night of Many Distractions around nine years ago?"

Bel laughed. Half of the partners had been drooling messes, all trivial knowledge lost to distraction as their beloveds rocked up in their finest, most risqué, most seductive outfits.

From the time his wife walked in with her team of seductresses, Hades hadn't spoken a single word. Just stared at his wife before hauling her out the door the moment the results had been read. Their resulting daughter was adorable.

Asmodeus had dropped his drink and only made carnal observations that were completely unrelated to any of the questions they'd been supposed to answer.

What animal breathes through its butt?

"Sariah's butt looks amazing in that skirt."

The correct answer had been "a turtle."

In a bingo game, what number is represented by the phrase "two little ducks"?

"Huh? What about ducks? I'll duck down to get Sariah to ride my face."

The correct answer had been "22."

Bel and Greg had been two of the few single members of their team that night and had been laughing too hard to get upset about losing so badly. Not a single team got a perfect score that night. The lines for the bathroom had been hysterically long and full of couples or groups.

"I seemed to handle it just fine last time."

"You didn't have someone you were half in love with last time."

It might be more than half . . .

What would Lily wear? Fuck, what would Lily *not* be wearing?

They hadn't progressed much beyond their kiss on the couch; no heated make-out sessions for them. Yet. Their pace had been restricted more by lack of opportunity than by lack of want. They'd both been busy, and Sharkie was wonderful and dear to his heart . . . but had a tendency to never knock and just appear places. Their stolen touches had just been fuel for the fire, adding detail to his fantasies bit by bit. The satiny feel of the sensitive skin on her neck. The curves of her body next to his.

He shifted his feet.

"I think I'll be able to control myself," Bel said, mostly to convince himself.

Greg shot him a pitying look right before he lunged forward, and Bel lost himself in the motions of sparring.

29

REASONABLE EXPECTATIONS

Lily

Sharkie sat at the kitchen table, thoughtfully chewing a chicken nugget. "You and Bel *and* Luci will be there?" she asked.

Lily looked up from her spot on the kitchen floor, Max sprawled across her lap. She'd convinced Sharkie to let her put her hair into a French braid in order to keep the messy blond strands from continually getting in her face, and it made Sharkie look both younger and like a very small Viking. Attending school and the field trip had been a huge step, but the slumber party would be a leap of faith. Lily had confidence in Sharkie's ability to thrive.

Sharkie added color to days and moments that otherwise would have been mundane, and Lily couldn't imagine what an existence without Sharkie would be like anymore. She woke up every morning excited to see what that day would bring, and one of her favorite parts of the day was sitting in the kitchen together while they had breakfast. One of her friends had once described parenthood as having a piece of her heart walking around outside of her chest. Lily understood that now.

"Yes, but we'll all have our phones, so if you need us, we're just a phone call away. Plus, the Underworld people are nice, and I trust them to keep you safe and treat you with respect. You saw the list of everyone who will be there, right?"

"Yep," Sharkie said around a mouthful of chicken.

"Do you want me to ask about having a room set aside for you in case you need a safe space?"

Sharkie mulled it over long enough to eat two more nuggets. "No thank you. I'll just call you. I'm really excited about all the games!"

"Yeah, those sound awesome," Lily agreed. "One last thing: Just in case you need a break, you can go to a bathroom. They won't bug you in there."

"Oh, that's a good idea."

Lily winked. "I've been known to have one of those every now and then."

Sharkie giggled and finished her food, holding the empty plate up with both hands like an offering until the house made it vanish into thin air.

"What about you?" Sharkie asked a moment later.

"Hm?"

"Are you going to have fun tonight?"

Lily ran her hand through Max's fur, a buzz zipping through her body at the thought of the night to come. She'd already showered after her shift in Hell, reveling in the never-ending hot water and taking her time to scrub and polish everything that needed to be scrubbed and polished until she felt like a new, glamorous person with silky smooth skin and fluffy hair. She'd thrown on comfy shorts and a worn button-up shirt, and, because the house refused to let her clean anything, plopped down in the library to finish a particularly filthy book that only intensified the anticipation she couldn't ignore.

She didn't expect anything to happen. But she sure as shit wasn't opposed to something happening.

She'd replayed that moment on the training fields over and over, often with a vibrator in hand, wishing that the silicone was Bel. She'd sat at her desk in between souls—and *during* a few souls, frankly—daydreaming about getting her hands and mouth on Bel's cock. She fantasized about bringing him to the edge and then making him beg for release. The secret part of her brain that she'd kept hidden away had a very different fantasy, inspired by the careful way he held her throat sometimes when kissing her goodbye. What if he held it a little *harder*—

Max chirped, bringing her back to the present, where she had done the inexcusable: holding but not petting a cat that wanted to be petted.

She tapped him gently on the nose and made up for her lapse of affection.

"I'm excited to see everyone, and I love trivia night," Lily said, finally replying to Sharkie. "So I think I'm going to have a blast."

"If you need us, call, but more than anything, have fun!" Lily said, giving Sharkie an extra squeeze before she let go.

Sharkie was practically bouncing, eyes gleaming with pure excitement as she gave Lily one last hug around the legs. "I wanna pet the big dog!" she announced, sprinting off toward the group of kids visible in a nearby courtyard.

Lily looked around for the dog in question.

Big dog. Underworld. Oh no . . .

"Don't worry," Persephone beamed, slipping outside with a giggle. "Cerberus is really good with kids." She wore a gloriously soft-looking, oversized, and masculine black bathrobe, her hair intricately woven with gold thread and studded with gems that sparkled like multicolored stars against the dark strands. Her makeup was only half done, but Lily still whistled.

"Damn. Hades is fucked."

"I certainly hope so. It's my turn." Persephone winked. "Speaking of fucked, that's what you're going to be once Beleth gets an eyeful of you."

Lily looked down at her casual outfit, gestured to her utter lack of makeup and styled hair and chuckled. "Are you *sure*?"

"Oh please, even if you went as you are, you'd still end up getting dragged out of the bar. Hey, that rhymed! Anyway, once Aphrodite gets her hands on you?" She laughed wickedly. "Their team won't be able to get a single point because they'll be otherwise preoccupied. Now shoo, or you'll be late!"

Lily made a face, but admittedly, did want to make Bel choke on his tongue.

It was the little things.

She waved goodbye and headed back toward the Universal Hallway, where her jaw proceeded to drop.

Aphrodite was causing something of a traffic jam.

Her olive skin glowed, pearlescent white dress draped over her lush body, hem brushing demurely against her knees. Long, perfectly curled hair hung to her waist, half braided up so intricately that it almost looked like lace. Simple gold chain earrings brushed her neck, complemented by a delicate necklace with a single diamond hammer as a charm.

Aphrodite shot her a seductive smile. "They don't call me the goddess of beauty for nothing, darling. Shall we? I don't want their drool to ruin my shoes."

⛤

30

MUTUALLY ASSURED SEDUCTION

Lily

Lily laughed over a drink that looked like liquid sunshine, the alcohol a warm simmer in her veins. She refused to look over to the guys' table, waiting for the almost tangible sensation of Bel's gaze to land on her again.

Luckyleaf had already been a hotbed of chaos when they arrived, with one half of the crowd shooting coy glances at their partners or ignoring them completely. The other half of the population seemed to have put in an effort to seduce as well, so it was to be a battle of wills.

Lily felt like she was floating, buoyed by the confidence and support of the fierce people around her. In the mortal world, she never would have dared go out baring so much skin, but in the safety of the Afterlife, she could have strolled down the Hall naked and not even been touched.

She'd seen Bel a moment after he'd seen her, just in time to watch him trail off mid-sentence to an equally stunned Asmodeus, whose eyes were locked on his wife. It had required effort to not pause in her tracks and stare, but she'd kept her wickedly high stilettos in motion.

Bel had cleaned up, and cleaned up *good*. His hair was smooth and braided back from his temples, cascading past his shoulders in a glossy curtain. In unrelieved black, he cut a sleekly intimidating figure. His pants were just slightly snug over his powerful legs and thighs, and a sleeveless tunic embroidered in faintly glittering designs hugged his powerful frame, leaving his thick arms bare. And *damn*. She wanted to sink her teeth into those biceps.

Just as his expression had gone from stunned to dark and hungry, she smirked at him, then turned to laugh at something someone had said that she hadn't actually heard. She'd thrown one more glance at him over her bare shoulder, slickness already gathering between her thighs.

A slickness that, an hour later, had only gotten worse.

Sariah fluffed her curly, shoulder-length charcoal hair and reached for her nonalcoholic drink, saying to the slight Fae woman at their table, "If I weren't already pregnant, the look he just gave you would have knocked me up just by sitting so close to you."

The Fae woman blushed, her gemlike skin glittering from within.

"How come you aren't tits in the breeze like the rest of us?" Muriel, a succubus with dark orange skin asked, her green eyes bright and drunk.

"Speak for yourself, Muri," Angel drawled, throwing back her drink. While there was an ample amount of cleavage on display at their table alone, Muriel had sauntered into the bar completely naked and covered in body glitter, except for a sparkly thong that nearly matched her skin tone perfectly. One of the servers had nearly dropped their tray.

Sariah's charcoal dress complemented her terra-cotta-red skin and might have been modest except for the truly magnificent amount of cleavage it displayed. It was otherwise innocent enough, draping over her baby bump and swirling around her knees, but all of them had noticed exactly how ravenous Asmodeus had been before his friends dragged him to their table.

"I'm putting in just as much work as all of you," Sariah said primly, golden eyes sparkling. "I'm simply using different methods."

"Explain." Persephone hiccuped.

"Azzy has a raging breeding kink. I am his wife, who is very obviously pregnant with his child, emphasized by the dress, and," Sariah said as if the final point was perhaps the most important, "I'm wearing an easily flip-up-able skirt. I'm also ignoring him. He's foaming at the mouth. Which is excellent news for me, because that means all I'll have to do is hold on for the ride later. Ladies"—she raised her glass in a toast—"to using our wiles."

Bel

"Ten more seconds," Lucifer said, "then it's Bel's turn."

"There's no way that was a minute," the man said, staring at his partner as if she were about to disappear.

Bel stared at the barely touched tray of food. He could *smell* the amount of sexual frustration at the table. But maybe that was just how Luckyleaf smelled, given the bevy of partners lusting after each other in public.

"If this turns into an orgy like last time, I'm going home and taking my actually useful contributions with me," Greg said, reaching for more nachos. It was true, he'd been one of the functional members of their team, while Bel had . . . not.

He'd only gotten to look at her four times since they set up their system. Operation: Don't Look Desperate involved a rotating schedule of getting to look at their partners for a minute each, in order to avoid being distracted and useless.

It had somewhat failed in its objective.

He'd barely believed his eyes when she'd entered the pub. The details were hazy, but her smoky makeup made her eyes even more mesmerizing and seductive than usual. Her long, thick hair had been pulled up into an effortlessly regal twist with a few loose, curled strands, baring her slender neck and drawing attention to the wet dream of a dress she wore.

He wasn't sure that what she had on could legally be called a *dress*, but he planned on finding its creator and offering them anything and everything they wanted out of gratitude.

Black silk poured over her body, the low cowl of the neck teasing at the upper slopes of her breasts, the delicate fabric doing nothing to hide the way her nipples had hardened under his gaze. It skimmed over her body, hugging just enough at her hips to make his hands twitch, before the hysterically short hem revealed the tattoos on her thigh, little slits on either side teasing him with hints of more skin. He wanted to wrap her long, bare legs around his hips—and that was before he saw the fuck-me heels that he immediately wanted her to press into his ass while he pounded into her.

"And time. Bel, your turn," Lucifer said, seemingly unruffled by it all.

Bel leaned over the table as if that small distance would ease the ache of not having her near, eyes locking on her.

The pressure at his groin verged on unbearable, and the glimpse of the back of her dress did absolutely nothing to help. Completely open, save for the tiniest strings for straps crossing over her upper back, it dropped down so low that he wondered whether if she moved just slightly he would see the cleft of her ass. A delicately wrought sword, twined with flowers and curls of filigree, was tattooed down her spine, framed perfectly by the drape of her dress. He wanted to trace it with his tongue.

Sure, their relationship was based on friendship and mutual respect, but there was a fucking lot of attraction there as well, and he was struggling. Not with control—he'd never do anything without her enthusiastic permission—but with the urge to beg, something he'd never done in his long life.

Beg her to stay. Beg to fuck her. Beg her to stay while he fucked her. Beg her to read to him in her lovely voice. Beg her to love him. Beg her to smile at him, just one more time. Always one more time. He'd better be the one doing the begging, because if she ever begged him, he'd lose his fucking *mind*.

As if on cue, she turned to look at him, sipping her drink as if she had no idea how close he was to coming in his pants like a teenager. Without breaking eye contact, she caught a drip sliding down the side of her glass with her tongue. Bel clenched his hands so hard the bones creaked.

Little vixen.

She knew it too. The little smile that played on her lips had his heart pounding. The lipstick she wore was only a few shades darker than her natural lip color, accentuating her smirk perfectly.

She arched an eyebrow.

Let's play, princess.

He arched his eyebrow right back and took his sweet time running his gaze down every inch of her body, catching the little hitch in her breath, the barest shifting of her thighs on her seat. When he met her eyes again, the mischief had been replaced with a heated, almost desperate expression that he understood intimately.

She set her glass down on the table and stood, the muscles in her legs and back flexing. Everything in him went still.

When she shot him another mischievous gaze, stuck out her tongue, and sauntered toward the bathrooms, he followed her without hesitation.

Lily

Lily had never had so much fun in her entire life. Sure, she was so horny she could barely form a coherent thought, but oh, it had been so worth it. Bel looked like every dark fantasy she'd ever had, the sweet, funny side of him replaced with something deliciously primal.

The hallway she'd been directed to had individual bathrooms on either side, and the line for them was surprisingly short. She didn't have those needs anymore, but she'd needed to leave the table before she orgasmed in public, figuring that she could hide in the bathroom until she'd composed herself. A woman in a tie-dye dress hurried out of a door, and Lily headed for it.

Just as she reached for the handle, she felt it. Felt *him*. He pressed up against her back, opened the door himself, and guided her forward with his body.

He locked the door behind them with a click that she felt down to her toes.

She'd been close to him before, so why was she suddenly realizing how much *bigger* than her he was? She'd never felt particularly delicate or feminine, but in that moment, she understood all her short friends and how they'd talked about their much taller partners. Protected. Dainty.

In the dim recesses of her mind, she almost laughed at that. She'd beaten a rapist into a bloody pulp with a bat the day before, then broken the jaw of a millionaire pedophile with a well-placed kick once she'd gotten him onto the ground, and here she was feeling *dainty*.

"Princess," Bel growled.

She closed her eyes and shivered. His voice was deeper than she'd ever heard it, rumbling against her back and humming through her over-sensitive body. His hands came to rest at her hips, claws pricking deliciously through the fabric.

"You've been playing games with me."

"Am I winning?" She aimed for cocky and ended up breathless. Gods, she could feel every inch of him, the hard bulge of his cock against her lower back had her leaning against him, covering his hands with her own.

He skimmed his nose up the side of her neck. She arched for him, gasping when he nipped at her earlobe and pressed her forward until she bumped against the vanity. Her eyes flew open, meeting his heated gaze in the mirror.

Fuck.

She'd always been visual, always liked to watch almost as much as she liked auditory stimulation. They painted a heady picture in the mirror—Bel looming behind her, every inch the demon with his arching horns, claw-tipped wings, and unearthly eyes, and her, looking like a heathen princess in her flimsy black dress and dark eye makeup, tattoos scattered over her skin. Their hands together at her hips were a study in contrasts. Rugged and feminine, dusky purple and fair, tipped with black claws and nails painted gunmetal gray.

His little finger trailed down the side of her skirt to trace the skin just below the hem. All of her attention zeroed in on that little touch. His other hand slipped out from under hers and ran up her body, grazing over a breast that felt heavy and hypersensitive, coming to rest around her neck, tilting her head back slightly.

The subtle scrape of claws had her reaching back with her now-free hand to grab at his thigh with what was dangerously close to a whimper.

She'd never whimpered in sexual abandon in her life. Any of her lives.

"Are you?" he asked, his breath fanning over her shoulder as he nipped at the whisper of a strap that held her dress up.

About to orgasm harder than I ever thought possible?

Yes.

"Am I what?" she breathed, having entirely lost the thread of conversation as she watched him move in the mirror, drunk on the sensation of his body around hers.

"Winning," he murmured.

"I don't care," she panted, arching her back to rub against that bulge. He groaned and pressed himself into her, grip tightening on her hip and tugging her dress up to nearly reveal her wicked little secret.

"You've been teasing me," he said, running his thumb up the side of her neck.

She managed to smile at that. "Only because you're so easy to tease."

He pressed an open-mouthed kiss to her shoulder, scraping his fangs ever so slightly and smiling at her reaction.

"Shall I return the favor, princess? Hm?"

Oh please, return the favor. Please return the fucking favor. Pull my dress up a little more.

"Please," she gasped, pulling him toward her, digging her nails into his thigh.

His wicked grin dropped, and the lines of his face tightened in delicious hunger. *"Fuck."*

Then he dropped his eyes to where his fingers were so, so close to where she most wanted him. Lily followed his gaze and blushed. Her arousal gleamed visibly on the inside of her thighs. Bel, the asshole, leisurely slid his hand to trace over it, inching higher, *higher*, the tension in his body ratcheting tighter behind her as he went.

"Bel," she murmured just as he brushed against her for the first time.

They groaned together, and Bel pressed his cheek against her temple, his breathing ragged.

"Nothing?"

"Surprise," she managed. "Claws?"

He flexed his hand to show her that his claws had blunted themselves, like they'd retracted, then cupped her fully and began to explore. Brushing, *teasing*. Lily let her head fall back, and her eyes slide shut, overwhelmed. The murmur of the crowd in the bar faded away. All she could hear were their ragged breaths, the slick sounds his fingers made as they moved against her. All she could feel was him, his wicked fingers, his massive hand collaring her neck, her back molded to every inch of his front.

Never end. She wanted it to never end.

The Universe had gotten it wrong. *This* was her real Paradise—

Bel sank a finger into her, and she arched her spine, panting, beyond words as he filled her, pumping once, twice, the heat of his palm cupping her entire sex, his thumb moving, seeking, brushing just there—

She keened, gripping his forearm to keep him there, possibly forever. He smiled against her hair.

"So responsive, princess. Look at me."

The hand at her neck cradled her jaw, tugging her head down. She opened her eyes and panted, watching him, watching them in the mirror.

"Watch me when I'm inside you. I want to see your pretty eyes when I . . ."

He added another finger, stretching, filling her more than she'd thought possible. She wanted to close her eyes, to drown in sensation alone, but she watched that hand move between her thighs, pumping, his thumb flicking her clit too fucking tenderly, she needed to come *now*.

"So impatient. Is this what you wanted? Is this what you imagined when you put this little dress on with *nothing underneath it*? All for me?"

"Yes," she nearly sobbed, releasing his forearm to reach up and grip the side of his neck, fingers tangling in his loose hair. "I just . . ."

He pumped hard and she momentarily forgot how to speak.

"I just . . . wanted to return the favor . . . for the training fields."

He paused and she almost killed him.

"Training fields?" He raised his head slightly to meet her eyes, brows furrowed.

She pulled on the hair in her grip. He pulled her tighter against him.

"When you wiped . . . your face with your shirt. I wanted to fuck you. Wanted you to fuck me . . . I've been suffering ever since."

"Probably about worn that vibrator out, huh?"

"You're entirely too smug about this—" Her scowl evaporated when he twisted his fingers deep.

"Let me apologize, princess." He traced the shell of her ear with his lips, hand going back to work.

Pleasure surged, winding tighter and tighter, building like a wave, more powerful than anything she'd ever felt before, almost terrifying in its intensity. But she had Bel. Bel wouldn't let her fall, or melt, or whateverthefuck was about to happen.

He seemed to sense her approaching climax, maintaining the steady pace, the deep pumps of his thick fingers, the gentle rub of her clit.

Lily would feel bad for the way she dug her manicured nails into him later. Feel bad for ripping at his hair, for probably clawing a hole in the side of his pants where she gripped his thigh. None of that mattered in that moment.

He twisted her head to the side and captured her lips with his own, *finally*, tongue tracing, asking. She opened for him just as his wicked, skillful hand sent her hurtling over the edge. Lights exploded behind her eyelids.

He muffled her cry with his mouth, swallowing it down, stroking her through wave after wave of bone-melting pleasure until she was sobbing, breaking away to gasp and plead for mercy. He stilled his hand and simply held her against him, face buried in her hair, panting, shaking with repressed energy and strength. Lily loosened her fingers, clumsily petting over his hair and neck with a shaky hand.

Her understanding of pleasure had been blown away.

A few long minutes later, Bel lifted his head and slowly pulled his hand away. She whined at the emptiness as his fingers left her, as the heat of his palm faded and the cool air rushed in. Bel raised his hand in front of them, fingers and palm gleaming with her wetness, then, holding her eyes in the mirror, sucked his fingers clean.

Lily twisted in his hold as he lowered his hand, taking his face in her hands and doing her level best to kiss him as senseless as he'd made her. The taste of herself on his lips was heady, powerfully erotic in a way that had her reaching for the waistband of his pants. She couldn't wait to return the favor, had dreamed about him on her tongue for days—

He caught her hand with a dazed grin. "I don't think so. This was about you, princess. For you."

"Can I make a royal request?"

He laughed, but it was strained. She could feel how hard he was, she *wanted* it, wanted him.

"Not here, princess. I don't want you on your knees in some bathroom." He kissed her long and deep, mollifying her slightly.

Only slightly.

She still wanted him. Wondered if she'd always want him, want more of him. She waited for the panic at that thought to wash in, but it didn't. She felt . . . settled. *Right.* Still horny, but right.

She slid her arms around his waist and pressed her cheek to his chest, mesmerized by his thundering heart while he held her close, resting his chin on top of her head, careful of the little spikes. They stood there for a long time, listening to the moderators ask unintelligible trivia questions over the microphone, until they'd both calmed.

She propped her chin on his chest, gazing up at him. "We're going to catch a lot of shit for this, aren't we?"

"Without a doubt," he said, kissing her nose, before he stopped dead, realization spreading over his face. He threw his head back with a groan. "Ah damn. I just lost one of my couches to Greg."

"Really? Which one?" Lily asked, straightening up a bit. *Not the one by his desk, not the one by his desk . . .*

"The one by the wall." He sighed, looking back down at her.

"Oh. Worth it, I'd say. I like the one by your desk."

"Totally worth it," he agreed, hugging her a little tighter.

31

STRIDE OF PRIDE

Lily

"Do I look like you just blew my mind in the bathroom?" Lily asked, fixing her smudged lipstick.

She didn't *think* it was obvious . . . but perversely, she rather wanted it to be.

Bel grimaced slightly, adjusting himself in his pants. A fresh wave of desire pounded through her veins like a drum.

She'd repay him soon. He might have noble compunctions about where she ended up on her knees, but she didn't.

"Not going to lie to you . . . yeah, a bit. I'm not mad about it though." Masculine pride dripped from every word.

"Me neither." She bumped him with her hip. "Ready to do the stride of pride?"

"Wait, is my ass 'prince' quality today or just 'decent'?"

Lily leaned back to get a better look.

Mmm.

She smacked it. For science.

His tail tip twitched.

"Seems pretty princely to me."

"Sweet." He rolled his shoulders. "Shall we?"

"Ten metaphorical bucks says that we are not the only ones missing from our tables when we get back," Lily said, heading for the door.

Bel reached around her to open it. "Not only that, I'll get specific. Fifty says Asmodeus is long gone."

Lily laughed and shook her head, stepping out into the dim hallway, ignoring the line of people and suspicious number of couples. "Fifty says he's still there. Sariah seemed pretty intent on making him suffer. Lovingly."

"Fair point," Bel said, weaving his wicked fingers through hers. "But Asmodeus can—and will—carry her."

They stepped to the side to avoid a collision with a pair of well-dressed male souls who practically ran toward the bathrooms, sexual energy crackling between them.

Things in the bar had grown palpably more desperate than before they'd left. The trivia rounds seemed to be more of a background occurrence than the main focus, and there were more than a few empty chairs at previously full tables. Lily fought to smother her giggles with marginal success.

She lost the battle entirely when she spied her table.

The Fae woman was gone, her chair sitting at a haphazard angle. Muriel had a pair of men, not souls but Afterlife denizens of some kind, flirting with her at once, while Angel made eyes at a particularly pretty woman with flawless dark skin. Persephone was notably absent from her seat, which had been carefully tucked back in to the table.

Sariah, Aphrodite, and another woman from the Summerland were the only ones at their table paying any kind of attention to trivia. Sariah, apparently unbothered, seemed to have elevated ignoring her husband into an art form. Bel's team had, for the most part, clearly given up the ghost of focus as well.

"That's fifty bucks, big guy." Lily cackled, nodding to where Asmodeus sat with his elbows braced on the table, hands folded as if in prayer and pressed to his mouth as he stared at Sariah with such heat it was a wonder her dress hadn't simply caught on fire.

Bel scoffed. "Does that look like a man who is mentally present in any capacity?"

"He might be thinking with his other head, but he is still, technically, here."

"In lieu of fifty bucks, how about I take you on a date?"

"Deal. But only if there's food involved at some point."

"Princess." Bel pressed a hand to his chest in affront. "I'm a growing boy, of course there's going to be food at some point."

Lily grinned at him just as Lucifer glanced their way and did a double take, reaching over to smack Gregorith's arm in excitement.

"Don't look now, but I think Lucifer just realized we were naughty in the bathroom." She nodded at them. Where Lucifer seemed almost childish with glee, Gregorith remained reserved, a raised eyebrow his only outward reaction.

"*Naughty* is such a strong word," Bel said smugly, flexing his hand at his side. "We were perfectly polite. You even said please—more than once, if I remember right."

Her cheeks flamed. She swatted him as he laughed.

She loved that laugh.

He held out his fist. "Stride of pride, princess."

"Damn right." She bumped his fist with her own and smacked his ass for good measure. "Go get 'em, champ."

She returned to her table to catcalls and whistles, dropping into a curtsy and raising a manicured middle finger.

Aphrodite smirked, propping her chin on a hand. "He didn't even mess up your hair. If you didn't look so blushy and satisfied, I'd be disappointed for you."

"As it is, I'd say that's a skill," Angel put in, glancing away from the woman who was nearly on her lap.

"He's very courteous," Lily murmured into her drink, blush spreading to her ears. *This was about you, princess. For you.*

"That," Sariah said cheerfully, "is the face of someone who is going to be absolutely useless for the last round of trivia."

"Unless it's about sex," Aphrodite said.

"If it's about sex, then someone needs to go find Persephone. Something tells me she's getting an education right now."

Lily swirled her glass. "Probably more of a refresher course."

"Never"—Aphrodite leaned across the table—"underestimate an immortal's creativity. Eternity presents a good opportunity to try lots of new things. And get shockingly flexible."

"Speak for yourself. I was flexible. Once. Now I'm pregnant with the child of a walking beefcake, which is great, but said child is currently kicking me in the ribs," Sariah said, pressing a hand to her side and shifting to a more comfortable position.

"And your point is?" Aphrodite asked.

"Downward facing dog got me into this, but downward facing dog is not going to get me out of it. Save yourselves. Screw fitness. Eat cake. Multitask and eat cake off of your partner, especially if you don't want to worry about dishes."

"Now feels like a great time to mention the many perks of being a lesbian," Angel said.

"Eating cake off of your husband is probably just a different road to the same result," Lily pointed out.

"True," Sariah said, rubbing her side. "But at least there's cake. Now, shut up and focus, we are *not* going to lose at trivia."

They lost at trivia.

Unsurprisingly, the top three spots were swept up by groups of asexual beings and souls who had wisely teamed up with each other. Lily's team—which they'd brilliantly named just as the alcohol had kicked in—had done respectably well, all things considered.

Team PigBenis beat the guys' team, Something Equally Stupid, which was really all they cared about. Especially after several more rounds of drinks.

The first-place team was announced, followed by an en masse scraping of chairs and stools and a collective burst of movement as people rushed to end an evening of teasing.

Asmodeus simply appeared by their table, picked up a smug Sariah with extreme care, twisted away, and disappeared through the crowd. Lily hadn't even seen him leave his table. He'd just been a blue-gray blur.

Aphrodite winked at Lily, demurely finishing her drink before she stood and spent an inordinate amount of time adjusting her dress just so, all while Hephaestus hovered patiently behind her. Not rushing, not saying a word, just watching her with reverence and enough heat to forge something. The moment she smiled at him and offered her hand, he towed her away with a speed belied by the presence of his cane. Angel winked at Lily and turned her full attention to the woman kissing down her pink neck.

Lily went to throw back the remnants of her bright blue drink, but paused to watch, impressed, as a four-armed, green-skinned being pushed a male soul wearing a three-piece tweed suit backward onto a table, one hand tugging his shirt out of his pants.

A wall of heat pressed against her back a moment before Bel's palms came to rest on the table on either side of her.

"This was about when I bowed out last time. Orgies aren't really my thing," he rumbled.

She downed her drink, carefully setting the empty glass on the table and tilting her head back to look up at him, ignoring the way the world spun slightly. "But you've tried it?"

He shrugged, dipping down to kiss her chin. "Once, barely into my time in the army. I like all genders and most positions, but it turns out I'm not fond of sharing. You?"

"I got propositioned by a couple once. They were a part of a swingers' club and old enough to be my parents. I turned them down, then spent a month reevaluating my entire life, because apparently, I was the kind of person creepy old swingers wanted at their parties."

"*Or* you were just hot, and they had eyes and no boundaries. How old were you?"

"Twenty-three. And I was at work too. Orgies are intriguing in theory, but frankly they seem like a lot of work. If I wanted to disappoint multiple people at once I would have talked about my reading habits at Thanksgiving."

Someone started moaning behind them.

They looked at each other.

"Time to go?" she asked.

"Time to go," he confirmed, making room for her to get up.

The Hallway was full of chatter, the asexual folks and the less desperate catching up with each other and laughing. Lily slid her arm around Bel's waist, careful not to brush his wings, hugging him as they walked. His arm was a pleasant weight around her shoulders, fingers tracing idle patterns on her upper arm.

Lucifer stood apart from the crowd, deep in conversation with an unfamiliar woman, their deadly serious expressions completely at odds with the jovial atmosphere of the night. Lily frowned and slowed, the haze of the alcohol lifting slightly.

Bel squeezed her shoulders. She met his eyes.

"Keep walking." He shook his head. "It's nothing for tonight."

Her chest tightened as a tendril of anxiety wormed in, but she nodded and turned her head forward, focusing on not falling in her heels. They'd seemed like such a fantastic idea sober. And while slightly drunk in the bathroom with Bel.

I regret nothing.

Firmly drunk and walking home, however . . . her feet didn't hurt, but the heels might not have been the best idea.

"Speaking of your reading habits," Bel said with a grin, his eyes glassy but coherent enough. "I must say, I've been taking notes."

"On which one? Is it the tail one?"

His mouth dropped open. "There's a *tail one*?"

"No . . ."

"You're a terrible liar."

"I'm a fucking fantastic liar. I'm just slightly drunk."

"Pounding the Fuzzy Navels, were we?"

"I don't like that mental image. And no, I didn't want to tempt you beyond reason."

"You existing is pretty damn tempting, princess."

"And yet," she said, squeezing him a little, "you wouldn't let me return the favor. Like a chivalrous asshole."

He chuckled.

"I've been thinking about it," she informed him. "I've been making plans."

"Oh?"

"Yep. Involving your cock and my mouth."

He choked and missed a step.

A woman who was even drunker than Lily pointed at her with enthusiasm. "*Yes!* Get it, girl!"

"I'm trying!" Lily said, then blinked. "I like your dress."

"I like *your* dress." The woman beamed. Her partner shook her head, smothering her laughter as she tried to tug the woman away. "We're friends now!" the woman called.

"Yeah we are!" Lily grinned, looking up at Bel. "See, she knows what's up."

Bel muttered something under his breath about something being up, a little smile on his face.

The Hallway grew quieter as they walked. Most realms operated on a fairly similar schedule, and it was generally night within them. Lily spied a certain arch and tightened her grip on Bel.

"What's wrong?" he asked, halting.

Lily opened her mouth, then closed it again, hating the slimy, dark sensation oozing over her skin, through her insides. Her chest had been so peaceful and full lately that the sudden hollowness was all the more jarring.

"Lily?" he asked gently, moving to see her face more clearly.

"Have you ever been to Heaven?" she asked, tearing her eyes away from the gleaming, hideous perfection of the arch and focusing on his handsome face.

"A few times. The souls there are nice, but a demon in Heaven can be a little jarring for even the nicest people, yeah?"

"That's bullshit," she muttered.

"True. I also don't like that much gold. I'm clearly more of a make-it-black kind of guy."

"You're trying to cheer me up."

"Yep. Is it working? Or do I need to start removing clothes?"

She squinted at him. "Yours or mine?"

"I haven't decided yet. Your shoes look uncomfortable. Incredibly sexy, but uncomfortable. However, I have more clothes on, so we have more to work with there."

"Mm." She glanced over his shoulder to the arch and sighed. "Seeing the arch to Heaven makes me feel small. Wrong. Like I'm this walking sinful flaw, and it's only a matter of time before someone notices. Which I know is bullshit, but I can't stop feeling that way. I hate it."

Bel nodded slowly, gazing down the Hallway while he seemed to consider his words. "You're not alone in that. It's shitty, but I've heard some souls talk about feeling the same way. That thinking, what they teach you, is wrong. You know that, and I know you know that, but sometimes it helps to have a reminder. You created and run the Hellp Desk in *Hell*. No one, not even Heaven or God or the Universe itself, gets to make you feel inferior, because you're not."

Lily wished her head wasn't so fuzzy. She rested her hands on his hips, toying with the embroidered edge of his tunic, savoring the solid strength beneath her palms. "You're making it very difficult to remember that I'm not supposed to have my way with you at the moment."

He arched his scarred eyebrow, a deliciously cocky smirk settling on his lips. "Princess, I think you're a horny drunk."

"Well, yes, but you're not helping. I keep thinking about what happened in the bathroom and my plans and you're *right here*. See my problem?"

He groaned, stepping a little closer. "Let's not talk about what happened in the bathroom, or your plans. If we do, I'm going to embarrass myself."

"You could embarrass yourself into my—"

He clapped his hand over her mouth with a laugh. "Let's get you home, Lils."

She shot a sour glare at the gleaming arch as they passed, then refocused on other plans that, sadly, did not include Bel naked.

"I have a proposition for you," Bel rumbled a few moments later.

"Go on."

"As much as I would love to explore other things tonight, I don't think we should. We're both drunk, and in no position to decide anything that important. So. We're not having sex. Yeah?"

"Yeah." She definitely wasn't pouting.

"However, I want to be with you. I don't want to just drop you off at Paradise. Would you like to stay with me? Fair's fair. I've seen your home, you are more than welcome to come see mine. Or we can stay at your Paradise. Or I can take you home. Whatever you want, obviously. But you're invited. To my home, I mean."

Lily hid her little grin. He was . . . rambling. It was cute.

"I'd love to see your home. And while we agree, no more hanky-panky tonight, making out can be really fun. I wouldn't be mad about making out like teenagers with you."

"Deal," Bel answered quickly. "Want me to sneak you in a side door so we get the full teenage experience?"

"How about we strut in like adults and then go full tonsil hockey?"

"Never call it that again. But yes."

32

SECOND BREAKFAST

Bel

Bel wondered if Lily had felt as nervous when she'd shown him her home. Just because a woman read about palaces and mansions didn't mean she'd actually *like* a palace.

Would she?

It had never mattered if previous partners had cared for it or not, because he'd liked them, but it just hadn't been the same.

Lily *saw* things.

His home stood in stark contrast to hers. They stood on the short walkway, staring up at the home he'd spent his entire life in. He looked at it and saw tall black walls, sweeping lines of architecture, and myriad tall windows lit up from within, offering peeks of the interior. Windows he'd snuck out of. Walls he'd bounced a ball off of in play. Twists and spires on the roof he'd used as a challenge course for flying.

What did she think of the carefully tended gardens? The flowers and vines shining with their own bioluminescence in an array of colors? The trickling creek of lava bubbling out of the ground and cutting a swath through the lawn, a shimmer of heat rippling in the air above it?

Would she think it ostentatious? Empty? Silly? Beautiful?

He braced for a less than positive expression—he'd seen them before—and turned to her.

She had a hand pressed to her chest, pretty nail polish reflecting the light, staring at the house in wonder.

He loved looking at her. Sure, she was stunning with the dress and makeup and whatever else, but more than that, *she* was radiant.

"Your house is *amazing*," she breathed. "Bel, you live in a beautiful fucking *palace*! Does it have a library?"

"Two, actually. A boring one in my office and another one on the main floor. The books aren't as interesting as yours though."

She glanced at him, a flicker of vulnerability, uncertainty in those eyes.

"I love your library," Bel told her. "And I am genuinely enjoying those books. I'd like to borrow more. After I've read the tail one, that is."

"If you need tail inspiration, big guy, I've got some books that would blow your mind. Stop trying to distract me." She tugged him forward, her smile bright in the dimness. "Show me everything."

So he did.

The foyer, with its pair of sweeping stairs and the beautiful, carved banisters. The library that she cooed over, running her fingers over the spines of the books, starting a small stack of ones that had more worn covers than the rest, clever girl. The small ballroom that he admittedly used for training purposes, the racks of weapons and weights and mats and other training paraphernalia a harsh contrast to the elaborately carved and painted walls and ceiling. The living room with its comfortable couches and chairs and a sweeping view of their level of Hell, the homes sparser in their area, the gardens more expansive. His father had liked the little bit of privacy, the separation, when he'd had the place built long before Bel had been born.

Bel guided her down the upper corridor to his wing of the house, explaining the entire time that he'd always thought it was ridiculous that he had an entire wing of the house to himself, but that he'd found it hilariously ironic when he was younger, given the wings on his back.

He opened one of the double doors and followed her inside his bedroom. He'd only gotten a glimpse of hers through the open door as he'd followed Sharkie to Lily's library, and he knew that while hers was a study of dusky purples and grays and blacks, elegant and cozy and feminine, his was much less . . . colorful.

Black walls rose twice the height of normal rooms, swirling subtle murals in glimmering gunmetal gray painted on certain sections. The shining mural of stars painted on the ceiling was a glimpse of the mortal night sky, thousands of years ago. Bel had never seen it, but the artist that his father had commissioned had painted it with such skill that, half the time, Bel was convinced that he lay under the open sky. The dark hardwood floor was broken up by a large gray rug that sat under his admittedly oversized bed. He'd spent years, decades, of his life sleeping in whatever tent or shack or shelter he could, wings clamped tight to his back in an exercise of basic, necessary rest. He liked the room to stretch out his wings and limbs, to luxuriate in sleep and rest his soul, as well as his body.

Lily grabbed his arm for balance, lifting one foot to work off her shoe. It clattered to the floor, and she sighed in relief before going for the second one.

"In the mortal world, those would have killed my feet before I'd even made it to the pub. I'd call this a success." Barefoot, she wrapped her arms around his waist and kissed his collarbone. "Your home is beautiful, Bel. I love it."

He didn't think he'd ever get tired of holding her, of feeling her body pressed against his or smelling her sweet scent. Being around Lily eased something in him. Holding her was like settling his feet on the ground after a long flight.

Relief.

Peace.

He tipped her face up, kissing her long and slow. She arched into him, lips soft and glorious.

He rested his forehead against hers, savoring the quiet moment every bit as much as he'd savored the events of the bathroom, a memory that had lust burning through his veins and tingling over his fingers.

"Pajamas, then canoodling?" he asked. She wasn't the only one with alternative terminology.

She laughed. "Canoodling confirmed. Can I borrow a T-shirt?"

Lily

Lily woke up warm, verging on too warm, and other than a faint headache, completely fine. She'd never get tired of the no-hangover development.

Paradise, baby. It has its perks.

She nuzzled closer to Bel, more than willing to deal with a little extra heat. He slept on his back, holding her close with one arm, her head resting on his shoulder. Her leg was thrown over both of his, his tail curled possessively around her calf.

She sensed a pattern there.

The night before, when a pair of her underwear had appeared on Bel's bed, he'd looked around the room as if it had a viper in it.

"Tell me this is a Paradise thing," he'd said, side-eyeing the door to his closet. "Because Carl is fine—great even—but I don't think I can deal with *this* house getting a personality too. It's seen too much."

"Please don't call my house Carl. I don't want to live in a *Carl*. I'll have to ask around, but maybe this is one of those 'soul who went to Paradise' perks?"

"Let's go with that."

She'd changed into her magic new underwear and one of his old band shirts, so oversized on her that it fell to mid-thigh, and laughed at the slits in the back that they'd both forgotten about. Then she'd used the second sink in his bathroom to wash off her makeup while he'd stood in his boxers and brushed his teeth, taking special care to check his fangs. It had been so casually domestic that she felt like they done it before, had been doing it for years. He'd made a face at her in the mirror while he'd brushed his hair. She'd crossed her eyes at him over a mouthful of toothpaste.

They'd crawled into bed and snuggled together under the glowing mural of stars, whispering like little kids about their days, asking random questions and giving random answers, reveling in the simple and powerful intimacy of just being together. A Paradise of its own.

To her delight, a swirling, vaguely geometric tattoo peeked out of the top of his boxers and crept down his right thigh. She'd discovered a primal fascination with his bare torso, the solid slabs of muscle with enough padding to fuel his body for hours of combat. She hadn't let herself explore it beyond gentle, sweeping caresses.

She opened her eyes and squinted at the red-gold light spilling into the room as Hell's day dawned.

Odd that the sheets were cooler and smoother by her legs, whereas from roughly her waist up, they were velvety and almost scorchingly warm, like suede left out in the sun.

Bel was laying on his back . . .

Fuck!

She eased upward, trying not to put too much pressure on Bel's chest with her hand, and looked down. Sure enough, his wings were splayed half open, draping over the extra-wide bed. And she'd been *laying* on one of them. She supposed that, if he'd been in pain, he would have woken up, but still. Careful not to crush his tail, she slid her leg fully over him, sitting up and adjusting herself to straddle his hips, taking pressure off his wing.

Gods, he looked like a painting.

Against silky black sheets, his form was perfectly delineated. The power evident in his heavy pectorals and faintly ridged abdomen marked him unmistakably as a warrior. A line of crisp black hair trailed down from his navel to disappear into his boxers, the waistband of which rode dangerously low on his hips. She licked her lips, itching to trace it. His nipples were tight and flat, a much deeper shade of purple-gray than the rest of his body, the thin line of a scar arcing dangerously near one.

If mortal artists had ever painted him, it would have caused a riot. Churches would have protested the image of a hot-as-fuck demon prince, though the internet would have gone buck wild for it.

Beyond his obvious beauty, it was his scars that caught her eye. They were scattered over his body—little ones, bigger ones, a couple of round ones that looked like puncture wounds from a gun or an arrow, though for some reason she suspected the latter. Each mark a reminder of how hard he had fought to protect what he cared for. His ashy black wings, paler near the thin edges, also bore faint evidence of old injuries. A fresher-looking patch of raised membrane made something in her chest twist.

Oh, Bel.

He looked so different from when he'd stayed at her house. The bone-deep exhaustion of that night was gone, allowing her to see the fine details of his face more clearly. His mouth had a slight natural downturn to it when he was completely relaxed, making him look rather stern. It was so at odds with his usual cheerful expression that she reached out and brushed her thumb over the corner of his mouth, wanting to see it twitch up in one of his smiles.

Bel's smile could power entire cities if someone ever figured out how to hook it up to a wattage thing.

Had she ever told him that?

Lily's smile faded. She hadn't, had she?

And yet how many times had Bel pulled her out of some emotional death spiral? How many times had he said the right thing to make her feel not so alone? To make her feel beautiful and precious?

She didn't know if she'd ever made him feel the same.

She wanted to. Someone should. Bel deserved to feel as wonderful as he made everyone else feel. He deserved the kind of peace and support that his mere presence gave her. She was determined to give it to him.

He just needed to wake up first.

She smoothed her hands over his chest and up his neck, cradling his angular jaw and leaning forward to kiss him with as much tenderness as she could manage. He inhaled slowly, his hands coming to rest on her thighs where they hugged his waist. She sat back as his eyes opened, the haze of sleep clearing away like mist in the sun.

"Good morning," he rasped, his already deep voice somehow impossibly deeper.

"Good morning." She smiled, catching one of his hands with her own and tangling their fingers together. "I realized something."

Bel blinked at her, seeming to still be in the process of orienting himself. "Oh?"

"Yeah, 'oh.' I've known that you are wonderful for a while now, and—"

"Lily," Bel said, a dark blush staining the tips of his pointed ears.

"Bel. Affectionately, shut up. I experienced a whole coherent thought before I had coffee, and you're going to let me say this. Please."

The last vestiges of sleep evaporated in an instant. A little smile played on his mouth, and his other hand left her thigh to press palm to palm with hers, fingers lacing together.

"Sorry. Keep going, princess."

"Thank you," she said primly, adjusting herself slightly. "I have known you are wonderful for a while now. From the beginning, frankly. But I realized that, for all the kindness and wisdom and support you have given me, I don't think I have ever once returned that favor. And if I have, it wasn't adequate."

Bel opened his mouth.

Lily squeezed his hands.

Bel shut his mouth.

"You," she said softly, "are many things. Patient. Kind. Steady. Strong, and not just because of your sexy muscles."

He brightened a little.

"I don't think I'm quite as gifted with words of wisdom and encouragement as you are, but I'm going to give it my best shot. I know, at some point, for some reason, in some way, you were left behind." He went utterly still beneath her, but she continued. "It's not your fault. Whoever and whatever it was, it wasn't your fault. For what it's worth, I'm proud of you. Proud of you as a general. Proud of you as a prince. Proud of *you*. That's not empty bullshit praise. I see you. I don't know all of you yet, but I know you, and I see you."

He didn't seem to be breathing. She untangled their hands, reaching up to cup his face. He stared at her with wide, unblinking eyes in wonder or horror or maybe both. The scattered strands of his hair were delicate against her fingertips, his cheeks nearly scorchingly hot.

"Bel, you are enough. You make existence better, just by being you." She swallowed. "And nothing about you feels temporary."

If she'd had a heartbeat, it would have been racing a mile a minute.

She'd never been so vulnerable in her existence, never taken a chance on sharing how she really felt with anyone.

So, she did the only thing left to do.

She kissed him. Hard.

His hands landed on her hips and gripped firmly, but not enough to hurt.

She broke away from his eager mouth, trailing kisses along his jaw, down his neck, over his thundering pulse. She lifted her head, emotions and lust swirling into a heady mix as she ghosted her lips over his, gripping his jaw with one hand. His glittering gray eyes were fever bright, the striations of silver gleaming as if they'd been polished.

"I want—" She teased his lips again. "To do something for you."

She leaned back, and he surged up to chase her lips. She put a hand on his chest, pressing him back down to the mattress.

"And I want you to lay back and enjoy it. Let someone be generous to you for once." She kissed him again. "Please."

He peered at her, as if determining how much she meant it, and then gave a single short nod. But it was the intensity in his eyes that surprised her. Gone was the lighthearted goof. Here, he was pure focus, pure heat, pure passion.

But behind the intensity she could see . . . something. A glimmer of insecurity.

That was unacceptable.

"You." She pressed a quick kiss to his mouth. "Are." She kissed his clavicle. "More." A kiss to the center of his chest as she moved back, scraping her fingernail lightly over one nipple for good measure. "Than." She nipped at his lower abdomen, then soothed it with her lips. She tugged at the waistband of his boxers, and he lifted his hips just enough for her to work them down, revealing his heavy, solid length and upper thighs. "Enough." She breathed, pressing a final kiss to the rigid muscle of his upper thigh, over a tattooed line at the junction of his hip.

"Understand?" she asked, looking up the length of his body.

Something in his eyes shifted. The glimmer she'd seen had disappeared, and in its place was exactly what should be there: trust.

With a grin, Lily turned her attention to her prize.

He was large enough that, when they finally did cross that line, taking him would be a delicious stretch. Thick and uncut, the shaft was the same deep, dusky purple as his nipples, the fat head even darker and already beaded with pre-cum. She danced her fingers over his heavy balls, and he groaned what might have been her name or a prayer. Maybe both.

She licked her palm and finally, *finally* touched him. Under the hot, satiny skin, faint ridges rippled along his length. Delightedly resolving to give him a little shit about being a walking sex toy later, she worked him, learning what he liked for a few moments before giving in to temptation. She licked up him in a long stroke, his hands flying to the sheets as he moaned, every muscle in his torso standing out in sharp relief.

Lily grinned and did it again.

"Tell me what you like, big guy. This is for you," she murmured, kissing just above his neatly trimmed patch of hair before returning to her treat.

Hoping to make him feel even fractionally as good as he'd made her feel, she took his tip into her mouth with a groan of her own. He was thick, silky skin blazing hot against her tongue, the salty taste strong but not unpleasant. She listened to his groaned instructions, paid attention to his growls and gasps, discovering that when she flicked her tongue just so, he let out moans that she'd be hearing in her fantasies for the rest of eternity.

She needed more. She needed to *give* him more.

She worked him with her mouth and one hand, cupping his balls with the other, rolling them gently in her palm. She took him as deeply as she could, until her gag reflex threatened to make an appearance. The fact that her lips had nearly touched the hand she used to work him mollified her slightly. When she ran a finger down the center seam of his sac as she sucked him long and hard, he swore so colorfully she was surprised the paint didn't peel off the walls. He seemed to be fighting the urge to grip her hair, continually returning his fisted hands to the sheets.

A naughty idea drifted through her mind. Bel was panting, apparently on the razor's edge of ecstasy, and as tempting an idea as it was to hold him on that edge for a little longer, it wasn't the time. She slipped a finger behind his balls and stroked—

Bel came apart with her name on his lips. Lily swallowed him down greedily, swirling her tongue to make sure she hadn't missed a drop. She eased off him, licked her lips, and pressed a tender kiss to his thigh. Bel sat up and pulled her roughly up his body, taking her mouth in a searing kiss before she even knew what was happening.

No one had *ever* kissed her after she'd gone down on them. She'd had no compunctions about it, but most people apparently found it gross. Bel, bless him, did not. She looped her arms around his neck and kissed him back, tongue tangling with his, the faint scrape of his fangs against her lip sending a lick of heat straight to her aching clit.

When they finally broke apart, Bel rested his temple against hers, hands under her borrowed shirt, making sweeping strokes up her bare back. Lily panted, her own sex humming with a need that she ignored, understanding Bel's words from the bathroom perfectly.

For him. For him and about him.

But beyond that, she could sense that something had fundamentally changed between them. They could be vulnerable with each other. She trusted him, and he trusted her, but more than that, she trusted them together. She ran her fingers through his hair, along the back of his neck, over his shoulders. She loved touching him; it was self-soothing as much as it was to show care.

"I don't think we need to wait anymore," she murmured.

Bel shifted back enough to meet her eyes. "Are you sure?"

"Yeah," she said quietly, offering a gentle grin.

"Okay," he breathed, a soft, precious smile gracing his lips.

She remained straddled over his lap as they simply held and watched each other, tracing little patterns over each other's skin as the room brightened with the dawn.

Until his phone buzzed.

And buzzed.

He slumped, closing his eyes with a sigh.

Lily pressed a kiss to his temple. "I've got to pick up Sharkie anyway. She's probably adopted Cerberus by now."

Bel chuckled and lifted his head, seeming brighter, surer of himself. He traced his thumb over her lower lip. "At least he's house trained."

Lily rolled her eyes and made to scoot off of him, but his grip tightened.

"My family is having a picnic party next week. My mom, my siblings, their families, and probably a few cousins will show up. Would you and Sharkie like to come?"

"Of course." Lily settled back onto his lap. "We'd love to. Should we bring anything?"

"Cinnamon rolls." His eyes gleamed, that impish grin reappearing.

Lily laughed and finally climbed off his lap.

Bel kissed her cheek as she went, then slapped her ass. "Perfect. Now that's settled, want a quick breakfast?"

Lily shot him a sly look over her shoulder and slid off the bed. "I could go for second breakfast."

❦

33

BEING BIRDS

Lily

L ily sat at her desk and swirled her tea, frowning as a teenage demon scurried from the Universal Hallway stairs toward the elevators, obviously trying to look unsuspicious and, naturally, looking incredibly suspicious. She'd seen it happen half a dozen times over several weeks. It was never the same kid twice, and most of the time she barely noticed them outside of a passing observation that it was odd to see young demons near the gate. She'd asked several shifts about it, and none of them knew anything. A few had suggested that sneaking into the mortal world for a prank or bragging rights was a bit of a rite of passage for many young demons.

She turned her attention to the soul stepping calmly up to the Hellp Desk, a quick glance at the desk confirming the lack of a soul file.

Lily shot the soul, a man, an easy smile. "How can I help you?"

"Hey," the man said, ducking his head slightly. He appeared mid-thirties, casually dressed, with dark brown hair pushed haphazardly back and a neatly trimmed beard. "I'm from Heaven, and I was wondering if it would be possible to visit my dad? The folks at the gate said you could help with that."

"What's his name?" Lily asked, sliding her computer closer and clicking on the disarmingly cute icon of a cartoon flame with smiling anime eyes, floating horns, and a little pitchfork. No one had fessed up to designing it, but they all adored it. There was a running list of name nominations on the whiteboard in the break room. Sharkie had climbed up on a chair to painstakingly write *Tim* in her best penmanship. It had a hundred and three votes, at least six of which were from Bel. Nine were from her.

"Henry Jones?" The man chuckled dryly. "I'm sure that narrows it down a lot."

Lily laughed with him, and a few questions later—*when did he die, where was he from, any outstanding identifying features*—found his father. The program on the computer offered a small bit of the full soul file. Thankfully, it offered pertinent information in written form, instead of delivering it directly into her mind.

Henry had certainly earned his place in Hell, but that wasn't what interested her. What had her softening was the impressive amount of work the man had done to learn and improve, working up from Level Five. His son, whom he had hurt so badly, had never visited before.

"Looks like he's made it up to Level One," Lily said kindly.

Quiet hope shone on the man's face while Lily scribbled down Henry's information and handed over the sticky note—cat-shaped this time.

"Good luck," she said, meaning it with every fiber of her soul.

He smiled and took it with fingers that trembled slightly.

"You can take the elevator or the stairs through that hall. Just give that to one of the demons and they'll help you from there."

With a quick murmur of thanks, the man stepped away, leaving her alone at her desk.

It had been a blessedly quiet few days, a fact for which Lily was grateful. Most souls were fairly content to go where they'd been told without causing much fuss, and the ones who did foray over to the Hellp Desk hadn't been too disgusting or argumentative. Lily hadn't touched a weapon since the day of the trivia tournament. Well, she'd used the blade Bel had given her once, to retrieve a paper that had fluttered to the ground just out of reach.

She cradled her mug of tea in one hand, kicked her feet up on the desk, and reopened a book she'd taken from Bel's library. Sci-fi was fairly hit or miss in her estimation, but she could understand why this particular book had such a well-worn cover. She ran her finger over a fingertip-shaped smudge of something on the bottom corner of a page, imagining the disgruntled look he must've had when he realized he'd left a mark.

Her chest went a little achy. Trivia night had been perfection, and she regretted nothing. Not that night, nor the morning after. She kept wondering if it had all been a dream. Surely she couldn't have been *that* happy? She'd had dreams a bit like that before and been immediately pissed upon waking up that no one was actually holding her hand or letting her kiss their neck. It was surreal to have actual memories of those things, along with the promise of more.

Oh, so much more.

The only thing that had kept her from grinning like a jack-o'-lantern the entire day after had been the nonstop buzzing of his phone and the expression he'd had when she'd come back from the bathroom. She'd found him sitting on the edge of the bed in full General Mode, staring at the screen.

The responsibility he'd carried was almost palpable. Not crushing him, but weighting his every movement with purpose and care. He'd still smiled when she'd walked over, but the way he'd pulled her to stand between his legs so that he could wrap her in his arms and rest his face against her chest had told her everything.

Playtime was over.

He'd called her later and told her he would be out of contact for a while, but that he'd let her know as soon as he got back. She'd heard his smile when he told her to text him like normal.

"I like seeing all your texts when I get a chance. It's like a little diary of your thoughts. Even if I can't respond, it reminds me that, no matter what, you're still out there doing things, being badass and *having* a great ass."

She'd told him to be safe and that her ass was adequate at best.

That had been two days ago.

Sharkie, when Lily had picked her up from the sleepover, had tried to convince her to let Cerberus, who turned out to be the size of a small bus, come home with them. Despite "Cerby's" very good "sit" and fiercely wagging tail, Lily had had to put her foot down. After giving all three heads a good scratch behind the ears, of course.

Sharkie had been cheerful but quiet ever since. Something was brewing in that little body, and Lily had almost no idea what. It wasn't about not taking Cerberus home with them; she'd noticed the shift in Sharkie the moment she'd arrived in the Underworld to pick her up. She'd tried to subtly get it out of her with some leading questions, but Sharkie hadn't taken the bait. She'd gone to school and skipped up to the Hellp Desk after, all smiles and stories, had done her homework in the break room with the assistance of everyone inside, but looked a little too long at the fire as it crackled in the hearth at home, or spent too long curled up on the couch, slowly and methodically petting the cat before going to her room for the night.

Lily didn't know what to do.

Five chapters away from the end of the book, her heart was in her throat over fear for her favorite character, until the sound of running feet pulled her out of the reading haze. She grinned as Sharkie scampered up and crawled onto her desk with zero hesitation. Ever since she'd had the additional consistency of school, Sharkie's confidence had blossomed.

Sharkie's eyes were wide. "Were you alive before cell phones?"

Oof. "Way to make me feel old, kiddo. Yes."

"I thought you died young though?"

"Relatively young, I was thirty-four. I got my first cell phone in high school, but I didn't get my first smartphone, like this"—Lily pointed to the one on the desk—"until college."

"How did you *do* anything?"

"I mean, we had dial-up and house phones, so we weren't completely in the Stone Age, but it was definitely a different time. What brought this up?"

"We learned about the mortal tech boom in school today. I thought it was weird," Sharkie explained, but something in her tone caught Lily's ear. She sounded . . . older somehow. "If you didn't have a screen, how did you know if you dialed the wrong number?"

Sharkie didn't *look* different, but she had no idea what a soul maturing looked like. Would she literally grow each time, or was it in spurts? Lily resolved to do some more research.

"The wrong person picked up the phone, which I always felt bad about, but hey, it happened."

"Ew. That's weird. Can we go home?"

Lily tucked her book under her arm and shoved her phone in the side pocket of her leggings. "Sounds like a good idea to me. Any ideas for dinner?"

"Bisque."

Lily stopped and stared at her. "Bisque?"

"Is it good? Nuuri said her mom's bisque was the best, and then Rimmon said that his mom's bisque was the best, and they ended up fighting over it and having to sweep the hallway together."

"We can try to make bisque. But maybe we make toasted cheese sandwiches too, just in case. I'd hate to have a repeat of the time we tried to do gnocchi from scratch."

Sharkie made a face of disgust that Lily couldn't replicate if she tried. "At least it made really good glue for my diorama though."

Lily texted Bel about their bisque disaster and sent him a picture of the splatters that somehow had ended up near the ceiling, along with a picture of the magazine-worthy crab bisque that had appeared on the counter moments after The Eruption.

Princess: *I don't know if the picture conveys how smug the house is right now, but it's smug. I can feel it.*

She held her phone for a few extra moments, then reached for the washrag. The otherwise fastidious house seemed more than willing to let her clean up after her own catastrophe. *Smug.* Lily hoisted herself onto the counter, hunting spatters of what could loosely be called bisque.

Loosely Called Bisque would be a great trivia team name . . .

Rain had been heavy and constant since they'd gotten home, the lights of the village barely visible through the gray haze. Huge puddles formed in the garden. She'd cracked a window to let the achingly familiar smell wash through the house, and she sucked it into her lungs like a drug.

The winters on the Pacific Northwest coast had been cold and wet and gray, with windstorms that howled and pounded at the windows. She'd loved storms. Loved the way the earth smelled when it rained. She especially loved the cozy days spent inside with a warm drink and a heavy blanket.

She inhaled long and slow.

Happy.

She seemed to be uncovering a remarkable capacity to be *happy*.

It was nice.

Lily slid off the counter and threw the washcloth in the sink, peering into the living room.

Sharkie leaned over the back of the couch near the big windows, arms folded, chin resting on top of them, staring out at the pounding rain. Max, never one to be left out, had loafed himself nearby, drowsing peacefully. Lily knelt next to Sharkie, propping her own hands and chin on the back of the couch. Sharkie's face was uncharacteristically flat, her eyes looking almost as soul tired as when she'd arrived.

"What'cha thinking, kiddo?" Lily asked quietly.

Sharkie shrugged.

Lily waited. Sharkie's hood slumped off her head and she twitched slightly. Lily reached over and brought it up again, carefully tucking loose hair behind Sharkie's ear. She followed Sharkie's gaze to a cluster of birds bathing in one of the puddles.

"Do you think they're having fun?" Sharkie asked, without looking away from them.

Lily watched the birds for a moment, splashing and dunking themselves in the water before shaking out their feathers. They seemed to be having a grand old birdie time, like little kids splashing in puddles.

Ah ha.

"I think there's only one way to find out."

Sharkie frowned at her. "How?"

"We should try it ourselves."

"But we can't do that," Sharkie insisted so quickly that Lily *knew* she'd heard it somewhere. Probably from her foster monster. The bitch.

"Why not?"

Sharkie hesitated, brows furrowed but eyes starting to get that glimmer of interest in them. *Come on, bug, play with me. Just* play.

"Because," Sharkie said.

"Says who?"

Sharkie looked out the window, a flash of excitement immediately followed by worry. She bit her lip and looked back at Lily, holding out her pinkie finger.

Lily took it and winked. "Come on, birdie, it's bath time!"

She pushed off the couch and headed for the door, bending down to pull off her fuzzy socks as she went. There was no reason to change out of her black sleep shorts and loose tank top, but she did pull the clip out of her hair and let it tumble over her shoulders.

"Do we need shoes?" Sharkie fretted as Lily pulled the large round door open, letting in a wash of damp air and the dull roar of the rain.

"Nope, not unless you want them. We're gonna go be birds, so if you don't want to be a bird in the rain with something, I'd leave it inside."

Sharkie hesitated for a moment, then unbuttoned her onesie. She wiggled free and carefully draped it on the nearby bench, standing uncertainly in her leggings and blue-striped shirt. Lily offered her hand, and Sharkie gripped it with a surprising amount of strength.

"On three?" Lily asked.

Sharkie nodded, the vulnerability fading slightly as she shifted from foot to foot, watching the rain come down in sheets.

"One," Lily started, squeezing Sharkie's hand.

"Two," they said together. "Three!"

They ran out into the dumping rain, immediately soaked to the skin.

Lily laughed, tipping her head back, then smiled down at Sharkie, who grinned back with bright, unburdened eyes. Lily let go of her hand, throwing her arms wide, spinning in a circle, kicking her toes through the grass and sending an arc of silvery droplets through the air. Sharkie's giggle was one of the most wonderful things Lily had ever heard.

Sharkie stomped into the nearest puddle, shrieking as a spray of mud dotted her face. Then she did it again. Lily took a flying leap into the nearest puddle but messed up the landing, her feet sliding out from under her. The soft ground squelched as she landed flat on her back, water flying in the air and mud oozing between her fingers.

Sharkie *cackled*, standing doubled over in the puddle, hair dark with water and plastered to the sides of her face, howling with laughter. Lily flopped onto her stomach and perched her chin on her hands, smearing mud all over her jaw. She grinned up at Sharkie and kicked her feet in the air behind her just for the hell of it.

Little hands seized one of her wrists, tugging her up. "Come on!"

They played together in the rain. Sometimes splashing in puddles, sometimes kicking water at each other, sometimes seeing how many times they could spin before they fell over laughing.

Lily pretended to chase Sharkie, sliding more than running, then turned and slopped away as chaser became the chased.

They lay side by side, mud soaking into their backs, staring up into the rain and making shapes with their fingers against the gray backdrop of the sky.

Sharkie jumped onto Lily's back with a triumphant howl, while Lily ran and spun them around the front garden in a victory lap.

Eventually, they staggered inside, giggling, soaked down to their bones and covered in mud, hair in snarls and clumps. Lily had shaken like a dog—or tried to anyway. Sharkie had followed suit, then peered down at herself and wrinkled her nose, which set Lily off on another round of laughter that Sharkie joined in on.

They separated to shower in their respective bathrooms and put on clean clothes. By the time Sharkie emerged in a set of polka dot pajamas, Lily was waiting with two mugs of cocoa and marshmallows. The house had already cleaned up all the mud and water they'd tracked in, so she'd dragged a few cushions into the entryway and plopped them in front of the wide-open door, along with a heap of blankets. She and Sharkie sat side by side, wrapped in blankets, sipping their cocoa in silence and watching the torrential rain as the sky grew dark, Max curled between them.

"Lily, I don't think I make a very good bird. I didn't get very clean."

Lily sipped her cocoa. "Maybe not. But you make a very good *you* though. And I think I make a very good me."

Sharkie rearranged Max, scooted closer, and rested her head against Lily's arm with a sigh that seemed to come from her toes. "I like you and me."

Lily wrapped her arm around her and kissed the top of her head. "I like you and me too."

"Lily?"

The tremulous little whisper had Lily's eyes snapping open, immediately at full consciousness. She sat up, taking in the brightly moonlit room, thankful that she was still wearing the T-shirt and underwear she'd put on earlier, having been too tired to strip naked for bed, as usual.

"What's up, bug?" She didn't bother asking if Sharkie was okay. Clearly, she wasn't, or she wouldn't be out of her sanctuary before the sun was up and the world felt safer to her.

Sharkie stood a few feet away from the bed, hunched in on herself, as if braced for a blow, arms wrapped firmly around a stuffed shark that was half her size. She sniffled, crawling up into Lily's lap without letting go of the shark, and buried her face in Lily's chest.

Lily wrapped her up in her arms, smoothing down her messy hair, and dropped a kiss on the top of her head, murmuring, "I've got you, bug. What's going on?"

Her little muscles seemed strung tighter than piano wire. Every fiber of Lily's being screamed that she *protect, comfort, make the monsters go away*, but she simply held the terrified child—*her* terrified child— offering what comfort she could and waiting. Lily had wondered, even after the joy of playing in the rain, what else was brewing in that little head. There'd been a residual tension in Sharkie as they'd gotten ready for bed, like she'd been ticking closer and closer to something.

Minutes went by. Then—

"Why didn't my mom love me enough to stay?"

Barely audible. A lifetime of pain in those words.

Lily's soul ached.

She closed her eyes and held her girl tighter. Ignoring the way her nose stung and swallowing hard to clear the lump in her throat, she smoothed Sharkie's hair.

"Sharkie—"

"At the sleepover," Sharkie said in a rush, as if a dam had broken and all her pain was flooding out, "everyone had moms and dads who loved them, moms and dads who were *nice* to them. They didn't worry that their moms and dads wouldn't come pick them up. And I knew you would, but . . . but I still wondered. You're not my mom, so I wasn't sure, but you're *not* my mom, so I thought maybe that's why you'd come back. But I wasn't sure. Why . . ." Her little sob made Lily's tears finally spill over. "Why am I so easy to leave behind? Why am I so easy to hurt? Why does no one love *me*?" She broke, clutching the shark and crying into Lily's neck.

All Lily could do was rock her back and forth. Hold her and rock her, waiting for her shattered sobs to subside. Lily fought the tide of her own emotions, knowing that Sharkie, sharp, empathetic, big-hearted Sharkie, would worry if she saw Lily weep too hard for her. Sharkie had worked her way into Lily's heart from day one, but with every passing day, she grew more deeply *hers*.

When Sharkie's crying had lessened enough for there to be more sniffles than outright sobs, Lily lifted her head and wiped at her wet cheeks with one hand, before offering her pinkie finger to Sharkie.

A sacred, unbreakable promise.

Sharkie gripped it with her whole shaking hand.

Lily drew her face up so that she could look her in the eye. Sharkie's breath hiccuped a bit, but she started matching Lily's deep, even breaths.

"You are lovable," Lily said gently but firmly. "You *are* lovable. You always have been, and you always will be inherently—that means 'naturally'—easy to love. Despite what happened to you in your mortal life, you are *not* easy to hurt. You are *not* easy to leave behind."

Lily fought to keep her voice even. "The people who hurt you were monsters, and you had more than your fair share of them in your life. They hurt you because you were there, not because of who you are or anything you did. Their evil was not your fault. Their actions were not your fault. You deserved a loving, safe, happy home, and the fact that you didn't get that is a crime. It's not fair, at all, but it wasn't because of *you*. As for your mother . . ."

Sharkie twitched.

Lily felt the echoes of her file in her soul. *A battered shark mobile, hung over a crib with care. A woman's smile filled with love and magic and wonder . . . a smile at war with the worn lines of her face, the world-weariness in her eyes. The shattered grief in the woman's wail as her baby was taken from her.*

"Your mother loved you as best as she could. From what I understand, she had her own monsters to fight. I don't think life had been very kind to her either. She had no idea what was going to happen to you in the system; she had no way of knowing. Maybe her life was so painful and scary that she thought you would have a shot at a better life if you weren't with her.

"I never had kids in any of my lifetimes, even though I wanted them. But if I'd ever had a child, I would have wanted them to be like you. Brave enough to bite a warrior in Valhalla. Kind enough to make sure everyone has a cinnamon roll, even if it means walking through a line of souls. Curious enough to try absolutely anything or go anywhere—even if it's a realm that most people find scary—and find the wonder in it. You are so fantastically, wonderfully, entirely *you*, and it is *amazing*. You are easy to love, and worthy of joy and protection."

Lily placed her free hand over Sharkie's, the one wrapped around her pinkie. "I might not be your biological mom, but, if you'll let me, I will love you as if you were my own child. I'll always pick you up from the sleepovers. I'll always hold you when you cry, and make you cocoa, and ask about your day. I'll have to set boundaries and enforce them sometimes, but I won't ever hurt you on purpose. I'll be here for you until you don't need me anymore."

Sharkie took a deep, shuddering breath. "What if I always need you?"

Lily smiled softly. "There's a part of us that always needs our moms, I think. But good moms help us be ready for life when they can't be in it. I will try—I *promise*," she corrected. "I promise to try and be that for you."

Sharkie squeezed her pinkie one last time, then let go. Lily let her hands fall as Sharkie sniffed, rubbing her forearm over her wet face, and then hugged Lily so tightly that she was glad she didn't need to breathe.

Lily hugged her back, feeling the tension ease out of her little body. Not entirely, but enough.

"Okay," Sharkie said into Lily's shoulder.

Lily gave her a little squeeze. "Okay."

They hugged each other for a long time. Max eventually made an appearance, trotting across the bed to chirp and nuzzle at Sharkie, who patted vaguely in his direction. He obligingly placed himself within the pat zone. A few minutes later, Sharkie sat up and scrubbed at her face with one hand, until Lily gently used a corner of the sheet to clear away the snot and tears.

Sharkie looked at her with cautiously bright eyes. "So, we can be a family?"

Lily smiled. "We *are* a family. Families aren't just a mom and a dad and kids. They can look a lot of different ways."

"Is the 'mom, dad, kid,' thing one of those stupid rules?"

"Yeah, a bit. 'Family' can be a pretty broad description."

Sharkie petted Max for a moment. "Can Bel be in our family too? 'Cause you're dating him and he's nice?" Before Lily could respond, Sharkie added, "And Luci! Luci is really, really nice and helps me to feel brave and promised to get me an actual shark someday."

Making a mental note to chat with Lucifer at some point—*seriously what the fuck, Lucifer, it better be a very cuddly Afterlife shark that is utterly harmless to souls*—Lily chuckled.

"Bel and Luci are our family too."

Sharkie nodded, relaxing further. "I like our family."

The warm, fuzzy, full feeling in Lily's chest was back. "Me too."

Sharkie crawled toward the middle of the bed and wiggled under the covers, Max following to perch against her side. Lily was momentarily stunned by the display of trust. Sharkie had never fallen asleep outside of the safety of her room before, not even for a nap. Pushing her shock aside, she folded the sheet to avoid the tearstained spot and lay down, rolling over to scratch behind Max's ears, then gently boop Sharkie's nose with the tip of her finger. Sharkie scrunched up her nose and giggled.

Family.

Lily's eyelids were heavy, but she stayed awake until Sharkie's breathing evened out, and even Max slept. Pieces were clicking into place. Slowly, steadily, the ugly, cold hollowness of her chest was fading, replaced bit by bit with warmth and light and understanding. By love.

I have my own family, and I'm not letting fear compromise who I am anymore.

She drifted off to sleep with a smile on her face.

34

FINDING BEAUTY

Bel

Bel wiped the mud and sweat off his face with a marginally clean rag, pacing around the tent they'd set up as a command post. The ragged hole the size of a fist that had been punched through his left wing throbbed, tendrils of fire shooting through his nervous system and exacerbating his foul mood.

Nine dead.

Unacceptable.

This was supposed to be a simple watch rotation. A simple line of defense to reiterate the point they'd made last time and deter the other Universe from any more violent bullshit. He was supposed to bring all his soldiers home a bit scuffed at *worst*, not in a fucking shroud.

He'd asked for their names. Maphias. Ingara. Dagon. Behe. Rihman. Uuli. Kikio. Ferneth. Jonereth.

Nine people gone. Nine families devastated. Children would grow up without a parent. Parents would bury their children. Lovers and partners would never again feel their warmth, hear their laughter, turn to them on a bad day.

All because one greedy fucking Universe couldn't take no for an answer and leave their Universe the fuck alone.

Bel closed his eyes, grief and rage crashing through him. It hadn't just been armed exploratory forces this time. It had been a planned attack, and they hadn't been prepared for the intensity of it.

"Sir, please, let me take care of your wing," a healer said firmly. Bel opened his eyes, and the healer pointed to a chair near the other commanders in the tent. Asmodeus had a bloody nose and a pissy expression but was otherwise fine. Morrigan had been outmaneuvered—a rarity—and was furious enough to make the air shake. One of her commanders was wisely giving her a bit of extra room. Bel didn't blame him. A deity in a mood was . . . unpleasant. Depending on the deity, the sensations ranged from static to sandpaper to oil to heat to cold and everything in between. Morrigan's wrath made Bel's teeth and skin ache, like the sound of nails being drawn over a chalkboard made manifest.

Knowing that his mother would give a lecture for the ages if she heard that one of her offspring gave a healer grief, Bel sat as directed and spread his wing, focusing on anything other than that particular part of his body as they went to work.

"I'm sorry," Asmodeus rasped, his voice uncharacteristically grave. "We didn't know about the gegony until it was on you."

Bel took the offered mug of water and downed half of it, grimacing as his wing *screeched* with pain, the fine muscles fighting his efforts to hold still.

Gegony. He saw them in his nightmares sometimes, had ever since his first brief encounter with them as a soldier all those years ago. Towering beasts with too-long limbs, razor-sharp claws, a twisted head set on a stubby, nearly nonexistent neck, with a maw that split their head vertically and almost completely in half. Fast, strong, vicious in the extreme, and damn near unstoppable. Their wet, shrieking roar sounded like babies wailing and flesh ripping, the latter a sound that had become painfully familiar thanks to their presence for a brief series of previous battles over some issue with an ambassador.

They'd killed it. Barely. It had taken nine lives to do it. Too many. The pain in his wing was nothing compared to the ache in his heart.

"Don't be sorry," Bel said. "There was no way you could have known about it. None of us did."

"How many?"

"Nine."

Morrigan and two of the other commanders began a heated discussion that, thankfully, didn't involve him or Asmodeus for the time being. They'd had their moment of battle. They'd conveyed the information they'd needed to convey.

"It could have been worse, for a gegony. I'm sorry all the same."

Bel just nodded. It *could* have been worse. Should have been worse. They'd all studied the reports of them through the millennia. Gegony could shred dozens, hundreds if they struck fast and hard enough.

The prickling, stinging pain of being healed scratched up his spine and dug into his brain like needles.

Find the beauty, Beleth. Even if it's small. Find it.

Bel focused on keeping his breaths steady, centering his mind, acknowledging the pain—physical, mental, emotional—without letting it consume him.

A flicker of movement caught his eye—Asmodeus, mindlessly running the pad of his thumb over the silvery shine of his wedding band, his gleaming black claws a sharp contrast against the delicate patterns engraved in the metal. Simple, quietly powerful, lovely.

Love enduring in a dark place.

The flickering light from a lantern reflected merrily in the ring of water on the table left behind by a glass. A dancing circle of cheerful gold against rough grains of dark wood.

Simple beauty, but no less precious.

Lily.

She sprang to his mind unbidden, and he immediately felt like he'd planted both feet on the ground.

Beauty. She was the definition of it to him. She'd been so ethereally glorious those mornings ago in his bed, rising above him in one of his old shirts, auburn hair rumpled from sleep and gilded by the morning light. She looked like she'd been crowned with fire. But her eyes . . . the expression she'd had—

"This last bit is going to hurt, sir," the healer warned.

Bel closed his eyes and thought of Lily's hands on his face instead. She'd touched him so delicately, as if *he* were some precious, fragile thing instead of a demon and a warrior. No one had ever done that. Looked at him with such tenderness. Lily saw him. Saw the warrior, yes, but she saw the rest of him too, and she hadn't curled her lip in disgust or treated him as less than. There'd been no pity in her eyes. Just understanding. One warrior to another.

You are more than enough.

He'd almost told her right then that he loved her, because for the first time in so long, he'd believed that he *was* worthy. Worthy of permanence and love, and that he truly had more to offer than his capability.

Then she'd told him to be safe.

His mother had stopped telling him to be safe while he'd still been in school. He'd never doubted that she cared, but telling him, a respected warrior, then a general, to be *safe*? She, like everyone, assumed that he was Beleth. He'd either be fine or he wouldn't.

It was nice to have someone . . . not worry, he didn't like the idea of Lily worried. Care. It was nice to have someone care, to express their care and recognize that he wasn't invincible.

He could practically hear her and Sharkie giggling together in the break room over something, could hear Sharkie cheering his name with the full force of her enthusiasm, and feel her flying over to give him a hug, shortly followed by Lily, who sauntered over with a sparkle in her eyes and a smile on her pretty lips. He craved those moments, even though they always made him wonder anew why his own young joy hadn't had the same grounding effect for its recipient.

He opened his eyes. The residual ache from his wing was minor compared to before, the new skin darker and far more tender than the surrounding membrane.

"Thank you," he rasped to the healer, who nodded and marched toward a resigned and sighing Asmodeus.

Bel drifted over to the rest of the meeting, offering his advice and insight when necessary. His and his legion's rotation had come to a close, but with Lily and Sharkie burning bright in his mind, he would be damned if he didn't do everything in his power to keep their Universe safe.

To keep *them* safe.

35

EXTREME FUSSITUDE

Lily

"**B**ut *why* can't the house be named Carl?" Sharkie insisted, homework abandoned on the kitchen table.

"It feels weird to say that we live in *Carl*. Why can't we call the house something else?" Lily asked, leaning against the doorframe.

"What's the name of the house in the hobbit book? Baggy End? Why don't we call the house Carl's Baggy End or something?" Sharkie said.

Do NOT form a mental image of that, and do not under any circumstances laugh about it.

Lily managed to hide her amusement by clearing her throat and biting her tongue hard.

"It's Bag End, and no, we aren't calling the house Carl's"—she coughed—"Baggy End."

Sharkie chewed on the end of her pencil, deep in thought. Kicked her sock-covered feet in the air. Wiggled. "Carlton?"

Lily couldn't keep herself from laughing that time. "Alright, I can work with Carlton. If you need any more help with your homework, let me know. I'll be in the library."

"'Kay," Sharkie chirped, leaning back over the table. As Lily headed down the hall, she heard Sharkie whisper loudly, "I'll still call you Carl though, don't worry."

The timbers in the kitchen groaned happily, and Sharkie giggled.

Lily shook her head, making a beeline to her nest of pillows and blankets on the window bed, eager to dive back into her book.

Several chapters and an indeterminate amount of time later, the door to the library swung open.

"Someone's knocking on the door," Sharkie announced. "I didn't answer it because I don't know if it's someone we like or not."

Lily kicked free of her blankets. "I don't think Paradise would let people we didn't like get in here."

Sharkie hung back in the hallway, just around the corner from the entryway and within sprinting distance of her room, wariness all over her round face while Lily approached the front door.

The latch clicked under her palm, swinging open on silent hinges and letting the cheerful sunshine spill over the floorboards.

"Hey, princess," Bel rasped.

"Fuck," Lily said simply.

"It won't be my best performance, but I'll give it a shot." His grin was weary.

Oh, Bel . . .

Lily raked her eyes over every inch of him, cataloging the armor that she would have drooled over if he hadn't looked so careworn. The weaponry, the filth, the new dark spot on his wing, the deep shadows under his eyes—oh, his eyes.

Sad. Exhausted. The silver of them dull.

"I didn't want to go home," he said quietly, shifting his weight. Vulnerability glimmered in those eyes.

"Come on, big guy, let's get you taken care of." Lily took his hand, tugging him inside. "Don't worry about your boots," she told him when he paused and started to bend over.

He straightened with a wince and a tiny wobble. Lily tucked herself against his side in an effort to support, mentally racing through what she had available and what might be helpful to the situation.

Sharkie peered around the corner, eyes widening when she saw Bel. She scampered across the foyer to take up a position on Bel's other side as Lily guided him toward her room. Sharkie could barely reach Bel's waist, but she tried.

"Hey, kiddo," Bel said, patting her on the shoulder. "How was the sleepover?"

"Fun. Lily wouldn't let me bring Cerby home with us, but that's okay. I don't think Max would have liked him very much."

"Max could have taken him," Bel said as they reached the door to Lily's room.

"Are you okay?" Sharkie's voice was small.

Please don't let this set her back. Please don't let this give her nightmares or something new to fear. I can explain everything, Baby Shark . . .

Bel crouched down slowly to smile at her. He gestured for her to come closer, leaning in to whisper in a pantomime of secrecy, as if Lily weren't standing right there. "I'm fine, I'm just tired and want Lily to fuss over me." He winked at her and stood, leaning dramatically against the doorway.

Sharkie's face lit up with understanding before she schooled her face into a mask of seriousness and turned to Lily. "I think Bel needs fuss-ing," she said with the gravity of a doctor in a hospital drama delivering bad news. Sharkie gestured to where Bel was blinking pathetically. "Look at him."

Despite her concern for the genuinely rough shape that Bel was in, Lily had to smother a chuckle at their performances.

"Well then. I guess you have your homework, and I have mine. Let the fussing commence," Lily said with equal seriousness, sliding under Bel's arm and tucking herself against his side. She felt him shoot Sharkie a thumbs-up behind her back, a gesture that Sharkie returned with both hands before the door shut behind them.

Bel immediately straightened and held her against him with a surer grip. Lily gave him a light squeeze, recalling how sore he'd been the last time she'd seen him after a mission/battle/whatever the fuck it had been, leading him into the cozy luxury of her bathroom. The shower had already started itself, and a plush oversized towel that Lily had never seen before hung on the heated towel bar.

"You don't have to actually fuss, princess. I'm fine."

"You signed up for fussing, you're getting fussing. From the look of it, you require some extreme fussitude, so suck it up, big guy," Lily said, mostly teasing.

Mostly.

She reached for one of his weapons and undid the straps, carefully setting it on the counter before reaching for another, while he took care of even more. After they'd amassed a small armory by the sink, they tackled his armor and his boots. She didn't miss the way his usually nimble fingers fumbled once or twice on a buckle, or the little exhalations of pain when his body moved a certain way.

Eventually, Bel stood in his pants and shirt, both made of a tough black fabric, rolling his neck and shoulders.

Lily started to pull the hem of his shirt free, but Bel stopped her and clucked disapprovingly.

"What do you take me for, Lils, a cheap date?"

"I'll feed you later. Strip, please."

"Maybe I don't want you to see what's under my clothes," he said, clearly hedging.

Lily folded her arms and arched her eyebrow at him. "I've had your cock in my mouth. I think I can handle seeing whatever bruises you're hiding under there."

He tried to scowl at her, but the effect was somewhat ruined by the way his lips tipped up at the corners. "I am not bruised."

She poked him in the side. He flinched and capitulated.

"Okay, maybe I'm a little bruised. Have your way with me."

"Thank you," Lily said primly, tugging his shirt free.

He took over, unclasping the panels around his wings and pulling it over his head, the heavy muscles of his torso working under his skin. Lily traced the outline of a particularly black bruise on his ribs with the barest touch of her fingertips, throat tightening in concern. Bel dropped the shirt and went still. She trailed her fingers across his stomach to a lighter mark, then up to a scrape near his collarbone, finally bringing her hands down to brace lightly on his hips. She pressed her lips to the center of his chest, feeling the reassuring thud of his heart.

Bel gently scooped her up, ignoring her murmur of protest, set her on the counter next to the pile of weapons, then leaned in and buried his face in her neck. She skated her palms up his back, tracing the dip of his spine, soothing the knots she could feel by his shoulder blades as the bathroom grew misty.

Her big-hearted warrior.

"I lost nine soldiers," he said quietly, not lifting his head. Lily held him a little tighter. "In the grand scheme of it all, nine soldiers out of the legion I had wasn't bad. Isn't bad. But it almost hurts worse when there're few enough to name. It's more personal. Losing soldiers always makes me feel . . . quiet for a while. But I didn't want to be alone. Being alone reminds me of . . ." He trailed off.

Lily smoothed over the snarl of his hair. "What were their names?"

He whispered them, and she felt the weight of their loss in every syllable. They curled together in silence, in acknowledgment. Bel eventually kissed her shoulder in quiet thanks. She slid off the counter and together they worked his stiff pants down his legs and over his tail. There was no heat in seeing him naked in that moment. She'd appreciate his glory later. He stepped into the oversized shower, and Lily took the opportunity to slip out, pressing a hand to her chest that ached in a new way.

Sharkie had settled cross-legged on the bed with her workbook in her lap, and she looked up when Lily sat on the edge of the bed.

"What's the finger trick for multiplying nines again?"

Lily showed her.

"That's what I thought," Sharkie said, scribbling down numbers. "Bel *is* okay, right?"

"Yeah, he's just tired and sore and a little sad, so he might be quieter than you're used to."

Sharkie nodded sagely and closed her notebook. "Can I fuss too, or is this a grown-up thing? Because I know exactly how to help."

"I think Bel can use all the help we can give him today."

"Cool. Bring him to the library," Sharkie ordered, sliding off the bed and running out the door. She ran back into the doorway. "Like, when he's done," she clarified, before running off again.

"Do you need help?" Lily called, trying to figure out what, exactly, Sharkie was up to.

"No!" Sharkie yelled.

Something scraped over the floor—a chair maybe?—and a cupboard banged. Something clattered loudly.

"Still no!" Sharkie called, then, quietly, "Shit . . . I think?"

Lily was waiting on the edge of the bed when he emerged from the bathroom wearing black sweatpants and a sleeveless gray shirt that Carlton had provided. He strode toward her, but she stood and stopped him just before he collapsed on the bed.

"Sharkie wants to fuss over you a little too. I told her you might be quieter today, but you don't have to if you just want to sleep."

His smile was tired but pleased. "I could use some Sharkie fussing."

"In that case, I have orders to take you to the library," she said, taking his hand and leading the way.

She pushed the doors of the library open and found Sharkie waiting on the other side. She immediately grabbed each of their hands, towing them over to the window seat that Lily had spent half the day lounging on. The pillows and blankets had been rearranged, and Lily's book had been set aside with a napkin stuck in it as a bookmark.

Sharkie released their hands and pointed at the window seat. "Cuddle. I'll be right back." She ran out of the room.

Lily looked at Bel.

Bel looked at Lily.

"You heard the shark, cuddle up, buttercup," Bel said.

"As the shark commands. I have an idea." Lily lay so that her shoulders and neck were slightly propped up and patted her chest. "You look like you need to be held, big guy."

Bel crawled over her, sparking heat low in her belly that she immediately quashed. He draped his heavy body between her legs, lowering to rest the side of his face against her abdomen. Thankfully, the vague C-shape of his horns lent itself well to the position, the upper curve of one horn just barely touching the underside of her breast, while his wings spread to drape against the sun-warmed window and down to the floor. Lily ran her fingers through his damp hair just as Sharkie hurried back into the room with a mug.

"Hot cocoa fixes everything. And it has extra marshmallows. And a straw so you can drink it lying down." Sharkie set it by Lily's leg, and Bel steadied it with one large hand. "I'm not done!" Sharkie ran out the door again.

Bel lifted his head to take a long drink through the chunky straw, then relaxed with a sigh that seemed to come from his soul.

Sharkie hustled back into the library, with a confused Max in her arms and a book in her teeth. She deposited the cat against Bel's side, just under his wing, then took the book out of her teeth and handed it to Lily before crawling over their legs and up their sides to snuggle between Lily and the window.

"Cuddles. Cocoa. Cat. Book. The three C's . . . and a B, that can solve almost anything. Aloud, please," Sharkie said, pointing to the book in Lily's hands.

Lily turned it over, the well-worn pages as familiar to her as her own face. *The Hobbit*. Her first bedtime story. Her dad had started reading it to her when she'd been five, and over the years, they worked their way through the *Lord of the Rings*, her dad's love of the story becoming her own. She'd given it to Sharkie and offered to read it to her, but Sharkie had always said "not yet."

Bel sipped his cocoa and patted Sharkie's foot. "Thank you, Sharkie." He curled his tail around Lily's calf. "Chapter one?" he rumbled.

Lily winked at Sharkie, who beamed brighter than the sunlight washing over them, then opened the book with one hand, running her other one through Bel's hair.

Family. My family.

"In a hole in the ground . . ."

36

FRIEND SHAPED

Lily

As the elevator slid downward, Lily glanced at Sharkie for the dozenth time since they'd left the house.

Something in her had shifted after the night she'd crept into Lily's room and finally voiced her fears. She carried herself with a bit more confidence, her eyes were brighter, and her smiles came quickly and lingered. Every moment of bravery and indicator of progress had pride and love swelling in Lily's chest.

Sharkie had even fallen asleep while Lily had read to her and Bel in the library a few days before. Lily had read more than a third of the book by the time darkness had fallen and the temptation of sleep had been too much to resist. Bel had, unsurprisingly, fallen asleep first. She'd just kept reading and running her fingers through his hair. Sharkie had lasted a bit longer, her head resting on Lily's shoulder more and more firmly until Lily heard the first soul-warming little snore.

The next morning, they'd all made Swedish pancakes and sat in the garden to eat. Bel had settled a wing against Lily's back, and Sharkie had sat between them while they'd watched a flock of birds as it twisted and turned over the hills and fjord.

Happy.

But back to Sharkie.

"Sharkie, I think you're taller," Lily said finally, adjusting her grip on the handle of the little cart they'd packed with food to bring to Bel's family get-together.

"What?" Sharkie squinted up at her.

"I think you're growing."

"I can *do* that?"

"Yeah, remember?" Lily chuckled, though she'd recently texted Siedah a barrage of questions to clarify. "We talked about this, and Siedah confirmed it. I think your 'growing up' is happening."

Sharkie pumped both fists in the air, shouting, "FINALLY!" just as the elevator doors slid open. Sharkie bounced with puppylike enthusiasm as they headed down the short hall to the gate, her hood flopping back.

"Moura!" she yelled, breaking away from Lily's side to sprint toward the demons and the line of souls. "Krun! Guys! I'm *growing*!"

The resulting cheer from every single demon wouldn't have sounded out of place in a sports stadium. Someone—Krun, probably, based on the height—had Sharkie held over his head, while the demons whooped and stomped their feet with such enthusiasm that Lily could have sworn the pens on her desk rattled. She tucked the cart behind the low wall—knowing better than to leave it in the break room—and walked over to join the celebration.

Sharkie was being tossed from demon to demon, laughing hysterically.

Lily's grin died when she spied a soul trying to sneak off in her direction. She stepped in front of the soul, a reedy-looking man with a hat pulled low over his brows, crossing her arms.

"I don't think so." She kept her tone and expression cool, silently daring the soul to be stupid.

The man gawked at her, glancing back at the celebrating demons, his confusion melting into anger. "Help me out here. We're the same," he hissed.

Something appeared between her crossed arms and her body. His file. Images and memories flickered across her mind.

"I think the fuck not. I certainly never beat my wife or children. Get your ass down to Level Four or it will get got for you." She kept her tone and expression frigid, silently daring the soul to be stupid.

Something flickered in his eyes. The rage and fear she expected, but the shame, guilt, and regret she did not.

Memories flickered from the file. He had been beaten before, for most of his childhood, and by most of his family—his parents, his older siblings, his grandfather.

A violent cycle. One he'd never brought himself to face, but only continued.

"You're a real bitch, you know that?" he said, but she could hear the faintest tremor in it.

"On a good day, there's no one who can do it better." She pointed to the tunnels. "Level Four. Move. And here's some advice: If you want to live again, the work is up to you. Face the consequences and learn, instead of trying to avoid them."

He stomped back into the line of souls. Lily snapped her fingers and pointed at another soul—a woman in an immaculately tailored, entirely beige outfit—as she scurried toward the employee hallway. "You too, BeigeWatch."

The woman stopped in her tracks, mouth falling open in protest.

"Does any part of my expression look like I'm open to excuses? You don't have to run in slow motion, but you do have to get back in line and go where you're told."

The woman huffed but turned around.

"Heeeyy, sexy," a male voice crooned with entirely too much confidence, just as another file appeared in her hand.

"You thought it was funny to kick animals and take naked pictures of unsuspecting girls through their windows and sell them on your website. You ruined *lives* with that shit, and you just kept doing it. I will send you to Level Five with no balls *or* penis."

The weight-room wonder stared at her as if she was an alien.

"Fuck around and find out, dickless." Lily let her hand drop to the hilt of the short sword Bel had given her. She'd taken to wearing it after hearing about the soldiers he'd lost. The threat loomed large in her mind, and some instinct, probably a holdover of preservation from being mortal, had her buckling the sword belt around her waist before she left the house. It looked slightly out of place paired with her leggings and fitted black T-shirt, but honestly, it felt right. Even if she had theoretical knowledge about how to use it at best, despite training with Bel in the afternoons. Enthusiasm and a vicious cutting edge seemed to make up for a lot though, especially against souls who fought with more audacity than brains or skill.

The soul flipped her off, spitting some choice insults as he went back to the line. Lily rolled her eyes.

The demons had put Sharkie down, and even though the general spirit of celebration persisted, most of them had returned to the business of making sure the souls got where they were supposed to go.

Sharkie skipped over to Lily with a grin that could outshine the sun. "I wonder how tall I'm going to be!"

"It's going to be cool to find out! Do you want to keep track of how much you're growing? Like on a wall?"

"YES!" Sharkie leapt clear off the ground. "Can we do it in the break room so everyone can see?"

"Sure! Let's get your first measurement real quick before you go to school."

Sharkie practically sprinted to the break room, then back to Lily, then back to the break room, urging Lily to walk faster. Eventually, Lily found herself being towed by the hand and laughing so hard she nearly tripped. It was the work of a moment to find a pencil and a book. While Lily had found those, Sharkie had selected the empty expanse of wall by the water cooler.

"This way," Sharkie explained, standing perfectly still while Lily made sure the book was level, "everyone can see it when they get their water."

Lily made the mark and Sharkie stepped away, turning to beam at the wall.

Lily handed her the pencil. "Here, sign it. No dates to worry about."

Sharkie stuck her tongue out with concentration, signing *Sharkie* with only slightly wobbly letters and adding a smiley face at the end. Lily draped an arm around her shoulders, every bit as proud of Sharkie as she seemed of herself.

"Do you think I'll be as tall as you?"

"Maybe. I was small for my age until I got to middle school, then I grew like nobody's business. And kept growing, always faster than my friends."

Flickers of a night she'd rather forget. Crying. Hating herself. Blaming herself for—

Lily blinked away the unbidden burst of memory, setting it aside to process later. She hadn't replayed that night in a long, long time, and didn't want to start now.

"Do you like being tall?" Sharkie asked.

"It has pros and cons. It's different in the Afterlife too. I never felt *short* in the mortal world, but ever since I started spending time with the demons? I'm getting used to feeling small, but it's still a fairly new thing for me. Well, in my most recent memories anyway. Pretty sure I was small in at least one of my lifetimes."

"Really? How did you feel about being small?"

The memories were hazy, with a slippery, dreamlike quality.

"Well," Lily said slowly, fighting to piece together cohesive information, "my first lifetime, I was a bit like you, actually. Only I'm pretty sure it was a long time ago, like, hundreds of years?"

The answering thought didn't quite feel like her own, but the information registered as accurate.

"Mid fifteen-hundreds, I think?"

North, rain, wind, cold, green, rough skirts, a tired mother who loved them, other children, hungry, a man's laughter, snow, cold, so cold.

"I was little when I died, probably six or seven? Froze to death, I think. It was winter and I got lost maybe? So 'kid small,' I remember. Being a short adult? I think I was a bit below average in the lifetime before this one, and it wasn't too bad."

As memories trickled, Lily frowned. Being short-ish hadn't been bad, but almost everything else had been. *Glimmers of happiness shot through with pain and fear and so, so much hunger.*

How the fuck was her happiest lifetime the one where she died young of cancer? How was the runner-up for that title the one where she was wrongly burned as a witch and had a husband who tolerated but didn't love her?

And she still wanted to go back?

Did she? Of course she did. Eventually. Right?

"Lily?" Sharkie's voice pulled her out of her reverie.

"Sorry, kiddo, got lost in thought there for a second. Guess we'll just have to wait and see how tall you get, and then you can see for yourself. Now come on, let's get you to school."

"And then we go to the party!" Sharkie wiggled with excitement. "Do you think I'll be taller by then?"

"I've never grown in the Afterlife, so it's up to you to find out. Don't be disappointed if you're not though, okay? Just because you don't notice-ably grow today doesn't mean you're not growing at all."

"Right," Sharkie said, adjusting the straps of her backpack and following her out the door.

A quick elevator ride, a short distance that, admittedly, they ended up running to make sure Sharkie arrived on time, a quick hug goodbye, and Sharkie was off to learn new things.

Lily headed back to the elevator quietly, turning things over in her mind.

I want to go back. Do I want to go back?

I want . . . What do I want?

The sweet memory of the three of them resting together on the window bed, the sun illuminating the pages, Bel's breath heating her skin, and Sharkie's warmth curled around her side felt like an answer.

But she'd never had the opportunity to grow old, and . . . she wanted to. What it would be like to laugh over her first gray hair, to see her face settle into age, instead of just starting to show the hints of it? She knew that aging wasn't for the faint of heart, that it could be frustrating and painful and scary to have your body fail. To worry about balance and falls. To say goodbye to more and more people.

What would she be gaining, really? There was no way to say that her next life would end better than any of her previous ones. She'd found peace in the Afterlife. Love, in various forms. Fulfillment. She *liked* waking up in the morning, was excited to get out of bed and see what the Afterlife had to offer, to see what Sharkie-isms would make her laugh.

And Bel.

Just Bel.

He was a friend, a confidant, a partner. Just being around Bel made existence better. Sex or no sex.

Though, she certainly couldn't wait for sex. The fact that she hadn't gotten to ride him senseless yet was like an itch under her skin. Like romantic idiots, they'd agreed that they didn't want their first time to be a stolen quickie in some closet. But between the tolls of his work, her obligations, and Sharkie's interruptions, stolen moments were all they'd been getting lately.

Though she knew that Persephone would happily arrange another sleepover, or that Sharkie could stay a night with Lucifer, who often picked her up after school and spent time with her before dropping her off at the elevators, Lily had found herself protective of Sharkie after her most recent breakthrough. Sharkie's idea of their family and trust in Lily's dependability were new, fragile things, and she didn't want to risk it just yet.

She headed toward the Hellp Desk, a line of souls waiting mostly patiently. She held up a finger to silence the first woman in line, who had sucked in a breath to start yelling the second Lily neared the desk.

Lily sat. Meticulously adjusted her chair. Reached for the file and flipped it open, running her finger over the first page.

"Given your history of mistreating service workers, especially your delivery drivers, in addition to your outspoken—and super fucking wrong—belief that Indigenous people are inferior to your bitchy ass, I'm guessing that you're about to yell at me and somehow manage to relay your racism while you do it."

The woman turned a fascinatingly mottled shade of purple and sputtered for a moment before screeching obscenities at a pitch that set the Hellhounds howling.

Bel was waiting for her when the elevator doors slid open, looking casual and delicious in his usual pants and a T-shirt with hacked-off sleeves.

He held up a hand to stop her before she could exit, glanced both ways, and stepped into the elevator, pushing the button to close the doors.

"What—"

He lifted her with ease, pressed her back against the paneled wall, and kissed her, long and hard and hungry.

Hello, stolen moment.

She hooked her legs over his hips while she fisted his hair with one hand. He growled against her mouth. In retaliation, she tugged his hair, hard, and his head fell back. She kissed and sucked along the column of his neck, careful not to leave any marks—this time—all while keeping a commanding grip on his hair.

"That kind of day, huh?" he asked with breathless excitement, hand skating up her side to cradle a breast.

"Mm." She took his earlobe between her teeth, and he groaned.

"*Princess.*"

She let him tip his head down slightly, scant inches separating their lips. The silver of his eyes gleamed.

He pulled against her anchoring hold on his hair. "Let me kiss you."

"Say please." She grinned, teasing herself as much as him. She gave the barest roll of her hips, grinding into him.

He hissed, and she clenched around nothing.

"Please," he breathed, eyes going hooded, pressing her even more firmly against the wall. "*Please* let me kiss you, sweetheart. Let me have just a taste—"

She silenced him with her mouth, releasing his hair. He slipped his tongue along the seam of her lips, and, when she moaned, he pinned her harder to the wall, devouring her in a searing kiss. He shifted the smallest bit away from the wall, settled his hands on her ass, and—

The elevator door slid open.

With a speed born of plenty of recent practice, they disengaged. She dropped her legs from his hips at the same time he set her down, turning to face their audience.

The older male demon stared in surprise over the potted plant in his hands. After a moment, he smiled knowingly at both of them, then reached inside, pressed the "door close" button, and stepped back with a wink. The doors slid shut again, leaving them alone inside.

"Shit," Bel muttered, rubbing the back of his neck.

"Yeah," Lily said, still reeling with arousal.

She met Bel's eyes, their heavy breaths filling the elevator as the pull between them grew tighter, like a rubber band stretched thin.

"He did give us more time," she pointed out.

"He did," Bel agreed, tipping her face up to his once more. The kiss shoved everything out of her mind except the sensations of his lips and tongue, his strong hands and warm skin. When he broke away to softly slide his fangs over the sensitive spot on her neck he'd discovered, she had to lock her knees to keep them from buckling with want. They had limited time, obligations to fulfill, and a family event to attend. But she wanted to scream that they needed a bedroom and at least half a day. *Immediately.*

"Bel." She wasn't sure if it was a groan or a moan or some hybrid of both.

He rested his forehead against hers, his voice raspy as he murmured, "I know, princess. Right there with you."

Lily wrapped her arms around his waist as they let the intensity of the heat fade, burying her face in his chest. He kissed the top of her head sweetly, the thud of his heartbeat against her ear reassuring in its steady rhythm.

For the hell of it, she bit him.

Gently. Ish.

He squeaked and stepped back, rubbing his pectoral.

Lily burst out laughing. "I've never heard that deep of a squeak before."

The strain of a long day filled with more-bombastic-than-usual souls melted away, especially when Bel's deep, rumbling chuckle filled the elevator.

"Spend some time with Cthulhu if you ever want to hear a super deep squeak out of something the size of an office building. He stepped on something squishy during a Hall party once, and my hearing wasn't right for days."

Lily giggled while she fixed her loose hair. Bel's massive hands cupped her face a moment before his delectable lips landed on hers, tender this time. She hooked her fingers into his waistband and pulled him closer, smiling into the kiss. He nipped carefully at her lower lip before pulling away with a twinkle in his eyes.

"You bite me, I bite you back, princess."

"Awesome, can I choose where?"

His eyes heated. "I'll accept suggestions, but I make no promises."

"Tease."

He winked, pressing the "open" button and slipping his hand into hers, calluses rasping against her skin as their fingers twined together. Lily had never really held hands before—it was a gesture of intimacy that hookups didn't tend to give each other—but it was honestly one of her favorite things they did together. She loved all of it, but the simple touch of their hands? Heady. Heady and delicious and so sweet she wondered if she deserved it half the time, but treasured it, nonetheless.

She grabbed the handle of her cart, and they walked toward Sharkie's school at a relaxed pace, since she'd come down extra early. The distance was barely noticeable as they talked about their days and swung their linked hands between them. While they waited, Bel gave her another quick rundown of the people he knew would be present at the party—mother, her current and previous partners, his siblings, their spouses and partners, their children.

"And," he added wryly as the first kids exited the school, "a bevy of cousins and some old family friends."

"I'm guessing Asmodeus and Sariah will be there, then, especially if food is involved," Lily said as the tide of kids rushed down the stairs.

Every shade of every color was on display, along with horns that were just starting to grow larger than nubs and take their various forms. She spied Sharkie immediately, and not just by virtue of the hard-to-miss onesie she still wore for comfort. She was almost a full head shorter than every other kid.

Bel seemed to be muffling laughter with his hand.

"What?" Lily asked, warmth suffusing her veins at the way his eyes had crinkled.

"I just . . . all I see is the fin on the top of her onesie moving through the crowd, like *Jaws*."

Lily looked to where, sure enough, the most visible part of Sharkie was the floppy little fin weaving through the sea of moving kids. She bit her lip and let out a long, measured exhale through her nose.

Don't laugh, don't laugh, don't laugh.

"See? It's . . ." Bel's voice wavered as he almost lost the battle to not laugh.

"Shit, pull it together," Lily hissed, waving at Sharkie. "And don't look at me, I'll lose it."

Sharkie dumped her backpack on the ground and threw herself at Bel, who lifted her as if she were weightless. "What's so funny?" she asked.

"Oh, Bel just made a joke about the movie *Jaws*," Lily said.

Sharkie wrinkled her nose and frowned at Bel. "What's funny about *Jaws*? It's not a very accurate movie, and actually it made a lot of people think sharks were bad and mean, when really, they don't like to eat people, they just have bad eyesight and get confused."

"Sharks and I had a lot more in common than I thought," Lily muttered, picking up Sharkie's abandoned backpack.

Both Bel and Sharkie gave her a puzzled look.

"People think you're bad and mean?" Sharkie asked.

"You don't like to eat people?" Bel asked innocently.

She cut Bel a heated look that made him cough awkwardly and shift on his feet—served him right—then turned to Sharkie. "That was a joke, by the way. No, in the mortal world, I had bad eyesight and got confused. Some people did think I was bad and mean though."

"Because you're tall." Sharkie nodded sagely.

"Yeah, and the resting bitch face didn't help."

"Oh, is that why you two get along? Because people think you're bad and mean but you're not?" Sharkie's face lit up in understanding.

Lily met Bel's amused and considering gaze. They had so much else meaningfully in common that she'd never picked up on that similarity before.

"I think," Bel said slowly, "we get along because we're similar in other ways, and we like, or at least tolerate, the ways that we're different. But it is nice to have someone see you for who you are, instead of who they think you should be. So, keep that in mind, okay?"

"Okay," Sharkie said, then asked to be put down.

Lily handed her the backpack and gave her a quick hug. "Ready for a party?"

"I think so. Are you *sure* there will be other kids there?"

"If there's one thing my family is good at doing, it's making kids," Bel said dryly.

Lily cut her reflexive sharp inhale short, praying Bel didn't notice.

He didn't seem to, as he continued speaking. "Don't worry, there will be plenty of kids there for you to play with. Plus, you're friend-shaped, so they'll love you."

37

FAVORITE UNCLE STATUS

Bel

Bel put an extra bounce in his step to make Sharkie giggle as she sat on his shoulders, hands gripping his horns like joysticks. He wasn't too worried about them meeting everyone, even though his cheerfully chaotic family was full of big personalities. Sharkie had displayed a remarkable adaptability to her various surroundings, making friends wherever she went. And Lily? Half his family was in awe of her for showing up and offering to work at the gate, and the other half liked her for no other reason than the effect she'd had on him.

His mother was especially eager to meet her, having heard about Lily from both Bel and Lucifer. Though the twinkle in her eyes when she'd said so had Bel wondering how his loving, cunning mother would test Lily.

Lily squeezed his hand, the full cart of food trundling along behind her. The red-gold light gilded her hair and cast a warm glow on her skin. The V-neck of her shirt offered a tempting glimpse of the upper swells of her breasts—breasts that he *still* hadn't gotten to explore with his mouth. It was an item high on his to-do list. Especially when she looked so *happy*. She was glorious when dealing with souls, when she had her nose in a book, when she scowled at the walls of Carlton, when she laughed, when she was focused. Her moments of sadness and self-doubt weren't what he would call glorious, but those glimpses into her brilliant, wonderfully complex mind were powerful. He treasured those moments of intimacy and trust just as much as he treasured everything else.

Every part of her captivated him.

Lily met his eyes with a little smile, her expression softening in a way that he'd learned was rare for her, the moment of connection washing through him like a warm breeze. Sharkie did something on his shoulders that made him hold her foot a little tighter to keep her from falling, and Sharkie and Lily laughed.

Something bloomed in his chest so powerfully that he sucked in a breath. Lily, perceptive as ever, raised her brows a bit, but before she could say anything, raucous laughter and music drew their attention.

His mother's estate was a study of jewel tones and silver and wide expanses of glass, reminiscent of—ironically enough for Lady Lilith—a cathedral. A high fence covered with bioluminescent vines kept the expansive lawn and garden private. The house had always reminded him of his mother—imposing in appearance, but a warm place to grow up, full of laughter and stories and mischief.

Lily and Sharkie had paused, staring up at the house. Lily seemed impressed, excited even, hazel eyes bright, and a smile playing around her mouth. He couldn't see Sharkie's face, but he could feel that she'd gone a bit still, so he pointed to the highest window on the tower.

"Sharkie, you see that window?"

"Yeah?" She rested her hands on top of his head.

"When I was about your age, my brother Orin dared me to fly between the spires on the tower, but I missed and flew into that window instead."

Sharkie gasped. "Really? Did it break?"

Bel nodded with exaggerated sadness, and Lily snickered.

"Yep, glass *everywhere*. But that wasn't the worst part."

"How was breaking a window not the worst part?" Sharkie leaned around his head to peer at him, wide-eyed.

"Because," Bel said gravely, biting back a smile, "behind that window is my mother's office. She was in it at the time." He paused for effect.

"And so was God, Parvati—a Hindu goddess—Lucifer, and Changxi, a Chinese lunar goddess."

He had to let go of Lily's hand to grip both of Sharkie's feet and keep her from tumbling sideways off his shoulders.

"What did you do?" Sharkie asked, completely ignoring the near fall.

Bel chuckled and grimaced, the memory of his mother's incredulous look of *are-you-fucking-kidding-me-child*, and the surprise and amusement of the other deities as fresh in his mind as the day it had happened.

"Said 'Hi, Mom,' apologized for the window, and asked if I could have a snack."

Lily snorted. "Now *I'm* surprised you lived to tell the tale."

"Frankly, me too. Needless to say, I did not get a snack, and I had to help replace the window the next day. I also had no dessert for a month, so I had an incentive to get better at flying."

"Was that a punishment for being wicked, or a . . ." Sharkie fidgeted a little on his shoulders. "A boundary?"

Wicked. He knew immediately that it wasn't her word.

"Making mistakes isn't wicked," he said gently. "Especially when you're a child and don't know any better, because you're still learning how to be a person. My mom didn't take my dessert away because she was mad *at* me and wanted to take something away from me. She was mostly scared for me. It's funny now, but I could have seriously hurt myself, or someone else, by flying through a window like that. I had to learn to be more careful. The no dessert was so I'd understand how important it was."

"So it *was* a boundary," Sharkie confirmed, a thread of relief entering her tone.

"Yeah, bug." Lily smiled up at her, pride shining in her lovely eyes. "That's exactly it."

"Good job recognizing that, kiddo," Bel said, shimmying his shoulders to make her laugh.

A moment later, Sharkie spoke up again. "Did Orin get in trouble?"

"Of course not. I wasn't a snitch, and Orin is a very good actor. Now," he said brightly, "how would you both like to get some food and meet my crazy family?"

He lifted Sharkie off his shoulders and took Lily's hand again, guiding them to the side gate that was always left unlocked for family events. It swung open on silent hinges, and a cheer went up from the fifty or so people in attendance. Sharkie stopped, twitching back toward Lily, who murmured something to her.

"UNCLE BEL!" A small stampede of kids shot out of the crowd like shards of metal being drawn to a magnet.

"Here they come." Bel grinned, letting go of Lily's hand to keep her from being tackled too.

His nephew Valafar was the first to reach him, barely slowing before he slammed into him. His nieces Nimmie and Lezzie were next, bouncing for his attention, followed by his cousin's youngest daughter. Soucri, his eldest brother's toddler, waddled as fast as his chubby legs could carry him, shrieking at the affront of being left out.

They all chattered at once, and he picked out maybe every third word. Nimmie grabbed his wrist, checking that her bracelet was still intact and crowing the news to her twin, who pointed out that her bracelet was still there too. Nimmie wrinkled her nose, abandoning Bel for more interesting company.

She walked up to Sharkie, confident as anything, and introduced herself. Sharkie beamed and said something back. Nimmie offered her hand, Sharkie took it and was pulled toward the crowd of adults and older kids. Sharkie went with a giggle, and Bel's heart swelled with pride for how far she'd come from that first day.

He picked up Soucri, who whined on the fringe of the pack of kids, tossing him into the air and catching him just in time to see the flood of adults, including his mother, heading their way. His sister made a beeline for Lily.

"Lils"—he gestured—"this is my sister Kasdeya; she's a hugger. Deya, this is—"

"Hello!" Kasdeya beamed, wrapping Lily in an enthusiastic hug. The two women began chatting as if they were old friends. Quiet pride hummed in his chest before he noticed the woman approaching him.

"Hey, Mom." He grinned.

"Hey, honey." Her smile radiated warmth.

Beautiful as ever, she was in her version of casual wear—wide-legged, comfortable trousers and a blouse with the sleeves artfully rolled to her elbows. On her hip, Bel's infant half sister fussed as usual, though admittedly with less volume. Bel adored his baby sister, but he—and his eardrums—were acutely aware that she could be . . . opinionated. She couldn't speak yet, but that didn't stop her from expressing her displeasure. Loudly.

Little spitfire.

With her free arm, his mother shooed away the kids and wrapped him in a hug. He hugged her back, leaning over to kiss Anyaet's little head between the pair of pigtails that stuck straight up like tiny antennas. She burbled at him with a gummy smile, so he kissed her again.

"You alright?" his mother asked, adjusting Anyaet. As one of the highest-ranking members of Hell outside of the six princes, as well as one of the oldest remaining beings of their realm, she was privy to most information, often knowing what Bel's orders would be before he did. Despite the fact that she had created and continued to manage the Healers Guild and had nothing to do with military operations, he knew she read every single tactical brief.

"Better than alright." He smiled, looking over his shoulder. *Getting better all the time. Except when I think about— Nope, not going there today.* "Would you like to meet Lily?"

He'd barely gotten the words out of his mouth before his mother waved them away, scoffing.

"Beleth. *Please.* What kind of question is that?" She turned, making to interrupt Lily and Kasdeya's conversation. Bel booped Soucri on the nose, set him down, and aimed him in the direction of his brother.

"Do you want me to take Anyaet?" he asked.

"No, no, it's fine," his mother said, entirely too casually. "She's a good judge of character."

Oh no.

He watched with fascination and concern as his mother briefly introduced herself. Then, to what could only be described as his horror, she handed Anyaet unceremoniously to Lily without warning, smiling the entire time, as if she hadn't just handed an infant time bomb to the love of Bel's life.

Lily

She loved Lilith's house.

At first glance, the cathedral-like appearance had sent a jolt of old panic down her spine, but then Bel had told the story of how he'd broken one of those beautiful windows. It was hard to imagine him as anything but massive, but she would have bet her Paradise that he'd been an adorable kid. She'd loved the story, but she loved how Sharkie had asked for clarification when she'd needed it even more.

Lily had braced to be intimidated by Bel's family, but when they'd cheered at their arrival, it felt like walking into a crowd of friends. Bel hadn't lied about being popular with the kids; they came belting from every corner of the yard to jump on him and clamber over each other for his attention. His love for each and every one of them was as obvious as the fact he had wings. Sharkie had a flare of hesitation at the noise, but the moment a little demon girl with lovely sage-colored skin and dark green eyes approached her, she lit up.

"I'm Nimmie! What's your name?" Her grin revealed a pair of missing front teeth.

"I'm Sharkie."

"Hi!" Nimmie beamed. "Wanna play a game with me?"

"Sure!" Sharkie grinned back, taking her hand and sprinting away, giggling without a shred of fear.

Lily watched them go, proud and relieved. Adults made their way over, laughing and chatting. More than a few of them eyed Lily curiously. She wondered what, exactly, they'd heard about her.

A beautiful female demon with ochre skin and striking emerald eyes practically bounced over to her. Despite her different coloring, Lily could immediately tell that this had to be one of Bel's half sisters. Their bone structure was too similar, even if the woman was built tall and thin and Bel was all solid strength.

"Lils," Bel called over the din, "this is my sister Kasdeya; she's a hugger. Deya—"

The woman, Kasdeya, scooped Lily into one of the most enthusiastic hugs she'd ever received, second only to the one she'd gotten from a drunk girl in a club bathroom to whom she'd given a hair tie.

"Hello!" Kasdeya squealed. "I am so excited to meet you! We all are! You are *so* beautiful!"

Lily blushed, laughing. "Oh, thank you, right back at you! That was your daughter Nimmie, right?"

Lily figured that brilliant smiles must be a family trait, as Kasdeya beamed.

"Yep, she and Lezzie have wanted to meet Sharkie ever since Bel first mentioned her. I can't promise that there won't be mischief, but we all keep an eye on the kiddos when we're en masse like this. Please, tell me all about your Hellp Desk! Every time we ask Bel, he ends up talking about how proud he is of *you*, which is sweet but doesn't answer the question."

Lily launched into the basic explanation that she'd begun to perfect. Kasdeya was incredibly perceptive, asking nuanced questions that Lily was delighted to answer. A few moments later, a tall, incredibly regal woman with a baby on her hip sauntered over to them.

Lily would have picked her out as Bel's mother anywhere. They had the same basic bone structure, but where Bel's features were rugged, hers were porcelain fine. Her skin was such a pale shade of purple that it could almost pass as a mortal skin color and carried the slightest hints of age in the lines of her face. Her inky tresses were untouched by time, however, and swept back into an effortlessly tousled French twist. Short, delicate horns curved back over her head, a less robust version of her son's. Immaculately tailored, wide-legged black trousers and a silvery blouse with the sleeves cuffed at her elbows hinted at a lush figure. Her eyes were warm but keen, the intelligence in her gaze a naked blade glimmering in bright green irises made all the more captivating by the black sclera surrounding them.

Lily wondered if Bel's father had black sclera too.

Lilith smiled, and yep, it had to be a family trait. "You must be Lily! I've heard so much about you!" She had a rich, smooth voice that was slightly deep for a woman but came nowhere near Bel's resonant bass.

"Hello, Lady Lilith." Lily smiled, trying to focus on the fact that she was Bel's mother, not the fact that she was meeting the Lilith of legend.

Be yourself, but not the self that loves to casually tell sex jokes, you filthy-minded gutter rat. This is his mother.

"Oh, please." Bel's mother smiled, waving an elegant hand. "Just call me Lilith. Here, have a baby."

Before Lily could process the words or even blink in surprise, she found herself with a chubby, wide-eyed baby in her arms. The baby's skin was a slightly darker shade of purple than Lilith's, and she had short, soft, black hair that had mostly been tied up into two little pigtails that stuck straight up. The eyes that stared at Lily were the exact same as her mother's. The baby huffed, clearly processing her new situation and deciding whether or not to start screaming about it.

Lily shifted her a bit so that her weight rested more comfortably, giving her a little half smile. "Hello."

It was then that she noticed the near-complete silence around them, as if all the adults and even some of the kids were holding their breath.

The baby blinked a few times, eyes locked on Lily's face, then cooed, breaking into a gummy grin, seizing a fistful of Lily's hair, and trying to grab her chin.

There was a collective exhale from the group, including Bel muttering in apparent relief.

"Look at that." Lilith's expression went soft. "It's not often Anyaet likes someone so quickly. You should feel special."

Bel emerged from the crowd to stand by Lily, shaking his head at his mother. "It's not often Anya likes someone at *all*, Mom. I can't believe you."

"What?" Lilith looked only mildly affronted.

"'Hi, Lily,'" Bel mimicked, his deep voice going comically high—for him, anyway. "'Welcome to the family, but before you even have a chance to eat, let's see if the Almighty Baby Grenade deems you worthy.'" He fluttered his eyelashes for good measure.

Lily swallowed her laughter and focused on keeping Anyaet from yanking out her hair. "You're a very cute little baby grenade," Lily told her.

Anyaet babbled in agreement and started nomming on a chunk of Lily's hair.

Something in Lily's chest loosened and ratcheted tighter at the same time. It was a sensation she was painfully familiar with. She'd rationalized it to hell and back when she'd been alive. She understood why she hadn't had the opportunity to have her own family, understood the ways her decisions had played a part in that.

But understanding it didn't mean it hadn't still fucking hurt though. Every time one of her friends or cousins had a baby she'd been beyond thrilled for them, loved that they were getting to fulfill that part of their dream, had offered her support and helped out when they'd needed a break.

But, *oh* how it had hurt, so quietly and deeply that it was like she'd swallowed little shards of glass into her soul. She'd ignored that feeling for a long time, until she'd realized that she could no longer do herself the disservice of pretending that it didn't matter. So she'd still loved those kids, still loved and supported her friends and cousins, but she would always allow herself a moment of selfish grief.

However, she sure as *shit* wasn't going to have that little moment in front of Bel—who was entirely too perceptive—and his entire family. Her momentary emotional slip had been dangerous enough, and she hoped no one—Bel—had noticed.

So what if he did? He'd listen. He'd understand.

The thought should have shocked the shit out of her, but instead it felt like the voice of reason had spoken into the situation.

Except.

Except how could she talk to him about the very thing that bound her so tightly to a possible reincarnation someday? The baby in her arms had reminded her starkly of that dream, even if it was in a far distant future, when Sharkie didn't need her anymore.

"You should have seen Bel," Lilith said, every inch the proud mother, "he was cute too, and he had those little bitty *wings*."

"You were chunky," Kasdeya told him. "Lily, I swear to you, his face was like eighty percent *cheek*. Although, unlike this one, he was almost indiscriminately cuddly. Just constantly needing to be held."

Bel snorted and shook his head, rubbing the back of his neck with one hand and making his biceps flex deliciously.

Down, girl.

"That does sound familiar." Lily smirked.

He raised an eyebrow, lips parting enough that she could see his tongue running over the tip of a fang. "What were you like as a baby, princess?"

"Oh, I wasn't fussy at all," Lily lied airily. She imagined that somewhere in the mortal world, her mom felt the sudden need to regale someone with the fact that Lily had raged passionately against nap time, even when she needed a nap, until she'd gotten old enough to win the nap time war.

Bel squinted, but before he could say anything, Lilith clapped her hands, announced that the food was ready when they were, and ushered them toward the ornate tables set on the lawn and piled with food. Someone had absconded with the cart of cinnamon rolls and added them to the hoard, so all Lily had to do was hold Anyaet and follow the crowd.

Bel's warm hand came to rest on her back, and he dropped a kiss into her hair. She hummed appreciatively, smiling up at him. He returned it, then shook his head at his little sister, who reached for him. Lily handed her over. Bel settled her against his shoulder like a pro, and Anyaet immediately reached for one of the little braids holding his hair back from his temples.

Bel looked so happy with the baby in his arms, and he'd been so excited to see all the kids. He was already so wonderful with Sharkie . . .

I wonder what our kids would look like?

She slammed the door on that thought so hard she was surprised it didn't audibly clang. It wasn't possible. Would never be possible.

She couldn't entertain the idea.

She could *see* it, though, see them raising more kids together.

The flash of warmth and pain was stronger than before.

She took advantage of Bel's distraction to have a moment, working through the fresh grief and settling into acceptance. Then, with a deep breath, she moved on, focusing on the laughter and all the wonderful new people she wanted to know better.

Laughter flowed freely and often among Bel's family. They had all piled plates high with food, scattering around the expansive lawn and the merrily crackling firepit to chat. She had already met two of Bel's siblings—Kasdeya and Anyaet—and was quickly introduced to the other four. She saw the pieces of their mother in all of them, but noted how wildly they differed from each other. Four of his five elder siblings had partners and children, and she'd met and adored them too. Then had come the wash of cousins, along with their families. Every single one of them had been friendly, and most had been exceptionally curious about the Hellp Desk. No one had looked down on her for being a mortal soul, and a few had even quietly thanked her for whatever she had done to make Bel "better."

Though, there had been a moment of weirdness when Bel had introduced her to the siblings' fathers. There was an odd tightness in his smiling expression, and he hadn't met her eyes for more than a second at a time during all six introductions.

Not seven.

One father had been conspicuously absent, and a reason had never been offered, or even hinted at. She noted it along with Bel's tension and didn't mention it, but curiosity simmered. Bel had never talked about his father, even obliquely.

The relationships in Hell, and among the Afterlife denizens in general, were all within the spectrum of healthy. She couldn't believe that Bel's father would ever willingly leave his incredible son's life. Perhaps his father died when he was little, like Asmodeus's had, and that was why he never talked about him? She was almost certain that that was the loss he'd referenced. But Bel had said "left behind," not "lost" when he'd talked about his experience with grief, so maybe he'd been talking about something else. She wanted to ask, but she also wanted him to share whatever it was when he felt ready enough.

Eventually, after they'd all been introduced, eaten, and settled into different conversations, Bel relaxed. They ended up sitting on the ground, Lily leaning back between his legs, his arms wrapped around her middle while they talked about various goings-on.

Asmodeus landed lightly on the lawn after everyone had sat down to eat, setting Sariah down as if she were made of glass. The kids descended on Asmodeus with almost as much enthusiasm as they had Bel and watched Asmodeus like hawks while he ate his plate of food. The moment he cleared his plate, they moved in. Nyso—one of the youngest, and Orin's youngest of four—was the first to convince Asmodeus that he simply *had* to have a "flight ride."

A ripple of laughter spread through the adults at the words "flight ride," several of them shooting Bel amused looks.

Bel smiled against her temple. "Oh boy, here we go."

Lily covered his hands with hers and twisted to kiss the underside of his jaw, the action as natural as breathing. "Are you being objectified by children for your wings?" she teased.

He squeezed her lightly and nipped at her ear, which sent an embarrassingly strong wave of arousal rocketing through her system. He clearly didn't miss the way her breath hitched, because he chuckled and did it again—

Right as a group of kids ran up to them, Sharkie leading the charge. Lily feigned a cough and took a long sip of the generously poured wine, hoping to hide her blush.

Sharkie had shoved her hood back, and her eyes were so bright and happy that Lily had to swallow a sudden lump in her throat. Lily marveled at the transformation from the terrified child she'd first met to this joyful, fiercely curious little person.

Lily was so proud of her. She didn't think she told her enough.

"Uncle Bellllll," Lezzie crooned, the picture of innocence, hands clasped behind her back and swaying back and forth. "Can I have a flight ride, pretty please?"

"Can I have one too?" Nimmie asked the moment her sister finished speaking.

"Can I be third?" Sharkie asked, hope shining out of her round face.

The other kids chimed in, talking over each other, each trying to be the loudest, best, first. Except Sharkie. She looked a little spooked as the other kids grew rowdier, but quickly regained her smile, quietly bouncing in place and waiting.

Bel's overly thoughtful hum was almost a growl, and it sent heat licking straight between Lily's thighs.

"A flight ride, huh?"

The near harmonious chorus of *pleeeeaaaasssseeee* set off another round of adult laughter.

"Since Sharkie has never had a flight ride before . . ." Bel drawled slowly. Sharkie's shuddered inhalation of excitement wasn't subtle in the least, but she looked so hopeful she seemed ready to burst. "I think Sharkie should get the first one."

"Oh yeah! Sharkie goes first!" Nimmie said brightly, then added with steel in her tone, "Then me."

"No, then *me!*" Lezzie argued. Across the circle, Kasdeya shook her head and shared a knowing look with her husband.

"Tell you what," Bel said, disentangling himself from Lily carefully, "if, by the time Sharkie and I get back, you guys haven't worked together *nicely* to figure out what order to go in, then no more rides. Can you do that?"

"Obviously," said a girl who was a bit older than the others, fixing the other kids in her stare. "We'll do that, right?" The *or else* was unspoken. The kids quickly agreed.

Bel offered his hand to Sharkie, who practically lunged for it. He guided her to an open stretch of lawn and crouched down to talk to her.

Lily braced a hand and leaned back, smile growing as Sharkie nodded enthusiastically to whatever Bel had said.

A chair dropped onto the grass beside her, and Lily looked up to see

Sariah easing down, one hand cradling the side of her ever-growing stomach.

"I love that man, and I love this kid, and I have honestly loved being pregnant until now, but fuck me, I'm starting to not have fun anymore," Sariah announced to the sympathetic laughter of everyone in the circle.

Several women started up a conversation about the joys and woes of pregnancy. Lily expected the men to launch to their feet and hurry away to talk about something—literally anything—else. Instead they seemed to settle, many of them sharing looks with their wives or partners; a few patted thighs and shoulders.

It still struck her to see affection given so casually sometimes, but she found that it was getting easier and easier to override that old programming. Especially since she'd always been fond of touch by nature. So many things had changed, she mused, watching Bel lift Sharkie in his arms.

"Here they go!" someone called.

The conversations paused as Bel spread his wings, holding them wide for a moment, then launched into the air. Lily watched them rise, whooping and cheering along with everyone else, her silent chest flooding with joy. Over the muffled thump of Bel's wingbeats as he circled high overhead, Lily could hear Sharkie's high, gleeful cackle.

"I don't know what your life was like," Sariah said, leaning over the side of her chair, "but, girl, you are having the coolest fucking Afterlife."

Lily squinted up at Bel and Sharkie as they flew high and far enough away to turn into specks and aimed a smile at Sariah. "My Afterlife is significantly cooler than my life was, though it wasn't bad."

Sariah nodded thoughtfully, a breeze ruffling her hair and blowing a charcoal-colored strand free of the clip she'd contained it in. She opened her mouth to say something, then winced and shifted, pressing a hand to her ribs.

"I was going to ask something profound, but my kid is starting to think they're running out of room," she said with an exasperated smile.

"Almost there, huh?"

"About five more months to go, but I'm closer to the end than the beginning, thank fuck. Is it true mortals are only pregnant for nine months?"

"Eh, it's more like ten, but there's usually a couple weeks of variance. How long for you?"

"A year. Possibly a bit longer if there are wings involved." Sariah sighed. "Did you ever have kids? This is obviously my first time."

Lily considered shrugging it off as usual, but . . . she was done being afraid. And part of not being afraid was being real. So, what the hell. Literally.

She gave Sariah a rueful smile. "Not in any of my lifetimes. Sorry, I'm not able to give you experience-based advice."

"Ah," Sariah said slowly, her golden eyes going sharp. "Did you want kids, then?"

Lily had known it was coming, but her throat tightened anyway. "Very much," she murmured, finding her wineglass particularly interesting.

"Then I'm sorry," Sariah said softly.

Lily met her eyes again.

Sariah's gaze flashed with a bit of the fire that must have drawn Asmodeus in so completely. "Not for asking. If you hadn't wanted to answer me, then you would have told me to fuck all the way off. I respect that. Then I would have apologized for asking. No, I'm sorry that you never got to have kids during your mortal life." Sariah glanced upward with a smile as Bel swooped overhead with Sharkie, who was shrieking with laughter. "But your kid is pretty awesome. I know it's not exactly the same, but—"

"We just skipped the pregnancy to preschool phase," Lily said, returning Sariah's smile with one of her own. She glanced upward, wondering briefly if Sharkie would ever ask about siblings.

Some of the kids in the nearby group raised their voices as their argument grew increasingly heated. Lily arched an eyebrow, happening to meet the gaze of Bel's oldest brother, Melchom. He rolled his eyes fondly.

Asmodeus landed, sending the cluster of kids sprinting toward him, shoving each other. He must have communicated with Bel at some point, because he shook his head, denying any more rides until Bel got back and saw that they'd done what he'd asked. The kids fell back into their argument while he stalked over to Sariah, running a gentle hand over the curve of her belly and kissing her forehead before nuzzling his nose against hers.

Lily looked away and listened to Lilith talking about her children.

"You'd think that Beleth would have been the most difficult because of the wings, but when they're born, their wings are just filmy little things plastered to their backs, so Bel's birth wasn't bad at all. Aludem"—Lilith pointed dryly at her fourth child, who grinned and laced his gray hands behind his head—"was the most difficult. And the biggest, *by far.*"

"But the most peaceful baby, right?" Aludem laughed.

People around the group chuckled. Lily caught Sariah glancing at her out of the corner of her eye and shot her a quick thumbs-up. *I'm fine.*

Sweet of her, though, to check in about all the baby talk.

"Very funny. Most peaceful baby award goes to Beleth or Orin. Though, Beleth was extra stressful because I'd never had a baby with wings before, and I was always worried that I would accidentally do something to keep him from flying."

"But noooo," Annika, the second-eldest child, put in, "Bitty Bel had to learn how to fly *early.*"

"And none of us knew a moment's peace from that day on," Orin drawled. "He'd just *fly off.*"

"*You* were the one who taught yourself how to pick the lock on the pantry and ate yourself sick on sugar. Multiple times," Lilith said.

"Mom! Keep your voice down, the kids will get ideas!"

"Too late," someone muttered.

"Sugar incidents aside, Bel was the one who flew into your office window," Orin said smugly.

Unwilling to let that one go by unanswered, Lily leaned forward innocently. "But weren't *you* the one who dared him to fly between the spires of the tower?"

There was a beat of silence during which Orin's deep blue face paled several shades. Then the circle erupted into laughter and catcalls. Sariah cackled like a Halloween witch, and Asmodeus laid fully on his side, howling.

"I *knew* someone put him up to that! You let him take the blame for that all these years?" Lilith's voice rose over everyone's laughter, which, of course, set them off again, drowning out Orin's attempts to explain.

A warm little body flopped against her side, catching her off guard.

"What's going on?" Sharkie asked breathlessly. Her shaggy blond hair was utterly windswept, and she practically glowed with excitement.

Lily wiped her eyes, chuckling. "Oh, we're just laughing about something Orin did. Did you have fun?"

"Yes! I'm gonna ask Bel to fly me everywhere now!"

A shadow fell over them, and she looked up.

Bel held his hand out expectantly. "Your turn, princess."

38

THAT'S THE GROUND

Lily

Lily followed Bel across the lawn to the open area that they'd used as a landing site, ignoring the wolf whistle from Asmodeus. She wasn't scared of heights, and she trusted that Bel would rather chop off his own tail than hurt her, but adrenaline crackled through her veins anyway. She paused to braid her hair. Sharkie might have been able to pull off the windswept look, but '80's hair metal wasn't a style she personally favored.

"I'll try not to make you scream too loudly." Bel smirked.

"Please," Lily scoffed, finishing her braid. "I seriously doubt you're going to make me scream."

Bel's heated *are-you-kidding-me* expression had muscles low in her belly clenching.

She smiled sweetly at him and patted his cheek. "With clothes on, anyway."

His scarred eyebrow arched higher. She could practically *hear* his mind coming up with a plan, or plans.

Dirty boy.

"Quit flirting in front of the kids." Someone laughed.

"Leave them alone, he needs the practice." This from a smug-sounding Asmodeus.

They both rolled their eyes, and Bel stepped closer, half shielding her from their onlookers.

"Ready?" he asked.

"Are you? You've already created one flying enthusiast today. Do you think you can handle having two of us on your hands?"

Bel's eyes crinkled. "I've got two hands, and I love flying. It'll be fun to share it with you both. Now, hold on." He dipped, swooping her into his grasp, one arm beneath her knees and the other around her back.

She reflexively threw an arm around his neck and gripped his broad shoulders. Being picked up was a deeply unfamiliar sensation. In fact, before Bel, her feet hadn't left the ground under someone else's power since she was small.

Oh, wait . . .

Hazy memories of being lifted from her bed or the couch in those last days of being sick swam to the surface.

Different. That was different.

She shoved the memories away, focusing on the solid feel of Bel's arms around her and the warm wall of his chest against her side. She hadn't been picked up for fun since she hit her big growth spurt at thirteen.

"On three, yeah?" he murmured, brushing his nose against hers. She stole a quick kiss that had his arms tightening around her. "Cheeky. Now, one."

Lily sucked in a preparatory breath, mortal instincts reminding her that flying wasn't a natural occurrence, the buzz of excitement in her veins beginning to shift to something less cheery. "Two—"

He launched into the air.

Lily yelped, gripping his shoulders with all the strength she possessed as her stomach was left behind on the ground. She buried her face in his neck, the wind whipping strands of her hair free. Over the wind and the thump of his wings, she could feel his chest shaking with laughter.

Her arms started to ache from holding him so tightly. They leveled out, his wings beating less frequently.

"What happened to going on three?!" she asked over the wind, refusing to open her eyes until she was certain that she could do so without having them pop out of her skull.

"It's like ripping off a Band-Aid. You can't overthink it too much, and I could see you starting to overthink it."

Lily bit him in retaliation. Gently, where his neck curved into his shoulder, tongue flicking over the soft skin. His whole body went taut, claws pricking through her clothes where they hadn't before. She kissed the spot and smiled.

"Do you feel properly avenged, Lils? Because, if not, tell you what, you can bite me more later. It's a bad idea to fly distracted." His laugh was deep and rumbling. "Now, open your eyes, princess. It's almost as beautiful as you."

Lily took a moment to mentally steady herself, then turned her head and opened her eyes.

She'd seen beautiful mortal places before both in person and in pictures, and visited incredible, impossible places in the Afterlife. None of them could compare.

The level of Hell stretched away into the distance on all sides, laid before them like a hauntingly beautiful map made up of fiery rivers and streams, with glowing red lava-falls tumbling down black stone. Bioluminescent vegetation glowed in a kaleidoscope of colors, breaking up the palette of blacks and grays and reds. Hundreds—thousands—of orderly and not-so-orderly gardens glowed around beautiful homes. Outside of the central "city," a feral tumble of colors and plants dotted the landscape, while a wide swath of forest gleamed in a hundred shades of green.

They were high, but the glowing ceiling of the cavern was still far above them, and the wind was pleasantly warm as it brushed over her skin. She couldn't tear her eyes away from the landscape before her; the darkness of the ground and the architecture that the demons preferred a stunning contrast to the light of the plants and ribbons of lava.

And she never would have seen it from the ground.

"Bel," she murmured, awestruck.

He chuckled softly. "Yeah, that was about my reaction when I was old enough to fly this high." He angled to fly over a wide river of lava that spat molten chunks into the air as it dropped over the edge of a ravine. The heat of the molten rock surged upward, and so did they, buoyed by the thermal air.

Another knot came loose in her chest, a sense of rightness similar to the one she'd experienced when she arrived in her Paradise. She rested her cheek against Bel's, loosening the grip of one hand to stroke over his chest, allowing herself to relax in his hold.

"Why do you ever spend time on the ground?" she asked, only half kidding. Tears—*tears*—of awe stung her eyes. Flying like this, with him, was about as close to a religious experience that she'd ever had. The motion of his wingbeats, of moving through the air had a soothing quality, like sitting on a porch swing.

"People I love are on the ground," he said, hands twitching a bit. "Life is on the ground. Flying is a gift; it's a part of myself that is intrinsic, necessary. But the things that are the most important to me? Those are on the ground. Besides, I'm sure this will shock you, but not everyone likes to fly." He chuckled. "It took Sariah years to really get comfortable with it. My mother refuses to fly unless it's practically an emergency. The little ones like it, for the most part, though there are a few outliers. I always dreamed—" He stopped himself and shrugged against her, muscles in his chest flexing as he beat his wings once. "Anyway, it's part of why I enjoy working with the aerial legions. Flight isn't optional for anyone there; it's our way of life."

He was quiet for a moment, flying them away from the river of lava and out toward the glowing forest. He kissed the corner of her mouth softly. "I love sharing this with you."

Lily tore her gaze away from the impossible beauty of Hell and focused on Bel, whose handsome face was more captivating and certainly more important than some glowing trees. He'd stopped himself. The little lines by his eyes were tight. She brought her hand up from his chest to cup his cheek, making his lashes dip. "I love sharing this with you too," she said softly. "But what did you always dream?"

There. A lightning-fast flicker of some powerful emotion rippled over his features before he steeled himself. He held her gaze as best he could mid-flight.

"We promised to be honest with each other, but I don't want you to feel bad."

"Tell me, big guy."

He swallowed hard. "I always dreamed that, if I had a partner who was willing and able to bear children, I'd have kids of my own to fly with. I loved flying with . . . with my father, and Asmodeus loves flying with his mom. My dad always talked about how much he enjoyed teaching me to fly, because it was like he got to rediscover the joy of it again through my eyes." He studied her face, thumb stroking up the side of her leg. "Having a family has never been a guarantee, and having winged kids certainly never was, but it was a dream."

Was.

Her stomach dipped. She didn't want him to think in terms of "was" because of her.

"I know the feeling," she said quietly, brushing away a piece of hair that was being especially annoying. She offered him a smile, praying that it looked genuine—because it was—but it also hurt badly. "I've always wanted to be a mom. Always wanted a couple of kids so they could have siblings, and so I could experience the full mess and joy of it all, every stage, every step, multiple times over. So, I get it. I know you'll be an amazing father, Bel."

His face whipped her way so fast she was surprised she didn't hear his neck pop, and they bobbled in midair. She gripped his shoulder again.

"Sorry," he said quickly, leveling out again. "I just . . . Are you . . . Fuck it, hold on." He tightened his grip just as she opened her mouth to ask what he meant, half folding his wings and sending them diving toward the ground.

Lily snapped her mouth shut to keep her shriek contained.

Bel knows what he's doing, Bel knows what he's doing, Bel knows—THAT'S THE GROUND!

He flared his wings, slowing their descent, and flapped hard to set them down gently in a clearing filled with tiny, softly shining flowers and grass gilded with its own light. He didn't set her down as expected, he just frowned at her.

Lily was fairly certain that her fingernails were embedded in his skin from the adrenaline rush of their dive, but she held his gaze. "What?"

"I 'will be' an amazing father? You're talking about Sharkie, right? We—souls can't have kids in the Afterlife, unless you've found some loophole I don't know about." A glimmer of hope flickered in his eyes. "*Is* there a loophole I don't know about?"

That vision of an impossible future flashed through her mind again. Her insides felt like they were made of broken glass.

She wished. Oh, how she wished for that.

"If there was," she said, voice cracking a little, "I would have told you about it. Sharkie adores you, and you are so good with her, so of course we're a family. But I was . . . After Sharkie grows up and I . . . I reincarnate, I want you to be happy. You don't have to give up your dream forever."

His frown verged on a scowl. "But *you* won't be there."

"You can't have the life you want with me," Lily said past the lump in her throat. The idea of Bel with anyone else made her simultaneously want to rage and cry.

"What kind of life do I want?" Bel asked.

She got the sense it was rhetorical and stayed quiet.

"I want to be a capable general to my legions. I want the other Universes to stay the fuck out of ours so that I have more time to spend with my family and friends. The role of 'fun and favorite uncle' is a title that requires effort to maintain. I want to read more of those smutty books from your library—I read the one with the tail, by the way, princess, and I took *notes*. I want to watch our Sharkie grow up and lose her fear and probably take over the Afterlife. But that's fine, I have confidence she'll be a wise and benevolent, if chaotic, ruler."

His eyes were intense, and she couldn't look away as his voice deepened. "I want you. I want you as my friend. I want to send you stupid texts. I want to make you blush. I want to fuck you and make love to you and do things with you that would probably get us sent to Hell by silly mortal standards, and I want to laugh with you during and after. I.

Want. You. For as long as I can have you. And"—he cleared his throat—"when it's time for you to go live the big, beautiful, amazing life you deserve, I want to cheer you on every step of the way, just like I promised I would."

"Bel, I want that with you too—" she started, but he stopped her with a single shake of his head.

"After you? After you, I'll focus on work, family, friends, and Sharkie, if she's still in the Afterlife. I'll do all the good I can, and I'll keep doing that, to the best of my ability, until I either die in combat"—Lily couldn't hide her horrified jerk—"or . . . the other option."

The Void. He was talking about the Void.

Lily tightened her grip on him involuntarily.

"Don't you dare feel fucking bad, because I had given up on the dream of *any* kind of family before you arrived and made my life better than it was ever going to be without you. You've given me a family, Lily."

Lily's nose stung. Dammit. "Bel . . ."

He had told her that he'd cheer her on if she left him, told her that he wanted to love like mortals. But he'd never mentioned this. Never told her that there would be no one else after her.

No one had ever made her so permanent a fixture in their lives. No one had ever felt so entirely *right* to her in every way.

Because I love him. Totally and completely.

As she finally admitted it to herself, every fiber of her being settled. Paradise had felt right. Kissing Bel had felt right. Their intimate moments had felt right. Playing in the rain with Sharkie had felt right. Working at the Hellp Desk had felt right. Flying with him had felt right.

But holy fuck, realizing that she was in love with Bel?

It lit her up like the first warm, sunny day after winter. It felt *right.*

Right enough to never go back? To give up all those dreams?

To give up life? Forever?

The idea of going back to the mortal world wasn't . . . soothing like it used to be. She tamped down the roil of doubt and fear hard, locking it away before Bel, with his eyes that missed nothing, could see and push before she was prepared.

I can love him and not know the whole future. Love like mortals, remember?

"You okay, princess?" he asked quietly.

"I just realized something," she managed. "I'm not ready to talk about it yet."

Bel watched her. She could see the curiosity eating at him, but he nodded.

"Is it about my butt?" he asked slyly.

His question jarred her out of her head and made her laugh so hard she leaned back to breathe. Bel spun her in a circle, laughing with her. A breeze riffled through the trees in a gentle susurration, the flowers and grass around them rippling like waves on a pond.

It seemed so glaringly obvious that she should have owned up to loving him for a while now, butt jokes and all. Or perhaps especially because of the butt jokes. She sat back up, wiping at her eyes while Bel kissed her cheek.

"Thank you for that. We're supposed to be having a fun flight, not going all heavy and deep," she said finally, smile still pulling at her lips.

"Princess, I'm always down to get *heavy* and *deep* with you." Bel sobered a bit. "But I'm sorry," he said quietly, meeting her eyes with a rueful smile. "I kind of dumped that on you, didn't I?"

Lily tilted his chin her way and kissed him long and slow, then rested her forehead against his. "You did not. We're honest with each other."

"One of my favorite things about you and I"—he tilted his head with a smile that carried a wealth of emotion—"is that we deal with stuff together. We like each other, we respect each other, we trust each other. Plus, we're both hot as fuck and have great senses of humor. Whatever it is, we'll figure it out."

She traced the point of his tattooed ear. "That's one of my favorite things about us too."

"Good," Bel said. "We will talk about it, when you're ready?"

"Yes," Lily promised, then spoke again. She *saw* Bel, and she was plenty observant herself. She'd picked up enough pieces to have an idea of what wounds he carried on his heart. "Just like you can talk to me. Whenever you're ready."

His eyes widened, a hint of vulnerability flaring before he collected himself.

She raised a playful eyebrow and leaned in. "In the meantime, we should probably get back to your family before they think I'm doing naughty things to you and send out a search party. Now that I'm a little more used to flying, I want to see if you can make me scream, because I have doubts."

All seriousness evaporated from his face. Lily had thrown a gauntlet, and had been fairly confident in doing so, right up until she saw the look in his eye.

"Princess, not only can I make you scream, I'm going to make you *beg*."

Bel

By the time he landed them on his mother's lawn, he was laughing so hard he could barely see. He was fairly certain that Lily's nails had made marks on his shoulders that would be there for days, and the primal satisfaction of that was eclipsed only by his glee at the sounds he'd gotten her to make. She panted and laughed as he settled her on her feet, her eyes bright and cheeks flushed, looking so damn kissable—

"UNCLE BEL!" A chorus of little voices interrupted his plans, and they both turned to watch the pack of kids sprint across the lawn.

"Did you guys do what I asked?" he said, running a critical eye over them.

There were grass stains where there hadn't been grass stains before, one of Lezzie's braids was wonky, and they aimed scowls at each other when they thought he wasn't looking. They all nodded, some with more enthusiasm than others. Behind them all, Sharkie's expression was cartoonishly wide-eyed and grim as she slowly shook her head.

Frankly, it was a relief to not have to give them rides. He felt . . . raw. Not from their conversation about kids and life, or even from the mystery of whatever had clicked in that brilliant mind of hers in the clearing. Her simple offer to hear him when he was ready had floored him. He wasn't surprised that she knew something. His princess was smart and sharp-eyed, and he'd been edging toward telling her the full story for some time. But it was his closest, most painful secret, and he had no idea how to share it.

"So, what order are you going in?" Lily asked mildly, threading her fingers with his.

Bel smothered his grin.

The cracks in the children's lie showed almost immediately. Two hands raised at the same time, followed by a brief stare-down that had one hand lowering slowly.

"Sorry, I forgot," Nimmie said through her teeth, tail lashing as she stared at her cousin. "I'm going second though."

This was apparently too much of an injustice for the rest of them to cover for, because they all erupted into arguments that, based on the sighs of some of the adults, had been thoroughly argued before.

"Well," Bel said with as much disappointment as he could muster without laughing, "I guess there're no more flight rides today. You guys will have to try and work together on a solution next time."

Their faces ranged from heartbreak to out-and-out betrayal.

"Uncle Bel, you're not the favorite uncle anymore," Furfur said with a pout that made him look exactly like his father, Orin.

"Is the new favorite uncle Asmodeus going to give you all flight rides?" Bel asked loudly.

"No, he is not!" Asmodeus called back around a mouthful of food.

More disappointed moans.

"Tell you guys what," Lily said brightly. "If you're not going on flight rides, how about we play a game?"

They all perked up.

"What game?" Sharkie asked.

"Have any of you ever heard of the game Ninja?"

A chorus of nos.

Lily squeezed his hand and let go, guiding the kids to a clear patch of the lawn and directing them into a circle, explaining the simple rules of the game. Bel watched her go.

I've always wanted to be a mom, always wanted a couple of kids.

He could see it. She was an incredible mother to Sharkie, her love for the kid palpable and fierce. He smiled. He'd met battle-hardened warriors, millennia old, who weren't as inherently fierce as Lily. The woman had a warrior's soul. Even Odin had commented on it during a tactical meeting. He held both Lily and Sharkie in fond regard, but Lily had his respect as a warrior. Warrior soul, mother's heart. Fierce.

Bel hadn't missed the little flicker of emotion on Lily's face when Anyaet had gurgled at Lily and grabbed a chunk of her hair. The flash of pain, of grief, in her eyes when she'd empathized about wanting to have multiple children had gutted him. Not just because he knew how it felt to want that so badly, but because he knew that she *could* have that. Just not in the Afterlife.

He'd cut off his own wings to have that chance with her. The real bitch of it all was that he could practically *see* it. He could see her, round with their child, or holding their newborn and probably still working at the Hellp Desk, wielding that gloriously sharp tongue with devastating effect. He could see Sharkie being the best big sister, teaching them her special brand of chaotic joy from day one. He'd already wondered a dozen times what their child or children would look like. Would they have human coloring? Would they have his eyes? Her nose? He hoped that they'd have her laugh.

He could see them both chasing toddlers, could see how his soldiers would adopt his kids when they came to the training fields like they adopted each other's. He wondered who their kids would grow up to be, what their passions would be, who, if anyone, they would love.

It wasn't like they couldn't be a family without that, they already were. The day he'd gone to Lily's Paradise and allowed himself the comfort that she and Sharkie had offered, he'd felt *safe* for the first time since he'd been small. They hadn't patronized. They hadn't made a production out of it. They'd both just been there. Them and the cat.

He rubbed at his chest and headed toward the chatting adults, aiming for the empty chair by Sariah.

Asmodeus squinted at him over his plate of food. "Interesting noises we heard from up there."

Bel smirked and mimed zipping his lips, locking them, and throwing the key away.

"Smart move," Sariah told him.

"Wait, before you sit down," Annika, his oldest sister said, handing him the squalling baby unceremoniously and beating a hasty retreat. "She's been fed and burped. Good luck," she called.

Anyaet was deep purple with what Bel assumed was blind rage. She'd stopped screaming like she was being skinned alive when Annika had handed her over and settled into tearful fussing. He checked her diaper, made sure nothing had worked through her onesie and was itchy or painful, pulled off her socks to make sure she hadn't gotten a hair wrapped around her toe again, and, finding nothing, settled her against his shoulder and bounced. She subsided to shuddering gasps, smushing her wet, snotty face into his neck and seizing his shirt in her chubby little fists.

He loved his little sister with every fiber of his being. However, the kid was incredibly particular about damn near everything, but especially who she was held by. He glanced over at his mother, who scolded a shamefaced Orin for something, and shook his head. His heart had nearly dropped out of his ass when she'd just handed Anyaet to Lily, oh so casually.

Luckily, Anyaet had decided that Lily was one of her people.

On his shoulder, Anyaet had stopped sniffling and rested her head on his shoulder with one fist in her mouth, watching the gathering with her bright green eyes.

"Did we miss anything?" he asked.

"The kids had a battle to do a general proud," Asmodeus said. "There wasn't a chance of them getting that one sorted out today. Valafar had great form on his takedown of Furfur though."

"He's been working on his grappling, remember?" Bel said.

"It shows."

Bel let the conversations ebb and flow around him, trying not to get too lost in thought. Eventually, some of the other adults joined in on the game that had the kids captivated, and Lily strolled toward him, shaking her hair out of the messy braid.

Anyaet squealed and launched herself sideways, reaching toward Lily with both hands and a big grin. Bel swore, catching her before she could slither out of his grasp, his heart threatening to pound out of his chest. Lily laughed and reached to take her from him, planting a big kiss on Anyaet's round cheek.

"You crazy girl, what was that?" she teased. "You trying to give us all a heart attack?"

Anyaet cooed.

"Of course she was. She thinks it's funny." Bel stuck his tongue out at her. She didn't see him, too absorbed with trying to grab as much of Lily's hair as she could.

Lily shot him a knowing look and reached to untangle Anyaet's hands, face flushed from playing the game with the kids, eyes bright as she teased the baby in her arms. Sharkie's laugh rose high and clear over the chatter.

"So, Lily, just remember if you ever have more kids—" Angra, his brother Melchom's wife, started cheerfully as she approached.

Bel shook his head, silently begging her to stop talking. At his side, both Sariah and Asmodeus also shook their heads; Asmodeus even made a slicing motion across his neck.

Lily smiled politely at her. Bel couldn't see physical evidence of a reaction, but he watched the walls go up in her eyes.

"—that while they might become the most important person in your life, you have to keep a space for who you were *before* kids. It's easier with just one, but once you have more, maintaining your own identity is so . . . important . . ." She trailed off, glancing between Bel, Sariah, and Asmodeus.

Lily glanced over her shoulder at them, and Bel did his best to look innocent, heart aching.

Lily adjusted Anyaet and offered her a finger to gum on, smiling at Angra. "Isn't that the truth? Seriously, some of the best advice out there. I saw a lot of my friends struggle with a sense of self back in the day, even before they became parents. Though, as for us—" Her voice grew regretful, and she didn't so much as look at him, strain easing into the lines of her body. "Unfortunately, as a mortal soul, I can't get pregnant in the Afterlife. If I could, I would. Without hesitation." She offered a genuine, gentle smile to a mortified Angra, who apologized profusely.

"You don't work with mortal souls. I don't expect everyone to know the minutia of mortal existence," Lily assured her. "Even I don't know that yet."

"True," Angra said, wringing her hands together. "But you know what? What I said still stands. You have that wonderful girl there." She nodded to Sharkie, who had her hood back and was laughing. "And you still have to remember to keep space for yourself."

Lily deftly and kindly guided their conversation to less treacherous ground, and the apprehension eased out of the people around them. Bel exchanged a glance with Sariah, whose golden gaze was gentle, then made a silly face at Anyaet, who grinned at him over Lily's shoulder.

Family gatherings. He loved them, loved the chaos and the fun and the conversations. But damn if they weren't at least a little bit stressful every time.

39

OLDIE BUT A GOODIE

Lily

Lily scrolled through emails on her computer without actually processing them, waiting for a soul to approach while working through the snarl of her thoughts.

The day after the party, while Sharkie went to the movies with Lucifer, she and Bel had gone on a date, getting dinner at a Moroccan restaurant and sneaking kisses in between sips of mint tea. Afterward, as they made their way back to his house to finally, *finally* indulge themselves in each other, he'd given her such a look of heated anticipation and joy that she'd been unable to resist temptation. Grabbing him by the front of his pants, she'd pulled him into a shadowy alcove in the Hall and kissed up his neck. He'd quickly turned the tables, the heat between them building and building, making her wonder how they'd manage to make it all the way to his house, when a new sensation had them both groaning.

"Please tell me that your cock magically vibrates and that isn't your phone," she'd sighed.

"Fuck, I wish." He'd pulled back just enough to dig his phone out of his pocket and read the message, not bothering to hide it from her.

URGENT! Reinforcements needed. Call ASAP.

Lily had gripped the side of his shirt so tightly her fist ached, forcing herself to think calmly and clearly as she studied his handsome, rugged features.

He'd dropped the phone to his side, bending to press his forehead against hers and take a few slow breaths. She'd cradled his face with her other hand, breathing his air, savoring their closeness.

"I'm sorry, princess," he'd murmured.

She'd pressed her thumb over his lips, stilling them. "Be safe," she'd said softly, kissing him one more time. Then he'd been gone.

The whole week since he'd left, she'd half kicked herself for not growing the fuck up and telling him she loved him right then and there, but she hadn't wanted it to be some clichéd "just-in-case." She wanted to have it stand on its own and matter.

She loved Bel, and was fairly certain he felt the same, which was both thrilling and terrifying. Despite the habitual fear, she knew in her bones that Bel was nothing like the people in her past. There was only one thing to do. One thing she wanted to do. Let him in.

He'd poured his heart out in that meadow. She wanted to give him the same.

Bel had some old, deep personal wounds of his own, clearly having to do with his father, and possibly something or someone else. She hurt for him every time she saw that flash of insecurity. Perhaps by her being vulnerable, he would feel more comfortable to share some of the pain that he'd carried alone for so long.

Tell him. Just tell him. Or should I wait until I decide—

"Excuse me, I seem to be lost, and I was told to talk to you." The young punk woman smiled politely at her, hands tucked in the pockets of her vest. One look at her eyes and Lily realized the youthful exterior was just a facade.

This soul was old. Very old.

She glanced at the desk. No file.

"Of course," Lily said, giving the soul her full attention.

The woman's mouth quirked up, lip piercing gleaming. "Love the name of the desk by the way, that's hilarious."

"Thanks! A little humor goes a long way in my book. So, how can I help?"

"It's been a while since my last visit down here. I like what they've done with the place." She paused, seeming . . . tired. "Anyway, I got a little turned around on my way to the Void."

Lily ignored the sad twist in her chest and smiled. "Yeah, the Void keeps itself pretty tucked away. They really should have signs for it. So, if you go back up the stairs, once you hit the main Hall, hang a left and keep going. At the second intersection, take a right, and you should be in a hall with no other doors. At the end of that is the arch of the Void. If you don't want to do the stairs to get back up to the Hall, you're more than welcome to use the elevator."

"Nah." The soul shrugged. "It's been a good, long run. I'd like to savor my last walk, ya know?"

Lily's throat went tight, but she nodded, remembering all the lasts that she'd tried to enjoy. "I do. Would you like some company?"

The woman considered it, giving Lily a long look, then gazing around at the gate, the line of souls, the little shark plushy that Lily kept by the computer—a gift from Sharkie "for emergency support in case the demons are busy"—before smiling and shaking her head.

"Thank you, but no, I'd like to do this one myself. Are you one of the new full-time residents? Like, are you staying in the Afterlife permanently?"

The question sucker punched her right in the gut. "I don't know. I'd like to, but . . ."

The woman tilted her head, propping her hip against the desk. "But what?"

Ah, what the hell.

Lily searched for the right words. "There are certain aspects of life and living that I'd like to experience. I think. But . . ." She looked at the black screen of her phone, where she knew that, if she tapped the screen, the picture of her, Bel, and Sharkie would appear. They'd all been in their pajamas for movie night, laughing at their hot cocoa mustaches when Bel grabbed her phone to get a selfie. Max was loafed on the arm of the sofa behind them, too proper for their nonsense.

Lily smiled. "But there are people here I care about. Very much."

"Ah, now that does complicate things. I get the love of life and living, obviously, or I wouldn't have gone back as many times as I did. But not all souls are meant for that. A few hundred lifetimes ago," the woman said casually while Lily tried not to choke on her tongue, "I considered giving it all up to stay and gain just as much. But in the end, living a mortal life felt right to me. I've gone back time and again, seen and done it all, or most of it anyway. I've had lives that were so brutal and awful that they are unspeakable, and I've had lives that were so incandescently wonderful that I could spend an eternity trying to explain them and fail. I've known souls who gave it up, stayed here, and had lives that were just as incredible and full of joy and pain. We're all made for different things."

The woman shrugged again, adding with a grin, "So, maybe you go back someday, maybe you don't, but in the meantime, I say let yourself be happy. With whoever and whatever 'happy' is for you. Anyway. Thanks for the directions." With that, she turned and walked back toward the stairs.

Lily watched her go, mouth slightly agape. She snapped it shut, mentally shaking herself and squinting down at the desk that had been a gift from Lucifer and the Universe, but mostly the latter, as Lucifer had confessed one day. Why, of all the moments and topics, had that soul arrived at that moment and talked about that?

"Are you trying to tell me something or what? Don't be coy, you fucking celestial coward."

A small mirror appeared in the same spot that files did, propped up to show her narrow-eyed reflection.

Shit. Pot, meet kettle.

"Yeah, okay, that's fair. I appreciate the honesty," she grumbled, scrubbing her hands over her face, then bringing one down to splay across her silent chest.

Silent, but not empty. Not anymore, and certainly not at that moment. Love. She had love filling her chest.

For Bel. For Sharkie.

For herself.

She'd thought she loved herself before, and she had, but in a defensive, prickly kind of way. This was a love of herself based on understanding. On forgiveness and empathy, the desire to love and be loved. To let people in.

A warm buzz of courage started in her chest, trickling out through her veins like electricity.

"I don't know how many times I have to say it," a male soul snarled, storming toward the desk, "I should not be here. I was a very successful, very influential—"

Lily ignored his ongoing tirade the moment his file appeared on the desk, a mucky whitish color, like spoiled milk, the letters of his name etched out in harsh lines of flat gray. She could feel the slimy sourness without even touching it.

"Shut up," she told him plainly. He narrowed his eyes while she pointed at his file. "You see this? This is your soul file. Your file goes where you belong or where it needs to be. Your file appeared here. In Hell. Because this is where you belong, for now. If you belonged anywhere else, it wouldn't be here. But here it fucking is." She gingerly lifted it without touching any of the pages and set it in the basket, where it promptly disappeared. She shuddered and fixed her bitchiest glare on the now purple-faced man. "Go to your level, before you find out what it's like to pick your own teeth off the ground."

He sputtered at her while she stared him down, until he finally turned and walked away.

She reached for her phone. Their smiling, hot cocoa–mustached faces beamed up at her before she pulled up the text thread with Bel. She'd sent him dozens of pictures and messages since he'd left, and he had yet to respond to a single one.

Princess: *I have so much I've been wanting to tell you.*

That sounded casual and totally not suspicious. Didn't it? Or was it too vague? Maybe vague was good in this situation? Lily tapped her nail on the desk to vent her nervous energy, then sent it and put her phone down, puffing her cheeks as she blew out a stream of air.

It was true, she had so much to tell him. Whether she stayed forever or not.

Bel

Bel clapped one of his soldiers on the shoulder in gratitude and watched her hurry off toward the elevators and home. The third-level training field, which served as one of their primary assembly areas before and after missions, was finally beginning to empty, bringing him one step closer to a clean change of clothes and seeing his girls. He'd kept his phone off, refusing to boot it up before he finished his debriefs, but his eyes kept going to the pocket of his bag.

Lucifer strode across the hard-packed earth, icy eyes glowing as he approached. "What news?"

"The rift hasn't grown, but they are slowly increasing their numbers. We're seeing more than just brutalizers like the gegony. They're sending more of the higher-intelligence ones through as well. Chittahi and kelatun, I think. It was Morrigan's people who encountered the latter." Bel shouldered his bag and pulled out his phone. "The attack patterns have changed, but they're still more or less predictable. We had a few injuries but thankfully no losses."

"I'm glad everyone came home. According to Freyja's reports they're still trying to rip the power of souls from the fabric of the Universe and remaining unsuccessful. I suppose since brute force wasn't working, they've sent in handlers to refine their efforts. Let's hope they give up and return home when they realize that it's impossible without a complete invasion."

"Let's hope." Bel started walking toward the elevators while his phone powered on, Lucifer falling in beside him. "What have I missed here?"

"Sharkie has grown another inch, and she seems to be closer to age ten than eight. She's doing very well in school. Lily continues to be her lovely self, though we all noticed that she's seemed a bit quiet since you left this time."

"'We'?" Bel tapped the elevator "call" button, debating if he really wanted to stop by his office first. He wanted to sweep Lily up and perhaps find a moment of privacy at long last, but he was filthy with old sweat, and his armor was itchy. And he would be remiss in his duty if he didn't send out at least a brief summary report for the next legion heading out and all the higher-ups, but that wouldn't take long.

"You were single for more than a century," Lucifer pointed out smugly, "and of all the people you could be with, you're with a mortal soul who is famous in her own right for revolutionizing the process at the gate. It's safe to say that many of us are aware of and invested in your relationship."

Bel grunted and stepped into the elevator, pulling up the message thread with Lily. He scrolled back through the pictures and notes she'd sent him, then read them in chronological order until he reached the most recent one, sent only a few minutes before. Something about it seemed off, lacking any of her usual wit or warmth. Her message sounded . . . contemplative? No, he was probably reading it wrong.

He nodded absently at whatever Lucifer was saying as he messaged her back.

40

PRINCE AND PRINCESS

Lily

Her phone buzzed.

Big Guy: *Hey, princess, I've missed you. So much. I'm just getting back, and I'm going to grab a change of clothes and a sponge bath in my office, and I have to do a quick report, but then I'll be right up.*

Big Guy: *Wait. Did you change my name???*

Lily half leapt out of her chair, but forced herself back down, resting her free hand at the base of her throat to steady herself. He was back and, most importantly, back safe. The mission must have gone well if he was chipper enough to ask about his contact name.

Princess: *Yeah, it was between Big Guy and His Royal HighnAss.*

Big Guy: *Ah, fair. Though, also in the spirit of fairness, my ass looks pretty great in armor, so it's not like you would have been wrong either way.*

Lily chuckled, then took a deep breath, thumbs hovering over the screen. The rush of courage fizzled slightly, and she set her phone down, scrubbing her damp palms over her leggings.

File. She needed her file for this.

She'd have to run home first to get—

Something landed on her lap. Her file had a slightly more purple hue to it than she remembered, but the metallic letters of her name glimmered with the same colorful sheen. She'd tucked it onto a shelf in her library soon after her arrival in Paradise and hadn't really thought of it since.

Good to know she could summon it.

I want and need to do this. I just wish I wasn't so chicken shit scared about it.

She swallowed hard. Then reached for her phone.

Princess: *Are you in the mood for a personal conversation in your office?*

The dots by Bel's name popped up and disappeared, popped up, then disappeared. She wanted to throw up.

Big Guy: *With you, princess, always.*

Her hands were shaking.

Princess: *Be rihgt diwm*

Princess: *Duck. Be right down.*

Princess: *F u c k*

Big Guy: *Ok*

Lily waved an arm to get Moura's attention.

"What's up?" Moura called.

"I need to step away for a bit. There's something I need to do."

"Sure thing."

Lily stood on unsteady legs, gripped her file so hard her knuckles turned white, and headed for the elevator. She barely registered the ride down and the walk to his office. There were other people on the stairs, but she didn't really see them. One of them might have even said something to her.

Suddenly, she stood in front of his door, the silly sticky note from her first visit still stuck to the wood, held in place by tape after the stickiness had failed.

Seize the ass.

What better advice to take than her own? She knocked twice, not waiting for an answer before opening it and trying to walk casually inside. Bel sat behind his massive desk, looking up with a smile, then freezing, his gaze darting over her face.

Shit.

His expression went carefully neutral, and he set down his pen with slow precision.

She kept moving, one step at a time, knees shaking like they were made of marshmallow. As she climbed the steps onto the dais and moved around his desk, she wondered if she was about to spontaneously develop a heartbeat just so that it could pound out of her chest. Or explode.

"No," he said mildly.

Lily paused mid-step as she rounded his desk. "No?"

"If you're here to break up with me, the answer is no. Obviously, if that's what you really want, I'll respect it, but not without a damn good reason. Lucifer said that you've been quiet while I was gone, and your last few texts have been unlike you. Then you asked for a 'personal conversation' and—"

She heard the little tremor in his voice toward the end of his speech, saw the tension humming off of him like a wire strung too tight.

"Honestly, Lily, if I dumped too much on you at the party, or if you feel like we're moving too fast, we'll slow down. We can figure it out, but I want us to try. Please, just—"

"I love you."

It was the "please" that had pushed through her fear. Her whole body might have been shaking, but her voice was steady.

Bel stopped breathing, eyes flying wide, body going so still he might as well have been carved from stone. His mouth opened and Lily rushed on.

"I love you. That's what I admitted to myself in the meadow." Her voice had lost its steadiness, but fuck it. She took the last few steps to stand beside him. "I've been in love with you for a while, Bel, and I was just too scared to own it. You feel more right to me than anyone ever has. And I still don't have everything figured out, but I realized that there was something I needed to do. We've been imbalanced. I haven't been as open with you as you've been with me. I haven't been as vulnerable, or as brave. This, the Afterlife, is your home. I get to share this piece of your life and meet your family, but you don't get to do that with me."

She held up the file, clearing her throat. "I haven't always been who I am now. The person in this file is very different than the person you know now, but I want you to know my story, because I trust you with it.

You're the *only* person I trust with all of it." She gave him a shaky smile that didn't last as she looked down at the file clenched in her hand, fighting the sting of tears. "And . . . and it's fine if you decide that it's—that *I'm*—too much after you see it. Really, it's okay. I'll be okay. But I want you to know." The first hot tear streaked down her cheek, her voice wobbling.

Before she could hold the file out to him, Bel pivoted and pulled her forward into his lap, straddling him. He held her tightly, hands splayed wide over her back, pressing her closer, molding their bodies together so there wasn't even a whisper of space between them. He pressed his face into the curve of her neck, his ragged breathing fanning over her hypersensitive skin. Lily gripped him, fingers digging into his back in a way that had to be painful, but he only held her closer.

He pulled back just enough to meet her gaze while one clawed finger gently wiped away the tears lingering on her cheek. A well of emotion lay in his glorious silver eyes, and for once she wasn't afraid of drowning in it.

"I love you," Bel said.

She opened her mouth to tell him that he might want to look at the file first, but he pushed her jaw closed with tender firmness, his gaze unwavering.

"I love you," he said more intensely. "Nothing in that file will make me love you less. Nothing. You got to meet my family, hear some stories about how I was as a kid, but you didn't get to watch the entirety of my life. You best believe that I was a little shithead, princess. There are parts of my life that I'm not too proud of either. None of that matters. I. Love. You. Now. I love who you are, and who you're becoming." His smile dimmed slightly, and he dropped his gaze to watch his thumb trace her lower lip. Heat sparked low in her belly, but she tamped it down.

Not yet.

His eyes met hers again, and the flare of pain in them had her sweeping her hands over the satiny skin of his neck and over his broad shoulders, offering what comfort she could without words.

He cleared his throat. "I haven't let you in entirely either."

Bel

Lily had his heart. Completely and utterly.

She'd looked like a woman walking the plank when she'd stepped into his office, and icy dread had doused his skin at the thought of her ending them before they had a chance. But then she'd inflamed him and brought him to his knees with three words.

I love you.

Said with surety and simplicity and conviction. With light in her glorious eyes, even though she'd clearly been terrified to say it.

He refused to allow her to be vulnerable alone. He wasn't afraid of telling Lily that he loved her; it was the highest honor of his life to do so. But he was afraid of telling the story and the secret he'd held on to for so long. He looked at Lily, his princess, watching him with patience and understanding and *love*, and knew he finally had the courage to do it.

"I'm sure you've noticed the lack of a father in my life," he started roughly, holding her gaze like the lifeline that it was.

She nodded, tracing the point of his ear and smoothing her hand down the side of his neck. A balm to his soul.

He leaned into the touch. "My father was Samael, one of the first beings made in the early days of the Universe and the Afterlife, before even the mortals existed. After the dawn of mortals, he was one of the first to believe in Lucifer's idea for the creation of a realm of justice and punishment. He'd seen what some mortals were capable of, and it didn't sit well with him that they all were granted the peace and privileges of what is now known as Paradise."

He traced a line over her shoulder blade. "This is what led to the early wars between realms. They weren't as long-lived as mortal religions might think, or true to how they've been portrayed in the mortal world. My father was never an angel, let alone a fallen one. Lucifer established Hell, and the Universe made him a deity, binding his essence to it and granting him additional power. My father was one of the first princes of Hell because he helped Lucifer set it all up and create the system.

"By the time he and my mom got together, he was *old*. So is my mom, but my dad was ancient. I *loved* my dad. He was my hero. He trained me, then trained with me, taught me to fly . . . He could be gruff with people, but never with me. Never with any of us kids. His younger sister, Agrat, was always over with Asmodeus so we could play together. Those days were fun. Dad was quiet but seemed happy. I never guessed . . .

"I was about a century old, the equivalent of a mortal in their early twenties, I suppose, and rising through the ranks of command, when Dad came to see me. He'd been kind of distant for years, especially after a short-lived but nasty conflict with another Universe, so I thought that him coming to train with me meant that he was getting better. He had me over for dinner—he loved cooking, he's the one who got Asmodeus into it—and we had a great time just swapping stories, talking about shit I got up to as a kid, talking about life. The whole time, he was happier and more peaceful than I'd ever seen him. He seemed *lighter*. Then, when we were winding down, he handed me an envelope and told me not to read it until I needed it.

"I had no idea what he was talking about. I thought there must be another war or skirmish firing up, but then he . . . then he just said, 'It's time.' Said he loved me more than I could imagine, that I was the best thing that had happened in his life, but that he was tired and it was time for him to find his peace in the Void. To us, going to the Void isn't like suicide is for the mortals. I suppose it's similar to dying of old age in your bed. Voluntarily. If we have to go, the Void is the best way."

His cheeks were wet, heart throwing itself against his ribs. He hadn't told the story to anyone in its entirety. Ever. Not his mother, his siblings, his cousins, any of his friends. No one knew.

He focused on Lily. The way she felt in his lap, her scent, the warm press of her hands as they moved over him, the softness in her teary eyes revealing that big heart she tried to keep hidden.

"I walked with him," he choked out. "Hugged him, wished him peace, and watched him walk into the Void. He was *happy*, Lily, and it shattered me because . . . I still wanted my dad. I wanted him happy, but I also wanted him to be here. He was supposed to be here. He said I was the best thing in his life, yet I wasn't enough to hold him here, for us to have more time. Almost everyone I know gets so much more time. I know I could have lost him to war, but that feels different, even though it shouldn't, even though I know the Void is our eventuality. I loved him, I still love him, still miss him, but sometimes I hate him for that, even if he felt like he had to go. I got back home and told my family, told everyone, that he was gone.

"My dad, meticulous to the end, had made provisions for his passing with Lucifer, and suddenly I was a prince. At least once the leaders of the legions convened and elected me to take my father's place as general, I had experience for that. I'd trained my entire life, and I'd been to war. I'd *earned* that. My father was one of the first princes. He earned that title. But then there I was, with a title and a crown that didn't feel like my own, mourning my dad and wondering why I was so easy to leave behind.

"So I threw myself into work, avoided the royal horseshit as much as I could, and tried to patch up the wound he'd left without letting too many people realize how fragile I felt. I'm not the fragile one. I'm the dependable one, when I need to be. And I did that for years. Centuries. I was happy enough for a while, but it all started to feel hollow, like a lie. The more battles I fought, the more of my soldiers and friends died or were savaged by some monster or other, the more . . . I understood my dad. He'd had experiences worse than anything I've ever seen, and he might have loved my mom in his way, and loved me, but he never really let people in, or let people close enough to help. Sometimes I'm *tired*, Lils, but that's when I go hang out with Greg, or Azzy, or Angel, just . . . anyone."

He smiled at her then, holding her a little tighter.

"I thought I was patching it well enough until Lucifer, king of Hell and matchmaker extraordinaire, apparently, came into my office one day spewing some crap about how he'd left a blade in the armory by the gate and needed me specifically to identify it. Then I saw you, met you in person, and realized that this voice I'd been crushing on for a month was going to be more to me than just a crush. I think I fell in love with you when you came here to share the apology pie I got from Greg and made me feel more seen than I ever have before. You're everything to me, Lily.

And I never wanted to tell you any of this, because . . ." He steeled himself for the final stretch of his confession that had been a long time coming.

Lily's soft voice was full of understanding. "Because you didn't want to guilt me into staying."

Bel nodded slowly, cradling her beautiful face with both of his hands. "*If* you chose to stay, I wanted it to be because it was what you really, truly wanted, not out of some misplaced sense of pity or guilt. If you go, I want you to go with a clear conscience. That opinion still stands." He ran his thumbs over the curve of her cheeks. "I will savor whatever time I get with you, and I will never ask you for more than you're willing to give. I came into this decided about that. I'll love and support you either way."

Lily's smile was watery. He wiped away her tears, memorizing the fine details of her face. If he lived twice as long as his father did, he would never forget this woman.

"I'm sorry," Lily whispered, pressing a kiss to his palm, covering his hand with her own. "I'm sorry that you've ever felt unworthy. You're not, Bel. I already told you, you're more than enough."

She leaned forward, resting her forehead against his. His eyes drifted shut. A weight he hadn't realized he carried lifted off his shoulders for the first time since his father had gone to the Void. Marveling at the sensation, he held her closer. He didn't know what Paradise felt like for the souls, but he imagined it was a bit like coming home after a long day. Even Paradise at its finest couldn't hope to compare with loving and being loved in return by Lily, holding her close in his office after they'd offered up the most vulnerable parts of themselves.

They stayed that way for a long while, sharing each other's air, holding each other close, settling into the peace that they'd found in each other.

Eventually, Lily's hands came up to his face and she sat back, eyes filled with so much love and passion that, if he hadn't already been sitting down, he would have ended up on his ass.

"I love you, Prince Beleth," she said quietly. Firmly. She brushed a kiss over his temple. "General." His hands tightened on her back as she feathered a kiss on the bridge of his nose. "Bel." She kissed the curve of his jaw. "FruitBat." He could hear the smile in her voice as her lips pressed to his cheek.

He smiled too, sparks shooting through his veins as the turbulent emotions settled into a new and better current.

She met his eyes, lips so close he could practically taste them. "Big guy." She leaned in to kiss him fully, but he stopped her with a gentle hand grasping her throat, just as his princess liked.

His nose brushed hers. "Yours," he rumbled.

Her eyes flared with some of that fire he loved more than his own life. "Mine," she said reverently. He tugged her closer, reveling in the sweet press of her lips.

Bel kept the kiss slow, languorous. It felt like a beginning. Of what? He had no fucking idea, but as long as it was with Lily, he didn't care.

He felt her smile. Then she nipped at his lip, and his hold on restraint snapped.

"Love you," he growled, before taking her mouth again with none of the softness of before. He was rewarded with a gasp and her kissing him back just as fiercely. Her hands slipped under the collar of his shirt, raking over his back, sending his hips grinding up against hers. She pressed herself against him, rolling her hips against his erection in a way that had him seeing stars.

"I wanted," he panted in between kisses, "to take you to bed properly."

"*Beleth*. If this is delayed again, I will lose my fucking mind," Lily said, kissing down his neck.

He threw his head back with a groan that turned into a growl when she raked his skin lightly with her blunt little teeth.

"I love you. You love me. You can fuck me properly on the desk, the couch, or the fucking floor, but you're going to do it now. You can take me to a bed *properly* later, okay?"

Bel couldn't stop the grin from spreading across his face, primal heat and desire ripping through him like a wildfire. He pulled her back, gripping her jaw just firmly enough to hold her in place. He hadn't missed the way her eyes always went molten when he was just a little bit rough.

"What about making love to you on the desk?" he asked, teasing her with little brushes of his lips.

She tried to chase after him to kiss him properly, but he held her in place. The heat of her body seared through her leggings and the front of his pants, and he nearly came on the spot.

Her slow, wicked smile had him falling in love with her all over again.

Lily

Lily wiggled off of him, bracing her hand on the desk for balance. Something warm buzzed under her palm, the sensation odd enough that it drew her attention away from him.

Her file.

She froze.

Shit. Bel had, once again, bared his soul, and while she'd handed him the entirety of her being, he still didn't know. She still hadn't really been vulnerable in turn. She loved him, he loved her, but they were *still* unequal—

He gripped her chin gently, pulling her gaze back to him while his other hand tugged her file out from under her palm. "I may not know what exactly is going on in that pretty head of yours, but I think I have a good idea. This"—he held her file up—"is important because you are important. But it doesn't define you, and it's not going to change a damn thing about how I feel. I will look at this, with you, later. But because it's not going to change anything"—he set it on the far edge of the desk, well away from them—"it can wait. Vulnerability isn't a race, it's a conversation. I said my piece, and we're going to celebrate that, then it'll be your turn, and we'll celebrate that too, yeah?"

Emotion clogged her throat. Love, joy, relief, trust . . . peace. The ripples on the pond of her soul settling.

She cupped his handsome face and nodded, kissing him long and slow, then with more heat.

"Stay," she purred, sauntering toward the door.

Bel

Everything in him roared to chase her, catch her, grab her around that pretty little waist and bury himself so deeply that they both forgot their names. But the princess had given an order, and he would obey it.

For now.

He wanted to see what that lovely, filthy mind of hers had come up with.

She grinned at him over her shoulder, reaching for the handle. He gripped the armrests of his chair so hard they creaked.

She flipped the lock with a quiet *snick* that he felt in his bones.

41

PARADISE

Lily

Bel's expression was hungry as she turned around and approached the dais. Excitement hummed through her body, sparkling through her veins and making her skin hypersensitive to the brush of her clothing as it shifted with her steps.

Bel, disobeying her order to stay put, stalked around his desk, tail swaying slowly from side to side, the tip flicking just a bit, molten eyes fixed on hers. She smothered most of her smile, pausing at the bottom of the dais.

He growled.

She arched an eyebrow.

"Princess." His deep rumble melted the rest of her will to tease him.

She climbed the first step. Then the second. She'd barely rested her foot on the dais when Bel seized her around the waist, lifting her with ease, tugging her thigh around his waist and pressing her against him. His kiss was searing, stealing away every thought in her head except for the endless pulsing chant of *more, more, more.*

She barely noticed that they were moving until Bel bent slightly, setting her down on something solid—the desk—his hand skating up her thighs to run just under the hem of her shirt. The brush of his fingers on her stomach had liquid heat pooling embarrassingly fast between her thighs. She ground herself against the heavy bulge of his cock, and his hand tightened around her thigh.

Off. Her clothes needed to be off *now*—

"Want me to take this off, princess?" Bel rasped, kissing down her neck and toying with her shirt.

"Yes," Lily gasped, burying her fingers in his half-loose hair and arching her spine. The seam of her leggings had lined up perfectly with her clit, but even that bit of extra friction still wasn't enough. "Take it all off."

They'd barely started, had gone so much farther than this before, but the anticipation, combined with the powerful release of emotions, heightened everything. She untangled her hands from his hair and reached to pull her shirt off.

Bel stopped her with a hum and a nip to her collarbone. "Let me," he murmured, guiding her hands to his chest. His heartbeat thundered under her palm.

His hands ghosted down her body, finally gripping the hem of her shirt and peeling the fabric away slowly, reverently. His knuckles brushed over her newly revealed skin, leaving goose bumps in their wake. Lily lifted her arms, and Bel finished pulling the fabric up with one hand, the other spreading wide and hot over her ribs, just below breasts that ached for his touch. The shirt fell to the floor, his silver eyes practically glowing as he took her in. He traced the line of the strap over her shoulder with a fingertip, grazing along the delicate edge of her black lace bra. Her nipples were so hard they almost hurt, but Lily wet her lips with a quick flick of her tongue and savored his slow exploration of her body.

Bel hooked his finger under the center gore of her bra and roughly pulled her forward, catching her surprised laugh with his lips, tongue flicking against hers. She opened for him, losing herself in the simple play of lips and tongues, his free hand smoothing up her back to palm the nape of her neck. Her hands had landed on his stomach, and she seized the opportunity to tug at his shirt before she remembered the tricky little bit around his wings.

She could feel Bel's laughter bubbling up in his chest, his lips smiling against hers before he pressed a quick kiss to her nose. "I'll get it."

"Don't you dare," Lily said, focusing on the decorative stitching under her fingertips as she searched for the way to open the slits at the bottom of his shirt. "This is my version of the 'unhooking a bra' test."

Bel chuckled, his smile soft as he watched her work.

She found the catch and started worming her fingers around to figure it out. Why the fuck hadn't she studied his shirts before?

"If you can unhook a bra, you can figure out my shirt." Bel grinned.

She bit her lip and frowned, staring sightlessly at his chest while her fingers worked at the catch.

"Are you sure?" she asked, seriously contemplating just ripping at the fabric until she got her way.

Bel flicked her bra hook open and it sagged forward. "I'm sure," he said smugly.

Lily pressed an open-mouthed kiss to the juncture of his shoulder and neck just as she figured out how to release the catch. She popped it open and bit him at the same time. Bel's hands flexed, pulling her closer while he ground his hips against hers. They made short work of his shirt, then her bra, and suddenly they were both bare from the waist up.

Bel ran the back of one finger down the side of her breast before cupping it and flicking his thumb over her nipple, sending electricity jolting through her body. Lily moaned softly and leaned back to give him room to play, bracing her hands on the desk.

He kissed her again, pressing her down with his body, the cool wood of the desk against her back a stark contrast against the heat of his body on her front. Her nipples grazed over his chest, and she gasped into his mouth. His kissed down to her chest, nuzzling her breast before flicking his tongue over the stiff nipple.

An unintelligible noise burst free as the sensation flooded her brain.

"Hold still while I make some new friends, princess." He moved over to the other breast as she laughed breathlessly. He plumped them up with his hands and set to work kissing and sucking her into a mindless, writhing mess.

She arched into his mouth, one hand tangled in his hair and the other skating over the heavy muscles of his back. Her hand brushed against something that felt like warm, ultrafine suede, and Bel growled against her skin, his whole body going taut.

His wing.

A pang of guilt for taking an intimacy that she hadn't asked for had her moving her hand away.

"No," Bel grunted, blowing gently on her wet nipple, the sudden coolness making sparks dance in her vision before he laved it with his hot tongue again. *"More."*

She mapped his back with both hands, sometimes with long, sweeping strokes, other times tracing delicate lines over the base of his wings and the decadent softness of the membrane until they were both slicked with sweat and Bel was desperate and gasping, his hands reaching, pulling her leggings and underwear down at the same time, his finesse forgotten.

She sat up, ripping at the laces of his pants, shoving them over his hips. He moved back out of her reach, pulling her legs up and shredding the laces of her boots with his claws before working them off her feet and throwing them over his shoulder. They hit something with a crash that neither of them cared about. Bel shoved his pants down and kicked his own boots off, and as he straightened in all his proud glory, eyes gleaming, Lily fell in love with him all over again. They'd had only stolen kisses and moments and touches for too long, and she had missed seeing all of him.

He was every inch a warrior; no one could ever mistake him for anything else. Every inch of him was built for power: broad shoulders and chest, solid, faintly ridged abdomen. The swirling black lines of his tattoo reached from his right hip down to mid-thigh, accentuating the lines of muscle. A slight dip over his hip bones worked in conjunction with the trail of crisp black hair leading down from his navel to draw her eye to his heavy, jutting cock and dark balls framed with a neatly trimmed thatch of black hair. Her core clenched around nothing, desperately wanting to be filled. She wet her lips, eyes roving over his thick, heavily muscled thighs, strong calves, even down to his bare feet and naturally black toenails. She leisurely dragged her eyes up his body only to find that he'd been staring at her with equal intensity.

He was beautiful and mighty standing before her, and she, completely naked and half splayed on his desk with her hair tumbling loose over her shoulders, had never felt more beautiful or mighty herself.

Lily held out her hand. Bel's mouth quirked into a smile, though his eyes lost none of their intensity. He took her hand and let her pull him close. She spread her legs to accommodate him, a thrill zinging through every fiber of her body as the cool air caressed her slick sex only for a moment before the heat of Bel's body replaced it and made her breath stutter. His cock slipped over her lower stomach, leaving a wet line of pre-cum behind. He lightly gripped her neck with his hand, and she couldn't stop her smile, tilting her head to meet his languid kiss.

"I love you," she murmured, nipping at his thumb as it traced over her lower lip.

"Love you," he breathed, giving her a quick kiss before he pushed her to lay down with a bit of pressure on her neck.

Then his hand smoothed down over her chest and stomach, and he dropped to his knees. He hooked one leg over his shoulder, kissing up her thigh to where she craved him. With anyone else, she would have been mortified to be so sloppily wet.

But he was hers.

The first stroke of his tongue had her arching nearly off the desk, gasping his name. His arm clamped over her hips and lower stomach, holding her in place as he worked her with sweeping strokes, pausing to flick her clit with the stiffened tip of his tongue. His other hand came up to toy with her entrance, his claws fully retracted, the combination of light, teasing touches and his sure tongue short-circuiting her brain. When he slid a finger deep and pumped, she sobbed for air, one hand gripping the arm he'd thrown over her hips and the other clawing at his head until she found something to grip. He added another finger, twisting and spreading them as he sucked on her clit and hummed.

Her pleasure built hard and fast—and somehow *kept* building. She might have been babbling, might have just been chanting his name, it didn't matter, she'd never been brought this high before, even when he'd shattered her understanding of what pleasure could be in the bathroom at trivia night. His fingers had been wicked, but his mouth was downright sinful.

Appropriate for a demon prince.

The thought had her half laughing, but that laughter quickly died when Bel flicked his tongue over her clit, wedging a third finger inside her at the same time his thumb circled and pressed against the pucker of her ass.

Lily shattered completely with a wordless cry, her hips writhing, grinding herself against his face, back bowing from the force of her orgasm. Bel kept working her with his hand, his tongue gentling against her clit as it grew almost painfully sensitive, and her orgasm kept rolling on and on, until she was sobbing and pushing him away. She dropped her head back onto the desk, trying to remember how to breathe.

Bel pressed a wet kiss just above her mons, his own breathing ragged. Lily opened her eyes to look down at him and realized that the thing she'd been gripping for dear life had been a horn. He grinned breathlessly at her. She pulled him up her body by his horn so that she could kiss him for all she was worth, her hands moving over his cheeks and his neck because she couldn't get enough. He settled over her, bracing his forearms on either side of her, wings flared slightly, ensconcing them both in a world of their own making.

Lily brought her legs up to cradle his sides, carefully sliding her calf across his lower back to hold him even closer. She could taste herself on his lips. She loved it, the tang of her orgasm a heady addition to the ecstasy of kissing Bel.

Her Bel.

"I want you inside me," she breathed, pulling back just enough to meet his eyes. His pupils were blown so wide his eyes were almost entirely black, only a thin halo of silver remained.

He smiled faintly and kissed her again, shifting his weight to one arm so that he could take her hand with his and guide it between them. His erection lay heavy on her stomach, trapped between their bodies. She slicked her hand with some of her own wetness before wrapping her fingers around his shaft, toying with the faint ridges under his skin. He groaned, dropping his head down beside hers as she stroked up him a few times. He throbbed in her hand, longer and thicker than anyone she'd ever taken before, but not a truly ridiculous size, even with those faint ridges she could feel under his skin. It wouldn't be impossible, but it would be delicious work to get him in.

She liked work.

Lily kept stroking him while she tugged on his hair with her other hand to get him to move back. He lifted his head, shifting until the head of his cock slipped over her clit and rested against her sex, making them moan in unison.

Lily rested her temple against his, and they both watched as she guided him to her drenched entrance; she was so wet that the broad head slipped right in, stretching her just enough to feel it. Her fingers tightened on the back of his neck. They panted in tandem for a moment, then Bel gave a slight roll of his hips and eased in just a bit more, enough that she could feel one of those ridges pressing sweetly against a sensitive spot. They both gasped. Lily let go of his cock and clutched his ass, pressing her nose against his cheek, reveling in the moment.

"Big," she breathed, her body adjusting to his size.

He smiled against her temple and pushed a bit deeper. "You can take it."

Lily gasped out a laugh, his cocky tone sending more heat crashing through her body. She loved him rough and cocky.

She wanted more.

So, she nipped at his earlobe. "Make me."

A brief grumble of a growl was all the warning she got before Bel surged forward smoothly, burying himself to the hilt and pushing all the air out of her lungs. He paused, breathing hard, giving them both time to adjust, moving to meet her wide-eyed stare with one of his own. Lily had never felt so full in her life. Any of her lives. Her entire existence.

It was exquisite.

It was *right*.

Bel brushed a strand of hair off her neck, a drop of sweat rolling down his brow. "Are you okay?"

She ran her thumb up the side of his neck and his lashes dipped. "Perfect," she said, sounding awed even to herself. "You?"

His eyebrows twitched up in surprise before one of his brilliant smiles took over his face. "Perfect." He bent to kiss her; their height difference had him sliding half out of her, and she felt every one of those little ridges like an erotic massage. Her exhale mingled with his. "Perfect, princess."

They were slow at first, learning each other, learning their rhythms, savoring each caress and kiss, the sweat-slicked glide of their skin and the mutual sound of their pleasure. Lily met every roll of his hips with her own, her hands moving proprietarily over his body, while Bel whispered lovely, filthy things in her ear.

"Look how well you take me, princess," he said, giving an especially hard thrust that had her leaving nail marks on his side. "Like you were made for it."

He'd pushed himself up so that he could watch her as she moved under him, with him, and she'd panted, watching his body work, muscles intended for combat being used to bring them both to new heights.

She managed to smirk at him, and he paused, a spark of something gleeful dancing across those solar eclipse eyes. She reached for the hand he had on her hip and pulled it up to her neck. "Fuck me, Beleth. We both know I can take you, so let's see what you can give me."

His hand was firm as he grasped her throat and leaned down with a smile that thrummed with danger, but the happy little crinkles around his eyes warmed her soul. His kiss was disarmingly sweet. The way his hand tightened was less so. She pressed against his grip with a grin.

He thrust hard, riding over a new spot inside her that had her seeing stars. "Hold on, princess."

Then Bel set about fucking every thought out of her head. Everything except for his name and every profane word she'd ever learned. She did her best to match him, to give as good as she got, but fucking hell, Bel had a lot to give.

Her first orgasm had come on fast and hard. The second was a slow, intense, inevitable build, shoved higher with every sensation and grunt and gasp and pant and slap of their bodies and a few screeches of the desk moving across the floor.

Lily's legs went shaky, and she ended up gripping Bel's wrist as he held her hip with his hand, her other hand clutching her breast because she *needed* it. Bel's rhythm grew uneven, his breathing gone ragged. His hand shifted on her hip, his thumb stretching over to roll over her clit, making her spine bow—

"Come for me, princess. Be a good girl and come all over my cock," he growled.

And that was it. Through the haze of ecstasy, Lily clenched around him, the fine muscles of her body milking him, pulling him deeper. Bel hunched over her with a moan, hips working in stuttered motions, face buried in her neck as he followed her over the edge, pumping inside her, prolonging her orgasm.

They lay like that for a while, still joined, coming down from their respective highs. Bel curled over her on the desk, cheek pressed against her hair while his thumb caressed the damp skin of her neck. His heartbeat raced against her chest, fast but steady, so strong it felt like it was beating for both of them. Maybe it was.

Lily had never known that sex could be transformative, but she knew with every scrap of her being that the Universe had shifted, the paradigm of her world had taken on a new definition. But that also hadn't been just sex. That had been *them*. Lily and Bel. Together. And it felt right. She felt right.

Her hands had been planted on his back, clinging to him as if he would disappear, and she let her grip relax enough to stroke up the groove of his spine, the ridges of muscle relaxing at her touch. When she reached the base of his wings, she ran her fingers along where they joined smoothly with his back. He chuckled into her hair, then lifted his head, brushing her sweaty strands off her face and smiling softly, searching her gaze. She smiled back, capturing his hand and pressing a kiss to his palm, tangling their fingers while losing herself in his silver eyes.

"Hi," she said softly.

He kissed her lightly. "Hi."

They watched each other for a quiet moment. Lily had no idea what he saw in her eyes, but she hoped he saw how much she loved him, saw that she was *happy*. His eyes were so expressive, and as she'd gotten to know him, been his friend, fallen in love with him, she'd understood more and more of that expressiveness. She'd seen Bel happy, seen him vulnerable, seen him exhausted and sad and goofy and grumpy.

But seeing him look lovingly at her?

"What?" he asked when she chuckled.

She shifted a little, feeling him growing soft inside her. "I was just thinking that you keep redefining Paradise for me." She smiled even wider when his eyebrows furrowed slightly. "I thought that the building I live in was my Paradise. But then I met you, then I met Sharkie, and I've had so many moments since then that I've thought put the physical location of Paradise to shame. You have no idea how many of those moments have been with you. Almost every time we're together, you redefine what is actually Paradise to me. And right now?" She ran her fingers down the side of his rugged face, and he leaned into the touch. "Paradise," she said quietly.

Bel

Lily had remade him.

He'd never be able to work at his desk again without seeing her sprawled naked across its surface, so beautiful his heart hurt and, most incredibly of all, *loving him*.

He'd never seen her look so settled, so languid and happy.

"You are my Paradise," he said, his voice rough but meaning every word. Demons weren't supposed to feel the pull and peace of Paradise like mortal souls, but with her, he did.

Her lovely hazel eyes softened, the understanding and love in her gaze nearly sending him to his knees.

Again.

He swallowed hard and glanced down their bodies before looking at her again. "I don't want to move, but I also don't want to keep you on the desk."

Her smile was coy as she reached her arms over her head in a languorous stretch that tipped her pretty breasts up like an offering that he eyed greedily. He loved every piece of her, but her breasts were now one of his favorite pieces. Just large enough to fill his palms and tipped with pert, rosy nipples that were so sensitive. He bent to pepper kisses over the satiny skin there—it would be rude to not accept an offering, after all—but the movement had his soft shaft slipping free of her. He didn't miss the stutter in her breath, smirking as he dropped one last kiss to the upper slope of her breast and straightened.

"Stay there, I'll get it," he said, hurrying over to the little kitchenette for a soft washcloth and wetting it with warm water.

Lily propped herself up on her elbows by the time he returned, and he carefully made sure she was clean of their combined mess. A dribble of his seed dripped free, and before he stopped to think about it, he caught it with a finger and pushed it back inside her.

"Fuck," she moaned, dropping her head back, eyes squeezing shut for a moment before her heated gaze captured his.

Bel arched an eyebrow and casually sucked his finger clean, rolling their taste over his tongue like a fine wine.

Thrillingly, Lily looked ready to eat him alive, sitting up slowly, her messy hair draped over her shoulders like a red-gold shawl. He waited to see what she would do, his body wanting to react to his arousal but not quite ready yet. She ran her eyes over his body, smiling a bit at what she saw, then reached for the cloth in his hand and set about cleaning him.

Something no one had ever done for him before.

He stood frozen while she worked, only twitching a bit as she ran the damp cloth over the head and hypersensitive ridges of his shaft. When she was finished, she set the rag on the desk and pressed a soft kiss in the center of his chest, looking up at him with a vulnerable expression.

"My turn?"

It took him a moment to remember the brief conversation they'd had before he'd lost his mind to pleasure and pleasing her. He couldn't keep himself from touching her, his hand settling perfectly in the dip of her waist, the skin of her cheek soft under his fingers as he traced the elegant arch of her cheekbone.

"If you're ready," he said softly.

Her nod was solid, that self-possessed surety of hers rising to the surface. Pride flooded his heart for this woman. She reminded him of so many of the warriors he'd known and knew. She had the same understanding of what needed to be done in a difficult situation and the grim determination to do it.

She turned to pick up her file, handing it to him with significantly more confidence than before. Her name was stamped cleanly across the front in metallic, colorful letters.

He took it reverently, the warmth of the pages spreading not just through his fingers, but his whole body.

"Alright. Couch?" he asked, tugging her hand.

"I can't," she protested. He blinked at her, not understanding. She clenched her bare thighs together, blushing. "I'll leak on it."

Aha.

Smug pride had him beaming and pulling her toward the couch anyway, explaining as they went. "Princess, if you knew the plans I had for you and that couch later, you'd realize how little I care for the upholstery. Now, the wings are going to make this a bit of a tricky entry, but I have a plan. Lay close to the back, on your side."

Still blushing a bit, she obeyed, pressing her back against the back of the couch and waiting to see where he was going with this, her cheek propped on her hand.

Bel settled himself half on his side, facing her, sliding his left arm under her head and down her back, pulling her half on top of him as he wiggled to get comfortable, then carefully coiled his tail around the leg she had thrown over him.

She hummed, shifting her head on his chest to look up at him. "I've been meaning to ask about the tail thing."

"Do you not like it?" Bel asked, a spark of worry flaring through the haze of pleasure.

"I love it," she rushed to assure him. "I was just wondering what tail etiquette is. I've seen demons winding tails before, but I wasn't sure what the cultural significance or protocol was. I guessed it's some kind of sign of affection?"

"Mm, to put it very simply, there's a friendly tail wind, very minor, very light, for close friends or family. Then there's a deeply affectionate tail wind, mostly done with lovers or partners." He tightened his tail's hold on her leg a bit for emphasis. "Prolonged, intensive, often done at rest, because it's a true twining and isn't easy to disengage quickly. I figured that you didn't have a tail, so I could just hold your leg a little."

"Bummer I can't tail wind you back. You can wrap your tail around me any time, big guy."

"Don't tempt me," Bel murmured, nuzzling into her hair. She made a contented little noise, relaxing into him. They cuddled for an indeterminate time, savoring each other.

Eventually, Lily sighed and reached for the file in his hand, easing it open. The seemingly blank pages were affixed to the back panel, their pristine surfaces seeming out of place in his moody, dark office.

Bel stared at them for a moment, then turned to kiss Lily's forehead and rested a finger on the first page.

42

WARRIOR PRINCESS

*L*ily had been a fussy baby. Her exhausted, confused first-time parents were products of a generation that hadn't been known for its emotional intelligence, and had often chalked her fussiness up to pure attitude. Baby Lily had been alert and vibrant, as if trying to cram as much living into life as she could, hence her vehement—and shrill—opposition to nap time.

She'd learned to walk early, learned to talk early, had definitive opinions early. She'd fought the reading lessons, not wanting to sit still for the endless repetitions of letters and sounds, but once she'd picked it up, she'd found her great love. She read voraciously, read everything she could get her hands on, even if she couldn't understand much of it. Her parents punished her by taking her books away, not knowing that Lily would have multiple books hidden, and that, in a pinch, reading the dictionary would do.

Her brothers arrived, and their family moved through the seasons of life.

Her parents were fairly religious and raised their children to be the same. Her mother was the more traditional of the two, and her father, for all his belief that he was incredibly progressive, enjoyed the benefits of a traditional marital household, and took steps to maximize that benefit.

Her parents had not been a particularly good match, not in Lily's opinion anyway. Lily had thought from a young age that their relationship was imbalanced. Her mother ran the house, raised the kids, did the shopping, the cooking, the cleaning, managed appointments, took them to school and to sports, helped them with their homework. Her mother could be critical, but Lily had always been eager to please, and she liked spending time with her.

Her dad worked, then he came home tired, and often didn't have the energy or time to play, so he watched TV in the living room, ate his dinner in front of the TV in the living room, preferred to spend most of his time in front of the TV in the living room. Her father was physically there, but he wasn't much of a source of emotional support, something that Lily, a deeply emotional child, had craved. Her dad had been happy to engage with them when it came to things that interested him though, and Lily had been just as enamored with fantasy as he had. He'd read her The Hobbit as a bedtime story, establishing her love of that world early. They'd often watched movies together, and occasionally shared books, but never been as close as she'd wanted.

Her parents fought fairly often over disagreements that Lily couldn't understand. A normal conversation would turn into a screaming match over nothing. So Lily stepped up and did more than her mother asked her to, because if they weren't stressed, then they wouldn't fight so much. Right? Lily became close to her mother, and always joined in on the shopping, the cooking, the cleaning. She tried to not need things because her mother was exhausted taking care of three kids, and when Lily needed things, it made her cranky. So Lily learned to try and take care of herself.

She figured that it would be good practice for when she got to be a mom, because moms figured stuff out. She'd always been praised for her maturity, for being an "old soul," but sometimes Lily was painfully aware of how young and confused and desperate to please she was. She was happy to help, but her brothers were never asked or expected to do the same. The imbalance bothered her.

The central part of their lives, church, was fun as a child, but as she got older, things got strange. The adults at the church had commented for as long as she could remember that her parents would have to watch her; Lily was so pretty—and a redhead!—that of course she was going to be trouble.

"She'll be a real temptress if you're not careful," a church elder had told her mom one Sunday, patting Lily on the shoulder.

A lot of the adults had laughed. Her mom had remained silent, lips pinching in disapproval, but not at Lily. She'd kept Lily close every Sunday after that. Lily, who had been eight and taken the lessons in Sunday school to heart, fretted about it for weeks. She didn't want to be one of those bad women who tempted men away from God. She'd been wearing a nice dress that her mom *had picked out, and her mom wouldn't dress her to tempt men, would she? Maybe adults just had odd senses of humor?*

Lily didn't want to be trouble, but as she grew up, she seemed to be anyway. She couldn't stop. She was too rambunctious, too curious, too mouthy, not friendly enough, not quiet enough, and she certainly asked too many questions.

Lily loved questions. She wanted to know everything. The world was so wide and wonderful, and people were so complex and interesting, and there were such amazing, fantastical stories, both real and fictional, she wanted to learn it all! She loved seeing how things fit together.

But as she grew from child to preteen to teenager, her questions were received with increasing hostility. Her youth leaders didn't like that she had questions about the Bible, about God, about things the church had done or things that alleged Christians had done in God's name. She wasn't supposed to question the Bible, and certainly not God. But she did. Because she wanted to know! She wanted the facts! The lack of answers bothered her, and even when she did get answers, she usually had questions about them too.

At school, when she learned about evolution, about science, about stars and space and history and other gods and belief systems, she loved how most things had an answer. And if not a definitive answer, at least people had gone to great lengths to discover one. People explained things. She spent most of her allotted computer time at home looking up things she'd heard or read, getting more information, ending up on new information trails. She soaked it all up like a sponge, but especially the information from the fantasy books she read and movies she'd seen. She had watched her dad's Jurassic Park VHS tape so many times she wore it out. Her dad had told her proudly that she was a nerd, like him.

She wondered if she wasn't built for blind faith. Problem was, that's what the church, and God apparently, wanted. But why would God have made her in such a way that it was hard for her to believe? Why had God made her to love physical touch when that was not something that was appropriate? Why had God made her difficult? That's what the youth leaders and her parents said she was, anyway. Difficult.

It all started to unravel as a preteen, when her youth group was separated by gender and the girls began their lessons.

Lily hated those fucking lessons.

Purity lessons. Spiritual warfare lessons. Modesty lessons.

Bare shoulders were a temptation. If they had to wear a tank top, they had to make sure it had thick straps. One-piece swimsuits only for youth group outings to the pool, and they had to wear a T-shirt and shorts over it anyway. As their bodies developed, if their youth leader, Suzanne, saw their nipples through their shirts because of the cold, she called them out of the water and had them sit in a towel until their nipples weren't showing anymore. Lily got into the habit of constantly pulling her shirt away from her body so that her hard nipples didn't show and she could swim longer. Skirts were dangerous. They made boys wonder what they had under them. Lily had pointed out that the boys already knew they had bodies, so obviously they already knew what was under there. She'd been told to sit in the hall for ten minutes.

She'd stewed about it the entire time.

The neckline of their shirts was another issue. One finger width of skin below their clavicle was fine, two was pushing it, three was "loose behavior." Lily's mother wore modest V-neck shirts all the time, but more than three fingers worth. When she'd asked her about it, her mother had told her that she wasn't showing any cleavage, and to remember that Suzanne didn't know everything. Lily didn't know what to believe, but she didn't want to be a temptress, and she still heard the comments from the adults at church about how she'd grow up to be a heartbreaker, so she figured that she'd err on the side of caution.

"Are you a target or a treasure?" Suzanne had asked them over and over. "If you dress and act like a target, you will be treated like a target. But if you dress and act like a treasure, you will be treated like a treasure."

Lily had rankled against all of it but kept it on the inside. Perhaps it all felt and sounded wrong because that was Satan's influence? Just like how seeing boobs on TV made her feel funny in the same way that seeing shirtless men made her feel funny. The boob thing was probably Satan's influence too.

Her world fell apart completely when she was fourteen and went over to a friend's house for a birthday sleepover. Her friend's older, sixteen-year-old boyfriend showed up for the fun night of movies and games, bringing over some of his parents' alcohol, and Lily had a glass of mostly margarita mix, rebellion crackling gleefully through her veins. The boyfriend drank more than that. Later, when most of the girls had gone to bed, Lily went upstairs to use the bathroom there, since the downstairs one was busy. The boyfriend was staying in the guest room up there, and when Lily had walked by . . . he'd grabbed her.

She remembered the smell of the alcohol on his breath. She remembered fighting him, asking him what he was doing, demanding that he leave her alone, telling him that she wasn't that kind of girl. He'd slapped her hard enough to make her see stars.

She hated herself for freezing, but she'd fucking frozen.

Scared. She'd been so scared. Hands on her body, grabbing, pinching, hurting in ways she couldn't understand. She'd snapped out of it when he started pulling her pants down around her thighs, fury roaring up inside her. How dare he?

When he gave up on her pants and started fumbling with his own, she kicked him hard enough to knock him on his ass. She bolted out and down the stairs, grabbing a blanket from the couch and sprinting through the sliding door into the backyard to hide in the playhouse for the rest of the night. She'd shaken and cried silently, terrified that he would find her.

She'd prayed. She'd asked God why. What had she done to deserve that? She'd been wearing her baggy jeans and a crew neck T-shirt from summer camp. She'd done everything right. She'd behaved. And yet . . .

The next morning, she snuck into the house early and found her bag, getting dressed and laying in her sleeping bag as if she'd been there all night, trying to warm up. When everyone woke up, she joined the other girls for a pancake breakfast, made by her friend's mom. They'd all yawned and laughed. Lily was quiet, ashamed. She didn't tell her friend, didn't tell anyone.

She didn't want to disappoint or upset her parents. Her mom might understand, but she also might be mad that Lily had let that happen, because she had, somehow, right? Her dad would be furious, but probably not at her. She didn't want him to do something that would get him in trouble, because that would be her fault too, and she wanted her dad around.

At church the next Sunday, she asked to talk to Suzanne, hoping that she might have some answer or comfort, help Lily understand. But when Lily explained, shaking and nauseous the entire time, Suzanne shook her head sadly, disappointment palpable.

"*You need to beg God for forgiveness, Lily. That only happened because your faith has been lacking. If you've really been living for Christ, that wouldn't have happened to you. God was trying to get your attention in a big way, because he loves you. You should really examine what's been going on in your heart that led to this happening. And,*" she'd sighed, "*you need to pray for your future husband's forgiveness for this. This is a stain on your purity as a result of your lack of faith. Pray that your husband is a forgiving man.*"

Lily's faith died in that room, withering further with each word out of her trusted youth leader's mouth until nothing was left.

Her whole life had centered around God and his teachings. She'd done everything, she'd followed the rules, she'd tried to behave, but it was never good enough. She was never good enough. Her whole life she'd been threatened with an eternity in Hell if she'd strayed from the straight and narrow path.

Fine. So be it.

If what had happened to her in that room had been an example of God's love, then she didn't want it.

What kind of love was that?

It wasn't.

She'd never heard God's voice like some people claimed to have, never felt his presence or comfort in her soul. She didn't know if he was real or not, but she'd had her doubts for years. Even if he was real, fuck him. Fuck him. If he was real—something in her soul told her that there was at least some kind of higher power out there—where was he?

Lily went home a different person. All the uncertainty and questions and fear she'd been taught for years, the hideous shame of failing to fight that boy back, of feeling his hands on her body against her will, all of it festered.

And she grew angry. Furious.

Lily had always been told that her emotions were too intense, and she'd tried to mute them. She stopped minimizing herself as much. Her head constantly felt like it was full of a whirlwind of coal dust, dark and howling and confusing. Everything felt too much. She hated everything, but mostly herself. She tried to be nice, but she hurt so badly, and no one saw it, or if they did, no one seemed to care. Her tongue was so sharp, cutting even when she didn't want it to, words flying out of her mouth before she could stop them.

Her parents wrote it off as teenage moodiness, and she got into fights with them over everything. Her clothes, her hair, the time she spent in her room, her refusal to go to church anymore. Her mom had insisted that the church might have its flaws, but that God was flawless and a relationship with him was necessary. Lily disagreed. She hated herself a little more every time she made her mom cry, but she wanted to do things differently! She'd tried to explain what had happened at the party to her mother once, but fear and shame had choked her when her mother asked why she hadn't come home as soon as someone pulled out the alcohol. She'd always hated disappointing her mom, knowing the stress and strain it caused, so she decided to avoid the subject.

Lily turned to her reading, learning life lessons from all kinds of books, but especially fantasy, and even romance. Before her assault, she'd found romance books fascinating. All she'd been taught about sex was that it was something married adults did, and it involved a bed and touching and was how children were made. She had no idea that sex was supposed to feel nice until she'd found a romance book in a thrift bin when she'd been eleven, and she'd bought it because apparently it was about saving a horse, and she loved horses. To her shock, there was a scene where the woman and cowboy had sex by a campfire—and they enjoyed it. Further research had been necessary. She loved the idea of unlimited pleasurable physical touch with someone she cared about, and who cared about her.

She didn't stop reading romance after her assault. Romance novels actually opened her eyes to the reality of what had happened, and what could have happened. The characters' traumas helped her understand what assault was, and that it wasn't God trying to get her attention. She inhaled story after story of characters falling for each other and going on adventures, choosing to love each other even when they were flawed.

Between romance novels, fantasy, and an assortment of other fiction, as well as time on the internet, she learned what she'd never been taught. That what had happened to her was not her fault. That asking questions was a very good thing. That other people had questioned the church and God. That the Bible wasn't a perfect translation like she'd been led to believe.

The foundations of her world cracked, and as she aged, she kept trying to rebuild them. Every time she thought she was solid, something would come along and rattle her. Inside, she still hurt so badly it felt like her heart and soul were shredding themselves. She couldn't understand it, couldn't explain it, it just hurt. She stumbled upon an article online about dangerous behaviors in teenagers that mentioned self-harm. So she'd looked up what that was and wondered if it might be worth a try.

Lily only harmed herself on her thighs and hips, where no one would ever see. She might have refused to go to church anymore, but she still wanted to be a good, nice girl. Good, nice girls didn't have scars where people could see. The pain on the outside was supposed to help the pain on the inside. It didn't. Lily just felt guilty and hated herself a little more.

She was fifteen and a half when she snuck into her parents' bathroom on a Friday night and grabbed a package of her father's sleeping pills. Her note was on her side table. She cried the entire time, until she fell asleep. She didn't want to go. It just all hurt so badly. She hated herself so much for failing to be good, to behave, to defend herself, to make herself better; she wanted it to end.

She woke up on Sunday afternoon. Woozy, nauseated, and chilly, but alive and . . . relieved. She'd often spent whole weekends alone in her room, so no one knew what she'd done. As she lay there, she was struck by a lightning bolt of clarity. She didn't want her life to end; she had shit she wanted to do. She still wanted to find real, supportive love. She still wanted to be a mom. She just wanted the emotional pain to end. There were options for that. There had to be.

So, she staggered to take a shower, then set about researching trauma and therapists, and discovered forums of survivors. She asked her parents if she could see a therapist, and her mom found one recommended by a lady from church. Lily was apprehensive and only went to one session, hating that the woman's main concern was her prayer schedule and faith walk.

So she fought to heal herself. She failed a lot and often, but she learned to forgive herself and seek out other coping mechanisms. She stopped hurting herself. She tried to be nicer, tried to work harder, tried. She flirted with boys, made out with a few, enjoyed their tentative, excited hands. Her heart raced like a chased deer the entire time, but she'd been determined to reclaim her body and discover sex and intimacy on her own terms. She graduated high school and headed off to college with optimism, ready to discover who she was away from her parents and family.

There, she made real changes. She found a nonreligious therapist through the college's counseling and psychological services and set about unpacking her life, realizing the positive and negative ways that she'd been impacted by her parents and religion. She picked up extra hours at her retail job to pay for her sessions, and for fun extra things, like a string bikini and her first tattoo. She threw up in the bathroom when she wore the bikini for the first time, confidence faltering and a childhood of shame training rearing up to condemn her from the past. But she rallied and went out to flirt with one of the girls in the hot tub, which had made her nauseated again, but had also been deeply arousing. Accepting her bisexuality had been a slightly long and terrifying process, but immensely fun and freeing too.

Her first tattoo, a stack of books entwined with flowers on her thigh, had felt right in a way that she'd never experienced before. The first step to covering her scars, but more than that, it felt like a step toward reclaiming her body. Like finally hanging pictures in an apartment to make it feel like home.

Her head didn't feel so messy and dark, but she still struggled with the fear and belief that her emotions were too intense for other people. Her friends didn't seem to have any problems dating, but Lily . . . well, she could find and usually enjoy a sexual partner easily enough, but she never had a mutual interest in someone.

Her friends started to get married, to build lives, and Lily was there to cheer and love and support them through it all, but it hurt. A different, quiet hurt, one that she, in her early twenties, was better equipped to process and understand than she had been as a teenager.

She graduated college and ended up working in customer service, as she always had, trying to laugh off the comments about a "real career" from family. She liked being social and helping people. She got her own apartment, delighting in filling it with books and decorating. She hadn't delighted in her mother's loving but backhanded comments every time she visited, but she and her mother had always had differing opinions about what was "clutter" and what was "decor." Her small home was hers. Her life was hers.

Lily moved through her twenties and past thirty with an increasingly strong *sense of self.* She usually liked working with people, but she hated having to cater to the whims of selfish, entitled idiots with no backup from management. She moved between jobs every few years, sometimes working as a secretary, sometimes in retail. Money was always tight; she spent hours poring over her budget, scrimping where she could while still trying to enjoy life. Her parents bemoaned every tattoo, but she loved them.

She started defining herself by what she was and what she liked, instead of who she wasn't and what she hated. She liked tight pants, ripped jeans, short shorts, corseted tops, low-cut shirts, tiny bikinis, and dresses that either hugged each curve or fluttered over her skin like a caress. She liked pretty lingerie, scouring the internet for sales. She loved her body, perceived flaws and all, and came to adore her red hair, letting it spill down her back and grow longer than she'd ever let it before. She liked sex, but wondered if emotional connection would amplify the experience. Her friends said that it did. When appropriate, she swore with ease and frequency. Fuck was such a nice, round, versatile word.

Her old church community had no idea what to do with her. Many tried to witness to her and bring the prodigal daughter back to the church family. She refused politely at first, then less politely when boundaries were crossed. Her parents tried to love her as she was, but Lily knew it was difficult for them to respect most of her life choices. Her brothers had long since left the church as well, and they all commiserated about their parents' attempts to redevelop their faith. She and her brothers had never once doubted that their parents loved them, but their dad hadn't been particularly loving, and their mother had cried at dinner more than once over her fear that her children would burn in Hell.

Lily tried to be kind, but she eventually realized that she would never be one of the sweet and gentle people of the world. She wanted to be, but, as a friend once told her, "There is teddy bear nice, and there is momma bear nice. You are momma bear nice."

A point that had been proved when a friend called her for help escaping an abusive boyfriend. Lily drove over with pepper spray and the baseball bat she kept by her bed for home defense, ready for battle. Hell, almost excited for it. She'd hated the fucker ever since he raised his drink at a barbecue and her friend flinched, terror in her eyes.

Her willingness to shed blood aside, the opportunity never presented itself.

Her friend had sprinted out of the house with a garbage bag of her belongings, thrown it into the back of Lily's car, and they'd sped away. Her friend, with a black eye and split lip, sobbed out the whole awful story. Once Lily got her settled with another friend in a different city, she sat in her car, seriously debating going back and "accidentally" running the bastard over. Repeatedly. Her Corolla was small, but anything at sixty miles an hour would hurt. Her friend hadn't known what she was thinking, but she begged Lily not to do anything, scared of what her ex would do after. Lily had little intention of leaving him alive, at least with working body parts, but decided that the jail time wasn't worth it. She went home, weeping for her friend and how scared she'd been.

At thirty-two, after a month of being fatigued and nauseated, with a constant low-grade headache, she went to the doctor. The random bruises that showed up with no rhyme or reason were what spooked her the most. Her doctor was mildly concerned but assured her that, since she was fairly young and seemed to be in good shape, it was probably something minor.

He ordered a batch of testing, and they'd waited to see if it would be covered by her insurance. Lily got the call that the health insurance company had denied coverage for the testing, as it had been deemed "not medically necessary." She grumbled and cursed the whole damn healthcare system, but especially the greed of her insurance provider—and had done it all again when she saw an article reporting record high profits for that particular company later that year. There was no way she could reasonably afford thousands of dollars' worth of testing, so she stocked up on over-the-counter meds and made some lifestyle changes, hoping that the problem would sort itself out.

She left her job when a new batch of management cut everyone else's pay and created a nightmarish working environment. Eventually, she landed a new job that she liked well enough. Her coworkers were cool, and the pay was decent, despite the lack of any additional benefits, but physically, she still felt crappy all the time.

It only got worse. And worse.

When she found the lumps in her armpit, she caved and paid for a doctor's appointment out of pocket, trying not to panic at the possibilities. One deeply concerned doctor and a hefty chunk out of her bank account later, they called her in for the results.

There, sitting in a scratchy blue chair, her heart racing like it was trying to cram in as many beats as it could before the end, Lily learned that she was going to die. Soon. Then her car didn't start, and she knew that, for the first time in her life, there was absolutely nothing she could do. Even with treatment, all she would do was buy herself a little more time. Miserable, painful, shitty time.

Everything in her screamed to fight. She'd always fought. She'd been born for it. Fought nap time, fought reading lessons, fought to ask questions, fought to defend herself, fought to be better, fought to learn, fought to love herself again, fought to live life on her own terms.

But she couldn't fight this.

The drive to her parents' house was the worst drive of her life, but she arrived with resolve. Her mother smiled when she walked through the door, certain that Lily would, at worst, need a minor surgery of some kind. Her dad emerged from the living room to give her a hug and ask how the drive had been.

Standing in the kitchen, with a voice that sounded stronger than she felt, Lily told them as gently as she could that she had an advanced and aggressive form of cancer, and she had perhaps a year to live. Her dad raged, furious at anything and everything, unable to handle or process anything other than anger. Her mom wept.

"There must be something," her mom sobbed, looking oddly frail as she sat on one of the stools. "Treatments."

Lily shook her head, throat tight. "No, Mom. They said, maybe if we'd caught it early, but not now. Now it would just"—she'd choked—"prolong it."

Fucking health insurance company. Fucking greedy CEO.

Her dating life was abysmal, but she'd still held out hope for love, for a family. All those times she'd held her friends' and cousins' babies and played with the kids, hoping that, one day, she'd have all that too . . . wasted hope. The little bitty pair of baby socks with tiny swords and cartoon dragons on them that she'd bought because they were too damn cute to resist, wondering if someday she'd put them on her baby's kicking feet . . . so stupidly optimistic and probably weird. Even if she hadn't gotten any of those things for herself, she wanted to be there to share them with the people she loved. She wanted to be the kick-ass auntie with cool stories, not the aunt who died young and none of the kids would remember.

"When do you start treatment?" her dad snarled, pacing back and forth like a caged tiger.

Lily fought to remember that he wasn't mad at her, he just defaulted to anger when things got hard. She couldn't manage his emotions for him at that moment. Her own were threatening to drown her.

"I don't."

Her mom made a keening sound that Lily would hear in her nightmares.

"I can't . . ." Lily bit the inside of her lip and struggled onward. "I can't afford it."

Perhaps if she'd gotten a roommate instead of living alone. If she'd never gotten tattoos. If she hadn't gone on that trip to the East Coast with her friends— No. No. She refused to think that way, to regret the life she'd lived. The decisions she'd made.

"We'll loan you the money. We'll get a second mortgage on the house—"

"No." Lily shook her head firmly. Her nose stung, but she battled back the tears. "I don't want that. I don't want to be in pain any longer than I have to, and there is no way in hell that I'm ruining your lives financially and destroying the boys' inheritance. B—" Lily fought to maintain her composure. "Burying me is going to be hard enough on all of you without . . . that."

"Please." Her mom sobbed, while her dad slumped against a wall, anger melting into grief, putting his head in his hands.

Lily walked over on shaky legs and knelt in front of her mom, taking her trembling hands, offering what meager comfort she could. Part of her wanted to scream with frustration at their selfishness—she was the one dying! She was the one in pain! But the rest of her understood them. She'd had a whole car ride to think about it. They were in shock.

All she had to do was die. They had to watch their child suffer and die. Lily wouldn't have wished that on her worst enemy.

"Please don't make me bury my baby," her mom wept brokenly. Lily was destroying her. She could see it in her eyes. "Please. Please."

Lily's tears finally spilled over. They clutched each other's hands for a long quiet moment, pain filling the air of the usually comfortable kitchen.

"I'm scared." Lily's quiet admission slipped free before she could stop it. Her mom's agonized gaze softened. "I don't want to die." Lily choked, tears running hot and thick down her cheeks. Her mom wrapped her in her arms. Lily gripped her back, her mother's familiar perfume filling her nostrils. She let herself sob. "I don't want to die."

Her dad came over to hug them both, and they all cried together.

Her brothers handled the news differently when she'd told them. Tommy went eerily still and silent, which she'd expected, given that he was the most emotionally reserved of them. What she hadn't expected was the silent tears and the fierce way he'd gripped her in a hug. Tommy didn't cry, and he certainly didn't like hugs. Ryan shook his head when she started explaining, and kept shaking his head until the very end, when he held her so tightly that her lungs ached while they cried together.

She gave up her apartment, moved back in with her parents, and got rid of most of her belongings. She went downhill fast after that. Her brothers were always coming to visit, and they'd play Mario Kart, talk shit to and about each other, revisit old stories, watch movies. Her friends had families and lives, and couldn't visit as much, but they called often. People from the church community reached out, with suggestions for faith healing, and one notable sales pitch for the efficacy of essential oils. Lily blocked them.

She tried to stay pleasant, tried to not be a whiny, miserable, bitchy patient, but on top of the increasingly awful way it felt to exist in her body, she was ashamed. Ashamed of the way she hadn't fought, ashamed of the way she just let it happen. She'd justified it emotionally, physically, financially, but the shame of surrender was a bitter taste in her mouth.

Old, conditioned guilt told her that she'd brought this on herself by pursuing passions and not wanting to do less enjoyable jobs for better benefits, by getting tattoos and enjoying her collection of smutty books, and a litany of other "sins." Common sense and two decades of deconstructing her faith told her that she'd done the best she could with what she had.

God wasn't punishing her for fucking a girl in a church parking lot that one time, or for anything else, but if he was . . . well then, Lily had a lifetime of anger to vent, and she figured she'd be seeing the big holy sonofabitch soon enough.

She'd known when death was coming for her. Something in her soul whispered that it was time, and that that bedtime would be her last. She called her brothers, said she felt ready. Told them she loved them and would see them again. She hugged her dad; as tense as their relationship could be, she'd always loved him. Her mom brought her water and sat on the edge of her bed.

"Thanks, Mom," Lily rasped softly, her hand too weak to do more than rest on her mom's. "For all of it."

Her mom gave her a sad smile, so Lily hugged her with all her meager strength and told her good night. When she left, Lily put on music, listening to a wide array of songs as she stared up at the ceiling, feeling her body shutting down, feeling the pain seep away bit by bit.

"Okay," she'd whispered, closing her eyes with relief. "Okay . . ."

43

KNOCK THE SOCKS OFF

Lily

Lily wiped Bel's tears gently as he blinked back into the present. There had only been a minute of silence since he'd touched the page, his body perfectly still except for the way his heart started racing after several seconds. It was simultaneously the longest and shortest minute of her existence.

She wanted Bel to know her story, and the whole ugly truth of it. She wasn't proud of a lot of it, of who she'd been when she'd been hurting, of the mean, biting things she said to people, of how scared and guilty she'd been for most of her life for no good reason. But it was her story, and she trusted him. She wanted him to understand.

Bel's tail tightened around her calf as he set her file on the floor. He cleared his throat, one hand smoothing up the curve of her back while the other came up to trace her jaw. "I'm so proud of you, Lily."

His gentle statement brought immediate and embarrassing tears to her eyes. She opened her mouth, but he cupped the side of her neck with his large palm.

"You have a warrior's soul. You've been a warrior from the very beginning. You fought to heal yourself from your trauma, and when asking for help failed, you did what it took to help yourself. You handled all of what you went through alone. You fought to grow and *live*. And at the end, you did the hardest thing any warrior could ever have to do: surrender."

"I gave up."

"No," he said with a firm shake of his head. "You were in a situation in which you could not win, no matter what you did. You chose the option that would spare others from suffering needlessly. I know how much it hurt your family and friends for you to die, and that should be acknowledged. But, Lily, if you had fought, knowing that it wouldn't have made a difference, and given false hope while draining your—and *their*—resources? That would have hurt them so much more. From one warrior to another, I'm proud of you."

A warm, fuzzy feeling filled her chest. "Thank you."

He smiled softly at her before those brilliant silver eyes, luminous in their intensity, lost their warmth. "As for your youth leader . . ." His jaw flexed, then he nearly snarled, "*Suzanne.*"

Lily scowled on reflex.

"She told you to pray that your future husband was a forgiving man. I'm not your husband, but I am *yours*, and I am not, in any way, shape, or form, forgiving about what that piece of shit did to you. You did nothing wrong; you did nothing that needs forgiving." Something dark seeped into his expression but it wasn't directed at her. Her resulting pulse of arousal was probably inappropriate. "But, Lily, I may need your forgiveness for what I'll do to him when he gets to Hell. I'll put Greg out of a job." His promise was harsh, dripping with the threat of violence. "Though, he'll likely be too busy with Suzanne to notice."

Lily smiled sweetly at him. "As long as you at least give me a turn, you can do whatever you want."

The little crinkles around his eyes deepened, harshness fading from his expression to be replaced with something soft and thoughtful.

He pulled her closer, nuzzling into her hair. "I . . . do have one more confession of my own."

Lily smiled against his chest, fully expecting something not only sexual but deliciously filthy—

"I have your brothers' socks in my desk."

Lily pushed herself up, staring at him. "You . . . *what*?"

"There's a drawer in my desk filled with your brothers' socks." Bel's cheeks stained a deeper shade of dusky purple. "You told me about the promise you made to your brothers, about stealing their socks from the Afterlife and how you felt bad that it was a lie. As an adult, I can't go to the mortal world without causing a bunch of problems. But teenage demons sneak into the mortal world all the time. It's like a rite of passage. So, I've been asking some of them to steal one of your brothers' socks every so often. I don't tell them why, but they bring them back to me, and I keep them in a spare drawer. You loved them so much, and I wanted you to be able to keep your promise."

Lily peered down at him, reeling from the flash of clarity. "Is *that* why I've been seeing those teenage demons go by the Hellp Desk?"

Bel shifted a bit under her scrutiny. "Probably. I tell them to act like they're running an errand for me so that no one questions them. There's a really good crack to the mortal world by Lua-o-Milu that I used to use that I tell them about."

Lily didn't know if she wanted to laugh or cry or both, so she settled for sliding her hand down his stomach. "I can't believe I'm about to fuck you senseless because of my brothers' *socks*. Have you ever been ridden by a hot redhead who loves you?"

Bel's eyes gleamed with interest, skimming the very tips of his claws down the length of her side. "No, but I'm thrilled that there's a first time for everything. And hopefully multiple repeats."

"Good. Floor? I don't want to crush your wings."

They wiggled off the couch and onto the floor without an ounce of grace, giggling the whole time as Bel leaned back on his hands and Lily straddled him.

Sobering slightly, she took his face in her hands, losing herself in his gleaming eyes. "Thank you," she said softly, kissing him. "I'm about to ride the capacity for speech out of you, but thank you."

Bel sat forward, bringing his hands up to brace her hips as he kissed her more deeply, just as someone tried to open the door, drawing both of their attention.

"Oh for crying out loud. They better not be doing what I think they're doing." Lev's annoyed voice was muffled. He jiggled the handle again. "Beleth! I *know* you received my memo about inappropriate office activities! We discussed this!"

Asmodeus's amused drawl chimed in. "Cut the guy some slack, Lev. What's he supposed to use that big desk for? It can't all be paperwork."

Lev snapped something in response, rattling the handle.

Bel was either choking or smothering laughter—Lily would bet on the latter—so she used Bel's shoulders as leverage to push to her feet, ignoring his huff of protest.

"I've got this," she said over her shoulder, searching for her clothes, which—other than her boots and one sock—were nowhere in sight. A pile of black fabric that turned out to be Bel's sleeveless shirt was her best option, so she pulled it over her head and padded barefoot to the door. It fell to her upper thighs, gaping open almost like a hospital gown at the back because of the wing slits.

Oh well. She was decent enough.

She threw the lock and opened the door just enough to smile with excessive politeness at an aghast Lev and an utterly delighted Asmodeus.

"Hey, guys, we're kind of busy fucking the sense out of each other right now—"

"Then fucking it back in," Bel added loudly from his spot on the floor.

"And then fucking it back in," Lily agreed. "I understand that you sent out a very well-written and clearly worded memo, Lev, but this is an important moment that couldn't wait. We're sorry."

"No, we're not," Bel called.

"We're just going to be a bit longer . . ." Lily glanced over her shoulder to where Bel lounged back on the rug, head cocked, a smirk playing over his features as the red-gold light gleamed deliciously over his naked body. "We're going to be *quite* a bit longer," Lily amended, pressing her thighs together and turning back to them. "So if it's possible to make it wait, please do so."

Lev huffed, looking pained. "I'll come back . . . later."

"Tomorrow," Asmodeus suggested. Lily shot him a grateful grin.

"I really appreciate your patience, Lev. I'll write you up a basic report on the Hellp Desk as soon as possible, how about that?" she offered, slowly closing the door.

Just before it shut completely, Lev sighed. "Make it double-spaced, please."

Lily smothered her laugh with her hand and threw the lock with a decisive click.

44

MEMO

Lily

"**L**ooks like someone had a rough night." Moura smirked as she walked by the Hellp Desk on her way to the break room.

Lily shot her a smug grin, fixing a typo on the long-overdue report for Lev. "Rough night, no. But this morning? Mm."

What had started out as a simple and sweet good morning kiss swiftly turned into Lily muffling her moans into a pillow while Bel pounded into her from behind, his powerful body curled over hers, fangs scraping along her neck and shoulder in a way that never failed to send electricity down her spine.

They'd ended up cackling when Max had cried plaintively for attention outside their door, prompting Sharkie to be deeply concerned for their safety because of their lack of response.

When they'd gotten up, Bel had taught Sharkie how to flip omelets while Lily went to Common Grounds to get their coffee—and hot cocoa. They'd all headed to Hell together, Bel and Lily with their arms around each other, Sharkie skipping along with her hand in Lily's. Bel took Sharkie down to school while Lily stayed at the Hellp Desk, wading into the waiting line of souls. Through every interaction, no matter how angry or shitty or lost the soul, she'd been *happy*.

The last two months had been the best of her existence. She and Bel loved each other, and with no more self-imposed limitations, they'd flourished. They hadn't spent a night apart since their confessions in the office, usually ending up at her Paradise, but occasionally at Bel's palace, where the three of them would chat over dinner, then watch a movie or play their respective games. Sharkie, who continued to age, had fallen in love with the aquarium version of *Zoo Tycoon*, and liked to perch at the table beside Bel, the pair of them glued to their laptop screens.

Lily could hardly believe it sometimes, given how they'd had to make do with snippets of time before. Of course, it helped that Sharkie was far more settled, and that their limitations were gone.

At night, whether they had sex or not, they always curled together and talked about something frivolous. Bel had made it his mission to hear the story behind each of her tattoos, picking a new one every few nights, and she did the same with his tattoos and scars. They bandied about ideas for future tattoos, and she secretly hoped that he would get the lower stomach one he'd mentioned, though he had no design in mind yet.

One afternoon, while Sharkie was out with Lucifer, Lily and Bel had sat down to have a nonsexual sex conversation, laying out and discussing their likes and dislikes, hard and soft limits, as well as their known kinks and curiosities. They'd established a set of sexual boundaries, agreeing to build up to the more intense of their interests with time and trust.

It had been incredibly freeing to talk plainly about something that she'd always had an interest in but had felt cautious being open about. Naturally, once the conversation wound down and had come to a respectable end, Lily made good on her promise to ride him again, this time with much less inhibition than she'd had in the office.

After all, the couch was easier on her knees than the floor.

Carlton had also sprouted a new room, much to everyone's delight: a personal gym with weights, a cardio section, and an open, mirrored area for sparring that had quickly been put to use. Sharkie had asked Bel to help her with her "combat homework" from the Valkyries and the Valhalla warriors. Lily got in on the lessons as well, wanting to learn how to properly use the short sword that had brought her and Bel together.

If they weren't sparring, Lily enjoyed lifting weights, but mostly liked to read and walk on the treadmill. If Bel was doing one of his insane workouts, she dropped the pretense of reading and shamelessly ogled him. They'd make faces at each other in the mirror, seeing how long they could tease until one of them couldn't take it anymore.

It was a good thing that Sharkie wasn't home all that often during the day—they always double-checked to make sure—because Lily and Bel christened the fuck out of that gym. And the foyer. And the hall. And the bathroom. And the living room. And the kitchen. And that was just in her Paradise. Lily was fairly certain that the only rooms in both houses they hadn't explored each other in were Sharkie's, and that would never change.

In every aspect, the two months had been steeped with a sense of peace and rightness.

As annoying as some of the souls could be, she loved what she did. There was a camaraderie among those who worked at the gate. Each day was a new adventure. The souls weren't all bad, though she got to interact with a disproportionate amount of the truly awful and entitled ones due to the nature of the Hellp Desk. She loved getting to see the souls who had spent time healing and growing improve enough earn a chance at reincarnation. Every day was a new adventure. She loved it.

She loved . . . everything.

The friends. The safety. The purpose. The family. *Her* family. Everything she'd ever dreamed of, and nothing she wanted to leave behind.

Stay.

The quiet whisper had only grown stronger with every precious moment. Every knowing eye roll from the gate demons as they dealt with the damned and the lost. Every little snuggle or giggle from Sharkie. Every sassy text in the group chat of deities and denizens that she called friends. Every crinkle of Bel's eyes and brush of his hand against hers.

Perhaps she would forget her silent chest in time, and the yearning for gummy smiles and little hands and more children to love would fade.

She was valued and loved and safe. Wasn't that what she'd always wanted?

She felt almost guilty for the sense of relief that the sheer safety of the Afterlife had given her.

She knew, thanks to Bel, that the other Universe continued to maintain a foothold in the pocket realm, but had failed to harvest the power of souls from their Universe. They would continue to fail, as she understood it, unless they completely invaded and successfully dominated their Universe.

Bel had quietly admitted one night as they were curled together that he felt like the long build to something decisive was coming an end.

"I still hope," he murmured, absently playing with her fingers, "that they will give up and go home, but this has dragged on for so long, I'm not sure they will."

Knowing that, she knew that "safe" was relative. But to her, for the moment, she was safe in the ways that mattered. She could wear what she wanted without fear of reproach or unwanted attention. Assault did not exist in the Afterlife. For that alone, she considered staying. But to exist without thinking like prey, while simultaneously having the freedom to do as she pleased? She didn't have to worry about money, or food, or shelter, or disease, or taxes. She had an unlimited supply of books and new friends and experiences available.

And if she stayed, she always would.

Lily watched as a soul approached, weeping hysterically. Her sobs were so intense that it was probably a good thing she didn't need to breathe. A flash of instinctual sympathy was quashed by the appearance of the soul's file, which, upon being opened, was clearly stamped with *Level Six*.

Ah, crocodile tears, then.

Lily rested her chin in her palm, flipping the file open and skimming her fingertip down the page while the soul continued to wail with increasing theatricality.

Tears were her weapon, and she wielded them like a master, refusing to accept any kind of accountability or consequences. A hypocrite of the finest order, she virulently condemned others for actions that she herself had done, setting out to elevate herself by debasing those around her.

She'd cheated on her first husband with a younger man, barely into adulthood, whom she'd threatened to ruin if he did anything other than comply with her orders. When she'd accidentally gotten pregnant and gone for an abortion, something she had loudly spent her life railing against, she had treated the clinic workers with vitriolic cruelty, even as she cried and they held her hand. She'd snarled at a glassy-eyed young woman in the parking lot as she'd left the clinic, calling her a baby killer. She'd taken sadistic joy in the young woman's tears, even as she noted that she looked around the same age as her daughter. When she found evidence of her husband's own affair a year later, she'd dragged his name through the mud for letting his eye wander.

Her second husband had been a timid man, whom she wrapped around her finger, then set about terrorizing the children that he'd brought to the marriage, as well as her own daughter. Her husband had been a businessman, and she'd enjoyed the social scene that his connections afforded her, cultivating a reputation as a generous hostess and a formidable enemy. When her daughter committed suicide, she'd wept for a night, but in the morning, she had refused to have anything more to do with it. She told her first husband that she would pay for cremation, but if he wanted anything more than that, he alone would be paying for the funeral, grave, and headstone. When he'd argued, asking her why, she told him the same thing she did to her friends.

"Suicide is a sin," she said with a carefully cultivated wobble to her voice. She'd artfully dabbed at a teary eye as her friends had comforted her. "Such a shame that she let the devil get ahold of her like that, but all we can do is try to protect the God-fearing children we have left." Their emphatic agreement had brought her glee. More glee than her daughter had ever given her. Her death was an embarrassment, but the attention and support that it had brought was something that she would happily exploit . . .

Lily blinked the file's information away, realizing that her nails were digging into her cheek with rage. She relaxed her fingers and flipped the file shut, coolly watching the soul's performance. The woman sagged against the desk, quickly glancing up at Lily to gauge her reaction while taking great shuddering breaths as she made a show of trying to compose herself.

"I am so sorry," the woman choked out. "It's just . . . this is all such a shock."

"Is it really."

The woman's eyes sharpened for a moment before she covered the slip with a sharp inhale and a swipe at her eyes. "Of *course*, I was a woman of faith all my days. Perhaps you saw that in my file? As a child of God, I am seventy times seven times forgiven."

The reference to a verse was dimly familiar. Lily tried to sound as bored as possible, knowing that a lack of reaction would rankle the woman more than anything else. "Yeah, I'm not too great at math, but I'm gonna say you ran out of those forgiveness points somewhere around . . . I dunno, coercing a young man into continuing to sleep with you and verbally abusing the clinic workers who were there to help you. You know, if I were going to make a ballpark guess."

"The devil works in mysterious and wicked ways—"

"He super doesn't," Lily drawled. "Like, he *super* doesn't. Bastard is about as obvious as a period stain on white pants, and he's less about blanket 'wickedness' and more about meting out justice. I'm not going to rule out wickedness entirely—maybe that's bedroom play for him, I wouldn't know. But the point is that bad acting makes me itchy, so knock it off."

The woman's tears dried up faster than a sponge in the desert. "Don't mock me!"

"Don't make it so easy."

"Listen here, you miserable little brat, I may have had some lapses in judgment, but I was baptized in a church and forgiven by God, so I should *not* be here."

Lily made a high-pitched hum of doubt, enjoying the way the woman seethed in response.

"I am—"

"Lucky you are only being sent to Level Six," Lily cut in, putting some steel in her tone. "The Universe and, I guess in your case, God, since you chose to be judged by Christianity's tenets, is a shit ton more merciful than I am. Because for the way you treated your daughter *alone*, I would have dragged your weepy ass down to Level Nine and let the really scary ones play with you. Matter of fact, if you don't go where you were so mercifully told to, I will."

The woman reeled back, hand pressed to her chest. Lily could see in her eyes that she knew she was outmatched. Interesting. A disgusting blot of a soul, but not audacious beyond all reason.

Lily watched the woman go, shaking her head. Just before she reached the archway to the stairs, a wailing sob split the air, echoing as the woman resumed her performance down the staircase until it faded entirely.

"Good grief," someone muttered in disapproval.

Lily turned to find Lev grimacing behind her. "Hey, Lev! Sorry about the delay on the report. Let me just print that out for you." Lily clicked the command on her computer and waited for the ultra-sleek printer built into the rock wall beside the desk to spit out the document. Even if the thing wasn't essentially a tray on the wall that produced papers, she was convinced that its real magic was the fact that it printed every time, without hesitation or fuss or suddenly dying. Sharkie had named it Prints Charming and made it a paper crown.

"Your outfit looks really good on you, by the way. I like the orange," Lily said, spinning her chair to face him.

He really did look good—the charcoal pants, button-down shirt, and vest were precisely tailored, with crisp embroidery in the demonic style picked out in a burnt orange that matched his eyes and tie.

Lev fidgeted, smoothing a hand over his vest and ducking his head in thanks, setting his briefcase—of course Leviathan had an actual, no-shit briefcase—on the Hellp Desk.

"Have you been able to formulate a clearly defined set of procedures for determining the best approach to deal with souls who act beyond the ordinary?" he asked.

Good ol' Lev.

"Not really," she said, waiting for his huff of annoyance and smiling when it came. "Sorry, Lev, it's . . . people. They're hard to clearly define and fit into a standard procedure. When it comes to these kind of souls—sorry, one sec. Either fuck off or get fucked up," she threw over her shoulder to a male soul who raged up to the desk.

He flipped her off. She held up her first two fingers in a V and licked between them. He huffed away.

Lev's olive-green skin was several shades lighter when she turned back to him.

"Anyway, as I was saying, these kinds of souls are clearly willing to deviate from the norm, because they're willing to ignore the perfectly good instructions that they're given. Some of them are going to beg. Some of them are going to barter. Some of them are going to threaten. Some of them genuinely need help or advice. There're a lot of people who just need someone to be there with them and guide them a bit. Mortal souls are fucking *complicated*. I'm not sure how I do it. I just do. But—" She pulled the freshly printed report out of the tray, stapled it, and handed it to him with a smile. "I tried to explain my process for you. It's double-spaced. With a reference page and citations."

Lev took the papers slowly, carefully groomed eyebrows furrowed in thought. He looked over the desk, to where the line formed when there was a rush of souls, over the stream of souls moving from the gate to the arches, then back at her.

"Mortals are complicated," he repeated thoughtfully. "I've never given much thought to them beyond the logistics of their numbers and maintaining the levels appropriately. Would you mind writing another report?"

"Um."

"Just a simple one on the nuances of mortal souls, please."

"Sorry, Lev, but there's no way to make that particular topic a 'simple' report."

"A detailed one would be fine, then."

"No." Lily laughed. "I don't think it's *possible*. Like, at all. Do you think that you could write a report on the nuances of all demon-kind?"

Lev considered it for a moment and sighed. "I suppose you're right. You're sure that you can't formulate some kind of preparatory material for this . . . Hellp Desk?"

"Preparatory material?"

He huffed again. "To give to your replacement after your reincarnation."

Hearing her possible reincarnation mentioned by someone else was completely different from when she mulled it over in her mind. Her own thoughts produced a dull ache in her chest. Lev's words felt like a sucker punch.

"How about we cross that bridge when we come to it, Lev." Did her voice sound raspy? It felt raspy.

He stared at her as if she'd suggested he dance naked on top of the desk. "I'll . . . consider it. Thank you for the initial report. I have something for you as well." He slipped her report into his briefcase and pulled out a single crisp sheet of paper. He cleared his throat as he handed it to her, then made sure his perfectly straight tie hadn't deviated from its position. "I deeply appreciate the changes you have made to Hell. They have been confusing but beneficial. It is also nice to see Beleth happy."

Lily skimmed over the brief blurb of text, then realized what she was holding and read it again more carefully.

> *From the Office of Prince Leviathan*
> *Subject: Workplace Decorum*
>
> *As a result of recent and ongoing events that have taken place in the workplace, it behooves me to remind everyone involved with all aspects of Hell's management of the importance of not sullying our professional spaces with sex. Office spaces afford occupants privacy so that they may focus on their tasks, not on carnal relations.*
>
> *Despite protestations to the contrary, and numerous attempts by certain members involved in the management of Hell to explain the opportunities for mutual connection afforded by the horizontal surfaces commonly found in an office (i.e., desks), I must insist on the renewed and fully clothed professionalism of all.*

Lev's angular signature and a round, metallic green seal embossed with what must have been his personal crest and motto took up the bottom third of the page.

Holy fuck.

The memo.

Lily slowly raised her head to stare at him, bemusement and vague annoyance melting away when she realized how deeply green his cheeks were. His tail twitched nervously behind him, despite his obvious attempts to still it.

Oh.

He was welcoming her. In his odd, Lev way, he was welcoming her to the team. Recognizing her contribution. Several pieces of Lev's character clicked into place. Sure, he was exacting and fussy and so damned fastidious that he'd probably refuse to eat his M&M'S until he found a way to organize them alphabetically, but it was all because he *cared*. Lev obviously cared so much about Hell and the proper management of it—and his coworkers too—even if he didn't seem to know how to show it with what most considered to be normal affection.

Lily set the memo down on the desk, stepped forward, and wrapped Lev's lean body in a hug. He made a sound like the air being slowly let out of a balloon for a few seconds, but just as she was about to let go, he brought his arms awkwardly around her.

"Yes," he said, flustered, "well. This kind of affection is fine."

Lily stifled her smile and gave him a little squeeze. "Thank you."

"You're . . . welcome." He was quiet for a few moments, then patted her back. "I understand that you and Beleth had a, *ahem*, very important personal moment in his office that day, and I'm sure you somehow had a lovely time. But really, Asmodeus and Sariah are bad enough. It all seems very . . . fluid, and there's only so much trauma I want to subject the janitorial staff to. So if you wouldn't mind heeding the memo? Please?"

Lily was still snickering several hours later when she rode the elevators down to the first level of training fields for lunch with Bel. He hadn't responded to the picture she'd sent him of Lev's memo, but he'd told her that morning that it was going to be a heavy training day, so she wasn't surprised he hadn't gotten to it yet. She couldn't wait to hear his reaction.

The elevator doors slid open, and she stepped out. But something felt off. She sobered, walking down the short hallway on quiet feet, hand creeping toward the sword at her waist, trying to place what was wrong.

Silence.

All she heard was the faint whiffle of a breeze over the accoutrement of the massive training field. No clanging weaponry, no grunts of exertion, no calls of orders or advice. She stuck her head out of the tunnel. It was eerie for such a massive place to be completely empty. Eerie, but nothing felt malicious at least. Where were they?

She headed back to the elevator just as her phone buzzed in her pocket. She waited until the doors were closed securely, the elevator remaining stationary, to look at her phone.

Big Guy: *Hey, Princess, the big thing I've been worried about happening just happened. We're mustering on TL3. I don't know if we can have lunch together, but I'd love to see you.*

Big Guy: *And your butt*

Princess: *Not my tits? On my way.*

Big Guy: *Bring them too.*

Lily shook her head, even as her stomach twisted into knots. Pressing the button for the largest and lowest training level, she took a moment to draw on her composure.

The big thing happened. An invasion had begun.

Mustering.

Bel was going to war.

The sound of commotion filled the air even before the doors slid open, a cacophonous dull roar that she felt in her bones.

The doors parted, revealing Bel leaning with his shoulder propped against the wall, clad in the matte black armor that made him look impossibly taller and broader. He clearly hadn't had time to braid his hair, as he'd pulled it back in a loose knot at the base of his skull, and he gazed intensely into nothing. He looked rugged and dangerous and like every morally gray fantasy love interest she'd ever crushed on.

"Someday I'm going to love the sight of you in that armor," she said ruefully, breaking him out of his reverie. Some of the intensity faded from his eyes, replaced with that gleam that was so quintessentially Bel.

"Well, we did both express an interest in role-play, and I seem to recall more than a few scenes in your books that involve tasteful stripping of armor."

Lily rested her hand on the odd metal covering his chest, hating that he couldn't feel her, and stretched up to press her lips to his. He sighed into the kiss, hands coming up to cradle her face. He rested his forehead against hers when they parted.

"This is it. They widened the rift and sent an entire army through. The Fae and Valhallans are holding them for the moment, but barely. We sounded full muster. We're all marching out; Lucifer's opened up the troop tunnels," he murmured against her cheek.

All. Lily swallowed hard, sliding her hand up to the nape of his neck, wondering how many of them would return. How many Fae and Valhallan warriors had already been lost.

"I don't know when we'll be back." His voice grew impossibly deep. "I hope it will be short and decisive—in our favor—but I don't know."

Lily pulled back to study him, to memorize his features. He seemed to be doing the same to her. Neither of them noticed the elevator arriving.

"Bel!" Sharkie cried.

They both turned in time for Sharkie to launch herself at him. Thankfully he caught her before she connected painfully with the metal armor, hoisting her up so that she could hug his neck. Lucifer was slower to make his way to them, his steps purposeful and eyes grim. He caught and held her gaze.

"Lily."

"Luci." She itched being so close to his roiling, unchecked power, but concern kept her voice soft. "Are you alright?"

Lucifer had been tense for the last several weeks, and lately, even Sharkie had commented on it. Lily had noticed some terse expressions on the warrior-like people groups of the Afterlife as she'd moved through the Universal Hallway, but Lucifer had been the most stormy.

He blinked at her once, twice. Some of the tension eased out of his face, replaced with weary resignation. The itch of his power faded. "As much as I can be. I don't march with them; I stay behind as a last line of defense." Something that clearly bothered him. "I am sorry," he said quietly, his electric-blue gaze sliding to study Bel and Sharkie as Bel murmured something to her.

"I know what and who he is. I'd never ask him to be anything less," Lily said with equal quietness. "If he was anything other than himself, I wouldn't love him so much."

"I always hoped you two would get along. You seemed like you would be good for each other. And I was right."

"Bel told me about the little errand you had him run to orchestrate our meeting." She arched an eyebrow. "Not exactly subtle."

"Worked though." Lucifer's smile had a bit more life to it. "Bel, go have lunch with your family. I'll make sure your legions don't need handholding for a bit."

They ended up going one level up, to a mostly empty training field dotted with other clusters of demons taking a few quiet moments to say goodbye.

Sharkie was quiet but had expressed utter confidence that all would be well and Bel was badass enough to deal with whatever needed dealt with. Her biggest concern was how long he would be gone.

The little bit of food that Lily managed to choke down sat like a rock in her stomach, but she tried to maintain the appearance of calm. She had faith in Bel's abilities, and the armies of Hell, not to mention the other Afterlife forces, but still. Bel ate with methodical ease, the underlying tension in his eyes belying the lightness of his tone as he answered Sharkie's questions about what it was like to wear armor.

"Heavy, but not too bad. Like clothes made out of your weighted blanket, you know?" He brushed a wayward piece of hair out of his face.

"Do you have a special way you like to do your hair so it sits under your helmet and stays out of your face?" Lily asked, wiping her hand on her leggings.

The corner of Bel's mouth quirked upward. "Not particularly, as long as it's out of my face, I don't really care. Feeling decorative, princess?"

"Can't have you going into battle with a shitty hairdo. Sit still and let me braid you like one of my French girls."

"What?" Sharkie asked at the same time Bel barked out a laugh that lit up his whole face.

"It's from a movie, Shark-a-doodle-do, but the actual line is 'draw me like one of your French girls,'" Bel explained as Lily circled behind the low rock he sat on.

"Draw, like makeup?"

Lily stepped between Bel's wings and loosened the tie in his hair. "Remember that documentary on art we watched, and how sometimes they draw people naked to practice different skills? It was like that: an art thing, not a sex thing. Well, in *that* scene anyway. Those characters in the movie we're talking about definitely had sex later. In a car. While it was on a boat."

"That just sounds like a lot of work," Sharkie mumbled into her sandwich.

Lily tugged lightly on Bel's hair when he opened his mouth. He shut it again, tail coiling around her ankle and warming her from the inside out. She focused on finger brushing his hair until it was smooth, then sectioned it and began to work, more conscious of what it needed to do than how it needed to look. Sharkie leaned against Bel's side, and after a few prompting questions, he got her talking about the growth spurt race happening at school between all the preteens.

He asked Lily about her day, and they laughed about Lev's memo, her fingers working quickly despite the fact that she felt like they should be shaking.

A braid down the middle between his horns, then a pair of braids on each side, all joining together into a single tight braid that she finished off, leaving it up to him what to do with it from there. Mindful of his horns, she leaned forward to press a kiss between them.

Then their time was up.

The orderly chaos on the third training level hadn't abated, so they lingered in the hallway near the elevators.

Bel crouched down to give Sharkie one last long hug, murmuring his goodbye and promising to get home as soon as he could.

When he stood and stepped close to Lily, his massive hands coming up to cradle her face, she leaned into him, covering his hands with her own, as it was the only skin of his she could easily touch. His silver eyes were intense, but she basked in it.

"Can I ask you a favor?"

"Anything," she said.

He pulled a little pouch out of a nook in his armor. "Will you wear my bracelets from the girls for me?"

"Every day." Lily tipped the glittery bracelets out of the pouch and slid them onto her left wrist, where they hung loosely.

"I love you," he said, kissing her long and slow.

"I love you," she told him, only retreating enough to meet his eyes. She stroked along his cheek and ran her thumb over his little chin spikes. "Be safe. Come home to us." She gripped his jaw firmly. "Come home to *me*."

He smiled at the order and nodded, kissing her again before he wrapped her in a hug, murmuring his love one more time. She buried her face in his neck, inhaling his warm, musky scent, embedding it in her memory. His lips ghosted over her forehead before he stepped away. Then he squeezed her hand and turned to leave, only to be blocked by Sharkie.

She held up her pinkie finger.

Bel looped it with his and gave a little squeeze.

"Okay," Sharkie said solemnly. "Go do general stuff."

Bel

Bel marched in silence, as did most of the tens of thousands of warriors who walked through long-unused tunnels to war and an uncertain future. Memories of Lily and Sharkie flickered through his mind, blurring his surroundings.

He would see them again. Even if it was as part of the fabric of the Universe, he would watch over them. Lily. Sharkie. His mother. His siblings.

His nieces and nephews. His friends. They made his life worth living, and he would give his life if it meant protecting them.

His fingers ran over the smooth bumps of his new braids. Tucking the thoughts of home and family away in his heart, he turned his mind to the job ahead.

"Time to do general stuff," he murmured.

45

MARGARITA COMPLEX

Lily

Sharkie plopped herself on the floor behind the Hellp Desk with a huff. "I know Bel is doing his job, but how long is that going to take? My teacher said she didn't know. And I miss him."

Lily, leaning back in her chair with her feet propped up on the desk, laid her book in her lap and lolled her head to give Sharkie a weary smile.

Two weeks had ground by with agonizing slowness since Bel and the legions had left. Two weeks since Hell had gone eerily quiet. Oh, demons still worked and talked and went about their days, but there were noticeably fewer of them around, and all the conversations seemed to have a hushed quality to them.

Lily had gone to Seven Deadly with a few of the gate demons the first week. There had been no boisterous laughter, no rowdy music or dancing, just the dull hum of conversation. Krun's wife, Naamah, had joined them, apparently with the sole mission of adopting Lily and fussing over her like a mother hen. A nearly seven-foot-tall, magenta-skinned mother hen whose solution for what she called the "missing your man blues" involved a large margarita, a brand-new vibrator in a pretty box, and a chocolate sheet cake decorated with fudge frosting and an enthusiastic application of rainbow sprinkles—courtesy of their daughter. The cake had come with instructions to not cut it into pieces, but take a fork directly to it, as needed.

"Now drink your margarita, dear," Naamah had said in her warm, motherly voice. "All the partners of soldiers have regular get-togethers, mostly by legion, but frankly, support is support, and in times like these, we need all the support we can get. I remember. Drink your margarita like you mean it. Here are tissues for when you want or need to cry; they're the kind that won't chafe."

Lily had dutifully inhaled the fishbowl-sized margarita and, once the tequila-horniness kicked in, headed home with the intention of using the new vibrator. She'd ended up crying on the bed as soon as she'd opened it, because it made her think of Bel's utter delight when he'd found her personal arsenal.

The tissues had come in handy then.

He'd been gone for stretches of time before and since they'd gotten together, but this time felt different. Bigger.

"I don't know either, bug. Wish I did. How are you doing with all this?" Lily said finally, fiddling with the beads of the bracelets.

Sharkie had been slower to laugh since Bel left. A semipermanent wrinkle of worry had taken up residence on her forehead. When she curled up next to Lily at the table or on the couch, she always glanced at Bel's empty spot with a little sigh before snuggling closer. When she and Lily sparred and trained with the demons, her glee wasn't quite as effusive. She still laughed, still got excited about new facts, still managed the aquarium on her computer with the intensity of a conservationist. She seemed more cautious, though, a bit less certain that good things were still good.

Sharkie shrugged and fiddled with her backpack. "I miss Bel a lot. I'm worried about him. Luci seems stressed and sad. You miss Bel, but, like, you're okay. As long as you're okay, I'm okay." Lily only had a moment to be awed by the trust in that statement before Sharkie squinted at her. "You *are* okay, right? Be honest."

Lily laughed, warmth spreading through her chest. "I miss Bel, and I'm worried about him too, but yeah, I'm okay. Here's why: I know that he's a badass warrior and general who knows what he's doing. He has all of his legions to help him, plus the other armies and legions too. So I hope that, all things considered, he'll be okay."

Okay enough. He can come back missing parts, as long as he just comes back.

"Yeah, that makes sense. But what if he isn't okay?"

Lily fought back a surge of nausea at the thought of a Universe without Bel in it. "Then I'll be devastated," she said quietly. "It will hurt like nothing I've ever felt before. But I also know that I will find a way to deal with it. I might want to fall apart, but I'll keep going. I love Bel so much, but he's not the only person I love. I've got you, and you are more than worth sticking around for."

Sharkie's concern melted into a soft smile. "I love you too. No matter what, we'll deal with it, right?"

"Right."

"YOU BITCH!" a woman shrieked at the demon who had checked her in, all while stomping her way toward the Hellp Desk and waggling her finger like she was trying to generate a breeze.

Lily exchanged a grimace with Sharkie before fixing her glare on the soul. *Can't we have a single uninterrupted special moment, for fuck's sake?*

Other than her mottled red face and the fact that she was quite literally spitting mad, the woman looked like a perfectly coiffed socialite. "Do you have *any* idea who I am? I—"

An awful, guttural shrieking noise cut through her tirade, bringing her up short. It took Lily a beat too long to realize that the noise was coming from the floor beside her. Sharkie slowly rose from the floor like an adorable Halloween decoration, eyes completely blank, mouth wide open, emitting the most god-awful noise that Lily had ever heard come out of a person. Lily bit her tongue and fixed her gaze indolently on the woman, as if this were a normal occurrence and she wasn't a blink away from crying with laughter. Several of the demons turned to watch, and more than a few of them, plus a few souls actually, seemed to be masking giggles.

"*Excuse* me—"

Sharkie's wail increased in pitch and volume, her arms raising to the sides in a T-pose.

Lily sucked her lips into her mouth and exhaled slowly through her nose, trying to maintain her composure. Sharkie shifted to a noise that sounded like some hybrid of Cthulhu and a husky throwing a tantrum, remaining completely blank-eyed the entire time. She abruptly honked like a goose, sucked in a dramatic lungful of air, and launched back into her croaky howl. Half the demons lost it, and Lily had to shut her eyes to keep from following suit.

Be serious. Help sell this. You're a professional, pull yourself together.

Lily opened her eyes. "Yes?" The one word was all she could manage, clenching her jaw to keep in the laughter.

The woman looked at her, looked at Sharkie, then hurried away, throwing disturbed glances over her shoulder as she went.

Lily caved, covering her face with her hands and laughing so hard tears streamed down her face, only to cackle even harder when Sharkie stopped shrieking as quickly as she'd started.

Sharkie cleared her throat and smacked her lips, her bland expression sending Lily into another round of hysterics. "That was fun."

Lily wiped at her eyes, still chuckling, and held her fist out for Sharkie to bump. "Nicely done. Couldn't have said it better myself."

"It felt like what needed to be said. Does this mean I can intern with you when I'm older?" Sharkie asked eagerly. Since hitting the milestone of "being eleven-ish," she'd learned that, starting at sixteen, demons began having short internships to help them decide what they wanted to do as adults. She'd immediately started asking Lily about the Hellp Desk.

"Of course, if you want to. But don't be afraid to try other stuff you might like doing. You don't have to do anything if you don't want to."

"I like hanging out with you and being sassy and funny and having fun. I like the gate demons. I like being helpful. I like the Hellp Desk. It's really cool, it has a procedure, but also it's not the same all the time, so it's not boring. I like your baseball bat. Like, I really, really like your baseball bat. I want it. You know, someday."

"Tell you what," Lily said with a smile, "that will be your internship present."

Sharkie pumped a fist in the air. "Yes! I'm gonna bedazzle it!"

A month went by, and for Lily everything seemed to blur together slightly.

Souls still came down to Hell. Still came up to the Hellp Desk to complain or threaten or rage or ask legitimate questions and seek actual help and advice. Lily got coffee in the mornings and chatted with the baristas and her friends. She and Persephone had a girls' night in the Underworld that involved drunken flower crowns. She had lunch with Aphrodite. She finally got that coffee with Angel. She parked herself in the Universal Library on one of her days off and didn't move from her couch the entire day. She sparred with Krun or Moura or one of the others. She brought pastries to the Front Desk and swapped stories about dealing with souls, good and bad.

She went with Sharkie to visit Cthulhu in his realm, and while the initial sight of a building-sized creature with a tentacled, unearthly face had been a bit of a shock, she'd quickly gotten over it when she saw how gentle he was with Sharkie. He was odd, but funny. Fist-bumping a hand the size of an SUV had been a new experience.

What wasn't a new experience was staring at her phone, twitching every time it rang or buzzed and quelling the flash of disappointment when it wasn't Bel. She still sent him messages, sent him a picture every day. Told him that she loved him. That she was proud of him. That she touched the bracelets on her wrist a dozen times a day.

The Universal Hallway grew a little tense as time and battles dragged on. The offshoot hall where the invaded realm lay had been cordoned off—not that anyone ventured that way much anymore. Lily found it one day, a prickle of danger itching through every fiber of her being as she stared grimly down the empty hallway.

She didn't know how long she stood there, but her reverie was broken by a cluster of soldiers carrying stretchers of the wounded toward their respective realms. Demons, Fae, Valkyrie, other warriors. She stepped out of their way and went back to the Hellp Desk, mechanically going about her work. She hugged Sharkie a little tighter when she picked her up from school.

A few days later, a gangly young demon with orange skin bashfully approached the Hellp Desk.

"Excuse me, Ms. Lily?"

"Hey, what's up?" Lily asked, all too happy to have an excuse to look away from the logistics report for Lev on her computer.

The young demon fidgeted a little, then held out a single black sock.

Lily's world narrowed down to that stupid sock, a cool sensation trickling over her skin.

"Prince Beleth asked me to give this to you. I, um, I made sure to get one of the ones in the dryer, so that it was clean and didn't . . . you know . . . smell."

Lily's breaths sounded loud in her head. "Bel asked you? Is he here?"

If he was back and hadn't said anything, she'd kill him. Kiss the sense out of him, maybe fuck the attitude and audacity out of him—how dare he come back and not say anything?—but then she would very much kill him. Then bring him back.

"Oh, no, I'm sorry, Ms. Lily, he, um . . . he set this up with a bunch of us before he, um . . . left."

"Ah." Lily said, her own voice sounding far away.

Sweet man. Sweet, thoughtful, beloved man, making sure she kept her promise, even while he was gone. She could practically hear her brother Ryan's exasperation as he dug through the laundry looking for his missing sock. One of his running socks, it looked like. It had to be Ryan's, because Tommy refused to wear ankle socks.

"Ms. Lily?" The concern in the young demon's voice snapped her out of her haze.

"I'm so sorry, I just got a little overwhelmed by this. Thank you." She smiled, taking the sock with fingers that trembled. It felt different than anything else in the Afterlife. Somehow it felt *mortal*. "This really means a lot to me. Did you have a good trip to the mortal world?"

The young demon ducked their head with a grin, slender tail twitching behind them. "Yeah. We pushed shopping carts around the parking lot when there was no wind. A bunch of people filmed it, but they couldn't see us. It was really fun. Then we got milkshakes. They taste different there."

Lily read between the lines of "got milkshakes" and interpreted that they must have "stolen" milkshakes, probably making them disappear right off the counter and confusing the shit out of some poor fast-food worker.

"I'm glad you had a good time. Thank you for this," she said, holding up the sock.

The young demon grinned and walked away, looking curiously at the line of mortal souls as they went.

Lily ran her fingers over the knitted fabric of the sock. The elastic was starting to loosen just a bit around the ankle. There were thin spots on the heel and the ball of the foot. This had probably been one of her brother's favorite socks. He always wore them until they were trashed, even when he complained constantly about how they didn't stay on his foot right anymore, or had holes in the toes . . .

Fuck, she wanted to cry. She wanted to break down and let it all wash over her in a tide, sweeping her away. Bel's absence was like a hole punched through her chest. She knew she'd see her brothers again, one way or another, but Bel . . . She'd seen the increasing number of wounded demons that had been brought back to Hell, and seen the mourning processions for those who hadn't made it back alive. The glittery, too-large bracelets weighed a thousand pounds on her wrist.

"Lily?" Crocell's voice was soft with worry, his hand warm on her arm. She hadn't even seen him approach the desk.

"It's all good, C. But I need to take the rest of the day off."

His eyes were knowing. "Do whatever you need to do. We've got your back."

A short time later, Lily knocked on the door of the house whose address she'd been sent. A female demon opened it wide, ushering her into a house full of voices. Children could be heard upstairs playing some kind of game and laughing.

"Thank you for having me," Lily said to the woman, Berte, whose husband was a colonel in Bel's Seventeenth Legion. One of the aerial legions, if she remembered right.

"Of course," Berte said. "You are more than welcome. It's a pleasure and an honor to get to meet you."

The large, open-concept house was filled with demons. They sat on couches and chairs; a few sat on the rug in a circle, their chubby babies—most of whom had tiny, delicate, gossamer wings—playing and having tummy time in the center. Everyone looked up, their greetings merging into a collective swell of sound. Their obvious welcome wasn't what lifted Lily's spirits though, it was the understanding in their eyes.

A female demon with shimmering charcoal-gray skin and wings rose from her chair and set her glass down. "Oh, darling, I see those eyes. We've all been there. We need a margarita, stat!" she called.

"On it!" a male voice responded from the kitchen.

"Actually . . ." Lily started, voice trailing off as her throat grew tight. Everyone zeroed in on it, and embarrassment burned over her face.

The gray-skinned woman looked concerned. "I'm so sorry, I should have asked if you drink! We have nonalcoholic options too."

"No, a drink sounds great, especially an alcoholic one . . ." Lily forced a rough laugh. Fuck it. Just . . . fuck it. "It's just that tequila makes me horny, and normally that's fine, but right now, it just makes me miss him even more because he's not here to help with that." Her voice and vision were suspiciously watery by the end.

The collective knowing hum that followed had her laughing through her tears.

"The bastards."

"Fucking hate it when that happens."

"I'm the same way with rum," the gray-skinned woman assured her warmly. "I had a bunch of daiquiris on their last long deployment, and I burned out my vibe. The good one. Didn't take the edge off, but it's a good story now, yeah?" She guided Lily to one of the chairs, yelling to the kitchen, "Forget the marg. This calls for a wine slushy."

"Thank you." Lily chuckled, wiping her eyes with one of the ultra-soft tissues someone handed her.

Then a large wine slushy was pressed into her hand, along with a decadently fudgy cupcake, and everything seemed a little bit more possible.

She'd be okay, she realized as the partners started chatting with her and each other, some with their own watery eyes. There was strength found in the simple and complicated act of understanding. First, she'd found it with Bel, in their honest conversations and their willingness to learn, understand, and accept each other, even the rough or ugly parts. Then, with other beings and souls of the Afterlife—Lucifer, Persephone, Siedah, Aphrodite, the gate demons, a dozen other deities and beings.

Sometimes the strength found in understanding was in acceptance, of and for herself, of and for others. Sometimes it was of a more brutal, combative nature, such as the way she wielded her understanding of souls to guide them to justice or accountability, or the way that Bel used his understanding of his enemies and soldiers to strengthen his tactics for battle.

Strength through understanding.

That would make a good motto for Bel. Lily sipped her wine slushy.

She'd tell him about it when he got home.

When.

Bel

Since the initial attack, it had been damn near nonstop action in one way or another for more than six weeks. Thanks to the sheer number of soldiers and legions at their disposal, they could keep themselves from complete physical fatigue, but the mental and emotional toll was steep.

The enemy Universe was throwing everything at them. Wave after wave of their brutal, vicious soldiers, gegony, and other monsters crashed against their lines with savage force. The death toll mounted high, too high.

And still they held.

And would hold. For as long as they needed to.

46

HAPPY TEARS

Lily

*B*el pushed her sleep shirt—*his shirt*—up her body, kissing his way up her back, tracing the lines of her spine tattoo with his tongue as she lay on her front, still mostly asleep. The satiny heat of his skin brushed over her body, his solid, reassuring weight an anchor for her mind and soul.

"Lily," he rasped into her neck, nipping at her earlobe. He smelled like he usually did after a long day on the training fields, his warm, musky scent edged with the tang of salt and sweat.

She arched into him as he caged her in from above. "Mmm." She twisted to steal a kiss from those wicked lips. "Morning."

"A good morning," he breathed, kissing her and grinding his solid erection against her ass.

She reached back to guide him into her and felt . . . nothing. His solid weight on the bed started to lift, as if he were floating away. Panic set in.

Lily twisted and reached for him, but paused when she saw his anguished, hollow-cheeked face, deep shadows of exhaustion smudged beneath eyes that glimmered with pain and regret. "Bel."

His massive body began disappearing bit by bit into tendrils of smoke. He reached for her, his fingers wispy and insubstantial. Lily knelt on the bed and ran her fingers over the more solid parts of his fading body to trace along his brow bone and over his lips.

"Come home to me," she told him. "Come home."

Lily woke up on her stomach, arm reaching toward what had become Bel's side of the bed, the sensation of his lips ghosting up her back and the empathy for his dream-self's duress weighing heavily on her.

More than two months—almost two and a half—had gone by. While the weight of his absence and the danger that he and all the others were in was just as heavy, her ability to deal with it had increased, making the burden more manageable. It was a bit like grief that way, she supposed. Or just life.

She pushed herself out of bed, not hearing any noises from the kitchen yet. Sharkie had found a podcast created by marine biologists who gleefully shared the absolute wealth of information about the ocean that they had access to in the Afterlife, and she listened to it every day, but especially in the mornings.

Lily tugged up her purple dinosaur shorts and some fuzzy socks, padding into the kitchen to stare into the pantry, waiting for inspiration to strike.

She was mindlessly staring at the flour, fiddling with her bracelets while Max smashed his face against her leg for attention, when Sharkie's door opened and her footsteps came down the hallway.

"Morning," Lily called.

"Morning, Mom. Can we have those scones with cinnamon sugar on top today?"

"Sure, that sounds . . ." Lily paused in the middle of reaching for the flour. Sharkie's words, said entirely too casually, sank into her brain. A strange floaty sensation took over her body. *Maybe it was a mistake.* She turned, staring at Sharkie, confusion warring with hope and a little bit of fear.

Sharkie stood half hidden behind the doorjamb, making her look too much like the child she'd been when she first arrived. She was clearly making a valiant effort to be casual, but her wide blue eyes were nervous. Apparently, Lily's direct eye contact was too much for her.

"Can I call you 'Mom'? I really want to call you Mom, because, like, you basically are, even though you didn't grow me, but you're helping make me into who I am, and that's a really mom thing to do, and also you're there for me and you love me and I love you and stuff. And I wanna call Luci 'Papa' and Bel 'Dad' too, but I wanted to ask you first because it was you and me first and that felt important," Sharkie blurted, barely pausing for breath.

Silence filled the kitchen. Well, silent except for Max, his purr was unending.

Lily smiled, tears leaping to her eyes with surprising swiftness. "I would love that. I would be honored." Her voice was more than a little choked, but she didn't care.

Sharkie's eyes lit up. "Really? These are happy tears, right?"

"Definitely happy tears. Come here." Lily laughed, wiping her cheek on her shoulder and holding her arms out for her girl.

Sharkie hugged her fiercely, burying her face in Lily's sternum, narrow shoulders trembling as she sniffed wetly. Lily held her tight, letting the tears flow freely down her face. Sharkie had changed so much—from the terrified little girl she'd first seen, to the confident, chaotic little badass she was growing into. Lily couldn't wait to see who she would become.

"Love you, Mom." Sharkie's voice was muffled.

Lily squeezed her tighter, dropping a kiss into Sharkie's shaggy blond hair. "Love you too, Sharkie. I'm so proud of you. And thank you."

Bel

Almost eleven weeks, and there'd been no let up from the seemingly endless enemy army. Even with rotations, exhaustion was beginning to set in, and Bel's body felt . . . brittle.

A broken arm, shredded wing, broken ribs, and a pike through his shoulder had all been fixed by the ever-busy healers, but anything less than a dire wound had been left to their own healing out of sheer necessity. Healers were already draining themselves dangerously low just to keep up with the critical patients.

Bel *knew*, could feel that the big one was coming, the attack that would either end the war or end them. He knew it as surely as he'd known that this last great campaign would begin.

He ducked his head into Asmodeus's tent. His wings had been shattered and his arm savaged by a gegony the day before. The healers had kept him out ever since. Bel listened to his cousin's even breaths, trying to do the math in his head. Sariah was due to give birth soon. A week to go, maybe? A tired smile pulled at his lips as he stepped inside the tent and tugged Asmodeus's blanket up, tucking it more securely around him. If Asmodeus were awake, he could tell him the due date without even having to think about it. He probably had the hour and minutes.

Bel stepped back out of the tent and headed to the mustering area. It was their turn on the front lines. His armor and weapons had always felt like an extension of him, but now he wondered if he actually had a body under there, or if he was just a war machine. The only things that kept him from believing that was all he was were memories of Lily.

Lily and Sharkie. His little family.

He grimaced, running his hand over his tangled hair. He'd kept Lily's braids in his hair for as long as possible, partially unbraiding and rebraiding to prolong them, but he'd had to take them out a week before. Ever since, he'd had the foulest fucking luck—

A deep, earth-shaking rumble shuddered through the air a moment before the horns blared with an urgency he'd never heard before. A horrifying, soul-quaking chorus of distant gegony screams—more than he'd ever heard at once—sent ice down his spine as he raced into action.

It was time.

47

LITTLE ONE

Lily

"You look weird. Did the holiday sauce turn out bad?" Sharkie asked over breakfast.

"Hollandaise sauce," Lily corrected absently, frowning as she tried to pinpoint the source of the *off* feeling she'd woken up too early with. "And no, the sauce turned out perfect, good job."

"Thanks, Mom. So, why do you have that funny look on your face?"

Fuzzy warmth suffused Lily at her new title. It had only been a few days since the first time, but she didn't think she'd ever tire of hearing it.

"I just feel . . . weird."

"Like bad weird or excited weird?" Sharkie's question was muffled by a mouthful of eggs Benedict.

"Just weird-weird. I dunno. How are the eggs?"

"Good this time."

Lily winced. She was pretty sure she'd used half the eggs in their realm of Paradise as practice, but she'd finally figured out how to properly poach a fucking egg.

Small victories. She chose to treasure each one.

They finished breakfast, Carlton whisking away the dishes before Lily could even reach to clear them. Having abandoned that particular battle with the house, she threw a quick "Thanks, dude" in the direction of the ceiling and patted the nearest cupboard, then stretched to loosen up her unusually tight shoulders.

"You want fancy cocoa today?" Lily asked as Sharkie set up her laptop.

"Actually, can I try the salted caramel latte?"

Lily quit stretching. Sharkie's eyes were bright and expectant.

"Please? Eleven-ish is totally grown-up enough for a latte. Or at least to try one."

It was true. Once she'd started growing, Sharkie'd seemed to make up for lost time, shooting up faster than a mortal kid would have. Lily's research in the Universal Library had confirmed that her physical growth had more to do with her mental and emotional growth than anything and had no set timeline. Sharkie's preference of attending school in Hell most of the time accommodated this, as she got to move around to different classrooms based on her learning needs, like all the other students. Today was a weekend and she'd been planning a daylong movie marathon and gaming session.

Sharkie's grin went impish. "It's not like it'll kill me."

Lily laughed. "Fair point. Alright, one *small* salted caramel latte coming your way. Anything else?"

"Nah, I'm good. Thanks, Mom!"

Lily blew her a kiss—which Sharkie pretended to be knocked sideways by—and headed for the door. The sword and belt Bel had given her hung on the weapons rack that had appeared when Bel had basically moved in. She brushed her fingers over the hilt of his "casual sword" before lifting hers off the pegs. She buckled it around her waist slowly, taking in the way the light seemed especially golden as it dappled through the windows, gilding the entryway in a way that was newly striking, and slanting one perfect beam on the myriad pictures that adorned the walls.

The picture of her and her brothers no longer sent bolts of pain through her chest every time she saw it, just the fond ache of love that had nowhere to go. The idea of seeing them on MortalTube was still too painful, but she saw the picture for what it was: an impossible gift memorializing a precious memory. One that no longer hung alone, surrounded now by more than a dozen pictures of various sizes.

A shot of her, Sharkie, and Max from behind, silhouetted in the open doorway the day they'd played in the rain, Sharkie's head on her shoulder, the pair of them wrapped in blankets, with soaking wet hair and steaming mugs, watching the rain pour down.

Lily and Bel tangled together on the couch the morning of their first kiss, before it had happened, still asleep and utterly peaceful.

The three of them, plus Max, in the library the day Bel had needed their fussing, the whole scene looking like a cozy renaissance painting.

A picture of her parents smiling on a sunny beach. She'd cried the day it had appeared. Their relationships had been complicated, but she still missed them.

Max on his back in the living room, basking in a particularly good sunbeam, legs completely stretched out to get the most out of the sun's heat.

Lily and Sharkie sitting in front of the TV playing *Mario Kart*, Lily with her head in her hands after getting blue-shelled at the last minute, while Sharkie leapt into the air with manic glee.

Lily, Bel, and Sharkie on the couch in their pajamas, all with different face masks on, watching a movie.

Bel in the new gym, shirtless and deliciously sweaty, holding a weight in one hand while he took a picture with his phone of Lily on the treadmill, who was not-so-subtly taking pictures of him.

She finished buckling on the belt and smiled at the collection of memories, marveling at how far she'd come in the Afterlife. A growing part of her wondered how far she could go.

Mulling that over, she reached for the door and paused, her sense of unease swelling up like a tide.

"Sharkie?" she called, heading back into the kitchen.

"Yeah?" Sharkie said, looking up in confusion as Lily stuck her head into the kitchen.

"I know you're already planning on staying home today, but seriously, don't leave Paradise at all until I get back. Okay?"

"Why? Is it your weird thing?"

"Yeah, I don't know what it is, but I just need you to promise to stay in Paradise. I can't explain why, but I wouldn't ask if it wasn't important, bug." Lily let a thread of steel into her tone. "Can you please promise me that you'll stay here?"

Sharkie's eyes rounded. "I promise," she said quietly, then again with more conviction. "I promise."

"Atta girl. Thank you." Lily winked, even though the light gesture required more effort than usual. "Be back soon."

Bel

Bel heaved in as much air as he could, half staggering from the command tent as every fiber of muscle screamed at him. The attack had flooded them. Thousands had died. Not just from the demonic forces, but from the collective mass of their Universal army, something he was grimly thankful for, though thankful seemed like the wrong word.

He had to make the best of the worst situation, he supposed.

In the days since the first wave of gegony and enemy soldiers crashed into them, he'd slept perhaps a total of ten hours. Broken, patchy, restless sleep, quick naps when he made it back to camp to give his reports, collaborate on tactics and strategies, and take a few minutes of a break from swinging his sword or axe.

He and his soldiers were tired, but they were holding. And it was time to go hold some more.

He left his sword in its sheath for the moment, hoping his hand might relax a bit from the claw it had frozen into after too many hours of gripping a weapon. As he walked back to the legion he'd be fighting with, he took stock of his body, cataloging aches and pains, factoring them into how he would need to adjust and compensate his fighting style to remain as deadly as possible and not make a stupid mistake. He did a double take at the familiar figure that caught the corner of his eye.

"What the *fuck* are you doing here? You should be in bed!" he snarled at Asmodeus as he limped toward him, wings wrapped tightly against his back with bloody bandages.

"I should be dead," Asmodeus rasped. The swelling around his eyes had gone down enough for his glare to be potent. "But I'm not. So, from one general to another, fuck you. Let's save the fighting for the real enemy."

Asmodeus was, unfortunately, every bit as stubborn as him, so Bel bit his tongue and let it go, knowing he would have done the same thing. Had done the same thing. On multiple occasions.

Bel briefed him as they walked, and Asmodeus split off to find his own soldiers, bumping his shoulder against Bel's before he left. Bel watched his cousin walk away, shredded wings half healed and wrapped up like mummies, every movement visibly taking more effort. But Asmodeus's head was high, and his mind was sharp.

Universe protect you, Azzy. And if that's not enough firepower to do the job, I'll ask your wife.

A different fierce woman flashed into his mind, the image so clear and vivid that for a moment he wondered if it was a hallucination.

Lily.

She could probably march her way across the battlefield and level one of her *looks* at the enemy. And if that wasn't enough, she'd give them a lashing with her gloriously sharp tongue and have them whimpering within minutes. Then she'd grab him by the front of his pants and tow him home, where she would dunk him in a bath, feed him, and tuck him into bed before marching up to the Universe itself and giving it a piece of her mind.

Fuck, he missed her, but he swallowed it down, pushing it aside with every step toward the curse of battle.

His world devolved into a nightmare of spraying blood and spit and venom and mud. His movements were automatic as he parried a strike and struck a blow of his own, then spun and drove his blade through the neck of a creature as tall as he was and bristling with needlelike spikes. Its overlarge mouth gurgled helplessly, hands with too many joints scrabbling at its throat. Bel didn't pause for even a second, ripping his blade free to twist and engage a new opponent.

Strike. Stab. Dodge. Parry.

Blood, not his own, was a bitter tang over his tongue. Something tried to take a chunk out of his leg. He bashed its skull in with the edge of his shield.

He couldn't feel individual rivulets of sweat any more. It soaked the padded clothing under his armor. His boots squelched, almost ankle-deep in gore and mud. There was no respite from any of it anywhere. Camp was a distant memory.

A pack of small, doglike creatures leapt on the soldier next to him. Her scream as she went down turned into a wet rasp as one of them ripped out her throat, tendons and ligaments stretching and snapping amongst spurts of vivid blood.

With a roar, Bel cleared the pack away with his blade, one of his strikes sending a creature shrieking through the air, where it landed on the pike of a distant soldier. The female demon's pink eyes were wide and pan-icked beneath her helmet, gloved hand fluttering over the gaping hole where her throat had been, lips covered in her own blood, silently form-ing one word over and over.

Please.

Bel locked eyes with her for only a second, but that second stretched into eternity.

Please.

He raised his sword over her. Mercy seldom seemed merciful on the battlefield.

The female demon's hand left her throat to point behind him. He swung blindly—judging the rush of air, the angle of her finger, the pounding thud of approaching footsteps—and scored a deep slash down the side of a rampaging gegony. It wailed, sounding entirely too much like his baby sister, and flinched, spinning toward its injured side as if it couldn't understand what had happened. Taking advantage of the dis-traction, Bel half chopped through the back of its stubby neck, and the thing collapsed into a twitching pile.

There was a momentary lull, and he spun back to the female demon—

one of his soldiers—who lay motionless, pink eyes dull and fixed, staring into an eternity that only she could see. Her hand, the one she'd pointed to save him, lay limply in the mud.

Bel crouched. Her fallen sword made a sucking sound as he pulled it out of the mud and laid it on her chest, then he lifted the hand that had saved him and rested it over the hilt.

He dipped his head and stood, a distant roaring heralding the coming end of the momentary lull. Something tickled at the back of his mind as he stared at the dead gegony. Something odd.

Several other soldiers frowned at it as well, looking up as he approached and making room for him.

"Sir, am I crazy or is that one . . . small?"

Bel studied the thing grimly. It *was* small. It didn't stand nearly as tall as the other gegony he'd seen. Its skin was paler, less knobby, and it had only a couple rows of teeth instead of several.

Then he realized. "It's young."

Every soldier who'd heard him cranked their head around to stare.

"That means they must be running out of the full-sized ones," someone said.

Something on the hindquarters drew his attention—dark, streaked marks that looked almost . . . charred. Like it had been intentionally burned.

Tortured? Why the fuck would the other Universe, or whoever was in charge of their forces, torture the young of their own creatures?

The answer came to him in a shrieking roar that had a layer he'd never heard to it. Grief and desperation and *rage*.

What fought with a fierceness unmatched by any force in any known Universe?

Parents protecting their children.

Bel bellowed orders, reforming the line and turning just in time to see the unbroken line of fully adult gegony charging toward them, wailing for all of their murdered offspring.

Overrun. They would be overrun—

The world devolved into a new nightmare, this time with bodies and body parts flung through the air like confetti as the gegony tore into them. Lungs screamed for oxygen. Muscles reacted and moved without conscious thought. Boots slipped in mud. Lines of pain opened up all over his body.

One gegony was killed. Then another. Bel was nearly knocked to the ground by the upper half of a soldier after a gegony had flung it aside. He regained his footing, spinning to face the source of the corpse.

A gegony nosed at the body of the little one, a high-pitched keening noise filling the air when the little one didn't respond. The parent threw its head back, vertical maw splitting wide as it screamed its loss.

A volley of arrows arched over Bel's shoulder, burying themselves in the exposed throat and chest, the scream shifting into a pained roar as the thing spun. Bel saw what was going to happen, and despite the fact that he was dripping sweat, he went ice cold.

It happened in slow motion. The gegony lunged directly at them, directly at *him*. The vertically slit jaws were wide open, something that the typical battle-hardened gegony never did, as it revealed one of their greatest weaknesses. Rows and rows of hooked, razor-sharp teeth set into a bloody mouth came right at him. He knew the press of soldiers behind him, beside him, their swords and spears all aimed for that same vulnerable target.

Bel rammed his sword down its throat just before the powerful jaws clamped around his entire body, one last blinding burst of pain and regret and love for his little family. His Lily.

Then everything was gone.

48

WHATEVERTHEFUCK

Lily

Lily stalked through the Universal Hall, noting the expressions of those around her. Most—no, not most, *all*—of the Afterlife denizens looked troubled, like they sensed the same nebulous, unknown bad thing that she did. Only some of the souls looked the same. Odd.

The Hall wasn't busy either, though it hadn't been as busy for a while. Given the baseline of wariness that had become common, most people preferred to stay within the relative safety of their realms.

And here I am, going for coffee.

Common Grounds came into sight, the usual line out the door nowhere to be seen, though people still went inside.

A sudden flood of sticky foulness crawled down her spine, stopping her dead in her tracks.

"What the *fuck*," she murmured, allowing instinct to take over, turning to scan the Hallway. A few others looked similarly disturbed. Maybe it was some kind of magic—

A wailing roar, like a chorus of terrified babies in pain, layered with something *wet*, like shredding meat but with volume behind it, echoed down the Hall, freezing everyone in place.

Bad. Wrong. Not supposed to be here. Wrong wrong wrong wrong—

Trust me, you'll know when something doesn't belong in this Universe. Bel's warning came rushing back to her.

"CLEAR THE HALL!" Lily bellowed at the same time as several other denizens.

Everyone burst into motion, a few screams and panicked calls adding to the chaotic thunder of feet and the horrible roaring that, Lily realized with horror as she launched into a sprint, was getting closer. People poured out of Common Grounds at the same time people started to run into it, only to be shoved back by the fleeing baristas.

"We're a fucking coffee shop, not a protected realm. Get the fuck out and run!" one barista yelled, shoving a panicking man back into the throng before hauling ass toward the nearest arch.

Going back to Paradise was not an option, the *whateverthefuck it was* would be coming from that direction. Hell. She could try to get to Hell. If she couldn't, she'd dive into one of the other realms. They would be better than nothing. Plus, she realized as she ran, souls were still trying to hide in stores and shops and restaurants.

"GET TO A REALM, NOT A STORE!" Lily yelled over and over, thankful she didn't need to breathe anymore as she urged her feet faster and faster.

People bumped into her from all sides, trying to get to safety. One woman was running the opposite direction, toward the thing, and Lily grabbed her arm, skidding them both to a stop.

"It's coming from there," Lily snapped, dragging the woman along by her arm.

"But my Paradise is back there!"

"Your Paradise is safe—"

"*I* want to be safe!" the woman wailed, beating Lily with her fist.

Fuck you too. Lily swallowed down the rage and fear, trying to tamp them down into something useful. "Get into a realm, then!"

"I'm an atheist—"

"You're a fucking idiot! *Your atheism doesn't matter right now.* If you want to be safe, find a realm and get into it, or you will experience pain you can't imagine. Now MOVE!" Lily threw her toward an arch—she didn't know which one, she just saw its occupants waving fleeing people inside—then kept running.

The Hallway was emptying fast. A few, like her, were running to help others, or trying to get to a distant haven.

Behind her, people started screaming in terror—not, thankfully, in pain. The wet, high-pitched roar was joined by something else that sounded almost hyena-like but bone-chillingly *wrong*.

Prey. She was prey, a deer fleeing from a predator she couldn't hope to outrun or outfight.

Whatever it was, it was too fucking close. The Hallway was mostly empty, the arches to the realms packed with people huddling together and trying to move back.

Lily rounded a corner as more screaming started, and she heard the first pounding footsteps of something large echoing up the Hallway.

Cold dread sat in her stomach like a stone. She wasn't going to make it.

A woman much shorter than her was hauling ass ahead, looking over her shoulder like an idiot in a horror movie. It slowed her down.

Lily caught up to her and grabbed her arm, guiding her toward the nearest archway, where people yelled encouragement and held out their hands.

Heavy, fast footsteps and more screeching—

Throat tight, veins buzzing, Lily shoved the woman forward, diving through the arch herself and skidding to a halt, half crashing into the wall of people just inside the gate.

Lily spun, pressing her back against them, hand automatically going to the sword at her waist.

Too close, she was too close to the arch, to the line where the gleaming floor beneath her feet met with the humble flooring of the Hallway.

The thing lunged around the corner and stopped, raising its wedge-shaped head to sniff at the air.

Nausea swam, every fiber, every shred of her rebelling at being in the presence of it. The thing ran on all fours, long limbs out of proportion with its comparatively stocky body. Its paws resembled long, slender hands with seven digits and too many joints. The claws flexing on the stone floor were long and curved, at least half as long as Lily's forearm.

The thing had to be eight feet tall at the shoulder, its head set almost directly into the bulky shoulders, with no mouth that she could see. Eyes the size of dinner plates were a pulsing shade that Lily had never seen before—the closest approximation she could give was a sick, toxic green. It reared back onto its hind legs, almost like a bear, and let loose another awful, shredding, baby's-wail roar that had Lily drawing her sword for comfort, if nothing else.

There was the mouth. Instead of lying horizontally, like every other fucking mouth Lily had ever seen, it split the creature's skull from forehead to throat vertically, opening its face like a book. If that book was lined with rows of teeth similar to sharks'.

Sharkie.

Fear like Lily had never known locked her body in place.

Sharkie promised. She promised. Paradise is safe, the safest place . . .

A distant horn split the air.

The horns of Hell had never sounded so damned lovely.

The thing launched itself forward and disappeared, presumably to do battle. Lily and everyone else breathed a collective sigh of relief.

Then she saw milky pale fingers curl around the edge of the arch. Three of them, overlong and multi-jointed, the flesh mottled toward the tips with sick gray, the glossy black claws set in nail beds that seemed red and inflamed. The fingers rested there for a moment, just long enough for a few others to notice them—

The other creature jolted into view, its round, lipless mouth overfull of jagged, black anglerfish teeth chattering with its awful not-hyena laughter.

The other thing had been terrifying. This? This was human nightmares made manifest.

Its limbs were wiry, at odds with its stumpy torso, pale white and gray flesh hanging off its bones. The head, though . . . The head and the face Lily would never stop seeing. When she someday went to the Void, she would see it still. The oval head was smooth, with two small holes that seemed to function as nostrils set high in its flat face. The huge eyes had no discernible difference between sclera, iris, and pupil—matte, and such a mottled, soulless black that it was like looking into a grave. They were rimmed with the same irritated redness as its claws, as was its twisted nightmare of a mouth, like its body was rebelling against its own existence.

Lily didn't even have time to flinch when it lunged for her, crashing face-first into whatever invisible barrier stretched across the archway.

The people behind her moved away, all of them pressing farther back into whatever realm they were in, leaving Lily standing alone in front of the arch, face-to-face with another Universe's evil. The instinctual revulsion and horror remained, but . . . safe. She was safe.

But the longer she stared at it, watching it test the barrier, gnashing those awful teeth when it couldn't get her, the angrier she got.

My Universe. My home. Our Afterlife. How many of my friends and my people did it kill to get here? This thing could have hurt Bel, my Bel. It would happily hurt Sharkie, my child.

The thing laughed, chattering its awful teeth in Lily's face, slamming its claws against the barrier before pressing its face against it and smearing its long black tongue across the shimmering wall of power. Laughing, laughing, laughing—

Lily cut its head off with one swing.

Her time working at the Hellp Desk had prepared her for the jarring sensation of a weapon making contact with a body. The crunch of bone snapping, the spray of blood, the slight drag of a blade as the friction of cutting through flesh slowed its path. Her time training with Bel and the demons had prepared her to have good form and strike true.

The head toppled to the floor, jaw still twitching, still chattering its teeth for a few seconds until whatever brain activity it had ceased. The body slumped in the other direction, spilling green-black blood all over the floor. It sizzled and burned away as it pooled against the invisible barrier of the arch.

Get fucked.

Lily stared at the line of sizzling blood, working the variables, trying to understand how they had gotten through.

Either it was a fluke of a particularly intense battle, in which their defenses had failed enough to allow not just one, but two, creatures into the Universal Hallway, or they'd lost completely. But if that was the case, there would have been more of them, right?

Someone came to stand next to her. The hum of power prickling over her skin told her without looking that it was a deity.

She kept watching the blood sizzle as it ran along the invisible barrier, smoking as it connected with the pristine mother-of-pearl surface—

Every thought, every feeling, eddied out of Lily's head.

She followed the line of the arch upward, took in every gleaming, heinously perfect inch, then looked at the deity at her side.

He dipped his head in acknowledgment, a small smile gracing his lips. "Your reputation is well deserved, Ms. Lily."

Lily stared resolutely at him. Small, she felt so small and wrong here. She didn't belong. Would never belong. A stain on the fabric of the existence of this place. A stain of a soul. She hated it. Hated this.

Her tone was flat, but her voice seemed very far away, as if it knew it had no business being anywhere near here.

"God."

--❦--

49

MAXED OUT
ON WEIRD

Lily

Made in God's image, my ass.

Lily was used to the paradoxical, dreamlike quality of certain things in the Afterlife, but every so often, something still struck her as especially odd.

Despite apparently being made almost entirely out of light, God was obviously human-shaped and incredibly tall, almost Bel's height. He had a face—eyes, nose, mouth—but the shape and color and other qualities of them were hard to discern through the steady white light emanating from his skin. Lily sensed more than saw his smile and gaze.

Not for mere mortals to see.

She scowled and stared harder. It was like looking directly into a light bulb, but features jumped out at her. His face had a shifting quality; one moment his nose was aquiline, then a few seconds later it was a pert button, then perfectly straight, the same with his jawline, cheekbones, and eyes.

God had all the markers to be unsettling as shit. The effect would have been much more potent if she'd encountered him before beheading the creepy whateverthefuck that still twitched on the floor. As it was, she'd maxed out on her ability to process weird, so if God was hoping to get some kind of reaction, he was shit out of luck.

Almost two decades of her life she'd spent living in fear and conditioned awe of this being. Trying to please him. Begging him for protection. For support. For love. Seeking those things in the community formed in his name and finding out exactly how conditional that protection, support, and love was. It was a lesson she'd carried the emotional scars of into death.

In many ways, God, as she'd been taught about him, reminded her of the worst parts of her father. There, but not *there for her*. Her father had watched TV in the living room, and God had watched TV in Heaven, both loving her but not being particularly loving in the way that mattered. Except God had never read her a bedtime story or checked her closet for monsters to soften that fact.

"All-knowing, all-powerful, and all-good," Lily said in a measured, neutral tone, gripping the hilt of her sword like a lifeline in a storm. "Which one or *ones* are a lie?"

God blinked.

Lily didn't.

"If you are all-knowing without being all-powerful, then watching the humans suffer and knowing that you can't change it is a nightmare of its own. If you are all-powerful but not all-knowing, then it's less your fault, but honestly, I've been in the Afterlife long enough to know that even a cursory glance through MortalTube will show you what's going on in the mortal world, so that excuse isn't valid."

She inhaled sharply. "And if you are both of those things, but not all-good, and you abandoned those who love you—the innocents who suffer in your name—then you are every bit the fucking monster I, and too many others, came to realize you might be."

The leather wrapping the sword hilt creaked in her grip, loud in the silence.

"So, God. Which. One. Is. It."

"I'm sorry." His words were soft.

"Answer me!" Lily snarled, temper fraying dangerously, eyes stinging. "I'll bet you're sorry, but that's not what I asked you. I was *lucky*. I didn't suffer nearly as much as some people did, not at all as much as

my daughter did, but *I still suffered*. It might not have been directly at your hand, but it was absolutely at the hands of people who claim to follow you, who have caused untold harm in *your* fucking name, and you weren't there."

The surge of fury burned away in a flash, leaving her with a lifetime of hurt and shame. "We were alone when we needed you. *I* was alone when I needed you. Where were you? And don't"—she held up her free hand, not bothering to hide how much it shook—"say you were there in the 'still small voice,' or that I didn't *listen* hard enough to hear you, because that's horseshit. You're a fucking deity, and I was a child who was crying too hard to hear much of anything. So, because the answer to this question will help me determine how to process all this, I want to know: Which of those three traits is a lie?"

The silence following her outburst was so complete, Lily felt its presence like another person as she and God stared at each other. Little sounds began to filter in. The sizzle of blood against the invisible barrier. The faint echo of confused, scared voices all along the Hallway. The whisper of her loose hair sliding over her shoulder. A distant clang of something metal, and an eerie, gurgling snarl.

"None of us are truly all-powerful, though we have incredible and inexcusable power," God said quietly, his voice layers of tones and pitches, as if multiple people spoke in unison. "And kindness, or goodness, is a choice that is easy for us to make. I am aware of all relevant information in the mortal world and in mortal lives, like an expanded version of MortalTube, though I do not use that ability to, as some mortals call it, snoop, without cause. Like all deities, my ability to influence the mortal world is limited. More limited than religions would have you believe."

The sorrow on his face, in every line of his glowing body, made her chest ache. She ignored it.

He continued. "We were supposed to help and inspire, but now? Now too many are subject to fear and shame and pain that never should have been theirs."

"And you can't do *anything* to change that?" Lily asked, skepticism dripping from every syllable.

"You remind me of my son."

"I'm sure he'll be flattered."

God's smile was weary. "He will. As I said, your reputation is well-known and well-deserved. While I can't make the spectacular change that you and I both wish I could, please know that I am doing all that I can to make amends."

"Explain."

"I work closely with Hell on the reeducation of those souls who claimed to live in my ideals, but either twisted them, or blindly followed twisted teachings. They are educated on what faith should be, and taught to think critically, especially about the teachings of church leaders. The hope is that, if enough of those souls reincarnate, the lessons they learned will echo through the mortal world and inspire change." He paused. "I recognize that the churches, especially the ones formed in my name but not my ideals, have turned into something that no longer truly helps humanity, but causes harm and provides a refuge for the harmful. And for that—"

God did something that at first made no sense, but then shocked her down to her toes.

He lowered his head, bent at the waist, and bowed to her.

"I am sorry. I am sorry that I was not there when you or others needed me. I am sorry for the harm and pain caused to you and your daughter by the followers of my name. And I am sorry for not being able to rectify the mistakes made in my name so that they will never harm another."

God, who'd ended up looking like a human-shaped light bulb, was bowing to Lily, sincerely apologizing for his shitty followers, while a monster from another universe that she'd decapitated in a fit of motherly and territorial rage lay dead only a few feet away.

"This is not how I expected this day to go," she heard herself mutter, unable to look away from the bowing deity, who smiled up at her with understanding.

"I offer only an apology, Lily, I do not seek forgiveness. My apology is not conditional."

That's a first. Lily bit her tongue to keep from saying it out loud. She wasn't sure what she'd expected, but it sure as shit hadn't been an apology.

It didn't make her or Sharkie's pain and experiences any less valid, but . . . she almost pitied God.

It was hard enough for her to see things on MortalTube in passing and not be able to do anything. But to constantly see more? To be charged with the care of mortals and have a limited capacity to do so? More than that, to watch pain and atrocities be committed in his name? Agony.

Lucifer flashed through her mind and clarity struck like a lightning bolt. He and God were two sides of the same coin. Though they had been cast in very different roles in the mortal world, both had been warped to fit a narrative, used as the carrot-and-stick of morality. Both had had their character and name used as a method of control.

She'd been wrong about Lucifer and Hell. And, though it was even more uncomfortable to admit, it seemed she'd been wrong about God and Heaven too.

"I accept your apology," Lily said, offering him her hand.

He took it, sending a scorching fizz through her body, and straightened.

"I can't . . . genuinely forgive you just yet"—*maybe not for a good long while*—"but I accept your apology."

The vestiges of her decades-long anger were still too searing for her to offer forgiveness, but she could recognize that God had never meant or desired for any of her suffering to happen.

"That is more than enough," God said quietly, releasing her hand.

Lily shook the impulse to scrub her hand on her leggings, instead wiping the blood off her sword with a sleeve. She still hated the conditioned feeling of smallness and impurity and whatever other icky garbage bullshit feelings the pearlescent arch and gleaming golden floor inspired in her. But the fear was gone, and there was a sense of grudging acceptance that the God she'd been raised to know was not the real God.

No, the real God had bowed and apologized.

Bowed.

She'd be tripping over that fact for a while. Possibly eternity.

Eternity . . . Bel. *Sharkie.*

"I have to go. I need to get back to Sharkie," Lily said, leaning through the arch to glance around, primed to leap back at the first hint of something *wrong*. Other than the thoroughly dead corpse, nothing seemed out of place. The prickle of intuition that something was off had faded, leaving behind the overwhelming drive to get home and make sure Sharkie was alright, then hunt down anyone who might have information about Bel.

"Of course. I can ask one of the angels to escort you, if you'd like?"

The instinctive "*Fuck* no" sat on the tip of her tongue. A lifetime of independence urged her to brush off the offer of help with her typical bluntness, because she certainly didn't need it. The newfound peace and groundedness she'd found in the Afterlife kept her mouth shut while she considered how to respond with a bit more tact than she otherwise might have.

"I appreciate the offer, but no. I'll be fine," Lily said, stepping through the arch and pointedly ignoring the resulting squelch.

"Yes, I believe you will," God said.

Lily looked at him. Really looked.

For a moment, eternity paused. They might as well have been statues frozen in time, the tapestry of the Afterlife a fixed backdrop behind them. A deity and a soul, seeing and understanding each other, recognizing the pain and the promise of all that had and could happen.

The weight of who she had been and who she was becoming seemed to hang in the balance before tipping . . .

"Thank you," she said plainly.

God inclined his head.

Lily adjusted her grip on her sword, the leather beneath her palm solid and comforting, then pushed herself into a jog.

She wove through the few brave souls and denizens who had left the safety of the realms, dodging debris from tables and carts that had been knocked over outside of shops, and goods that people had dropped in the rush to safety.

At the sound of her running footsteps, people either froze or dove for the nearest cover, the ripple of fear passing from person to person like a virus as they frantically looked for what she was running from.

So, even though every scrap of her soul screamed at the delay, Lily dropped into a purposeful walk.

The sounds of people crying echoed out from the various arches, mingling with clipped orders from unseen authority figures and the rumble of the more creature-like denizens of the Afterlife. High above, near the sky-like ceiling, a horde of wisps in various sizes and colors hovered out of harm's way. What was the collective term for the wisps? A covey? A flock? A host? A folly? A poof? Until she found something more accurate, she'd call them a poof. It was ridiculous enough to keep the situation from feeling overwhelming.

Numerous footsteps drew her attention away from the poof of wisps and toward a distant juncture in the Hall. Bel wouldn't be among them—as a general he'd be one of the last to leave—but maybe someone knew something—

She made it all of one step toward them and froze. Fear like she'd never known, not even when facing down the *thing* outside of Heaven, scribed itself onto her soul.

The soldiers were barely recognizable as living beings. They shuffled more than walked, every inch of them covered in filth and Universe knew what else. Some of the ones in better shape dragged the now-familiar carts filled with those too wounded to move under their own power. A shredded wing, recognizable as a wing only because she'd spent so much time studying Bel's, nearly dragged on the floor beside one cart, leaving a trail of blood. The membrane almost completely gone and the supporting bones jutting out through tears in the skin.

She managed a breath that felt like shards of glass and lurched forward, following the line of the ruined wing to the equally battered body it was attached to. *I don't care if he's in pieces, as long as he's alive. I don't care if he's in pieces, as long as he comes back.*

The female demon wept with the eye that wasn't covered by gauze, her other wing a bloody mass of hastily applied bandages.

Not Bel.

None of the walking wounded moved like him, were built like him, had his horns. From what she could see, none of the ones on the carts bore him either, though there was a stump of a tail dripping blood from soaked wrappings that was about the right skin color.

Too purple. It's too purple-purple. Bel is gray-purple, and if he'd lost blood, he'd be more gray. Not purple. Right?

A few of the soldiers glanced at her as they passed, but if any of them recognized her, they didn't show it. Whatever mortals thought Hell was, whatever incomprehensible evil and suffering and struggle they expected, these soldiers had seen it. Lived it.

Mortal Hell was in their eyes.

Lily watched them go, watched denizens from other realms run up to take the weight of the carts, to offer water. A Roman woman sprinted out of an arch with an armful of stola and a knife, then began cutting them into strips as she strode alongside a cart.

Fuck walking. Lily *bolted.*

She skidded around a corner and hurtled toward the massive Paradise arch, breath sawing in her throat. A group of souls milled about behind the safety of the invisible barrier. Standing apart from them, next to a leg of the arch, was a tiny figure with a distinctive shark fin sticking up crookedly from the top of their hood.

Relief hit Lily so hard she half tripped and slowed to a jog. Sharkie made to run to her but stopped, blue eyes wide and worried. Max scurried back and forth along the invisible barrier with an urgency he usually reserved for begging for tuna, his tail puffed up to twice its usual size.

"Mom!" Sharkie launched herself at her just as Lily swooped down to scoop her up.

Sharkie was almost too big to pick up, and their bodies collided almost painfully hard, but Lily didn't care. She held Sharkie tight, swaying to soothe Sharkie's shaking and her own jittery nerves. Max screeched at her feet, front paws braced on her thigh, claws none-too-gently digging through her leggings. Lily hushed him, blindly patting at his fuzzy head and placating him enough to stop yowling. The small crowd of souls murmured to each other, and a few called out questions, but she ignored them. For now.

"What are you doing here?" Lily tried to ask, but the adrenaline of decapitating a monster and confronting God, along with the horror of seeing what might have happened to Bel, *her* Bel, had the question coming out as more of a demand. "I told you to stay inside!"

Sharkie remained plastered to Lily, arms tight around her neck, speaking so fast her words slammed together. "You told me to stay in Paradise, not stay *home*! I was worried about you because of your weird feeling thing and so were Max and Carl, but Carl couldn't come because it's a house, so I thought I'd wait here, but then there was this noise and this scary thing—*two things*! Mom, there were two different things! A bunch of people ran into Paradise, and we all saw the things and they saw us, but they ignored us and kept going toward where *you* were, and then there was *screaming* and—and—"

"Okay, I'm okay, you're okay, we're okay. They're gone, they're dead. It's safe."

"It's safe?" one of the souls called. "Is that what she said?"

Lily leveled a look at the concerned crowd, guessing that the significantly more frazzled people were the ones who had run to safety.

"Both of them are dead, yes, and the weird feeling is gone too, so I'm pretty sure that means it's safe." *For now,* she added mentally.

The expressions were a mix of relief and confusion.

"What weird feeling?" someone asked.

Lily frowned. It confirmed what she'd noticed before—not all souls had been unsettled, but all denizens had been. What it meant, she didn't know. Perhaps it was because she worked at the Hellp Desk? Like an employee-only alert? She'd have to ask someone later.

"Don't worry about it."

"Weird," Sharkie said, frowning.

Word of the day, apparently.

"Well," Lily said to everyone, setting Sharkie down and tucking her under an arm. "As far as I know, it's safe. Paradise is the original stronghold of the Afterlife, so if you're worried about it, don't leave, but if you do leave, just know that you can dive into any realm for safety. It might not be as good as this, but it's better than nothing."

"How do you know?" someone yelled from the back.

"She's the Hell lady, dude. She knows stuff," someone else called back.

Lily pointed at the responder with confidence she didn't feel, but was flattered nonetheless. "That."

"What are we going to do?" Sharkie asked as the crowd broke apart.

"What I want to do is go home, pack up some stuff, and get us both down to Hell. We can stay in Bel's house while we wait for"—*information, something, anything*—"him."

"Bel's coming home?" Sharkie asked.

"I don't know, bug, but maybe. It looked like a lot of soldiers are. But we'll be practically as safe that deep in Hell as we would be here, and we'll be in the best place to stay informed."

"Bel's fine, though, right?"

Sick. She felt fucking sick. She'd been worried about Sharkie, but deep down she'd known that as long as Sharkie had stayed in Paradise, she'd be fine.

She had no such reassurance about Bel.

"I don't know." She managed to say it calmly, honestly, but it ravaged her. Fear could be useful. Fear could be informative. Panic was nothing but a fast track to freezing up, being useless, being reckless, and making mistakes. She might be scared out of her mind, but she refused to fucking panic. She was Lily, of Paradise, of Hell, of whatever she fucking felt like, and she was going to handle this.

Because that's what princesses did. Handled shit.

"Carlton," Lily said into the quiet of the entryway, the thumps and bumps of Sharkie quickly packing in her room the only sound other than the birds singing outside. Max had laid himself directly across her feet and seemed to have no intention of moving. The house didn't groan, but she felt its awareness.

Not all Paradises were so sentient, she'd learned. It depended on the preference of the soul, which was why Carlton had only gotten more . . . communicative when Sharkie arrived. Now she couldn't imagine wanting to have anything other than their quirky, personality-packed home anymore.

"This isn't an indictment of you, buddy; I know you would keep us safe and comfortable and as happy as possible. But if anything happens to Bel—shit, even if something *doesn't* happen to Bel—the first place he is going to go is Hell. And Hell is the best place for us to stay close to the action and in the know, so we're going to leave for a little bit." Her nose stung. Why did her nose always sting right before she got emotional? She rested her hand on the nearest wall. "I'm really going to miss you, miss being here, but I'd just be worried sick about Bel the whole time. We'll come back no matter what, I promise."

Carlton groaned sadly, the pictures rattling on the wall. The closet door swung open, and Bel's "casual sword" floated free as if carried by invisible hands, hovering in front of her until she grabbed it, dipping with the weight. Movement on the wall drew her attention. The paint finish shifting to form matte letters.

Be safe
Stay together
Defend all
Stay happy
Come home
Find peace

The to-do list presentation was a little weird, but she got the message. It was the same sentiment she'd sent Bel off with.

"Will do, buddy. We'll see what kind of shape Bel is in, but we'll do what we can to be happy and at peace again."

A pair of books zoomed out of the library and plopped onto her bag. One was a sci-fi fantasy series she'd been meaning to suggest to Bel. The other she hadn't read yet, but the blurb on the back promised a deliciously filthy read, with a male love interest who had a tail that, according to one of the reviews, was used *very* creatively.

Lily snorted. "I'm not sure if that will be quite what the doctor calls for, but I'm— Ack!"

The wad of fabric smacked her directly in the face with extreme speed and an incredible amount of sass. She barely managed to catch it before it hit the ground. Lily registered what it was and quickly shoved it into her bag along with the books, just in time for Sharkie to pop around the corner.

From there, they proceeded in silence. Lily shouldered her bag and took Sharkie's hand, patting farewell to Carlton on their way out the door. The house groaned its own goodbye, sending a blue scarf to drape over Sharkie's shoulders. Max trotted beside them until they reached the arch to the Hall, then begged to be picked up. Lily cradled him against her shoulder.

The Hall remained quiet, despite the fact that midmorning was one of the busiest times. Almost no souls were out and about, and the few denizens they saw kept a sharp eye on their surroundings and were quick to look over their shoulders. Lily followed a path close to the wall, acutely aware of their proximity to each arch.

Clawlike gouges in the stone of the floor by the well-guarded arch to Hell were the only remainders of the monster that had sounded like a chorus of agonized children. The newly posted guards were unfamiliar and grim-faced, but nodded politely as they went by. One of them returned Sharkie's little wave.

Things at the gate were business as usual, except for the demons' tight expressions and the lack of usual tolerance for souls and their bullshit.

Lily tucked that away in her mind, hurrying Sharkie to the elevator.

Bel's house shouldn't have felt any emptier than it usually did. After all, it was a big fucking house, and the trio of housekeepers were tending to it with care and pride just like they did every other day, but Bel wasn't there filling the house with his steady, mischievous, loving energy. Without him, the house felt like a furnished Grand Canyon.

The head housekeeper, Lecti, clucked over both of them upon their arrival, making a batch of colorful, delicious cookies that were apparently a common treat in demonic households. She soothed Sharkie with an entire plate of them while Lily perched on a nearby stool, wondering exactly how much of her bullshit Lucifer would tolerate before turning her into goo.

One way to find out.

50

DAMNED COFFEE

Lily

Two hours later, Lily stared out of the window of Luci's Admin Level office, watching the play of shifting red-gold afternoon light and listening to the harried secretary outside explain something to someone in the same decisive tone that Lily had ignored on her way in.

Lucifer's massive office felt a bit like an uber-luxurious cigar lounge, with black-and-gold paneled walls, deep, rich colors, and elegant decor. She'd been here several times before with Sharkie, but never on her own. She shifted her shoes on the desk, settling more deeply into the deliciously comfortable chair.

The muffled voice grew clearer, like the secretary was approaching the towering double doors of the office. "I am *so* sorry, sir. She refused to wait outside. I told her that I would have you call when you had a moment, but she insisted . . ."

Oddly clear-minded and composed, Lily dragged her eyes away from the window and stared at the door.

"It's alright, Vitan, thank you," Lucifer said just before the door swung open on silent hinges.

He looked like shit. Not a thread of his clothing was out of place, but his face was gaunt and weary, the opalescent sheen of his copper skin had dulled, and shadows smudged under his eyes. His hair was only slightly rumpled, like he'd run his fingers through it a time too many, but it said enough about what was going on in his head.

He closed the door smoothly. "I believe you're supposed to sit *behind* the desk," he said, voice rasping like he'd been talking too much.

"Not that one."

A smile played at the edges of his mouth. "I heard you read God the riot act and did it with grace. Not to mention how you so kindly relieved the chittahi of its head. I'd say you'd do just fine behind that desk."

Chittahi. That must be the name for the *whateverthefuck*.

Good to know.

"Gossip travels fast, I see." Lily shook her head with a quiet smile. "My perspective is all wrong for that chair. I am neither wise nor kind enough to sit behind that desk and do what you do. I'm far too mortal for it."

"I don't know if anyone feels wise or kind enough," Lucifer said, pushing his fingers through his hair and rubbing his hand down the back of his neck. "I'm sure you'd like some information—"

Lily stopped him with a noise, holding out the coffee cup she'd kept in her hand because the warmth and weight of it was soothing.

"Here. It's not Common Grounds, but it's still pretty good. Just sit and drink this. We can talk when you're done."

Lucifer took the cup but shook his head. "I'd love to, but there is so much to do—"

"You're in a very important meeting right now. That's what you're doing. Drink the damn coffee."

He blinked, then eased himself into the chair beside hers, leaving the opulent office chair behind the desk empty. His feathered wings rustled as he settled them into a comfortable position around the specially designed back. "A moment. It's all I can spare."

Lily picked up her own coffee cup, which she'd set on the floor beside her chair. She'd only managed a sip or two thanks to the nerves fluttering in her belly, but the practice of holding a coffee cup was familiar and comforting.

She needed familiar and comforting.

A minute ticked by as Lucifer sipped his coffee and tilted his head back against the supple burgundy leather of his chair. Lily looked back to the window, the quiet wrapping around them like a blanket.

It was ethereally beautiful on this level of Hell. Bioluminescent ivy crawling up the side of the window fluttered in a breeze, glowing flowers in a myriad of colors dancing amongst the leaves. The pulsing veins of light on the high ceiling outside were less numerous in this particular area, but more intense, making them all the more striking. Bel wouldn't struggle to find beauty here.

Her fingers tightened on her cup, the warmth of it somehow failing to seep into her skin. Wherever he was, she hoped the beauty was as easy to find, but she doubted it.

She'd heard about the massive wards already being set up on the training fields for the injured. And heard they were filling up fast. Hell had long-established systems and procedures in place for such an event, and things were happing at a speed that never would have been possible in the mortal world. The elevators had been crammed with healers and supplies on their way up.

If he's hurt, then they'll take care of him, while I make sure Luci doesn't fall apart. If he's missing, then he won't get any less missing if I lose my shit. If he's fine, he's fine. If he's dead . . . The sips of coffee threatened to make a reappearance. *If he's dead, then he's dead, and I refuse to make the Afterlife a worse place to be just because I'm hurting.*

She swallowed.

I will never regret kindness.

But if Luci could drink that coffee a little faster, I'd really fucking appreciate it.

It was probably only three minutes, but it felt like an eternity by the time Lucifer sighed and rested the empty cup on the armrest.

"What happened?" Lily asked, turning to study his weary profile.

"I have no definitive information on Bel specifically."

Fuck.

"Before dawn this morning," Luci rasped, "there was a major attack. The definitive attack, as it seems. A small portion of our forces were overrun—hence the gegony and chittahi—its handler—that made it all the way into the Universal Hallway. Following that wave, we broke their lines and forced them back enough to close the rift. Preliminary reports are saying that it's over. We are mopping up the ones that were trapped when the rift closed and have begun bringing most of our people back."

"So we . . . won?"

Lucifer studied his empty cup, eyes sad and lips tight. "So it seems. As much as a war can be won."

Lily leaned her head against the back of the chair, feeling too many things at once. "I was American in my last life, Luci. I remember watching 9/11, and all the wars afterward. I had friends who left to serve and never really came back. Trust me, I know that 'won' is a very subjective term when it comes to war."

A faint smile flickered over his face. He glanced at the door, then his phone, and sighed. "In five minutes, this room will be filled with people and become a logistical headquarters."

Lily nodded.

Lucifer rolled his empty coffee cup in his hand. "How is Sharkie?"

"Worried," Lily replied, then added with a somber smile, "Less worried than me, but worried. About Bel. About you. She saw the creatures go by Paradise, but she's fine. Pretty sure she's being doted on by all of Bel's housekeepers at the moment."

"What do you mean she *saw* the creatures?" Lucifer's voice was sharp.

"I had an off feeling this morning, not knowing what it meant, so I told her to stay in Paradise while I went for coffee anyway, thinking she'd stay *home*. Turns out she's a fan of loopholes. Technically, she never left Paradise," Lily said darkly, letting her tone convey exactly how she felt about that. Every time she thought about what could have happened, terror pulsed through her body like a racing heartbeat.

Lucifer muttered something about limiting school field trips to the Fae realm, then asked, "You felt the warning?"

"Yeah. I know not all the souls did."

He looked at her, considering. "Mortal souls who have a certain connection to the Afterlife are typically the ones to feel things as its denizens do."

Maybe it was the Hellp Desk, then. Or maybe it wasn't. It was an issue for later; her time with Lucifer was running out.

"Which . . ." Her voice cracked and she cleared her throat. "Which portion of our armies was overrun? Which legion, do you know yet?"

"Bel's Fourteenth, according to early reports," Luci said quietly. "But all my most recent information says that he was fighting with the Thirty-Fourth."

I was thirty-four when I died.

Information can be wrong.

Where is he?

How long did his braids hold up?

Is he safe?

A kaleidoscope of thoughts, most of which made little sense, spun through her mind until they combined in a continuous mental scream.

"And how hard was the Thirty-Fourth hit?" Lily asked levelly, grounding herself with the warm coffee cup, the buttery leather of the chair, the bite of her nails into her thigh.

"All the legions seem to have been hit hard." The words seemed to be pulled out of him. "There are going to be many casualties."

Lily closed her eyes. Steady breath in. Hold. Steady breath out. Repeat. Repeat again. Perhaps spend eternity repeating.

"Lily." Luci's voice was gentle.

"I don't want to freak out without a reason to," she said tightly, not opening her eyes. The dark was soothing until it wasn't. She opened them, composing herself. "So I won't. All I ask is that you let me know as soon as you hear *anything*. Good . . . good, bad, or otherwise."

"You'll be the first to know."

She should have demurred and insisted that his mother, his family, actually be told first. But she was selfish. Bel was hers, and she was his, and she didn't want to wait a single fucking second longer than she had to out of some purely performative sense of decency.

And that's why I'm too mortal to be behind that desk.

She stood to leave.

"Thank you. I also—" She cut herself off, realizing that barging into Lucifer's office was one thing, telling him how she thought he should handle any element of this crisis was another. But she wanted to help. "I also know that you've done this long enough that you know how to best handle this, and I want to help, not be in the way. But I do have an idea, if you wanted to hear it."

"Your last idea went rather well for us, Lily." Lucifer gave her a small smile.

"The healers are swamped. A lot of the demons at the gate, especially the ones that are former military, have medical knowledge or other relevant skills. If I can help cover the gate, you can ask them to go help."

Lucifer frowned. "I know that the Hellp Desk makes things easier, but do you think it's enough to free up that many demons?"

Lily could hear voices in the hallway.

"Maybe. Maybe not. But maybe some of the demons on the levels could help cover the gate for a little while? I've seen the lower levels. They can throw some souls in a cage until things settle down."

Lucifer nodded thoughtfully, scrubbing a hand over his mouth. "It didn't occur to me to change anything about the mortal function of Hell. We cannot stop doing what Hell was made to do, but we can adjust it. Temporarily."

Someone knocked on the door.

"I'll head up."

Lucifer touched her arm as he rose to his towering height, his eyes a bit brighter than they'd been when he first stepped into his office. "Thank you," he said quietly. "I will learn what I can as quickly as I can."

Lily offered him what smile she could. She had an answer—for now—and she had something to do.

She could work with that.

"You've got this, Luci. I know you know that, but you've got this."

At the door, she stepped aside to let the secretary and a dozen professional-looking demons pass. She glanced back at Lucifer standing tall behind his desk, then headed for the elevator, phone already in hand.

51

MASTER OF LEVEL NINE

Lily

Lily tossed the soul file into the little basket on her desk and watched it disappear, rubbing at the small of her back. She'd been keeping an eye on the trickle of demons coming from the Universal Hallway entrance all afternoon. One of them explained that they were the ones who were uninjured enough to return home under their own power, and didn't want to clog up the direct routes to the infirmaries.

She desperately wanted to see Bel among them.

Her attention was drawn to a dozen demons that stalked out of the elevator hall and toward her desk. From Level Eight or Nine. Had to be. The demons that worked there had a certain feel to them. None of them came close to the primal eeriness of Gregorith, but they could be plenty unsettling if they wanted to be.

Over the last few hours, she'd learned that what the demons from the lower punishment levels lacked in procedural experience, they made up for very effectively through varying styles of intimidation.

"Ms. Lily, Gregorith sent us up to help however we can. Where would you like us?" one said smoothly.

"One moment please— Don't *even* think about it," she snapped mid-sentence to an approaching soul that already looked wary of the new demons. They scurried away.

Moura had left to help, along with Krun and a dozen others who had served, so Zagan had stepped up with quiet efficiency.

She waved him over. "Zagan, what do you think about relieving some of the ones who have family they're worried about? Parents, siblings, kids?"

"I think they'd appreciate that."

"Would you like to take off?" Lily asked, remembering the charcoal sketches that Zagan had shown her of designs for the Hellp Desk. They'd been done by his brother, who served in Asmodeus's legions.

"I already know what happened to my brother. Me being there won't change anything. I'd rather have something to do." Zagan ducked his head, expression neutral. "I'll get a dozen people who are worried about immediate family members and let them know."

A hole punched through her chest. "I'm so sorry, Zagan."

He met her eyes, nodding tightly in thanks, as if it was all he could manage while maintaining his composure.

"You can get at least twenty," the Level Nine demon who seemed to be in charge said. "We're nothing if not good at controlling souls, and our people deserve to have that peace of mind. I'm sorry for your loss."

Zagan searched the other demon's face, then adjusted his grip on his spear and nodded. "Twenty. Thank you."

The Level Nine demon bent deeply at the waist to him, then nodded at Lily, heading toward the gate with the others.

Lily pressed a hand to the base of her throat, aching for Zagan and his loss. The designs his brother had done were beautiful, including options for expansion. Later, when the pain of grief was more manageable, she'd ask Zagan for them and make sure it wouldn't bother him to see his brother's designs come to fruition.

She reached for her phone, which she'd been on and off all afternoon. When she hadn't been coordinating volunteers, she'd been texting with Sharkie, who was now at Lucifer's, having decided to wait there for him in case he needed fussing at the end of the day. Lily's messages to Sharkie had been boring and brief. Sharkie's had been a play-by-play of her aquarium game, interspersed with inspirational quotes that Lily was certain she'd looked up a master list of. Each one made her smile and kept the screaming in her head from becoming deafening.

The phone buzzed in her hand, screen lighting up—

Lucifer.

She couldn't answer it fast enough, already running for the elevator. "Luc—"

"They found him. He's alive—"

Oh, thank fuck—

"—but barely. They're doing everything they can."

Lily stumbled against the wall, jarring herself so hard her teeth clacked. She smashed the elevator "call" button over and over, Lucifer's grim voice continuing in her ear.

"They're taking him home. Lilith initiated a standing emergency protocol with the Healers Guild as soon as we received word of the attack this morning, and they're on their way to treat him there. How fast can you get to his house?"

"I'm in the elevator." Lily hit the button for Bel's floor so hard it should have cracked. Mercifully, the doors closed quickly, and she felt the drop in her stomach as the elevator started moving. "Tell me everything."

"It was a gegony that got him, though Asmodeus says that he was already in pretty bad shape before the battle started. They couldn't get to him, because he was so close to the front line, right in the thick of the fighting."

Of course he was.

"Asmodeus is okay?"

"He's alive and talking."

"Good enough. Sariah . . . ?"

"Is with him."

The second the elevator doors started to open, Lily dug her fingers into the gap and pulled, squeezing herself through. "Thank you, Luci. I have to go."

She hung up without waiting for a response, pouring every ounce of speed she had into her feet. Hell blurred around her. She lunged through the front gate of Bel's house and ran up the wide stairs, slowing when she saw a lone figure sitting on the step just below the landing.

Gregorith sat quietly, arms crossed, elbows braced on his knees, his angular face neutral at first glance, but his eyes were strained and staring into nothing.

He spoke before her panic choked her.

"They just got him here. They're doing surgery. Lady Lilith is inside. I was with her when she got the news." His words were cool and clipped, belying the vibrating tension that hummed through his body. Every mortal instinct she still had told her that Gregorith was an injured, cornered predator, who would strike and strike hard if provoked. But the part of her that didn't seem so mortal anymore whispered that he was Bel's friend—one of his *oldest* friends—and dangerous or no, he was hurting.

"Why are you out here?" she asked softly.

Gregorith's grip on his arm tightened, jaw clenching. He still hadn't looked at her, red eyes fixed on something distant. He reminded her of . . . herself. When she was younger and feeling too much and didn't know how to handle it because she thought her feelings were too overwhelming for *anyone* to handle.

"I'm not family," he said.

"Bullshit."

His eyebrows twitched downward.

"You've known him since you were both, what, four? You're like a brother to him," Lily reasoned, hoping that would spur some reaction.

Gregorith said nothing, but his shoulders grew tighter.

"Thank you for sending those demons from Level Nine to the gate," Lily tried gently. "They helped a lot."

Tiny nod.

Lily ran through what she knew about Gregorith, which, in reality, wasn't a lot. She knew he was a skilled manipulator because of *Invaders*. He had a quiet, dry kind of humor based on the few interactions she'd had with him, and she knew what Bel alluded to in their conversations— that he was witty, serious, and lonely. His bloody, brutal work isolated him, even among demon-kind, and he cared about his few friends quite a bit in his own quiet way.

Lily sat, keeping a respectful, but not fearful, distance between them.

His eyes shifted a bit, tracking her movement out of the corner of his eye. "You should go inside," he said finally.

Lily nodded, watching a pair of gleaming birds flit around the front garden. "He's in surgery. It's not like it'll matter to him where I wait. This seems like as good a place to wait as any."

Such a fucking liar. I want to be in there next to him more than I want a heartbeat.

But she couldn't be next to him yet. And Gregorith needed a friend, even if she doubted she'd be his first, second, or third choice.

Gregorith's tail twitched once before he stilled it. Then it twitched again.

Lily kept her tone soft and understanding, despite the edginess coiled in her belly. "I can go inside if you want me to, but it doesn't feel right to just leave you out here. You care about him, and Bel wouldn't want you sitting out here in exile. *I* don't want you sitting out here alone, unless that's really what you need. But as someone who's used isolation as a self-harm technique, I'll tell you that, even though it's what you think you want, it's not going to help anything."

She let the words hang between them, waiting.

Gregorith's breathing went a bit ragged as he stared into space.

Someone raced toward the house, crashing through the gate in a whirlwind of pink skin and white-to-black hair. Angel paused on the steps beside them, panting for breath, red eyes wide and scared.

"*Why* are you out *here!*" she cried, holding her fists to her chest, then pressing her hands to her cheeks, eyes brimming with tears. "Please tell me he's not dead. You'd be crying if he was dead." She said the last part to Gregorith in a tone that was half reprimand and half plea.

"He's in surgery," Lily answered, when Gregorith didn't.

"Oh, thank the Universe. We can work with that," Angel said in a rush, bolting into the house.

Lily blinked after her, a bit whiplashed by the extreme differences in emotional reaction she'd encountered in the last few minutes.

She sat with Gregorith in silence for a while longer before he sighed.

"I'm not in exile. I just . . ." His voice caught, a sharp contrast to his usual effortlessly smooth cadence. He flexed one hand. "I heard some of the things that happened to him, when the healers were telling Lady Lilith. I know how much similar injuries hurt. I inflict them on evil souls *because* they are so painful. Knowing that, knowing that my *friend* is experiencing that level of pain without deserving it . . ." He shook his head tightly. "I felt . . . I don't know what to do. How to handle it."

Lily slowly lifted her hand to his shoulder, giving him every opportunity to signal that comfort would be unwelcome. His shoulder was surprisingly muscular given his leaner build, and she could feel the stress humming through him like an electrical current.

"There's nothing any of us can do except wait," she said gently, to herself as much as to him. "And we handle it together. As family, as friends, as people who care about one another and care about Bel."

Gregorith's breathing evened out a bit and he cleared his throat. "How are you holding up?" he asked.

"I've been screaming inside ever since I realized something was wrong, and I feel like I'm one wrong move away from completely losing it, but I can still be mostly rational. So, better than I expected, really."

A beat of silence.

"I see why Bel loves you so much," Gregorith said quietly.

The wave of emotion came crashing down, immediately sending hot tears down her cheeks.

"Oh fuck." She choked, pressing the heels of her hands into her eyes and trying to fucking *breathe*. "Yeah, I love him too," she sobbed. "Gregorith, you asshole, I was doing so well."

He patted her back, murmuring an apology and letting her cry.

It felt . . . good. Good to cry, to let it all out, like releasing pressure from a valve that had been dangerously over capacity. She couldn't afford to lose it completely, though, so she focused on taking deep breaths until the tears stopped.

"You can call me Greg," he said. "I prefer Gregorith with most people, because it's more professional, but my friends and people I'm close to call me Greg."

And Lily was crying again.

She and Greg sat outside for another hour and watched the light start to dim before finally going inside. Lilith swept her up into a hug, followed by Angel, as well as Kasdeya and Orin, who had arrived with Lilith earlier.

In addition to a spate of already brutal injuries from previous stints on the battlefield, Bel had been crushed between the gegony's jaws and savaged by its rows of sharp teeth, then clawed and stomped on as he lay on the battlefield. Unconscious, they thought. She hoped.

Heavy bruising, strained ligaments and muscles, broken ribs, wings shredded and broken, broken arm, broken collarbone, extreme lacerations over a significant portion of his body, a staggering amount of blood loss, and . . . a bruised tail.

Perhaps it was the stress, but after the list of horrifying injuries, the additional mention of a *bruised tail* had Lily exhaling sharply through her nose to hide a laugh.

Four of the healers that formed the medical team for the princes and other higher-ups in Hell worked on Bel with the extent of their skill. Another four were at Asmodeus's house. At that news, Greg shook his head.

Lilith, pale-faced but composed, smiled. "Asmodeus is quite possibly the worst patient I've ever seen. At least this time he has a good reason for it. When I saw him earlier, he was trying to get up to aid his soldiers that are scouring the battlefield and making sure everyone is brought home. Even though he's not as injured as Bel, unless he's unconscious, his healers have their work cut out for them."

"Not if Sariah is there," Lily pointed out, proud of how steady her voice seemed. "She'll keep him in line."

Everyone had a little chuckle over that, even if it seemed a bit forced.

And then they waited.

And waited.

Lily called Sharkie and gave her the update. Lucifer had already gone home to sit with her and explained that there had been an emergency Lily needed to deal with, so Sharkie was concerned but not blindsided.

"But he's not dead?" Sharkie clarified.

"No, bug, but he's really, really hurt."

"Hurt can heal, right? Like, it's *Bel*, he'll be okay. He's huge. You'll be okay, because you're smart and strong. And Luci will be okay because he's Luci and he has the whole Hell thing. We'll be okay. Like, eventually. We just might need some fussing."

If I only had a shred of the faith in myself that this child has in us to figure things out and deal with stuff, I would be unstoppable.

It was fully night by the time a healer came downstairs, gaunt-faced and looking like she hadn't slept in a month, but relieved.

"He will live."

Lily had to lock her knees to keep them from buckling in pure relief.

"We managed to satisfactorily repair his wings, all broken bones, and close up the worst lacerations, as well as replenish some of the blood volume. Most of the muscles and ligaments have been repaired; however, we, as well as the prince, ran out of safely usable energy. After a recovery period, we will return for a full, final healing, but we estimate that he will need to be in bed, or"—the healer smiled grudgingly—"at least *resting* for a week, minimum."

"Oh, that's going to go over well," Orin muttered.

"But he'll fully recover? Physically?" Lily asked, hand resting against her throat.

"Completely. He'll have a few new scars, but physically, he will make a full recovery." The healer's eyes were knowing. Healing the body was the easy part. The mind and soul were different animals entirely. "He should sleep through the night and wake up at some point tomorrow. One of us will come by to check on him."

They all said a discordant thank-you, then again when the other three healers—one of whom nearly collapsed with exhaustion—came down the stairs.

Greg's sigh of relief seemed to come from his soul.

"Well," Lilith said crisply, "it's a big house. You are all more than welcome to stay . . ." Her eyes snagged on Lily. "I'm sorry, I shouldn't speak for you. Those months before the war, you were here as often as Bel."

Lily'd had way too many shocking things happen in one day to process that statement, so she just waved her hand. "It's fine. Please feel welcome to stay. It *is* a big house." She smiled at Lilith, who returned it softly. Now that the urgency had faded, a trickle of guilt for her insistence that she be one of the first people notified when they found Bel wormed through her. "May I go up and see him, or would you like to?"

Lilith settled her arm over Lily's shoulders, the scent of her perfume bright and clean. "He's my son, but your love. Together?"

They climbed the stairs in silence, heading down the familiar hall to Bel's room. She didn't bother with a dramatic pause before opening the door. Dramatic pauses were for people with different priorities. She hadn't seen Bel in more than two and a half months, and he'd just almost died on her. She was getting through that door. Immediately.

The healers had propped him up on his side with pillows so that his wings could rest comfortably behind him and give them easy access to the splayed expanse. He was shirtless, the sheets pushed down to his waist, and completely passed out. His whole body seemed leaner, his muscles standing out in sharper relief, and even in the dimming light, Lily could see the mottles and ridges of bruises and mostly healed gashes.

His face—oh, how she'd missed that face. The rugged, rough-hewn features, his little chin spikes, the broad sweep of his cheekbone, the point of his ear, the scar through his eyebrow that now had companions on his cheek and nose. She watched his chest rise and fall. Once. Again.

He was *alive*.

Just being in the same room made breathing easier. Made everything seem a little more bearable.

Lilith approached the bed and brushed a hand over Bel's slightly damp hair, pushing it away from his face—they must've washed it, Lily realized—before silently sitting on the edge of the bed, a strangely vulnerable expression on her regal features.

Lily waited for her to say something, but she remained silent, watching her son, soaking in the fact that he was still breathing. Finally, she leaned forward and pressed a kiss to his temple. Lily could see it, like a vision from the past, how Lilith must have tucked little boy Bel into bed after one of his rambunctious days and kissed him good night just like that.

Lilith walked toward where Lily waited by the door, taking her hands and dipping to kiss Lily's forehead. She squeezed her hands lightly, then closed the door behind her.

Lily sucked in a deep breath, held it, and let it go. The cadence of Bel's breathing was as familiar as her own. Every fiber of her being wanted to curl against him and listen to his steady heartbeat, bask in his warm scent, his quiet strength. Hold him. Take the pain away. Take the awful memories away.

She kicked her boots off before she even got close to the bed. Then she stripped down to her T-shirt and underwear, lifted the sheet, and slid in, careful not to disturb him, even though the bed was massive. She lay an arm's length away, facing him, tucking one of the many spare pillows against her chest so that she would cuddle it and not his healing body. Her hand slid over the cool sheets toward his, heat radiating off him like it always did. It made her want to cry.

Here. Alive.

Her fingertips brushed over the back of his broad hand, and a tear leaked free. She could hold his hand. That was safe. That wouldn't hurt him.

She curled her hand over his and simply lay there, soaking in every detail of his face, how grumpy he looked when he slept, the cadence of his breathing, letting it lull her to sleep.

Something woke her up in the middle of the night. Her hand still curled over his, and Bel lay in the same position, breathing the same deep breaths. It took her a moment to realize what had woken her up so suddenly.

Something warm tightened around her calf.

His tail. Firm and unyielding.

❧

52

NOT BACK YET

Bel

He'd always wondered what it was like to die.

He'd asked Lily about it once, as they'd lain tangled in each other, all sweat-slicked skin and gentle, exploring touches, coming down from their respective peaks.

"Death itself isn't bad," she'd said, her beautiful eyes soft in a way she rarely allowed herself to show. *"Dying though, that's a bitch. You can fight it, but there's a sense of inevitability that just swamps you, no matter how hard you fight. There comes a moment, or it did for me anyway, when you're more dead than dying, and it stops being so bad and it was just . . . a relief."*

She was right, his Lily. Dying was a bitch.

He fucking *hated* it.

Lying on the muddy battlefield, in the dim in-between of consciousness and unconsciousness after the gegony had flung him aside and clawed helplessly at its own throat, where he'd made sure his sword had embedded itself deep, Bel had been swamped with pain like he'd never known. He'd felt his body fighting to keep him alive, fighting a losing battle. Every pump of his heart, every pulse of blood through—and out of—his body had felt like one step closer to the moment when the sense of inevitability would set in and—fuck that.

Fuck that.

He was Beleth, a general and a prince. He loved a mighty woman, and she loved him, and he loved a child who had more bravery than an entire army as if she were his own—*their* own. He was the son of Lady Lilith and Samael, two of the original great beings of the Afterlife, of Hell, and his siblings were all incredible in their own rights. He had a life. He had a family. He had a purpose. They were waiting for him, and he had only the faintest opportunity to fight against death.

He would be taking it.

So he'd gone deep within himself, and during brief flickers of consciousness had done everything he could to stem some of the bleeding before black spots blinded him to the world. Even overwhelmed by the black nothing, he'd snarled at it, clinging to his memories of all the things that made his life beautiful and worth fighting for.

The sensation of being lifted had ripped him away from the internal battle, and he'd come to vague consciousness *furious* that death was taking him against his will.

He still had fight in him, dammit!

He'd swiped at the sneaky fucker—or tried to—before the white-hot pain of his broken arm had him choking. Strange hands firmly kept him down on something, while voices said urgent words that he should have been able to understand, but everything had been so garbled.

Then there'd been nothing but numb blackness and the thud of his heartbeat. Brief flashes of other sensations. Being carried. Being on something solid and moving. Hands. Voices. Lying on something soft. Then *agony*.

The agony of healing was unique—like the pain of getting the injury, of his body being forced apart, combined with the unnatural pain of having his body forced back together again far faster than it naturally wanted to heal. It drove him into nothingness again, to only blackness and his heartbeat.

He'd been little, barely old enough to form memories, but he remembered crying at bedtime because his wrenched wing hurt so badly. The stupid little kid with the dark red skin and the stupid name in his first-ever combat class was terrible at wrestling, but had managed to twist his wing when they'd both lost their tempers and attacked each other.

Greg. The meanie.

Bel had gotten in a good stomp on Greg's tail before the teachers had pulled them apart. They'd sat in time-out together until they'd grumpily made peace and grudgingly realized they could help each other learn. Bel couldn't figure out the stupid rubber knife, and Greg couldn't follow the wrestling instructions to save his life. Bel happened to be very good at wrestling, and Greg had picked up the knife with disgusting ease. They'd agreed to help each other.

His wing still hurt, though.

His mother tucked him in and smoothed his sticky-uppy hair back from his face, her cool fingers soothing on his forehead, through his hair, around the itchy nubs of his horns, as she murmured comforting things until his wing didn't hurt so much and his eyes grew heavy. He barely registered the kiss on his forehead before he dropped completely into sleep.

Old memories and new sensations blurred together as the darkness lifted. His wing hurt. *Both* his wings hurt, as did most of his body, but not as sharply as before. A deep ache had settled into every fiber of muscle, every tendon and joint, every bone. His skin felt raw in places, not exactly painful per se, but oversensitive. It was too disorienting.

Death was supposed to be peaceful nothing.

The pain was his first clue that maybe, just maybe, he wasn't dead yet.

If this was real.

Was it real?

His tail was wrapped around something warm and smooth and familiar, something that kicked his brain into gear. He knew that thing. He knew that feeling. It was important. He needed to follow that feeling. *It* was real. It would guide him up out of the nothing.

It took a moment for his brain to catch up with his eyes opening, to make sense of the colors and shapes and shadows. The first thing that came into focus was deep-auburn hair splayed over black silk, glinting faintly in the dawning red-gold light.

Lily.

His throat grew tight.

Lily slept on her side a few feet away, curled around a pillow instead of him, her arm reaching out, fingers resting on the back of his hand. Under the sheets, her leg rested near him, his tail curled firmly around her calf, just as he liked. His anchor. He studied her face with the intensity he usually reserved for the battlefield. Her brows were slightly furrowed, dark lashes fanned across her pale cheeks, soft lips parted slightly. A tiny spot of drool on the pillow told him everything he needed to know about how tired she was. She drooled a little when she slept hard. He loved it.

Too far away. He needed her in his arms. If his tail around her leg had brought him out of consciousness, maybe holding her would keep him in his body, keep death away.

He reached for her, ignoring the flaring ache that pulsed through his arm, shoulder, and back, then paused.

Lily. He was with Lily. He ached. He *felt*. The room around him, it was *his* room, his bed, his sheets that they were lying on. His heart still beat, pounding away in his chest, the rhythm picking up as the realization sank in.

Alive. He was still alive. And he was *home*.

Bel's hand shook as he traced a line down the arch of Lily's cheek with the backs of his fingers, over the soft line of her jaw, down the satiny skin of her neck, then back up again to cradle her lovely face, trace those lips with his thumb. She was so *real*.

A contented little hum was all the warning he had before Lily's eyes eased open, obviously not fully awake. She pressed into his touch with a little smile, just like she had so many other mornings.

She went rigid, eyes snapping fully open.

He loved her eyes. So bright and pretty, her intelligence and heart shone through them, capturing him every time. Her gaze darted over his face before meeting his, a whirlwind of emotions dancing across her features in a heartbeat before settling on concerned relief. Her hand came up to cover his, hazel eyes going glassy. Beautiful.

"Hi," she whispered.

"Hi," he said, his voice a broken rasp. Clearly his vocal cords had been low on the priority list of the healers. He opened his mouth to say something—*everything*—to her, but his throat couldn't make a sound.

Emotion welled up. The battle, the whole damn war, the blood, the death, the horror, the pain, the loss, the *fear* . . .

"I'm alive," he rasped, not sure if he was saying it for clarification or in wonder.

Lily nodded slowly, not looking away, reaching out to skim her fingertips over his jaw. "You're alive."

His eyes burned, breath catching. "I'm home."

"You're home," she said. A tear dripped down the side of her nose.

"I . . ." His heart raced, breath stuttering in his lungs, mind swirling. She saw it. She always saw him. "Princess," he choked, and then the dam of his composure collapsed. The sobs seemed to come from his soul. He wasn't sure if he pulled Lily to him or if she moved under her own power, or both. It didn't matter. Somehow, he ended up with his face buried in her chest, arms gripping her too tightly, but it didn't matter because she was gripping him just as tightly back. She'd ended up higher on the bed, curling herself protectively over him as he wept, her own tears dampening his hair.

Bel wept for the soldiers, the friends he'd lost, the orders he'd given that had led them there, the things he couldn't control. He wept for their families. For their pain. For the grief that he knew all too well would never fade but would become more bearable with time as it wove itself into the tapestry of their lives. For the nightmares. For the scars that the survivors would bear, inside and out. He wept for the gegony, the little ones who had been tortured and their parents, forced into a war that was not their own. He wept for himself. For the parts of himself that had been irrevocably changed on that gory battlefield.

No matter how many times he'd seen combat, he always came back changed again. And he wept for that too. For the echo of the times before, and the fresh pain of the now.

Lily held him through all of it. She never moved, never wavered, just held him, wept with him, her quiet strength and understanding the only thing keeping him from spiraling into a place that was harder and harder to come back from.

It could have been hours later when the mountain sitting on Bel's chest lifted. Not entirely—a lifetime of experience told him that it would always partially be there—but he could breathe easier than any other time he'd come back before, thanks to Lily and her grounding presence. He wasn't alone. He would never be alone. Not in this.

He smoothed his hand up the small of Lily's back, pulling in a lungful of her sweet scent, mixed with the salty tang of his tears in her shirt. She kissed his head.

"Asmodeus?" he asked, his voice more broken than before.

"Alive and in slightly better shape than you. Your mom said he's an ornery patient."

"Understatement," Bel mumbled, more weight lifting off his soul.

Lily's fingers ran through his newly clean hair, her voice soft. "It's over, apparently. Luci said you managed to push them back enough so that they could get the rift sealed up."

"Not me."

Her fingers paused in his hair.

"I was . . . injured before the final push."

"Your armies," Lily said softly, lightly tugging on a strand of hair.

Bel grunted, letting the information soak into him like a balm.

Over. Done. Safe.

"The healers had their work cut out with you yesterday." Her voice went oddly tight. "But they fixed you up enough that you're out of the woods. They're going to send someone over today to check on you, then come back tomorrow or the day after and do the final healing."

Bel mulled that over. He felt like he could spend another three days sleeping, but he needed to deal with bringing the injured home, bringing the dead home, organizing the funeral pyres, preparing to meet with the grieving families even though it would rip at his heart. Maybe he could ask Lily to go with him—

"They also said you're going to be on bed rest for at least a week."

"*What?*" Bel went to lunge upward, but at the last second remembered his horns and how Lily was curled over his head, so he carefully maneuvered himself onto an elbow to stare at her.

"I'll be completely healed after the second session. Other than a nap, there's no justifiable reason for me to lie in bed for a week when there's so much that needs to be done!"

Lily propped her cheek on her fist and raised an eyebrow. The effect of her arch expression was somewhat ruined by her puffy, red eyes. "I feel the need to remind you that you almost died."

He winced. "Fair. But by the time I've had two sessions with a healer—"

"Four," Lily said plainly, though her voice wobbled. "There were *four* healers working on you all day yesterday, and they drained themselves and you completely dry of healing energy. Whatever that means. One of them practically fell down the stairs when they left."

Oh. Bel frowned, indignation fading. Four of his mother's best healers. Drained. And he still felt as bad as he did.

"I don't need to be in bed for a week," he said slowly, not actually sure but too worried about his soldiers to rest without a fight.

"I seem to recall more than a few promises to spend an entire week in bed with *me*," Lily said smoothly, and then her expression softened. "I know you want to take care of your soldiers, Bel. I get that. But you won't be any use to them if you don't heal. You'll end up right back in bed again anyway. Hell is rallying to support them; they're not being abandoned."

The pounding ache in his body grew worse. Just holding himself up on one arm had the first sharp prickles of pain piercing through the dull soreness. She was right. He knew she was right. But . . .

"Well, if you're going to be in bed with me all week," Bel said, lowering himself down with a groan he couldn't stop and which Lily pointedly ignored.

"Until you can fuck me in the manner to which I have become accustomed—and have been cleared by a healer to do so—you're not getting any," she said, a smile in her voice. "Guess you'd better focus on healing real quick."

Bel sat up with a pained wheeze and stared at her. "Are you . . . Lily, are you blackmailing me into resting by putting me into sexile?"

Lily stretched on the pillows with an indolent smile. "Worked in *Lysistrata.*"

As right as it felt to banter with her again, there was a piece of him that wondered if he was disrespecting those who had fallen by engaging in something so light so soon after their time in the dark. What right did he have to a nonserious conversation when too many lay dead?

Survivor's guilt.

The thought brought him up short. They'd all heard about it, studied it, seen it in various forms throughout their training. Bel had felt it before, but not so intensely as he did now. His father had had it; Bel had read so in his journals. It had played a major part in Samael's reclusion, which had then made living that much more unpalatable for an already hurting soul.

Bel grieved the ones that they had lost. Would grieve them until the day he joined them. But he would not do them the disservice of scorning the gift of life that they had fought and died to ensure for others.

Lily's hand on his cheek brought him back. He'd been quiet too long, and she must have seen the processing on his face.

He kissed her palm and eased his increasingly painful body back down. "'Fuck you in the manner to which you've become accustomed.' Which manner is that, princess?" He slid his hand up her bare, tattooed thigh. "Rough? Slow?" He skimmed his claws along the hem of her panties.

Lily grabbed his chin firmly, tilting his head up. "Well." She kept her lips just out of reach. "Until you can fuck me *well*, you're shit out of luck, big guy."

She was right, but he pouted anyway.

She snorted. "And your mother said that *Asmodeus* was the worst patient she'd ever seen."

"It's true. They'll have to keep him out until he's healed enough to get out of bed." He ran his hand down toward her knee, letting any heat from the moment fade. "He's really okay?"

Lily wiggled down so that they lay face-to-face on the pillow. "Yeah. You're the one who . . ." Her nose went red, and she seemed to be fascinated by the little spikes on his chin. "You're the one who scared the shit out of us."

"Sharkie?"

"With Luci. She was worried, but she always thought that you would be fine. I believe her exact words were *He'll be okay. He's huge.*"

He chuckled, able to hear Sharkie's voice in the words.

"She's going to be really excited to see you." Lily smiled. "Your mom's here, or at least she was last night. Kasdeya, Orin, Angel, and Greg are here. As far as I know they stayed overnight, and I'm not sure if anyone new has arrived. As soon as the healers left, I came up here."

"Greg?" Bel asked, surprise overriding his other thoughts.

She smirked. "Yeah, your best friend? Runs Level Nine, quiet and a little creepy sometimes, but he's actually pretty nice. Has red skin, wears a lot of black—"

Bel snorted. "Yes, I'm aware you're talking about *that* Greg. I'm just surprised you're calling him Greg and not Gregorith."

"He gave me permission yesterday. We had a little moment on the stairs outside."

"Was he upset?"

"He tried not to show it, but yeah."

Bel huffed a laugh, wondering how Lily had gotten Greg out of a mood. His moods were notorious.

"Do you want me to let everyone know you're awake?" Lily asked.

"Did they hear what the healers said yesterday? That I'm out of the woods?"

She nodded.

"Then not yet," Bel said, his voice cracking almost into nothingness. *Damn it.* "I'm not . . ." He slipped his hand under a chunk of her hair and watched it slide free, gathering himself together. "I just want to be quiet with you. I'm not . . . back yet."

He would admit that to no one but her. It didn't feel right, like he was trying to get out of the responsibility of being him.

Lily brushed his nose with hers, then pressed a sweet, powerful kiss to his lips. It felt like the first full breath he'd taken in months.

Alive.

Home.

Lily

They lay in simple quiet together for hours, tracing slow patterns over each other's skin, savoring the closeness and being together again. Eventually, Bel drifted back to sleep, but Lily stayed, her hand over his heart, every beat against her palm chipping away at her uncertainty until only a thread remained. Eventually, a knock on the door woke Bel up so abruptly it was like he'd been jolted with electricity.

Lily kissed him, slid out of bed, and pulled her pants on before opening the door for the healer, as well as a parade of Bel's family and friends. With one notable absence. She exchanged a look with Bel, who gave her a knowing nod, and went downstairs to let the others have their time.

She leaned against the bottom banister, hand curled around the phantom sensation of his thudding heartbeat, and took a long, deep breath.

"Okay," she whispered, pressing her closed hand to her chest.

She found Greg in the living room, sitting in a chair with a casual elegance that reminded her of a tiger at rest. Though, speaking of tigers . . .

"Your cat has no sense of self-preservation," he told her smoothly, running a single finger down Max's head as he purred away in Greg's lap.

"You're friend-shaped," Lily said, dropping into a nearby chair.

"Demons run warmer than humans. He probably just likes the heat."

"Has he sat on anyone else's lap since yesterday?"

Silence.

"He might seem like a feckless cuddle slut, but he's actually quite picky. Always has been, even when he was a kitten. He picks his good people."

"Good people," Greg muttered, scratching under Max's chin. "He's awake?"

"Yes. There're lots of naps in his future, and he might give Asmodeus a run for his money in the difficult patient department, but he's awake."

Greg nodded, carefully petting Max with hands that seemed awfully uncertain for being so capable. "How is . . . he?"

Lily wondered how to say it in a way that explained without betraying trust. That wouldn't make Greg relate the torture he meted out to deserving souls to the experiences of his friend.

"He's a general who lost a lot of soldiers. He's a man who lost a lot of friends. He's seen and done and experienced things that you and I will never see, do, or experience, no matter how big and bad we are." Lily took a deep breath. "But he came home. He didn't come home the same, but he came home. I remember talking to active-duty soldiers in the mortal world who'd come home from deployment, and all of them said that coming home was the hard part. Our war was different, but Bel came home when others didn't. He's probably going to struggle with that."

"He has before," Greg said. "Nothing too bad, but it was there. But this war . . . We haven't lost so many people in a long time."

Her chest ached. "Patience and understanding can accomplish a lot. And so can you, O Great Master of Level Nine, if you're there for him."

Greg's smile was faint and wry, but he looked like he could breathe easier as he nodded.

Voices floated down the stairs. Bel's wasn't among them, wrecked as it was. She hoped the healers made a point to fix that soon. She could tell it bothered him to sound so broken.

A few minutes later, people began to trickle down the stairs, chatting quietly amongst themselves, but looking more relieved.

Greg watched them all, glancing down at Max in his lap, a whisper of frustration flickering across his stoic face.

Oh, for fuck's sake.

Lily stood and picked the cat up, cuddling him against her chest. His warm fluff was as comforting as it had been when she'd cuddled him for moral support during exam season.

"Go," she told Greg, "be free."

He stood, checking himself for cat hair. "I thought you weren't supposed to disturb a resting cat?"

"I wasn't supposed to do a lot of things," Lily said, giving Max a little smooch. "And now I'm here. Though, of my 'sins,' that's probably the one that would send me to Level Nine. Quit stalling. He missed you."

BEEF

Lily

The day after Bel woke up, Sharkie walked into the room with her hood pushed back, messy blond hair sticking up in all directions, and stopped at the edge of Bel's bed, folding her arms.

Lucifer trailed her, weary but bemused. Greg glanced up from where he'd settled with his laptop by the window after returning from Asmodeus's house. He hadn't said anything, just shaken his head with exasperation. Bel had nodded knowingly.

Lily leaned beside the door, while Sharkie squinted at Bel as he sat up.

"Did you do what you said?" Sharkie asked.

"I did." Bel's voice sounded slightly less fractured than it had.

"Are you missing any parts?"

The beat before Bel responded made Lily's heart ache.

"Nope."

"Not anymore," Greg muttered.

Bel's head cranked around to stare at him. "The fuck do you mean *not anymore*? Oops, sorry, Sharkie."

Sharkie shrugged lightly. "It seems like a swearing situation to me."

"They had to regrow half of your ear," Greg said too neutrally, staring at his laptop.

Lily stiffened. She must have missed that part of the conversation with the healers. Bruised tail, she remembered. Missing chunk of his ear? Not so much.

"Oh." Bel relaxed, then tensed again, hands flying up to the points of his ears. "Wait, which one? Not the right one!"

"It was the right one," Greg said.

"Fuck."

"Was that your favorite ear?" Sharkie asked, cocking her head.

"It was the one with a tattoo on it," Bel groused, fingers tracing the newly formed ear. "And if they had to regrow it, that means the tattoo is gone."

"Fuck." Lily winced in sympathy. When she'd been alive, she'd had an irrational fear of losing one of her limbs. Not because of the loss of the limb, but because of the tattoos that would go with it. The limb was free. The tattoos? She'd *paid* for those. Bel hadn't paid for his, but the principle of the thing was the same.

"Right?" Bel sighed, catching her gaze with his silver one.

It hit her again how much she loved him. Even when he was exasperated and verging on cranky, she'd never get tired of seeing those eyes.

He focused back on Sharkie, tone gentling and hand dropping down to rest on the sheets. "I'm okay, Sharkie. I did my best, I'm home now, and . . ." He glanced up at Lucifer before continuing. "It's over. The war is over. We're safe."

He said it all with a smile, but Lily saw the effort it took.

"Are you gonna stop being a general?" Sharkie asked, arms dropping to her sides.

"Nah, kiddo, I like swinging swords around too much."

"Then we'll always be safe," Sharkie said decisively, crawling onto the bed and wrapping her arms as far around him as she could.

Bel blinked rapidly with suspiciously shiny eyes. The arm he wrapped around her made her look tiny, but every movement was infinitely gentle.

"It's a good thing you kept your promise," Sharkie told him, "or else you would've gotten smitten by the pinkie promise gods. I'm not sure who they are, but I'm sure they take their job seriously."

Lily smiled. "I think you mean 'smote,' Sharkie."

Sharkie made a noncommittal noise and hugged Bel a little tighter.

He pressed a kiss into her messy hair, combing through it delicately with his claws. Lily caught Greg staring at Bel and Sharkie with a little smile before he shut it down and returned his stoic focus to his laptop.

Lucifer clasped Lily's shoulder as he headed out the door, heat searing through the thin fabric of her shirt.

She covered it with her own, pausing him. "Thank you," she whispered.

He inclined his head, the shadows under his eyes not as pronounced as they'd been in his office. The time he spent with Sharkie always did him good. He'd seemed less aloof and lonely since she had arrived to the Afterlife.

She released his hand, and he made it all of one step before Sharkie cried, "Wait!"

Every eye turned to her.

She sat up and turned to Bel. "I was gonna ask you, like I asked Mom," Sharkie started, and both Bel and Lucifer's eyebrows hit their hairlines at the title, "but then you almost *died,* apparently, and I was worried about you, so now I'm just going to call you Dad without asking, because you are." She turned to Lucifer and beamed. "And you're Papa. Because calling you both Dad would be confusing." Her gaze darted to Lily's with a flash of concern. "That's okay, right? That I didn't ask first?"

Lily grinned, taking in Bel's and Luci's glistening eyes and matching awestruck expressions. She patted Luci's shoulder. "I think they're honored. Aren't you, guys?"

They launched into hurried—and choked—profusions of pride and love, both rushing to reassure her how honored they were to be called Dad and Papa.

"You can call me anything you like, Sharkie, just as long as you don't call me late to dinner," Bel said with wet eyes and a brighter grin than Lily'd seen on him since he'd woken up.

Ah, the dad jokes were going to be next-level now.

Luci wiped at his eyes and strode over to the bed, reaching down to scoop Sharkie into a hug.

Worried that he was feeling left out, Lily checked on Greg just in time to watch Max jump onto the arm of his chair and saunter across his keyboard before lying down on top of his hands. Greg stared sternly at him, then looked to Lily for guidance.

She shrugged, mouthing *Cats* as an explanation.

The front door closed with a thud, and voices echoed up the stairs, along with footsteps. Luci ruffled Sharkie's hair and walked out without another word, just a nod of acknowledgment as he passed Lily, a new light gleaming in his eyes.

A few moments later, Lilith arrived with a baby in her arms and a pair of healers in tow. Anyaet squirmed, twisting around in an effort to see everything and fussing with frustration when she couldn't. Lilith shifted her with the effortless ease of a well-seasoned mother, turning her to face the front. The second Anyaet's eyes landed on Bel, she squealed happily.

"BEEF!"

"Beef?" everyone except Lilith and the healers asked in unison.

Anyaet reached for Bel, a big gummy grin, complete with two new teeth, lighting up her chubby little face. "Beef, Beef, Beef!"

"It's as close as I could get her to 'Beleth.' If it makes you feel any better, she calls Melchom 'Mum-Mum.'" Lilith handed Anyaet to Bel and kissed his forehead, ignoring his confusion. "How are you feeling, sweetheart?"

"She's *talking* already? And I'm fine. Why did you go with Beleth? Bel is so much easier for the little ones to say."

"I wanted her to know her siblings' proper names. I had a picture of you laminated so she could carry it around and not forget you, so you've been Beef for a while now."

"Beef!" Anyaet agreed, reaching for the little spikes on Bel's chin. He caught her little hands before they could make contact and wiggled her fists, making her laugh.

"Bel," he told her. *"Bel."*

"Beef," Anyaet said happily.

Greg snickered.

"I'm not the one being held captive by a cat," Bel shot over his shoulder. "Anya, say 'Bel,' it's easier."

"Beeeeeeefff," Anyaet cooed.

Bel resigned himself to his beefiness, exchanging a conspiratorial glance with Sharkie. "Anya, how about Sharkie? Say 'shar-kee.'"

"Sha-we!" Anyaet said, eyes bright.

Bel exchanged a look with Sharkie, who nodded. "I'll accept it."

"Beef," Bel muttered darkly, then looked between his mother and the healers. "Please tell me I can get up sooner than you originally estimated."

"Not a chance," Lilith informed him, leveling him with a look that had even Lily feeling chastised.

"Given the severity of your injuries when you were brought in, sir, we feel that even with an additional healing session, you should remain in bed for at least another four to five days," the male healer said.

"Four to five—" Bel burst out.

"Beleth," Lilith said sternly.

"Beef," Anyaet mimicked her mother's tone.

Lily coughed and found a spot on the floor that was *tremendously* interesting all of a sudden. *Do not laugh. Do not laugh.*

Lilith shook her head. "You sound like Asmodeus, who is also arguing with perfectly reasonable *advice*. It's like you're racing each other to see who can get out of bed the fastest."

"Dad," Sharkie said confidently. Then seemed to consider it. "I mean, probably."

The healer cleared his throat. "You need time to recover, not only from your injuries, but from the toll that being healed has had on your body. As long as you cooperate, after bed rest for another four days, you can start easing back in to your usual activities. We'll trust you to know the limits of your own body at that point."

Lily looked up from the floor, knowing how hard that would be for Bel to take. Asking him to lie low, especially at a time like this, was like asking a bear to relax in a cat carrier. During berry and salmon season.

Lounging in bed for hours was not his thing.

Shit, they barely even had sex in beds. When the mood struck, they were seldom patient enough to find a mattress. Any horizontal surface would do. Or vertical, really. She rubbed at her cheek, hoping it wasn't too red.

"When can I get my ear re-inked?"

"As soon as you are off bed rest," the female healer said.

"What am I allowed to do on bed rest?" Bel asked, catching Lily's eye with a gleam she knew all too well.

She ignored the swoop of heat and arched an eyebrow at him, shooting a pointed glance at Sharkie and *his mother*.

"You can move under your own power to the bathroom, you can shower, you can spend time on the couch, do things that you normally do when you're relaxing. Nothing physically strenuous, of course."

"Uh-huh."

"Not that," Lilith said smoothly. Knowingly. She fixed Lily with a look.

Lily shrugged, aiming a smug grin at a glowering Bel. "I already told him I have standards he's not medically cleared to meet."

This is payback for edging me for two days that one time.

Out of the corner of her eye, Greg twitched and whipped his head to the window, but not fast enough to hide the entirety of his shit-eating grin.

"But medically able to," Bel put in.

"No," Lilith said.

"Yes."

"I think not."

"I think—"

"BEEF!"

"Thank you for your contribution, Anyaet. Clever girl," Lily said cheerfully. Anyaet cooed at her in delight. Bel scowled.

"So . . . are you not allowed to play *Invaders* because it stresses you out, or what?" Sharkie asked.

A wheezing sound came from Greg's direction.

"Something like that," Bel said mutinously.

The next day, Bel lay on his stomach while Lily read *Pride and Prejudice* aloud, his wing stretched over her legs like a leathery heated blanket, tail curled firmly around her calf. He traced lazy patterns over her bare thigh with his fingertips, listening with his eyes closed. Greg had gone back to work, and Sharkie had declined their offer to stay home from school; there was a guest speaker that she was incredibly excited about.

Lily treasured all her moments with Bel, but she found herself oddly fond of the quiet ones in particular. Moments where they both got to just *be*.

So far, he was the picture of cooperation. The combination of his desire to get the fuck out of bed and his desire to beat Asmodeus to the finish line of health had quashed most of his rebellion.

Most.

Lily poked him in the shoulder and called him "Beef" every time his fingers crept under the hem of her shorts and grazed the edge of her underwear. His hand would scoot right back down to the relatively safer skin of her middle thigh.

Her phone buzzed on the nightstand, and she leaned over to retrieve it, tapping the screen.

"Hey, Sariah, Bel's here. You're on speakerphone. How's it going over there?"

"He's feeling well enough to be ornery, so I'm oddly thankful for that. How are you doing, Bel?"

"I can't believe I'm saying this when I have Lily in it with me, but I want out of this fucking bed."

"Does it run in the family, do you think? Or is this just a warrior thing— *Get back in bed!*" Sariah snapped.

Asmodeus's voice rose from the background. "What are you doing on the phone? You should be focused on labor right now!"

"Are you in labor?" Lily and Bel blurted in unison, exchanging wide-eyed glances. Bel rolled to the side and sat up, hunching over Lily and the phone as if he could peer through it. Lily shivered at the loss of her "blanket" and leaned against his chest.

"No, I'm not in labor— *ASMODEUS!* Get. The Fuck. Back. In. Bed. Or you will never see me naked again."

Asmodeus grumbled something incoherent, and there was a muffled *whump* of a body landing on a mattress.

"Thank you. Anyway, no, I'm not in labor. I'm one day past my due date, which happens during pregnancies all the time, and *somebody* is using it as an excuse to ignore the advice of medical professionals."

"To be fair, Sariah, of the excuses he's come up with in the past, it's not bad," Bel rumbled.

"This is true."

"Sariah," Asmodeus said earnestly in the background, "Bel's fine. You know who isn't fine? Our child. All squished up in there. I heard that certain things can kickstart labor, and listen, baby, I'm already in bed—"

"Asmodeus."

"For the good of our child—"

"Asmodeus!"

"Can you at least take off your bathrobe?" His tone was cajoling. "You're *so* beautiful . . ."

Bel buried his face in Lily's shoulder to muffle his laughter, his whole body shaking.

"Stop, I'm gonna lose it," Lily breathed, covering the beginnings of her giggles with a hand.

"When our child is born, do you know what the first thing I'm going to tell them is?" Sariah said sweetly. "That we love them. The second thing is going to be an explanation of why their father is *chained to the bed*."

"Aw, baby, they won't need to know the details of their conception—"

Lily dropped the phone in her lap and muffled her laughter with both hands. Bel wiped at his eyes—

Then he snorted.

Lily doubled over, half flopped across Bel's legs, laughing so hard her stomach ached. Bel's deep laugh rolled through the room like thunder, a glorious counterpart to her higher tone, right up until Lily choked on her own spit trying to breathe and set them off again.

Dimly, Asmodeus and Sariah continued their bickering, Sariah laughing at them. Bel lay against the headboard and pulled Lily back against his chest, trying to stem the hysterics. She leaned her head against his shoulder, trying to take deep, shuddering breaths, feeling lighter than she had in days.

"Where's the . . ." Bel tried, and his deep giggle nearly set her off again. "Where's the phone?"

Lily patted around the blankets until she came up with it, leaning back against him and holding the phone up for both of them to hear.

". . . how much do they really know anyway?" Asmodeus said.

"You don't trust them to give you medical advice, but you trust them to birth our child?"

"Okay, yeah, I see your point, but that's different—"

"Azzy," Bel said, only laughing a little.

"Hey, Bel, good to hear you, man. Hey, have you apologized to Lily for the fact your voice goes deeper than your—"

"*I will chain you to the bed and birth this child on the street.*"

"Never mind!" Asmodeus said with too much enthusiasm. "Totally kidding, Lily, he's the deepest guy around. Go, Beef."

"We're hanging up," Bel grumbled, reaching for the phone.

"Wait!" Lily said, holding it out of reach. "Asmodeus?"

"Yes, O Lady of the Hellp Desk?"

"Did they give him medication but not me?" Bel muttered.

"Just so you know," Lily said with a smirk, "Bel's going to get cleared to go back to normal before you. Because he's been behaving."

There was silence on the other end of the line.

Then an indignant: "I think the absolute fuck not."

Bel leaned over, taking the phone from her. "It's true. I've entered my era of cooperation, and I'm going to kick your ass. I'll visit you."

~~~❧~~~

54

DEATH BY REVERSE STRIPTEASE

Lily

Bel's era of cooperation lasted all of one day before the irrationality of boredom set in.

Lily ran up to the Hellp Desk to check in on the gate demons and the surprising number of fill-ins from Level Nine, and went to Paradise to visit Carlton. She grabbed coffee from Common Grounds as a treat, reveling in the lightening atmosphere in the Universal Hallway. It was tinged with grief, and perhaps always would be given the losses, but it felt . . . hopeful. Just like she did.

She pushed open the door to Bel's bedroom—their bedroom, he insisted—coffee cups in hand, to find him lying flat on his back, limbs akimbo, tail twitching, staring intensely up at the ceiling. The bulge at his groin tented the sheets and made her mouth water.

Down, girl.

He lolled his head to the side and stared at her with a heated gaze she felt like a caress.

"Sit on my face." The order, given in that dark tone, with his deep voice, had moisture gathering between her thighs. She could picture it. Hell, she could imagine how it would feel, and it had been so long . . .

Near-death experience. Healers. Not cleared for sex.

"I think not. I got you a matcha chai," Lily said lightly, hyperaware of her body with every step she took toward the bed, fine muscles fluttering low in her belly. Gods, her breasts felt so *heavy*, she'd never been more aware of them in her life. Any of her lives. Falling in love with a hot-ass demon who fucked, well, like a demon, followed by more than two months of celibacy had her feeling like a woman in a shitty romance novel written by a man who thought breasts were their own characters.

"Thank you, I appreciate it. It's not technically sex."

Lily set the cup down on the side table, standing just past his reach. "'C'mon baby, just the tip, it won't even count,'" she mimicked.

"Ride my face," Bel said again, eyes darkening.

"Nah." *Yet.*

"It's medicinal."

"Is it really."

"One way to find out."

"Or," Lily said, taking a step back and sipping from her cup with a casualness she didn't feel in the slightest, "we don't do that, and you get to get out of bed possibly tomorrow or the day after."

"I'll lie very still," Bel promised, eyes running leisurely down her body.

Fucking liar.

He was never still when he went down on her. She'd seen him grinding himself into the mattress, making little thrusts like he couldn't help it, like he couldn't wait to thrust into *her*. And if he didn't have anything to grind against, like that time in the shower, he had his fist pumping leisurely around his erection, enjoying himself, biding his time . . .

For fuck's sake, Lily.

"What about beating Asmodeus?" Lily threw out almost desperately.

"Fuck Azzy. He can have it. Consider it a 'congrats on having a baby' present."

She was saved by a knock on the door. Bel sat up with a curse, bringing his knees up to hide the evidence of his arousal and reaching for his latte.

Lily opened the door for Lucifer, Lilith, and two other important-looking demons. She smirked over her shoulder at Bel, who looked remarkably composed given their prior conversation, except for a slight stain of color along his cheekbones.

"I hope you don't mind, but we'd like to have a quick meeting," Luci said.

Bel gestured them toward the assortment of chairs that had made their way into his room with various visitors. Lily took the opportunity to bow out, citing her genuine desire to spend some time at the Hellp Desk.

Bel shifted his bent legs on the bed and sent her out the door with a look that was molten.

The next day, Bel scowled at her around the fogged-up glass panel of his shower. Lily envied the water droplets trailing over his skin. She wanted to catch each one of them with her tongue.

She perched on the counter next to the sink, sipping her coffee from a shop not far from Bel's house and enjoying the torturous show of him in the shower.

"You didn't even come cuddle," he said accusingly. Then, softer, "All you had to do was say no, and I would have dropped it."

She'd slept in one of the guest rooms the night before. Well, "slept" was a generous term for tossing and turning most of the night, trying not to make bad decisions.

"That's the problem, big guy. I didn't *want* to say no. I always want you."

Bel grunted, loading up a washcloth with body wash.

Lily wetted her lips and watched the bubbles run down his solid abdomen. "Just like I really want to join you in that shower right now. But—" She sighed, the hormonal part of her brain vaguely disgusted with the rest of her. "I want you healthy more. *Then* I want you to fuck the common sense out of me so we never have this conversation again."

"I like your common sense, though. It's part of what makes you *you*," Bel said, turning into the shower spray.

Lily bit back a pathetic whimper of appreciation. She'd always appreciated guys with nice backs, but adding wings and all the muscles required to support him in flight? Delicious.

And then there was his ass . . .

"Are you objectifying me?" he teased as he turned to face her again.

"Mm." Lily sipped her coffee, pointedly appreciating the way his thick thighs flexed with each motion, drawing her attention to that beautiful cock of his. It started to harden under her gaze.

"Now see what you've done," Bel said with a half grin, ducking back under the water. "It thinks it's playtime. I'll be half hard all day."

"I've been wet for you since yesterday," Lily said mildly. Bel whipped around, looking almost pained. "We're suffering together."

Bel shook his head, a smile playing over his lips. "As long as we're together, princess." He twisted his arm to scrub at his back, shadows creeping into his eyes again. "I'm glad . . ." He trailed off, silently rasping the washcloth over his body for a few moments before turning to put the suds under the spray.

"You're glad what?" Lily asked softly.

He was quiet, the lines and details of his massive body obscured by the steamy glass, but she could tell he was motionless, the long, inky strands of his hair plastered over his shoulders, back, and chest.

"I'm glad the scars don't bother you," he said quietly.

Lily set her cup on the counter and slid down, the tile warm under her bare feet as she padded to stand in the opening of the shower. Bel looked up from where he'd been staring at the wall, looking young and old and vulnerable and fierce all at once. He stepped out of the spray and stood in front of her, their chests almost touching. She tilted her head back to look at him, loving how tall he was.

She took his hand, threading their fingers together. "You've always had scars, Bel. They're just markings on your skin, mementos of a life lived, just like tattoos. They're a part of you, but they're not the sum of you." She searched his eyes. "Do they bother you?"

His free hand ghosted over a newly healed patch on his side, lingering, before it dropped. "No." His tone was soft. "Do you miss your scars?"

Lily blinked, almost rocking back at the immediate answer that sprang to her mind. "I do," she said, "very much. The stupid ones, the ones I gave myself, the ones I was lucky to walk away with. They were mine."

She pressed her lips to the center of his chest and gazed up at him. "Just like you are."

He dipped to kiss her softly. "And you're mine."

She smiled.

He kissed her again, more firmly this time, then brushed his lips over hers, whispering, "Thank you." He glanced down her body and winced. "Sorry, princess, I got you all wet."

Lily stepped back, arching an eyebrow in the way she knew drove him crazy. "I told you, I've been that way since yesterday, big guy. It keeps being your fault."

He huffed a laugh, returning to his shower.

Lily crept into the bedroom and dug into her bag, pulling out the outfit she'd planned for this kind of day, along with Carlton's parting gift, and headed back into the bathroom. She pulled her sleep shirt over her head and let it drop. Bel turned. Then wiped a clear spot on the glass.

She shimmied out of her shorts, kicking them to the side with a flourish. Bel was motionless. She reached for Carlton's gift and shook it out.

Bel groaned. "Lily . . ."

The deep purple bodysuit was completely sheer. Mesh in places, iridescent lace in others, vaguely obscuring certain places, while artfully placed seams emphasized other ones. It skimmed up her body, the fit immaculate. She carefully settled the straps on her shoulders, making sure her breasts rested in the cups to best effect.

Bel leaned around the glass to see more clearly and groaned. "Princess, my cause of death is going to be 'reverse striptease.' The healers are going to keep me in bed for another month because they'll think I'm dying of something other than sexual frustration."

Lily stepped into the floaty, short, black skirt and worked it up her legs. "Consider this your incentive to think healthy thoughts. What do you think, shirt or no shirt?"

Bel's hungry expression dropped into a murderous look of *are-you-kidding-me?*

"Shirt," he growled.

Lily licked her lips at the thrill that growl sent through her, reaching for the tight, black, V-necked T-shirt and pulling it over her head, tucking it in.

She gathered up her discarded clothes and turned for the door.

"What about hair and makeup?" Bel asked, hanging half out of the shower. She knew he adored watching her do her makeup, even though, when she wore eyeliner, she'd get frustrated with it half the time.

"You know, it's pretty humid in here and not the best conditions for that. I'll just do it in the break room. The final look can be a surprise." She grinned.

Bel hung his head dramatically. "Lily, the healers won't be here until at least *noon*."

She spun on her heel and walked over, careful to avoid the water dripping off of him, giving him a quick peck and smiling brightly. "I know. Think of the anticipation."

He pouted. "You're mean."

She laughed as she headed for the door. "You love it."

"I really do," she heard him say warmly before she closed the door.

Bel

It took every ounce of willpower not to squirm as the elder female healer settled her hands on his shoulder, sending the radiating warmth of her power coursing through his body, testing and prodding as it went.

Lucifer, far more well rested than he'd been when Bel had last seen him, sat in a nearby chair and watched the proceedings while giving updates on the situation.

The funeral pyres would be lit in three days, allowing time for the families to conclude their private services and rites, and for the most injured of the survivors to heal enough to attend. The rift had been sealed so completely that there was no evidence of it, save for the scarred pocket realm where the battles had taken place and the thousands upon thousands of enemy dead that lay there. Their bodies wouldn't rot; they would simply dry out and eventually fade from existence. As for the pocket realm itself, the heads of each realm were in agreement to petition the Universe to close it off and seal the entrance, leaving the filled-in archway as a memorial to those who had lost their lives there.

"When?" Bel asked, eye twitching as the healer's power prodded the tender area at his side.

"Not for some time. A month, at least, in order to respect the rite of mourning."

The rite was nothing official, nothing required of anyone, but it was common practice among not only the warriors and warrior families of Hell, but the whole Afterlife. To go in peace to a place that had been one of war and remember. Why they'd fought. The fallen. The living. What they'd lost and what they'd gained.

"Are you going to ask Lily to go with you?" Lucifer asked, propping a foot on his opposite knee.

Bel glanced at the healer, seeking some kind of sign that her perusal of his health would be over soon, or at least that it was going well. Nothing. Her expression was serene, the healing energy prickling through his body.

"I . . . don't know. There are things on that battlefield that I don't want in her head. It's bad enough that they're in mine."

Lucifer seemed to choose his words carefully. "Given her work at the Hellp Desk, I doubt the blood will bother her. She's not exactly . . . unaccustomed to violence. And the bodies will be mostly, if not completely, dry by then."

"Well sat, sir," the healer told Bel warmly, lifting her hands. "As I'm sure you've felt, you're not quite back to full health, but I feel comfortable releasing you from bed rest and allowing you to use your discretion as to your own physical limits."

Bel threw the covers back—he'd pulled on a pair of boxer briefs in anticipation and out of the desire to not flash some poor healer—and swung his legs over the side of the bed, planting his feet on the rug.

"However," the healer's voice grew firm, and the look she fixed on him was so similar to his mother's pay-fucking-attention expression that he froze, "freshly healed is not fully healed, as you are well aware. You do have greater limitations than you otherwise would. I understand that this will be annoying to you, but I ask that you respect that. If you don't, you'll end up right back in this bed."

Like fuck he would. They'd have to catch him first.

He nodded respectfully and thanked the healer for her time as she headed for the door. The second the door clicked shut behind her, he strode into his closet.

"So will you ask her?" Lucifer called, resuming the conversation.

Bel yanked his pants up to his thighs, pausing to thread his tail through the hole at the back. "She'd probably handle the gore just fine," Bel admitted, pulling his pants up the rest of the way. "It's the creatures I'm worried about her seeing."

"She handled the gegony and chittahi just fine," Lucifer said.

Bel huffed a laugh, reaching for one of his casual athletic shirts. "Of course she did—" He stopped, the meaning and *implication* of what Lucifer said filtering through his brain.

He lurched out of the closet, gripping the door frame in one hand while the other crumpled the shirt. "When the *fuck* did she see a gegony *or* a chittahi?"

Lucifer's eyebrows arched, realization dawning across his angular face before his eyes gleamed. "During one of the final attacks, a single gegony and chittahi broke through the lines and made it all the way into the Universal Hallway. My understanding is that Lily was getting coffee at the time and was one of the first to realize something was wrong. She ended up taking refuge inside Heaven's arch. The gegony passed by and was killed by some of ours, but the chittahi . . . Well, it was taken care of by our lovely Lily. With the very sword you gave her, actually."

"She WHAT?"

55

❦

REMEMBER THAT

Bel

The elevator door dinged with disgusting cheerfulness as it settled on the gate floor, and Bel half shoved the doors open in his hurry to get by.

Getting coffee.

Of course she'd been getting coffee. Of course she'd beheaded a fucking chittahi. Of course she'd given God a piece of her lovely, wicked, wise mind.

She didn't even give herself a break afterward.

No, Lucifer had informed him that she'd brainstormed and coordinated the temporary modification of the gate process in order to better support the wounded and their families.

And *then* held her vigil over him that very same day.

He marched out of the tunnel with singular focus. A young demon pressed themself to the wall as he approached, watching him storm by with wide eyes.

There. Standing behind her desk, talking to Crocell and Krun without a care in the world. As if she didn't have naughty lingerie on under her plain skirt and shirt, as if she hadn't edged him for days as an incentive to behave and get healthy, as if she hadn't beheaded a monster from another Universe and *failed to fucking mention it.*

Crocell and Krun saw him coming. Crocell's eyebrows nearly hit his hairline at the same moment that Krun's expression dropped into a knowing smirk. Lily, noticing the direction of their stares, started to turn toward him a moment too late.

He bent and wrapped his arms around her legs, bracing his shoulder near her ass and lifting her straight up. She flailed for balance, sitting back on his shoulder and grabbing one of his horns to steady herself. He turned without a word and headed toward the stairs to the Universal Hallway.

She laughed. "Bel, what—"

"I can't throw you over my shoulder, otherwise your skirt will flip up and show everyone your pretty ass, so this is how it's going to be."

"I can walk!"

"Your legs are too short," he growled, taking the stairs two at a time.

She grabbed both of his horns as they lunged upward. "Never heard that one before." She chuckled, wiggling a bit. "Obviously, you're off bed rest, but maybe you should put me down and take it easy, big guy."

Bel's grip tightened on her silky legs. "There's nothing easy about the way I'm about to take *you*, so consider this a warm-up."

He strode out of the arch, ignoring the stares aimed their way. The Hall seemed to be decently busy, if a bit somber. He set Lily down, careful that his shoulder didn't flip her skirt up as he stood. She spun to face him, and he scooped her into a much more secure hold and launched them into the air so fast that, even if he'd somehow missed securing part of her skirt, no one would have been able to see anything anyway.

Lily gasped, throwing her arms tightly around his neck for just a moment before she got over her shock. He leveled out, pouring all his effort into speed, dimly noting the muscles that still ached. The people and arches below them blurred.

Good.

The first shake of her body snapped him out of his single-minded focus on getting her to Paradise, and he slowed.

Shit. Was he being too rough? Was he scaring her?

Lily's laughter bubbled over, and she threw her head back, auburn hair flying in the wind, laughing so freely and joyously that he felt like he could fly without wings. She curled into him, kissing along his cheek to nip at his earlobe.

He flew faster.

She pressed her cheek against his, watching where they were going, fingers playing with the collar of his shirt. There. *Finally*. The Paradise arch loomed. Bel dipped, not bothering to check his speed, even though his wings were beginning to properly ache. *Limitations are for later.*

Lily went a little stiff. "We're landing, right?"

Bel adjusted the angle, making minute calculations that were second nature after a lifetime of flight.

"Oookay," Lily said, her voice a little higher than normal, her fingers going still on his collar.

At the last moment, he folded his wings, and they skimmed just a few feet below the highest part of the arch, the pristine white stone whipping by in a blink. He flared his wings and angled gently downward, adjusting to the left when he spied a familiar round door. The landing was as gentle as he could make it, but it still jarred his body and jostled Lily ever so slightly in his arms.

He set her down and immediately grabbed her hand, towing her through the door and across the lawn. A cool, lovely, sunny day greeted them, the grass damp underneath their shoes. Beautiful—and irrelevant. Outside was not where the bed was. Or the mirror. He had plans for both.

Bel shouldered the door open, kicking it shut behind them and made it all of two steps across the entryway before the house shimmied and groaned in delight. He patted a wall, making a beeline for their bedroom.

"Good to see you too, buddy. We're a little busy right now, so maybe go chat with other houses for a bit."

He ushered Lily ahead of him and heard Carlton's faint rumble of what he hoped was assent before he slammed the door and pushed Lily up against it, taking her mouth with feverish intensity.

She tasted like sweetness and coffee and life and *her*. He wanted to sink into it, weave it into his veins, never be apart from it again. He ignored the bitter tang of fear at the reminder that Lily might not always be with him and kissed her more deeply, slicking his tongue along hers, cradling her face, growling when she nipped at his lower lip and ground her hips against his.

The angles didn't quite line up, and that was just fucking unacceptable. Gripping her thighs, he hoisted her up and pressed his cock against her core, separated only by his pants and the flimsy lace of her bodysuit. She gasped into his mouth. He released one of her thighs and held her throat firmly but without any real pressure, her dazed eyes snapping open to meet his.

"You beheaded a fucking chittahi and *didn't tell me about it*," he growled, barely an inch between their noses. He could see every striation of her hazel eyes, the minute widening of them at his words, could practically listen to that mind of hers going to work.

"Heard about that, did you?" she asked breathlessly, a smile flickering over her reddened lips, even as her eyes searched his, calculating, assessing. Her breathing steadied a bit as she pulled herself together, her slender hand smoothing up his back from where she'd dug under the collar of his shirt to cradle the back of his neck. "Are you mad?" she asked softly, thumb stroking over his skin. "Is that what this is about?"

"Mad?" Bel rumbled, pinning her back against the wall and holding her up with his body. He shifted his grip to her lower jaw, and the flicker of vulnerability in her eyes made his heart ache. "You stood in the archway of Heaven—which I know how you feel about—saw a gegony, beheaded a chittahi with the sword I gave you, then turned around and gave God—who I also know how you feel about—a piece of your mind. And then you haven't stopped doing incredible and thoughtful and loving things since, and you think I'm *mad*? Princess, I'm so fucking proud of you I could burst."

Her soft inhale was a thing of beauty. The tension in her body seeped away, her fingers digging into the back of his neck, holding him closer.

He tilted his head, not bothering to hide his intensity. "Always have been, always will be." He kissed her, hard. "So fucking proud of you," he murmured into her mouth. Bel broke away to kiss down her neck, scraping his fangs as he went and making her arch against him. "Admittedly, I'm not thrilled that *you* didn't tell me any of this."

"You were supposed to be healing," Lily breathed, grazing her nails over his biceps. "I didn't want you to freak out. I was going to tell you once you were cleared."

He felt her swallow hard, throat flexing under his lips, and raised his head to study her again. "I'll accept that. I'm cleared. Anything else I need to know?"

"My safe word is *Kennedy*."

There she was.

Bel's grin felt wicked, and so did he, heat sparking through his blood, every filthy, depraved thing he'd ever wanted to do with this woman springing to the forefront of his brain.

"Bratty princess," he growled, circling her neck again and brushing his lips teasingly over hers. Her eyes lit up with the challenge. "*So* fucking proud of you. I want you to tell me the whole story in exquisite detail later. You know how proud I am of you, right?"

"Yes." She tried to capture his lips, but he stayed just out of reach, pulling back to make solid eye contact with her as he gave a slow roll of his hips.

"You know how much I love you?"

"Yes," she breathed.

"Good." He turned to drop her on the bed, following her down before she could even bounce. He caught her laughter with his mouth, losing himself in the play of lips and teeth and tongues until he broke away for air. "Remember that, princess. Because I'm about to fuck you like I don't."

Lily

Bel yanked her skirt down, tugged her shoes off, and had her shirt halfway up her torso with a speed that made her breath catch. She sat up to free the bunched fabric, and he sent it flying across the room. His hands were warm and rough as they landed on her thighs, smoothing upward until he gripped her hips, and then she was being lifted, flipped over, and shoved across the bed.

She got up onto her hands and knees, glancing over her shoulder in time to see him kick free of his pants and prowl across the bed, eyes gleaming. He came over her like a beast, pressing her upper body down to the mattress with most of his weight, his cock sliding over her inner thigh, leaving a trail of dampness in its wake. One arm braced on the mattress to keep from crushing her. His face buried in the juncture of her neck as his free hand slipped around her hip and down her belly, his fingers dipping under the lace to find her slick and wanting as he teased her with the barest of touches.

Yes, yes, yes. Missed you so much.

"I remember your little list of fantasies, princess. I've been thinking about them for months. So, here's what I'm going to do," he growled into her ear, holding her still as two of his fingers slid deep, easing some of her emptiness but not nearly enough. "You want primal? I'll give you primal. I'm going to mark you up just like you wanted, and I'm going to play with this pretty little ass, maybe even use my tail to do it."

She clenched on his fingers, scrabbling in the blankets to push back against him, seeking more—always more with him. Immediately.

His cock was *right there*. She nearly hissed in frustration.

Bel chuckled darkly and bore down on her with more weight. "I'm not done, greedy girl."

Not done? She was about to come from his words alone. How the fuck was he not done?

"Go on," she murmured. He shifted his forearm that had been braced on the mattress, bringing his hand over to capture her jaw and lift her head, forcing her gaze forward. Into the mirror.

Oh.

"I'm going to make you come apart for me, princess," Bel growled, holding her gaze in the mirror, "and you're going to watch while I do it."

The pleasured tension that had built in her core with every lazy pump of his fingers and every word out of his filthy mouth jolted right to the edge of a climax at the sight of them in the mirror.

His wings were flared slightly, the gleaming talon at the apex glinting along with his horns in the cool golden light. He was every inch the battered demon prince—beautiful, all muscles and scars and barely leashed power, and she *adored* it. Her own reflection showed flushed cheeks, kiss-swollen lips, and eyes gleaming with excitement.

His claws pressed ever so slightly into her jaw, angling her head to allow him better access as he licked and nipped his way up her neck to rake his teeth over the shell of her ear. She shivered.

"Is there any part of that you have a problem with?"

His thumb flicked over her clit, once, twice, drawing the entirety of her focus to the brink of ecstasy she was so close to plunging over . . .

His fingers stilled, and she did hiss this time, trying to find any friction, any contact at all to push her over.

"Answer me." Bel's voice was guttural.

"I want all of it," Lily gasped, twisting the blanket in her fists. "Now."

"So bossy." Bel's fingers slipped free of her body, and she almost sobbed at the loss. She'd been so close . . .

His hand moved from her jaw to between her shoulder blades, pushing her upper body back down into the mattress, even as his other hand hauled her hips up. His hand began to slide down her spine, calluses catching on the flimsy fabric of her bodysuit, pulling it taut against her front before it sagged . . .

No, not his calluses.

His *claws.*

The lace and mesh gave way with a faint susurration, the very tips of his claws trailing down her skin with a light sting. He pushed and tugged the fabric away from her body until it tangled around her legs, keeping her from spreading her knees too far apart. Every time she moved to help him, he pressed her down with a firm hand and a deep rumble. He shifted away completely, the sound of her bedside drawer sliding open.

Lily lifted her head to peer into the mirror, confusion melting into a heady throb centered between her thighs.

The bottle of lube was tiny in his hand, and he set it on the blanket with intent precision, like he was staging the scene just so. His eyes caught hers in the mirror, and he slid his hands over her hips with a smirk. She was completely open to him, completely at his mercy.

Habitual insecurity flickered through her mind at the exposure, only to be quickly chased away by the absolute confidence she had in Bel. In herself. In them.

So she stretched her arms forward and arched her back, offering herself to him, preening at his attention, raising an eyebrow as she smiled daringly at him in the mirror. His tail lashed against the pillows.

One hand left her hip, only to come down on her ass with a resounding smack that jolted her forward and stole her ability to breathe properly. Before the pain even registered, his hand massaged her cheek, turning the sting into buzzing warmth.

"That's for not telling me about the chittahi," he said darkly, then repeated the process with the other side.

Lily moaned, pleasure tingling up her spine, inching her back toward the edge of the orgasm that had eluded her.

"That's for taking care of everyone except yourself afterward." A series of spankings and massages followed, until her entire backside was burning with pleasure-pain, and she could see the redness of her skin in the mirror. Still, she lifted her ass for more, needing just one more to go over that edge, but Bel simply bent to nip at one reddened cheek, kissing his way up her lower back, tongue dancing along the lines of her tattoo.

"Bel, please," she almost sobbed, the crescendo slipping away again.

He smiled against her skin and moved away.

Then he reached for the bottle.

She watched him drizzle a line of lube over her ass, but the coolness of it still jolted her as it dripped between her cheeks. His finger, claw fully retracted, caught a dribble and followed it up to circle lightly around her puckered entrance.

Circling and pressing, circling and pressing until he pressed just a bit harder—

She exhaled in a wordless burst of sensation.

It was unfamiliar but definitely not unpleasant, a new type of fullness she certainly wasn't opposed to. She squeezed her eyes shut, letting her head drop, all of her focus on that wonderful new sensation.

Bel tsked disapprovingly, pumping his finger once, then adding more lube and pumping again, working her open. "Eyes open, princess. I know how much you like to watch."

She forced her eyes open, panting and dragging her eyes to the mirror where Bel loomed behind her. She couldn't see exactly what he was doing, but she could see the way his forearm flexed with each movement, movement that she felt down to her toes. His finger eventually eased away, though she moved back, chasing it, begging with a wordless moan for *more*, pausing only when she saw his long, prehensile tail curling around his thigh.

Yes. Yes, yes, yes . . .

"How well did you pay attention when you read those books of mine, big guy?" she asked breathlessly, pushing up onto her forearms to get a better view.

His smirk was wicked. "Guess we'll find out."

Bel flicked the cap of the lube closed and set it aside, fist slicking over the very tip of his tail and making it glisten before guiding it down.

It was blunter and slightly thicker than his finger. She dropped her chest to the twisted blankets, one hand reaching back to claw at his thigh but unable to gain purchase at that angle. It pressed in, hot and thick, stretching without straining, and her body *sang*.

Her climax barreled into her like a freight train, lights scattering across her vision as she gave a wordless cry.

It had been so fucking long, and he was being so delicious and filthy, and his tail tip was in her ass, and it felt so good that she never wanted it to end and yet wanted more, all at once.

She writhed, pushing back, clawing at him, gasping his name. He hissed, scraping his claws down her side, not drawing blood but leaving a sting in their wake, as well as leftover smears of slickness from the lube.

Lily panted through the aftershocks, trying to reorganize her understanding of pleasure and desire around the fullness still in her ass when she felt something hotter and thicker and gloriously familiar being guided between her thighs, his ridged cock thrusting slowly and coating itself in her dripping heat.

"Did I pay enough attention for you?" Bel kissed between her shoulder blades and bit just hard enough to be on the right side of pain.

Lily pushed herself into the bite, rolling her back against his chest, another orgasm already building.

"Good enough," Lily gasped, trying to focus her vision, which was hazy but clearing by the second. "There's always room for improvement, and I'd hate for you to get cocky—"

He filled her in one jarring thrust, the shock and dual fullness of her lower half sending her into another crashing, mind-rending climax. His forehead pressed into her upper back, his ragged breaths hot against her hypersensitive skin as he fought for control, to hold himself still and allow her to adjust as she shuddered underneath him.

"Kennedy?" he asked hoarsely.

"Get fucked," Lily mumbled.

She panted, open-mouthed, caving to the urge to close her eyes and bask in the zips of lighting that seemed to comprise her body. Whatever he had, she could take.

His growl rumbled through his chest, and he withdrew slowly before slamming back home, balls tapping against her oversensitive clit. "I said, *eyes open.*"

Her eyes were open—*were* her eyes open?

She was pretty sure they were, but everything was dancing lights and other irrelevant shit, like walls and blankets—the mirror, she needed to see the mirror. She lolled her head to the side, resting her sweaty cheek against her upper arm, searching in the vague direction the mirror might be.

There. Oh gods, there they were.

And they were glorious.

Bel's eyes held hers in the reflection as he moved over her like a tide, the slap of their bodies joining together and their combined gasps and moans a music of their own making.

Suddenly, he reared back, seizing her around the throat and pulling her up with him, banding his other arm around her to press every inch of her back to his chest as he pounded up into her.

"Look at us, princess. Look at *you*," he half snarled into her ear, his motions shallower at that angle, but his thick, ribbed cock riding over a spot inside her that had her chanting his name like a prayer. He didn't need to tell her to look.

She couldn't look *away.*

His hand that splayed over her belly moved down over her sopping curls. His fingers spread in a V around where they were joined, his rough palm pressing against her swollen clit at the same moment his tail shifted a little deeper into her ass.

Lily tried to climb out of her skin, clutching at his forearm, at his muscular ass as it flexed, driving him deeper.

Too much, it was too much. She'd shatter into pieces, she'd become something else, something new. Her body couldn't handle this much pleasure, she didn't know what would happen—

Bel pressed his temple into her hair, every line of his face utterly feral as he flicked her clit with his thumb.

Lily exploded. Nothing existed before them, maybe nothing would exist after them, who fucking cared. Every nerve ending crackled with energy, sparking and humming and pulsing, the heady image of them in the mirror twined together like colliding galaxies was replaced by snowy whiteness. Nothing else mattered but their pleasure—the heat of Bel's skin against hers, and his shout as he followed her over the edge.

Lily came back to the world in a haze, cheek pressed into the mattress, Bel draped over her like a panting blanket, his face resting alongside hers. He still pulsed deep inside her, but the pressure of his tail was gone. He, like she, was absolutely dripping sweat, his eyebrows furrowed over his tightly shut eyes.

Lily sucked in a full breath. Her body still buzzed, actually felt a little shaky in the best way, but the cataclysmic sexual frenzy had passed.

Bel's eyes opened and he blinked several times, like he also had to reorient himself in his body. Worry sharpened his expression. "You okay?"

She smiled softly, chest full and aching all at once. "Never better. You?"

Bel brushed some of her hair back, pressing a gentle kiss to her lips and settling his cheek more comfortably on the mattress with a smile.

"Now I'm really home."

56

WHAT'S THE MOTTO

Lily

Lily half dozed, running her fingers through Bel's hair. He lay on top of her like a living weighted blanket, the bulk of his body resting between her legs and his cheek pressed to her abdomen, wings flopped carelessly over the bed. Peace washed over them, seeping into her bones.

They'd come together again, the second time slower, and sweeter, re-acquainting themselves with each other's bodies and focused more on the enjoyment of each other than on reaching a climax, but grateful for the gentle climax anyway.

They'd gone to the shower to rinse off and wound up just holding each other under the hot water before drying off and cuddling together on the bed, where they'd been for several hours, judging by the changing sunlight.

Bel was right, Lily thought, tracing her fingers over the newly regrown tip of his ear.

Now we're home.

Something—two somethings—dropped heavily onto the bed, jolting them both upright at the same time. Bel snarled, going rigid as he twisted toward the threat. Lily leaned over to peer past his loose hair.

A tray loaded with fruit, cheese, and crusty bread perched on top of the twisted blankets, and next to it lay Bel's "casual" sword.

Bel's eyes were wide when they met hers.

She shrugged, not sure what else to do. "Thanks, Carlton."

A pitcher of icy water, fogged with condensation, and two glasses appeared on the side table with a thump. Carlton gave a happy little rumble from what sounded like the living room.

"Glad to see you too, buddy. We really appreciate it." Bel reached for the tray warily, glancing up at the ceiling.

Lily pulled the sheets over her lap, eyebrows furrowed. The tray looked delicious, but something about the house's semi-sentient activity in their bedroom felt . . . awkward. Like they'd had a pet watching.

"Have you been here the whole time?" Lily tried to ask neutrally, eyes darting to Bel, who put an undue amount of focus into smearing compound butter on a slice of bread. Lily searched the ceiling, as if Carlton would write its confession there.

What sounded like the whole house rumbled and groaned, but inside their bedroom, not even a board creaked.

"Ah," Bel said, tension seeping out of his shoulders. "Well, thanks for the room service, Carl." He handed her the buttered slice, and she appreciated the scents of fresh bread, herbs, and butter before tearing into it.

The house gave a happy little shimmy before silence fell again and Lily sensed its awareness fading away, like a waiter leaving a table.

"Why the sword?" Bel murmured, slathering butter on another slice of bread.

"I think Carlton is very excited that you're back," Lily said, holding out her slice of bread like a wine glass. "Cheers, big guy."

He tapped his bread against hers. "Cheers, princess."

Just as Lily took a bite, she realized the absolutely golden opportunity that she'd let slip by. "Fuck."

"What?"

"I should've said 'Let's make a toast,'" Lily said in disgust. "How could I miss that?"

Bel shook his head solemnly. "Rye would you turn that opportunity down? You're baking my heart."

Lily grinned. Challenge accepted. "It was pretty crumby of me, I know. It was a no-grainer, and I still missed it."

Bel snorted, fighting for his composure. "Well, at yeast we still have each other."

"I loaf you." Lily giggled. "Even when you're being kneady."

"I loaf you too. You're my butter half," Bel managed to say with a mostly straight face.

The butter and the loaf of bread disappeared from the tray, confiscated by Carlton, and they collapsed into laughter.

They sat in comfortable silence, propped up against the headboard side by side, the half-empty tray resting on their extended legs. Bel had gone quiet while they'd eaten, and she'd noticed him glancing at the sword, a furrow between his brows. Despite the moment of levity, something in the air had shifted. It didn't feel *bad*, just heavy. Lily didn't want to push, giving him the time and space to sort through his own mind, and her patience was eventually rewarded.

"The funeral pyres are in three days," Bel said, gaze distant.

Lily chewed a grape slowly, chest aching, studying his profile, his hands lying limp on the sheet. She knew better than to ask him if he was going, or if he wanted to go. His sense of responsibility would allow nothing else.

She swallowed, reaching for his hand. "What do you need to do, and how can we help?"

He kissed her knuckles and tipped his head back, eyes closing with a sigh, lines of weariness bracketing his eyes and mouth. She reminded herself that he might be physically healed, but his heart and mind were an entirely different matter. The scars on his skin were nothing compared to the ones that scored his soul.

"The healers are the ones who perform the body of the rite. Since it's a military burning, the commanding officer and general of the deceased have a part to play. But since there are . . ." He trailed off, jaw flexing.

"Since there are so many," Lily said softly for him.

He squeezed her hand. "All the generals and remaining officers will be doing it together." He paused, something brewing behind his eyes, but it was gone before she could name it.

"Afterward, I usually pay a visit to the family or families of any of the fallen. But in times like these, we'll hold receiving lines for those who wish to speak with us." Bel opened his eyes, gazing at her. "As for how you can help? Be there. I'll try, but . . . I'm sorry if you have to be patient with me."

"Nothing to be sorry for, Bel. We're there for each other. If you need to cry, I'm here. If you need to vent, I'm here. If you need space, you'll get that too. If you want to talk to someone professionally, there are plenty of therapists on Levels One and Two who specialize in dealing with survivor's guilt and military trauma, and I will support you in that every step of the way. If you need me to show up to your office wearing nothing but peanut butter to keep your head from feeling so dark and inescapable, I will fucking do it." She put every ounce of her love for him into her next words. "Nothing about *us* feels temporary, and things that aren't temporary require effort. I can't do this for you, Bel, but I will do it *with* you, and I am honored to do so."

With every word out of her mouth, Bel's eyes brightened, then the little crinkles at the corners deepened, and finally, toward the end of her speech, he'd smiled. Softly, but he'd smiled, the worst of the nightmares fading from his eyes.

And that was all she cared about.

He pressed a kiss into her hair, murmuring a thank-you and resting his cheek on the top of her head, his powerful body relaxing.

Lily smiled and rested her head on his shoulder, cradling his hand in both of hers. The Afterlife was brighter with him beside her. The colors and scents and sounds even more potent, her own monsters seeming like simple challenges instead of insurmountable obstacles.

"Am I limited to just peanut butter?" he asked quietly.

Lily snorted and turned her face into his shoulder to bite him. He squirmed and chuckled, nuzzling her hair.

"I'm open to suggestions," she said, settling against him.

"Honey?"

Her mind presented her with the intriguing image of Bel lapping drips of golden honey from her breasts, fangs grazing over her skin in the way she adored. She shivered.

"I could do honey. It's a bit drippier than peanut butter, though, so Lev will have a stroke when he follows the trail of drips and catches us being 'unprofessional.'"

"Mm, but either way, we'll be making a mess of my office, and I like honey more than peanut butter."

"Honey it is." Lily grinned, then abruptly remembered her gift and grabbed his thigh. "Oh! Speaking of your office, I have something for you."

She sat up and reached for her side table where she kept a notebook and pen to write down late-night ideas or thoughts. She had no idea where her phone was—probably still at the Hellp Desk—but she'd memorized the phrase just in case.

"Lube?" Bel asked smugly.

"You want to play with my ass in your office, that's more than fine, but my house, my lube. Your office, your lube," Lily said, seizing the notebook.

"Fair."

"So," Lily explained, clicking the pen, "when I was hanging out with some of the partners of your legions for the first time, I saw how powerful it was to be around people who just *understood*. Though you were the first one who taught me that and helped me realize it in the context of our relationship, I realized it on a bigger scale with them. Then I thought about you and how, from a tactical standpoint, understanding is one of the best weapons you can have. Understanding your strengths and weaknesses, as well as your enemy's. That's when it hit me that that could be a great motto for you, even if it was just a sticky note on the door for a week. 'Strength through understanding.' I even got one of the linguists in the Universal Library to translate it into Latin for me." She slid the notebook over for him to see what she'd written.

VIRES PER INTELLECTU

He took the notebook from her and studied it, tracing each letter with the tip of a claw, but was otherwise utterly still.

Suddenly nervous, Lily bit her tongue to keep from babbling about how he didn't have to pretend to like it, and he could tell her she was fifty kinds of sentimental idiot if he wanted to.

The silence stretched, the only sound their breathing. Bel's breathing mostly. Lily was fairly certain she hadn't breathed since she handed him the notebook. Finally, she couldn't take it anymore.

"You don't have to like it," Lily assured him, reaching for the notebook. He held it out of her reach, blinking at her with suspiciously shiny eyes.

Oh.

"I love it," he rasped, setting the notebook carefully to the side. He then moved the empty food tray, cupping the back of her head and kissing her deeply. Every thought eddied out of her head, the twisting worry in her chest replaced with warm, happy buzzing.

"I love it," Bel repeated, kissing down her neck. He threw the sheet off of them and backed down the bed, pulling her with him until she lay flat, trailing kisses between her breasts and over her stomach, the silver in his eyes a thin halo around his blown-out pupils.

Well, then.

Arousal pulsed between her thighs, and she let them fall wide to accommodate his broad body. The calluses on his hands rasped over her hips as he eased downward, nipping at the skin of her lower belly.

"Are you sore?" he rumbled, lifting his head, the furrow back between his thick eyebrows. Lily smoothed it away with her thumb.

"A little," she admitted, then smirked and added, "You did solid work."

His responding grin was unrepentant. "Ah, well, let's see if I can kiss it better."

Bel lowered his head, warm breath fanning over her increasingly sensitive skin—

The front door slammed open with enough force to rattle windows.

"Hi, Carl! I missed you!" Sharkie's excited cry turned them both into statues, staring at each other in mute horror for the briefest of moments before launching themselves off the bed.

"Pants, pants, pants . . ." Bel muttered in a panic, throwing loose blankets back on the bed in search of his long-lost pants.

Lily half fell off the bed, wincing at the thump, scrambling into the closet for something—*anything*. Out of the corner of her eye, she saw Bel yank up his pants and lean his shoulder against the door while he fumbled to thread his tail into the hole at the back.

She almost didn't bother with underwear, but the thwarted moment of intimacy and the resulting dampness had her rethinking that idea. She had no idea if the underwear was on inside out or not, but she hopped and cursed her way into a pair of leggings and reached for a shirt at random, yanking it off the hanger so hard the hanger bounced to the floor.

The door rattled, and her stomach dropped to her toes, but Bel leaned against it with wide eyes and a guilty expression.

"What's wrong with your door?" Sharkie asked, and the doorknob jiggled.

Bel winced, gesturing for Lily to hurry up. "It seems like Carlton is playing a little joke," he lied.

"*Carl!*" Sharkie laughed. "I know you missed Bel, but come on!"

Lily yanked the shirt on. Finding and securing a bra would take too much time, and Sharkie had seen her wander around braless plenty of times before. Bel pointed at the bed, still bracing himself against the door, mouthing, *What do we do?*

Oh shit, the *bed*. They'd destroyed it. The blankets were mostly on the floor, except the ones Bel had thrown back on in his search for pants, and the fitted bottom sheet was completely pulled off one corner. Pillows sat at haphazard angles, and there were very distinctive claw marks on the top sheet.

"Fuck," Lily breathed. *Um* . . . "Carlton!" she whisper-yelled up at the ceiling. "Can you please make the bed? Please please please, thank you so much for the privacy and the food and I'm sorry we're blaming you for not opening the door right now, but I need just this one thing from you, buddy, *please* . . ."

With a soft *whump* the bed was instantly remade, the pillows plumped up and in their proper place.

Lily whirled and kissed the door frame of the closet. *"Thank you!"*

"Good house!" Bel whispered, shifting his weight to move away from the door.

A wad of fabric smacked him in the shoulder as Carlton chucked his shirt at him, and he snagged it before it hit the ground. Lily took over bracing the door with her hands, allowing Bel to pull the sleeveless shirt over his head. She didn't bother giving him time to close the wing flaps but made a show of jiggling the handle before opening the door.

Sharkie lunged forward, wrapping her arms around Bel's middle with an excited laugh. "Papa said you were allowed out of bed! Why didn't you text me?"

There was more than a little accusation in her tone.

"We're sorry, Sharkie. We should have texted you, but something kind of distracting came up and we didn't handle it well," Bel said, hugging her back and shooting a guilty look at Lily.

Shame ate at her. She'd completely forgotten to give Sharkie an update. Sharkie shouldn't have heard it from Luci, but from them, especially knowing how excited Sharkie was to see Bel on his feet. Lily was usually so on top of keeping an open dialogue with her that the failure to do so was all the more jarring.

As much as she felt like a bad parent in that moment, she also knew they'd just made an honest mistake. All she could do was apologize and do better.

"We're really sorry, bug. I know that doesn't change it, but we won't do it again."

Sharkie shifted to keep one arm wrapped around Bel while she blinked up at Lily. "Did you guys get it figured out? Was it one of those monsters again?"

"No," they both hurried to assure her.

"No, there won't be any more monsters like that," Lily said. "It wasn't *that* serious, but we, uh, had to have a serious conversation about our relationship."

"Very serious conversation," Bel said seriously, though Lily saw his eyes crinkle.

Sharkie whipped back toward Lily, horror all over her round face. "Are you reincarnating?"

"No!" Lily said vehemently, then again, more gently, "No. I'm not going anywhere, bug."

Sharkie visibly relaxed. "You talked it all out, though? Whatever it was?"

"Yep."

"Okay, cool. So, what fancy dinner are we having to celebrate Bel being home?"

Lily let herself be swept up in the joyful whirlwind of being with her family for the rest of the day, but something tickled at the back of her mind, like a grain of sand in a shoe.

Bedtime involved Lily and Bel sitting in the hallway outside of Sharkie's room while she snuggled in bed, listening to Lily read a chapter from a fantasy series that Sharkie was obsessed with. Lily and Bel had gone to their newly made bed hand in hand, cuddling naked together just because they could.

Bel had dropped off to sleep before she did. Lily lay in his arms, listening to his breathing, to the rustling of leaves outside their window, and asked herself the question again.

Reincarnation. Did she still even want it?

The logistics side of her decision was easy. The Afterlife had no money, taxes, disease, rape, assault, violent crime. She not only had her own home, she had her own Paradise, with a semi-sentient house that she grew fonder of by the day, as well as a job she enjoyed. Logistically, the Afterlife won by a mile.

But something in the fiber of her being craved *life*.

The dreams she'd held for so long were still dreams, but perhaps they no longer looked the way she'd expected them to. She'd always wanted a family of her own. Now she had one. She'd wanted a loving partner and a relationship built on mutual trust, respect, communication, and affection. She had that too. Children? She had one—one incredibly bright, strong child whose courage and curiosity never stopped awing her.

There was also still a bolt of pain when she thought of being pregnant, having Bel's child, getting to watch them grow up with Sharkie. Ever since the picnic at Lilith's house, Sharkie had talked about siblings, and asked endless questions about what it was like to be the oldest child. Lily had caught her beaming up at the picture in the entryway, head cocked and eyes brimming with curiosity. It'd hurt every time.

But . . . that was new, wasn't it? It wasn't some faceless person she was having children with; it was Bel. It wasn't just torturing herself, wondering what her and Bel's family might grow into, if the impossible was possible; it was being unable to imagine having children with anyone else. There were so many precious milestones that she'd missed sharing with Sharkie, moments that she'd dreamed of: First time rolling over. First steps. First tooth. First word. But when she indulged in that dream, it was with Bel.

She slid a hand up to her chest, resting over where her heart should beat. Such a silly thing, to miss a heartbeat. She hadn't realized how intrinsically important it was until it was gone. She still waited for her heart to skip a beat when Bel gave her a heated look, to pound when a soul yelled at her, to steady when Sharkie hugged her. Yet her silent heart was more filled with love and belonging and joy now than her beating one had ever been.

Being alive was one thing, but she'd fought to *live*, to savor every heartbeat and take in every experience. Life had been difficult and flawed and stressful and beautiful and surprising and glorious. But she'd died. Over and over and over again she'd died young. In painful, sad, tragic ways. But she'd had hope, had dreams.

Almost all her dreams had come true here. In that moment, in Bel's arms, in her Paradise, with her adopted child sleeping in the next room while her beloved cat watched over her, Lily had everything that mattered.

The old soul who had come to the Hellp Desk flashed into her mind, the one who'd lived hundreds of lives and finally been ready to rest. Lily thought of her often, wondering if, someday, she would ever be that wise and kind, wondering what kinds of things a soul could see in hundreds of lifetimes, what things she knew.

"I considered giving it all up to stay and gain just as much. But in the end, living a mortal life felt right to me."

To stay and gain just as much.

Lily hadn't fully understood her then. She did now.

Because the Afterlife felt right to her.

Bel shifted, pulling her back closer to his chest. "You're thinking too hard," he slurred deeply, obviously still mostly asleep.

"How do you know?" she asked the room, moonlight through the curtains giving the room just a hint of light.

"You're stiff. I can feel you thinking. Stop it," he mumbled, relaxing back into sleep.

Lily smiled and rolled over so that they were face-to-face. She studied the stern droop of his mouth, the way his brows had lowered into a hint of a scowl, the line of his cheek and the new scar, warmth suffusing every inch of her body. So unlike she'd expected him to be, and she loved him with her whole heart.

And wasn't that just the best metaphor for the Afterlife?

She smiled softly to herself.

To stay.

To stay.

57

OH, BABY

Bel

Adrenaline pumped through his body, hand reaching for the weapon that should be right next to his cot—

Lily grumbled under her breath, shifting to a more comfortable position before relaxing once more.

Lily.

Home.

Safe.

Bel sucked in a deep breath, held it for a few seconds, trying to steady his racing heart and thoughts, then let it out slowly. He dropped his head back down on the pillow, reaching to settle his hand over Lily's hip, her solid warmth acting as an anchor as he repeated the process until his heart no longer thudded out of control. The morning light was golden instead of gray, but it still felt too early.

The buzzing phone that had jolted him awake stopped, only to resume a couple of seconds later. It was coming from his side table, he realized, rolling onto his stomach to reach for it, blindly tapping on the screen and holding it to his ear.

"What?" he grunted, dropping his forehead onto the pillow.

"Sariah had the baby!" Asmodeus whisper-yelled.

Sariah. Baby. Had—HAD?

Bel's head snapped up, all the residual panic of waking up blown away by his excitement. He pushed himself up to a sitting position. "Really?" He shook Lily, heart racing for a much better reason.

She rolled over, squinting grumpily at him.

"Sariah had the baby." Bel grinned.

Lily bolted up with a gasp, and he put the call on speaker.

Asmodeus's pride and awe filled every word. "Osmodai was born exactly two hours and nine minutes ago, and he looked so gross and so beautiful. Bel, nothing that slimy and squished up should be that *beautiful*, but he's the most beautiful thing I've ever seen. Sariah was a fucking badass. She did so well, birthed a whole baby, and didn't even yell. I married *all* the way up. And she only threatened to kill the healers twice. Mom and baby are both doing great—"

An earsplitting wail cut him off, followed by Sariah's soothing murmur and the unintelligible words of a healer.

"He's not thrilled that the healers took him to get measured. The kid's got some lungs on him," Asmodeus said, and Bel could practically see his cousin beaming with pride. "Sariah and I talked about it, and do you guys want to visit us around noon? I want you to meet your new coolest nephew."

Bel's throat grew tight. He cleared it roughly, only for it to immediately close again. Cousins they might technically be, but he and Asmodeus had always been more like brothers, and he was so proud of and happy for his brother that he could burst. He just couldn't fucking speak. It was more than just excitement that had him speechless, it was the wave of hope that blindsided him.

Lily kissed his shoulder and rested her cheek on it, her hand rubbing soothing circles over his back as she answered for him.

"We'd love to." Her voice was suspiciously choked as well. "Do you guys need anything?"

"Just bring yourselves," Asmodeus said, his voice fading as if he moved the phone away from his face for a second. When his spoke again it was hushed, like he was trying to be secretive. "Actually, can you guys bring Sariah a cinnamon mocha from Common Grounds? No whip. She gave up coffee during pregnancy, but I asked the healers earlier, and it's okay if she has some now."

"Of course we can," Bel rasped, wiping at his eyes with a corner of the sheet. "Do you need anything?"

"I'm good."

"Allow me to rephrase, do you *want* anything?"

There was a beat of silence, then, softly, wondrously, "Bel, I'm a *dad*. I'm here and I'm a dad."

A tear ran hot down Bel's cheek. He got it. After so much horror and pain and grief, it was hard to wrap his mind around the fact that they were home.

He'd had one of those moments the night before, while they'd all been watching a movie after dinner, and Lily and Sharkie had both cried on him. Such a normal thing, in theory, to watch a movie with his new little family, but he'd had a brief moment of wondering if it was real, if he was actually there, relaxing in his sweatpants, holding Lily, holding Sharkie, a cat on his lap, no battles to fight. He'd had to consciously accept that moment, to grieve that such a thing was no longer as easy for him to enjoy as it once had been. Perhaps it had been the sheer brutality of the war that had it affecting him more than previous ones had, or maybe it was because he'd had so much more to lose this time. But he understood Asmodeus's awe at just being alive and here.

Asmodeus had practically burst into flames with excitement when they'd found out Sariah was pregnant. When he'd called Bel, he'd still been so excited that Bel had barely understood a word coming out of his mouth. On every training mission, Asmodeus had a picture of Sariah with her increasing baby bump, and would regale everyone with what fruit the baby was of a comparable size to. He'd doted on Sariah to the extent that she'd let him. He and Sariah both liked to cook, but he'd tried to take over more days, and when the smell of a certain food made her gag, he'd banished it from their house as if it had personally offended him. When Sariah had gotten a craving for that exact food three weeks later, he'd hurried out to get plenty of it. He'd only groused a little bit when some of her cravings resulted in culinary nightmares, like the time she cheerfully stuffed chocolate chips into black olives.

Asmodeus had agonized over finding the softest socks and knit caps in the baby stores. He had, on more than one occasion, dragged a committee of his friends, Bel included, with him to get multiple opinions. They'd made a hilarious picture—half a dozen massive demon warriors, still in their training gear, huddled together among the racks of itty-bitty clothes, arguing over which onesie was of superior quality.

"You made it, Azzy," Bel said. The words too small for what they meant. "Go hold your son and wife. We'll see you at noon."

Shortly after they'd hung up, a picture had arrived of a tiny bundle in a blanket with a scrunched-up face, tiny pointed ears, and wispy, dark hair plastered to his head. The little bumps where his horns would someday grow were barely visible. Osmodai's little face and the single chubby fist they could see were a reddish gray, and his eyes were closed, keeping their color a secret. Bel ghosted his fingers over the screen, awed as he always was at each new addition to their family.

"That nose is all Sariah," Lily murmured warmly.

"Mm, he got Azzy's mouth, though. I love the little newborn cone head," Bel mused, an envious pang shooting through his chest.

At that realization, he glanced over at Lily, knowing how badly she'd wanted that for herself too. Still wanted. She looked up from the screen and met his eyes, confusion flickering across her face before understanding set in.

"It's okay," she said softly. "I'm where I want to be and I'm happy. Are you happy?"

Bel smiled at her, thinking of how Sharkie would have been with younger siblings. "I'm happy." He kissed her forehead. "You would have looked amazing pregnant, though."

Old grief ghosted over her face, and his heart ached for her, for them. Then he watched as she drew on that inner strength that so amazed him.

Her smile went impish. "Well, *obviously*. You wouldn't have been able to keep your hands off me."

"Like I can keep my hands off you *now*?"

She had the audacity to hum doubtfully, taking the phone from him and setting it aside. "The effort I have to put in to get your attention," she tsked, and he smirked, lacing his hands behind his head to wait for the rest. "Breathing in your direction? Objectifying you when you look good? Sleeping *naked*? All you have to do is exist vaguely in my orbit, and I'm off to name a newly formed river."

Bel raised his eyebrows. "Well," he said slowly, scooting down to lie flat. "Breathing in my direction is unnecessary. Just breathing is enough. I can't have all your effort going to waste and making you feel unappreciated. So, here's what I want you to do: Come ride my face."

"Is that all?" Lily asked, already pushing the sheet back and crawling toward him, breasts swaying temptingly. "But I'm breathing *and* naked."

"Ah, yes. Double the effort, double the reward," he murmured, capturing her waist in his hands and laving a nipple with his tongue before giving it a leisurely suck that made her arch and gasp. He released her, skimming his nose up her neck. "I want you to hold the headboard and ride my face. Then I'm going to fuck you—lovingly—until you come again."

He pulled her legs to straddle his head, shifting so that the tips of his horns would press into the mattress and not threaten her thighs. She caught herself, grabbing the headboard with a laugh. He smirked, lightly pulled her down to his mouth and went to work.

True to her word, she was drenched, and he ran his tongue along her in a single sweep from ass to clit, savoring the taste of her. It was a drug, *she* was a drug, and his cock throbbed as he flicked his tongue over her clit, her thighs clenching on either side of his head. Too fucking far away . . .

He gripped her pretty ass with both hands and pulled her *down*. Much better. He teased her entrance with his tongue before stiffening it and thrusting it inside, fucking her with it. Her resulting moan went straight to his cock. He half considered freeing up one of his hands to give it a stroke but reconsidered as she lifted herself up. He needed his hands.

He nipped the inside of her thigh, growling. "Get back down here."

"You need . . . to breathe," she panted above him. "And I don't want to wake Sharkie up."

"Then let's be nice and quiet." He tugged her back down. *More. Always need more.* "And I'll fucking tap if I need to breathe. I want you to come on my face. Now sit."

He lost himself in pleasuring her with his lips and tongue, gauging what made her simply gasp and what made her muffle her cries with a hand. When her thighs started trembling, he nearly came undone. He pumped two fingers deep into her clenching heat, curling them to press against the spot that always made her make one of those breathy gasping cries at the same moment that he sucked her clit, flicking it with his tongue once, twice—

Lily came apart above him, one hand clutching the headboard, the other clamped firmly over her mouth, muffling but not muting the delicious sound of her orgasm. Bel kept pumping his fingers as her slick muscles clenched rhythmically around them, kept working her clit with gentle taps of his tongue, prolonging her climax until she fought to pull herself upward.

He relented with a kiss on each of her inner thighs, lifting her and guiding her to lie on top of him. She pushed herself up to kiss him, no doubt tasting herself as she stroked her tongue along his and nipped at his lower lip. He took a careful fistful of her hair and angled her head back, kissing along her jawline.

He held her close as he sat up, carefully twisted so as not to catch his wings, and rolled her back down, catching her laugh with his mouth. She twined her arms around his neck, pebbled nipples brushing against his chest and driving him even more insane for her, and gasped as he drove into her in one smooth stroke.

The first slide of being inside her always felt like molten lava was surging up his spine. Wet, hot, tight, inside Lily was his favorite place to be. They fit each other perfectly.

Her hazel eyes were dazed when they met his, her pretty lips parted as she panted, a smile curling the corners of her mouth. He braced one forearm on the bed to keep from crushing her, sliding his other hand down the center of her chest, over her navel, slowing as his palm moved over her lower stomach. He imagined it rounding slightly, imagined it growing, full with their child, and his hips pressed him deeper inside her.

He looked up at her, worried that he'd overstepped, made it awkward, made it sad, but saw what he felt reflected in her eyes. She moved a hand between them to cover his.

"I wouldn't have been able to keep my hands off of *you* if I was pregnant," she said with a little smile.

"Like you can keep your hands off of me now?" he sassed, sliding their hands a little lower on her abdomen, pressing just slightly and giving a slow thrust that had both of them catching their breath. Her hand left his, clutching at his hip, pulling him into her.

They found their rhythm, slow and heady, each stroke sending ecstatic pleasure crackling throughout his body. A flush worked its way up her skin, from her chest up to her cheeks, her nails digging into his skin, the little hitch in her breath that always happened right before she came apart around him. She arched up, her body going taut as she buried her face in his neck. He followed her right over the edge, hips stuttering in their rhythm, release crashing through him like a tide, pumping—

The door swung open.

On reflex, Bel dropped flat, intending to cover Lily's nakedness and hide their joining, his wings sweeping out in a mantling gesture. There was an odd croaking noise in his ear, but he barely processed it once he realized who stood in the doorway.

❦

58

THE FLIP SIDE OF THE SEX COIN

Lily

Lily couldn't stop her loud guttural wheeze as Bel's full body weight crushed her into the mattress. No, not just his full body weight. He'd thrown himself downward with *force*, ejecting all air from her lungs in possibly the least sexy noise she'd ever made.

She fought to clear away the decadent high of her orgasm, to think around his bone-crushing weight, the fact that he still filled her, the pulsing of his own climax fading by the moment. She pressed her head back into the pillow, twisting to stare at the door, then immediately wished she hadn't.

Sharkie's face went from blank shock to horror in about a second.

"Are you doing adult stuff?" she asked, words slamming together in her rush to get them out.

Fuck. What was worse? Lying? Telling the truth? There was no good way out of this, was there? *Was there??*

"Just a little," Lily said breathlessly at the same moment Bel said, "I mean, yeah?"

Sharkie's expression went from horror to outright revulsion, followed by a gag that came from her soul. She spun, slamming the door behind her. Another gag sounded in the hallway.

Lily grimaced.

"I didn't hear a knock. Did you hear a knock?" Bel asked, looking down at her. His eyes widened and he pushed upward, guilt written all over his face. "Shit, sorry."

She sucked in a lungful of air that, really, she didn't need, but it felt nice anyway. "I didn't hear a knock either, but then I wasn't listening super hard."

Bel sighed, dropping his head onto the pillow beside hers.

Lily blew out a long breath, closing her eyes. *Oof. Well, sometimes kids walk in on their parents.*

She had when she was younger, and her reaction had been about the same, except she hadn't said anything, just immediately shut the door. Her parents had never addressed it, which hadn't been great, honestly. It'd made her feel worse about it.

They needed to start locking the door. Knocking or not, they'd nearly been caught twice in as many days. She attributed the uninterrupted months before Bel had marched out to a stroke of luck.

Bel lifted his head, silver eyes back to their normal dilation. "So. Breakfast will be fun."

Lily curled into him, smothering her mortified laughter in his chest.

Lily handed Sharkie her cocoa, then poured two mugs of hot water and added a tea bag to each while Sharkie squinted at her. She'd told Bel to grab a quick shower if he wanted and said that she would take care of talking to Sharkie. She thought it might be better coming from her.

Lily steeled herself and tried to deliver her little speech as naturally as possible. "Hey, so I'm sorry you walked in on us while we were having a private moment. It's totally normal to feel uncomfortable seeing that. We felt uncomfortable too. Sex can look and sound a little weird, so I'm sorry if that upset or scared you. We have a lock on our door for a reason, and we should have used it. In the future, let's have a house rule where, if the door is shut, we knock first and wait until we get permission to enter."

She hadn't been blushing and bashful about explaining sex to Sharkie before, but it felt a bit different when she was talking about her and Bel together. Thank *fuck* Sharkie hadn't walked in on them in the middle of celebrating Bel's release from bed rest . . .

"Okay," Sharkie said slowly, moving the melting marshmallows in her cocoa around with a spoon. She seemed to start asking a question and talk herself out of it several times.

"You can ask me anything, bug," Lily said gently.

Sharkie nodded, stirring her cocoa.

Lily swished the tea bag in her mug around a bit, waiting.

"You and Bel do that for fun, right? For the 'because it feels nice' reason, not the . . . other one?"

Oh, Sharkie . . .

One day after school, Sharkie had come home concerned and jittery with a panicky kind of energy that reminded Lily of when she'd first met her. They'd gotten the school version of the sex talk, and while demon school was wonderful for many reasons, it failed to take into account the sole mortal soul in attendance and what mortal ideas and trauma she might have about sex. Demons and denizens of the Afterlife in general had a much healthier attitude toward sex and sexuality than most people in the mortal world. That healthy attitude had caused a lot of confusion and fear for Sharkie.

Lily had explained, pinkie promising the whole time, that there were normal, healthy kinds of sex, like what the school had been talking about. Sex for pleasure, connection, fun. That was what most people had. There were some people who didn't like sex, for one reason or another, people who were on a spectrum of asexuality and people who just preferred not to. Then there was the other kind of sex, the kind that had been warped and twisted, weaponized to hurt people, to exert power in a cruel way. (Lily had figured that power play dynamics in healthy sex and BDSM were a bit much for Sharkie's maturity at that point.) Weaponized sex was what had happened to Sharkie, and to herself, and it was not, and never would be, their fault.

Sharkie had soaked up all that information like a sponge. She usually did when people took the time to explain things properly and had been relieved that there was a positive side to the sex coin.

It made sense that, given the shock of walking in on Lily and Bel, she might need a bit of reassurance and clarification.

"Do you think Bel would want to hurt me?" Lily asked.

"No."

"Do you think I would ever want to hurt Bel?"

"No," Sharkie said, relaxing a bit. "So you do it for fun."

"We do it for fun," Lily confirmed, pulling her tea bag out before her tea got bitter. Bel liked his a bit stronger, so she left his in.

Sharkie huffed a sigh and took a hearty gulp of her cocoa, licking the chocolate mustache it gave her.

She wrinkled her nose. "It seems very messy."

Bel pushing his seed back into her as she lay on his desk. Their combined release dripping down her thighs after she'd ridden him. The way he'd carefully wiped her clean with a damp cloth, just as he always did, after he'd bent her over the bench press in the new home gym.

Lily, thankfully, had only just raised her mug to take a sip, so she was spared the indignity of spewing tea across the kitchen. Even so, her face felt hotter than the magma rivers in Hell.

"It is."

"And noisy. It sounded like you guys were dying in there. Like, again."

"Only one of us in that room has died, and I did so in silence, thank you very much. But yeah, it can be."

"And you *like* it?" Sharkie couldn't have been more disbelieving if she tried.

"We do, but that's a personal preference." Hoping for some relief from the Sharkie Inquisition, Lily decided to offer a new topic of conversation. "Hey, by the way, Asmodeus and Sariah had their baby last night and they want us to visit at noon."

"They *did*? And you didn't tell me that first?!"

Sariah's face went from "happy to see them" to tearful joy when Lily presented her with the cinnamon mocha. She lay in one of her and Asmodeus's guest rooms that had been prepared as a birthing suite, propped up in a nest of pillows that Lily would have bet her Paradise had been carefully and fussily built around her by Asmodeus.

"Oh," she breathed, taking a deep sniff of the steam, "how did you know?"

"Two guesses," Lily said, dropping down into the chair next to the bed.

Asmodeus sat on the couch, his son draped across his bare chest, Bel and Sharkie sitting on either side of him while he talked quietly.

"Not only did I marry the right man, I married up," Sariah said, taking a sip and moaning. "Who cares if he's the reason our kid has a big head."

"Yeah, how was labor?"

"Mercifully, not as long as I was afraid it would be. Nothing went wrong, even though it hurt like a bitch. My mother was right—active labor was the worst part. You're not pushing, you're just contracting, and it doesn't feel like you're getting fucking anywhere, even though you know you are. Pushing I was fine with, because it meant there was a light at the end of the tunnel. Then"—Sariah smiled over at her boys, cradling her coffee—"he was here, the most beautiful thing in the world, and screaming his head off."

Lily followed her gaze to where Asmodeus was carefully transferring Osmodai to Bel's arms, and he looked even tinier than he had with Asmodeus. An itty-bitty tail curled as he scrunched up his little legs, and Lily had to focus to realize that there, plastered to his back, were delicate, filmy little wings, disproportionately small for his body compared to the powerful wings of his father and uncle.

Sariah must have seen her expression and line of sight. "The wings are like that when they're born. They'll unstick from his back in about a week, and then grow to be more proportionate. I knew from talking to the healers about what to expect if he came out with wings, but I still have to keep reminding myself that it's okay." She took another sip. "This mocha tastes like sex."

"See, that's what got you into this position," Lily said dryly.

"Speaking of which, turns out that a lot of the positions that got the baby *in* are the same ones that help get the baby out. Asmodeus thankfully withheld that little observation until after Osmodai had been born."

"Because he wanted to live." Lily chuckled.

Sariah hummed in assent, and they watched Asmodeus show Sharkie how tiny Osmodai's feet were.

"That baby is going to help Asmodeus get through the funeral, I think," Sariah said softly.

Lily tore her gaze away from the scene on the couch. Sariah's features were soft, and her eyes bore a grief that Lily had seen in the other partners of warriors who had been in the recent war.

"He and I will turn to each other as we always have, but Osmodai . . . he'll be a tangible piece of hope, a reminder that there are always endings, but there are beginnings too."

"Lily!" Asmodeus called carefully, glancing sideways at the baby. "Quit seducing my wife with coffee and come meet our son."

"Joke's on you. She knows you put me up to it."

"She's seducing me for you, babe," Sariah added, cradling the cup in both hands.

"Well, then she's doing a shit job of it. Swap places with me, Lily, so I can flirt with my wife properly and tell her what a fine baby she cooked up."

Sariah and Lily rolled their eyes at each other, but Lily rose, bumping Asmodeus's fist as she passed. Bel had stood and was swaying a bit, staring down at Osmodai so tenderly it melted her. Sharkie stood on the couch to keep an eye on the baby, her eyes sweetly curious, a little smile on her mouth.

Lily had asked Bel about people visiting a newborn so soon, but apparently, since they didn't have to worry about germs in the Afterlife, except for occasional colds once they hit adulthood, visitation was based more on the social preferences of the parents and not medical concern.

Osmodai stared up at his uncle with wide bronze eyes, clearly taking after his mother in that regard, though Sariah's were more golden. His little tail was curled around Bel's forearm as far is it was able to go, which, considering Lily needed both hands to wrap the thickest part of it, wasn't all that far. Those bronze eyes blinked in her direction while he yawned.

Lily nudged his delicate little hand with her finger, and he gripped it with surprising strength. Joy surged through her veins. Such a tiny, powerful little life.

"I can't believe I was ever this small," Sharkie said, carefully touching the downy hair on his head.

"You were probably smaller. He's a bit bigger than the average mortal baby," Lily told her, running her thumb over the tiny little fingers gripping her own and marveling as she always did at the teensy fingernails, which happened to be black.

"Really?"

"Mm, I'd say so. Though birth size isn't really an indicator of where you end up. I was on the small end of average for humans when I was born. Then I got tall."

"This may shock both of you, but I was a big baby," Bel said.

"You're still big," Sharkie said.

Lily bit her lip to let that golden opportunity pass.

"Only when I'm not next to someone bigger," Bel murmured, smiling softly at the baby socks with bats on them.

"Which is why, when he gets his ass handed to him in wrestling, it's deeply amusing for me and humbling for him," Asmodeus called across the room.

"What happened to flirting with your wife?" Lily asked.

"We disagreed and it became less flirty and more conversation-y," Asmodeus explained while Sariah shook her head.

"Nothing to disagree over, I'm going. The healers agreed to spend extra time with me—"

"Healing wears you out. Ask me how I know." Asmodeus scowled at her.

"The healers," Sariah said more firmly, "agreed. Frankly, even if they hadn't, I would have gotten someone to carry me there. I'll have a chair for the ceremony and come home early, but I'm going."

"Sariah—"

"If the roles were reversed, what would you do?"

Asmodeus subsided, looking more serious and general-like than Lily had ever seen him. The funeral. That had to be the ceremony in question.

"Lily, if you had *just given birth*, would you, two days later, go to a funeral?" Asmodeus asked in a sweet but deeply misguided attempt to make a point.

"Try to fucking stop me," Lily said. "To be there for Bel when he needed it and pay my respects to those who died to protect all of us? You couldn't keep me away."

Asmodeus exchanged a long look with his wife, who, for all her fire, seemed soft at that moment. She leaned in to say something to him that none of them could hear, and Lily returned her gaze to the baby still gripping the life out of her finger. Bel, his finger held captive by Osmodai's other hand, nudged the back of her hand with his. His silver eyes were searching, quietly intense.

Lily smiled at him. "Try to fucking stop me."

The corner of his mouth tipped up in a smile, then he slid that look to Sharkie, who kept petting Osmodai's little head with extreme gentleness.

"You can try to fucking stop me, but you'd have to catch me first."

59

TO HONOR
THE FALLEN

Lily

It felt odd to slip into the deep purple gown Carlton had provided. It seemed more appropriate for a gala of some kind, but everything Lily had researched—and Bel had confirmed—had told her that color and elegance were not only appropriate, but respectful. Demonic funerals were colorful, yet somber, affairs.

She'd brought the dress from Paradise the day before, hanging it on her side of the closet in Bel's house. His light ceremonial armor had starkly contrasted with his remaining set of combat armor, which loomed on its stand near the back of the closet. Beautiful and deadly, perfectly clean but lightly scuffed in places from use. She'd run her fingertips over one of the scuff marks, giving silent thanks to the armor for protecting him from whatever had made it, heart aching for those whose armor hadn't been able to do the same.

He kissed her that morning as he rolled out of bed but had otherwise been silent as he went to take his shower and get ready. By the time she'd gotten up and headed to the bathroom for her own shower, he was brushing his teeth, a towel slung around his waist. He squeezed her hip when she kissed his shoulder on her way by but said nothing. When she reentered the bedroom, he and his armor were both gone, leaving her to dress alone and worry.

Lily smoothed her hands over the subtly shimmering fabric of her dress, studying herself in the full-length mirror. The high neck of her gown glimmered with ornate embroidery the same shade of silver as Bel's eyes, as did the decorative sweep of fabric that draped over her upper arms, leaving her shoulders and the rest of her arms bare. The fabric skimmed over her body, fitted until it flared gently at her hips, cascading to brush over the floor. The dress was otherwise unadorned, but the elegantly placed seams and the shimmer of the fabric as she moved kept it from looking bland.

She tweaked a piece of her hair, wishing she'd been able to craft a sleeker chignon, and fiddled with one of her long earrings.

"Hey, Mom?" Sharkie lingered in the doorway of their bedroom, toying with a brush.

Lily had told her what she'd learned about the funerals but allowed her to make her own decision about what she wanted to wear. Lily'd assured her that if the now-iconic shark onesie was what would make her comfortable, then she was more than welcome to wear it, but Sharkie had just gone quiet for a moment, then asked if they could go shopping.

They'd found a long-sleeved, dark blue tunic in the demonic style and matching leggings that tucked into black ankle boots. Sharkie had worried that it was too plain, but the shopkeeper, a sweetly understanding man, had offered to stitch a design on it to make it better. The metallic teal thread curled and twined against the backdrop of dark blue, looking a bit like the surface of the sea. Intrinsically Sharkie, but with a Hellish twist.

"Hey, bug." Lily smiled. "You look nice."

"Thanks, you too. Can you braid my hair?" Sharkie held up the brush.

Lily guided her over to one of the chairs and stepped behind it, running the brush through Sharkie's shoulder-length blond hair. "What kind of braid are you thinking?"

"Like the ones you gave Dad before he left, please."

Lily stilled. "I didn't braid his hair today, but if you describe it, I can give it a go."

"Oh, I haven't seen him today. I meant like before he went to war. Dad said they were good luck, and I dunno if we need luck today, but you never know. Better safe than sorry, right?"

"Right," Lily murmured, swallowing hard and willing the stinging in her eyes to subside. Bel had told her how much the braids had meant to him, and the fact that he'd shared the sentiment with Sharkie, as well as Sharkie's logic for wanting them, was unexpectedly touching.

Her fingers only shook a little as she sectioned out Sharkie's hair, modifying what she remembered doing for Bel to suit Sharkie's shorter style. "You've grown up so much, you know. I've always been proud of you, but I'm really, really proud of you for that."

Sharkie waited for her to finish and secure the braid down one side of her head before twisting to grin up at her. "Thanks, Mom. Hariti thinks I'm still short, though."

"You're a mortal soul, not a giant demon, so obviously you might be a bit shorter than them. Hopefully, you won't have as rough a time going through puberty as I did."

"Yeah, so I was reading about that, and it sounds sucky. Do you think it will actually be puberty, since I'm technically dead, or is being dead a cheat code to get the height and maturity without the grumpy-and-acne-and-awkward part?"

"That," Lily said, finishing the braid on the other side of her head, "is a question for either the Front Desk or the librarians at the Universal Library."

"Well, I know what I want the answer to be."

"As someone who went through puberty, I don't blame you." Lily pressed a kiss to the top of Sharkie's head, just like she'd done for Bel that awful day. "All done."

Bel's deep voice rumbled through the room like thunder. "Time for one more?"

Lily snapped her head up, cautious relief soothing the worst of her worry. The sight of Bel in his ceremonial armor was a study in lethal beauty, of honed strength and power ready to be unleashed. Where his combat armor covered nearly every inch of him, the ceremonial armor consisted of a light breastplate, pauldrons, tassets, bracers, and greaves.

The matte-black metal was embossed with symbols that had become familiar to her in her time with the partners of his warriors—the insignia of each of his legions. Beneath the sparse armor, his black pants were tailored immaculately to his powerful legs, and his shirt was a similar shade to her dress, but more complementary to his skin tone. He held an ornate box in his hands that Lily didn't recognize. Something for the ceremony, probably.

His eyes made her chest ache. Brighter than they'd been when he'd first woken up, but with a soul-deep grief that only time, love, and patience could soothe.

"Always time for you," Lily said as Sharkie made to get up and move to a different chair.

Bel sat in front of her, settling his wings around the specially designed back and allowing his tail to rest against her skirts.

Lily ran her fingers through his already smooth hair, scraping her nails lightly over his scalp the way he liked. "What are you wanting?"

His tail brushed over the floor, finding its way under her skirt, tip coiling around her ankle. She tugged his hair lightly.

"Like what you did the first time, but leave the bottom loose," he said, head turning toward Sharkie as he spoke to her, voice warming. "I want us to match."

Lily worked quickly, taking care to not leave a hair out of place, bringing the three braids together in the back and binding them off. She gave a final cursory swipe of the brush through the loose parts of his hair, ensuring there were no hidden tangles, before pressing a kiss to that same spot between his horns.

"Done," she murmured, setting the brush down.

"Not quite," Bel said roughly, then cleared his throat.

He twisted and set the box beside the brush, his clawed hand resting on the top. It was nearly the size of a place mat, and as tall as the width of his hand, inlaid with gunmetal gray in a lacelike pattern.

Whatever it was, it felt *old*. Like the deities and certain souls felt old.

Sharkie hopped off her chair, eyes bright with curiosity.

Everything inside Lily went still as he flipped the catch and slowly lifted the lid.

A crown rested on a bed of charcoal velvet, masculine in form but delicate in execution. The gunmetal gray strands twined together to create a series of five small spires, each studded with a gloriously vibrant black opal, and perfectly in line with the center spire, the band dipped into a shallow V that held its own larger stone. It wasn't a massive, ostentatious piece, but a simple, powerfully elegant symbol befitting a prince of Hell.

"I was wondering," Bel said quietly, lifting the crown from its cushion, "if you would mind helping me put this on."

Lily took it from him carefully, a slight hum tingling up her arms and a sense of occasion seeping into her bones.

"There's a catch at the back, I think," Bel continued, his voice carefully neutral, but his shoulders tight.

"You *think*?" Sharkie asked, poking a finger into the plush velvet inside the case, then petting it like it was a cat.

"I've never worn it before." Bel cleared his throat, and Lily squeezed his shoulder.

She knew what this meant for him. For so long, he had avoided any reminders that he was a prince of Hell, yet here he was, about to wear the crown, *his* crown, not only for himself, but for all to see. She didn't know where he'd been or what had happened that morning for him to decide to claim his title, but she recognized that it was a huge step in facing an older, deeper grief and hurt.

She tucked her swell of emotion away. He'd share it with her when he was ready.

"Never?" Sharkie asked.

"Never. But I remember my dad always needed help closing the catch at the back when he wore it. Helps get it around the horns."

Lily found the catch and opened it.

"Did your dad have horns like you?" Sharkie asked.

"His curled more, like ram horns," Bel said, and Lily could hear the smile in his voice. "He always teased Lucifer about not having any."

She lowered the crown around his horns and settled it carefully on his head, making sure not to snag any hair when she closed the catch.

It fit perfectly.

Lily smoothed her hands down his shoulders and across his chest, pressing a kiss just in front of his ear.

"How does it feel?" she asked.

Bel leaned his head back against her, covering one of her hands with his and taking a long, slow breath before nodding. "It feels . . . right." He lifted his head and winked at Sharkie. "Helps that it looks good too."

Lily ran her thumb against his palm, whispering only for him to hear. "It's beautiful. You're beautiful."

Bel kept a firm hold of their hands from the moment they walked out the door. He guided them not to the elevators but to the stairs, where they joined the seemingly endless crowds of demons in bright finery walking downward to the Hearth.

Thousands and thousands of people moved in one direction. No one spoke. The only sounds were the rustling of clothes, the scuff of feet, and the occasional sniffle or sob followed by a quiet murmur of comfort.

Down.

Down.

Down.

They gathered more with every level until the stairs ended, opening out onto a massive expanse similar to the other levels of Hell, but with an entirely different feel to it. The air was quieter. Peaceful.

A place of rest.

The ceiling of the giant cavern was still incredibly high, but not nearly as distant as everywhere else. The pulsing veins of magma and golden light were far denser above them, like lace rather than latticework, and trickled down the walls, peeking out from a lush growth of bioluminescent plant life that climbed the walls into the distance.

They'd emerged onto a massive expanse of open, bare ground, the black soil packed down so tightly that at first, Lily thought it was stone.

A huge crowd had already formed—a beautiful kaleidoscope of every color of fabric and skin, a sea of horns in all shapes and sizes.

Bel led them through the crowd, people stepping aside to let them pass. Lily squeezed his hand once, and he gripped hers a little tighter, tension stealing into the lines of his body as they approached the open space beyond the crowd. When they reached the edge of it, Lily understood why.

It took a moment to process exactly what she was seeing. Dozens, perhaps hundreds, of raised stone structures reminiscent of waist-high plateaus in varying sizes. All of them far too large, and all of them covered in rows of lumps wrapped in shrouds, a banner hanging from the end of each structure with a different symbol on each—

Oh.

Tears sprang to her eyes, mind spinning and stomach plummeting at the sheer number of warriors wrapped lovingly in shrouds by their family and friends.

Strong. Be strong. Think strong. Don't fucking cry. Don't you dare fucking cry.

Lily reined in her whirling emotions. For Bel. For the fallen. For their families. For their friends.

At the front of the crowd, she barely recognized Lucifer without his black clothing. He stood in regal, deep teal finery that offset his skin and eyes, a larger and more ornate crown made of red-gold light resting on his head. Beside him stood four of the six princes, each wearing their own crowns and accompanied by their families. Lev was the one she knew best, and he nodded a greeting. The other two she recognized from brief interactions in Bel's office were Mammon and Zee—Beelzebub—each of whom raised their eyebrows at Bel, glancing at the crown on his head. Zee's eyes moved immediately to Lily, then to Sharkie, a ghost of a smile playing over his stern mouth before he nodded and returned his gaze to the pyres, grief written all over his face. The fourth must be Tanael, who Lily had never met, but she knew his name from passing mentions.

Lucifer stared out at the fallen, a sense of age pouring off of him. More than when she'd cornered him in his office, she saw the weight of his responsibility bearing down on him. While he seemed to be managing it, the toll of that burden was carved into his bones. Bel positioned them so that Sharkie stood next to Lucifer, and she immediately let go of Bel to hug him. It took a beat for Lucifer to blink back into the present, but when he did, he wrapped an arm around her, some of the pain leaving his expression.

More demons came, and folk from other realms too.

Someone came to stand on Lily's other side, and she turned her head to greet them. It was Asmodeus, in ceremonial armor similar to Bel's, with a shirt several shades darker than his skin tone, and a silver crown with five gleaming sapphires resting on his brow. Sariah, on his other side, cradled Osmodai, secure in his swaddle of blankets. Lily touched Asmodeus's arm, and he nodded to her, glancing at Bel before turning to look at the pyres.

Asmodeus did a hard double take, whipping his head to look at his cousin so fast that Lily half expected to hear his neck crack. He stared at Bel, who was lost in gazing at the bodies of his warriors, eyes darting from the crown to Bel's profile and back again. To Lily's absolute shock, tears welled up in his eyes. He clamped his mouth shut, turning to face the pyres, blinking rapidly. His hand fumbled to pat at her arm, and she caught his wrist, giving it a gentle squeeze. He exhaled slowly, eyes fixed forward, relaxing by degrees.

On her left, Bel held her hand tighter.

Bel

He'd always expected the crown to crush him, to weigh his head down until he was bowed beneath the weight of the responsibility and the memories it carried.

After he'd walked with his father to the Void, he'd returned home feeling like his entire being was a paper-thin shell waiting to crack and found the box with the crown set on his bed. He'd left it there for days, knowing his father had put it there himself, needing to keep that one little piece of his father's presence around just a little while longer. Eventually, he'd taken the letter, set it on the box, and put both on the highest shelf in his office, stacking books he'd never read in front of them. He didn't look at it again.

Until that morning.

He'd slept badly, and woken up long before Lily, but lay there listening to her breathing, feeling her skin against his, marveling in the awe of who she was. This mortal soul who had been through so much, who had walked straight into Hell on a whim and found her place in it, not because of the pain in her life, but because of the heart she had for others. She'd taken Sharkie in as her own, opening her home and her heart to a child who needed her, despite her fears that she wasn't good enough for the job. Lily faced her fears with a bravery that astounded him. And . . . inspired him.

So, he'd kissed her and gotten up, leaving her to shower and get ready while he put on his armor and headed to his office, locking the door and reaching for the highest shelf. Of course, Lecti, his housekeeper, had kept even a speck of dust from gathering on it without ever saying a word about her knowledge of its whereabouts.

The box felt smaller in his hands than it had before, lighter. He'd set it on the desk and picked up the thick envelope with his name scrawled in handwriting both familiar and long forgotten. He'd never forget seeing that envelope in hands broader and meatier than his, the gray skin scarred and starting to show signs of age.

Bel had paced to the window, staring out at the garden, soaking in the beauty of the morning light starting to dim the glow of the plants before he sliced the letter open with a claw, just like how his father used to, and pulled out the pages.

My beloved son . . .

He'd had to stop, tears blurring his eyes so that he couldn't read. He could *hear* him, his voice as deep as Bel's but with a slightly different tone and an older pattern of speech. Memories long repressed swam to the surface, sparked by those three words.

My beloved son. Spoken through laughter because Bel had successfully pranked him.

My beloved son. Spoken with exasperation after he'd been told Bel flew through the tower window.

My beloved son. Spoken with such pride whenever Bel mastered a new maneuver or was promoted.

My beloved son. Spoken quietly and softly as he'd tucked Bel into bed.

Bel had braced his hand against the window frame, knees threatening to buckle, but after a moment, he wiped his eyes and kept reading his father's bold handwriting, a hard copy of his voice.

My beloved son,

Never doubt that you are, have always been, and always will be, my beloved son. I know that the decision I have made has caused you unspeakable pain, and I ask not for your forgiveness. How could I ask that of you? However, I will ask you for one thing. I ask that you keep your courage. Not for me, but for yourself.

There are many things in this world both terrible and beautiful, and all of them require courage. The courage to stand on a battlefield, to command soldiers, to come home from that battlefield and dare to carry on is a powerful thing. The courage to love, to let others see you at your most vulnerable, to allow joy in is just as powerful, but, for me at least, has always proven the most difficult.

I want better for you.

You are the best and bravest parts of your mother and me, and better than us both. Do not be afraid of error. Make mistakes, and many of them. You learn much about yourself through them, often more than you learn from your triumphs.

And, oh, my son, you have so many triumphs. I have been proud of you since the day you were born and nearly split our eardrums announcing your own arrival . . .

The rest of the letter had blurred, words of encouragement and apology, of hope, a reminder to stretch more, and always, pride in his son.

Bel only managed to read it once in its entirety.

He'd forgotten what his father had sounded like. He'd forgotten that he *was* a beloved son, was his father's beloved son. The pain of being the child Samael had left behind had overwhelmed the joy of being his child in the first place.

His grief had obscured that love. Buried in pain and anger and doubt and fear. And he'd let himself forget.

He'd been enough. He had always been enough. His father had loved him as fiercely as any parent loved their child. When he'd gone to his final battles, protecting the entire Universe had been too heavy of a burden for his wearying soul. His motivation to fight had been to ensure the safety of his son.

His father's decision had nothing to do with some kind of inadequacy or failure on Bel's part but had everything to do with his father's own limitations, his own pain and exhaustion. His father had been ancient and weary and had lost the tethers tying him to life and living. But he'd stayed longer than he would have, longer than he could have otherwise borne, for Bel alone.

Reading his father's words on the page, hearing his voice echo in his head once more, had shattered the incorrect beliefs he'd been holding on to.

The grief for his father and the years he'd expected to share with him would linger, as grief always did, but it would no longer be emblematic of his perceived failure. Because it hadn't ever been true. It had been a result of confusion and sorrow and fear that he'd let grow and fester, but not anymore.

A chapter had ended. A new one had begun, and it was starting with hope and understanding.

It had taken several minutes for Bel to compose himself, but there was a noticeable weight that had lifted. His father's letter had loomed over him for more than two centuries, heavy with the fear of what was in it, along with the weight of his own disgust at that fear. But finally, he had faced it, knowing that no matter what was in the letter, it wouldn't crush him, because he wouldn't let it.

He'd gone to Lily then, box in hand, wanting her to crown him that first time. When Lily had placed the crown on his head, he hadn't expected the memory it sparked as it settled onto his brow.

He remembered being a little boy, laughing hysterically with his father when he'd tried to put it on his head and it had slipped down to rest on his shoulders instead, digging in uncomfortably.

"Not yet, my beloved son," his father said with a laugh, gently lifting the crown over his head and cradling it in his hands. "But one day. And I will be just as proud of you then as I am now."

Keep your courage.

The memory did not crush him.

Just as the crown would not.

Bel watched the healers sweep forward to stand amongst the pyres, focusing on breathing through his nose and not crushing Lily's hand.

Several of his legions had made it through with no fatalities, but all of them had had soldiers with grievous injuries. Out of the two hundred and sixty-eight pyres, seventy-nine were for his soldiers. Nearly twelve thousand lost from his army alone. So many. Too many.

The worst war Lucifer had seen in millennia.

The healers began to hum in unison. Goose bumps rippled up his arms, just as they did every time he heard the beginning of the chants. The humming swelled into a wordless undulation of song, the healers swaying like trees in the wind, voices raised in lyrical grief. His heartbeat pounded in his ears, as if it wanted to make itself known, reassure him that it was still there. That he was still there.

He pressed his arm against Lily's, and she leaned into him.

Some of the healers continued their wordless song, while the rest began the gentle, heartbreakingly beautiful song of the fallen. Sung in no language commonly spoken, but understood nonetheless, the funeral chants were both an expression of purest grief and of peace, sung as much for the living as for the dead.

His throat grew tight, and he cleared it roughly. *Not now. I won't be able to sing if I cry now.* Lily sniffed next to him, but he didn't dare look at her, no matter how much he wanted to as the healers' song faded.

Silence fell. It was time.

He squeezed Lily's hand twice, the signal they'd agreed on, and with a soft squeeze back, she let go.

As one, Bel, Asmodeus, the other generals, and the surviving commanding officers stepped forward out of the crowd, striding across the black soil until they stood equidistant between the crowd and the fallen. Beside him, Asmodeus's breathing was ragged; all seventy-two of his legions were represented on the pyres. They sank to one knee in a line, a second line forming behind them. Bel clasped his cousin on the shoulder, and Asmodeus looked at him, eyes glassy but resolved. Asmodeus gripped Bel's shoulder in return, and something settled in him.

Not alone.

Bel glanced at the officer next to him and clasped him on the shoulder as well. The idea rippled down the line, hands on shoulders, some holding hands. Grief was intensely personal, but in their grief, they would not be alone.

Like the healers, their song started slowly, an upswell of sound, wordless, contemplative, seeking. Like the first moments after learning of a loss, building to a more resonant and emotive tone the longer the loss set in. When words finally came, they were not of battlefield glory. They were not there to sing of myths. None of them loved battle, they were there for something far bigger than that. They loved what battle protected.

Flames crackled to life uniformly over the pyres, lit by the inherent power of the funeral grounds, of the Universe they called home. There was no smell, no sound other than their song and the crackling of the flames. The Rising began. Embers far larger than those from a normal fire floated upward slowly, a few at first, then more and more until there was a shower of embers raining upward. The souls of the fallen returned to the fabric of the Universe—of Hell—becoming a part of all of it.

So many.

Bel closed his eyes, anchored by the hands of his fellow warriors on his shoulders and the crown placed on his head by the woman he loved, and sang his grief. Sang honor to the fallen for giving their lives to protect all that was good and wonderful in their world. Sang peace for them, for their loved ones.

He didn't notice until Asmodeus's hand tightened on his shoulder that their voices had been joined by the crowd behind them.

Then he let the tears fall.

❦

60

LILIES

Lily

Lily stood next to Bel in the receiving line, an oddly calm tension sitting in her chest that she couldn't really identify. Her role in the line was mostly a supportive one for Bel. She spoke to the partners and families she recognized and offered what comfort and thanks she could where it was welcome to those she didn't.

Berte, the first woman to welcome her into the support group of warriors' families, had arrived on the arm of her husband, her damp eyes gleaming with equal parts relief and grief as she'd hugged Lily. A younger man from a different group had arrived alone, hollow-eyed and lost. His tears had dripped on her shoulder when she hugged him. He'd been waiting for his partner to come home and give him an opinion on how to redecorate their living room, knowing how much she enjoyed designing their home. Lily wondered if he would ever move their couch to a different wall now. If he would ever shop for a new rug without waiting for an opinion that would never come. Perhaps someday he would, but as Lily held his shaking body, she knew that day was a long way off. Bel had bowed deeply to him and hugged him, murmuring words that Lily couldn't hear.

She'd been braced for anger, for the same helpless rage that she'd seen at too many mortal funerals for those who had died as a result of tragedy. There was grief and there was pain, but no one seemed to blame Bel or any of the other demons in the chain of command. Loss recognized loss, and respected that each pain was different.

Bel's fingers brushed against her skirts for the dozenth time, not solid enough to be a caress, but a subtle, grounding gesture. She stroked her thumb up the side of his hand. *I know. I see you.*

He had settled after the haunting beauty of the warriors' song and the upward rain of embers from the bodies of the fallen. The Rising, it was called. Despite being wreathed in flame, the bodies hadn't technically burned, but had instead simply and slowly disintegrated into embers and sparks. There was no ash left on the raised platforms, not even a single scorch mark. The entire time, the long line of warriors had knelt together, connected through touch and through their song, singing their fallen friends to whatever peace came next.

After several hours, and what had to have been tens of thousands of people, the line dwindled. Sariah and a crying Osmodai had left a bit earlier, accompanied by an older female demon, who appeared to be Sariah's mother. Asmodeus had relaxed a bit but watched every step they took until they were out of sight. Lily checked on him every so often, and despite his weariness, he seemed to be all right.

A small arm wrapped around her waist, Sharkie's body pressing against her side quietly. Lily hugged her, scanning her round face for any hint of her being overwhelmed and finding nothing.

"How are you doing, bug?"

Sharkie shrugged, her grip around Lily's waist tightening a bit. "I'm okay. But, um . . ." She trailed off, hunching her shoulders a little.

Lily turned to give her her full attention. "But?" she asked gently.

Sharkie lifted her eyes to hers, concern glimmering in their depths. "Can I ask you something that may be bad?"

"Always," Lily said, holding her pinkie out to prove it.

Sharkie stood a little straighter and looped it with her own.

"We're all sad," Sharkie said softly, "but, um . . . Dad has you and me to fuss over him, but Papa doesn't have anyone, and I don't want him to be sad *and* alone. I mean, if he wants to be alone, he totally can be, but I don't think that's what he wants right now. I don't want Dad to feel like I love him any less because I'm not there for him today, though. I don't know what to do."

Love and pride washed through Lily. She clasped Sharkie's shoulders with a smile, considering the best way to approach this.

"Bel knows that you love him, and that you can only be in one place at once," Lily started. "So does Luci. But it is true that Bel has me too. How about you talk to Luci and see if he wants company today? Then you can go from there."

Another thought occurred to Lily, memories of feeling responsible for her parents' emotional state. Oh, how she'd wished someone had explicitly freed her of that responsibility then.

"But, Sharkie? Just so you know, it's not your job to take care of either of them. They're grown men, and you are a child—our child—even if you are growing up. Kids shouldn't have to take care of their parents like parents take care of their kids. Absolutely be there with him, spend time with him, all of that, but it's not your job to make him happy or feel better, okay?"

Sharkie nodded slowly, pinkie finger tightening around Lily's.

"We get through things together, not just because of one of us, yeah?"

"Yeah," Sharkie said, eyes brightening a bit.

"So, with that in mind, you can talk to Luci and see if he wants company today, or you can hang out with me and Bel, or you can do whatever *you* need to in order to process and be okay with all this. I know it's a lot."

"I think . . . I want to talk to Luci. Not," Sharkie said with a bit of relief in her voice, "because I think he needs to be taken care of, but because I want to spend time with him so we can be sad together. You and Bel can be sad together, then we can all just be together at home."

"Sounds like a plan." Lily smiled.

Sharkie scurried off, weaving through the scattering crowd in the direction Lily had last seen Luci.

Bel spoke softly to a winged warrior with a bandage over one eye and what appeared to be her husband at her side. A few other demons milled around like they might be waiting for their chance to approach, but there was no longer a definitive line.

Just as Lily turned to stand properly by Bel, someone tapped her shoulder.

Lev stood behind her, wearing a deep blue demonic-style suit adorned with an abundance of intricate orange embroidery that matched his eyes and contrasted with his olive-green skin. A female demon hovered a bit behind him with her arms crossed, eyes fixed on the back of Lev's head. Her skin was a few shades lighter than Lev's, and her features were a perfect female replica of his. Those details, combined with the look she was aiming at him, all pointed to her being Lev's sister.

"Hey, Lev," Lily said, then nodded at his sister, who gave her a smile that was surprisingly soft.

"Hello, I have a—"

His sister poked his back, and he snapped his mouth shut, cleared his throat, and started again.

"Hello, how are you?" Lev asked with almost robotic politeness. She could practically hear him chafing against the small talk.

"Not bad for being at a mass funeral," Lily said, suspicious of the gleam in his eyes that had nothing to do with the dampness still clinging to his lower lashes.

"Ah, yes. Here, have a tissue. I brought extra." He produced a neat packet of tissues that had obviously been fuller at one point, tugging a couple free and holding them out with awkward sweetness.

She took them slowly, deciding that bluntness might be the best approach. "Thank you. What's up, Lev?"

He visibly perked up. "I have a report for you to look over that I believe will be most beneficial to the efficacy of the Hellp Desk and ensure its long-term success."

Lily blinked slowly. He couldn't be serious.

But it was Lev. He was always serious.

Deep breath. Respond, don't react.

Wrestling the "Kindly fuck off" she would have given to anyone else under control, she took a slow breath.

"Lev. Honey. We are at a funeral," she said as gently but firmly as she could.

He winced, but rallied. "Yes, I know, but ever since I received your report, I've had my assistants researching and compiling options and suggestions that I believe would benefit you and cheer you up. If you're happy, Beleth will be happy, and if the gate runs smoothly, then so will the rest of Hell."

She knew that Lev was Lev and probably genuinely thought he was being helpful, but she had to repeat it to herself a few times.

"Universe's mercy, Leviathan," his sister hissed, "what happened to 'offering comfort'?"

Lev shot a worried look back at her, then hurried to produce the packet of tissues again, this time holding the entire thing out as an offering, his orange eyes anxious. "I'm sorry. Personally, I find knowledge to be very comforting. It's a very nice report, the options and suggestions given in order from what I believe to be most optimal to the least. It's double-spaced—"

Lily wrapped both her hands around his extended one, tissue packet and all, silencing him. It was still inappropriate to be discussing a work report at such a devastatingly powerful funeral, but she understood him. Lev was comforting her in the way he found comfort. He just happened to find reports and work soothing in a way that few others did. He was trying. Trying her patience, and apparently his sister's as well, but he was *trying* to be helpful, bless him.

"I would love to read and discuss that report, Lev, just not right now. You are more than welcome to deliver it to the Hellp Desk, and I will read it as soon as I can. Thank you for having all that work done for me. I really do appreciate it. But right now, I need to focus on today."

Relief flickered over his face, as if he'd been worried she would outright reject his gift. She released his hand and offered him a smile that she hoped looked genuine.

He nodded, giving her a quick little hug.

She returned it and stepped back, waving goodbye to his sister, who dragged him away by his arm. Lily watched them go, shaking her head slightly. Just because she understood Lev and the heart behind the conversation didn't mean that she wasn't annoyed. It had been an intensely emotional day.

A large, warm hand settled on her lower back, followed by Bel's lips pressing into her hair. She leaned against him, slipping her arm around his armored waist with a sigh.

"Tell me he didn't just ask you to read a report," Bel rumbled.

"He was trying to help in his own way." She sighed. "He's sweet, but he needs to work on his timing."

Bel grunted, shifting so he could search her face for something inscrutable.

"What?" she asked.

He was silent for a moment, brow furrowed in thought, hands gently wrapping around her own. "Today has been a lot."

"Yeah," Lily said slowly, knowing there was more.

Bel studied their joined hands, then lifted his gaze to hers. "Will you do one more difficult thing with me today?"

No one looked twice at them as they walked through the Universal Hallway in their finery.

Bel pulled Sharkie aside before they left, assuring her that he understood and appreciated why she was spending extra time with Lucifer, and that he loved her always. She hugged him with every fiber of her strength, and had done the same with Lily, adding a quick peck on the cheek.

It shocked Lily down to her bones that Bel wanted to partake in the rite of mourning today. That he would want to go back to the battlefield so soon, let alone after the funeral, had left her a little speechless. But that jittery tension that had been welling up in him ever since he'd woken up from his injuries was nowhere to be seen. If he wanted—if he *needed*—to do this, then she would trust his judgment. He would have her love and support in it.

Their trip out of Hell had been silent. She wasn't sure who'd reached for the other's hand first, but it didn't matter. Neither of them was letting go anytime soon. Even when they'd stopped at a florist shop, after Bel had had a crisis of confidence about which flowers to get, they'd tucked their massive bouquets into their free arms and still held on to each other.

No one else was in the hall leading to the now-ruined realm. The arch was nondescript and dull, the vitality that pulsed through every other archway nowhere to be seen. There was no seeping sense of wrongness like there had been every time she'd peered down that hallway before, only a weary resignation, like an abandoned old house that couldn't wait to collapse.

Bel paused before the arch, not looking up at it but into its depths, hand tightening around hers. She studied his profile. The hard set of his jaw. The bump on his nose where it had been broken. The gleam of his silver eyes. The black opals in his crown gleamed with their own fire, yet the crown seemed just as much a part of him as the arch of his horns.

"I couldn't tell you anything about this realm other than what it was in the end," he said roughly, without looking at her. "I know that it was a minor fringe realm that belonged to no one and everyone, like a public park. But beyond that . . . ?" He shook his head. "I wonder if it was beautiful once. I wonder if it was someone's favorite place. What small, precious moments happened here."

They were silent for a long moment, then Bel tugged her forward.

Lily had expected something a bit more . . . realm-like. The soil was bare and relatively flat, studded with chunks of rock that almost looked like they'd fallen from the ceiling. Perhaps they had. The ceiling looked just like that of a cave, but much farther up and illuminated with the same nebulous, sourceless light that was present in most realms. The distant walls of the massive space were bare, rough rock. No plants, no animals, not even a whisper of a breeze. The ground from the arch sloped downward like a massive ramp, offering a grandstand view of what remained of the camp. Ragged tents of all sizes were covered in what looked like dried mud. A handprint was smeared on the side of a large tent by a half-open flap that hung limply. Bel guided her through all of it, heading for a small rise.

He'd explained that the bodies wouldn't rot, that they would dry out and either crumble to ash or be pulled out of existence when the realm was collapsed, but something in her brain still told her to expect the stench of corpses. The air had a bit of a bitter tang to it, but nothing particularly pungent.

They crested the rise, and her head went oddly silent.

Just below them lay the desiccated bodies of multiple unidentifiable creatures, shriveled up like mummies, dried blood in black spatters over their leathery skin and pooled on the ground. Beyond them?

There had to be tens of thousands of them scattered across the expanse. Some in clusters, some as lone lumps, increasing in quantity the closer they were to the giant scar that cut across the far wall. It had to be at least three miles away, but it seemed as tall as a small skyscraper and wide enough to drive at least a dozen buses through side by side.

She could see where the ground had been turned to mud with blood and churned up by countless feet. The brutality of what had happened there, a battle the likes of which she couldn't hope to accurately imagine, was evident in the ground itself, which was blotchily stained a darker color than the bare soil in camp. The utter stillness made it surreal, almost like a movie set.

Bel squeezed her hand. She snapped back to herself, squeezing in return.

They picked their way down the rise, and she allowed him to guide her across the eerie landscape, curious what exactly he was looking for. She recognized more of the creatures she'd beheaded—chittahi—and dozens of gegony of various sizes and states of dryness. Bel seemed to be checking the gegony for some reason, his grip on her hand tightening the farther they went across the field.

They were nearly halfway to the scar when Bel stopped, his hand clenching hers almost painfully.

She didn't have to wonder what she was supposed to be looking at.

A large gegony, riddled with arrows and bone-deep gashes, curled protectively around a much smaller one with pale green skin marred with scorch marks.

Protectively.

Oh. Oh no.

"Bel?" she breathed, understanding but needing confirmation.

"It happened toward the end, when they ran out of the ones willing to go to battle, I guess. I realized it just before I was . . . injured. They must have tortured the little ones, driven them mad with pain, then turned them loose on the battlefield for us to kill, giving the parents the incentive to do what every parent would do for their child."

Tears spilled free, running hotly down her cheeks. She'd found the gegony in the hallway to be monstrous, and it had been. But what made a monster? A real monster? She saw monsters every day at the Hellp Desk, made monstrous by their actions, their cruelty. Perhaps some of the gegony were monsters through and through, perhaps they'd enjoyed being unleashed in battle. But this? There were many, many levels of brutality before the one that called for young to be tortured in order to force their parents into battle. Into a slaughter.

"What kills me," Bel choked, "is that I'll never know if *any* of these creatures wanted to be here. Were they tortured too? Were their people being threatened? Could they even think, or were they just animals who couldn't even try to fight for something better for themselves? I'll never know. But I do know that, no matter their intelligence or where they came from, those parents and their young wanted nothing to do with the fight they were forced into. They deserve more than to lie forgotten on some battlefield."

He let go of her hand, swiping his palm roughly over his tear-streaked cheeks, then pulled a single flower free of the bouquet cradled in his arm, placing it so that it rested on top of the young one and against its parent.

He took a deep, shuddering breath, pressing his hand over his face while he composed himself.

The white lily should have been a stark contrast against the two bodies, and in a way, it was, but there was a softness to the curl of the petals that seemed . . . right.

"I don't know how many there are," Bel said finally, dropping his hand to brush against hers.

Lily reached up and cradled his wet cheek, gently tugging him down for a soft kiss that tasted of both of their tears. "We'll find them."

They split up, though not without a brief flash of hesitation on Bel's part, his eyes flickering to the twisted scar on the wall before he took a deep breath and nodded.

They spent hours picking through the battlefield, leaving a lily with each of the young and their fallen parent. Every time she found a new pair, fresh tears would fall. They were always in pairs. Always one adult, one young. She'd found one that, at first glance, looked like an abandoned youngster, but then she'd spied the adult twisted up in a net several paces away, where it had been straining toward the little one, the one foreleg it had managed to free from the net stretched toward its young.

Lily had set down her bouquet and dragged the little one over to its parent, pushing it up against its side and laying a flower on them. It had been heavy and unwieldy—and she suspected she'd only managed it because the body was dry—but she couldn't leave them apart. It could have been her or Bel and Sharkie. Lilith and Anyaet. Sariah or Asmodeus and Osmodai.

She knew that they had killed people from her Universe, had killed Bel's soldiers, that one of them had almost killed Bel himself. But if not for the twisted whims of whatever powers ruled that other Universe, they never would have set foot on that battlefield. Bel, with his big heart, had forgiven them, mourned them. So would she. She already had.

They met in front of the scar on the wall, their bouquets dwindled down to a few flowers each. Bel looked exhausted, but there was peace in his eyes. Lily took his flowers and joined them with her own, then set them on the ground in front of the scar.

"For the ones we don't know to mourn," she said hoarsely.

"For the ones we don't know to mourn," he murmured.

Bel slipped his arm around her, pressing his nose to her hair and letting out a long breath.

Bel's rite—their rite—was done.

They lingered in front of the scar for a moment before they turned and began the long walk back to the rise. To her surprise, other figures dotted the battlefield, some moving alone, others in pairs or groups. Some cried, some sang, some were silent, and there seemed to be people from many different realms partaking in the rite of mourning.

They passed by one of the pairs one of them had left a flower for, and Lily pulled Bel to a stop, pointing.

Beside their lily, someone had laid a yellow chrysanthemum.

61

SYMPATHY, CONDOLENCES & APOLOGIES

Bel

B el sat statue-still while the tattoo artist worked on his ear, the minor thrum of pain a familiar and welcome sensation.

It had been nearly a week since the funeral. They had spent a few hazy, restful days at home before inaction had itched at him. From then, the days had blurred into a whirlwind of reports, meetings, coordinating an inventory, and beginning to ease back into training.

Nausea had clenched his stomach the morning he'd decided to go to the training fields, enough that he'd balked and told Lily while they'd been having lunch that he'd be putting it off another day.

"Okay, big guy," she'd said, adjusting her grip on her sandwich. "I'll ask Krun, then."

His curiosity had spiked. "Ask Krun what?"

"Oh, I was trying to remember how to smooth out that combination you showed me right before you left, so I was going to head down with you after lunch. But Krun gives me pointers sometimes, so it's okay. I'll ask him when I go back up."

"Krun forgets the size difference, so what works for him might not work for you. Here—" He'd reached for one of the swords on the display rack by his desk, worried that Lily might start forming fighting habits that would be hard to break. "Let's work it out real quick."

"Now?" she'd asked, putting down her sandwich. "Okay."

It had taken him entirely too long to realize what she'd been doing.

She usually picked up on techniques quickly and was always good about implementing instructions, but for some reason, she kept making little mistakes and asking him to demonstrate again, then asking him to act as her opponent for practice. He'd lost himself in the dance of combat, the sword in his hand no longer a separate thing, but an extension of his arm. The tension had seeped from his muscles as they warmed up, moving by memory instead of conscious thought.

When Lily had suddenly stopped making mistakes and pressed her advantage, he'd had to hop up onto the dais to avoid her strike, laughing as he realized that he was having *fun*.

He'd lowered his sword, understanding dawning. "I see what you're doing."

"My best?" came the cheeky reply.

He'd swatted at her ass with the flat of his sword, but she danced out of the way, sheathing her blade and propping her hands on her hips.

"I'm not going to tell you how you should heal, or when you should do things. But I know you. You're so *physical*, Bel. You're a warrior to your core, and sitting around staring at paperwork isn't going to do you"— she'd tapped her temple—"any favors. Maybe you don't spar today, maybe you go and just work out. As much fun as it would be to try, you can't fuck your way to better mental health. You can fuck part of the way there, but at some point, you need to have another outlet."

He'd smirked at the last bit, but then sobered. "I didn't struggle with this. After the other conflicts." *I've never seen so much death at once.* "I've never felt hesitant to go back. But you're right. I know you're right."

So, he'd gone.

Several other warriors had been there, all of them looking just as hesitant and just as determined as him. They'd all been a little stilted at first, but soon they'd been sparring like they had before the war, laughing, teasing each other, calling out advice. Bel had sparred until his arms had

gone shaky and he'd been half blinded by dripping sweat, elation pumping through his veins.

Instead of showering, he'd gone up to the Hellp Desk, where Lily had
been listening to an especially shrieky soul, tugged her out of her chair,
told her again that she was right, and kissed her with every ounce of passion he felt for her. It was only when she lay back on her desk, pulling him
down after her, and the gate demons had burst into a chorus of whistles
and catcalls that he'd remembered where they were. He'd pressed an innocent kiss to her cheek, thanked her, bowed to the hooting demons,
and sauntered back to the elevator as if nothing had happened.

He'd spent time on the training fields every day since. More and
more demons showed up each day, and all of them found peace in the
controlled violence of training. They talked to each other about their
struggles, about the guilt, about the nightmares that ripped them awake,
about things that had helped them. Bel floated the idea of asking some
of the therapists on Levels One and Two to come down and have either
group sessions or to organize schedules for individual meetings, and it
was well received.

"Ear is done," his artist announced, the prickling pain of healing fading
into nothing. "Which one do you want to do next? Your hand, or . . . ?"

Bel had asked Lily about mortal tattoos, and while the overall process
was the same, he'd been mildly horrified at the healing time. All demonic
tattoo artists either had healing abilities, or they had a healer they worked
in tandem with, resulting in a process that minimized inconvenience and
maximized the quality of the art.

"Hand," Bel answered.

The artist nodded, reaching for the stencil.

If his artist had been initially surprised at his request when he'd made
the appointment, he hadn't showed it in the slightest. He'd only nodded
and begun sketching.

When Bel had mentioned to Greg what he was planning, his friend's
face had gone carefully neutral.

"For fuck's sake, what?" Bel asked.

Greg hadn't even twitched. His stillness often made him difficult for other people to read, but Bel knew him too well. Greg felt things deeply, and the less he showed, the more tended to be going on under the surface.

"She's it for you, isn't she? No matter if she reincarnates or not," Greg said.

As always, the mention of Lily's reincarnation sent razors tearing through his insides, but he'd nodded.

Greg's features had softened, a smile playing at his mouth. Relationships had never come particularly easy to either of them—meaningful relationships, anyway—but even less so to Greg. Bel had seen the quiet longing in Greg's eyes before, but the flashes of it had become less frequent over the years as Greg had settled into his work on, and then mastery of, Level Nine. He suspected that Greg had convinced himself that not only would he spend eternity alone, but that he and everyone else were better off if he did. Bel hoped that, someday, someone would convince him otherwise.

"If you were anyone else, I'd say you were a hopelessly romantic idiot," Greg said, "but it's you. So, hopefully, you're just a romantic."

Bel watched the artist place the stencil on the back of his hand and wrist, then gave his approval.

A moment later, the artist lowered the needle to his skin, the hum of the tattoo gun buzzing through his bones and making his fingers twitch. He forced them to still.

The image of Lily on the battlefield during the rite was seared into his soul. He'd spent his life looking for the beauty in the world, from the tiny and mundane to the grand and overwhelming, but in that moment, she had been the pinnacle of all of it. She'd been utterly regal in her sweeping gown and upswept hair, the large bouquet of lilies cradled in one arm as she gazed down at a fallen gegony and its young with quiet empathy. Her loveliness had been so at odds with the torn-up, barren surroundings and the bodies of creatures, yet she *belonged*. She'd bent to place a flower with a tenderness that had made his heart ache, resting her palm on the shoulder of the adult gegony for a moment. An acknowledgment, from one parent to another. Then she had risen and swept forward, her shimmering purple gown a beacon of color, of *life* in the desiccated realm.

As the lines of ink sank into the back of his hand, forming a small piece of beauty during the rite, he smiled.

Maybe he *was* a hopeless romantic.

Though, at the moment, he was a worried one too.

Lily had been quiet for the last several days, and acting off. He'd caught her staring out the kitchen window, lost in thought. He'd caught her watching him or Sharkie with a soft but slightly sad expression. The look had worried him. He'd asked about it, but she'd just said that she was "soaking it all in." He didn't know what to make of that, and admittedly fear had lanced through him when he wondered *why* she'd need to soak them in. They kept an open dialogue with each other, so he knew she would talk about it when she was good and ready, and there was really no point worrying about it until then.

Because Greg had been right. She was it for him. His life was and always would be better for having her in it, even if she was just there for a little while in the grand scheme of his eternity. Even if his heart clenched every time he thought of her leaving, as much as it clenched when he thought about what she'd have to give up in order to stay.

A hopeful romantic.

He was definitely that.

Lily

Her hands had been shaky all day, despite the sense of rightness that had settled into her soul that morning. She'd never been more certain of anything in her entire existence, but her damn hands seemed to have missed that memo.

Today, she made it official.

Permanent.

No more reincarnation, no more mortal world, no more heartbeat.

All things she would miss, sure. But she would gain *everything* that was actually important.

She would go to the Reincarnation Office, tell them to put that note in her file, and finally tell everyone she loved that she wasn't going anywhere, and never would.

Bel had noticed that something was up—because of course he had—catching her in moments of wonder and a little bit of grief. She hadn't told him what it was, because she'd been allowing herself to *feel*. She'd known she wanted to stay, and if she was being honest, she'd known for a while that reincarnation was no longer an option for her.

But that decision? It needed its own grieving too. She'd spent days working through her feelings, not wanting to burden Bel with them because she knew how guilty he already felt for wanting her to stay. It seemed important for her to do it for herself.

As she processed, it struck her that before, where she would have gotten overwhelmed and frustrated with herself for having strong emotions, she was now able to acknowledge, accept, and work with her feelings. Her feelings weren't too big or inconvenient or ugly. They just *were*, and she wasn't afraid of them anymore.

Her decision that it was time had crystallized that morning. While Bel and Sharkie were making eggs Benedict, she had gone outside to sit on a chair in the front yard with Max on her lap, watching the sunrise gilding the wisps of mist that lingered in between the hills. The air had been crisp but not cold, the songbirds filling the quiet with their myriad songs, distant trees rustling in a breeze.

Then Sharkie and Bel had laughed together about something, and she'd known. Known that she had to go to that office today and close off that path, because she'd truly chosen another.

She hadn't told them yet. She didn't want to tell anyone until she'd been to the Reincarnation Office and told them to put a note in her file. She was staying for them, but she was staying for herself too. She loved the Afterlife, the people in it, and, oddly enough, her work at the Hellp Desk, chaotic though it might be.

But damn, she couldn't wait to share the news with them.

She'd decided to go to the Reincarnation Office during a lull that she was still waiting on.

Lily drummed her fingers on the desk, waiting for the male soul to stop slamming his palms against the invisible protective barrier that had manifested itself across the front of her desk. She liked the upgrade. Before, the barrier had only applied to the souls' irate spitting, which she'd very much appreciated, but it'd meant that they could still come over the desk to invade her personal space. Which had been annoying.

The new barrier was more expansive, and seemed to apply only to the souls, as she'd had no problem throwing her stapler at a particularly entitled soul earlier. They'd tried to throw it back at her, but it had ricocheted off the barrier and smacked them in the chest.

Lily considered her options with scientific detachment as the man slammed his hands against the barrier so hard she heard joints pop. His purple-faced litany of insults and threats were woefully uninspired—*Ugly bitch? Fuck you up?*

Really? Where was the creativity?

Her bored lack of response seemed to infuriate him. Perfect. His file indicated that he'd given himself a heart attack having a tantrum after his sports team had lost, and since he'd driven everyone in his life away due to his abusive behavior, no one had been there to help him. As hilarious as it was to watch him froth himself into a truly spectacular hissy fit and not worry about the consequences, she had more important things to do.

She stood, reaching for the spear the gate demons had cut down for Sharkie. It was slightly too short for Lily, but it was long enough to whack the idiot with.

"I have the report for you, but first, please make that stop." Lev's voice pulled her attention away from where the man was throwing his shoulder at the barrier, trying to break it down like a door. Horrified disgust was all over Lev's face as he stood a few feet behind her chair.

Lily blinked, then swung the spear with all her might as the man connected with the barrier again. The strike jarred up the shaft of the spear, followed by a splintering crack that, at first, she thought was just the man's bones. He toppled backward to the floor, unconscious, while the first third of the spear clattered against the stone beside him.

"Oops," Lily muttered, staring at the broken wood in her hand. Thankfully, there were plenty of extra spears around. All she had to do was get another one cut down. But still, she felt bad.

She used the stick to wave and get Krun's attention. "Could you take care of him, please?"

"Of course," Krun rumbled, grabbing one of the man's legs and shooting her a grin. "At least he's quiet now."

"Small mercies," Lily agreed, watching Krun drag him away like a doll before turning to Lev. "Sorry about that. A report?"

"Yes," Lev said, hurrying to set his briefcase on the desk and clicking it open. "The report that I mentioned at the funeral. Also a card."

"A card," Lily repeated, not following.

"Yes, my sister advised that an expression of sympathy and condolences would be appropriate, given the emotional toll that the war and the funeral have taken on you and Beleth, as well as an apology for perhaps not choosing the best moment to mention the report, so I'll lead with that." He handed her an envelope, then clasped his hands together a bit impatiently.

She took pity on him and ripped it open, ignoring his little gasp, and pulling out a deep purple card with a gold filigree pattern across the front. She flipped it open. Inside, it was plain white and completely empty, except for five words in Lev's neat little script.

Sympathy, condolences, and apologies.

Leviathan

Lily managed to smother her laugh to a sharp exhale through her nose, but she couldn't keep herself from smiling. Sweet Lev, so quintessentially himself.

"Thank you," she said. Before she'd finished speaking, Lev nodded, lunging for his briefcase.

"Yes, yes, you're welcome. Here." He held up an immaculately bound report that was as thick as a small book. "This is the comprehensive report on options to maximize the efficacy of the Hellp Desk, as well as ensure its continued success in the long term. I took the liberty of having my assistants arrange the options available to us in order of the most to least helpful, in my opinion. I was deeply concerned with the idea that your reincarnation would leave us bereft of this valuable addition to the functionality of the gate, so, since apparently a comprehensive training manual and codified set of procedures is not possible—"

"Lev, honey," Lily said, rubbing at her forehead, "I promise I'll read the report, okay?"

"Well, obviously." Lev frowned, fumbling uncharacteristically to flip through the pages of the report. "But, please, I believe that I have found a solution in the Archival records that would eliminate the need for training materials for any possible replacement, while simultaneously compromising on all possible concerns. I would like to know that you are at least considering it. Even if it does, um, require a sacrifice on your part." He held the open report out to her with wide, pleading eyes.

Lily looked between him and the open report, reaching for it slowly, only to have Lev shove it at her.

"If this sacrifice involves a virgin or some kind of vow of chastity, then we're shit out of luck," she warned him.

"Read." He tapped the top of the page.

While never a common or well-known practice, the yielding of reincarnation has been known to offer mortal souls a chance to experience life without mortality. By Universal definition, mortal souls in the Afterlife are said to "exist," not "live." However, a true and permanent yielding of the ability to reincarnate could, upon approval by the Universe, result in a mortal soul being deified, and therefore becoming a denizen of the Afterlife, though not a full deity.

Application for deification is not a guarantee of acceptance. According to Archival records dating from approximately the beginning of time to present, 1.9 billion souls have applied for deification, with an approval rate of less than 10 percent. The majority of these approvals occurred early in the dawn of civilization. Most of these deified souls have since gone to the Void with their partners or families or have become reclusive in their Paradises. An application for deification has not been received in at least three millennia, and knowledge of this process seems to be fairly uncommon, even among deities and elder denizens.

It is imperative to note for consideration that deified souls may never return to the mortal world. Deified souls are, for all intents and purposes, no different from natural-born denizens of the Afterlife, though they retain their mortal physical characteristics. Deified souls may reproduce with born denizens of the Afterlife, as well as other deified souls, though it seems that some deified souls struggled with fertility . . .

Lily reread the last paragraph. Then read it again.

And again.

Her breath sawed in her throat, hands shaking so badly that she nearly dropped the report. It couldn't mean that. She had to be reading it wrong. There was no way that was even an *option*. Sure, she'd caught the bit about rare applications and approvals and all that shit, but was there really a *chance*?

Breathe. She couldn't breathe. Did she need to breathe?

"Lev?" she rasped. "Does that say what I think it says?"

"Oh good, you got to that part. Yes, I know it requires you to forgo returning to the mortal world, but if your deification was approved, your experience would be very *like* the mortal world, according to my research, though I think arguably our world is—"

"*A baby,*" she interrupted, tapping the paragraph in question. "Does that say that if I get deified, I could have a baby?"

"Well, yes," he said reassuringly. "But it doesn't have to be with Beleth if you don't want to. Though you do make each other very happy and seem to like, ahem, *being* with each other. Though I do appreciate that you don't make a habit of partaking of carnality in his office—"

Lily dropped the report on her desk and gripped Lev's upper arms to shut him up and steady herself. "Where do I apply?"

Lev blinked, then his eyes lit up hopefully. "The Reincarnation Office. So you'll consider it?"

"*Consider it?*" Lily laughed. "Lev, I could kiss you—"

He blanched. "Please don't."

"I know. Thank you. *Thank you*, even for the chance." Lily spun away from him, bolting for the stairs. She took them two at a time, hurtling through the Universal Hallway, grinning so hard her face hurt.

Bel

"It is not. You haven't even seen it." Bel rubbed his hand over the new tattoo in question, scowling at Asmodeus, who swayed in place, Osmodai napping in his arms.

"The location tells me everything, I don't need to see it to call it what it is. And what it *is*, is a ridiculous tattoo."

"This from the man who has a line that is his wife's exact height along with the words *must be this tall to ride* tattooed on his back," Greg drawled from the couch.

"At least I'm not afraid of needles," Asmodeus shot at him.

Greg snorted but didn't say anything. He'd gone with Bel to get his original ear tattoo when they were younger and had hurried out of the artist's studio the moment the tattoo gun had touched Bel's skin. Bel had pretended not to hear him dry heave on the way out the door. The irony of that was hilarious, but also not worth pissing Greg off to point out.

"Think what you want," Bel growled, dropping onto the other couch. "I like it, no matter what you chucklefucks say."

"Okay, but what if *Lily* thinks it's a ridiculous tattoo?" Asmodeus said smugly.

"She won't," Greg said.

I hope she won't. Oh, Universe, I hope she won't.

"It's on Bel," Greg continued. "Ergo, she's going to love it, because she loves him. Unless it's something truly stupid, like a portrait of her face."

Bel said nothing.

Greg lifted his head, eyebrows furrowing together. "It's not her face, is it?"

"Look at his hand! The man is in *all* the love. It might actually be her face—wait, is it her *name*?" Asmodeus said.

"For fuck's sake," Bel exploded. "It's not her face and it's not her name. It's something very personal to both of us, and if you had a romantic bone in your body, you'd respect that, you dick."

Asmodeus covered Osmodai's exposed ear. "Excuse you, there is a child present."

"And Osmodai," Greg and Bel said at the same time, then grinned at each other.

There was a brief knock before the door to his office swung open to reveal Lev, who studied his door with interest.

"Beleth, the sticky note mottos are beginning to go too far."

"I didn't notice the new one. What is it?" Asmodeus asked, making it all of one step before Osmodai woke up with a squawk and started fussing, drawing all of Asmodeus's attention.

Lev glanced at the bundle in Asmodeus's arms with concern and pointedly stayed by the door. "I have news that may interest you," he said, fixing his orange eyes on Bel.

"Try to use words with three syllables or less," Asmodeus said, then quickly returned to trying to soothe Osmodai, who sounded like he was working up to a tantrum. Bel had heard Anyaet make those noises enough times to start fearing for his eardrums.

"Ignore him," Bel told Lev, who probably thought Asmodeus meant it. "What's up?"

"I visited the Hellp Desk to deliver the report on how to maximize the efficiency and long-term success of said desk," Lev said, as if that explained everything.

I bet Lily loved that, Bel mused, waiting for Lev to keep going. He didn't.

"What did Lily think?" Bel prompted finally.

"She went to the Reincarnation Office."

Time stopped. His heart stopped. Someone had dumped ice water over his head and somehow it had crashed over his insides too. His hearing hollowed out. The last time he'd felt this way, he'd been a young man watching his father walk into the Void, understanding why but screaming inside for him to turn around.

Beside him, Greg had gone eerily, perfectly still.

Lily.

Reincarnation Office.

The way she'd cooed at his fussy little sister. Her face when Osmodai had gripped her index finger while Bel held him. The wistfulness when they'd talked about kids . . .

Her cuddling with Sharkie on the couch. Sharkie asking her about siblings while they made breakfast. The picture of her and Sharkie silhouetted in the door looking at the rain. The way she and Sharkie looked at each other with love and pride. The way she looked at him. How she would press a kiss to the center of his chest. The way she left him funny and naughty sticky notes on his desk when they had lunch together.

All the tiny and incredible moments of their friendship and relationship told him one thing.

She wouldn't.

Lily, his princess, fucking *wouldn't*. She was no coward, and if she'd been thinking of leaving—the timing of which made no sense if it was true—she would have talked about it. Disappearing into the ether of the Universe wasn't her style.

It *wasn't*.

It *couldn't be*.

Bel went to stand up, intending to corner Lev and interrogate him until he told him every-fucking-thing, but Osmodai chose that exact moment to let out a shrieking grunt and release a loud, large, and sticky-sounding load into his diaper that practically echoed in the silent room. He then launched into a screaming fit. The obscenely noxious smell dispersed itself with surprising swiftness, making even Bel wrinkle his nose.

Lev, standing closer to the source, gagged so violently that he bent double, staggering away, retching the entire time. A frazzled Asmodeus hurried after him in the direction of his own office and the diaper bag, calling Lev ten kinds of dramatic.

Bel's surge of adrenaline dropped as swiftly as it had risen, leaving him shaky and weak. He dropped back onto the couch, all his thoughts happening at once, but only one remaining clear.

She wouldn't.

Lily wouldn't. Not like this.

"That can't be all," Greg snarled, launching to his feet. "He can't fucking leave it there. I don't care if he pukes up a lung, there has to be more to the story, and he needs to get back here and tell it." Greg ran—actually ran—out of the room in pursuit.

Bel sat numbly on the couch, then lurched to his feet and stumbled to his desk. Her file. If he could just hold her file, hold that little piece of her close until this all got sorted out, he would feel better. They would laugh about this later.

In several decades, when it finally became funny.

Or maybe never.

He kept her file in the same drawer that he'd kept her brothers' socks in, and he'd added several of her favorite books to keep the file company. The paper was warm beneath his touch, radiating the same soothing energy that Lily gave him. He pressed it to his chest, choking on his own breaths. Still there. Still happy and strong and safe.

Just a misunder—

Her file disappeared, leaving him alone.

Again.

62

VENI, VIDI, VELCRO

Lily

Her feet barely touched the ground as she raced through the Hallway, weaving through people, skidding around corners, hope propelling her forward faster and faster.

A chance.

A small chance, but holy shit, it was a *chance*.

The Reincarnation Office was close to the Front Desk, separated from the Entry Hall by an invisible barrier that only applied to souls who hadn't gone through Judgment. Lily stopped so hard in front of the office that her boots squeaked in protest, dimly remembering the place. The Reincarnation Office wasn't an arch, it was a massive alcove separated from the Universal Hallway by a towering wall of smooth rock that, despite its height, came nowhere near the ceiling. From a distance, it looked like a silly half wall, but up close, it stood all too solid and imposing.

A huge set of permanently open double doors was the only entrance, and she took a moment to pull herself together before she walked through them. Inside, it looked a bit different than she dimly remembered, more like the lobby of a fancy bank. Souls stood patiently in orderly lines, chatting amongst themselves as they waited to be called to one of the many elegant office pods for a private conversation. The long, bank-style general information desk only had a few souls waiting to speak to an attendant, and Lily figured that they would be the ones to help her figure out the best course of action.

She'd taken all of one step forward when an elderly man and woman caught her eye as they walked hand in hand through the doors, bright smiles on their weathered faces.

Oh. It was him. The man who'd been waiting for his wife.

When she'd first seen him, she'd envied him for experiencing that kind of love and hated herself for feeling unworthy of the same. She knew better now. She'd always been worthy. And that love? She'd found it too. Everyone in the mortal world had made such a fuss about finding someone you were willing to die for, and there was a dramatic power to that, she supposed. But finding someone you were willing to *live* for? To fall in love with over and over again through lifetimes, or to love for the whole of an eternity? She'd take that kind of love any day.

Lily smiled and nodded at them as they went past. They beamed at her, the woman shooting her a knowing wink, joy recognizing joy. They joined the line of souls waiting to reincarnate, moving together with the ease of familiarity. Lily's own palm felt empty and cold while she waited for her turn at the general information desk. She curled her fingers, missing the sensation of Bel's massive, callused hand, recalling the warm pulse of his heartbeat when she pressed her hand to his chest. He'd be so happy when she told him she was staying, and if she was granted deification, he would be ecstatic. Either way, a new and glorious chapter of their lives would begin.

A smiling Inuk man gestured her forward, a buzz trickling over her skin as she stepped up.

"How may I help you?"

"I would like to yield my ability to reincarnate and apply for deification," Lily said, the rightness of that statement settling into her bones.

The man, however, blinked once, twice, then rapidly while he processed what she'd said. "That's . . . not . . ." He cleared his throat. "I'm sorry, but I don't think that's possible."

"It is. I'm not saying that I expect the application to be approved, but I want to try. And whether that application is approved or not, I still want to have a note put in my file that I will not be reincarnating again. Ever." She paused for a moment, racking her soul-deep memory for clues. "I'm sorry, would it be better for me to wait in the other line?"

"No, no, that's for reincarnation only," the man said, more than a little flustered. "Let me find one of the older souls; they'll probably know more about this."

He hurried off, leaving Lily to wait under the curious stares of the other attendants. She offered them all a neutral smile and reached for her phone to give Bel a heads up that she would want to see him soon, only to realize that she'd left it at the Hellp Desk. Oh well, it would be more of a surprise.

It was odd to be so excited, yet so calm. It felt similar to getting home and walking in the door after being gone for a long time, but on a much grander scale.

The man returned, accompanied by a soul that reminded her of the one she'd helped find the Void. The soul's age was obvious with every tiny motion of his body. He moved with perfect fluidity, so used to existence and *being* that everything he did looked effortless. The Inuk man had relaxed a bit and seemed curious as he slipped back into his seat.

"Lily," the ancient soul said smoothly, his near-black eyes missing nothing. "I have heard much of you."

"That seems to be a running theme," Lily said. "Hopefully not a bad one."

The ancient soul smiled. He was tiny in stature compared to her, but he carried himself with the same easy confidence as seven-foot-tall demons.

"Not bad at all. No one with sense could think poorly of the lady of the Hellp Desk. We admire you too much. I wondered if you would ever come here, even if only to spend some time behind a less hostile desk, but you have come for a better reason, it seems." He tilted his head, a smile playing on his thin lips. "No one has asked about deification since my younger days. And even then, the price was too steep for many."

Yielding her ability to reincarnate, giving up her inherent mortality, was a scary concept at face value, but she'd already decided to stay no matter what. To let herself love and be loved with abandon.

The opportunity to have all that and more? She'd do anything.

"For what I could gain, my mortal life seems a worthy price. I understand that it's not a guarantee, but even the chance is worth it," Lily said.

"If you apply and are rejected, you will remain as you are and would be able to reincarnate if you so choose."

Lily smiled softly, thinking of quiet mornings with Bel, playing in the rain with Sharkie, kissing Max on his fuzzy little head. "I wouldn't. No matter what happens, the mortal world isn't for me anymore."

"It could be."

"It could," she agreed, "but it's not. Just like Heaven could be for me, but it isn't."

"An immortal heart made by the mortal world," he mused with a smile. "A curious and powerful thing. If you are certain, far be it from us to stop you."

Warm paper pressed against her fingertips, and she clutched it on reflex. The color of her file had shifted to lilac, the metallic letters of her name glimmering. All that she had been. All that she would be.

She held it out to him.

"You'll have to walk me through the application process," she said.

He studied her gaze, not taking her file. "You understand what you would give up and what you would gain?"

"My ability to reincarnate in order to become like the denizens of the Afterlife and have a true life here."

His eyes sharpened. "Why do you wish to do this? What is your motivation?"

Watching the sunrise while Bel and Sharkie laughed. A shower of sparks rising as Hell sang. Helping souls who were lost. Placing flowers on fallen creatures. Watching warriors from Valhalla teach a small child how to be less scared. Helping souls who were lost. Distracting unpleasant souls so that the gate demons could breathe easier. Playing in the rain. Making faces at Bel in the mirror. The way his eyes crinkled at her.

All the quiet and grand moments.

"Love," she said simply, setting her file on the desk.

The ancient soul's eyes dipped to watch her soul file disappear, then gave her a look she couldn't interpret. "It seems your application is being considered."

Lily went hot and cold at the same time. "Well . . . that was . . . easy."

"Was it?" The ancient soul angled his head.

"Yeah," Lily said, wiping her palms on her thighs. "Except for when it wasn't."

A few of the eavesdropping attendants chuckled. Even the ancient soul cracked a smile, which Lily returned.

Done. No matter what, it was done. The ancient soul hadn't told her when or how she'd know if her application had been accepted, and she figured that he knew the answer to that as well as she did.

As much as she wanted to spin on her heel and haul ass down to Hell and tell Bel everything, there was something else she needed to do for herself.

"Can I look at it one last time?"

Despite the fact that souls reincarnated all the time, and there was only one gate back, thanks to Universal magic, no other souls were visible as she walked through the hallway toward it. Something about each journey being a personal one unless intentionally embarking on it with others.

She'd been warned not to step off the solid stone, as that marked the point of no return for reincarnation, so she stopped a few feet away from where the stone ended and the colorful swirling mist began. The gate was deceptively small, a bit bigger than an average door, but it hummed with just as much power as any other arch in the Afterlife.

Lily stared into the mist, her throat clogging with emotion.

Life. She could practically taste it. For all its faults and evils and pain, the mortal world was a beautiful thing. Mortality was a beautiful thing. The curious uncertainty, the boldness both quiet and brash that *living* required, all of it.

Beautiful. Powerful.

A part of her would always miss it.

She took a long, deep breath, watching the colorful mist twist and curl around itself, the power of the gate reaching out to brush over her soul with all the potential of mortality.

A dozen different children, all of them somehow identifiable as different incarnations of herself growing up with a dozen different lives. Parents who loved each other. Parents who hated each other. A single mother. Siblings. An only child. Foster care. Different hobbies, but always she loved reading. Athleticism. Chronic pain. Average in every way. Red hair. Brown hair. Blond hair. Curly, straight, long, short.

Life of love. Life of fear. Life of everything and nothing. Boyfriends, girlfriends, always single. A fancy wedding, a backyard wedding, never her own wedding, a domestic partnership, a vow of celibacy. A child, children, infertile, had a baby but lost it, miscarriage after miscarriage, twins, another negative pregnancy test. Died old. Died young. Car crash. Heart attack. Childhood cancer. Laughter. Crying. Happiness. Grief. Joy. Pain. Adventure. Hope. Beauty.

Complicated and wonderful and awful and simple.

Life.

Always life.

Lily let the hot tears run down her cheeks as she smiled at the gate, thankful for all the time she'd ever had in that beautiful world of uncertain potential.

But love called.

"Goodbye," she whispered.

The mist swirled in response.

Lily shoved the door to the building of Bel's office open, a chord of nerves thrumming alongside her excitement. She'd never felt surer of herself and her decision. Halfway across the cavernous foyer, a commotion in one of the halls drew her attention. She almost chose to ignore it, right up until Greg hauled a wriggling Lev out of the hall and toward the stairs.

"*You* don't feel good? Imagine how *he* feels. Whatever it is, you're going to explain everything," Greg snarled, fighting to drag him backward across the floor.

"Let go, I'm going to be sick!"

"You think bodily fluids bother me? Puke on yourself, for all I care. After this shit, you deserve—"

"What is going on?" Lily snapped, marching toward them.

Greg spun to face her, not letting go of a dry-heaving Lev. His red eyes burned with intensity as they scanned hers, relief flickering over his angular features. He opened his mouth, closed it, nodded once, and silently ushered Lev back into the hallway they'd come from.

What the fuck?

Whatever *that* was, it was a problem for later.

She raced up the stairs, growing warmer with every step. Bel's office door was shut, so she raised her hand to knock but paused. The sticky note she'd given him that morning hung just below his name. She'd written it as a personal joke, but also as a hint.

Veni, Vidi, Velcro.

I came, I saw, I stuck around.

Obviously not a literal translation, but Bel had gotten a kick out of it when she'd handed it to him. She brushed her fingers over the note, nerves dissipating, and knocked.

Silence.

Lily frowned, reaching for the handle anyway.

Bel stood facing the floor-to-ceiling windows, wings clamped tight to his back, arms folded, every line of his body taut. Even his tail was stiff, only the tip twitching slightly. Worry shredded her excitement.

Please don't let there be another war. Please. Not so soon. Not now. He hasn't recovered from the last one.

He didn't react when she shut the door, or when she slowly approached, pausing between the couches.

"Bel?"

He jolted like he'd been shocked, whipping around to stare at her with wide eyes, his breath catching in his throat.

Lily's chest squeezed. "Hey, big guy," she said soothingly, closing the distance between them. Bel watched her approach, desperation all over his face. He dropped his arms to his sides, fingers twitching.

Something had happened.

"What's wrong?"

"You're here," Bel rasped, eyes never leaving hers.

"I'm here," Lily said, pieces clicking into place. Greg threatening Lev, who had given her the report and, bless his sweet dumb ass, had probably shared that information in the worst possible way with no other context.

Lily smoothed her hands up the heavy muscle of his chest and he melted. "I don't know what Lev said, but I'm here to stay."

"I know," he said, voice wobbling. He cleared his throat and rested his hands on her hips with surprising gentleness. "Lev said you were going to the Reincarnation Office, and it scared the shit out of me. But I knew you wouldn't just leave like that. You wouldn't do that. I *knew* that, but I was still . . ." His voice dropped to a ragged whisper, and she reached up to cradle his handsome face, wiping at a tear with her thumb. "I was still scared," he admitted quietly. "I held your file to feel better, but then it disappeared, and I . . ." He clenched his eyes shut, pressing his cheek into her palm. "I knew you wouldn't leave like that. I figured you probably needed your file for a very good 'Lily' reason. But I still needed to come to the window."

With every word out of his mouth, Lily wanted to shred herself into a million pieces. She'd been so caught up in the excitement that she hadn't realized how it would look to him, especially if Lev simply told him that she was going up to the Reincarnation Office. It was the worst possible thing she could have done to him, short of actually reincarnating on a whim. His utter faith in her made her love him all the more, but in that moment, she hated herself just as much.

She brought his face down to hers, pressing their foreheads together so they could breathe each other in. His hands tightened on her hips, holding her closer.

"Why did you have to go to the window?" she murmured, resting her hand over his heart.

He brushed his nose against hers. "I needed to find beauty in a moment that had none. But now you're here." A tear ran down his nose and dampened her cheek, his heart beating solidly against her palm.

She cupped his face with her other hand and pulled back just enough to meet his silver eyes. "I'm here." She kissed him once, softly. "And I'm staying. Forever."

Hope dawned on his rugged features, but his eyes were still glassy.

Lily smiled softly at him, excitement fizzing through her veins again. "I'm guessing Lev left out why I went to the Reincarnation Office."

Bel nodded slowly, searching her eyes. She fought a losing battle against her tears.

"I was already going to tell them that I wouldn't be reincarnating. I was going to have them put a note in my file, make it official, and then I was going to tell you about it. But then Lev brought me that report he mentioned at the funeral." She smoothed her hands across the breadth of his shoulders. "He found a possible loophole for us, big guy. Some souls can apply for something called deification, where, if they get approved, they yield their ability to reincarnate forever and, in return, they become denizens of the Afterlife, and all that that entails." She smiled softly. "Including the ability to possibly have kids."

He froze. "What? *Lily.* That's . . ."

Her tears spilled over, even as her smile broadened enough to hurt her face. "I know! I—I ran all the way there and I applied. But whether I get approved or not, I'm staying with you. With Sharkie. The mortal world isn't for me anymore. I was so excited, and I didn't know Lev would say anything, but I'm so, so sorry that I scared you like that." She kissed him long and slow. "I love you, big guy."

"You're staying," he murmured, almost to himself, then he kissed her again, harder. "I love you, and you're staying."

She kissed him again, his hand sliding up her back and threading through her hair in the way that made her stomach swoop pleasantly.

"Forever," she added, pressing herself against him.

He grinned at her, all traces of his earlier fear vanishing until he looked like his normal self again, except happier than she'd ever seen him.

"Princess," he murmured, tenderness radiating from him as he brushed his lips over her cheek and pulled her into a hug. She gripped him back with every ounce of strength she had, nuzzling into the curve of his neck, reveling in his quiet strength. He was, as always, infinitely careful with her, but he held her as hard as he dared, molding her body against his.

If they spent eternity just like that, she would spend eternity the happiest woman in the Afterlife. But, she realized, her existence would be better than just this moment. They had *forever* to have more moments like this one. To have different moments, better moments, and all of them together.

Bel's heart beat so strongly against his ribs, against her, that she felt it in her own chest. She pressed against him even harder, reveling in every line and ridge of his body, in every piece of *him*. Perhaps it was just the heightened emotion of the moment, or the culmination of several lifetimes of experience and pain and dreams, but there, in the Afterlife, holding her demon prince, she'd never felt more alive.

Thump.

Lily opened her eyes.

Thump-thump.

Thump-thump.

She'd never heard Bel's heartbeat in her ears like that before. Something was different. Not wrong, but different. Warm, she was warm, and she felt . . .

She shoved back with a gasp, giving herself just enough room to press her hand to her chest.

There, under her palm—*thump-thump.*

Lily grabbed Bel's hand and pressed it over the center of her chest, his look of utter confusion evaporating in a moment. Her heart—her *heart*—beat steadily under his touch, pulsing its rhythm throughout her body.

She was *alive*.

She met Bel's shocked expression with one of her own. "It worked," she breathed, the implications of that statement sinking in. Deified. Alive. She was home forever, and they could . . .

"It worked," she managed to say before crumpling into happy tears.

63

TOUCHING MUSIC

Bel

The beat of Lily's heart against his palm was exquisite but paled in comparison to the glory of her joy.

Staying. Forever.

Bel held her a little tighter. Forever to hold her, to nuzzle into her hair, to hear her laugh and see her scowl, forever to *live*. All that, and the possibility of expanding their family.

His throat clogged again, and he kissed the curve of her shoulder. She smiled against his neck as she tightened her hug, fingers stroking over the sensitive bases of his wings.

Forever.

"Fucking Lev," she murmured, smoothing one hand up the heavy arch of one wing. He shuddered at the heady prickle of sensation that fizzed up his spine. "This was supposed to be a completely good moment."

"It *is* a completely good moment. Now, anyway. I don't know if we should thank him or kill him. That is, if Greg hasn't already gotten to him first," Bel grumbled into her neck, unwilling to let her go.

She hummed. "Greg got to him first. I think he was dragging him up here when I arrived, but he backed off when he saw me."

She pulled back a bit, and he let her go with reluctance. Thankfully, she gave herself just enough room to slide her hands up his chest and smile softly at him, so radiantly beautiful and *his* that he had to remind himself that the moment was real.

"I could never leave you." She brushed her thumb over his cheek. "Heartbeat or no heartbeat, I was always going to choose you. You're worth dying for," she said, smile broadening, "but more than that, you're worth living for too."

His skin felt too small to contain his emotions. They closed his throat and made words impossible, his heart threatening to beat out of his chest.

Worth living for.

Of all the praise he had ever received, that was the highest.

He kissed her palm, clearing his throat enough to rasp, "Princess . . ."

That was all he managed.

"I know," she said gently, an impish gleam entering her eyes. "I had the whole elevator ride to come up with that. You can knock me on my ass with something romantic later, but let me have this one."

He barked a laugh, running a hand over his too-warm face. "Alright, you can have this one. Besides, I have better plans for your ass."

"Go on."

"I'm not sharing them *now*. This is your moment, remember?" he teased, settling a hand on her hip while the other came to rest over her beating heart.

The rhythm of it under his palm was like touching music.

Forever. The idea of it kept washing over him in waves of astonishment.

"Can I see the new tattoo?" she asked a few moments later, brushing her fingertips over the back of his hand resting on her chest. He held it out for her inspection, a thrum of nerves cutting through his elation. He swiftly pushed the fear down. She'd yielded her ability to reincarnate to stay and have a life with him in the Afterlife. One tattoo wasn't going to change her mind.

Well, two tattoos . . . But he'd mention that later.

Done in black and gray, the lily was delicately crafted of clean, sweeping lines and intricate dot work, spanning the entire back of his hand and creeping slightly up his wrist and the backs of his fingers. A furled bud was tucked amongst the few abstract lines of the background, nestled close to the flower in full bloom.

His reasoning for it had been multifaceted, and he hadn't wanted to explain it to Greg and Asmodeus when they'd seen it. They had both correctly surmised that Lily had been the inspiration and that he'd wanted to get something to remind him of her, but it was more than that. They hadn't commented on the furled bud, perhaps assuming that it was just a way to fill in the background. It wasn't.

He explained it to her quietly, her fingers tracing each element as he spoke.

He'd been specific about the imagery he'd wanted. A lily like the ones they'd laid on the battlefield. The flower and the bud. Lily and Sharkie. A parent and a child. In honor and in remembrance. He'd hoped that it wasn't too cheesy to get a tattoo for her and Sharkie, and in the same breath worried that the second half of the tattoo's meaning would render it too morbid.

"Asmodeus gave me some loving shit for it, but not nearly as much as he gave me for the, uh . . . other one," Bel said, segueing brilliantly, in his opinion, into his next big reveal.

Lily peered up at him, arching an eyebrow. "The other one? I've seen Azzy's back tattoo, and he still had the audacity to give you shit?"

"It's Asmodeus," Bel said in explanation.

Lily rolled her eyes, bringing his hand up to press a soft kiss to the center of his new tattoo. "He shouldn't have given you any shit about this one. It's beautiful, Bel. For all of your reasons."

He squeezed her hip and murmured a thank-you. He'd felt fairly confident right up until his shithead cousin started giving him grief for both of his new tattoos. Greg had been supportive, though Bel hadn't expected anything less. Greg and Lily were more similar than either of them probably cared to realize, but Lily was—with Bel anyway—the softer of the two.

Bel stepped back to give himself a bit of room and reached for the fastenings of his pants. Lily's eyebrows rocketed upward, surprise giving way to blatant interest that had him focusing on *not* getting fully hard. A worthy distraction from the nerves.

"You know how everyone keeps telling me I need to pick a motto?" he asked, fingers undoing the laces while he studied her expression.

She watched his progress with rapt attention but met his eyes at the question.

"Yeah," she said, a smile quirking the corner of her mouth. "Don't tell me you're sticking with 'Veni, Vidi, Velcro.'"

"Funny, but no," Bel said, loosening the last lace. "An artisan will add my new motto to the door next week, but it resonated with me so much that I wanted to get a tattoo of it too. And because it was a result of your brilliance, I wanted to get it in a spot you'd appreciate." He eased the front of his pants down just far enough to reveal the tattoo that Asmodeus had given him such grief over.

Across the lowest part of his stomach, stretching nearly from hip bone to hip bone in a single line of clean, simple font:

Vires Per Intellectu

Lily went wide-eyed, lips parted slightly as she stared at the words in complete silence.

Shit.

He'd always liked the idea of a tattoo on his lower stomach for sexual and aesthetic reasons—and Lily had agreed with him when he'd mentioned it in bed one time—but perhaps Azzy had been right about the subject matter.

Heat scorched his cheeks and ears as he fought not to fidget under her stare.

"Princess?" he managed, hands twitching with the urge to pull his pants up.

"That's fully healed right? Like, *fully* healed?" Lily asked with the same neutral tone as someone inquiring about the readiness of a meal.

Bel was fairly certain his face was about to burst into flames, but something in her expression . . . he'd seen that before. Hope sparked, along with arousal.

"Yeah," he said, then added cautiously, "I can always get it removed—"

"Don't you *fucking* dare." Lily glared at him in affront, dropping her eyes back to the tattoo and reaching for the hem of her shirt. "Asmodeus gave you shit for that? What an idiot," Lily said, hauling her shirt over her head and kicking off her shoes. "I love it. It's sexy and thoughtful and I want to lick it. Think of it as celebrating my heartbeat, which I'm currently feeling between my legs for the first time in too fucking long. Pants off now. Please."

Well, then.

Nonexistent crisis averted. In hindsight, he'd been an absolute and utter idiot to ever worry.

"So bossy." Bel smirked, reaching behind him to undo the clasps of the wing slits in his shirt instead, enjoying the sight of her shimmying out of her leggings and kicking them aside. He pulled his shirt over his head and dropped it.

Lily prowled toward him in nothing but her underwear, the black lace contrasting beautifully with her hair and skin. She'd always been so stunningly beautiful, no matter if she was covered in blood spatters from some evil soul or wearing sweatpants or dressed like a walking wet dream, but she seemed somehow . . . *more*.

Alive.

His.

Forever.

She grabbed him by the front of his undone pants, the backs of her fingers brushing against the base of his erection and driving the breath from his lungs, pulling him closer. Heat boiled up his spine.

He resisted the urge to take her like a primal beast. Again. This wasn't the time for that. Probably. He skated his hand up and down her side, following the flare of her hips, the dip of her waist, up to the fullness of her pretty breasts, leaving goose bumps in his wake. Lily tipped her head back, offering her mouth, eyes gleaming with passion and love, fingers lingering so damn temptingly close to where he ached for her.

With his tattooed hand, he cupped a breast, not missing the way her breath caught and her grip on his pants tightened. Electricity hummed over his skin, prickling over his nerve endings in a way that should have been painful but only brought exquisite sensitivity, similar to the adrenaline rush of combat but infinitely better.

He lightly pinched her stiffened nipple, then rolled the pad of his thumb over it to soothe away the small hurt. Her eyes fluttered closed, the soft noise that escaped her parted lips like a tangible stroke along his cock. His breathing hitched, and she half opened her eyes to smile indolently at him.

He released her breast, watching it settle with a small bounce, and moved his hand to press flat on the upper slope of her chest. *Thump-thump. Thump-thump. Thump-thump.* The rhythm was faster than the first time he'd felt it, but no less wondrous. He understood why she always seemed to like resting her hand over his heart. Her heart was his new fascination, its beat his favorite song.

Lily's hand slid from his neck down to his chest, some of the hazy arousal fading from her eyes to be replaced with soft wondrous joy, an expression he felt mirrored on his own face, in his own chest.

Thump-thump.

"Ah, princess," he rasped, shifting his tattooed hand to trace up the side of her neck with his fingertips. "You've always had a beautiful heart; now you have the heartbeat to match."

"And an equally beautiful new necklace if you hold my throat with that hand," she breathed, leaning in to kiss the center of his chest.

She let go of his pants and brought her hand up for a quick lick, then slipped it into his pants to wrap around his aching cock. Whatever romantic thing he'd been planning on saying flew out of his brain as his vision went white. She squeezed his base lightly, moving her fist as far along his ridged length as she could within the confines of his pants.

Should have taken the pants off, really should have—

She twisted her grip as she stroked down to his base. He dropped his head back and groaned.

When synapses started firing again, he kept his hand right where it was, holding her hip to keep her in place as he dipped to capture her mouth. She arched into him with a little laugh that he felt in his bones.

"How," he murmured in between deepening kisses, "committed are you"—he nipped at her lower lip, careful not to catch it with his fangs—"to licking the tattoo?" He groaned into her mouth as she worked him in her grip, and he shoved her soaked thong out of the way to slick his fingers against her core.

"Floor," she gasped, hips working as she rode his hand. "I'm licking the tattoo."

Somehow he ended up on his ass, wings splayed, leaning back on his elbows as Lily kissed, licked, and nipped her way down his torso, pausing to nuzzle his hip bone like a fucking tease.

"Princess," he growled, shoving his pants down around his hips. She shot him a wicked grin, gripped his thigh with one hand to brace herself, lowered her head and . . . planted a feather-soft kiss on the first letter.

When he regained his ability to think and form a plan he was going to—

She ghosted her tongue over his skin in delicate motions, carefully tracing each letter and leaving behind a damp trail. Her hand seared against the skin of his thigh. She held his cock in a loose grip, the head occasionally brushing her breasts and leaving gleaming traces of his arousal on her skin. The dark, possessive part of his brain purred.

She finished tracing the first word and paused. Every molecule of his body paused with her, waiting for the next touch of her tongue to his skin. She blew over the dampness she'd left behind, his already sensitive skin crackling with an overload of sensation and pleasure, robbing him of every rational thought he'd ever had except—

"More," he snarled, hauling her up his body to devour that smartass mouth he loved so much. "Ride me?" He managed to make it a request, though the way her ass filled his grip was more than a little distracting.

She sucked on his lip, making a breathy noise of assent, fumbling to reach down to guide him to her entrance. He half tugged her thong out of the way just as she notched the head of his cock inside her. The first slide into her silky, wet heat always reordered his understanding of the Universe, and this time was no different. *Home.* They gasped into each other, adjusting, reorienting themselves to the new paradigm of ecstasy. Different. Being inside her was always Paradise, but somehow it was *different.*

"Oh, fuck . . ." Bel ground out, eyes squeezing shut as he fought not to rut up into her. "You feel so . . ." He could swear that he felt her pulse, that she was warmer, silkier wrapped around him than she ever had been before.

"I feel it," she panted, half laughing.

He sure as shit felt *that*. He couldn't help thrusting slightly, working more of himself into her. She pushed back, supporting herself by splaying her hands on his abdomen, her legs spread wide over his broader hips, framing the place where they were joined with her thighs. *Fuck.*

He gripped her hip, urging her into motion. Nothing else mattered after that. His whole world narrowed down to the slick grip of her around his cock, gliding, stroking him into a frenzy as he met her thrust for thrust. Her hair gleamed, tumbling over her shoulders and chest in a spill of silky decadence, lush breasts bobbing with each movement, muscles in her stomach and legs flexing as she worked.

A ball of tension coiled at the base of his spine, tingling down his tail, spooling tighter and tighter, threatening to explode at any moment. He sat up, hips working as hard as they could as he pressed his lips to her chest, to her incredible racing heartbeat, his arm banding around her lower back to guide her movements. Her face got that lovely, almost desperate expression that told him she was teetering on the edge of a climax, and he slid the hand on her back down her ass, spreading his fingers to press on either side of where they were joined—

She came apart around him, curling forward with the force of her orgasm and burying her face in his shoulder like he fucking *loved*, her breathing stuttering as her core rippled around his cock, pulsing, clenching, driving him over the edge right after her. The explosive energy at the base of his spine raged through his whole body with enough force to stun him, though he tried to keep his hips in motion until it all became too much.

He held her as they panted together. She ran her hands over his wings while he moved his trembling hands up and down her back, inhaling the salty tang of her hair, still buried in her tight heat. Long minutes later, a cohesive thought managed to form and he almost chuckled. What a picture they probably made, tangled up on the dais in front of his floor-to-ceiling windows, his pants around his knees, her thong twisted around her hips, both of them sweaty, disheveled . . . the happiest people in Hell.

"I think I still have a sock on," Lily muttered breathlessly.

"Do you?" He thought she'd been thong-only, but he admittedly had been a bit distracted by her breasts. And hips. And thighs. And everything else. Everything except her feet, apparently. He kissed the spot on her neck that always made her shiver and savored her shuddered inhale. "You know who fucks with one sock on, princess?"

"People with one cold foot."

He pinched her ass. She tickled him where the membrane of his wing met the bone. He squirmed, and they both gasped as his softening cock shifted inside her.

"People who are *alive*."

She shifted back to grin at him, her lips red and kiss-swollen, the blush of exertion still fading from her pale skin. He grinned back, dipping to press his lips over her heartbeat.

"You know," she said, toying with the newly tattooed tip of his ear, "I didn't get to finish licking your tattoo. Which, by the way, I'm a huge fan of, in case it was unclear."

A flicker of arousal hummed through his veins, but he tamped it down, unwilling to celebrate such a momentous occasion entirely in his office.

"I picked up on that, eventually, but you might need to remind me again sometime. You can finish your little project later. We've got eternity to fill, after all."

He couldn't keep himself from grinning like a lunatic at the last bit. Forever. Together. As a family. And, someday, with more kids. He could see them, hundreds of years in the future, wedding rings on their fingers, watching Sharkie teach her siblings how to live with fearless joy.

Eternity.

He was going to savor every moment of it.

64

HOME

Lily

"I think the thong is a lost cause," Lily said, wrinkling her nose at the sad piece of black lace that had tried so valiantly to hold up to the combined lusts of a demon prince and his deified princess.

She headed toward the garbage can by his desk, but Bel snatched it out of her hand before she could make it more than a few steps.

"It did its best. I think we should keep it to remember today."

"Thong or no thong, I think I'm going to remember today for at least a few reasons." Lily laughed, finding her shirt and tugging it over her head.

Bel's expression went so achingly tender that her heart skipped a beat.

"Yeah," he said softly. "Me too."

Unable to stand even the few feet of distance between them, she crossed the room and slid her arms around his waist, kissing his pectoral, then resting her chin on it, gazing up at him. His tail curled around her calf, free hand coming up to trace the line of her nose before he nuzzled it with his own.

A tentative knock at the door drew their attention.

Bel sighed, squeezing her calf with his tail before easing away and heading for the door, completely unbothered by his lack of shirt, her damp, ruined thong casually in one hand.

I'm going to marry the hell out of this man someday, she thought with a smile, warmth washing over her at the thought.

The office door swung open to reveal a fretful Lev and a completely neutral Greg.

Lev's orange eyes danced between her and Bel, eyebrows furrowing slightly at Bel's shirtless torso and her slightly messy hair, but even though he looked slightly pained, he just swallowed hard and began speaking.

"I wanted to apologize, um, to both of you. Beleth, I'm very sorry for misrepresenting the situation in a manner that caused you distress. I should have carefully and thoroughly explained the situation"—he coughed awkwardly, flushing a deeper shade of olive green—"once I had committed to even saying anything. Though, I realize now that I shouldn't have said anything, which is where I begin my apology to you, Lily."

Beside him, Greg simply folded his arms and gave a tiny nod.

Lev, to Lily's shock, horror, and amusement, bent deeply and formally at the waist and stayed there.

"I offer you my sincerest and most heartfelt apology for my actions. In my excitement, I shared news that was yours to share, not mine. In doing so, I robbed you of the opportunity to tell your story in your own way and time and caused great emotional distress to those who care deeply about you. There is nothing in my power to undo what I have done, but please know that I will do everything in my power to not repeat this mistake. Should you ever need assistance in the future, I offer all the help I can give."

Lily blinked. Then blinked again. She glanced at Bel, whom she expected to look exasperated, but instead he was staring at Lev with a curious expression that she didn't have time to fully interpret.

"I . . ." Just telling him to stand up didn't feel right. Lev was always a bit formal, but that apology had been *formal*. There was meaning there that she couldn't fully appreciate without more information. She collected herself quickly, deciding that formality was probably the best approach.

"I thank you, Lev . . . iathan, for your apology. You may stand."

She felt like a fucking idiot, but Lev stood, looking a bit relieved, yet still more than a little worried. So she kept going.

"I accept your apology," she assured him. "And I forgive you. It happened, and it wasn't great, but you are genuinely sorry and have a chance to learn and grow from this. You . . ." The immensity of what Lev had done for her, for all of them, before he'd gotten excited about it, struck her. She rubbed at her stinging nose. "You're the reason I get to have the future I dreamed of—that Bel and I dreamed of. You're the reason the Afterlife really feels like home now. I know I said thank you before, but holy shit, Lev." She chuckled wetly. "*Thank you.* Can I give you a hug? Or would you prefer something else?"

"Um. I . . . well, a hug would be fine. You're clothed."

Lily ignored the wheeze from Bel's direction and wrapped Lev in a careful hug.

His lean arms eased around her slowly, patting awkwardly at her back while he whispered, "Lily, I don't mean to be a terrible pedant about this, but I know that the chances are slim to none of you being approved for deification, and I'm concerned that you all are celebrating prematurely. Statistically—"

"Lev, honey, can you feel my heartbeat?"

His hand stilled on her back. "Yes, of course. A healthy heart rate. A tad elevated, perhaps, but that makes sense considering the excitement."

"Lev."

He paused. "I've missed something, haven't I?"

"Souls don't have heartbeats."

A long pause. Then he hugged her with actual enthusiasm. "Oh, thank the Universe, this will make so many things easier."

Lily laughed and hugged him back.

"The translation there is that he's glad you're staying, because not only do you make soul management easier, but he's actually rather fond of you and would have missed you," Greg said dryly, leaning against the door frame.

Lev released her, ducking his head and squirming a little. "Your reports are thorough without being needlessly dense and are formatted very nicely."

"Benefits of having a bachelor of arts degree." Lily smiled, letting Lev off the hook.

"What *Greggles* is trying to say is that he would have missed you too," Bel drawled, nudging his friend's shoulder with his fist.

Greg nodded, the barest hint of a smile playing at his lips, his long tail flicking behind him. "Welcome home."

Lily was debating whether or not to ask him if she could hug him too when her phone rang. She'd grabbed it on her way down, then completely forgotten about it. She fished it out of the pocket of her leggings and studied the name flashing on the screen.

"It's Asmodeus," she said.

"Put it on speaker," Bel said. "I want to hear his reaction when you tell him the news."

She swiped the screen. "Hello—"

"Where are you?" Asmodeus snapped.

Everyone in the room went still. She wasn't sure if she was imagining the swift rise of the guys' tempers and attitudes along with her own, but she pushed those distractions aside and reached for her control. No one outside of souls at the Hellp Desk had spoken to her that way since she'd arrived in the Afterlife, and the biting response that danced on the tip of her tongue was instinctive.

Just as she opened her mouth, she remembered that it was Asmodeus. Azzy. Badass and goofy and good-hearted, if a bit clumsy on the delivery of that good-heartedness sometimes.

She took a measured breath. "Excuse me?"

"*Where are you?* I am standing at your desk and there are souls here being shitty, and I have an infant who is also being shitty, but in a far more literal way, but no you. I came here because Lev said you were going to the Reincarnation Office, and I thought, Lily wouldn't do that to Bel without so much as a *decent fucking explanation*, so I came here to—"

"Asmodeus, stop," Lily said. To his credit he went silent immediately. "I understand that you're upset and worried about Bel, but you don't get to speak to me that way. You can either treat me with respect, or we can hang up and have a different conversation later."

She knew he was terrified for his cousin, his brother in all the ways that counted, but there were boundaries that she refused to allow violation of. Even Greg and Lev frowned darkly at her phone.

"Shit. You're right. I'm sorry. I—"

"Of course she's right. What the fuck, Asmodeus?" Bel growled. She'd never heard Bel sound like that, darkly protective and tightly restrained all at once, like a bow at full draw with an arrow on the string, waiting to be released. It was more than a little sexy.

Focus.

"Bel? You're with Lily?"

"Yes. And I better be about to witness your apology," Bel said, glowering between her and the screen as if he could convey his displeasure to his cousin with just a look.

"You are. I was in the middle of it," Asmodeus said seriously. "Lily, you're completely right, and I'm sorry for talking to you that way. I . . . got really emotional and didn't think, but that's no excuse for snapping at you like that. I never should have done it, and I won't do it again. I'm really sorry."

Lily's pique faded at the sincerity in his voice. He was a good man, and she appreciated his apology more than words could say. It would take some more getting used to, all these genuine, unflinching apologies.

"Thank you. I forgive you and accept your apology." She paused, wanting to lighten things up, because today was too good of a day, and he'd been sincerely sorry. "At least you'll be able to tell Sariah that."

Bel grinned delightedly. "Sariah is going to *murder* you when she finds out, Azzy."

Asmodeus groaned. "I deserve that."

"Also," Lily continued, "I went to the Reincarnation Office to let them know that I'm not leaving. Ever. I'm staying in Afterlife and managed to get full denizen status. Someone's got to shake you heathens up and love Bel properly."

Relief dripped from every word of Asmodeus's response. "Oh, good. Congratulations! And welcome home forever! I want to hear how you managed the denizen thing. We should have a celebration dinner, like a little-ish one at our house before the big family party you *know* is going to happen . . . and before my wife kills me."

Lily smiled at Bel, then at Greg and Lev.

"I'd like that."

Not long after she'd hung up with Asmodeus, her phone, along with
Bel's, had blown up with calls and texts. Asmodeus had, with her bless-
ing, made the announcement to the gate, and it'd flown from there. The
first call she'd answered had been from a downright giddy Lucifer, who
sounded suspiciously choked up despite his glee. He'd apologized for
not thinking of deification, explaining that he hadn't worked with souls
who hadn't been sent to Hell closely enough to know much about it. His
obvious pride in Lev and his discovery warmed her heart.

A bombardment of texts and phone calls from Persephone had followed. Her first few voicemails were mostly excited shouting of things
Lily couldn't quite make out, but what she did understand—ribald suggestions of how to celebrate her newfound deified status—scorched
even Lily's ears.

More messages, from Siedah and several other workers at the Front
Desk, along with Athena, Aphrodite, Freyja, Cthulhu, Thanatos, Brighid,
the Morrigan, Pele, several of the librarians from the Universal Library,
baristas from Common Grounds, deities and beings she'd never met.
The best, though, were from the demons she'd befriended in Hell. Apparently, the entire contingent of gate demons was celebrating like they'd
won a major sporting event, sending her blurry videos of absolute chaos
as they whooped and cheered.

It had been a long, winding road to arrive where she belonged. Her
mortal life had happened the way that it had, and no one could change
that. But she couldn't be mad about how things had unfolded. She, for
one, wouldn't change anything about how she and Bel had come together,
or how she and Sharkie had found each other and grown. Well, except
maybe the near heart attack Bel had had after Lev's well-intentioned but
badly delivered announcement.

That realization, along with Lev's and Asmodeus's apologies, had settled something in her heart. So, before they left Bel's office, she'd pulled
up a contact on her phone, took a deep breath, and typed out the message

that had been a long time coming. The pain of her past no longer defined her, and the future was bright with promise.

Lily: *Thank you for your apology, God. I forgive you.*

A few whirlwind hours later, Lily leaned back against Bel, basking in his steady strength as they waited for the flood of kids to burst through the front doors of Sharkie's school. He had his arms banded over her chest loosely while she traced aimless patterns over his forearms.

"Still processing?" he asked, resting his chin on top of her head.

"Mm." She took a deep breath, hearing the first threads of kids chattering in the halls. "I didn't realize how much it would matter to other people. To you, me, and Sharkie, sure. I thought your family would be excited, along with the gate demons and our friends, but I didn't . . . I didn't realize how much *I* mattered to people. They're not just happy because I'm useful, though that's a part of it. They're happy for *us*. It's been a long time since I've had a community like that. Like this."

"Forever," Bel reminded her teasingly in a deep singsong.

She bit his forearm. Lightly. Ish.

He laughed just as the door to the school burst open, releasing the torrent of kids, younger ones first, then gradually increasing in age. Sharkie and the young demons around her were all on the cusp of becoming teenagers, but Sharkie, though still growing, was getting outpaced in the growth spurt department.

She saw both of them and lit up, breaking away from her friends with a cheerful wave.

How far Sharkie had come. How far they'd all come.

"Both of you?" she asked, eyes bright. A flicker of concern danced over her features. "Wait, did something bad happen?"

"Something did happen today, but it was nothing bad," Lily assured her, stepping out of Bel's hold to wrap Sharkie in a hug. "It's actually really, really good. How was school?"

"Fine, not nearly as interesting as whatever has you both looking so sappy." Sharkie giggled, gripping her tight and resting her cheek against Lily's chest, just like she always did.

Lily waited with bated breath to see if she'd notice. She didn't doubt that she would. Sharkie was one of the most observant people she'd ever met.

Sharkie froze, then jerked back, staring at Lily's chest in shock. Her wide eyes jumped between Lily's gaze and her chest, then she pressed her ear against Lily's chest again.

"You have a heartbeat?!"

Lily explained what had happened, what she'd done, and Sharkie's grin grew brighter and brighter with each word.

"I'm staying, bug." Lily grinned.

"So, you get to stay *and* have kids?"

"That's the plan and hope." Lily laughed.

"Heck yeah! Siblings! They're gonna be so cool! This is going to be great! We get to always stay a family, and it's going to get even better! When do your powers come in?"

"I don't think I'll be getting powers, beyond what I've already got."

Sharkie wrinkled her nose. "Well, that's stupid. Are you sure?"

"Pretty sure." Lily laughed again.

"There're pros and cons for everything, I guess." Sharkie sighed, then went right back to her enthusiasm. "How are we celebrating? We *are* celebrating, right? This is not a situation that calls for being chill. I say we do something that either involves food or fire. Or both."

"We can do both." Bel grinned, taking Lily's hand. Lily draped her arm over Sharkie's shoulders, and her heart kicked happily, the last piece of her soul settling into place.

Home.

EPILOGUE

A few years later . . .

Lily

Sharkie huffed a bored sigh, spinning in her office chair with a bedazzled baseball bat lying across her lap like a safety bar on a carnival ride. "Cowards, all of them."

"Wise cowards," Lily said bemusedly, turning the page of her book.

"I'm going to have time to bedazzle *myself* at this rate." Sharkie grimaced.

Lily grinned at her, a familiar rush of pride washing through her heart.

The years since she'd decided to stay had been wonderful. Thankfully, they hadn't been perfect. After all, life wasn't perfect, and the joy of living again was a precious gift that she savored every day.

Bel's mental recovery from the war hadn't been linear, and some days were still better than others, but he and the other warriors had pointedly banded together to support each other through all of it. Sometimes he would come up behind her at work, or home, or wherever she happened to be, wrap his arms around her and bury his face in her neck or hair, taking measured breaths until whatever nightmares he'd been battling eased their assault. But those moments were growing fewer and farther between. More often than not, he sought her out just to give her a kiss and smack her ass lovingly. She always kissed him back and pinched him in return.

Every moment with him was a balm to her soul, even when they were having a rare disagreement. She'd been terrified when they'd had their first moment at odds with each other that their patient, loving relationship would disappear and become a tumultuous battleground like her parents' marriage. But those fears had been unfounded. They both respected and cared too much about each other and their relationship to speak to each other the way her parents had. They worked together to solve the problem instead of attacking each other. Then they had heated, mind-blowing sex to burn off any extra energy and celebrate the fact that they were "nailing the relationship thing"... and each other.

Being together was *fun*.

Sharkie had moved out a couple of years prior, when she'd aged to fifteen or sixteen and accepted the offer of her own Paradise right next to Lily's. Ever the proud papa, Lucifer had personally come up to show it to her and give a housewarming gift. Her Paradise was a gorgeous, palatial aquarium, the likes of which would have been impossible to re-create in the mortal world. There was an abundance of sharks, of course, all of them happy, healthy, and adoring of Sharkie. How she kept their names straight, Lily would never know, but she knew each shark by sight.

Lily had no idea where Lucifer had found an actual no-shit Megalodon, but Bruce was a seventy-foot-long present from the king of Hell, who glided through the vast expanse of the aquarium with languid grace. Sharkie cooingly described him as a water puppy, and had nearly given Lily a heart attack when she'd arrived at the aquarium just in time to watch Sharkie give the massive shark scritchies with a plastic leaf rake.

It had been the joy and honor of Lily's existence to watch Sharkie grow up and find her voice. She marveled at the sheer brilliance that Sharkie, now a very young adult, displayed on a daily basis, and laughed until her stomach ached at her hilarious antics. Sharkie had ripped through her schooling with fierce glee, inhaling every drop of knowledge sent her way. She loved attending scientific presentations and debates at The Theater and paraphrasing them for Lily, Bel, and the demons at the gate.

When she'd matured enough to start an internship, as all demonic teenagers had to do as a part of their education, she'd skipped up to the Hellp Desk and made herself right at home. The desk had grown to accommodate her, bulging farther out of the wall in a larger semicircle and dividing itself in half with a small stone partition, just like in the drawings Zagan's brother had made. Sharkie's internship had turned into a passion, and the Hellp Desk was no longer Lily's alone. She loved it.

Sharkie spun in another bored circle, tapping her fingers on the sparkly bat in a hectic rhythm.

"We need bait."

"There're waffles in the break room," Lily said mildly.

Sharkie groaned.

Lily's world went dark as a giant, warm hand covered her eyes, Bel's familiar scent tickling her nose. From the orientation of his fingers, she knew it was his tattooed hand over her eyes.

"Which lover of mine is this?" she teased, tipping her head back. His hand moved with her to keep her blind.

"The really hot but not jealous one."

"Well, that doesn't narrow it down at all. Is it the sweaty gym one? The demonic metalhead one? The cuddly one? The one who cheats in *Invaders*? The one easily distracted by lingerie?"

"The one with a sexy voice, who's into redheads but not in a creepy way," Bel rumbled. She could hear the smile in his voice.

"Oh good, I love that one."

"He loves you too, and also happens to be fantastic in bed," Bel went on.

"And the storage closet, apparently," Sharkie muttered darkly.

Lily's cheeks went warm. It was true, as she'd found out several times. Though she could have sworn they'd pushed something against the door, Sharkie had walked in on them a time or two.

"Dad, you're scaring the idiots away," Sharkie said plaintively.

Bel laughed an apology, pulling his hand away from Lily's eyes and easing into the spare chair they kept behind the desk for friends and family who stopped by. He was deliciously casual in his black pants and boots, with an old sleeveless AC/DC shirt draped over his powerful torso. A thin, scraggly braid hung behind his ear, clearly his younger sister's work. Her heart squeezed happily.

They'd decided to wait a bit before trying to grow their family, much to Sharkie's chagrin. Bel wanted to get his head put back together for his own sake, but also for the sake of any kids they might add to the mix. And Lily had wanted to settle into deification and her new life, as well as savor all the precious moments that eternity had to offer them. They'd talked about getting married, but, for the same reasons, they'd decided to wait. Though Lily had caught Bel staring at her empty ring finger—and she at his—more than a few times. Their claim on each other was permanent, but there was a growing, primal need to throw a huge party, stand in front of the Universe, and make vows she'd heard and dreamed of her entire life.

Lily kissed him lightly. "What are you up to?"

"I was on Two for a little therapy session, figured I'd stop by and see my favorite of Hell's Belles." He grinned, pointing at his shirt. "Get it?"

"Jingle-jingle," Sharkie drawled, making jazz hands as she spun.

"No, like b-e-l-l-e, which is French for 'beauty' or something. I looked it up before I came here."

"Ah, that's actually kinda cool. Did you have a good session?" Sharkie asked, stopping the spin of her chair by dragging her scuffed sneaker on the ground.

"Yeah, nothing too intense, just a little mental tune-up."

"Swaggity." Sharkie nodded.

Sharkie had spent plenty of time on Levels Two and One, talking with professionals to work through some of the more snarled and painful parts of her trauma. Lily had gone up too, grateful to have someone impartial to talk to and to offer a different perspective. It was odd to struggle with guilt for being so happy, but after so long fighting for survival, she supposed it made a bit of sense.

Bel's hand caught hers, tangling their fingers together and bringing the back of her hand up to his lips. Their easy physical affection lit her up every time, even though it had drawn the ire of more than a few souls at the Hellp Desk, as well as the cheerful teasing of some of their friends. Asmodeus had absolutely no room to talk, but that didn't stop him.

Lev, shockingly, hadn't said a word about it. Sure, he still sent regular memos about "cessation of all workplace fornication," but he'd never so much as looked twice at them when they'd leaned into each other or given each other chaste kisses. She used to suspect that it was guilt over the stress he'd caused with his little announcement, or that he probably felt like he owed her for saving his life from whatever Greg had been about to do to him that day. But, eventually, Lily came to the conclusion that it was just their unique little friendship that had relaxed Lev a little.

The tiniest bit.

Her regular double-spaced reports—which admittedly were often the same paper with a few scant details changed—helped her stay in his good graces.

"Any luck on the hunt?" Bel asked, silver eyes gleaming.

"Alas, the bat remains bedazzled and unbloodied," Sharkie said with her usual sardonic flair. "But if this doesn't pick up soon, I've got a plan to change that."

"If it involves Level Nine, I'd steer clear for a bit. Greg is in a mood," Bel told her.

Lily gave a tiny shudder. When Greg was in a mood, things got bloody. Creatively, viciously bloody. For whatever reason, recently, his moods had been more frequent and long-lasting.

"Who showed up on Nine?" she asked.

Bel shrugged. "No one, but beyond the general weirdness with him lately, Asmodeus borrowed Greg's bolt cutters and never gave them back."

"Oh, so he's *pissy* pissy," Sharkie said.

Bel grimaced. "Hence, if you're going to break in the bat, go to Level Eight. Choose life."

"No thanks, I'm never reincarnating." Sharkie grinned. "I'll take the tip about Level Eight, though." She stood, leaning the bat against her shoulder. "I'm gonna get some of those waffles. Want some?"

Bel declined, and she sauntered away to the break room, striking up a conversation with a newer gate demon as she went.

"How goes *your* hunt?" Bel asked, stroking his thumb up the side of her wrist.

Lily wrinkled her nose, tipping her head from side to side in a wishy-washy gesture.

She and Sharkie had discussed growing the Hellp Desk even further by adding more people, but so far, no one had been willing or crazy enough to spend even a moment of their Afterlife dealing with a wide range of Hell-bound souls. Lily explained that, unlike customer service, talking back and calling bullshit was not only allowed, but encouraged. It hadn't changed any minds. Surprisingly, that seemed to be a bigger stumbling block for people than the fact that they would possibly be viewing soul files for some of the worst people to ever exist.

That was what she and Sharkie struggled the most with, and she'd warned Sharkie about it before she let her anywhere near dealing with souls. The images and details of the soul files faded away, but, like a flash of light, sometimes there was a hazy afterimage of the flash for a while. Some days they both went home quiet, or Sharkie would roll her chair over and ask for a hug with no further explanation. Those hugs were a lifeline for Lily too. On those days, she threw herself into living a little more. She savored every bite of food, every glimpse of art and beauty, every note of music. She kissed Bel a little longer, a little hungrier, and held him a little tighter when they curled together in bed.

And yet, despite sharing all that during her pitch for a trainee, people still were more worried about the pseudo–customer service aspect of the job than anything else. Go figure.

"Sharkie and I remain the only resident badasses of the Hellp Desk," she said.

"Mm, bummer. You'll find the right one eventually, and then the whole Universe will tremble in fear and awe," Bel teased with a grin.

"If I want the Universe to tremble in fear and awe, I'll wear a cute outfit and skip my coffee in the morning."

"I said 'fear and awe' not 'blind terror and drooling over your pretty ass.'"

Lily smirked, arching an eyebrow. "What else can that silver tongue of yours do?"

She knew full damn well what that tongue of his could do. It had done it to her that morning as a wake-up call.

Bel was the picture of smugness as he leaned forward. Her heart sped up in anticipation of one of his delicious kisses, but he merely brushed a featherlight kiss on the tip of her nose and stood.

"Guess you'll have to wait and find out," he said airily, though his eyes smoldered. He kissed her fingers before releasing her hand. "See you at home, princess."

Lily scowled halfheartedly at him as he turned to go before movement caught the corner of her eye. A dazed-looking man shuffled toward the desk, taking his time moving across the glowing floor.

Her heart skipped when Bel's hand wrapped around her throat from behind, tilting her face up for him to plant a searing, upside down kiss on her mouth, the little spikes on his chin grazing her cheek. As he pulled away, she nipped at his nose, and he gave a baritone squeak that made her laugh. Bel ambled away then, tail swishing lazily behind him, wings held effortlessly against his back.

Mine, Lily thought warmly before turning her attention back to the man, who finally approached the desk.

His file appeared just as he came to a stop in front of her, *Level Seven* stamped boldly across the top of the first page. Lily quickly sifted through the opening lines. She and Sharkie had begun to develop more elaborate and ridiculous opening statements as a way to entertain themselves, when appropriate.

"Hi, welcome to Hell, this is the Hellp Desk, where I might be built like a frog that stood up and put pants on, but I can still kick your ass. How can I help you today?" Lily managed to say with a straight face. A boy had told her that in middle school once, and it had been so ridiculous that she'd never forgotten it.

"I'm . . . here?"

"Yep."

"I wasn't supposed to actually die, though. I was supposed to almost die, and that would have solved everything."

Not entirely understanding but inferring enough to avoid touching his file, Lily arched an eyebrow. "Well, good news, bad news time: Good news is, whatever you were worried about, you no longer need to worry about. Bad news is, well, the obvious." She waved a casual hand at their surroundings.

"That's . . . stupid." The dazed expression faded with each blink, replaced with a cold shrewdness.

"Not nearly as stupid as getting yourself killed trying to avoid consequences for actions you did and knew you shouldn't be doing. Anything else?"

"Bitch."

"Bless you." Lily set his file in the basket and watched it disappear.

He stomped away, revealing a timid-looking woman in an oversized red hoodie. Her brown eyes were wide, and she had medium-length dark hair framing a heart-shaped face with full lips and level brows. She looked solemn in a way that didn't seem natural, but more like a habit.

Lily wanted to make her laugh, or at least crack the facade before she sent her down to Level One or Two or wherever she was supposed to go. She seriously doubted that the woman would go any lower than that.

"Hi, welcome to Hell, this is the Hellp Desk, where both the 'welcome' and the 'Hellp' part of that statement are up for debate. What can I do for you?" Lily asked cheerfully.

"Hi," the woman said in a soft voice, trying for a smile, "I just need you to tell me where to go, I, um . . . got lost."

Lily's hand just started to lift off the desk but paused an inch above the surface. There was no file. She didn't belong there.

"You shouldn't be here," Lily said slowly, staring at the soul in confusion. "I don't have a file for you."

"I should be here. Really." The woman fidgeted a bit, tucking a hand inside her long sleeve. "I was pretty sure I wasn't going to make it anywhere good when I got to the, um, lobby thing, so I just decided to come straight down here. Besides," she added with an attempt at brightness, waving a hand tightly, "I'm from Florida, so I'm used to the heat already."

Comprehension dawned, along with a strange sense of déjà vu. If anyone could relate to sending themself to Hell, it would be Lily—and Sharkie—but Lily hadn't made her trip with the genuine belief that she *belonged* there. At one point in her life, sure, but not by the time she'd arrived. This was different. Deeper. Like Sharkie on her first day, except this soul was a full-grown adult, and a chat with Luci was not going to remedy her deep-set beliefs that she needed to be here.

Fucking great, Lils. Way to joke around with the sweet little trauma bean.

"If you really belonged down here, you wouldn't have been able to just wander around. You have options," Lily said gently, suddenly intensely focused on keeping this soul from suffering any more than Lily suspected she already had.

"I mean, maybe. Someday." The woman shrugged, but it did nothing to hide the fact that she was wilting into herself. "But I'm not . . . I'm not comfortable assuming that I, um, deserve that . . . just yet."

A wry smile tugged at Lily's lips. It took a certain amount of guts to send yourself to Hell, even if it was a decision fueled by trauma. She wanted to help her. Sometimes people just needed . . . a chance.

"I get that. It's a process we all have to go through in our own time," Lily said, smiling gently at her. "In the meantime, would you like a job? I've been looking for a trainee. We can get you set up with a room on Level One if you like."

"Really?" The first hint of a true smile ghosted across the young woman's face. "I can work down here?"

I think you can.

"Yeah, it can be pretty fun, actually. There's a good amount of emotional labor involved, but you get to mouth off to morons all day. Plus, the demons are big sweeties; they help keep an eye on us. You're more than welcome to give it a try, but you don't have to commit."

A tentative, tiny smile curved the woman's full lips. "I'd like that."

"Excellent." Lily beamed, holding out her hand, and making plans. "I'm Lily."

The woman shook her hand, a little light entering her eyes. "Penny."

ACKNOWLEDGMENTS

Writing—much less publishing—a book has been a lifelong dream, and this story is part of an adventure that I never in a million years could have expected.

On October 4, 2021, I decided to film a silly little skit that I'd come up with while working at one of my retail jobs during COVID. As an AC/DC fan, I decided to call it "Hell's Belles." I never expected the skit to get the attention it received. As the series progressed far beyond where I had expected to end it, another story started to come to me. One day, I sat at my chart table aboard *Venturess*—the sailboat that I lived on—wrote the first chapter, and for the first time in my life felt brave enough to share it online. That led to a weekly chapter on Patreon, where the first draft of this story took shape week by week.

Without the enthusiasm and support of fans of Hell's Belles on TikTok, as well as my supporters on Patreon, this story never would have been told, and my life would look drastically different. I thank all of you, no matter how long you've been at the Hellp Desk with me.

This book wouldn't be what it is without Katrina, my developmental and line editor, and now a friend. Katrina, I cannot thank you enough for tackling this beefcake and guiding a baby author so gently and wisely through this process. You give the best, funniest, and most powerful notes! Sorry for giggling at some of the notes you made indicating your emotional duress at certain moments (you know which ones). Getting to know you has been a gift and an honor.

Thank you to my family, who have all supported me in their own ways.

Dad, thank you for being a good sport when I accidentally showed you the worst possible scene, and for teaching me to always be curious. Mom, thank you for making sure that I remembered to eat when I was lost in editing, and for always emboldening me to pursue the adventures of life. Benjamin, thank you for making me laugh and encouraging me to forge a new path, even if it's scary. Jonathan, thank you for sharing your quick wit and for asking me about the Cloud Thing all those years ago. It's a conversation and lesson I'll never forget.

Thank you to the baristas of A-Town Coffee, and especially Maddie, Aurora, and Rachel! You are all incredible, kind, and make a damn good cup of coffee! I wouldn't have been nearly as productive a human being without getting coffee from you each morning, and your unending kindness was often a highlight of my days. Your awesomeness inspired the creation of the cosmic baristas of Common Grounds.

To my younger self, who decided to stick around out of spite, thank you for your stubbornness and all the work you did that led us here. We made it, bug.

And finally, to you, the reader! Thank you for taking a chance on this book. I hope you enjoyed it! Getting to share this journey and world with you has been the adventure of a lifetime, and I cannot wait to share what comes next with you.

ABOUT THE AUTHOR

Jaysea Lynn was born and raised in the Pacific Northwest, and has always been a lover of fantasy and storytelling. After graduating from college, she purchased and lived aboard a thirty-five-foot sailboat for eight years. During that time, she found success with Hell's Belles, her comedy/drama skit series on TikTok, and gained the confidence to share her writing, which had been a lifelong but private passion. When she's not writing or pursuing other creative endeavors, she can be found with her nose in a book, going for walks, finding random adventures, or trying to perfect a cup of coffee (with mixed success).

Please visit her at www.jaysealynn.com.